Praise for *The*

"Fully fleshed-out characters living in an immaculately imagined and executed near-future world, lush prose, crystal-sharp dialogue . . . unreservedly recommended."   —*Interzone*

"Reaches another level of excellence . . . brilliant."   —*Locus*

"A cracking good story, full of action and adventure . . . unputdownable."   —*Critical Wave*

Praise for the Greg Mandel Books

"The plotting is tight and ingenious."   —*Interzone*, on *Mindstar Rising*

"Reads like a collaboration between William Gibson and Ian Fleming."   —*Publishers Weekly*, on *Mindstar Rising*

"Thoroughly engrossing . . . immensely satisfying. An excellent book. One that engages the intellect as well as the emotions. A tale that drags the reader on a corkscrew rollercoaster ride of dazzling imagination and electrifying excitement."   —*Starburst*, on *A Quantum Murder*

Praise for Peter F. Hamilton

"Hamilton is the clear heir to Heinlein in my view. Large-scale space opera told through a shifting and interlinked cast of people from various walks of life, [his writing is] amazing storytelling."   —Marc Andreessen, founder of Netscape

"Sweeping in scope and emotional range . . . carried me with rapt attention to the end."   —*San Antonio Express-News,* on *Judas Unchained*

"Breathlessly entertaining . . . Hamilton tackles SF the way George R. R. Martin is tackling fantasy."   —SF Reviews

"Dozens of scenarios, a surprisingly well-delineated cast of thousands, plotting enough to delight the most Machiavellian of readers and, this time out, a far leaner and more purposeful product: a real spellbinder from a master storyteller."   —*Kirkus Reviews* (starred review)

"Peter F. Hamilton [is the] owner of the most powerful imagination in science fiction, author of immense, complex far-future sagas."
—Ken Follett, *New York Times* bestselling author of
The Pillars of the Earth

"Packed with great storytelling . . . just about everything a reader could hope for in the middle book of a trilogy."   —SFF World

"The author's mastery of the art of the 'big story' earns him a place among the leading authors of dynastic SF. A strong addition to any SF collection."   —*Library Journal*

"With intimate storytelling threads woven through a grand tapestry of epic adventure, the tale will . . . captivate returning fans who can dive right in."   —*Publishers Weekly*

BY PETER F. HAMILTON

Pandora's Star
Judas Unchained

THE VOID TRILOGY
The Dreaming Void
The Temporal Void
The Evolutionary Void

THE NIGHT'S DAWN TRILOGY
The Reality Dysfunction
The Neutronium Alchemist
The Naked God

THE GREG MANDEL TRILOGY
Mindstar Rising
A Quantum Murder
The Nano Flower

Fallen Dragon
Misspent Youth
A Second Chance at Eden
The Confederation Handbook

THE MANDEL FILES

Volume 2

THE NANO FLOWER

THE MANDEL FILES

Volume 2

THE NANO FLOWER

PETER F. HAMILTON

BALLANTINE BOOKS   NEW YORK

A Del Rey Trade Paperback Edition

Published in the United States by Del Rey, an imprint of The Random House Publishing Group, a division of Random House, Inc., New York.

DEL REY is a registered trademark and the Del Rey colophon is a trademark of Random House, Inc.

Originally published in hardcover in the United Kingdom by Pan Macmillan, an imprint of The Macmillan Group, a division of Macmillan Publishers Limited, in 1995 as *The Nano Flower*, and in hardcover in the United States by Tor Books in 1998.

This book contains an excerpt from the forthcoming book *Great North Road* by Peter F. Hamilton. This excerpt has been set for this edition only and may not reflect the final content of the forthcoming edition.

ISBN 978-0-345-53314-2
eBook ISBN 978-0-345-53466-8

Printed in the United States of America

www.delreybooks.com

2 4 6 8 9 7 5 3 1

THE MANDEL FILES

Volume 2

THE NANO FLOWER

1

Suzi crapped the Frankenstein cockroach into the toilet bowl, then pushed the chrome handle halfway down for a short flush.

She concentrated on the neural icon which seemed to hover at the periphery of her consciousness, and marshalled her thoughts into a distinct instruction sequence. **Activate Sense Linkage and Directional Control,** she ordered her bioware processor implant.

When she closed her eyes the ghostly image from the cockroach's infrared-sensitive retinas intensified to its full resolution. There was a moment of disorientation as she interpreted the picture being fed along the optical fibre plugged into her coccyx ganglion splice. It was a hazy jumble of Mobius topology, shaded red, pink, and black, a convolution through which green moons fell. The cockroach was clinging to the bottom of the sewer pipe directly underneath a shower of droplets from the toilet down-pipe. Directional graphics superimposed themselves across the picture, resembling an aircraft pilot's command display.

Suzi guided the cockroach up the side of the sewer pipe until it was out of the water channel, then set it walking. Optical fibre began to unspool behind it, thinner than a cobweb.

Perspective was tricky. She allowed herself to believe she was walking through some baroque nether-world cathedral. The fluted walls had a black-mirror sheen, carved with a fabulous abstract glyph. Above her, the curving roof was punctured by elliptical ebony holes, all of them spitting phosphene-green globules. A small river slithered down the concave floor, bearing away unidentifiable lumps of pale fibrous matter. She was suddenly very glad Jools the Tool hadn't stitched any olfactory receptors into the Frankenstein cockroach when he was putting it together for her.

Pressure-sensitive cell clusters detected the rush of air, warning her of the approaching flush. She scuttled the cockroach right up to the roof of the sewer. The burst of water churned past underneath her. A turd the size of a cargo ship rode the wavefront, trailing ribbons of disintegrating paper.

She waited until the surge had gone, then brought the cockroach back down the curving pipe and carried on forwards. Fungal growths were blooming out of cracks in the concrete, moonscape mattresses of slime. The cockroach clambered over the humps without even slowing, all the while spinning out its gossamer thread.

Up ahead, where the pipe contracted to a black vanishing point, she thought she saw something move.

*

In a way, Suzi considered the Morrell deal as a vindication of the way she had lived the last twelve years. There was no violence involved, not even a hint of it. Violence had launched her into the tekmerc game after she got out of prison. Organized violence, deliberately and precisely applied. It was her trade, all she knew.

Her teens and early twenties had been spent in the Trinities, an anti-PSP gang operating out of the Mucklands Wood estate in Peterborough during the years when the People's Socialism Party controlled the country, a long dark decade of near-Maoist dictatorship just after the Greenhouse Effect ran riot.

She had joined up the day after a squad of PSP Card Carriers ransacked her parents' hotel, stripping out the fittings, stealing the booze. Her father had been pistol whipped, a beating which left him partially paralyzed down his right side. Her mother had been gang-raped, a trauma she never recovered from. They were middle-aged middle-class suburbanite innocents, well-to-dos who couldn't believe what was happening to their green and pleasant England, and didn't know how to stop it.

The only reason Suzi had been there when it happened was because the PSP had shut down Welbeck College, the British Army's officer cadet boarding school. A military career was all she had wanted for as long as she could remember. An ambition subtly reinforced by her slightly disreputable maternal grand-father who spun enticing stories of glory and honour back in the days when he'd served in the Falklands and the Gulf. Gaining one of the fiercely contested places at Welbeck, despite her physical stature, had been the zenith of her young life.

She had wanted to fight that afternoon when the Party militia came, young struts with their red armbands and bright new cards that had President Armstrong's signature bold along the bottom to say whatever they did was official. Fresh from her four terms of unarmed combat classes and rifle shooting and square bashing she considered herself invincible. But her father, bigger and stronger, had forced her into a storeroom and locked her in. Suzi hammered on the door in rage and humiliation until sounds of the looting penetrated, the crash of breaking glass merging with anguished screams. Then she shrank into a corner, hugging herself in the dark, and praying nobody smashed down the door to find her.

The police discovered her the next morning, all cried out. As she saw the wreckage that was once her home and her parents, rage turned to demonic hatred. She could have prevented it, she knew. If she'd just been given the chance, been given the weapons hardware to complement her determination and amp-lify her size.

The Trinities were led by an ex-British Army sergeant, Teddy La Croix, called Father by the kids under his command. He put her to work as a runner.

Peterborough in those days had a raw frontier-town edge to it. Over fifty thousand people had descended on the city, one step ahead of the rising sea that was slowly devouring the Fens, and more were on the way. The polar melt and thermally expanded oceans eventually sent the muddy water to lap at the city's eastern suburbs, turning the lush Nene valley into an estuary. This on top of an indigenous population still struggling to adapt to the year-round heat, the imminent collapse of public gas, electricity, and water grids, food rationing, and austerity economics.

Suzi flittered about the congested streets, soaking up the buzz of grim determination everyone seemed to possess. She watched the old temperate vegetation die in the steambath atmosphere exhaled by the Fens quagmire, only to be replaced by the newer more vigorous tropical plants with their exotic blooms. She walked entranced along the rows of stalls which sprang up along each road as the traffic faded away, stealing often, eating well, and fighting with the barrow boys.

Nobody noticed her, one more kid running wild in a city teeming with thousands of her kind. She thrived in her environment, but all the while she moved with purpose, keeping tabs on Party members, watching who went in and out of the town hall, acting as a sentry for raids on Party offices. At nights she would be there in the riots organized by the Trinities, an incongruously small skinny figure compared to the rest of her platoon, which aimed for muscle bulk and favoured combat fatigues and leathers.

She learned tradecraft from Greg Mandel, another ex-Army man working with Father to overthrow PSP oppression; how to make Molotovs that didn't go out when they were thrown, how a platoon should deploy to jump a police snatch squad, what to use against assault dogs, the correct way to break riot shields, a long interesting list of tactics and weapons no one had ever mentioned at Welbeck.

She killed her first man at sixteen; a People's Constable who was lured out of a warm pub on to a dark building site by a halter top, a mini skirt, and a smile that promised. The rest of her platoon were waiting for him with clubs and a Smith and Wesson. They were all blooded that night.

Suzi threw up afterwards, with Greg holding her until the shudders subsided.

'You can go home now,' he said. 'You've had your revenge.'

But she glanced at the broken body, and answered, 'No, this is just the hand, not the head. They've all got to go, or what we're doing will be pointless.'

Greg had looked terribly sad, but then he always did when anyone talked about vengeance, or let their grief show. It wasn't until years later she found out why he always seemed to be hurt so much by other people's pain.

The next morning she cut her hair, spiked it, and dyed it purple. Standard procedure; a lot of people in the pub would have given her description to the Constables.

The Trinities taught her discipline and self-confidence, as well as a hell of a lot about weapons, filling in all the technical gaps Welbeck had left. She was young enough to be good at it, and smart enough to use her anger as inspiration rather than let it rule her.

There were gangs like the Trinities in every town in the country, battling to overthrow the PSP. Suzi considered herself to be part of a crusade, making everything she did right.

Then they won. President Armstrong was killed, the PSP was routed, the Second Restoration returned the royal family to the throne, the first elections gave the New Conservatives a huge majority, and everything suddenly became complicated. The PSP relics, their Constables and apparatchiks, banded together as the Blackshirts, went underground, and turned to ineffectual civil disobedience that petered out after a few years. The Trinities fought them, naturally. But it wasn't appreciated any more. They were too crude, too visible; people were looking to cut free from the past.

It ended as it had run on for ten years, in bloodshed. A two-day firefight between the Trinities and the Blackshirts that left Mucklands Wood and Walton in ruins. The government had to call out the army to put a halt to it.

Suzi survived to be picked up by the army. Her barrister was the best available, paid for by sympathizers of the anti-PSP cause, of which there were plenty. She got a twenty-five-year sentence, because the New Conservative government wanted to demonstrate it was showing no favouritism. On appeal, held quietly and unpublicized by a co-operative press, it was reduced to five. She served eighteen months, fifteen in an open prison that allowed weekend leave.

*

The closed universe of the sewer was familiar enough now for any abnormality to register; Suzi had almost forgotten the limp reality which lay outside. And there was definitely something else in the pipe with her. A cool pulse of excitement slipped along the optical fibre as the cockroach hurried onwards.

In front of her the bloated hump which was blocking a quarter of the pipe glowed a rich crimson, flecked by weaker claret smears. It was a rat, gnawing at some fetid titbit clasped between its forepaws. Huge glass-smooth hemispherical eyes turned to look at Suzi, the nose twitched.

She remembered all those fantasy quest novels she used to read as a child, princess sorcerers and fell beasties. Grinning wryly, none of them had ever gone up against dragon-sized rodents.

Initiate Defence Mode.

A pair of flexible antennae deployed on either side of the cockroach's head, swinging forward, long black rods curved like callipers. The rat hadn't moved, staring seemingly in surprise at the intruder in its domain. Suzi halted twenty centimetres away, antennae quivering at the ready.

It came at her with a fast fluid grace, mouth widening to reveal serrated tombstone teeth, forepaw reaching out to pin her down, black talons extended. The descending paw brushed against the cockroach's erect antenna tips. Suzi's vision was wiped out in an explosion of sparkling white light as the electroplaque cells below the cockroach's carapace discharged through the antennae.

When the purple mist cleared she could just see the rat's beefy hindquarters pumping furiously, tail held high, whipping from side to side.

A quick systems check showed she had enough charge left in the electroplaque cells to fend off two more assaults. Guidance graphics told her there was another twelve metres to go before she reached the junction she wanted.

Suzi moved forwards. This underworld was no different to her own, she thought, except it was more honest. Down here you either ate or got eaten, and everything knew where it stood in relation to everything else, the knowledge sequenced into its DNA. In her world nothing was so simple, everybody wore a chameleon coat these days, status unknown.

*

After prison she had picked up work on the hardline side of tekmerc deals, the combat missions which were launched when covert penetrations and clandestine data snatches had failed.

At first it had been as part of a team, then as word got around about her competence and reliability she commanded her own. She began to add dark specialists to her catalogue – hotrods, 'ware spivs, pilots, Frankenstein surgeons, sac psychics. Companies with problems sought her out to organize the whole deal for them. She was the interface between corporate legitimacy and the misbegotten, the cut-off point.

She had picked up the Morrell deal four months ago. It was straightforward enough, a simple data snatch. Morrell was a small but ambitious microgee equipment company in Newcastle, a subcontractor supplying components to the giant kombinates for their space operations.

Space was in vogue now, the new boom industry; ever since the Event Horizon corporation had captured a nickel-iron asteroid and manoeuvred it into orbit forty-five thousand kilometres above the Earth.

Because Event Horizon was registered in England, the rock came under the jurisdiction of the English parliament, who named it New London and established a Crown Colony in the hollowed-out core. New London ushered in an era of ultra-cheap raw materials, which were eagerly consumed by the necklace of microgee factories in low orbit above the equator, doubling their profitability virtually overnight. Mining chunks of rock from New London was easy enough, but refining metals and minerals out of the ore in a freefall environment presented difficulties, that was where the real money lay.

It was a problem which had led Suzi to a second-floor bistro in Peterborough's New Eastfield district on a muggy day in January. She was thankful for the bistro's smoked-glass windows and air conditioning; the building opposite was buffed white stone, inlaid by balconies with mock-Victorian ironwork. It gleamed like burnished silver from the low sun. The street below was a flux of people, men in spruce shirts and shorts, salon-groomed women in light dresses, most of them with wide-brimmed hats, all of them with sunglasses. Silent cars glided down the rain-slicked road, bumper to bumper Mercs, Jags, and Rollers. New Eastfield had been ascendant even in the PSP years, but since Event Horizon cracked giga-conductor technology and reindustrialization went into overdrive the district had become a beacon for the smart money and the brittle, propitious lifestyle which went with it.

'Morrell have developed a cold-fusion solution to ionic streaming,' said the man sitting opposite her. He was in his late thirties, with a gym-installed muscle-tone to complement his salon manicure. An image as tabloid as his power-player attitude. The name he gave her was Taylor Faulkner.

Suzi's tame hotrod, Maurice Picklyn, had run a tracer on him for her, and that actually was his name. Working for Johal HF in their orbital refinery division, executive rather than technical.

'Cold fusion?' Suzi asked.

'Pie in the sky,' Faulkner sighed. 'Too good to be true. But somehow they've done it, boosted efficiency and lowered power consumption at the same time. Old story; small companies have to innovate, they don't have the research budget that shaves off a percentage point each year.'

She sipped at her orange juice. 'And you want to know what they've got?'

'Yes. They've finished the data simulation, now they're starting to assemble a prototype. Once that's been demonstrated, they'll be given access to kombinate-level credit facilities by the banks and finance houses. They've already asked for proposals from several broker cartels; which is how we found out what they're working on.'

'Humm.' Suzi used her processor implant to review the data profile Maurice Picklyn had assembled on Johal HF; a fifth of their cashflow came from refining New London's rock. 'What's my budget?'

'Four hundred K, New Sterling.'

'No, seven hundred. The licence alone would cost you that, even if Morrell grant you one, and then you'd be paying them royalties straight out of your profits.'

'Very well.'

She took a week to review Morrell's security layout. The company had taken a commercial unit on a landfill site that used to be one of the Tyne's shipyards. Its research labs and prototype assembly shop were physically isolated, a cuboid composite building sitting at the centre of a quadrangle formed by offices and cybernetics halls. And there was a lot of weapons hardware in the gap. The only way in to the research section was through the outer structure, then over a small bridge, clearing five security checks on the way. A team of psychic nulls working in relay prevented any espersense intrusion. The research division mainframe wasn't plugged in to any datanet, so no hotrod could burn in. She had to admit it was a good set up. The only way to breach it physically would be an airborne assault. That lacked both finesse and an acceptable probability of success.

She started to review personnel, which led to the discovery of the company's blind spot. Because it was impossible to physically carry data out of the research building, Morrell security only vetted the workers once a year, a full data and espersense scan.

Maurice Picklyn found her three possibles from the ionic streaming project's research team, and she selected Chris Brimley, a programmer specializing in simulating vacuum exposure stresses: unmarried, twenty-nine, unadventurous, a Round Tabler whose main interest was fishing. He lived by himself in Jesmond, renting a flat in a converted terrace house. A perfect pawn.

Suzi did a deal with Josh Laren, a local small-time hood who owned a nightclub, L'Amici, which had a gambling licence. She set up Col Charnwood, a native Geordie and one of her regular team, with a stash of narcotics any pusher would envy. Paid Jools the Tool to stitch together the cockroach. Then to complete the operation, she called Amanda Dunkley up to Newcastle. Amanda Dunkley had a body specifically rebuilt for sin, with a small rechargeable sac at the base of her brain which fed themed neurohormones into her synaptic clefts. The psychic trait which the neurohormones stimulated was a very weak ESP, giving her an uncanny degree of empathy. Maurice Picklyn manufactured a fresh identity for her, and Suzi got her a secretarial job at the city council building.

Three days after Chris Brimley bumped into Amanda in his local pub, his old girlfriend had been dumped. Two days after that Amanda had moved into his flat. In the house on the other side of the street, which Suzi had leased as a command post, she and the rest of her team settled down in front of the flatscreens and enjoyed themselves watching the blue and grey photon-amp images of Chris Brimley's bedroom. It took Amanda a week and a half to corrupt his body with her peerless sexual talent. After long nights during which his whole body seemed to be singing hosannas he told her he wanted them to be together for ever, to get married, to live happily in a picturesque cottage in a rural village, for her to have ten babies with him. Corrupting his mind took a little longer.

Chris Brimley slowly came to the realization that his life

didn't offer much in the way of interest to his newfound soul mate. They began to venture out at the weekends, then it was two or three nights a week. They discovered L'Amici, which Amanda loved, which made him happy. Col Charnwood introduced himself, so delighted to be their friend he gave them a gift. Nibbana, one of the most expensive designer drugs on the market, though Chris Brimley didn't know that.

He tried a few chips on the table, egged on by an excited Amanda. It was fun. The manager was surprisingly relaxed about credit.

After two months Chris Brimley had a nibbana habit that needed three regular scores a day to satisfy, and a fifty-thousand-pound New Sterling debt with L'Amici. They couldn't afford to go out any more, and now Amanda cried a lot in the evening, showering him with concern. Chris Brimley had actually slapped her once when she found him searching her bag for money.

Josh Laren's office was a dry dusty room above L'Amici, the only furniture his teak desk, three wooden chairs, and an antique metal filing cabinet. Ten cases of malt whisky, smuggled over the Scottish border, were stacked against one wall.

Col Charnwood spent an hour going over the room with a sensor pad, sweeping for bugs. It wasn't that Suzi mistrusted Josh Laren; in his position she would have wired it up.

The trembling Chris Brimley who walked into that office was unrecognizable as the clean-cut lad of two months previously. Suzi even felt a stab of guilt at his condition.

'I thought—' Chris Brimley began in confusion.

'Sit,' Suzi told him.

Chris Brimley lowered himself into the seat on the other side of the desk from her.

'You came here to discuss your debt, right?' she asked.

'Yes. But with Josh.'

'Shut the fuck up. For a welsh this size Josh has come to me.'

'Who—'

Suzi split her lip in a winter grin. 'You really wanna know?'

'No,' he whispered.

'Good, maybe you're beginning to realize how deep you're in, boy. Let me lay it out for you, we're gonna get that money back, every penny. My people had a lot of practice at that, never failed yet. Why we get called in. Two ways, hard and soft. Hard: first we clean you out, flat, furniture, bank, the same with that little slut you hang out with, then we start working down your family tree. We see that Morrell gets to know, they fire you, you're instant unemployable.'

'Oh, Jesus.' Chris Brimley covered his face with his hands, rocking back and forth in the chair.

'Think maybe I'd better tell you the soft before you piss yourself,' Suzi said.

*

Suzi halted the cockroach below a toilet downpipe. Her implant's time function told her it was eleven thirty-eight. Ninety seconds behind schedule, not bad at all.

Climbing up the downpipe was slow going. She had to concentrate hard, picking ridges for a secure foothold. Two metres. There was a rim where the concrete pipe slotted into a stainless-steel one.

She stood the cockroach on its back legs, pressing it against the smooth vertical wall of stainless steel. Her perspective made it seem at least a kilometre high. Three snail-skirt buds on the cockroach's underbelly flared out and stuck to the silvery metal. It began to slide up the featureless cliff face.

*

'Pull the ionic streaming data from Morrell's research mainframe and squirt it into your cybofax,' Suzi told an aghast Chris Brimley.

'What? I can't do that!'

'Why? Codes too tough?'

'No. You don't understand. I can't take a cybofax into the research block. Hell, we're not even allowed to wear our own clothes inside; security makes us change into company overalls before we enter. We're scanned in and out.'

'Yeah, Morrell security's got a real fetish about isolation. But you've got the use of a cybofax in the research building, aintcha?'

'A company one,' Chris Brimley answered.

'Good. And you can pull the data from the terminals no sweat?' Suzi persisted.

'Yes, my access codes are grade three. My work is applicable to every component of the refiner. Loading it into a cybofax would be unusual, but nobody would question it. But I can't bring it out.'

'Not asking you to. Point is, you can move that data around anywhere you like within the research building.'

*

Without the directional graphics providing constant guidance updates, Suzi would never have made it round the U-bend. The water confused the cockroach's infrared vision, and there were too many curves.

It was eleven forty when the cockroach rose out of the water, clinging to the side of the stainless-steel toilet bowl. She wondered what it must look like to Chris Brimley, a demon insect sliding up silently to bite his arse.

The infrared cut out, leaving her at the bottom of a giant silver crater; a uniform sky of pink-white biolum light shone overhead. She saw something moving above her, dark and oblong, expanding rapidly. Brimley's cybofax. There was a flash of red laser light way down on the borderline of visibility. An answering pulse from the Frankenstein cockroach.

Loading Data, her implant reported; its memory clusters began to fill up.

Suzi knew Chris Brimley was saying something, the cockroach's pressure-sensitive cells were picking up a pattern of rapid air compression. But there was no way of telling what the words were, not without proper discrimination programs. She just hoped there was no one in the next cubicle.

Loading Complete.

She slackened the snail skirts' grip on the stainless steel. There was a blurred swirl of silver and pink-white streaks as the cockroach fell back down to the bottom of the bowl. Chris Brimley pressed the flush, and the world vibrated into black.

Initiate Internecine Procedure.

The electroplaque cells discharged straight into the body of the Frankenstein cockroach, roasting it in a millisecond.

Disengage Optical Lead.

Suzi's coccyx interface sealed. The end of the optical fibre dropped into her toilet bowl. She pressed the chrome handle for a full flush, then tugged her panties and skirt back up.

The elapsed time was seven minutes, her bioware implant told her as she left the toilets. Outside she was Karren Naughton again, one of eight hopeful candidates for a job on Morrell's main reception desk.

She rejoined the other girls sitting in the personnel department waiting-room. It was in the outer ring of buildings, a low-security area where visitors came and went all day.

It was still the tea break. Earlier on the candidates had been given assessment tests, now it was the separate interviews. Suzi wanted to skip them, plead a queasy stomach and leg it out on to the street. The stolen data seemed to gleam like a sun-lanced diamond in her brain. Everyone would be able to see it. She held her place, discipline was something Father had drilled into her all those years ago. Unless you are about to be blown, don't ever break cover. Chris Brimley didn't know it was her on the other end of the optical fibre, didn't know where the Frankenstein had been infiltrated into the sewer system.

Karren Naughton was third to be called. She sat in a glass-walled office being sincere to a woman whose big lapel badge said her name was Joanna.

Twenty minutes later, after being told she was first-rate material Suzi walked out of the sliding glass doors and into the wall of humidity rolling off the Tyne.

Col Charnwood picked her up, driving a navy-blue low-slung Lada Sokol with one-way glass.

'Well, pet?' he asked after the gull-wing door hinged down.

Suzi allowed herself a smile, breath coming out of her in a rush. 'In the bag.'

'All right!' Col Charnwood flicked the throttle and accelerated into the thick stream of traffic along the base of the river's embankment. The huge slope was covered by the thick heart-shaped leaves of delicosa plants that had twined around the rocks.

'I'll squirt it down to Maurice, let him give it a once-over first,' Suzi said.

'Ya think he'll know if it's kosher?'

'Maybe not, but he'll know if it's connected with ionic streaming. I'm no 'ware genius. Brimley could've palmed us off with the data construct of a steam engine for all I know.'

There was a serpent of red tail-lights growing in front. Col Charnwood swore at them as he slowed. The road was contra-flowed ahead, long rows of cones stretched across the thermo-hardened cellulose surface. Suzi could see heavy yellow-painted contractors' machinery moving slowly along the embankment. They were stripping the shell of rock and vegetation from the mound, exposing the dark blue-grey coal slag underneath.

'Canna leave anything alone,' Col Charnwood muttered.

Suzi didn't say anything. She knew Col had been one of the thousands who had built the embankment over a quarter of a century ago. A third of Newcastle's population had signed on with the city council's labour crews as the West Antarctic ice-sheet went into slushdown, and most of the rest had contributed at some time or another. Men, women, and children using JCBs, wheelbarrows, spades, picks, sacks, anything they could lay their hands on to haul the slag out of the barges, dumping it on the fifteen-metre-high mounds along the Tyne's banks. They rolled the rocks into place on top of the slag with ropes and pulleys, a protective crust against wave erosion. Working round the clock for a solid nine months to save their city from the rising sea level.

'Never been anything like it,' Col Charnwood had told Suzi and the team late one night when they had tired of Amanda's gymnastic antics. 'Like something out of the Third World, it was. Bloody thousands of us, there were. Swarming like flies over the muck. Didna matter who you were, not then. We all worked ten-hour shifts. The money was the same as you'd get paid by the benefit office for being on the dole. But it was our city we were protecting. That meant something in them days, ya know?'

Now the embankment was being refurbished, centimetre by centimetre. Tracked machinery that crunched up the rock, heated it, spun it into fibres, then laid it down over the slag mounds which had been re-profiled for improved hydrodynamic efficiency, a glassy lava flow that would hold back the Tyne for a century.

'Cutting our heart out of it,' Col said sadly.

Suzi looked closely at the machinery as they passed, seeing the small Event Horizon logo on each of the lumbering rock smelters, a blue concave triangle sliced with a jet-black flying V.

'We unplugging from the deal, pet?' Col asked.

Suzi visualized Chris Brimley, shorn of all dignity, helpless eyes pleading with her. A victim of deliberately applied psychological violence. 'Not straight away, no. I want Amanda to put Brimley back together again first. The money from this will pay his debts to L'Amici. She can get him to break his habit. After that I'll pull her out. He'll have a chance at life again.'

Col shot her an uncertain glance.

'Where's your sense of style, Col?' she asked, smiling. 'We make a soft exit. This way Morrell doesn't find out for at least another five months. Maybe never. People have a way of forgetting the worst, glossing over the nightmares. Morrell's security psychics might not spot his guilt next time they vet him. Be nice to think.'

'Well, you're paying, pet.'

'Yeah, I'm paying.' An expensive treatment to wipe the

memory of that broken man with the bowed head in Josh Laren's dim echoing office. Buying off her own guilt.

*

This time it was a pub in Longthorpe, a long wood-panelled, glass-fronted room originally built to serve the Thorpe Wood golf-course as a clubhouse. Now it looked out over the Ferry Meadows estuary where the golf-course used to be. Taylor Faulkner had taken a window table, staring across the grey-chocolate mud-flats which the outgoing tide had uncovered. He was dressed in an expensive white tropical-weave suit, toying with a tall half-pint glass of lager.

Suzi slid on to the bench opposite him. The barman had glanced at her when she came in, drawn by her size, about to object to a schoolgirl waltzing in, then he met her gaze.

'We hadn't heard,' Taylor Faulkner said. 'It's been very quiet in Newcastle.'

'You want combat, find yourself a general.'

'No offence.'

'For seven hundred K, offend away.'

Taylor Faulkner looked pained. He held up a platinum Zürich card, and showed it to the Amex which Suzi produced, using his thumb to authorize the transfer. She watched the Amex's grey digits rise, and smiled tightly.

'May I see what I've bought?' he asked.

'Sure.' She scaled a palm-sized cybofax wafer across the table to him. 'The code is: Goldpan. No hyphen. Anything else will crash wipe, OK?'

'Yes.' He pocketed the cybofax.

'Nice knowing you, Mr Faulkner.'

He turned to the window and the gulls scratching away at the mud.

Suzi rose and made for the door. The sight of the figure in black cotton Levi's standing at the bar drinking German beer from a bottle made her stop. Leol Reiger, another tekmerc commander. They'd worked together on a couple of deals, hadn't got on. Not at all. Leol fancied himself as very big time. He was into running spoilers on kombinates, burning Japanese banks. Rumour said he'd even snatched data from Event Horizon. Suzi knew that wasn't true; he was still alive. And he hadn't been there when she came in.

She sat on a stool next to him, feet half a metre off the floor, putting their heads at almost the same level. Ordinarily she didn't mind having to look up at people. But not Leol Reiger.

'Slumming, Leol?'

Leol Reiger lowered his bottle, amber eyes set in a pale face stared at her. He had designer stubble and a receding hairline, oiled and slicked back. 'Never learn, do you, Suzi. Four months for a soft penetration, that's four months' worth of exposure risk.'

'Bollocks. What the fuck do you know about it?' she asked, feeling a kick of dismay. How the hell did Leol Rieger know about her deal with Johal HF? He would never work for a company like Morrell, they were too small, too insignificant.

'Know you checked the wrong people. You were looking down, Suzi. Then, down is where you come from. Once a Trinity, always a Trinity. Nothing more. You don't have what it takes to make tekmerc, you never did.'

'Lifted my data, and the target doesn't even know it's gone. Not like you. Your deals, all that's left is smoking craters in the ground and bodies. Your catalogue's getting pretty thin these days, Leol, right? Word's around, not so many troops want in on your deals.'

'That so?' Leol Reiger gestured with the beer bottle.

Two men were sitting with Taylor Faulkner. Both of them hardline troops, Suzi could tell.

Leol Reiger took another sip. 'You should've looked up, Suzi. A real tekmerc would've looked up. A real tekmerc would've seen how much that ionic streaming trick is really worth to Johal HF.'

She looked at Taylor Faulkner again, seeing how relaxed he was, smiling wanly out of the window. With sick certainty she knew she'd been switchbacked, the knowledge was like bile.

'You were real careful looking down,' Leol Reiger was saying. 'Went through all Morrell's personnel. But you should've been looking up, maybe got your hotrod to crack a few Johal HF files open. Done that, you'd have found our Faulkner here. Not a perfect specimen of humanity, our Faulkner.' Leol Reiger finished his bottle, putting it on the bar.

Suzi had to look up at him.

'Five million New Sterling, Suzi. That's what me and my partner are going to get from Johal HF this afternoon when we deliver the ionic streaming data. I paid you out of petty cash.' He turned to the barman. 'Get the little lady a drink, whatever she wants. My treat.'

She watched Leol Reiger walk over to Taylor Faulkner, clap him on the shoulder. The two of them laughed. Fury and helplessness rooted her to the bar stool. That shit Leol Reiger had been right, that was the real source of the pain, not the money. She should've checked, should've ripped Taylor Faulkner a-fucking-part, built a proper profile, not just a poxy ident check.

'What'll it be?' the barman asked.

Suzi picked up Leol Reiger's empty beer bottle and hurled it at the row of optics.

2

Monaco at dusk was bathed in thick copper-red light as the dome diffused the last rays of the sun into a homogeneous glow, banishing shadows. Buildings seemed to shine of their own accord.

Charlotte Fielder admired the town's tasteful stone-fronted buildings through the window of the chauffeured Aston Martin. Monaco's architecture was a counterfeit of the late nineteenth century, a blend of French and Spanish; hacienda mansions, apartment blocks with elegant white façades, black railings, red clay tiles, verandas festooned with scarlet-flowering geraniums growing out of pots.

It was the kind of flawless recreation which only truly idle money could achieve. Hardly any of the town was more than twenty years old, so little had survived the razing, when the citizens of Nice had marched on the principality in search of food. Charlotte had been three years old when it happened. But she'd seen AV recordings of the aftermath at school; they reminded her of bombed-out towns from some war zone. Dunes of rubble, where a few walls and archways had endured the maddened assault to jut skywards like pagan altars, soot-blackened bricks, burnt spikes of wood, wisps of smoke twisting lazily. The heat-expanded Mediterranean sea had risen to swirl around that part of the town built on landfill sites, its filth-curdled water pushing a grisly tideline of bodies and seaweed along the crumpled streets. Even the colours had leached out of the images, fixing the scene in her mind as grainy black and white desolation.

The destruction had been spectacular even by the standards of a Europe which had almost collapsed into anarchy in those first few years of climatical tumult engendered by the Warming.

Charlotte retained only vague recollections of her early childhood when the world was plunged into chaos, dream sequences of places and faces, a seemingly endless procession of days when it was too hot and there was never enough to eat. Half of her waking hours had been spent roaming London's wide bicycle-clogged streets, scavenging food from markets and street stalls. She had lived with her aunt Mavis, a woman in her late forties, with a round haunted face, always wearing floral-print dresses and pink slippers. Aunt Mavis never had a job; by design a lifetime dole dependant, she only took Charlotte in for the extra food allocation. Charlotte never saw any of it; her ration cards were traded with the spivs for bootleg gin, which Aunt Mavis would sit and drink in front of the big flatscreen on the lounge wall, curtains perpetually drawn.

The woman had exchanged reality for Globecast's soaps, where formatted plots always rewarded a hard life with the glitter trappings of materialism and golden sunsets, love and caring. The channels offered her a glimpse of salvation from the Warming and the PSP, a world twisted out of recognition, becoming an electronic religion-substitute. Worshipped ceaselessly.

One evening, when she was seven, Charlotte had returned home to find her aunt pressed against the flatscreen, knocking on it tearfully and pleading with the handsome smiling characters to let her in. She had been put in an orphanage not long after. The hunger ended then, replaced by work in the kitchens, peeling vegetables, washing crockery.

That was when her life really began, the normality of school and other children. The only link with her past was a solid thread of determination never to be hungry again. Then Dmitri Baronski had come into her world when she was fifteen, and he made his offer, opening a door into a semi-magical realm where nobody ever lacked for anything.

The Aston Martin reached Monaco's perimeter road, where the seamless translucent shell of the dome rose out of the concrete sea wall, curving gradually overhead, massive enough to hold up the sky. She could see a couple of jetties on the outside, sleek white-painted yachts bobbing gently at their moorings. Large circular tidal-turbine lagoons of gene-tailored coral mottled the quiet sea all the way out to the darkening horizon. Monaco still refused to plug into France's electrical grid, remaining resolutely independent.

On the other side of the road were dignified hotels with black-glass lobby doors and long balconies. She watched them go past, feeling a vague sense of amusement that a town which had so meticulously recreated the ambience of long-lost imperialistic elegance in its fabric and culture should seek shelter by huddling under a hyper-modern structure like the dome. It was a failing of the set she moved through, she thought, that they never strived for anything new. The talent and resources deployed here could just as easily have been used to create something bold and innovative. Instead, they turned automatically to the past, drowning themselves in the safety of their genteel heritage.

Yet, for her, the replication was less than perfect. She recognized the quality of crispness in the lines of the buildings, a cold efficiency in the determinedly handsome layout which betrayed the mentality of its originators. Monaco was a compact bundle of wealth, its borders jealously guarded. It had become an enclave, a fortified castle of the rich, complete with drawbridge.

Even with her whiter than white passport and prepaid hotel reservation the Immigration officials had taken their time before allowing her in. Permanent residency within the principality was strictly limited; you had to be proposed by three residents and demonstrate assets in excess of four million Eurofrancs before you could even register for consideration.

So Charlotte stood in the airport arrivals lounge in a queue of impatient, nervous people watching enviously as resident card holders zipped through their channel without any fuss. She had been afraid the hard-nosed woman behind the customs desk would open the flower box in her flight bag, ask questions about it. But the customs and immigration setup seemed more like a ritual than anything else. The wait, the questions, underlining that Monaco was different, not some common tourist resort or gambling state.

It was while she was standing there that she saw the man for the second time that day. He was in the same queue, ten places behind her. There was something about him, the way his cool eyes were never looking at her when she turned round, his phlegmatic indifference to queueing, which set him slightly apart, creepy almost. At any other time she would have guessed him to be a hardline bodyguard for some Monaco plutocrat, coming home after a holiday. But she had seen him earlier in the day at the Cape Town spaceport, mingling among the crowd of friends and relatives that had greeted the other passengers on her spaceplane flight. If she had seen him in the departure lounge, waiting for the connecting flight to Monaco, then it would only be natural for him to be standing in the queue behind her. But what had he been doing in the crowd waiting for the spaceplane?

Finally, her passport had been cleared, her invitation and hotel reservation validated by the Immigration officer, a matronly woman in a stiff blue uniform. Charlotte obediently thumbprinted the declaration on the officer's terminal, confirming that she had read and would abide by the principality's laws. She received her temporary visa from the unsmiling woman. Their eyes had met for a second, and Charlotte read the uniquely female contempt for the thousandth time. She had worn a scarlet Ashmi jumpsuit for her flight back to Earth, tucked into black leather cowboy boots, gold Amstrad cybofax wafer clipped into her top pocket, Ferranti sunglasses. About as expensively casual as you could get; she enjoyed the look in the mirror, a designer test-pilot. Then the Immigration bitch went and smashed her mood.

It was an appropriate entrance to Monaco, she thought later; scorn and suspicion dogging her steps.

The El Harhari hotel wasn't much different to the others ringing the inside of the dome. A little larger, perhaps. Its colonnaded frontage a pearl-white marble that glowed pink in the directionless sunset. The Aston Martin swept smoothly up a looped drive lined by tall, bushy-topped palm trees. There was a stream of cars ahead of it, disgorging passengers outside the hotel's main entrance.

The El Harhari was hosting the annual Newfields ball, a charity that sponsored educational courses for underprivileged children throughout Europe. There was nothing remarkable about the charity, or the ball. At least half a dozen similar fund-raising events were held in Monaco every night. But Newfields rose far above the ordinary by having Julia Evans on its board of trustees, making its ball the social event of the month. Tickets were seven thousand Eurofrancs apiece; touts charged twenty and cursed their scarcity.

Dmitri Baronski, Charlotte's sponsor, had managed to get her one, shaking his head in dismay when she phoned him with the request. 'What on Earth do you want to go to that function for?' he'd asked. His thin, lined face seemed more fragile than usual, white hair drooping limply. The valley outside the Prezda arcology where he lived was visible through his apartment's picture window behind him.

'I just want to see Julia Evans,' Charlotte had replied equitably. 'I've always admired her. Meeting her would be a real treat.' She didn't like holding out on the old man, but it was a harmless piece of fun, exciting too, in its own way. That was the real reason she had agreed to make the delivery. She had spent years striving to bring stability into her life, overlooking the fact that it was the partner of monotony.

'All right,' Baronski had grumbled. 'But all she'll do is shake your hand and thank you for supporting the charity. Same as everybody else. You won't be invited back to Wilholm Manor for tea on the lawn, you know.'

'I don't expect to be. A handshake will suit me fine.'

It had taken him six hours to track down a ticket for her. She never doubted he could do it. Then when he called her at the Cape Town spaceport to confirm, he also told her to introduce herself to Jason Whitehurst as soon as she reached the El Harhari. 'He's a nice enough old boy; and he's English, too, so you should get on fine.'

'OK.' She had kept her face perfectly composed, just as Baronski himself had trained her, not letting her disappointment show. But it would have been nice to go to just one ball as a regular guest.

Baronski squirted Jason Whitehurst's data profile into her cybofax for her to study during the flight to Monaco, and signed off chuntering.

She smiled fondly at the cybofax screen after his image had faded. Nothing ever seemed to faze the old duffer, no request too obtuse for him to handle; his shadowy web of contacts rivalled a superpower's intelligence agency. It was a job Charlotte would love to take over when he retired. She suspected most of his girls shared that ambition.

The footman who opened the Aston Martin's door was dressed in smart grey livery. Charlotte alighted gracefully, careful not to smile when she caught his eyes straying to her legs as her skirt rode up on the car's cushioning. She'd had ten-centimetre bone grafts put in her legs, six centimetres above the knee, four below. Her muscles had been recontoured around the extensions. It was an expensive treatment, but well worth it. Her new legs were powerfully athletic, beautifully shaped; designed to make men wish.

Five huge aureate chandeliers hung in the El Harhari's lobby, throwing a silver haze of light over the guests as they filed into the ballroom. The men wore formal dinner jackets, although some of them had military-style regalia complete with swords. The women were all in long gowns, dripping with diamonds.

Charlotte moved easily through the crowd, holding the flower presentation box in her left hand. Her gown was made from navy-blue silk with a décolleté neckline; with her long neck and short clipped sandy hair it looked as though she was showing more skin than she actually was. She felt rather than saw several of the men watching her.

She accepted a glass of champagne from the waiter, taking a sip as she looked round. The plush ballroom was nearly full, long stalactites of freshly cut flowers floated above the milling partygoers, a large orchestra occupied the raised stage. She saw a pair of matched Mercedes coupés on the side of the highly polished wooden dancefloor, the raffle's grand prize.

Julia Evans was standing at the centre of a small group of Newfields' committee members, greeting a long queue of guests. A dinner-jacketed channel gossipcast cameraman covered each introduction. Charlotte studied her closely. The owner of Event Horizon was thirty-four, tall, with an attractive oval face and light complexion; her chestnut hair was worn long and straight, falling halfway down her back. Her dress was emerald green, a fabric as smooth as oil, stylish rather than ostentatious. Even her jewellery was modest, a few small intricate pieces; making the elderly gem-bedecked dowagers in the queue seem absurdly gauche in comparison.

It was almost as though Julia Evans was using her own refinement to mock the crass flamboyance around her.

Charlotte found it difficult to look away. Julia Evans's reputation exerted an intrinsic fascination. She had inherited Event Horizon, aged seventeen, from her equally famous grandfather, Philip Evans, and had gone on to run it with the kind of barbed efficiency which was beyond any of its rivals. The company's fortune was based on its giga-conductor patent, a universal energy-storage system used to power everything from household gear to spaceplanes. Julia had shrewdly exploited the money which licensing brought in to expand Event Horizon until it dominated the post-Warming English economy. There were just so many legends, and rumours, so much gossip connected with this one woman, it was hard to relate all the allegations and acclaim to the slim figure standing a few metres away.

Watching her, Charlotte decided there was something different about her after all, a kind of glacial discipline. Julia's small
polite smile never faltered as she was introduced to the torrent
of eager dignitaries. It was almost a regal quality.

'Genuine power has an attraction more fundamental than
gravity,' Baronski once told Charlotte. 'No matter whether it is
an influence for good or supreme evil, it pulls people in and
holds them spellbound.'

The effect Julia Evans had on people made Charlotte realize
just how true that was. The snippets of conversation she'd
overheard so far in the ballroom were all mundane, small talk.
Everyone knew that Julia Evans didn't like to talk shop at social
functions. It was faintly ridiculous, the whole Mediterranean coast
was talking about the new alliance between Egypt and the Turkish
Islamic Republic, worried about how it would affect regional
trade, whether a new Jihad legion would rise in North Africa. And
the people here must be the most interested of all, they stood to
make or lose fortunes on the outcome. But there wasn't a word.

She remembered a midnight conversation with one of her
patrons, a high-grade financier, two or three years previously.
He had confessed that his children were deliberately conceived
to be the same age as Julia's two children in the hope they would
prove acceptable playmates. That all-elusive key to the innermost
coterie. At the time Charlotte had shaken her head in bemused
disbelief. Now she wasn't so sure.

Julia Evans's tawny eyes found Charlotte across the ballroom.
With a guilty start Charlotte realized she must have been staring
for well over a minute. She hurriedly took a sip of champagne
to cover herself. Gawking like some adolescent wannabe who'd
unexpectedly bumped into her idol. Thank heavens Baronski
wasn't here to witness such a lapse.

Charlotte quickly scanned the faces in the background. Before
the party she had reviewed Julia Evans's data profile, the one
Associated Press assembled, looking for someone close to her.
She had sifted carefully through the information, deciding on
three names which might provide a short cut to access.

She walked round the end of the queue, towards the knot of people behind Julia Evans.

Rachel Griffith was chatting to one of the Newfields committee members. A middle-aged woman trying not to let her boredom show. The data profile had said she'd been with Julia Evans for nineteen years; starting out as a bodyguard, then moving over to personal assistant when she got too old for hardliner activity.

She gave Charlotte a quizzical look. There was that instant snap of recognition, condescension registering. 'Yes?'

'Would you see Julia Evans gets this, please.' Charlotte handed over the box. It was twenty-five centimetres long, ten wide, with a transparent top showing the single mauve trumpet-shaped flower inside. A white bow was tied round the middle.

Rachel Griffith took it in reflex, then gave the box a disparaging frown. 'Who's it from?'

'There is a card.' It was in a small blank envelope tucked under the ribbon. Charlotte didn't quite have the courage to open it and read the message herself. As she turned away, she said, 'Thank you so much,' all sugary pleasant, to show how indifferent she was. Rewarded by Rachel Griffith's vexed expression.

The box wouldn't be forgotten now. Charlotte felt pleased with herself, making the connection with so much aplomb. How many other people could hand-deliver articles to the richest woman in the world and be sure they'd reach their destination? Baronski had taught her a damn sight more than etiquette and culture. There was an art to handling yourself in this kind of company. Perhaps that was why he had selected her. His scout in the orphanage staff must have recognized some kind of inherent ability. Character was more important than beauty in this game.

*

Charlotte let herself be talked into a couple of dances before she started looking for her new patron. She'd be damned if she didn't get some enjoyment out of the party. The young men were charming, as they always were when they thought they were conversing with an equal; both in their twenties, one of them was at university in Oslo. They were good dancers.

She thought she saw the creep from the airport while she was on the dancefloor, dressed in a waiter's white jacket. But he was on the other side of the ballroom, and he had his back to her, so it was hard to tell, and she certainly wasn't going to stop dancing to check.

She located Jason Whitehurst in one of the side rooms; it was a refuge for the older people, with plenty of big leather armchairs, and waiter service. The data profile from Baronski said Jason Whitehurst was sixty-six, a wealthy independent trader with a network of cargo agents all across the globe. She thought he looked like a Russian czar, straight backed, a pointed white beard, wearing the dress uniform of the King's Own Hussars. There was a discreet row of ribbons pinned on his chest. She recognized the one which was for the Mexico campaign. His eyes must have been implants, they were so clear, and startlingly blue.

According to the profile Jason Whitehurst had a son, but there was no wife. Charlotte was relieved about that. Wives were a complication she could do without. Some simply ignored her, others treated her like a daughter, the worst were the ones who wanted to watch.

Jason Whitehurst was in conversation with a couple of contemporaries, the three of them standing together with large brandy glasses in their hands. She walked right up and introduced herself.

'Ah yes, the old Baron told me you'd be here,' Jason Whitehurst said. His voice was beautifully clipped and precise. He left his friends with a brief wave.

She liked that, there was no pretence, no charade that she was a relative or a friend's daughter. It spoke of complete self-confidence; Jason Whitehurst didn't have to care what anyone else thought. He could make a good patron, she thought, people like him always did. A man who had made a success of his life wasn't inclined to quibble over trivia. Not that money ever came into it. There was an established routine, no need for vulgarity. And Baronski would never tolerate anyone who didn't play by the rules.

While she was with him, the patron would pay for all her clothes, her travel, incidentals; and there would be gifts, mostly jewellery, perfume, sometimes art, once a racehorse (she still laughed at Baronski's consternation over that). After it was over, after the patron had tired of her, Baronski would gather in all her gifts and pay her a straight twenty per cent.

'Are your bags packed?' Jason Whitehurst asked.

'Yes, sir.'

'Jason, please, my dear. Like to keep an informal house.'

She inclined her head.

'Good,' he said. 'We'll be leaving Monaco right after this blessed fandango.'

'Baronski said you were voyaging to Odessa,' she said. Always show an interest in their activities, make them think everything they do is important.

Jason Whitehurst stared at her. 'Yes. Have you been to Odessa before?'

'No, I'm afraid not.'

'Beastly place. I do a little trade there, no other reason to go. Lord knows what'll happen now Turkey's plugged in with Egypt, though. Still, not your concern. Phone your hotel, tell them my chauffeur will pick up your luggage; he'll take it down to the airport for you.

'Pardon me?'

'Now what?'

'I thought we were voyaging on your yacht?'

Jason Whitehurst pulled at his beard. She couldn't tell if he was amused or angry.

'Ought to read your data profiles a little closer, dear girl. Now then, I've got some people to see here first. So, in the mean time, I want you to find Fabian, get acquainted.'

'Your son?'

'That's right. Do you know what he looks like?'

She remembered the picture in the data profile, a fifteen-year-old boy with thick dark hair coming down over his ears. 'I think I can recognize him, yes.'

'Excellent. Just go where the noise is loudest, that's where he'll be. Now then, a few words of caution. Little chap doesn't have many real friends. My fault, I expect, keep him on board the *Colonel Maitland* all the time. Not terribly used to company, so make allowances, yes?'

'Certainly.'

'Good. I've told him you'll be meeting us here. Splendid girl like you is exactly what he needs. As you can imagine, he's looking forward to your company enormously, so don't disappoint him.'

'You want me . . .?' Charlotte trailed off in surprise.

'You and Fabian, yes. Problem?'

The idea threw her completely. But in the end, she supposed, it didn't make any real difference. 'No.' She found she couldn't look Jason Whitehurst in the face any more.

'Jolly good. I'll see the two of you in about an hour in my car. Don't be late.'

Jason Whitehurst marched off, leaving Charlotte alone with the realization that no matter how well you thought you knew them, the ultra-rich were not even remotely human.

*

Fabian Whitehurst was easy enough to find. There were only about fifteen boys and girls in their early teens at the ball, and they were all clustered together outside the entrance to the disco. They were giggling loudly, red faced as they swapped jokes.

Charlotte made a slow approach across the ballroom, taking her time to study them. She was only too well accustomed to the inherent brattishness of the children of the rich. Spoilt and ignored, they developed a shell of arrogance early in life, treating everyone else as third-class citizens. Including Charlotte; in some cases, especially Charlotte. Her throat muscles tensed at the memories.

These seemed no different, their voices grated from ten metres away, high pitched and raffish. The girls had been given salon treatments, fully made up, their hair in elaborate arrangements. They nearly all wore white dresses, though a couple were in low-cut gowns. There was something both silly and sad about the amount of jewellery they wore.

The boys were in dinner jackets and dress shirts. Charlotte was struck by their similarity, as if they were all cousins. Their cheeks chubby, moving awkwardly, making an effort to be boisterous. She imagined someone had told them *this* was the way you had to behave at parties, and they were all scrabbling to conform.

Then she caught sight of Fabian Whitehurst, the tallest of the group. His face didn't have quite the pampered look of the others. She could see some of his father's characteristics in his angled jawline and high cheekbones. Handsome little devil, she thought, he'll be a real handful when he grows up.

Fabian suddenly looked up. For the second time in one evening, Charlotte felt flustered. There was something *demanding* in his gaze. But he couldn't keep it going, blushing crimson and dropping his eyes quickly. She waited. Fabian glanced up guiltily. She lifted the corner of her mouth gently, a conspiracy smile, then let her attention wander away.

Julia Evans was dancing on the ballroom's wooden floor, with some ancient nobleman sporting a purple stripe across his tailcoat. Maybe there were penalties for being so rich, after all.

Charlotte knew that if she had that much money, she would've taken her pick of the handsomest young blades, the ones who could make her laugh and feel all light inside, and screw protocol. She took another sip of champagne.

'Er, hello, you look awfully bored,' Fabian said. He was standing in front of her, an oversize velvet bow tie spoiling the sartorial chic of his tailored dinner jacket. His shaggy hair was almost falling in his eyes as he looked up at her, he flipped it aside with a toss of his head.

'Oh dear, does it show?' she asked encouragingly. Out of the corner of her eye she could see all the other youngsters watching them with eager envious expressions.

'No. Well, sort of, a bit. I'm Fabian Whitehurst.' His eyes darted down to her cleavage, then away again. As if it was a dare.

'Yes, I know. Your father said I'd find you over here. I'm Charlotte Fielder. Pleased to meet you.'

'Crikey!' Fabian's gasp of surprise was almost a shout. He blushed hotly again at the solecism, his shoulders hunching up in reflex. His voice dropped to a whisper. 'You? You're Charlotte?' And for a moment every aristrocratic pretension was stripped away, he was an ordinary incredulous fifteen-year-old who didn't have a clue.

''Fraid so.' Training halted the giggle as it formed in her throat. But he was funny to watch.

'Oh.' A spark of jubilation burned in Fabian's eyes. 'I wondered if you would care to dance,' he said breathlessly.

'Thank you, I'd like that,' she said, and drained the glass.

Fabian's grin was arrogant triumph. They walked into the disco together, past Fabian's astonished friends. He gave them a fast thumbs up, lips curling into a smug sneer. Charlotte's serene smile never flickered.

3

Julia Evans's office occupied half of an entire floor in the Event
Horizon headquarters tower. When she sat at her desk the
window wall ahead of her seemed to recede into the middle
distance, a delusory gold band sandwiched between the expansive
flat plains of floor and ceiling.

The office was decorated in beige and cream colours, the
furniture all custom-made teak; work area, informal conference
area, leisure area, separated out by troughs of big ferns. Van
Goghs, Turners, and Picassos, selected more for price and
pretension than aesthetics, hung on the walls. It would have been
unbearably formal but for the crystal vases of cut flowers
standing on every table and wall alcove. Their perfume perme-
ated the air, replacing the dead purity of the conditioning units.

After her PAs politely but firmly ended her conference with
the company's senior transport division executives, Julia poured
herself a cup of tea from a silver service and walked over to the
window, turning down the opacity. Virtually the only reason
she had an office these days was for personal meetings; even
in the data age the human touch was still an essential tool in
corporate management, certainly at premier-grade level.

When the gold mirror faded away, she looked down on
Peterborough's old landbound quarter lazing under the July
sun, white-painted walls throwing a coronal glare back at her.
The dense cluster of brick and concrete buildings had a kind of

medieval disarray to them. She rather liked the chaos, it had an organic feel, easily preferable to the regimented soulless lines of most recent cities. Meticulous civic concepts like town planning and the green belt were the first casualties after the Fens had flooded; the refugees swooping on the city had wanted dry land, and when they found it they stubbornly put down roots. Their new housing estates and industrial zones erupted on any patch of unused ground. A quarter of a century on, and legal claims over land ownership and compensation were still raging through the county courts.

The old quarter had an atmosphere of urgency about it; there was still excitement to be had down on those leafy streets. From the few local newscasts Julia managed to see, she knew that smuggling was still a major occupation for the Stanground armada, a mostly quaybound collection of cabin cruisers, house-boats, barges, and motor launches that had flocked to the semi-submerged suburb from the Norfolk Broads. Unlicensed distilleries flourished; syntho vats were assembled in half-forgotten cellars, causing a lot of heat for the vice squad; brothels serviced visiting sailors; and tekmercs lived like princes in New Eastfield condominiums, ghouls feeding off company rivalries.

There was a certain romance about it all that appealed to a younger part of Julia's personality, the girlish part. Peterborough served as a kind of link to her past, and the few brief years of carefree youth she had been allowed before Event Horizon took over her life. She could have it all shut down, of course, if she'd wanted – ended the smuggling, sent the madams packing, banished the tekmercs. It was her city well enough; the Queen of Peterborough, the channels called her. And she did make sure that the police stamped down hard on any excesses, but held back from all-out sanitization; not so much out of sentiment these days, but because she recognized the need for the escape valve which the old quarter provided. There was no such laxity in the new sector of the city which was rising up out of the Fens basin.

Seventeen years ago, when Event Horizon returned to England

after the PSP fell, Peterborough had been approaching its infra-structure limits. It was becoming increasingly obvious that the kind of massive construction projects Julia and her grandfather envisaged just couldn't be supported by the existing utilities. The city's eastward sprawl was already up to the rotting remnants of the Castor Hanglands wood, and threatened to reach the A1 in another decade even without Event Horizon's patronage; there simply wasn't room for their proposed macro-industry precincts on land.

The solution was easy enough: the Fens basin was uninhab-ited, unused, and unloved; and west of Peterborough the water was only a couple of metres deep. So fifteen years ago the dredging crews and civil engineers moved out into the quagmire, and began to build the first artificial island.

From where she was standing, on the sixty-fifth floor of the Event Horizon tower, Julia could see all twenty-nine major islands of the Prior's Fen Atoll, as well as the fifteen new ones under construction. Event Horizon owned twelve of them: the seventy-storey tower which was the company's global head-quarters; seven cyber-factory precincts churning out household gear, cybernetics, light engineering, and giga-conductor cells; and four giant arcologies, each of them providing homes, employment, education, and leisure facilities for eleven thousand families.

Kombinates had followed Event Horizon to Peterborough, lured by Julia's offer of a lower giga-conductor licensing royalty to anyone who set up their production facilities in England. The subsequent rush of investment helped reinvigorate the English economy at a rate which far outstripped the rest of Europe, and allowed Julia to consolidate her influence over the New Conser-vative government.

It was those same kombinates and their financial backing combines who had built the rest of the Atoll she was looking down on, adding cuboidal cyber-factories, dome-capped circular amphitheatre apartment complexes, the city's international airport, and the giant pyramidal arcologies. Prior's Fen Atoll was now home to three hundred and fifty thousand people, with an industrial output ten times that of the land-bound portion of the city.

She could see the network of broad deep-water channels which linked the islands. Their living banks of gene-tailored coral were covered in sage reeds, showing as thin green lines holding the mud desert at bay. Container freighters moved along them, taking finished products from the arcologies and cyber-factories, and sailing down the kilometre-wide Nene to the Wash and the open sea beyond. The new expanded river course had been dredged deep enough so that the maritime traffic could even sail at low tide, most of the mud winding up as landfill on the airport island.

A thick artery of elevated metro rails stabbed out from the landbound city, splitting wide like a river throwing off tributaries. Individual rails arched over the deep-water channels to reach every island. Blue streamlined capsules slid along the delicate ribbons, slotting in behind one another at the junctions with clockwork precision. In all the time she had watched from her eagle's vantage point she'd never seen a foul-up.

But then, that was the way of this new conglomeration, she thought, no room for failure. That was why she preferred to gaze at the old quarter. The mega-structures of the Atoll, with their glossy lofriction surfaces bouncing the sun like geometric crystalline mountains, were a pointer to the future. It looked like shit.

The nineteen-sixties paranoids were right; the machines are taking over.

She shook her head as if to clear it, and finished her tea. The knowledge of her own power did funny things inside her brain. Whatever she looked at, she knew she could change if she wanted to – give that neighbourhood better roads and services, improve the facilities at that school, stop that tower block from being built. So much she could do, and once she did it without even stopping to think. There hadn't been so much as a tremble

37

of hesitancy when she began Prior's Fen Atoll. Now though, some of the old assurance was beginning to wear thin. Or maybe it was just age and cynicism creeping up on her.

Julia returned to her desk, a big teak affair with a green leather top. Her hands slid across the intaglio edges, feeling little snicks of roughness in the deepest insets. At least someone in England still knew how to work with wood. Cybernation hadn't engulfed everybody. She caught herself, frowning disparagingly. What a funny mood.

She touched the intercom pad. 'Is Troy here yet?'

'Reception said he's arrived,' said Kirsten McAndrews, her private secretary. 'He should be up in another five minutes. Do you want him to come straight in?'

'Call me first,' Julia said.

'The Welsh delegation is still here.'

'Oh, Lord, I'd forgotten about them. How's my schedule for this afternoon?'

'Tricky. You said you wanted to be home by four.'

'Yes. Well, if the last meeting doesn't run on I'll see them.'

'OK, I'll tell them.'

'And for Heaven's sake don't let them know my stylist has preference. If they do see Troy come through, tell them he's some kind of financial cartel president.'

'Will do.' There was an amused tone in Kirsten's voice.

Julia sank back into the chair, resignation darkening her mood further. The Welsh delegation had been laying siege to her office for over a week now; a collection of the most senior pro-independence politicians who urgently wanted to know her views on their country's bid for secession from the New Conservative-dominated Westminster parliament's governance. Event Horizon was currently considering sites for two new cyber-precincts, and Wales, under New Conservative rule, was one of the principal contenders. The referendum was due in another five weeks; it was a measure of their desperation that they were prepared to sit out in the lobby rather than hit the campaign trail. So far she had managed to avoid any comments, on or off the record.

Open Channel to SelfCores, she instructed her bioware processor implant.

Her view of the office was suddenly riddled with cracks, fracturing and spinning away. It always did that if she didn't close her eyes in time.

Everyone thought she ran Event Horizon with her unique sang-froid flare because of her five bioware node implants. They reasoned she simply plugged herself directly into the vast dataflows the company created to act as some kind of omnipotent technophile sovereign. Given that the nodes with their logic matrices and data storage space gave her an augmented mentality able to interpret reports in milliseconds and implement decisions instantaneously, it was an understandable mistake. Companies and kombinates gave their own premier-grade executives identical implants in the belief they could boost their own managerial control in the same fashion. None of them had ever come close to matching Event Horizon's efficiency.

Julia's consciousness slipped into a dimensionless universe; the body sensorium of colours, sounds, touch, and smell simply didn't apply here. Even her time sense was different, accelerated. She hung at the centre of three dense data shoals, like small galactic clusters, observing streams of binary pulses flash between the suns. They were bioware Neural Network cores, brains of ferredoxin protein: Event Horizon's true directorate. Their massive processing capacity enabled them to keep track of every department, follow up every project with minute attention, directing the company along the policy lines she formulated. Her confidence in them was absolute. All she did was review their more important decisions before authorization, a human fail-safe in the circuit.

Two of the NN cores had been grown by splicing her sequencing RNA into the ferredoxin, duplicating her neuronic structure. After that she had downloaded her memories into them. They echoed her desires, her determination, her guile, crafting Event Horizon with loving vigilance, uninterrupted by the multiple weaknesses of the body's flesh.

Calmness stole into her own thoughts, as if the rationality which governed this domain was seeping back through the linkage. Here, there was a subtle boost to her faith that all problems were solvable. It was just a question of correctly applied logic.

Good morning, she said.

You seem a bit peaky today, NN core one replied.

Yes, last night's Newfields' ball was a wash-out.

Total surprise. I don't know why you keep going to those dos.

To keep up appearances, I suppose, she answered.

Who for? NN core two asked.

There was a difference between the personalities of her two NN cores, slight but definite. Core two assumed a stricter attitude, more matriarchal. Julia always thought she must have been very up-tight the day she downloaded her memories into it.

Self-delusion is what makes the world go round, she said.

If other people believe everything's all hunky-dory with you, you might even begin to believe it yourself, said NN core one.

Something like that, yes, she admitted.

There's still no sign of him, then? NN core two asked.

Sensation penetrated the closed universe, a sliver of cold dismay trickling down her back. Royan had been missing for eight months now. Her lover, confidant, partner in crime, joy-bringer, keeper of the key to her heart, dark genius, father of her two children, haunted soul. Deliberately missing, as only he could be. Eight months, and the pain was still bright enough to hurt. And now worry was its twin.

You would know that, she said. *Best of all.* Their awareness was spread like a spectral web through the global data networks, alert for facts, whispers, and gossip they could use to Event Horizon's advantage. There were patterns to the flow of information, tenuous and confused, but readable to entities like the three NN cores. Everybody in the world betrayed themselves through the generation of data; you could not move, eat, wash, or make love without it registering in a memory core somewhere. Except for Royan, whose flight left no contrail of binary digits, mocking the most sophisticated tracker programs ever constructed.

What could someone with Royan's brilliance build in eight months? And why keep it a secret from her?

Shadow wings of sympathy folded round her, a sisterly embrace by two of the NN cores.

Don't fret yourself so, Juliet, the third NN core said gruffly. *He'll be back. Boy always was one for stunts, little bugger.*

Thank you, Grandpa, she said.

The thought patterns of Philip Evans reflected a brisk gratification.

He was a perfect counterbalance to her two NN cores, Julia thought, his cynicism and bluntness tempering her own gentler outlook. Together they made a truly formidable team. And one which was unlikely to be repeated. She knew of some kombinates who'd loaded a Turing managerial personality into a bioware number cruncher, hoping to recreate Event Horizon's magic formula that way. They hadn't met with much success. Instinct and toughness, even compassion, weren't concepts you could incorporate into a program. Neural Networks could possess such qualities, because they weren't running programs, they were genuine personalities. But at sixty million Eurofrancs apiece, an NN core wasn't the kind of project to be attempted on a speculative basis. And even if one was built, there was the question of whose sequencing RNA to use as a template, whose memories to download. If the person selected didn't have the right mindset to run the kombinate, it would be too late to change.

Philip Evans had done it because he was dying anyway. He had nothing to lose. It worked for him because he had a lifetime's experience of running the company in a dictatorial fashion. And it wasn't until she'd been in the hot seat for seven years that Julia had grown her first core.

I'm all right now, she said.

The intangible support withdrew.

My girl, her grandfather said proudly. At moments like this, he could be absurdly sentimental.

Let's get this morning's list crunched, Julia said. She opened her mind up to the stack of data packages the three NN cores had prepared over the past forty hours. There was no conscious thought involved, no rigorous assessment; she let the questions filter through her mind, instinct providing the answers.

They started with subcontracts; company names and products, their quality procedures, industrial relations record, financial viability, bid prices, and finally a recommendation. Julia would say yes or no, and the profile would be snatched away, to be replaced by the next. She couldn't remember them afterwards; she didn't want to remember them. That was the whole point. The system only involved her thought processes, not her memory, leaving her brain cells uncluttered.

Personnel was the second category. She handled the promotions and disciplining of everyone above grade five management herself. If only divisional managers knew how closely their boss really followed their careers . . .

Divisional review came next. Start-up factories' progress, retooling, enlargement programmes, new product designs.

Cargo fleets, land, air, rail, space, and sea.

New London biosphere maintenance.

New London second chamber progress.

Microgee materials processing modules.

Finance.

Energy.

Security.

Prior's Fen Atoll civil engineering.

That's the lot, said NN core one.

Julia consulted her nodes. Over eight thousand items in six and a half minutes. She couldn't remember one of them, although her imagination lodged an image of hard-copy sheets streaming by on a subliminal fast forward.

Any queries? she asked.

Only two, said her grandfather.

Says you, NN core two rebuked. *How you can think Mousanta is a problem I don't know.*

What are they? Julia asked, forestalling any argument.

Well, the three of us share a slight concern about Wales, NN core two said. *You are going to have to make a decision about who to support some time.*

I know, she said miserably. *I just don't see how I can win.*

So choose the option which causes the least harm, said her grandfather.

Which is?

For my mind, the Welsh Nationalists have promised Event Horizon a bloody attractive investment package if you go ahead and build the cyber-precincts. I say see the delegation, they are bound to improve on the offer. It would be a fantastic boost for them to come out and announce they've swung you over. Bloody politicians, never miss a trick.

In order for their promises to mean anything they have to win the referendum first, NN core two said patiently. *They're terrified you won't commit to a site until after the vote, of course. People won't vote for secession unless they're sure it will be beneficial. Which is what the Nationalists have been promising all along. Catch twenty-two, for them anyway. If they win the referendum and can't produce the jobs independence was supposed to bring they'll be lynched.*

Dead politicians, her grandfather chortled. *If I had a heart, it would be bleeding.*

Our civil projects development division has been getting daily calls from the New Conservatives' central office, NN core one said. *And the Ministry of Industry is pledged to Lord knows how much support funding if you build the precincts around Liverpool.*

What sort of concessions have they been offering Event Horizon if I do site the cyber-precincts in Wales?

Almost the same support deal, her grandfather said. *Officially. But Marchant has been playing his elder statesman go-between role to some effect; he's made it clear that the offer only stands providing the Nationalists lose the referendum, and you announce a cyber-*

precinct for Wales after that. It'll show the New Conservatives aren't neglecting the area.

Which is precisely why the Nationalists have been getting so much support in the first place, NN core one said. *Because Wales hasn't received much priority from this government.*

What would a Welsh secession do to the New Conservative majority? Julia asked.

Reduce it to eighteen seats. Which is why they're taking Wales so seriously for once. Chances are, with an independent Wales they'll lose their overall majority at the next general election.

After seventeen years, Julia mused. *That would take some getting used to.*

It wouldn't affect us much, NN core two said. *Not now, Event Horizon is too well established, in this country and abroad. And it's not as if any new government is going to introduce radically different policies. The party manifestos are virtually all variants on a theme; the only differences are in priorities. This new breed of politicians are all spin doctor bred, they don't pursue ideologies any more, only power itself.*

Whatever you do, Juliet, it wants to be done soon.

Yes, I suppose so.

We recommend one cyber-precinct is sited in Wales and one somewhere else, presumably Liverpool, NN core two said. *It's a compromise which makes perfect sense, and de-emphasizes your role in the referendum.*

Fine, I'll notify the development division.

That just leaves the question of timing the announcement.

She massaged her temple, wishing it would ease the strain deeper inside. *Yes, OK, leave it with me, I'll think about it. What was the second query?*

An anomaly I picked up on, Juliet.

A data package unfolded within her mental perception. Julia studied it for a moment. It was a bid which Event Horizon had put in for a North Italy solid state research facility, the Mousanta labs in Turin. Event Horizon's commercial intelligence office noted that the molecular interaction studies Mousanta was doing would fit in with a couple of the company's own research programmes. The finance division had made a buy-out offer to the owners, only to be outbid by the Globecast corporation.

Julia saw she'd turned down a request to make a higher bid. *So?*

So, why, Juliet, is Globecast, a company which deals purely in trash media broadcasts, making a too high offer for a solid state research lab?

Oh, come on, Grandpa; Clifford Jepson probably wants it to help with his arms sales. The chairman of Globecast had a profitable second occupation as an arms merchant. She knew that he handled a lot of extended credit underground sales to organizations which the US government didn't wish to be seen showing any open support. In consideration, Globecast's tax returns weren't scrutinized too closely.

Clifford is a middle-man, Juliet, not a producer.

You think there could be more to it?

It doesn't ring true, that's all.

Yes. OK, Grandpa, get commercial intelligence to take another look at Mousanta, what makes it so valuable. Perhaps they've got a black defence programme going for the North Italy government?

Could be.

Sort the details, then.

OK, girl. There was no mistaking his eagerness.

Exit SelfCores.

Julia was back in the office, grinning at her grandfather's behaviour. He did so love the covert side of company operations. One of the reasons he and Royan had got on so well, closeheads.

She was just refilling her teacup when the door opened and Rachel Griffith came in.

There weren't many people who could burst in on Julia Evans unannounced. And those that did had to have a bloody good reason, invariably troublesome.

Julia took one glance at Rachel's thin-lipped anxiety and knew it was bad. Rachel didn't fluster easily.

'What is it, Rachel?' Julia asked uneasily.

'God, I'm sorry, Julia. I just didn't pay it a lot of attention when she gave it to me.' Rachel Griffith held out a slim white flower-presentation box.

Julia took it with suddenly trembling fingers. The flower inside was odd, not one she'd seen before. It was a trumpet, fifteen centimetres long, tapering back to what she assumed was a small seed pod; the colour was a delicate purple, and when she looked down the open end it was pure white inside. There was a complex array of stamens, with lemon-yellow anther lobes. The outside of the trumpet sprouted short silky hairs.

She sent an identification request into her memory nodes' floral encyclopaedia section.

The envelope had already been opened; she drew out the handwritten card.

> *Take care, Snowy,*
> *I love you always,*
> *Royan*

Julia's eyes watered. It was his handwriting, and nobody else called her Snowy.

With her eyes still on the card she asked, 'Where did it come from?'

'Some girl handed it to me at the Newfields ball last night.' Rachel sounded worried. 'I don't know who she was, but she knew me. Never gave her name, just shoved it in my hands and told me to pass it on to you.'

Julia looked up. 'What sort of girl? Pretty?'

'She was a whore.'

'Rachel!'

'She was, I know the type. Early twenties, utterly gorgeous, impeccably dressed, manners a saint couldn't match, and lost eyes.'

There was no arguing, Julia knew, Rachel was good at that kind of thing, her years as a hardline bodyguard, constantly vigilant, had given her an almost psychic sense about people. Besides, Julia knew the sort of girl she was talking about, courtesans were common enough at events like the Newfields ball.

Her nodes reported that the flower species wasn't indexed in their files.

Open Channel to SelfCores. *Get me a match up for this, would you?* she asked silently. It was important she knew what he had chosen for her.

She looked back to the card, its bold script with over-large loops. She could remember him perfecting his writing, sitting at a narrow wooden table in her island bungalow, the sea swishing on the beach outside, his brow furrowed in concentration.

And the flower, the flower was the sealer. Royan adored flowers, and she always associated them with him, ever since the day when they finally met in the flesh.

Access Royan Recovery. She had node referenced the memory because she knew it would always be special, wanting to guard the details from entropic decay down the years.

*

Six of them had walked into the Mucklands Wood estate that afternoon fifteen years ago, all of them wearing English Army uniforms. Morgan Walshaw, Event Horizon's security chief at the time, who was quietly furious with her. It was the first (and last) time she had ever defied him over her own safety. Greg Mandel, who was as close to Royan as she was, and who'd agreed to lead them as soon as he'd heard she was going in. Rachel, who was her bodyguard back then, and two extra hardliners, John Lees and Martyn Oakly.

Mucklands Wood was the home of the Trinities, a bleak tower block housing estate which the city council had thrown up in the first couple of years after the Fens flooded. It stood on the high ground to the west of the A15, looking down on Walton where the Blackshirts were based. Two mortal enemies, separated by a single strand of melting tarmac and the luckless residential district of Bretton.

Rescuing Royan was more than a debt. Two years before, he

had saved Philip Evans from a virus that PSP leftovers had squirted into the NN core. One of the best hackers on the circuit, he had written an antithesis which purged the virus. He had never asked for payment. A strange kind of bond had developed between them afterwards. Both of them powers in their respective fields, both feared, both near friendless, both wildly different. The attraction/fascination was inevitable, affection wasn't, but it had come nevertheless. There was nothing sexual about the relationship, given the circumstances there couldn't be. Neither of them ever expected to meet in the flesh. But the association was mutually rewarding. Royan had helped Julia safeguard Event Horizon's confidential commercial data from his peers on the circuit, while Julia supplied the Trinities with weapons to continue their fight against the Blackshirts. She hated the Blackshirts almost as much as Royan did.

But only now was she seeing the real cost of sponsoring the Trinities. Nothing like the intellectual exercise of arranging shipments through Clifford Jepson. An action whose only reaction was the occasional item on the evening newscasts. She didn't have distance between her and the Trinities any more. Mucklands Wood wasn't the adventure-excitement she had expected, the little scary thrill of visiting the darkside. This was raw-nerve fear.

The struggle was all over now. There were no more Trinities, no more Blackshirts. Fires still burnt in both districts, sending up pillars of thick oily smoke to merge with the low bank of smog occluding the sky above the city. Half a squadron of Army tilt-fans orbited the scene slowly, alert for any more trouble.

Peterborough's usual dynamic sparkle had vanished, shops closed, factories shut. The city's frightened, shocked citizens were barricaded in their homes, waiting for the all-clear to sound. Both sets of protagonists had known this was the last time, the showdown, they hadn't held back.

Julia walked over hard-packed limestone. The whole estate was a barren wasteland. There were no trees or shrubs, even weeds were scarce; a greasy blue-grey moss slimed the brick walls of abandoned roofless employment workshops. The Trinities symbol was sprayed everywhere, raw and challenging, a closed fist gripping a thorn cross, blood dripping.

Two of the estate's high-rise blocks had been razed in the battle, toppling over after a barrage of anti-tank missiles had blown out the bottom floors. Julia's little group threaded its way past one, a long mound of broken twisted rubble, with metal girders sticking out at low angles. Squaddies picked their way over it gingerly, helping city firemen with their thermal-imaging sensors. Futile gesture really. She could see pieces of smashed furniture crushed between the jagged slabs of concrete, torn strips of brightly coloured cloth flapping limply, splinters of glass everywhere, dust thick in the air. A long row of bodies lay at the foot of the tower, covered in blankets. Some had dark wet stains.

Morgan Walshaw looked at her as they marched past. But she forced herself into an expression of grim endurance, and never broke stride.

A two-man patrol halted them. The squaddies in their dark-grey combat leathers and equipment webs didn't even seem human. Sinister cyborg figures cradling stub-barrelled McMillan electromagnetic rifles, bulbous photon-amp lenses giving their helmet visors an insect appearance, there wasn't a square centimetre of skin visible. She couldn't understand half of the gear modules clipped to their webs, and didn't bother consulting her nodes. She didn't want to know. All she'd come for was Royan.

Greg and Morgan Walshaw exchanged a few words, and the squaddies waved them on. They had been guarding the approach to a field hospital, three inflated hemispheres of olive-green plastic. Land Rovers and ambulances stood outside, orderlies hurrying between the bloody figures lying on stretchers. The empty white plastic wrappers of disposable first aid modules littered the ground; the oddest impression of the day, a dusting of giant snowflakes.

For the first time, Julia heard the sounds of the aftermath. The moans and screams of the wounded. Guilt sent icy spikes into her belly.

'Morgan,' she said in a small voice.

He glanced back at her, and she saw the genuine worry in his face. Despite the forty years between them, she had always considered him one of her closest friends.

'What?' he asked. There was an edge in his voice. He was ex-military himself. She wondered, belatedly, what sort of memories their visit must be raking up.

'I'd like to do something for the survivors. They'll need proper medical treatment after the Army triage. Lawyers too, probably.'

'I'll get on to it when we're finished here.' He dropped back to walk beside her. 'You holding out all right?'

'I'll manage.'

His arm went round her shoulder, giving her a quick comforting shake.

'Tell you, this is the one,' Greg said over his shoulder. He was indicating the high-rise block straight ahead.

It was identical to all the others left standing. Twenty storeys high, covered in a scale of slate-grey low-efficiency solar cell panels. Most of its windows had blown out. Fires had been extinguished on several floors, she could see the soot stains, like black flames, rising out of the broken windows, surrounding solar panels had melted and buckled from the heat.

'Been one hell of a scrap here,' Greg muttered.

The burnt-out wreckage of an old-style assault helicopter was strewn on the ground fifty metres from the tower. She stared at it, bewildered. Assault helicopters? In a gang war? Three military microlights were crumpled on the limestone around it, wing membranes shredded by laser fire.

There were several squaddies on sentry duty outside the tower, under the command of a young lieutenant who was waiting for them near the entrance. An intelligence officer, Julia knew; the Minister of Defence had assured her the lieutenant would be briefed about the need for total security.

The lieutenant snapped off a salute to Greg, then his eyes widened when he saw the Mindstar Brigade badge on Greg's shoulder. If anything he became even stiffer. Julia wondered what he would do if she lifted up her own silvered vizor to let him see who she was.

Greg returned the salute.

'Nobody has entered the tower since the firing stopped, Captain,' the lieutenant said. 'But apparently some of the Blackshirts penetrated it on the first day. There was a lot of fighting around here, they seemed to think it was important. Do you want my squad to check it out?'

Morgan Walshaw glanced up at the blank grey cliff in front of them. 'No, thank you. Give us forty-five minutes. Then you can commence a standard securement procedure.'

'Yes, sir.' The lieutenant had found the brigadier's insignia on Morgan Walshaw's uniform.

'At ease, lieutenant,' Morgan Walshaw said mildly.

Greg led them into the tower, leaving the lieutenant behind outside. He moved like a sleepwaker, eyes barely open. Julia knew he was using his bioware gland, neurohormones pumping into his brain to stimulate his psi faculty, espersense washing through the tower to detect other minds, seeing if anyone was lying in ambush. He always said he couldn't read individual thoughts, just emotional composition, but Julia never managed to feel convinced. His presence always exacerbated her guilt. Just knowing he could see it lurking in her mind made her concentrate more on the incidents she was ashamed over – losing her temper with one of Wilholm's domestic staff yesterday, twisting Morgan Walshaw's arm to come to Mucklands, the two boys she was currently stringing along – running loose in her mind and bloating the original emotion out of all proportion. An unstoppable upward spiral.

The inside of the tower was stark. Bullet craters riddled the entrance hall walls, none of the biolum panels were on. A titan had kicked in the two lift doors, warping and tearing the buffed metal. The shafts beyond were impenetrably black.

'Through here,' Greg said reluctantly. He put his shoulder to the stairwell door. John Lees and Martyn Oakly had to lend a hand before it finally juddered open wide enough for them to slip through.

There was a jumble of furniture behind it, and two bodies: Trinities, lads in their late teens. She looked away quickly. They had been trying to get out, pulling at the pile of furniture. Their backs were mottled with laser burns.

By the time they reached the eleventh floor, Julia was sweating hard inside the heavy uniform, her breath coming in deep gulps. Nobody else was complaining, not even Morgan Walshaw who was over sixty, so she kept quiet. But he could see the difference between being genuinely fit like the hardliners, and her own condition, which was arrived at by following a Hollywood celebrity's routine to keep her belly flat and her bottom thin. It was damn embarrassing; she was the youngest of the group.

Greg held an arm up for silence, he pointed to the door which opened on to the corridor. 'Someone a couple of metres inside. They're in a lot of pain, but conscious.'

'What do you want to do?' Morgan Walshaw asked.

'Bad tactics to leave a possible hostile covering your escape route.'

Morgan Walshaw grunted agreement, and signalled John Lees forwards. The hardliner drew his Uzi hand laser and flattened himself against the wall by the door. Greg tested the door handle, then nodded once, and pulled the door open. John Lees went through the gap with a quick professional twist.

Julia was always amazed by how fast her bodyguards could move. It was as if they had two sets of reactions, one for everyday use, and accelerated reflexes for combat situations. One time, she had asked Morgan Walshaw if it was drugs, but he'd just laughed annoyingly and said no, it was controlled fear.

'All clear,' John Lees called.

It was a boy in his early twenties, dressed in a poor copy of Army combat leathers. He was sitting with his back propped against the wall, helmet off. Both his legs were broken, the leather trousers ripped. A thick band of analgesic foam had been sprayed over his thighs. Blood covered the concrete floor beneath him. His face was chalk white, covered in sweat, he was shivering violently.

'A Blackshirt,' Greg said in a toneless voice.

The boy's eyes met Julia's, blank with incomprehension. He was the same age as Patrick Browning, one of her current lovers. She had never been so close to one of her sworn enemies before. Blackshirt firebombing was a regular event at her Peterborough factories, the cost of additional security and insurance premiums was a real curse.

'Don't hurt him,' she said automatically.

The boy continued his compulsive stare.

'Your lucky day,' Greg told him blandly. 'I've gone up against a lot of your mates in my time.' He pressed an infuser tube on the boy's neck, and his head lolled forwards.

'The Army will pick him up when they comb the tower,' Morgan Walshaw said. 'He ought to live.'

They carried on up the stairs to the twentieth floor. Greg halted at the door which opened into the central corridor, his eyes fully closed. Julia could hear her heart yammering. Rachel caught her eye, and winked encouragement.

'Is he alive?' Julia asked.

Greg's eyes fluttered open. 'Yeah.'

Julia let out a sob of relief. This hardly seemed real any more, it was so far outside her usual life. She thought she would feel anticipation, but there was only a sense of shame and despair. It had taken so many deaths to bring about this moment, mostly people her own age, denied any sort of future, good or bad. And all for an indecisive battle in a war which had ended four years ago. None of this had been strategic, it was basic animal blood-lust.

The corridor was a mess. There were no windows, the biolum strip had been smashed. Greg and Martyn Oakly took out powerful torches.

There was something five metres down the corridor, an irregular hump. At first she thought one of the tower's residents had dropped a big bag of kitchen rubbish, there was a damp meaty smell in the air. Then she saw the ceiling above had cracked open; three smooth dark composite cones poked down out of the gap. A battered helmet lay on the floor, alongside a couple of ammunition clips, and a hand. It still had a watch round the wrist.

Julia vomited violently.

The next minute was a blur. Rachel Griffith was holding on to her as she trembled. Everyone else gathered round, faces sympathetic. She didn't want that sympathy. She was angry with herself for being so weak. Embarrassed for showing it so publicly. She should never have come, it was stupid trying to be this macho. Morgan Walshaw had been right, which made her more angry.

'You OK?' Rachel Griffith asked.

'Yes.' She nodded dumbly. 'Sorry.'

Rachel winked again.

Bloody annoying.

Julia got a grip on herself.

Greg turned the handle of room 206, the door opened smoothly. There was a hall narrower than the corridor outside, then they were in Royan's room.

That was when she saw the flowers. It was so unexpected she barely noticed the rest of the fittings. Half of the room was given over to red clay troughs of flowering plants. She recognized some – orchids, fuchsias, ipomoeas, lilies, and petunias – a beautiful display, lucid colours, strong blooms. Not a dead leaf or withered petal among them. The plants were tended by little wheeled robots that looked like mobile scrap sculptures, the junked innards of a hundred different household appliances bolted together by a problem five-year-old. But the clippers, hoses, and trowel blades they brandished hung limply. For some inane reason she would have liked to see them in action.

Past the plant troughs a wall had been covered by a stack of ancient vacuum-tube television screens, taken out of their cabinets and slotted into a metal framework. Julia ducked round hanging baskets of nasturtiums and Busy Lizzies. She saw a big workbench with bulky waldos on either side of it. The kind of 'ware module stacks she was familiar with from Event Horizon's experimental laboratories took up half of the available floor space.

A camera on a metal tripod tracked her movements. Its fibre-optic cables were plugged into the black modem balls filling Royan's eyesockets. He sat in a nineteen-fifties vintage dentist's chair in the middle of the room.

Julia smiled softly at him. She knew what to expect, Greg had told her several times. When he was fifteen, Royan was a committed Trinities hothead, taking part in raids on PSP institutions, sabotaging council projects. Then one night, in the middle of a food riot organized by the Trinities, he wasn't quite quick enough to escape a charge of People's Constables. The Constables' chosen weapon was a carbon monolattice bullwhip; wielded properly it could cut through an oak post three centimetres in diameter. After Royan had fallen, two of them set about him, hacking at his limbs, lashing his back open. Greg led a counter attack by the Trinities, hurling Molotovs at the People's Constables. By the time he got to Royan, the boy's arms and legs had been ruined, his skin, eyes, and larynx scorched by the flames.

Royan's torso was corpulent, dressed in a food-stained T-shirt; his arms ended below the elbows; both legs were short stumps. Plastic cups were fitted over the end of each amputated limb, ganglion splices, from which bundles of fibre optic cables were attached, plugging him into the room's 'ware stacks.

The bank of screens began to flicker with a laborious determination. The lime-green words that eventually materialized were a metre high, bisected by the rims of individual screens as they flowed from right to left.

JULIA. NOT YOU. NOT YOU HERE.

''Fraid so,' she said lightly.

NEVER WANTED YOU TO COME. NOT TO SEE ME. SHAME SHAME SHAME. Royan's torso began to judder as he rocked his shoulders, mouth parting to show blackened buck teeth.

Julia wished to God she could interface her nodes direct with his 'ware stacks here, they normally communicated direct through Event Horizon's datanet. Speedy, uninhibited chatter on any subject they wanted, arguing, laughing, and never lying; it was almost telepathy. But this was painfully slow, and so horribly public. 'The body is only a shell,' Julia said. 'I know what's inside, remember?'

OH SHIT, A RIGHT SMART-ARSE.

'Behave yourself,' Greg said smartly.

HELLO, GREG. I KNEW YOU WOULD COME. GOING TO HAUL ME OUT OF THE FLAMES AGAIN?

'Yeah.'

HIDE ME UNTIL THE ARMY HAS GONE.

'No,' Julia said. 'It's over, Royan.'

NEVER. THERE ARE STILL THOUSANDS OF PSP OUT THERE. I'LL FIND THEM, I'LL TRACK THEM DOWN. NO ONE ESCAPES FROM ME.

'Enough!' she stamped her foot. Tears suddenly blurred her vision. 'It's horrible outside. You Trinities and Blackshirts, all lying dead. They're our age, Royan. They could have had real lives, gone to school, had children.'

STOP IT.

'I won't have it in my city any more. Do you hear? It stops. Today. Now. With you. You're the last of the Trinities. I'm not having you start it up again.'

I CANT HAVE A LIFE. I'M NOT HUMAN. BEAST BEAST BEAST.

Julia's resolution turned to steel. 'And the first thing you can do is stop feeling so bloody sorry for yourself,' she said coldly.

SORRY. YOU THINK THIS IS SORRY? BITCH BITCH BITCH. WHAT DO YOU KNOW? COSSETTED PAMPERED BILLIONAIRESS BITCH. HATE YOU. VILE.

'You're coming to the Event Horizon clinic,' she said. 'They'll sort you out.'

Royan began to twist frantically in his dentist's seat. NO. NOT THAT. NOT HOSPITAL AGAIN.

'They won't hurt you. Not my doctors.'

WON'T WON'T WON'T GO. NO!

'You can't stay here.' Julia was aware of how unusually quiet

Morgan Walshaw was, the other hardliners, too. But they didn't understand, deep down Royan wanted to be normal again, she'd seen his soul, its flaws, weeping quietly to itself. The fear barrier stopped him, the time he'd spent in the city hospital after the riot had been a living medieval hell, blind, voiceless, immobile. It had taken a long time for the health service to release funds for his ganglion splices and optical modems.

STOP HER, GREG. YOU'RE MY FRIEND. DON'T LET HER UNPLUG ME.

'Julia's right,' Greg said sadly. 'Today was the end of the past. There's no more anti-PSP war to be fought.' He took an infuser out of his pocket.

NO NO NO. PLEASE GREG. NO. I'LL BE NOTHING WITHOUT MY 'WARE NOTHING NOTHING NOTHING. BEG YOU. BEG.

Morgan Walshaw moved to stand in front of the camera on the tripod. Royan was shaking his head wildly. Julia pressed her hand across her mouth, exchanging an agonized glance with Greg. He discharged the infuser into Royan's neck.

The letters on the screens dissolved into bizarre shimmers of static. Royan worked his mouth, wheezing harshly. 'Please, Julia,' he rasped. 'Please no.' Then the infusion took hold, and his head dropped forwards.

Julia found herself crying softly as Rachel Griffith hugged her. Greg and Morgan Walshaw hurriedly unplugged Royan's optical fibres from the 'ware stacks.

They trooped up the service stairs to the roof, Greg and Martyn Oakly carrying Royan on an improvised stretcher. Julia held his camera, careful not to get the cables caught on anything.

One of Event Horizon's tilt-fans, painted in Army colours, picked them up. It rose quickly into the overhanging veil of filthy smoke, away from curious squaddies, and the prying camera lenses of channel newscast crews. Julia looked down through a port at the broken landscape below, emotionally numb. The damage was dreadful, Mucklands Wood's desolated towers, Walton's smashed houses. So many bystanders made homeless, she thought; and this was the poorest section of the Peterborough, they didn't have much clout in the council chamber. She was going to have to do something about that, not just rebuilding homes, but bring hope back to the area as well. That was the only real barricade against the return of the miasmal gangs.

*

Now, fifteen years later, she could allow herself some degree of comfort with the result. From her office she could just make out the heavily wooded park and prim white houses, there were schools and light manual industries, an open-air sports amphitheatre, a technical college, the artists' colony. The residents of Mucklands and Walton could believe in their future again.

We can't find any reference to the flower, NN core one told her.

She focused slowly on the presentation box in her hands, her mind still lingering on the showy array of blooms in Royan's room. He told her later he grew them for their scent; smell was one of the few natural senses he had left. He put a lot of weight on flowers.

Are you sure? she asked.

Absolutely, it's not in Kew Gardens' public reference memory cores. They are the most comprehensive in the world.

Access all the botanical institutes you can. It has to be listed somewhere.

She frowned at the delicate enigmatic mauve trumpet. Why, after eight months without a word, would he send an unidentifiable flower?

4

For ten months of the year Hambleton village slumbered tranquilly under the scorching English sun, the rural idyll of a nineteenth century that existed only in wishful daydreams and apocryphal historical dramas. It was nestled at the western end of a long whale-back peninsula which jutted out into the vast Rutland Water reservoir, surrounded by a quilt of lush citrus groves which had sprung up in the aftermath of the Warming. Through those quiet ten months the groves were maintained by a handful of labourers who lived locally. But twice a year the trees fruited, and the peninsula played host to an invasion of travellers which quadrupled the population overnight. Such an influx could never be anything other than a rumbustious fiesta, awaited with a mixture of trepidation and delight by the residents.

This July the convoy of travellers hunting work at the groves stretched the entire length of the road which ran along the peninsula spine. There were genuine horse-drawn gypsy caravans, brightly painted in primary colours with elaborate trim; twentieth-century vans with long strips of bright chrome, bulky custom-built trailers towed by four-wheel-drive Rangers, converted buses, and sleek ultra-modern land cruisers. Kids screamed and ran among the stationary vehicles, playing their incomprehensible games. Dogs barked excitedly and tripped the children. Goats and donkeys added their querulous cries to the hullabaloo. Adults stood in groups round the cabs talking in quiet murmurs. Smells of cooking drifted through the stifling air.

From where Greg Mandel stood at the gate of the camp field it looked like a real carnival. He always enjoyed the first two weeks of July, blistering heat, fruit hanging ripe in the groves, the campfire meals, music and dancing under the stars. There were even the odd days when they got some picking done.

'Roll it through,' he yelled up at the driver in the trailer cab. The vehicle had been converted from a redundant Army AT Hauler chassis, eight metres long, with six wheel sets. It rumbled into the field, leaving deep ruts in the mud.

'How many is that?' he asked Christine, his eldest daughter.

'Nineteen. Room for lots more yet, no messing.' She grinned happily. The twice-yearly picking seasons were dizzy times for the four Mandel children. New faces, old friends, no school, late nights, extra money for helping with the crop.

'How many teams do you want this year?' Derek Peters asked. He was standing beside Greg, a grizzled old family chief, wearing dungarees and a porkpie hat. He was the first traveller to arrive looking for work when Greg and Eleanor moved into the rundown farm sixteen years ago. Since then he'd been back each time, in summer for the oranges and limes, and November for the smaller tangerine crop. He knew most of the travellers, advising Greg who to take on, who the trouble makers were.

'About thirty-five,' Greg said. 'That ought to see us through. There was a lot of blossom in the east grove this year.'

'You'll make it to kombinate level yet,' Derek said.

Greg shrugged, inwardly pleased by the compliment. The year he and Eleanor began converting the farm's old meadows, he had struggled to plant two groves in time for his first crop; now he had nearly fifty hectares of the Hambleton peninsula covered with gene-tailored citrus trees. All of them on the prime southern slope where they received the most sunlight.

There were eleven other citrus plantations on the peninsula, taking advantage of the reservoir's superabundance of water to irrigate the thirsty trees. But the Mandel plantation was easily the largest, which meant Greg was invariably elected chairman of the local Citrus Growers' Association. His cosy lifestyle, his respectability, was something he looked upon with a strong sense of irony. Not that he would ever consider abandoning the groves, not now.

When he and Eleanor set up their new home on the peninsula he hadn't been at all sure of the idea. Up until then his life had been given over almost exclusively to combat or conflicts of one kind or another. A professional soldier, he had joined the Army at eighteen, serving in a paratroop regiment until the joint services' psi-assessment test found him to be esp positive; where-upon he wound up with a hurried transfer to the newly formed Mindstar Brigade. After the Army came the Trinities, and a hot brutal decade slugging it out against the People's Constables on Peterborough's streets. But unlike the majority of the Trinities he made an attempt to cut free once the PSP fell; living in an old time-share estate chalet on the shore of the reservoir, trying to make ends meet as a private detective. A role his espersense made him ideal for.

Two years spent grubbing away on desultory poorly paid cases and enduring lonely bachelor nights. Two years trying to build a reputation for professionalism and competence. And ultimately it paid off. He was hired by Event Horizon to track down the source of a security violation in their orbital factory. The case grew in size and complexity until he was finally con-fronting some PSP relics who had squirted a virus into Philip Evans's NN core. At the same time Eleanor came into his life. The two events combining to change his mundane world out of all recognition.

An extremely grateful Julia paid him a ridiculously lavish fee for resolving the case. They could have lived quite comfortably off the interest alone, which made the prospect of carrying on as a detective seem stupid. But they had to do something, aristocratic lotus-eating, endless parties, and global tourism didn't appeal to either of them. So they bought the farm: Greg had been a picker before often enough, a good supply of ready cash during the PSP years; and Eleanor grew up on an agricultural kibbutz.

By and large, it had been a good choice. Apart from one relapse, when Julia had used something approaching moral blackmail to coerce him into helping the police with a murder investigation which threatened to tarnish Event Horizon's esteem, his previous life drifted away from him. He was happy to let it. The old memories of violence and sorrow grew progressively more inaccessible, veiled by a cold discouraging fog.

The next vehicle trundled up to the camp field's gate. Greg reckoned this year's convoy was the largest yet. With the New Conservatives giving road repair a high priority, traffic in general was on the increase. Another ten years would have people worrying about gridlock again – he had to explain the word to Christine, a relic of his own youth. To someone who had grown up with roads that were little more than moss-clogged tracks it was an unbelievable concept. But three years ago the big Transport Department remoulder vehicle had laid a thermo-hardened cellulose strip over Hambleton peninsula's crumbling tarmac road, and she had fallen into thoughtful silence. That was one part of the post-Warming boom he could do without. But with each of Hambleton's plantations taking on pickers the convoy families should all find work this summer. He ought to bring that up at the next Association meeting; if they ever had to start turning away large numbers it could lead to resentment. Maybe he could sound Derek out about it first. He scrawled a quick note on his cybofax wafer.

'Hey wow,' Christine growled.

Greg looked up at the new arrivals. Two boys driving an old blue-sprayed ambulance, he could just make out the words Northampton Health Authority down the side.

'Alan and Simon,' Derek said. 'Cousins.'

Everybody was a cousin or an in-law, if they weren't they didn't get past the gate. Greg never could work out what qualified them as family, it certainly wasn't anything as simple as genetics.

'First year by themselves,' Derek added.

Greg could see that for himself, they were both about twenty, fresh-faced and apprehensive. The ambulance's tyres were bald. 'You ever done any picking before?' he asked.

'Yes, sir,' the driver said. 'Ever since I could climb a ladder, maybe before, too.'

'And you are?'

'Simon, sir.'

'Can you do anything else?' Christine asked. There was a purring challenge in her voice.

Simon broke into a sudden ingratiating smile. From his position in the passenger seat, Alan was craning over Simon's shoulder, staring.

Greg sent out a silent prayer. Christine was fifteen years old, and developing a figure as grand as her mother's. The lime-green cap-sleeve T-shirt she was wearing proved that; and now he thought about it, her cut-off jeans were high and tight. None of her clothes were exactly little-girlish any more. He supposed that one day he really ought to talk to her about boys and sex, except that he had always sort of assumed Eleanor would do that. Coward, he told himself silently.

Simon's mouth had opened to answer her, but then he took in Greg's impassive expression and Derek's scowl, and decided not to chance it. 'We can help with the cooking. And I have an HGV licence,' he offered.

'Any mechanical problems, and I'm your man,' Alan added. 'City and Guilds diploma in transport power systems.'

Greg made a note on his cybofax.

'Mr Mandel lets you in, then you work from dawn to dusk,' Derek said. 'I told him you was good boys; you fuck up, you make me a liar, you disgrace your family.'

From anyone else it would have been absurdly over the top. But Simon and Alan suddenly looked panicky.

'We want to work,' Simon insisted. 'We didn't drive two hundred klicks for fun.'

Greg ordered a low-level secretion from his gland. In his imagination it was a slippery lens of black muscle, pumping away enthusiastically, oozing milky liquids. It was an illusion he had somehow never quite managed to shake off. Reality was far more banal. The gland was an artificial endocrine node which the Army had implanted in his skull, absorbing blood, and refining a devilish cocktail of psi-enhancing neurohormones to exude into his synapses.

The Army saw psychics forming a super-intelligence-gathering task force, pinpointing enemy locations, divining their generals' strategies, opening up a whole chapter of information that would ensure victory. The Mindstar Brigade never quite lived up to those initial hopes, although it retained a fearsome reputation. Psi wasn't an exact science, human brains were stubbornly recalcitrant, and not everybody could take the psychological pressure.

After his encouraging test results, the project staff had expected Greg to develop a formidable sixth sense, seeing through brick walls, seeking out tactical data over twenty kilometres. Instead, he wound up with the ability to perceive people's emotions, their fears and hopes, knowing instantly when someone was lying. It was useful for counter-intelligence work, but hardly justified the expense.

His gland also cultivated a strong intuitive sense, although official opinion was divided on that. Greg knew it was real. One time in Turkey during the Jihad Legion conflict, he had tried to convince his company commander it was too risky crossing a valley floor. The major hadn't listened, putting it down to the usual squaddie superstition about open ground. Eight of the company had been lost when the Apache attack helicopters swam out of the cloudless sky, another fifteen were stretcher cases.

Greg felt his perception altering as the neurohormones bubbled through his brain, the world receding slightly, becoming grey and shadowy. The tightly wound thought currents of the two boys in the ambulance shone out at him. It was like watching fluid neon streamers swirling in surreal patterns, a cryptic semaphore message he alone could read.

He always checked over newcomers, just to make sure he wasn't letting any vipers into Hambleton's rustic peace. But neither of the boys were harbouring anything sinister, no malice or secret disdain, there was just a flutter of nerves as they waited for his answer, a genuine urge to work. And in Alan's case, a high-voltage sparkle of admiration for Christine.

The one thing Greg never used his espersense for was checking up on his own children. He'd always promised himself that. Paranoid parents were the last thing a growing kid needed. So he stopped short of seeing how interested Christine really was with the two boys, preferring trust instead. Besides, she already had three serious boyfriends that he knew of.

Christine brushed some of her long titian hair aside, tucking it behind her ear. 'Two hundred kilometres; where have you come from?' she asked the boys.

'York,' Alan said.

'Oh, I think that's such a wonderful city. I always love visiting it.'

'We'll give it a shot,' Greg said hurriedly, trying to regain control.

'Thank you, sir,' Simon said, grinning broadly. 'We'll show you haven't made a mistake.'

'Right. Park down beside the torreya tree. Make sure to put some wood underneath your wheels, the ground's wet. OK? And don't cut down any trees in the copse.' He pointed at the block of Chinese pine saplings beyond the groves. 'We provide logs.'

'Yes, sir.'

The ambulance's hub motors engaged with a light whine.

'And don't you piss in the reservoir,' Derek yelled after them. Simon's hand waved from the open window.

'You've never been to York,' Greg said to Christine.

She started giggling. 'Oh, Dad, what's that got to do with anything?'

Greg gave up. 'Right, that's twenty. Who's next?'

A pair of hands were placed over his eyes. 'I thought you always told me it was impossible to creep up on a psychic,' a woman's voice said in his ear.

Christine squealed. 'Aunty Julia!'

Greg turned round to see Christine hugging Julia Evans. He gave her a lame grin. 'Listen, you, it's more than possible when a psychic is having a day like this one.'

'I know the feeling.' Julia gave him a kiss, just a little bit longer than politeness dictated.

Greg slapped her bottom. 'Behave yourself.' When Julia was seventeen she'd had a mild crush on him, a psychic detective and ex-hardline resistance fighter was so far outside her usual experience she thought it terribly romantic, the ultimate in mysterious strangers. Greg was suddenly aware of Derek shuffling uncomfortably. He introduced Julia, privately amused by Derek's consternation when he realized that, yes, it really was *the* Julia Evans. 'Did you bring Daniella and Matthew with you?' he asked.

'Yes, I've just picked them up from Oakham School. They went on into the house.'

'Picked them up from school,' Greg chuckled. 'Just an ordinary working mum, huh?'

Julia grinned. 'Looks like you've got a good crop this year,' she said.

'Best yet.' He caught sight of Victor Tyo, Event Horizon's security chief, standing respectfully a couple of metres behind Julia. A slender Euroasian with an adolescent's face and thick black hair, he had slung his suit jacket over one shoulder, white shirt undone at the collar. At forty years old, he was young for the job, but Greg had worked with him on the virus case, Victor Tyo had what it took. That too young face was a misdirection, the brain behind could have been made from solid bioware.

66

There weren't many tekmercs who chanced going up against Event Horizon these days.

Greg shook Victor's hand warmly. 'Where are Julia's bodyguards? You're far too old for hardlining now.'

'Hey,' Victor Tyo spread his arms. 'You speak for yourself.' He gestured with one hand. A nineteen-fifties Rolls Royce Silver Shadow was parked on the drive just above the farmyard, two sober-faced hardliners in ash-grey suits standing beside it.

Greg rolled bis eyes. 'My God, it's the camouflage detachment.' On the road at the top of the drive a flock of children was forming, plotting dark misdeeds.

A horse-drawn caravan had pulled up in front of the gate, painted bright scarlet with yellow and blue trim. Greg recognized Mel Gainlee holding the reins, a spry pensioner who'd been coming to Hambleton for almost as long as Derek. He waved hopefully to Greg.

'Christine.'

She was staring across the field to where the ambulance was parking.

'What?' she asked guiltily.

Greg handed her his cybofax wafer, glancing at the logo on the bottom right corner. Thankfully it was Event Horizon's triangle and flying-V. That could have been embarrassing. 'You and Derek sort the rest of the teams out for me, OK?' His intuition had been sending out subtle warnings since he saw Victor Tyo had accompanied Julia. Victor was a good friend, but he didn't make social calls in the middle of the working week. Neither did Julia, come to that.

Christine's face coloured slightly. 'Sure, Dad,' she agreed seriously.

Greg felt a burst of pride. She really was growing up.

*

'She's quite something,' Julia said as she and Victor Tyo walked with Greg down the rough track back to the farmhouse. Her bodyguards had fallen in a regulation ten paces behind. The kids on the road were letting off wolf-whistles.

'Yeah.' Greg couldn't stop smiling.

'Sorry if we interrupted. I'd forgotten what a pandemonium Hambleton is at picking time.'

'No problem. Derek knows who to let through. I only put in an appearance for form's sake.'

'Where do they all come from?' She gazed back towards the heat-soaked convoy.

'From all over, of course.'

The E-shaped farmhouse had been added to and extended over the years, bricks and stone and composite sheeting were all in there somewhere, hidden under a shaggy coat of reddish-green ivy. The steeply angled roof was made entirely from polished black solar panels. A couple of satellite dishes were mounted on the western gable end, pointing into the southern sky. The larger of the two was faded and scratched, obviously second hand, with a complicated-looking aluminium receiver at the focus.

A gaggle of geese scattered, honking loudly as the five of them walked into the farmyard.

'That's new,' said Julia, pointing at the satellite dishes.

'Oliver put it up,' Greg explained. 'The boy's gone astronautics crazy. He picks up all sorts of spacecraft communication traffic on it. Wants to go and live in New London. So Anita's decided she's going to live in a Greenland commune.' Oliver and Anita were eleven-year-old twins, and took a savage joy in trying to be total opposites.

Greg had planted evergreen magnolias around two sides of the farmyard, the third side was defined by a long wooden barn. The planks for which had come from the dead deciduous trees in Hambleton Wood. It was full with white kelpboard boxes ready for the picking, the stacks reaching up to the roof. Three tractors were drawn up outside, their wheels thick with mud.

Julia looked at them pensively. 'I really ought to have remembered this was the main fruit season.'

'No reason why you should. Fruit picking isn't something Event Horizon has cybernated.'

'Oh, you!' She poked him in mock exasperation as Victor Tyo laughed.

It was cooler inside the house, conditioners filling the air with a slightly clammy refrigerated chill. Greg led Julia and Victor Tyo into the sun lounge, checking quickly to see if any of the children's toys were lying about underfoot. The room had a white-tile floor, furnished with a pair of twisted-cane frame chairs and a three-seater settee. Benji, the family parrot, was climbing delicately over the outside of his cage.

A broad bay window looked out over the huge southern prong of Rutland Water. White wooden hireboats from the fishing lodge at Normanton bobbed about on the blue water, windsurfers and sailing yachts zipped round them. Red-faced cyclists pedalled along a narrow track just above the far shoreline, sweltering in the tropical heat of the English summer.

Greg relished the view, he had grown up in the small arable county, lived on the shore of the reservoir for over twenty-five years. The Berrybut time-share estate was almost directly opposite the farm; in the evening he and Eleanor would watch the nightly bonfire blaze in the centre of the horseshoe of chalets, remembering earlier, simpler times.

Eleanor came into the sun lounge, walking carefully, stiff-backed from her seven-month pregnancy.

Greg caught Victor Tyo throwing him a startled glance as Eleanor and Julia embraced. It added to his growing sense of unease.

'Victor.' Eleanor was smiling as she kissed the security chief. 'Never see enough of you. Found a girl you can settle down with yet?'

'Eleanor,' Greg protested.

'There is someone,' Victor agreed defensively.

'Good, you can bring her round to dinner. We'd love to meet her.'

'You never mentioned her to me,' Julia said.

Victor Tyo sent a silent dismayed appeal to Greg.

'Sit down,' Greg said. 'And you two, behave; stop trying to embarrass Victor.' He snagged Eleanor round her waist and urged her over to the settee.

'Oliver, Anita and Richy are out in the stables,' Eleanor said. 'I sent Matthew and Daniella out to find them. One of the mares has just foaled.'

Julia groaned. 'They'll only want to bring it back to Wilholm with them.'

Greg put his arm around Eleanor, enjoying the feel of her as she leant in against him. 'So what did you come for?' he asked.

Julia had the grace to look mildly guilty. 'Royan.'

'You've heard from him?' Eleanor asked.

'Sort of.'

She handed Greg a slim white box, explaining about the unknown girl at the Newfields ball.

The trumpet flower inside was drooping, its light fuzz of hairs curling up. Greg's intuition strummed a quiet string of warning. Something about the flower was desperately wrong. He couldn't begin to guess what.

'And there was just the one card with it?' he asked.

'Yes.'

He gave the box to Eleanor.

'I don't recognize it,' Eleanor said. 'What sort is it?'

Julia shot Victor Tyo a nervous questioning glance. The security chief shrugged.

'That's where the real problem begins,' Julia said. 'My NN cores ran a search through every botanical memory core they could access. Nothing. They drew a complete blank. No big deal about that, there are a lot of new gene-tailored varieties on the market; can't keep track of everything. So I sent it down to the lab for genetic sampling, see if we could find what it was derived from, the parent species.' She drew a breath, pressing her palms together. 'It's extraterrestrial.'

'Alien?' Greg felt a fast twist of cold fear. Gone. With his sensitivity, no wonder the flower had triggered a mild wave of xenophobia. He stared at the flower; intuition shouting loud and clear what Julia was going to ask him to do next. Eleanor's weight pressed against him, she was giving Julia a doleful accusing look.

'It can't be,' Eleanor said. 'It's no different to any other flower.'

Greg could sense a stiff form of revulsion growing in her mind; she wanted to reject the whole notion.

'A flower is a very simple organism,' Julia said, the slightest quaver in her voice betraying the severe fright Greg was observing in her thoughts. 'It attracts insects to assist in pollination, nothing more. Naturally an alien flower will look similar to our own.'

'So this planet it came from has bees as well, does it?'

'The individual species of plants and animals won't resemble ours, but given a planet with anything remotely approaching Earth's climate they will certainly be analogous. Evolutionary factors will remain pretty constant throughout the universe, the simplest solution always applies. Think how many plants have developed since life began on Earth, all of them variants on a central theme.'

'What rubbish.'

'Please, Eleanor,' Julia said painfully. 'I wish you were right, I really do. I wanted the geneticists to be completely wrong. But the flower has nothing like our DNA. The chromosome-equivalents are toroidal, arranged in concentric shells. My geneticists say the sphere they form is unholy complex, and definitely not from this solar system.'

'For complex, read "advanced",' Victor Tyo said. 'The geneticists estimate the source planet could be anything up to a couple of billion years further up the evolutionary ladder than Earth. The gene sphere is much larger than terrestrial DNA strands.'

It didn't really register with Greg, nonsense numbers. He ordered a gland secretion, concentrating inwards. There was no truth to be gained from intuition, only a sense of what might be, hints. He scrambled round for a sign of fear, that the flower was dangerous. But there was only the original tremendous unease, amplified to a cloying presence. He imagined this was what being haunted must be like.

He rose from the near-trance state.

'The flower,' Greg said. 'It's not lethal, but I get a sense of weight behind it, a pressure building up.'

'The aliens?' Victor Tyo asked.

'No,' Greg gave him a wry smile. 'No spaceships, no Martian invasion fleet. But there's something . . . biding time.'

'There is a ship, something had to bring it here,' Victor said. 'They're close, watching us, hell they're probably even down here among us. How would we know? We've no idea what they look like, what they're capable of. God Almighty, entities from another planet.' Perhaps it was just the emphasis his boyish face gave to any deeply felt emotion, but Victor's dismay seemed to be on the point of crushing him.

'Aliens might have the technological advantage over us,' Greg said. 'But I'd be very surprised if they could land on Earth without the strategic defence networks picking them up. Am I right, Julia?'

She gave a subdued nod. 'Yes. The sensor coverage is good, it has to be given the potential for kinetic assaults. You could orbit a ship two hundred thousand kilometres out without being spotted, fair enough, but the chances of detection increase with every kilometre you travel closer to Earth. Once you're within fifteen thousand kilometres of the surface you're visible. It doesn't matter how good your stealth technology is, any physical body passing through the planetary magnetosphere generates a flux that the sensors will pick up. We're tracking hundreds of thousands of objects up there, anything from discarded solar panels to composite bolts.'

'So where did the flower come from?' Eleanor asked.

Julia shook her head slowly. 'I don't know. And that's what really worries me. I can't believe even aliens have the ability to circumvent our technology to that extent.'

'You said you could feel a pressure,' Victor said. 'What kind of pressure?'

Greg shrugged, uncertain how to express it in words. 'Something waiting.'

'Look,' Julia said. 'We know there's been some kind of first contact; that there is, or has been, a ship visit the Earth, or at least the solar system. That's your presence; no big mystery there. What I want to know is, how is Royan tied in? That's what I came for, Greg. Where is he?'

'I don't know. But you were right about the flower being a message. It might even be a warning.'

'Then why didn't he say so?' she asked hotly.

Greg realized how much worry and concern was bottled up behind her tawny eyes.

'Wrong question,' he said. 'We should be asking: what's he warning us about? And why such a baroque warning? If he had enough liberty to send off flowers, why not just give you a call? At the very least he could squirt us a data package.'

'Bugger your questions, Greg! I want to know what's happened to Royan.'

'Well, what did you expect? A seance?' He cursed as soon as he said it.

Julia blushed.

'No,' Eleanor said levelly, her eyes never leaving Julia. 'You want the girl, don't you? The one who gave Rachel the box.'

The blush deepened, she nodded once. 'She's the link. The only one we've got.'

Greg looked at Eleanor, then back to Julia. 'I can't,' he said, appalled at how much it cost to say. 'Not me, not any more. Sorry.'

'Bloody right you can't,' Eleanor said coolly. She fixed Julia with a stare. 'Look around you; four children, a fifth on the way, the farm, the picking season.'

'I know,' Julia whispered. 'But ... *aliens*, Eleanor. It goes beyond me and Royan, though I wish to God it didn't. Who else can I trust? Who would you trust? You want these aliens to contact the religious fundamentalist movements first? One of the South American dictatorships? We have to find him, quickly and quietly. Greg's a gland psychic, worth ten of these new sac users, and he's had proper training. The best there is, and my friend, Royan's friend. Who else can I ask?'

Greg narrowed his eyes. Julia's compulsion had always been stronger than any psychic power. And combine it with logic as well . . .

'Give me a name, Greg, someone better; Lord, someone your equal would do.'

'How the bloody hell would I know?' he snapped. 'I left that game sixteen years ago. Victor? You must have whole memory cores full of psychics.'

'I do,' Victor said quietly. 'And we reviewed them, that's why we're here. I'm sorry. These modern sac users are good, but they don't have your training, your strength. Mindstar hunted out people with the highest potential. Today, anyone who has a minor flash of talent can take a themed neurohormone and think he's some kind of warlock. In a lot of respects themed neurohormones are a step backwards; and no one ever developed one to boost intuition.'

'Jesus wept!'

'Royan's out there, Greg,' Julia said. 'Negotiating with aliens, holding them off, leading them in. Lord, I don't know which. But I have *got* to find out, Greg. Please?'

He looked helplessly at Eleanor. She fumbled for his hand, and gave him a squeeze. He tightened his grip round her shoulder.

'He is a friend,' Eleanor said in a tiny voice. She sounded as though she was trying to convince herself and failing miserably.

'Yeah, he is that.'

'You're not hardlining, Gregory,' Eleanor said firmly. 'Not at your age.'

He twisted under the look in her eyes, wanting to object, or at least have it said in private. The trouble was she was quite right. At fifty-two he would be hopelessly outclassed by today's youngsters. Logic and intuition were in concord over that, worst luck. And if there was one certainty about all of this, there was going to be trouble. Royan's method of contact alone was evidence of that.

Nothing ever simple, nothing ever straightforward. His bloody life story.

'No problem in that direction, at all,' Victor said smoothly. 'One of Event Horizon's security crash teams will be on permanent alert to assist you. With hypersonic transport, they can be anywhere on the globe within forty minutes. And of course you'll have as many of my hardliners accompanying you as you want. All you have to do is ask the questions.'

'No,' Greg said. 'If I'm doing this then I want someone I know watching my back. Someone who's reliable, someone who's good.'

'Of course,' Victor said.

'I'll take Suzi.'

'What?' Julia sat upright in her chair.

Eleanor stiffened inside his encircling arm.

Greg resisted the impulse to smile.

'She is one of the more competent tekmercs,' Victor said grudgingly.

'Yeah,' Greg said. 'She ought to be. I trained her.'

Victor raised an eyebrow. 'I think you'll find she's grown a bit since those days. Reputation-wise, that is.'

'I'm sure Event Horizon can afford her,' Greg said.

'We certainly can,' Julia agreed. 'There will be one of Event Horizon's executive jets here for you first thing tomorrow morning. I've already cleared your entry into Monaco.'

Eleanor's features hardened, spiking Julia with a voodoo glare.

'Fine,' Greg said phlegmatically. Had there ever been a time when Julia didn't get her way? 'We'd better visit Suzi this afternoon.'

'You might find you need more backup than Suzi by herself,' Julia said.

Greg gave her a hard look, he was rapidly tiring of revelations. 'Why?'

'The girl at Newfields, or somebody else, they took a sample out of the flower as well.'

'You sure?'

'Yes. The lab pointed it out as soon as they saw it. One of the stamens had been cut off. And it was definitely a cut, not a break.'

'Would a stamen be enough for a genetic test?' Greg asked. 'I mean, this unknown who took it, are they likely to know the flower is extraterrestrial?'

'Yes. Theoretically, all you need is a single cell. A stamen is more than sufficient.'

Greg rubbed a hand across his temple. 'I doubt it would be the girl who took the sample.'

'Why not?' Eleanor asked.

'Purely because she is just the courier, especially if Rachel is right about her being a whore.'

'Courtesan,' Julia corrected. 'Don't fall into the mistake of thinking she's a dumb go-between. Believe you me, at that level there's a difference. She'll be smart, well educated, and know-ledgeable.'

'OK,' said Victor. 'But smart or not, courtesans don't own genetic labs.'

'I agree,' said Greg. 'Somebody else apart from us knows about the alien. But until we know more about the girl, I couldn't even begin to guess who.'

'Exactly,' said Julia. 'So will you take some extra hardliners?'

'Maybe a couple. But they stay in the background.'

'I'll brief them myself,' said Victor.

Eleanor rested her head well back on top of the settee's cushioning, eyes slitted as she stared at the ceiling. 'What did the government say about the alien?' she asked.

Greg watched Julia flinch at the question. He'd never seen her do that before, not in seventeen years.

'They don't know yet,' Julia mumbled reluctantly.

'When were you planning on telling them?'

'As soon as the situation requires it.'

'You don't think it does yet?' Eleanor asked.

'All we have is supposition, so far.'

'And the genes. They convinced you.'

'The point is, what could the government do that I can't? Order a strategic defence network alert? I really don't think neutral particle beam weapons and pulsed X-ray lasers are going to be an awful lot of use against the kind of technology which moved a ship between stars, and did so undetected. Besides, think of the panic.'

'All right,' Eleanor said uncertainly. 'But we have to make some preparations.'

'Event Horizon is preparing,' said Victor. 'We're assembling a number of dark specialist teams, spreading them through our facilities, kitting them out with top-line equipment.'

'What use is that?' Eleanor demanded indignantly.

'Listen, I can't believe we're facing some kind of military action,' Julia said. 'But so far these aliens have been acting in a very clandestine fashion. If push comes to shove, then Earth is going to lose. No question about it. So we roll with the punch; if we can't fight interstellar technology, we acquire it for ourselves, and fire it right back at them.'

Greg turned to watch the sailors on the reservoir. There was something cheerfully reassuring about the brightly coloured triangles of cloth slicing across the water. A nice homely counterbalance to this vein of raw insanity which had erupted into his life.

He didn't like the connotations interstellar technology was sparking off in his intuition. Though he had to admit Julia had the right idea. If they couldn't be beaten with hardware, use innate human treachery against them.

And what does that say about us as a species?

5

Jason Whitehurst was right, she should have paid more attention to his data profile. He did have a yacht, of sorts, the *Colonel Maitland*; it was an old passenger airship he had bought and converted into an airborne gin palace.

After the Newfields ball, Whitehurst's limousine had driven the three of them halfway around the Monaco dome's perimeter road before turning off. A covered bridge linked the dome to the city-state's airport, a circular concrete island fifteen hundred metres east of the Prince Albert marina. They'd driven past the terminal building and across the apron to a Gulfstream-XX executive hypersonic. The plane was a small white arrowhead shape, with a central bulge running its whole length, twin fins at the back. With its streamline profile, embodying power and speed, it would have been easy to believe it was some kind of organic construct.

Charlotte ducked under the wing's sharp leading edge and climbed the aluminium stairs through the belly hatch. The cabin was windowless, a door leading forwards into the cockpit, another at the aft bulkhead for the toilet, there were ten seats. A smiling steward in a dark purple blazer showed her how to fasten the belt. Jason sat at the front; and Fabian sat opposite her, his greedy smile blinking on and off.

And that was it. There was no passport and immigration control, no customs, no security search. Jason Whitehurst's money simply overrode the mundane protocols of everyday existence, an intangible bow wave force clearing all before his path. Even so, she thought there should've been some kind of formality. But at least she didn't see the creep with the cool eyes this time.

Charlotte had actually dozed on the short flight. She woke as the steward touched her shoulder. The back of Fabian's head was descending through the hatch.

She glanced about in confusion as she came down the hypersonic plane's stairs. The Gulfstream had landed on a circular VTOL pad. A stiff chilly breeze plucked at her gown. They were definitely out at sea, she could taste the freshness of the air. But all she could see past the lights ringing the pad was a band of night sky, stars twinkling with unusual clarity, there was no sign of the sea, no sound of water. A bright orange strobe light was flashing two hundred metres ahead of the Gulfstream's nose, seemingly suspended in space. That was when she started to realize where they were.

'Welcome to my yacht, my dear,' Jason Whitehurst said with a touch of irony.

Charlotte lifted her mouth in a smile. 'Thank you, sir.'

He wagged a finger.

'Jason,' she corrected.

'Good girl.'

We must be right on top of the airship, she thought. But it's so stable, even in the breeze, it must be massive.

Fabian had disappeared through a door at the rear of the pad. Jason guided her courteously towards it.

Charlotte yawned widely, covering her mouth quickly. 'Excuse me,' she apologized.

'Tired, my dear? You were out like a light on the plane.'

'I'm sorry, you must think me dreadfully rude. I've been on my feet for thirty-six hours. I've only just returned from my holiday. It's been planes and airport lounges all day, I'm afraid.'

They went through the door into a well-lit corridor. Fabian was waiting by a lift.

'That sounds most interesting,' Jason Whitehurst said. 'I shall enjoy hearing all about your travels tomorrow over lunch.'

Charlotte's heart sank.

The lift door hummed open. Everything was made out of composite, she noted – walls, floor, ceiling.

'Fabian, I think you had better see your lady guest to one of the spare cabins for tonight,' Jason Whitehurst said. 'Dear Charlotte is terribly tired. I think she needs a night's rest. She can move into your room tomorrow.'

And that cleared up any possible ambiguities about the situation, Charlotte thought. Clever of him, reassuring his son in front of her.

Fabian's face fell. 'Yes, Father.'

She shared the lift with Fabian. He kept giving her fast glances, suddenly nervous again. She thought she'd succeeded in putting him at ease while they were dancing. 'How old are you?' he asked quickly. 'I mean . . . you don't have to say. Not if you don't want to.'

'I'm twenty-one, Fabian.'

'Oh.' He stared at the stainless-steel control panel beside the door. 'I was fifteen a few months back, actually. Well more like nine months, really.'

According to the data profile Baronski had squirted over to her, Fabian had celebrated his fifteenth birthday barely a fortnight ago. 'That's nice.'

Fabian blushed. 'Why?'

'Because people will still treat you like a kid. But you're not. It means you can get away with murder.'

His jaw worked silently for a moment. 'Ah, yes, right.'

The lift doors opened on the gondola's upper deck. He showed her down a long corridor to her cabin. She began to wonder again about the size of the *Colonel Maitland*.

'Thank you, Fabian,' she said when the cabin door slid open.

'Sleep as long as you want. There's nothing rigid about meals on board. The cooks will always get you something to eat whenever you ask them. That's what they're here for.' He flipped the hair from his eyes. 'Would you like to come swimming with me tomorrow?'

'Swimming? In an airship? What do you do, jump into the sea?'

Just for a moment a genuine fifteen-year-old's grin flashed over his face. 'No, nothing like that. I'll show you.'

'Sounds fun. That's a date, then.'

*

She woke to the faintest of buzzing sounds, having to concentrate hard to be certain she wasn't imagining it. It seemed to rise and fall in some strange cycle of its own. There was no accompanying vibration. She thought it might be the propellers.

Her cabin was stylish and luxuriant, vaguely reminiscent of a nineteenth-century steamship. Wooden dresser and chests, mossy sapphire carpet, biolum globes like giant opals, pictures of pre-Warming landscapes on the walls. Three sets of mulberry curtains along one wall emitted a dull glow. A remote unit was sitting on the bedside cabinet.

She found the button for the curtains, and rolled off the bed as they drew apart, revealing long rectangular windows with brass frames.

Colonel Maitland was cruising three or four kilometres above the Mediterranean. The water below shone with a rich clear blue hue, while wave-tops shimmered brightly creating a silver glare. She had never flown over the Mediterranean like this before. Hypersonics flew so high and fast that details blurred to non-existence, seas were reduced to a formless blue plane. But this view was hypnotic. She could see ships down there, trailing long V-shaped wakes; bulk cargo carriers, rusty splinters no bigger than her thumb nail.

There was a light tapping on the door. Charlotte looked round the cabin, and saw a towelling robe on the foot of the bed. She slipped into it.

'Come in.'

It was a maid, a woman in her early thirties, dressed in a

plain black knee-length tunic, her mouse-brown hair wound into a neat bun. She curtsied. And she got it right, too, Charlotte noticed.

'Did madam have a pleasant rest?' The maid's English was slightly accented. Slavonic?

'There's no need for that nonsense in private,' Charlotte said.

'Madam?'

That hurt. Formality was the way a patron's household staff told her they thought she was on a social stratum way below them, about equal to the family pets. Dumb, pampered, and good at tricks. 'I had a very pleasant rest. Is the rest of the ship up and about?'

'It is nearly eleven o'clock, madam.'

Charlotte blinked in surprise. When she looked out of the windows again she saw the sun was well up in the sky.

She cocked her head at it, finding something vaguely disconcerting about its appearance. Whatever the anomaly was, she couldn't quantify it.

'Mr Whitehurst is expecting me for lunch,' Charlotte said. 'What time is that?'

'Twelve fifty, madam.'

Charlotte ran her hands through her hair. 'I'll take a shower first. Where are my clothes?' The gown she'd worn to the Newfields ball was draped over a chair. She'd been so tired last night she couldn't be bothered even to find a hanger for it. Now the material was probably creased beyond rescue.

The maid opened a drawer. Charlotte recognized some of her clothes folded neatly. When had that been done?

'Would madam like me to assist in the bathroom? I am a trained manicurist.'

'You know how to do hair as well?'

A slight bow.

'Good, in that case you can give me a hand.' And get that nice clean tunic all wet and soapy as well.

The maid slid open a varnished pine door to reveal a

bathroom. It was all marbled surfaces and extravagant potted ferns.

The marble must be fake, Charlotte decided. They couldn't possibly afford the weight, not even in this airship. Jason Whitehurst giving his guests fake marble. She grinned.

'Mr Jason said to be sure your choice of day attire was a suitable one for a companion of Master Fabian's,' the maid said. Her face was beautifully composed. 'I took the liberty of laying out one or two of the briefer items from madam's wardrobe. I hope they meet with your approval, there were so many to select from.'

'Why, thank you, I'm sure your knowledge in that area is unmatched.' Charlotte swept regally into the bathroom. One all. But it was shaping up like a long dirty war.

*

Lunch was difficult. They ate in the aft dining-room on the gondola's upper deck; looking out at the stern of the airship. Charlotte discovered she had been quite right about the *Colonel Maitland*, it was vast; seven hundred metres long, a hundred and twenty in diameter. Its fuselage was made up from sheets of solar cells, a glossy black envelope reflecting narrow ripples of sunlight in mimicry of the sea below.

Jason Whitehurst sat at the head of the table, with his back to the curving band of windows. Charlotte and Fabian sat on either side of him, facing each other. Fabian was doing his best not to stare. But once or twice she thought she caught that glint of anticipation on his face again.

As she worked her spoon into the avocado starter Charlotte watched the translucent blur of the contra-rotating fans at the stern. The *Colonel Maitland* was making a hundred and fifty kilometres an hour. She hadn't known airships could travel so fast, her mind classing them as lumbering dinosaurs.

'Oh no, not at all,' Jason Whitehurst said when she mentioned it. 'Even the previous generation of rigid airships in the nineteen-thirties were reaching speeds around a hundred and twenty kilometres an hour. Flat out, the *Colonel Maitland* can make a hundred and eighty. It used to cruise at about a hundred and fifty when it was on the trans-Pacific passenger run.'

'This was a passenger ship?' she asked.

'Yes. Airships came into their own after the Warming and the Energy Crunch. Damnable era, that one, the whole world went positively insane for over a decade. Still, I expect that was before your time, my dear. And very fortunate you were too, missing it. But after the jet fleets were grounded by impossibly expensive fuel, beauties like the old *Colonel* were all we had until Event Horizon cracked the giga-conductor's molecular structure. After that, of course, everybody went bloody speed mad. Hypersonics, spaceplanes; nothing but rush and bustle. One shouldn't complain, one supposes; the world is a better place now, so everyone says. But airships have such class. That's why I couldn't resist buying this old chap when it came on the market.'

Charlotte took a sip of her white wine. This assignment was turning into a complete waste of time. Jason Whitehurst spent most of his time on board the *Colonel Maitland*, so he said, only touching the ground for parties like the Newfields ball and other social events, the occasional business meeting. His trading empire was mostly handled by his cargo agents, and ninety per cent of his financial business conducted via private satellite relays. That didn't bode well at all. A large part of her arrangement with Baronski was listening to table talk. It was amazing what premier-grade kombinate executives and company chairmen would say when they were relaxed in a convivial atmosphere, safe amongst their own. Of course, they didn't expect her to follow a word of what they were saying. Youth, a pretty face, and a perfect figure equals no brain at all. So the next day she would call up Baronski, and he played the bytes of insider knowledge on the stock markets. Charlotte only got two per cent on that deal, but it would often come to more than the price her patron's gifts brought in.

Except now there were no guests on board, nor any prospect

of them before they reached Odessa. And Fabian was supposed to be her patron; the only gifts she was likely to get from him would be rock concert tickets and a Playboy channel subscription.

One of the waiters brought her a chicken salad. Charlotte waited until Jason Whitehurst started eating, then tucked in. Her usual patrons, with their overhanging bellies and multiplying chins, tended to become irritable when they saw her nibbling at her food while they chomped their way through five-course meals, it showed them up. So she had had her digestive enzymes alerted with biochemicals to reduce her digestion rate; now it didn't matter how much she ate, she didn't put on weight. With slenderness guaranteed, a simple regimen of light exercise was all she needed to keep her ballerina muscle tone.

'So where did you take this holiday of yours?' Jason Whitehurst asked.

'New London.'

'No, really?' Fabian stopped eating, his fork halfway to his mouth. 'You mean the asteroid?'

'Yes.'

The boy's eyes shone. 'What's it like?'

Charlotte moistened her lips with the wine again. 'Formidable. The flight out leaves you with a most peculiar impression; it's both big and small at the same time. On the approach you see this huge mountain of rock adrift in space halfway out to the moon. Then, inside, it's a tiny little worldlet, the centre hollowed out and planted with trees and grass and crops. Yet even that is big, because you can see it all, and know how small you are by comparison.'

'Crikey. I'd like to get up there myself sometime.'

'When you're older,' Jason Whitehurst said.

'Yes, Father.'

Jason Whitehurst reached over, and ruffled the boy's hair. 'Ah, impatience of youth. Just wait a few more years, Fabian, you can do what you like after that. Tell your poor old father to get stuffed then.'

Fabian did a half-squirm below his father's hand, glancing anxiously at Charlotte, so obviously fearful of how she would interpret the gesture. Daddy's little boy.

'I imagine there can't be very much to do up there,' Jason Whitehurst said.

'Oh no, there's much more to it than the microgee industries and Event Horizon's mineral mining operation,' Charlotte said. 'They're trying to develop it as a finance and tourist centre.'

'Good heavens, a sort of Disneyland in orbit, that kind of thing?'

'Not quite, it's rather more exclusive than that. They have casinos, nightclubs, if anything it's rather like a giant cabana club.'

'Sounds ghastly,' Jason Whitehurst muttered.

'And there's zero gee, as well,' Charlotte said.

'From what I've been given to understand, it makes people sick.'

'Not much nowadays, the medical people have got the anti-nausea drugs worked out fairly well. They had to. Sports form a big part of the attraction. There are a lot of games that you can play in the various low gee terraces. Tennis, badminton, squash, handball; they're all a lot of fun up there. The ball travels completely differently, you have to develop a whole new set of reflexes to cope. And then there's the fall surfing, that's worth the price of the ticket alone. You must have seen it on the channels.'

Jason Whitehurst dabbed at his mouth with a linen napkin. 'Yes. Well that settles it, I certainly won't be going. I'm far too old to learn anything new.'

'Oh, come on, Father. It sounds terrific.'

'Maybe for your sixteenth birthday.'

'Great!'

'I said maybe.' Jason sat back as the waiter removed his plate. 'You obviously enjoyed yourself up there, my dear?'

'Yes. I'd like to go back.'

Jason Whitehurst pulled thoughtfully at his beard as he looked at her. 'How long were you up there for?'

'Ten days.'

'I see. And then straight from the spaceport to the Newfields ball. You were in a bit of a rush, weren't you?'

Charlotte didn't like the way he was asking her questions, it wasn't polite conversation-making any more. 'I support the Newfields charity, it means a lot to me.'

'Dead boring, though,' Fabian said. 'Except when we were dancing,' he added hurriedly.

'Thank you,' Charlotte smiled at him.

'Do you still want to come swimming?'

It was the third time he'd asked. Charlotte had finally twigged why he was so persistent: swimming meant bikinis. Devious old Fabian. 'I certainly do, yes.'

'Not until you've digested your lunch,' Jason Whitehurst said. 'Why don't you show Charlotte round the old *Colonel* first.'

*

The gondola was a hundred metres long, thirty wide, with two decks containing all the cabins, lounges, and staff quarters. Fabian led her down the central corridors, opening various doors. The flight centre was at the front of the lower deck, a big room with panoramic windows; three bored officers monitored the airship's systems on five horseshoe consoles. Fabian introduced her to them, then they went up into the main hull.

'This is where it gets interesting,' Fabian said as they climbed a short flight of stairs at the rear of the gondola, right above the dining-room they'd had lunch in.

The stairs came out on to a narrow composite walkway with a rail at waist height, illuminated by a row of biolum strips. Charlotte was standing in a three-metre gap between a spherical helium balloon and the solar cell envelope. Long girders made from improbably thin monolattice carbon struts curved away on both sides, disappearing into darkness. The walkway was a narrow thread of light which stretched out into infinity fore and aft.

She shivered from the cool air. The gap seemed to suck sound away.

Fabian started walking towards the stern. 'There are nine of these big spherical gasbags,' he said, pointing up, 'and two smaller ones in the conical sections at both ends.'

Charlotte pressed her hand against the blue-grey roof of plastic. It felt tacky, slightly cooler than the surrounding air.

'Then there's these ten doughnut-shaped ones spaced between the spheres, so we don't waste any volume,' Fabian continued. They were underneath a deep curving valley where the spherical gasbag pressed up against a doughnut, taut wires securing both of them to the monolattice spars.

Charlotte let him guide her, not really listening to the details of what she was seeing. Fabian found a walkway leading off at right angles to the main one. It began to curve upwards. She was soon climbing a ladder to another walkway halfway up the side of the fuselage.

'I'm sorry about the way the staff treated you,' Fabian said. 'It was jolly rude.'

Charlotte watched him flip the hair out of his eyes. She hadn't realized he'd noticed the chill of the waiters as they served her at lunch, not many did. 'They don't count,' she said.

He considered this. 'Oh. Does it happen to you a lot?'

'Sometimes.'

There were more turns, another flight of stairs. They arrived at a doorway. Charlotte didn't have a clue where they were any more, except the unending buzz of the fans was slightly louder.

'Here we are,' Fabian said happily, and showed his card to the lock.

Charlotte looked round as biolum strips covered in protective grilles came on. The room had an industrial feel to it; a gloomy high ceiling, the walls covered in big thermal insulation panels. It had housed some heavy machinery in the past; the mountings were still there, jutting out of the walls, two rows of thick pipes rose out of the floor like stumpy chimneys, capped by metal plates, a spiderweb of empty cable ducts arched around the door. But it was a teenager's den now. A rich teenager. There were flatscreens screwed to the walls, several hardware terminals and display cubes on old tables, piles of cushions, a music deck, a couple of electric guitars, large speakers, clothes scattered round, empty boxes, and ten large tanks full of tropical fish.

'This chamber used to hold the MHD units,' Fabian said. 'When it was an ordinary passenger ship on the Pacific run the *Colonel Maitland* burnt hydrogen for power. The solar cell envelope doesn't catch enough energy to power the fans, you see. But when Father had it refitted, we switched the giga-conductor cells. Saves an awful lot of weight.'

'So where does the power come from now?' she asked.

Fabian fell back into one of the beanbags, hands behind his head, beaming. 'The Gulfstream has extra cells fitted, they charge up from the industrial grid every time it lands, then it transfers the electricity when it gets back.'

'So this is where you hang out, is it?' She peered at one of the fish tanks, admiring the vivid rainbow patterns on the guppies, suspecting genetic engineering featured prominently in their heritage.

'Yep.'

'Doing what, exactly?'

'I'll show you.' Fabian jumped up, limbs jerking erratically, as though he was operated by wires. He tugged his T-shirt off. 'This is really the most scorching game on the market. I love this. I'm good at it, too. Really good.'

She frowned, slightly bemused as he started to delve through a pile of junk. He pulled on a sleeveless shirt that was stained and torn, then started to clip on what looked like body armour. A metal breastplate painted in jungle camouflage; it had a small spotlight that stood above his left shoulder on a stalk.

'That screen,' Fabian told her, urgently. 'Watch that one.' He was typing quickly on a complicated-looking terminal. 'Please, Charlotte.'

'Sure.' Your daddy's paying for it, after all. She saw he had acquired a GI helmet with a small radio mike hanging down. He picked up a bulky gun, some sort of cross between a shotgun and a semi-automatic rifle, and stood in the centre of a circular black mat.

There was something weirdly familiar about the costume. Then the theatre-sized flatscreen on the rear wall lit up.

A cramped room illuminated by dull red lighting, metal lockers forming walls and narrow aisles. Figures frozen in an alert pose, all of them holding the same kind of rifle as Fabian, all looking up at the ceiling with expressions of worry and concern. Charlotte recognized the woman in the centre: Sigourney Weaver. 'I know this,' she said. 'It's from *Aliens*.'

Fabian laughed. He was abruptly engulfed by a two-metre bubble of holographic light, a shadowless pearl haze. Faint coloured lines flickered around him, an exoskeleton drawn in blue, as though he had been cocooned by a computer graphics display.

The scene on the flatscreen came alive. And there was Fabian, one of the space marines, firing his gun wildly as the aliens crashed down through the command centre's roof. He had obviously perfected his chosen role, screaming obscenities, blasting the creatures apart in eruptions of green and yellow gore, covering the retreat back to the medical centre. Then one of the aliens punched up through the floor at his feet, and he went down firing defiantly until a black skeletal hand clamped over his face, dragging him to oblivion. A last terrified scream and he was gone.

Charlotte laughed delightedly, clapping and whistling. 'Encore!' She didn't have to fake it. Almost all of her patrons tried to impress her, showing off their sophisticated art collections or delicate antiques, lecturing her extensively on every piece, demonstrating how cultured and refined they were, always hoping for an admiration which wasn't entirely bought. No one had ever tried to woo her with anything remotely like this before, not simple enjoyment. It was all so gloriously childish.

She couldn't help wondering how she would look up there on the big screen.

Fabian clambered back to his feet, and slung the chunky rifle over his shoulder. His face split with a rich happy smile. 'See, told you I was good. You can pick whatever character you like. I love playing Hudson; he's a real fighter. He's scared the whole time, but he's tough too when it counts. I know his dialogue off by heart.'

'You were brilliant.' She went over to the terminal he had activated, there were three times the usual number of keys. 'What is this?'

'Videoke. All the companies and kombinates say it's going to be their supernova sales item this Christmas. Father got me this deck in advance; he's trying to buy a big consignment of them for Central America. The software houses have only remastered fifty movies for interactivity so far. I've got them loaded in the deck's AV memox; all the real classics since cinema started, even some black and white ones.'

'It's wonderful, Fabian.'

'Do you want to try it?' he asked generously. 'You could be Ingrid Bergman in *Casablanca*, or Laura Dern in *Jurassic Park*, you're easily beautiful enough.'

'Thank you, flatterer. I will some time, once I've learned the lines. If I'm going to do it, I want to do it properly, like you. I'll have to find the right clothes, too.'

'I could do the Humphrey Bogart part with you.'

'Yes.' She read the list of films the videoke deck's flatscreen was displaying. Snow White in the Disney cartoon would certainly be a challenge. And which dwarf could Fabian be? She chuckled quietly to herself.

Fabian slowly took his helmet off. His hair was all sweaty, clinging to his scalp. 'Charlotte.'

She looked round at him, surprised by his serious tone.

'I meant it when I said you were beautiful.'

'Thank you, Fabian.'

'I couldn't believe it the first time I saw you.' His pose of assured confidence crumpled, shoulders slumping inside the green armour. 'I thought I was dreaming. I knew you'd be pretty, but—'

'Give you a tip, never oversell.'

His head came up, lips pressed together defiantly. 'Are you laughing at me?'

'No, Fabian. I'm not laughing at you. Life is cruel enough without people deliberately adding to it.'

'Oh. You're nothing like . . . I don't mind what you do, you know.'

'What do I do?'

Fabian blushed, the invisible wires tugged his shoulders into a lopsided shrug. 'You know. The others, before me. Hiring yourself out.'

'Cars and flats are hired out, Fabian. They're objects.'

'You mean you want to?'

'I mean there are limits. I have a choice.'

His youthful uncertainty had returned. He looked almost fragile, she thought.

'So you only came on board the *Colonel* because you wanted to?' he asked.

'More or less, yes.'

'With me?' his voice was disbelieving.

Charlotte was strongly tempted. Revenge for all the shit she'd been made to eat over the years. She could hit him now, beat him with words, sarcasm and derision, cripple him up inside. He was one of them, the indifferent rich, floating effortlessly through life. Never caring, that was their real crime.

His face hovered halfway between pride and trepidation. The kind of innocence she'd never had.

She couldn't do it.

It wasn't often like this. She was supposed to be a passing fancy, an interesting diversion. Not someone who could leave a lasting impression. But with Fabian, she knew she'd be a wonderful memory for the rest of his life. The greatest present a fifteen-year-old could ever be given – judged from a fifteen-year-old's viewpoint. And who knows, I might even alter his perspective on life.

Charlotte twitched her lips sensually. 'You won't like this.'

'What?'

'When I saw you back at the Newfields ball. I thought you were kind of cute.'

'Cute?' he blurted in dismay.

'Told you.'

'Oh.' Fabian dropped the rifle back on the junk pile and scratched his neck. 'Really?'

'Yes.'

'So you must like me a bit.'

'I suppose so.'

He seemed to inflate with purpose. 'All right! Can we go swimming now?'

*

There really was a swimming-pool on board. A surprisingly large one, fifteen metres long, six wide. The room had a small bar at one end, and Solaris spots shining out of a hologram sky. Sun loungers were set out along one side of the pool, the other side was flush with the wall, the windows ten centimetres above the water.

Charlotte tested the water with one foot, then shrugged out of her towelling robe. She was wearing a bright scarlet crossover-back swimsuit underneath. Fabian watched her with a bold face and timid eyes as she dived cleanly into the pool.

She swam over to the windows, and looked out at the Mediterranean below. Floating in water that was floating through air. How strange. And there was that feeling of something being out of kilter again. It was mid-afternoon, with the sun sinking towards the horizon ahead of the *Colonel Maitland*. She decided that when she got to Odessa she'd call Baronski and tell him to find her another patron. Fabian could nearly be classified as sweet, he was certainly gullible, and easily controlled. But there was no way she was going to spend the next month cooped up in an airship with no one else to talk to.

'Do you want the wave generator on?' he asked.

'Maybe later. I'm still getting used to the idea of a pool in the air. Waves would be pushing it.'

He turned onto his back, and drifted away. 'The pool makes a lot of sense, you know. It weighs less than the hydrogen the ship used to store; and water is the best kind of ballast, quick to dump.'

'Are you telling me that if there's an emergency we're going to go down the plug hole?'

Fabian laughed. 'No, course not, stupid. There's a grille over the drain.'

Charlotte pushed off from the windows. 'Fabian, where do you go to school?'

'Here, I use flexible rate learning programs on my terminal. But I'm going away to university. Father said I am. Cambridge, I hope. That's where he went. I want to do economics so I can take over the trading company from him.'

'So when do you get out?'

'Out?'

'Of the *Colonel Maitland*.'

'Oh, when we reach a port where Father has some business. Or if we go to a party.'

'So how do you make friends?'

Fabian's good humour faded. He stood up in the middle of the pool. 'There are the other kids on the party circuit. And I talk to people on the phone chatlink.'

She swam over to him, and stood up, the water coming up to her elbows. His head tilted up to look at her.

'That's nice,' she said. 'You must meet a lot of varied people.'

Fabian nodded. His gaze dropped to the scoop of her swim-suit and stayed there. She eased her chest forward a fraction. Regretting it almost immediately as Fabian became very still;

teasing him was such a delicate business. He was on the verge of panic.

'Yes?' she said gently.

'Charlotte . . .' He visibly gathered courage. 'Charlotte, can I kiss you now? You don't have to say yes.'

She took a slow step forwards, amused by his suddenly startled expression. Her hands held his shoulders, and she gave him a long kiss, finishing by sucking his lower lip as they parted.

If anything Fabian looked even more confused and lost than usual.

'Didn't you like that?' she asked.

'Crikey, yes! It's just—'

She gave him a fast impersonal kiss on the tip of his nose. 'Don't feel guilty, Fabian. Never that. I'm here for you.'

'I didn't ask for you to be brought on board,' he said defensively.

'I know. So, friends?'

'Yes.' He gave an anxious nod, then experimented with a grin.

'Good.'

'Why did you want to know about my friends?' he asked.

'Just curious.'

'Where do you live?'

'I have a flat in the Prezda, that's an Austrian arcology.'

'But you can't live there much.'

'No. I don't suppose I do. But it's nice to have somewhere to call home. Somewhere you can always return to and shut the door on the rest of the world. Everybody needs that.'

'If you don't live there much, then you can't have many real friends either. Not steady ones.'

Charlotte couldn't manage to summon up her usual smile. 'Fabian, have you got a bioware processor implant?'

His satisfied expression dissolved into perplexity. 'No. Of course not. Why?'

'Because you're a very bright boy, that's why.'

His grin reappeared. 'Really? You really think so?'

'Yes.'

'I didn't want to be rude,' he said contritely. 'I thought—'

'Go on, I don't bite.'

'Well, I thought that might be why you decided to come with me, because we were both the same. Neither of us has anybody really close.'

She let the water flow back over her, twisting idly. 'Could be.'

*

Charlotte waited for an hour after dinner before she tapped on Fabian's door. The meal had been another exercise in high discomfort; the three of them sitting in the aft dining-room as the twilight faded into night. Jason Whitehurst had asked about New London again. Where she stayed, who she'd met, actually wanting to know which flights she'd used, for Heaven's sake. Even Fabian had begun to shift uncomfortably in his seat.

'Busy?' Charlotte asked.

Fabian shook his head, and backed away from the door. The flatscreen on the wall was showing a Western. His cabin's layout was similar to hers, but pesonalized, with clothes scattered about, real books piled on the dresser, shoes underfoot. Biolum panels glowed dully, reddish pink embers.

Charlotte closed the door. Fabian gave the impression of wanting to jump on her, and flee at the same time. He stared miserably at his bare feet.

'I wasn't sure if you'd really turn up,' he said in a thick voice. 'I still think you might be a dream.'

Charlotte turned the flatscreen off, deepening the shadows. 'Fabian?'

'Yes?'

'Am I really so hard to look at?'

When he lifted his head she gently pushed the lock of hair from his forehead, then put her hands on his cheeks and kissed him. His skin was singularly smooth under her fingers.

She let go, slightly disturbed by the amount of adoration in his gaze. 'Before we go any further, I just wanted to thank you.'

'Me? What for?'

'For not trying to order me about.'

'I wouldn't do that. Honestly.'

'Yes. I know.' Charlotte showed him a slow enticing smile. 'And now you don't have to.' She slipped the straps off her shoulders in an easy motion and let the gown slide to the carpet with a silky rustle. Her self-control nearly cracked at the sight of the outright astonishment on his face as he stared at her breasts. Baronski had said they were big enough not to need enlarging, but she'd taken a hormone course to strengthen the Cooper's ligaments which supported the ductal lobes, keeping them high and firm.

Fabian flipped his hair aside, and scrambled for his shirt buttons, his eyes never leaving her.

'No,' she said, and the huskiness of her tone surprised even her. 'I'll do that.'

She started at his collar, kissing his skin as it was exposed, moving down his chest on to his belly. There were no blemishes, nor spots, it was baby-flesh. She reached his shorts, and pulled them down along with his pants.

Fabian was biting his lower lip, drawing breath in judders when she rose to stand in front of him. She slithered quickly out of her panties.

'Bed,' she said, and took him by the hand.

He lay down on the rumpled sheets, an almost fearful expression on his face. Charlotte sat across his hips, her gaze holding his eyes for a long moment, then slowly leant forwards.

It was a strange sensation, to be in bed with someone so inexperienced, having to guide and whisper encouragement. But she discovered a secret miscreant pleasure in being dominant for once, bigger and stronger. It was exciting listening to him whimper as her fingers dug into his hard buttocks, tongue making love to his erection. She let him play with her breasts for a long time.

Then finally he was up between her legs, pumping wildly. It was over quickly, Fabian crying out as he fell on top of her.

She held him until his shaking passed. Kissing his brow as she gently stroked his spine.

'I got it all wrong, didn't I?' he said wretchedly.

'No, not at all. I've known of some people who get so wound up the first time that they just freeze. That hardly happened to you, now did it? You'll learn how to make it good for both of us.'

'So it wasn't good for you, then?'

She sighed. Even now his mind functioned like a 'ware chip. 'This was your night, Fabian.'

'But you let me do anything I wanted to you. Anything. You never stopped me.'

'Was that so terrible? Didn't you like it?'

'God yes, you're so beautiful. It's brilliant enough just being able to look at you and touch you, but sex with you is like going to heaven.'

She had to strain hard not to laugh. He really was cute. 'Sex is whatever you enjoy, providing it doesn't hurt your partner.'

He raised himself on his elbows, looking down on her body with a sheepish awe. 'Please, Charlotte, show me how to make you enjoy it. I want to thrill you, I want to make you as excited as I am, I want to be the greatest lover you've ever had. Please. Just show me how. Please, Charlotte.'

Now how long had it been since she'd had a request like that? If ever. She grinned lazily, and stretched her arms above her head, arching her back. 'Do you know what an erogenous zone is?'

'Course I know!'

She giggled. 'Ah, but where are they?'

His indignation faltered.

Charlotte caught one of his hands; she gently kissed the tip of each finger, licking with feline provocation, then guided him across her abdomen.

6

Suzi was sunbathing on the balcony when she heard the piccolo hiss of the executive hypersonic's compressor fans. Darkness swept over her, accompanied by a wave of half-imaginary cold as the boiling afternoon sun was eclipsed by the little arrowhead plane.

Suzi opened her eyes and squinted up, but there was too much glare to make out the fuselage insignia. Andria sat up beside her, long hand shielding her eyes from the sun as she watched the hypersonic settle on the condominium's roof pad two storeys above them.

'I don't recognize it,' the girl said.

Suzi turned on to her back, shuffling her shoulders until the lounger's cushioning was comfortable. 'It's an Event Horizon Pegasus CV-188D,' she mumbled with her eyes closed again. 'Their latest marque.'

Andria laughed. 'No, Suse, I meant, I don't know who it belongs to. I don't think it belongs to any of the residents.'

That laugh did things to Suzi's brain that could normally only be achieved by a hefty infusion of proscribed substances, it was carefree and warm, amazingly sultry. She lifted her head to look at the naked girl on the lounger beside her.

Andria was nineteen, her body lean and long limbed, dark wavy hair falling below her shoulders. She had a heart-shaped face with a flat nose, and wide ever-curious eyes that never seemed to stay focused on anything for more than a few seconds. The whole world was a constant delight to Andria, she had to try and see all of it at once. Then there was her shyness, which was a provocative aphrodisiac.

Her pregnancy didn't show yet. Six weeks after the private London clinic specializing in parthenogenetic reproduction had fertilized Suzi's ovum and planted it securely inside Andria, the girl's coffee-coloured belly was still flat and firm.

They had met in a New Eastfield nightclub last October, Suzi celebrating a finance sink deal with some of her team, Andria on a night out with her boyfriend.

It took Suzi three weeks to lure Andria into bed, shamelessly exploiting the girl's sunny, trusting nature. She hadn't pursued anyone with such determination since her Trinities days; it was like being drunk on raw lust. Their first night together was worth every agonizing second of the wait. She used Andria's body to work off fantasy after fantasy, only to find it just left her wanting more. It meant that for the first time in a long while Suzi had been forced to tell someone how much she felt about them.

Andria had moved in permanently at the start of December, though she insisted on keeping her datashuffling job in the office of a local shipping agent. It was that kind of quiet pride which was such a puzzle and fascination to Suzi. A girl who would surrender every inhibition to her at night, yet still refused to become a dependant. Andria was more than erotic satisfaction, she filled the soul's longing.

So in January, just before she started working on the Johal HF deal, Suzi screwed up her courage, and asked Andria to consider having her child.

'But why?' Andria had asked as Suzi lay on top of her.

The air-conditioned darkness of the penthouse's bedroom revealed only the faintest of silhouettes, but Suzi knew the girl had a frown on her face. 'Because it's a way out for me,' she answered, shrinking inside for showing her vulnerability. 'This shit I'm in, I know it's bad, but it's addictive. It gives me a high.

I can't get out. There's nothing outside tekmerc territory that can give me the same buzz. I've seen 'em all, dopey bastards who say they'll quit when they've made their wad. Never do; they live wild for a few months, even a couple of years, then they come crawling back, and when they do their edge is all screwed up.'

She felt Andria's fingers running lightly round her chin. 'You could always set up as a corporate security consultant, your experience must count for—' the girl began.

'Bollocks. Kombinate security wouldn't touch me with a bargepole. Besides, I want right out, the whole way. Got the money, too.'

'But what would you do?'

'Get conventional. Shit, I know it sounds fucking stupid. Right? But I'd like to give convention a go. I thought a pub or a hotel, maybe a club.'

'If a consultancy wouldn't give you the excitement, then I don't think a pub would be what you need.'

'I know someone,' Suzi whispered. 'Someone who used to do this kind of crap, a real hardliner. He got out, clean and sweet. Jesus wept, one person. One out of all the thousands.'

Andria kissed her throat lightly, trying to give comfort through intimacy. 'And he did it through being conventional?'

'Yeah.' That image came back to spook her again. Greg and Eleanor walking down the aisle of Hambleton's dinky little church, both of them smiling radiantly at each other, not seeing anyone else. Suzi hadn't wanted to go, hadn't known what to wear, hadn't known what present to get. Like a fucking savage figuring out a cybofax. It had come as a harsh shock, finding out just how far she'd regressed from society. 'He's got a wife, kids, farm, the whole fucking works. And he never came back.'

'Was he your lover?'

'No. Yes. Not really. Good mates, that's all.'

'And you think you can follow him?'

Suzi stroked the damp strands of hair from Andria's forehead. She always wanted to be tender afterwards, make up for her earlier fierceness, show the girl she really cared. She knew sex was another of her failings, needing to be on top when it was boys, making the girls submit. She wanted to stop, to be normal. Didn't know how; couldn't figure how the other ways could possibly work like everyone said, all that giving and sharing bollocks. Sex was power.

'Fuck-all chance of doing anything else,' Suzi said. 'I mean, tekmercs, we screw convention, deliberately. That's what we are. But this jobs and family bullshit, it works, for billions of people, it sodding works. If I just had something that I could commit myself to, something I could feel a bit of pride in.' Her voice had risen without her realizing. 'Shit, maybe Leol Reiger was right about me when he said I haven't got what it takes. Sometimes I hope he is. But I need something to anchor me to that kind of world. Kid would do that.'

'Yes,' Andria said simply.

'You'll do it?'

'Of course I will. I love you, Suse.'

Andria was still watching the hypersonic above them. The balconies on the eastern end of the Soreyheath condominium looked out over New Eastfield's marina and the gleaming structures of Prior's Fen Atoll away in the lazy distance beyond. They were arranged in tiers, which meant Suzi could see any of the balconies below her, but not the two above. A concrete-enforced statement about social position, she always thought.

The tip of the hypersonic's nose was sticking over the end of the roof, like a bird of prey crouched ready to pounce on the supine bodies laid out invitingly below it.

Access Concierge. Identify Incoming Plane Ownership. Suzi took a drink of orange from her glass. She was skipping alcohol right now, it wasn't fair on Andria.

Pegasus G—ALPH Registered with Event Horizon Corporation. Suzi glanced thoughtfully at the white nose cone.

The phone shrilled.

Andria pressed the sound-only button. 'Yes?'

'Guests for you, Miss Landon,' the concierge 'ware's construct voice said. 'Julia Evans and Greg Mandel.'

Suzi heard Andria's indrawn breath at the mention of Julia, she smiled at the girl's innocent enquiring gaze, and began hunting round for her robe. 'Well, send 'em in, then.'

*

Suzi hadn't seen Greg for over six months, though she did make an effort to stay in touch. Sort of. Julia she hadn't talked to for nearly three years. The multibillionairess was only a couple of years older than Suzi. When she came through the front door, Suzi couldn't find any appreciable signs of ageing. Julia still looked like a young twenty-five-year-old. And she didn't possess the kind of conceit which would send her scurrying to the surgeons. Rich *and* youthful; there just wasn't any justice.

Greg gave her a quick hug and a kiss. Julia seemed at a loss what to do, kiss, shake hands, wave . . .

'I thought you aristo types always knew what to do in every social situation,' Suzi scoffed. 'Inbred etiquette along with all the other deviances.'

Julia screwed up her face and stuck her tongue out.

*

Suzi turned the white presentation box over in her hands. Flowers weren't her thing, though she had to admit it was a bid odd. But— 'Extraterrestrial?'

'Yes.' Julia was sitting on one of the lounge's white-leather pillow chairs. A real close look showed she had stress lines around her eyes and mouth.

Suzi shot Greg a look. 'And what do you make of it?' She'd always been awed, and not a little envious of his intuition. If she had anything like it, no way would Leol Reiger ever have taken her so easily. What Greg said about the flower she'd be happy to go along with.

Aliens were something so far outside her norm she hadn't got a clue how to react at all – except maybe scream and run. But if Julia was right about them arriving in the solar system, they were behaving fucking odd. And what did they look like? More important, what did they want? Why all this secrecy?

Just thinking about it made her ache inside.

'The flower is real enough,' Greg said. 'But as to what the aliens are like, I've no idea.'

'Shit. You're a big help.'

'Forget the implications, if it makes you feel any easier,' Greg said. 'Concentrate on the immediate. All we're going to do tomorrow is track down the courier girl, find out where she got the flower from. Julia takes over from there.' He kept glancing out at the balcony where Andria was lying on the lounger.

'I'll bet you take over,' Suzi muttered. 'Starship technology should bring in a bundle, even by your standards.'

Julia played nervously with her fingers in her lap. 'I just want Royan back,' she said. 'That's all.'

That name was an omen, all bad. Suzi could feel it shackling her to the past, reeling her in. Greg was the same, she figured, all edgy underneath. He really wasn't up to any of this any more, not at his age, he'd been out of it for too long, things had changed. Respect was gone, violence was on the up. Trouble was, they all owed Royan in a big way. Without him, his hotrod expertise, the Trinities would have been wiped off the map.

'You really going looking for the little pillock?' she asked Greg.

'Yeah.'

'Oh, bollocks, count me in.'

7

On top of everything else, this. Julia came down the hypersonic's stairs in a foul mood. It was the children's speech day at school, she never missed that, and wasn't about to start now.

The wind on the top of the Event Horizon tower was cool, blowing off the land. Down below, a thick milky mist covered the quagmire and the deep-water channels, even rising high enough to claim the interlocking metro rail lines. The sun was an anaemic pink nebula hovering somewhere out over the Wash.

Kirsten McAndrews waited for her at the side of the landing pad. 'Is Mutizen's negotiator here yet?' Julia asked her.

'Yes, he arrived on the metro right after you called to set up the meeting.' Kirsten cleared her throat delicately. 'The Welsh delegation are waiting as well.'

'Bloody hell! What do they do, sleep here?'

Kirsten maintained a diplomatic silence.

Julia glanced back down at the Prior's Fen Atoll, where the Mutizen kombinate's arcology lifted out of the oily mist, up-draughts around its sloping walls stirred slow-moving eddies all around the base.

Open Channel to SelfCores. *You three had better be right about this,* she told them crisply.

We are, NN core one replied levelly. *The Cambridge laboratory team has been up all night assessing the data; the concept is radically different from any current technology.*

Julia paused at that. *Different, or just more advanced?*

Different, there's a whole new set of principles involved. Mutizen have come up with a real breakthrough, by the look of things. That's why we gave Peter Cavendish's message a priority one grading.

Right, thanks. She screwed some of the sleep out of her eyes with her knuckles. The Fens Basin was so much quieter at this time of day, passive and clean, less fraught. 'I'd forgotten how refreshing a sea dawn can be,' she told Kirsten McAndrews as they walked into the lift.

*

Royan had loved to sit on the beach and watch the dawn creeping up out of the Atlantic.

It had taken Event Horizon's Bristol clinic twenty months to rebuild him. They cloned his muscles, blood vessels, tendons, nerves, skin, and bones, a hundred diverse glands, organs, and cell clusters, then painstakingly stitched the components together into entire limbs. It was a hugely expensive procedure, not that the money meant anything to her. She had to buy the clinic an extra thirty clone vats, draft in a regiment of specialists. Their so-called Frankenstein department was already one of the most advanced in Europe, but they didn't have anything approaching the necessary capacity. None of the medical team had heard of a case where all four limbs had to be replaced. Normally amputees used kinaware prosthetics, but she wanted him whole again, human. She knew that was the only way he could ever hope to truly banish the past.

Julia visited once a week, never shirking, closing her ears to the pitiful pleas and wails, his demands just to end it all. Royan hated the clinic, it was a constant reminder of the time he had spent hospitalized after the riot, a helpless pain-racked dependant. At least in Mucklands Wood he had been somebody; Son, the one the Trinities depended on for information and technology, an electronic guru. Vital. Venerated. Now she had reduced him to a slab of meat again.

When the process of grafting his new limbs began, the clinic kept him in a near-permanent state of induced somnolence. The few times she visited when he was awake he hadn't been lucid, crying out at the pain, trapped in a looped nightmare of flames and black whips.

Then one day, more than a year after they rescued him from Mucklands, she walked into his room to find him standing, skinny paper-white hands gripping a zimmer frame, blue veins bulging. Pride and wonder illuminated his face. The nurses had to catch him almost straight away, but he'd wanted her to be the first to see him upright again. She had to turn quickly so he couldn't see her tears.

After that, the physiotherapists went to work on him, building the muscles, teaching him co-ordination. Even something as simple as lifting a spoon to his mouth had to be relearnt from scratch. They spent another two months bringing him up to full health with exercises and high-protein diets, massages and deep-heat toning. All the while, Royan's complaints growing louder and crabbier.

Then, when the last medical team had completed their final checks, Julia took him away from the clinic. They went to a small island she owned off Mahone Bay in Nova Scotia, her retreat from the world.

She had bought it a couple of years earlier. A desolate uninhabited place, barely two kilometres across. Grass had survived the Warming, as it always did; but all that remained of the stunted windswept trees were parched white branches lying on the marly soil. She got the island for a song; the hard-pressed Canadian ecological teams were still absorbed with reseeding the continental biosphere, replacing the forests and replanting the prairies. It would be decades before they got round to isolated regions like Mahone Bay.

Event Horizon's botanical crew moved in to reshape the island's habitat, transforming it into the kind of pre-Warming Bahamian paradise she'd seen on the channel shows.

There was a simple wooden bungalow set back from a long sandy beach, the only building. The two of them walked aimlessly along the shore the afternoon they arrived, exploring the gentle bluff behind the beach. A small dense selva forest was spreading out from the island's core, broad-leaved trees draped in pale grey and green epiphyte mosses, tied together by a filigree of vines. The company crew had hatched families of small colourful birds to fill out the ecology. Julia laughed in delight at their antics as they swooped in and out of the branches. Royan was entranced by the profusion of flowers in a natural habitat, smelling their exotic scents, picking them and holding them up to the sun. He reminded her of a child let loose in a spring garden after a long icebound winter.

They ate supper on the creaking veranda, and slipped off to bed as the last fragments of light drained from the day.

Royan had been moulded by her subconscious desire, tall, strong, broad-shouldered, exactly how she imagined the shell of his mind to be in her fantasies, a physique to match the intellect. There was something strangely enticing about a power which could incarnate a lover exactly as envisaged, making sure neither of them would be disappointed. Royan had never argued about the rehabilitation programme she'd selected, it was an anodyne to his previous state. Like her, he wanted his new self to be as far removed from the crippled husk in Mucklands as it was physically possible to get.

For three months they did nothing but laze in the sun and make love. Royan learned to swim. Julia learned to cook, or at least barbecue. Then she found she was pregnant with Daniella.

They returned to England flush with optimism and an inflated sense of omnipotence. It was the future they laid claim to; rich, young, and data smart, digital godlings forging their new bright empire.

She often thought, later, that they were both slightly crazy, the kind of hubristic crazy that always came when the power to build dreams was granted. But they had been a unique combination: her money, his hotrod talent; the result was synergistic. She gave him access to 'ware coming out of Event Horizon's research divisions, so new the security programmers didn't even know it existed. He rewarded her with the personality package, a digital micro-entity capable of functioning within any processor core, self-contained and self-determinative, its purpose reflected in its originator's thought processes.

Together they unleashed a deluge of the sprite-like composites in the global data networks, raiding the research cores of rival companies, adding to Event Horizon's technological base. Then they went for the big one, the electron-compression warhead. Their super-compressed packages squirted into the Sandia National Laboratories processor cores, established themselves within the management routines, and downloaded every file they could find.

The channels called electron compression the rich man's nuke; an explosive which produced a megaton blast without the radio-active fallout of nuclear weapons. Only America, the Russian republic, and China had mastered the technology, though there were rumours of Japan making a successful test under the Pacific.

Julia built the electron-compression warheads on a cyber-factory ship floating in international waters, and used them to knock New London into Earth orbit. The asteroid's mineral reserves, coupled with the giga-conductor royalties, gave Event Horizon a financial primacy which the kombinates could never match.

She gave Royan challenges he could never have conceived of back in Mucklands Wood, she gave him a love he'd never known before, she gave him the most exquisite pair of children. Then she had to stand beside him and watch him lose interest in each one of her gifts. It made her feel so small and destitute, for she had nothing else left to give. Finally, when he walked out without any explanation, she was left clinging desperately to the children in a reflex defence. They were all she had left of the good times, and her sole hope for the future.

*

Two men were already in the office waiting for her. The first was Peter Cavendish, the director of Event Horizon's collaborative ventures office. A bulky fifty-year-old with snow-white hair, his charcoal suit showing signs of being worn too long. Accompanying him was Nicholas Beswick, a physics professor who unfailingly managed to set Julia's nerves on edge with his combination of eagerness and timidity. Nicholas Beswick was basically a complete nerd, but one whose understanding of quantum mechanics was unsurpassed, making him tremendously important to Event Horizon. It was his research team which five years ago had finally produced a processor that utilized one-dimensional wire to carry single electrons. The technology had invigorated the global 'ware industry to a degree which hadn't been seen since the late nineteen-eighties. The amount of money licensed production of quantum-wire processor chips raked in for Event Horizon was second only to that of the giga-conductor royalties.

Nicholas Beswick half bowed, half flinched when Julia entered the office. She gave him a gracious smile as she sat behind her desk, and turned down the window's opacity to let the wan early morning light flood the big room. There were no flowers in the vases yet, the tower's daytime maintenance crew were only just starting their shift.

'Thanks for coming in so quickly, Julia,' Peter Cavendish said. 'I know it was short notice, but I really do think this is important enough to warrant your personal attention.'

'Yes, so I understand. Can you give me a summary of where we stand before Mutizen's negotiator arrives, please.'

Peter Cavendish settled into one of the high-backed chairs in front of her desk. 'Mutizen came to us yesterday with what is a pretty standard proposal. They claimed they have made a break-through in atomic structuring, and asked if we would go into partnership with them to develop and market the technology. They offered us a look at their data under a confidentiality contract. If we decide not to join them we can't research or sell the same technology for five years. Since we don't have any atomic structuring projects right now, I agreed. We were in a no-lose situation. That's what I thought.'

'This atomic structuring process,' she asked. 'You mean they can just assemble blocks of atoms in any pattern they want?'

Nicholas Beswick rocked forwards in his chair, an eager schoolboy grin on his face. 'Yes, that's exactly it. We didn't quite comprehend the implications until after we reviewed their data. At first we were under the assumption that it was just an improved method of our current solid-state assembly techniques; as you know quantum-wire construction is still fairly laborious even with today's ion positioners. But it turned out that Mutizen was talking about a method of locking atoms into place with coherent emissions of gluons, the field particles of the strong nuclear force. They operate directly on the quarks which make up neutrons and protons. If it is possible to manipulate the force like this you could literally solidify air, turn it into a block stronger than monolattice filament.' He sighed, breath hissing through his teeth. 'Ms Evans, I'm not kidding, the potential of this thing frightens the living shit out of me. My staff have been working out applications more or less nonstop ever since they got Mutizen's data package. It can strengthen metal to make it impregnable, harden a bubble of air over a city to withstand a nuclear attack, squeeze deuterium together for fusion, manipulate weather fronts, heck, we could probably even produce lumps of neutronium—'

'Have Mutizen actually physically demonstrated it?' she asked sharply.

'If they have, they haven't told us,' Peter Cavendish said. 'This was just a taster to gain our undivided attention.'

'And believe me it worked,' Nicholas Beswick said. 'All we've been given so far is the force's behavioural equations. No word on the method of generation.'

'Humm.' Julia stared at Nicholas Beswick until he started to redden. 'You're the best I've got, Nicholas, can you see how to build a nuclear force generator?'

He made a farting sound with his lips. 'No way, sorry. It's totally beyond me. In fact, gluon emission of the type they describe isn't even explainable with our current understanding of quantum chromodynamics. They must have something totally and radically new.'

'But the rest of it makes sense to you?' she persisted.

'Absolutely, the maths checks out perfectly. That's not difficult at all, we do know enough about quark properties to confirm their predictions.'

'Interesting.' Julia switched her gaze to the ceiling. **Open Channel to SelfCores.** *What do you three think?*

Mutizen hasn't built a working nuclear force generator, her grandfather said. *It stands to reason. If they had, they wouldn't be offering you a partnership.*

Yes, but why offer me a partnership anyway? They have a lead in a field which no one else even knew existed. Why not just keep plugging away?

Mutizen is a heavy industry kombinate, NN core one said. *Their production is geared towards cars, ships, civil engineering plant, macro-cybernetics, more or less anything mechanical, with mining and foundry divisions. Interesting that a kombinate like that should have a research team working on such fundamental physics in the first place.*

I concur, NN core two said.

Me too, Juliet. The obvious conclusion is that the data isn't theirs. And they don't have the means to develop it themselves, which is why they've come running to you. No skin off their nose. You say yes, and crack the generator; they're plugged into a whole new technology with a minimal outlay. Trouble is, if Event Horizon commits funds and research teams to developing the technology, and in the mean time the real owner emerges with the completed system, you're going to be out in the cold. The giga-conductor and New London aren't going to be worth bugger-all if this atomic structuring is half as good as Beswick reckons.

You mean I've got a little more bargaining power than we thought originally?

Damn right, m'girl. Screw the bastards for every penny you can get.

A smile touched Julia's lips. Good old Grandpa, they weren't made like that any more. *Yes, you're probably right. What I can certainly do is buy us a breathing space. In the mean time, I think it would be a good idea to try and track down the source of this atomic structuring concept. Assemble the most comprehensive profile of Mutizen possible, turn over their financial backing consortiums, review their research personnel for a likely candidate in the atomic structuring field – someone like Beswick. The works. Then get our economic intelligence division to see if any of the other kombinates are building up an investment reserve. If one of them is working on atomic structuring they're going to need some hefty production facilities when it's perfected.*

My girl.

We'll initiate now, said NN core two.

Julia pondered whether to squirt a personality package into Mutizen's management cores to see what it could find, and decided to wait until the preliminary findings were complete first. She refocused on Peter Cavendish and Nicholas Beswick. 'Tea, please, Kirsten, we might as well do this properly. And have Mutizen's negotiator come in now. What's his name, anyway?'

'Eduard Müller,' Peter Cavendish told her. 'He's one of Mutizen's vice-presidents, in charge of their Prior's Fen Atoll power engineering division. Top notch.'

'Power engineering,' Julia mused. 'It has a certain ring to it, I suppose.'

Eduard Müller was a professional premier-grade executive, London suit, Italian shoes, French shirt, sado smile. He had a ginger crew cut, and carefully shaded tan, cloned clear green eyes; his age was indeterminately forty.

Julia hated the sight of him, his manners would be as smooth as his clothes, his English unaccented, they might as well have sent her a cyborg.

He sat in a high-back chair beside Peter Cavendish, radiating friendliness. Two young assistants stood behind him, one male, one female, blank courteous faces. The woman kept a slim black leather briefcase folded under her arm.

'I'll come straight to the point,' Julia said as she left her big breakfast cup of tea to cool on the desk. 'As you can tell from the priority I've assigned this meeting, I'm extremely interested in acquiring atomic structuring technology. Nicholas here is full of praise for its potential.'

Eduard Müller's eyes flicked to an embarrassed Nicholas Beswick, then back to Julia. 'We had every confidence you would be. Obviously we are strongly in favour of an association with Event Horizon, your size and technical ability would make you a perfect partner to help us exploit this technology. A partnership would be most rewarding for both of us.'

'You are envisaging a fifty-fifty split?' Julia asked.

'Yes, although we would expect you to perform most of the final development stage given that we have provided a theoretical framework for you to work from. Your solid-state research division is second to none, whereas it is no secret we lack in that direction. After that, production and marketing would be a joint effort, perhaps handled by a newly created subsidiary, with Event Horizon and Mutizen each holding fifty per cent of the stock.'

'So far all you have shown us is a sequence of interesting equations. I shall require far more substantial data before I can even begin to make a decision.'

'What sort of data were you thinking of?' Eduard Müller asked.

'Your complete research findings on the practicality of a nuclear force generator.'

'It is within my brief to offer you such additional data in return for a certain level of commitment visible on your side.'

'Good,' said Julia. 'Because unless we see some proof that the force generator is theoretically possible, there can be no deal.'

'The data we have assembled concerning the force generator does indicate that it is possible to construct one. It can be made available, providing Event Horizon deposits two hundred million New Sterling in a neutral account as a guarantee of confidentiality. Please understand, I do not ask this lightly. But I'm sure that by now you appreciate the implications of this technology.

It is quite capable of instigating a profound revolution in the pattern of our lives. Its defence applications alone would bring in a revenue far in excess of Event Horizon's annual turnover.'

'Oh, yeah,' Julia drawled. 'I'm aware of the implications. So aware I'm surprised you're prepared to share atomic structuring with anyone.'

Eduard Müller was good, she had to admit that. His face could have been machine-milled steel for all the expression he showed.

'As I said, we have the theorists, you have the facilities; strengths and weaknesses corresponding, the basis of all mutually profitable ventures.'

'Humm.' Julia sipped her tea. She'd been expecting Eduard Müller to spring something like the deposit. A standard business tactic. Mutizen would want to know exactly how keen she was to acquire the atomic structuring technology.

'I will give you an answer in two days,' Julia said.

Eduard Müller inclined his head, the first hint of emotion he had betrayed. 'Of course.'

'Providing you do not make a similar offer to anyone else during that time. You will thumbprint an agreement to that effect before you leave.'

'Ah.' He offered a reluctant smile.

'It will give my assessment team time to draw up a full report based on the data they already have. That's reasonable, surely? Two days isn't going to make any difference to a project of this undertaking. Besides, it will take that long for you and Peter to thrash out the confidentiality clauses; even I don't put two hundred million on the line without reading the small print first.'

'Very well, Ms Evans. I think Mutizen can agree to that.'

*

'Odd,' Peter Cavendish said after Eduard Müller and his two assistants had left.

'Yes,' Julia agreed. 'They produce a few giga-bytes of data, and we embark on an open-ended research project for them.' There was something else, the way Eduard Müller had been wanting a decision straight away. Even if he had wanted it, he shouldn't have shown her that he did. Either he wanted her to know, which made even less sense, or he was under a great deal of stress. Whatever the answer, she had more cards to play with than she'd started with.

She got up and walked over to the window. The mist had melted away under the first rays of the sun, exposing the chocolate mud of the quagmire. Tepid oil-rainbows shivered across its surface. 'He was right about one thing, though. I can't afford not to be involved.'

Peter Cavendish rose from his seat. 'You think they have solved the generator problem?'

'No. At least, nothing past a fundamental theory, a notion how it might be built; that's why they want to bring in Nicholas and his team.'

'So what do you want me to do?'

'I'll need you to draw up two sets of contracts. The worst case, where we have to agree to Mutizen's current terms. The second, I want Mutizen paying half of the development costs with us, and Event Horizon owning fifty-one per cent of the marketing subsidiary stock.'

Peter Cavendish let out a whistle. 'Do you think you can get them to agree to that?'

Julia abandoned the view of Prior's Fen Atoll. If she closed her eyes she could see hologram-colour data streams like arched fairy bridges looping around her. She was woven into the web via her implant nodes, digesting and contributing, but never controlling. The topography of the global data net had long left human understanding behind.

The key to the modern world is retrieval, Royan had told her. All the answers you could possibly want exist somewhere within the world's data cores.

She didn't know what questions to ask. The glowing data web was contracting. Smothering.

Julia opened her eyes, seeing Peter Cavendish's concerned face.

'We've got two days to find some leverage,' she said. 'In the mean time, I've got a speech day to attend.'

8

Greg slipped his leather jacket over a sky-blue sweatshirt. The black leather was thin enough to move easily, thick enough to shield him from the chill of early morning. It had been a present from Eleanor a couple of years back when his old one had finally torn.

'You're going to wear that in Monaco, are you?' Eleanor asked. She was sitting on the edge of their bed, wrapped in a quilted housecoat. Hands fidgeting in her lap, knotting and un-knotting the belt.

Greg glanced at himself in the bedroom's antique full-length mirror. Flat stomach, sideboards frosted with grey, a hint of excess flesh building up on his neck. Not bad for fifty-four. He managed to get down to the gym in Oakham twice a week, *the* fitness bug was something he'd caught during his Army days. After surviving the war in Turkey and the street violence in Peterborough, it would be silly to succumb to clogged arteries and wasted muscles.

'I thought it was all right,' he said. 'Fits the image of an English gentleman farmer.'

Eleanor *tsk*ed in disapproval.

'It's not as if I'm going to a social function with the Prince.'

'Don't I know it,' she mumbled.

Greg went and sat beside her on the bed, his arm going round her shoulders. Eleanor's head remained bowed, focusing on her hands.

There was none of the old pre-mission exhilaration that used to fire his blood. He'd thought there might have been, the one final deal, proving he could still hack it. He knew plenty of married officers in the Army, combat deployment was something their wives accepted. But family had come after that stage of his life, there was no way the two could be reconciled now.

'If you don't want me to go, then I won't,' he said.

'That's blackmail, Greg. Putting it off on me. You know you have to go.'

'Yeah.' He kissed her on the side of the head, tasting hair.

'And you behave yourself around that Suzi.'

Greg laughed and gave her a proper kiss.

Eleanor responded hungrily, then pushed him away. 'Don't, you know where that sort of thing leads.' She looked down at her belly, smile fading.

'Tell you, it's funny,' he said quietly. 'Even five or six years back I would probably have pleaded with Julia for the chance to do this. I mean, Royan missing, in trouble. What could be more important? But now . . . I resent it, this being ruled by the past. And I think Suzi does, too. That was a nice girl she's living with. Pregnant, as well.'

'Suzi?' Eleanor exclaimed.

'No, the girl, Andria. Not that Julia and I were actually told. But you can't hide that from a psychic.'

'Oh. That ought to be interesting. Suzi, a parent.'

'Yeah.' He went over to the dresser and picked up the Event Horizon cybofax Julia had given him yesterday. 'For your own safety,' she'd said. 'It's got a locater beacon for the security crash teams to keep track of you. If you need hardline help, just shout, they'll be there in minutes. And I've loaded one of my personality packages into the memory. You never know, I might actually be of some use to you.'

Greg slipped the palm-sized wafer into his breast pocket. God alone knew what else her security division had squeezed into its 'ware.

He drew back the honey-coloured curtains. Cool early

morning sky, halfway between grey and white. A narrow spire of smoke rose from the dead ashes of the Berrybut estate's bonfire on the opposite shore. Heavy dew coated the grass of the paddock. The pole jumps for Anita's pony made sharp splashes of colour among the pale blades. They wanted a fresh coat of paint, he saw, and the grass was too long.

'I'd better get off,' he said. 'This is going to be a long day.'

*

Rutland Water's high-water level was marked by a thick band of quarried limestone blocks thrown round the entire shoreline to prevent erosion when the reservoir was full. But it had been a hot summer, the farms and citrus groves of the surrounding district had siphoned off a lot of water for irrigation. The vertical water level was already two metres below the bottom of the limestone; on the Hambleton peninsula that produced a broad expanse of mudflats which had dried as hard as concrete under the relentless sun.

Greg and Eleanor walked down the slope from the farmhouse to the limestone, and stood on the top of the crumbling blocks. The travellers' camp was just beginning to stir.

They heard a shout as Christine came running down the slope after them. 'Dad, you were going to leave without saying goodbye,' she accused.

Greg saw the Event Horizon Pegasus hypersonic sink out of the wispy cloud band and skim across the reservoir towards him.

'I'll only be gone a couple of days, at the most,' he said.

Christine threw her arms round him and gave him a wet kiss. Eleanor's peck on the cheek was more demure.

The three of them watched the arrowhead-planform Pegasus slowing; a hundred metres from the shore its nose pitched up. Slats opened in its underbelly, venting the compressor fans' efflux straight down. The undercarriage unfolded, and it settled on the rusty-coloured mudflats in a swirl of dust. A flock of swans drifting on the water behind it rose into the sky, wings pumping frantically.

Greg gave Eleanor a final kiss, and clambered down the nettle-swamped limestone.

There were two security division hardliners waiting for him at the bottom of the hatchway stairs. Pearse Solomons and Malcolm Ramkartra; depressingly young, healthy, and respectful.

'Good morning, sir. We've been instructed to provide you with backup should you request it,' Pearse Solomons told him.

Greg's espersense picked up a hint of resentment in the man's mind. Not a total cyberg after all, then. He went up the stairs in an improved frame of mind.

The windowless cabin had fifteen seats, a compact rosewood cocktail bar at the rear, and a flatscreen on the forward bulkhead beside the door into the cockpit.

Suzi and Rachel Griffith were sitting at the back. Suzi lounging lethargically in her chair, dressed in a dark purple shellsuit. Her mousy hair had been given a crew cut. At least she didn't dye it mauve these days.

'Christ, you look keen,' she said.

Greg sat in the seat beside her. 'You know me.'

'Yeah. Me too. I feel like I've been press-ganged.'

Greg gave Rachel an apologetic shrug.

'I gave up hardlining ten years ago,' Rachel said. 'Exec assistant suited me just fine.'

'Just point her out to us,' Greg said. 'Your job ends there.'

'Yes,' Rachel said; she looked troubled.

Pearse Solomons and Malcolm Ramkartra came up the stairs and sat in the front two seats. The belly hatch slid shut.

Malcolm Ramkartra picked up a slim phone that was built into his armrest. He turned to Greg and Suzi. 'Is Monaco still the destination?'

'Yeah,' Greg said. 'And tell the pilot to put the nose camera image on the screen after we lift.'

'Yes, sir.' Malcolm Ramkartra spoke briefly into the handset.

'We travel on these planes when we go on holiday with Julia,' Greg said. 'I never can get used to not having a port. I grew up with aircraft that you can see out of.'

There was a gentle whine from the fans as they spun up. The deck tilted back slightly.

Suzi grunted. 'Didn't know you went on holiday together.'

'Sure. The kids are all big mates. And I sometimes think Eleanor and I are the only ordinary people Julia knows.'

'You're ordinary, huh?' Suzi grinned evilly.

'More than you, dear, that's a fact.' He felt a press of acceleration as the Pegasus surged upwards. The flatscreen lit up, showing blue sky, splashes of white cloud piling up in the south, and a big pink-gold sun lifting over the horizon.

'It was bad at the start,' Greg said. 'People thought we were an easy route to her. The rich and the social climbers. We couldn't move for presents and invitations. The way they behave, it's ridiculous, disgusting really. Say hello to one, and you're a lifelong friend. They don't know what shame is. One birthday the drive looked like the end of a car factory production line; Jags, Ferraris, Lotuses, MGs. Two of them had a ribbon tied round, for Christ's sake. I sent them all back to the garages. That type just don't know when to give up. And I couldn't count how many times I've been asked to be a non-executive director—' He became aware of Suzi's silent unsympathetic stare.

'It's a hard life, isn't it?' she said.

*

The Pegasus flew at an altitude of twenty kilometres, turning south above the North Sea and passing over the English Channel at Mach two. They hit Mach four heading into the Bay of Biscay, then went subsonic to cross the Pyrenees.

Greg watched their approach to the tiny coastal principality on the bulkhead flatscreen. Circles predominated below, almost as if some weird genealogy of symmetrical aquatic creatures was surfacing to storm ashore. The pink rings of the tidal turbine lagoons, flat dusty-grey field of the airport. Then there was the Monaco dome itself, a faintly translucent golden egg that had driven itself into the cliffs. Two thirds of it extended out into the rich blue water of the sea, radiating white jetties like wheel spokes. He could just make out shaded rectangular outlines through the monolattice shell.

The Pegasus settled on to the airport island. Over half of the parked planes were similar white arrowhead executives, the passenger jets were long flattened cones with narrow fin wings.

Pearse Solomons and Malcolm Ramkartra stood as the belly hatch popped open.

'Are you carrying?' Greg asked the hardliners as he came forwards.

'Yes, sir,' Pearse Solomons said. 'A Tokarev IRMS7 laser pistol.'

'OK. Load up with a second, and come with us. Malcolm, you stay here, and maintain constant contact.'

'I've got a Browning, fifty-shot maser,' Suzi said as she slung a canvas Puma flight bag over her shoulder.

'I sort of took that for granted,' Greg said.

It was hot outside, the expansion joints on the concrete apron creaking in protest, barely audible over the ever-present piccolo hiss of compressor fans. Greg slipped on a pair of Ferranti sunglasses.

Commissaire André Dubaud was waiting at the foot of the stairs, Monaco's deputy police chief.

'Trust him,' Victor Tyo had told Greg. 'He's good at his job, and he understands the politics involved with corporate cases. He's also totally paid for, so there shouldn't be any trouble.'

They shook hands, and Greg introduced Suzi and Rachel. Commissaire Dubaud was in his mid-forties, wearing an immaculate black uniform with a peaked cap.

'Mr Tyo informs me you are looking for a girl,' he said.

'That's right,' Greg said. 'We don't know her name, but she was definitely at the Newfields ball three days ago.'

'May I enquire why you are hunting her?' André Dubaud nodded pointedly at the Pegasus. 'This seems rather a large operation to track down one good-time girl.'

'Certainly. She was in possession of a certain item which interests us. We'd like to ask her a few questions about it.'

André Dubaud glanced at his polished shoes. 'Very well. Are you intending to extradite her?'

'No. She will answer everything I ask her.'

'So?'

'No messing,' Greg said.

*

They drove into the dome in André Dubaud's official car, a black Citröen with fold-down chairs in the rear. Greg thought it was the kind of limo a head of state would normally ride in. He looked hard at a thick white pillar sticking out of the water halfway across. It was made of metal, topped by a petal-segment composite hemisphere. There was another one five hundred metres past the first, heat distortion above the sea made it impossible to see if there was a third.

'What are they?' he asked.

'Tactical defence lasers,' André Dubaud said. 'If Nice comes knocking again, those bastards will wish they hadn't. The principality is impervious to all forms of attack now, from rioters with stones all the way up to KE harpoons. It has to be done, of course. Our inhabitants are the natural targets to certain kinds of diseased minds. But they're entitled to live like anyone else. Inside our dome civilization is total. The one place in the world where you can walk down any street at any time, and never have to look over your shoulder.'

'It sounds as if your department is doing an excellent job,' Greg said. He glanced at Suzi, but she was hunched down in the Citröen's leather seat, staring out of the tinted window, her size making her appear like a sulking child. She hadn't spoken since being introduced to the Commissaire. They were total opposites; Greg reckoned Dubaud knew it as well. If she hadn't been operating under Julia's aegis, he doubted Suzi would even have been allowed to land at the airport.

'There is a degree of fraud perpetrated by our financial community,' André Dubaud said. 'But physical crime – property theft, the act of violence – that is unheard of.'

By banishing the poor, Greg thought, the people who commit robbery and muggings. Monaco hadn't solved crime, they'd just dumped the problem on someone else. Not even New Eastfield in Peterborough went that far. He could sense the stubborn pride in André Dubaud's mind, mingling with a trace of what seemed suspiciously like paranoia. He held back on the urge to inject some sarcastic observations. Maybe that's why Suzi had kept silent, instinctively recognizing the futility. Trying to reason with someone like André Dubaud about basic human dignity would be like pissing in the wind.

The covered bridge from the airport island dipped down, and the Citröen drove through an arch in the base of the dome, coming out on the perimeter road. Clean, that was the impression he got from the tidy rows of white buildings bathing under a tangerine glow, clean verging on sterile.

'Where's the casino?' Suzi asked.

André Dubaud pointed to a cluster of white-stone buildings on the cliffs. She peered up at them curiously.

The Citröen took them right up to the marble front of the El Harhari. A footman opened the door for Greg, and he followed André Dubaud up the stairs into the lobby.

A troupe of cleaners were busy inside, polishing the mirrors and dark wooden furniture, drone vacuums moving up and down the carpet. Claude Murtand, the hotel security manager, met them under one of the chandeliers. With his handsome face and perfect hair he looked like a channel star, dwarfing Suzi.

'A picture of a girl?' he asked after André Dubaud explained what they wanted.

'Yeah,' Greg said. 'She was here for the Newfields ball, name unknown. Attractive, early twenties, short fair hair, wearing a dark-blue gown, possibly silk. We think she's on the game.'

'This is Monaco,' Claude Murtand murmured. 'Who isn't?'

André Dubaud scowled at him.

The El Harhari's white-tiled security centre had a long bank of monitor screens along one wall relaying scenes from around the hotel. Two big flatscreens showed the floorplans, red and yellow symbols flashing in rooms and corridors. There were two island consoles, with three operators each. Claude Murtand had a small glass-walled office at the back.

'We compile a profile on each guest,' Claude Murtand said as he led them in. 'In so far as we can, just what is available in public memory cores. Obviously it's only a secondary precaution. Customs and Immigration filter out anyone genuinely dangerous.'

'That true?' Greg asked André Dubaud.

'Certainly,' the Commissaire said. 'Our passport control is the most stringent in the world. Nobody with a criminal record is allowed in.'

'You and the wife must get lonely here all by yourself,' Suzi said in an undertone.

Rachel smiled faintly. Greg shot Suzi a warning glance. 'What about the Newfields guests, did you put together a profile on them?' he asked Claude Murtand.

'No. We have a complete list of those who originally bought tickets. But unfortunately tickets for these events change hands all the time, especially when someone like Julia Evans is attending, there's no way of knowing in advance exactly who's going to turn up.'

'OK.' Greg switched a finger at the monitor screens. 'Did you record the ball?'

'Of course.'

'Right. We'll start with the lobby camera memory for the night.'

*

There were six cameras covering the lobby. Rachel chose the one giving a head on view of the door; Greg watched over her shoulder.

He recognized the people coming in, the category, not the names. The type that used to pester him and Eleanor during the first years after their marriage. Anybody over twenty-eight had their facial structure frozen in time with annual trips to discreet clinics, until they reached fifty-five, then they were allowed to age with virile silver-haired dignity. Appearance wasn't just important to them, it was everything.

He watched Julia make her entrance a quarter of an hour after the official start. The jockeying to greet her. One statuesque redhead beauty in a shimmering black dress quite deliberately screwed her stiletto heel into the foot of a rival to be sure of being on the front row as Julia walked by.

The faces blurred together. Beauty was a quality which ebbed when it became monotonous, and none of the women lacked it. He concentrated on the dresses, looking for blue.

'That's her,' Rachel Griffith said.

Greg halted the memory playback. The girl had sharp cheekbones, broad, square shoulders held proud. Judging from her build she could have been a professional athlete, except . . . He stared at her. An indefinable quality. Something lacking, perhaps? Rachel was right, she was a pro.

Suzi whistled softly. 'Some looker.'

Greg restarted the memory, and watched the girl walk down the lobby towards the ballroom. He stopped the memory again when she was just under the camera. The white flower box was clasped in her hand. 'Bingo. Can you get me a better shot of her face?' he asked Claude Murtand.

'Certainly.' The security manager slid on to a chair beside Rachel. He checked the memory's time display, and began to call up corresponding memories from the other lobby cameras. He found an image of the girl staring almost straight into one camera above the reception desk, and squirted it into André Dubaud's cybofax. The Commissaire relayed it to the police headquarters central processor core.

'Two minutes,' he said proudly. 'We'll have her name for you.'

'The name on her passport,' Suzi said.

'Madame, nobody with a false passport enters Monaco.'

Greg reversed the memory, watching the girl walk backwards to the door, halted it. She seemed to be by herself. 'Can I see the memory of the outside camera, a couple of minutes before she comes in, please?'

The girl was the only person to get out of a dark green Aston Martin.

André Dubaud's cybofax bleeped. He began to read the data that flowed down the wafer's little screen. 'Charlotte Diane Fielder, aged twenty-four, an English citizen, resident in Austria. Occupation, art student.'

Greg felt a grin tugging his face. Suzi was chording.

'She checked in to the Celestious at four-thirty p.m. three days ago,' André Dubaud continued. 'Then checked out at nine-forty p.m. the same evening.'

'What time did the Newfields ball end?' Greg asked.

'Julia packed up around one o'clock,' said Rachel. 'It was still going strong then.'

'Most had left by four,' said Claude Murtand. 'There was a party of about thirty who stayed on to have breakfast. That would be about seven o'clock.'

Greg closed his eyes, sorting out an order of questions. 'André, would you find out if she's still in Monaco for me, please?'

'Of course.' The Commissaire began to talk into his cybofax.

'Rachel, would you and Pearse review the lobby door camera memory for the rest of the night, please. I'd like to know what time Charlotte Fielder left the hotel. And whether she was alone.'

'Sure thing,' said Rachel.

'What about me?' said Suzi.

Greg grinned. 'You come with me to the Celestious. Make sure I don't get into any trouble.'

'Bollocks,' Suzi muttered.

André Dubaud slipped his cybofax into his top pocket. 'Immigration have no record of Charlotte Fielder leaving the principality, so she's still here,' he said firmly. 'But there is no hotel registration in her name. That means she's staying with a resident.'

Greg ordered his gland to secrete a dose of neurohormones, shutting off Claude Murtand's office, the turbulent thought currents of nearby minds, concentrating inwards. It was his intuition he wanted; now he had a face and an identity to focus on, he could scratch round inside his cranium for a feeling, maybe even an angle on her current location.

But he didn't get the certainty he wanted, not even a sense of mild expectancy, which he would've settled for; instead there was a cold emptiness. Charlotte Fielder wasn't in Monaco, not even close.

*

Back in the Citröen, Greg used his cybofax to call Victor Tyo, and squirted Charlotte Fielder's small file over to him.

'See what sort of profile you can build,' he said to the security chief. 'She's gone to ground somewhere. Be helpful to know friends and contacts. Her pimp too, if you can manage it.'

'You got it,' Victor said. 'Is she still in Monaco, do you think?'

'Commissaire Dubaud believes she is.'

The cybofax screen had enough definition to show a frown wrinkling Victor's forehead. 'Oh. Right. Can you get me her credit card number?'

Greg looked across at André Dubaud, who was sitting on one of the fold down seats, his back to the driver. 'Can we get that from the Celestious?'

'Yes.'

'Call you back,' Greg told Victor.

The Celestious had a faintly Bavarian appearance, a flat high front of some pale bluish stone, a tower at each corner. Windows and doors were highly polished red wood, with gleaming brass handles. The principality's flag fluttered on a tall pole. Greg looked twice at that, there couldn't be any wind under the dome, someone had tricked it out with wires and motors. Utterly pointless. He put his head down, and went through the rotating door. It was the politics of envy. Monaco was getting to him, he was finding fault in everything. Always a mistake, clouding judgement. Never would have happened in the old days.

There was a strong smell of leather in the lobby, the decor was subdued, dark wood furnishings and a claret carpet. Biolums were disguised as engraved glass bola wall fittings.

André Dubaud showed his police card to the receptionist and asked for the manager.

'You think she's made a bolt for it?' Suzi asked Greg in a low voice.

'Yeah. She came here for one thing, delivering the flower to Julia. When that was over, her part in all this finished.'

'Snuffed?'

'Could be.' He scratched the back of his neck.

'But you don't think so.'

'Not sure. My infamous intuition doesn't say chasing her is a waste of time.'

'So how did she get out? This gold-plated rat hole is worse than a banana republic for security.'

'You're the tekmerc, you tell me.'

'No. Seriously, Greg, I'd never take on a deal inside Monaco. Use hotrods to burn data cores in the finance sector, maybe, but only from outside terminals. It's like Event Horizon; something you just have to learn to accept as untouchable.'

'I thought you left Event Horizon alone because Julia owned it.'

Suzi made a big show of shifting the weight round on her shoulder strap. 'Yeah, well. That, and I've seen what's left of people after our angel-face Victor has finished with them. Sometimes there's enough to fill a whole eggcup.'

'He's good, isn't he? Julia and old Morgan Walshaw knew what they were doing giving him the job.'

'Too fucking true.'

'So you don't reckon our Miss Fielder could get out on the quiet?'

'Put it this way, I've never heard of anyone else doing it. And

I would've done. It's the dome which is the problem. A one hundred per cent physical barrier. The only holes are the official ones. Nobody needs to create smuggling routes into Monaco, see? Drugs aren't illegal here. They actually have two pharmaceuticals licensed to produce narcotics. Any kind you want.'

'I didn't know that.' Somehow he wasn't surprised.

André Dubaud walked over to them with the manager, a tall old man with thinning grey hair, who actually wore glasses, round lenses with silver rims. He must do that for effect, Greg thought. It worked too; he had the kind of old-world dignity anyone would trust.

He listened to Greg's request, and beckoned one of the receptionists over. Greg was given Charlotte Fielder's American Express number, which he squirted direct to Victor.

The porter who was on duty the night of the Newfields ball was summoned from the staff quarters. Greg didn't learn much. Charlotte Fielder had phoned the hotel and told them to pack her bags, a car would be sent to collect them. The porter couldn't remember any details, it was a limousine of some kind, black, maybe a Volvo or a Pontiac.

'Not a green Aston Martin?' Greg asked.

'No, sir,' said the porter.

'You seem very sure, considering you couldn't remember the make.'

'We have a complimentary fleet of Aston Martins at the disposal of our guests,' the manager explained. He consulted his cybofax. 'One was booked by Miss Fielder to take her to the El Harhari for the Newfields ball. But that's the only time she used one.'

'Right, can you show me the memory for the camera covering the front of the hotel please.'

The manager gave a short bow. 'Of course.'

They viewed it in his office, sipping coffee from delicate china cups. Greg watched the porter put three matched crocodile-skin cases into the boot of a stretched Pontiac, a chauffeur helped him with the largest.

'Progress,' said Greg. He leant forward and read the licence plate number off to André Dubaud. 'Can we have a make on the driver as well, please.'

'It's a hire car,' the Commissaire said, as his cybofax printed out the vehicle registry data. 'I'll have my office check the hire company's records. The chauffeur's identity won't take a minute.'

Greg and Suzi walked back out into the dome's filtered tangerine light. One of the Celestious doormen was holding the Citröen's door open for them. André Dubaud followed slowly.

'Problem?' Greg asked.

A muscle on the side of André Dubaud's cheek twitched. 'There seems to be a glitch in our characteristics recognition program.'

'Meaning what?' Suzi asked.

'It's taking too long to identify the Pontiac's chauffeur.' He gave the cybofax a code number, and began speaking urgently into it.

Greg met Suzi's eyes as they sank down into the Citröen's cushioning, they shared a sly smile. He knew André Dubaud wasn't going to trace the chauffeur, it wouldn't be a program glitch, that was too complicated. The simple method would be to wipe the chauffeur's face from the police memory core, or make sure it was never entered in the first place. Either way, it would take a pro dealer to organize. His cybofax bleeped.

It was Julia. She appeared to be sitting in Wilholm's study. The walls behind her were covered with glass-fronted shelves, heavy with dark leatherbound books. The edge of a window showed sunny sky.

'How's the speech day coming along?' Greg asked.

Julia smiled. 'You'll have to ask her when she gets back.'

'Right.' He was talking to an image one of the NN cores was simulating. He wondered how many of her business deals were made like this, flattering the smaller company directors with what they thought was a personal interview.

'Rachel was right about Charlotte Fielder,' Julia said. 'She's quite well known, at least to us. She's one of Dmitri Baronski's girls. Security keeps a fairly complete list of his stable in case any of my executives should stumble.'

'Who's Dmitri Baronski?' Greg asked.

'A first-class pimp, although that doesn't do him justice, he's a lot more than that. Clever old boy, lives in Austria. Runs a stable of girls who aren't quite as dumb as they like to make out to their clients. He's made a fortune on the stock market based on loose talk they've picked up for him.'

'No messing?' For the first time, Greg began to feel a certain anticipation. 'So this Fielder girl was a good choice as courier, then?'

'Yes. After all, would you know how to deliver a present to me, and be sure I'd see it?'

'Royan would,' Greg said. 'But you're right; method is one thing, carrying it off is another. Fielder must be bright enough to realize some of the implications of what she was doing.'

*

Rachel, Pearse Solomons, and Claude Murtand were sitting round the El Harhari security centre's desk drinking tea. A plate of biscuits rested on top of the terminal. The monitor screens were dark.

'Got her,' Rachel said. 'She left at five to eleven, and she was with someone.'

Greg didn't like the dry amusement leaking into Rachel's voice, it suggested a surprise.

Claude Murtand called up the memory, and Greg watched Charlotte Fielder walking out of the El Harhari with a young teenage boy. The kid kept sneaking daunted looks at Charlotte Fielder's low-cut neckline, his smile flashing on and off.

Greg halted the memory and studied the boy's eager, wonder-struck face. There was something not quite right about him. It was as if he was a model; everything about him, the awkward-ness, the slight swagger, a designer's idea of teenager.

'She'll eat him alive,' Suzi snorted gleefully. 'He won't last the night.'

'Way to go,' Rachel said.

'André, can you get a make on that boy for me, please?' Even as he said it, Greg knew the boy would defy identification, just like the chauffeur. Judging by the apprehensive way André Dubaud was ordering the make, he thought so too.

'What car did they leave in?' Greg asked Claude Murtand. The hotel security manager tapped an order into his terminal's keyboard, and played the outside camera memory on a monitor screen.

Greg and Suzi groaned together. It was the Pontiac.

He got Claude Murtand to run the outside camera memory, and watched the Pontiac rolling up to the El Harhari's front door; the same chauffeur who'd driven it at the Celestious hopped out and opened the doors. Charlotte Fielder and her boy companion climbed in. Greg asked to see it again, a third time. His intuition had set up a feathery itch along his spine.

'Freeze it just before Fielder gets in,' Greg told Claude Murtand. 'OK, now enlarge the rear of the car.'

The image jumped up, focusing on the open door and the boot. Charlotte Fielder's raised foot hovered over the door ledge.

'More,' Greg said.

The image lost definition badly, black metal and darkened glass, fuzzy rectangular shadows stacked together. He peered forward.

'Suzi, look at the rear window, and tell me what you see.'

She sat in Claude Murtand's seat right in front of the monitor screen, screwed up her eyes. 'Shit yes!' she exclaimed.

'What?' Rachel demanded.

Greg tracked an outline down the left-hand side of the rear window, a ghost sliver of deeper darkness. 'There's someone else in there.'

*

Greg could sense André Dubaud's growing anger; there was worry in there as well, churning his thought currents into severe agitation.

'It would seem that my office is unable to identify the boy at this time,' the Commissaire said.

Greg knew how much the admission hurt him. The Nice sacking was burned into the psyche of Monégasque nationals, everything they'd done since had been structured around safeguarding the principality. Now people were coming and going as they pleased. The wrong sort of people.

'No shit,' Suzi said, and there was too much insolence even for her.

'Madame, everyone who comes to Monaco is entered in the police memory core. Everyone. No exceptions.'

'Wrong. You squirt my picture into this characteristics recognition program of yours, or Greg's, or Rachel's, or Pearse's. You'll get bugger-all back, just like the chauffeur and the kid. We never showed our passports to anyone, never thumbprinted an Immigration data construct.'

'Certainly not,' André Dubaud said. 'You are here as Madame Evans's guests. I know how much importance she attached to your mission. Though I might question her judgement in your case. Naturally, considering the urgency, you were spared the inconvenience.'

'And that's it,' Suzi said. 'Greg asked me how I'd pull someone from this pissant lotus land. Said I couldn't. I don't have what it takes, I'm hardline and covert deals. What you need for this is money. That's what jerks your strings, Commissaire. Money. You people have turned it into a fucking religion, you fawn over the stuff. Christ, all Julia's got to do is speak, and you roll over and spread your legs. All 'cos she's loaded.'

André Dubaud had reddened, lips squashing into a bloodless line, taking slow shallow breaths through his nose.

'Yeah, thank you, Suzi,' Greg said. 'How about it, André? Is there anyone else in the police department apart from yourself who has the authority to waive Passport and Immigration controls?'

'There are some others who could sanction such a courtesy.

But it could only be done if the circumstances justified it,' André Dubaud said sullenly.

'How many people?'

'Please understand, money is not all that is required. The person making such a request would have to be of impeccable character.'

'How many?'

'Twenty-five, thirty. Perhaps a few more.'

'Oh, great.'

*

Victor's face formed on Greg's cybofax as soon as he entered the code.

'Charlotte Fielder was lifted out of here,' Greg said. 'No doubt about it. This is a real pro deal; lot of money, lot of talent. The Pontiac that spirited her away from the Newfields ball was hired, the bloke who paid was the chauffeur. There's no trace of him, he wasn't entered in the police memory core. Same result for the boy she left with. As for the other person in the car, I couldn't even tell you if they were male or female.'

The other three, Rachel, Suzi, and Pearse Solomons were sitting quietly round Claude Murtand's office, happy to let him summarize. The air conditioner was humming softly, sucking out the accumulated moisture. Claude Murtand and André Dubaud were on the other side of the glass wall, talking in low tones, and casting an occasional unhappy eye in his direction.

'I can't add much,' Victor said. 'Fielder hasn't used her Amex card for the last three days, so no leads for that. But then she hadn't used it for a ten-day period prior to booking into the Celestious, either.'

'What did she use it for ten days ago?' Greg asked.

Victor glanced at something off screen. 'It was in Baldocks, that's a department store in Wellington, New Zealand. A bill for forty-three dollars; but it wasn't itemized.'

'Not important,' Greg said. 'So what was she doing for the ten days between Wellington and Monaco?'

'That's what you're supposed to tell me,' Victor said.

'Meeting Royan,' Suzi said.

'Right. But where?' said Greg. 'I have two questions, based on what we've found out so far. Firstly, why take so much trouble over a courier? Given that all she had to do was deliver the flower box to Julia, someone has gone to a hell of a lot of effort to stash her away.'

'Because she can lead us to Royan,' Suzi said.

'Fair enough. So that means the people behind her, the ones with the Pontiac, don't want us to know where Royan is. Ordinarily, I'd say that pointed to a kidnapping.'

'But there's the flower,' Victor said.

'Yeah, and also the eight months that Royan's been missing. Holding someone for eight months without a ransom demand is ludicrous.'

'Who knows how alien minds work?' Suzi asked.

'Not me,' said Greg. 'But the chauffeur and the kid were human—' he broke off, remembering the boy's perfection. 'Make that humanoid.'

'Oh, bollocks,' Suzi said. 'Fucking aliens walking round Monaco.'

'They might have the technological know-how to enter and leave the dome whenever they wanted,' Greg pointed out. But he couldn't bring himself to believe it. Too complicated, especially now they had established money could do the job just as easily. 'The thing is, someone powerful is moving Fielder around. That's the second question. Why not bring her in to Monaco the way she was taken out? Letting her come in through the normal channels, going through Passport control, thumbprint, the legal construct, then booking into the Celestious; all of that let's us find out who she is. Why? When they could obviously have handed over the flower to Julia, and left us completely in the dark?'

Suzi stretched in her chair. 'Go on. You've obviously got an answer.'

'Two different groups,' Greg said. 'She came from Royan, to deliver the flower. Then afterwards, someone else nabbed her.'

'If it was a tekmerc squad, could you find out, Suzi?' Victor asked.

'Maybe. But it would take time. Week, maybe two. Then longer to find out who put the deal together.'

'Not good enough,' said Victor.

'Fuck you too.'

'If you want my opinion,' Greg said, 'the group that arranged for Fielder to be lifted are the ones who took the first sample from the flower.'

Victor nodded. 'That fits. You think they'll have found Royan by now?'

'If they had a psychic interrogate Fielder, it would take a minute to find out what she knew. Drugs and a polygraph, that's about thirty minutes. They've had her for nearly three days now.'

'Bloody hell.'

'There's one easy short cut we could try,' Greg said. 'Phone Fielder's cybofax number, and use whatever clout Event Horizon has with English Telecom to find out the co-ordinate.'

'Good idea,' said Victor.

His image on Greg's cybofax slid smoothly to one side. Julia appeared on the other half, sitting in her study again. Nothing behind her had moved, even the sunlight shining through the window was at the same angle.

'No need to make it an official request,' she said. 'I'm infiltrating the location response targeting software in Intelsat's antenna platforms. Calling Fielder's number now.'

Greg waited.

'No reply,' Julia said. 'There isn't even a signal from the transponder.'

'Keep trying.'

'If all they wanted from Fielder was Royan's location, then she's probably been snuffed,' Victor said.

'No, she hasn't,' Greg said.

'OK.' Victor subsided with good grace. He had seen Greg's intuition at work before.

Greg wondered what young Pearse Solomons was making of

all this. The security hardliner had been sitting at attention ever since Victor had come on the cybofax. After Julia appeared he hadn't taken a breath.

'That just leaves us with Baronski,' Greg said.

'What can he tell us?' Suzi asked.

'Charlotte Fielder left the party early, with a rich young boy, in an expensive car. She walked out of the El Harhari freely, I'd almost say happily. That means the boy was either someone she knew, or more likely the son of a client. Either way, Baronski should be able to tell us.'

9

It was the sun again, inexplicably wrong. Charlotte finally twigged the reason when she was having a latish breakfast in the *Colonel Maitland*'s aft dining-room.

Fabian sat opposite her as usual. He acted dazed, almost in shock, barely eating his cereal. Every time he looked at her it was with an unsettling degree of reverence.

But then Fabian was a boy in lust. He was also a remarkably fast learner. She had spent a strenuous two hours last night coping with his enthusiasms and demands before he finally drifted off into an exhausted sleep, then he'd been ready for more this morning. Which was why they turned up late at the table.

Jason Whitehurst was already sitting at the table waiting for them. He greeted them with an unabashed smile. 'Ah, glad to see you young people are getting on so well.'

Fabian blushed hot crimson.

Jason Whitehurst had chosen his cereal, unperturbed, and ordered his cybofax to display the London *Times*, which he read as he ate.

Charlotte could hear the waiter squeezing fresh orange juice at the side table behind her. She started in on her own cereal bowl. The sun was filling the dining room with a liquid rose-gold light, rising into view directly behind Jason Whitehurst. She stared at it, feeling cold despite the thick cotton of her summer dress.

Jason Whitehurst looked up from his cybofax. 'Something wrong, my dear?'

'West,' she said numbly. 'We're heading west.'

'That's right.'

'But Odessa is east of Monaco. I thought we were going around Italy, then up into the Black Sea.'

'No.' Jason Whitehurst inspected a slice of toast, then began buttering it. 'My agent has taken care of my business in Odessa. There's no need to go there now. Great relief all round, one expects. I told you what it was like.'

The waiter put a glass of orange down in front of Charlotte. She ignored it. 'Where are we going, then?'

'Going?' Jason Whitehurst affected puzzlement. 'Why, my dear girl, the *Colonel Maitland* simply drifts. On a whim and a prayer, I always say. I had a notion that South America would be nice. You and Fabian could laze around on the beach, that sort of thing, whatever it is a boy and a girl do together these days. How does that sound, young man?'

'Great, father,' Fabian said cautiously.

'Which country in South America?' Charlotte asked. It was hard to maintain her pose of polite seminal interest.

'Oh, I don't know. I really hadn't given it any thought, to be woundingly honest. Why, have you got any preferences?'

For once she was stuck for a reply. There was a small part of her mind thinking that Baronski would be shaking his head in dismay; questioning her patron's intent, letting her own disapproval show. It simply was not done. But either Jason Whitehurst was the most carefree soul she'd ever met, or he was being deliberately obtuse.

She'd heard of patrons like that, not that there were many, thank heavens. Instead of physical mastery, they went in for nasty psychological games. Mental kinks designed to rip the sense of order from a bewildered girl, reduce her to a disorientated nervous wreck. It gave them a sense of power. A mind set which got its bang from destruction.

Charlotte remembered talking to one of the women tutors

that Baronski had sent her round to learn the extras which put her so far above the others of her trade. The woman had told her it was all down to age and bitter jealousy; the patrons wanted to punish the girls for their youth and beauty, something their money could never bring back to them.

Charlotte reckoned that no one with a trading empire as large as Jason Whitehurst could have the kind of slapdash mind he alluded to.

She ran quickly through her options. 'French Guiana is supposed to be nice,' she said with cheerful enthusiasm. 'It has some wonderful beaches. Then there's the tropical nature park we could tour; that has some of the oldest original rain forest on the continent. And they're still discovering new insect species each year.' French Guiana was also one of the closest South American countries to Europe; which meant the voyage would be over as quickly as possible, and she could skip out.

'I can't somehow imagine Fabian being vastly interested in bugs; is that right, young man?'

Fabian looked at Charlotte, then at his father. Trapped, not wanting to disappoint either. She felt sorry for him.

'Isn't French Guiana where Devil's Island is?' Fabian asked.

Jason Whitehurst pulled at his beard. 'Yes, do you know, I think you're right there. The jolly *Île du Diable*. I might have guessed a red-blooded lad like you would show an interest in the totally macabre. Still, can't be helped, all part of growing up. So, French Guiana it is, then.'

*

Charlotte dived straight into the *Colonel Maitland*'s pool and started doing lengths, a smooth easy freestyle with a neat flip at each end. It was one of the best ways she knew of working off frustration, losing herself in the mechanical spin of limbs, not having to think. She stopped after thirty lengths; the pool was smaller than she was used to. There wasn't the distance to work up a decent speed, or maybe she was just spoilt.

'Crikey, is there anything you're no good at?' Fabian asked. 'I thought I was a good swimmer, but you just left me standing.'

'Sorry. I was a bit wound up over Odessa.'

'Oh.' The corner of his mouth depressed. 'Father can be a bit, well, casual, at times. I suppose it must be unusual unless you're used to it.'

She swung her legs up, and floated on her back. Now probably wasn't a good time to ask what happened to his father's previous girls, if they left in floods of tears.

'Now I know where we're heading I'll be all right.' She began to swish her feet, heading for the window. 'You didn't have to say you wanted to go to French Guiana, you know. I wouldn't have been offended.'

'No, really, I wanted to go.' He started swimming beside her. 'Well, all right, not the trees and caterpillars and things. But I would like to see Devil's Island. And the beaches, with you.'

Charlotte steadied herself on the side of the pool by the window. She looked down thoughtfully on the water below. 'Where are we now, do you think?'

Fabian held on to the side, eyes on her rather than the water. 'It's the Atlantic, we're west of Africa. I can get you the exact co-ordinates if you want.'

'No, thank you Fabian, that's all right. It's just a pity we missed seeing Gibraltar. Have you ever been there before?'

'No.'

'If the *Colonel Maitland* comes back to the Mediterranean some time, then remember to ask your father to show you. The Straits drop flow is quite something; that tiny little gap is the only place the Mediterranean basin can fill up from. Thermal expansion didn't raise the Mediterranean's level as high as the oceans, the water was warmer to start with. So the Atlantic is still a good couple of metres higher, and that's after nearly twenty-five years. They won't reach equipoise for a long time yet.'

'Did you ride it?'

'No. I was too scared, the drop flow is over five kilometres long. I watched the macho loonies doing it, through. You sit in one of the overhang cafés on the rock, and your bones shake from the turbulence round the base, the sound is like one continual thunderclap. They reckon the rock itself will be gone in a few more decades. Nothing can resist that sort of pressure.'

She remembered more, the sleek canoe-like capsules that people rode the Straits drop flow in, like phosphene dots zipping across her vision as she watched that incredible surge of white water from the safety of the café. Two of the people in her group had wanted to try it, knowing full well the drop flow claimed a couple of lives a week.

She thought at the time how little regard they had for their own lives. There was a degeneracy building in the world's rich, becoming more advanced with each generation. There used to be a kind of adventurism in the excitement they sought, the power boat racing, desert car rallies, polar trekking. But now the element of calculation was missing from the risks they took, superseded by recklessness, a return to the live fast die young ideal. She supposed it was an answer to the increasing jadedness of their existence, in this world so much pleasure could be bought on the cheap. Their urge towards self-destruction set them apart from the poor again.

'Sounds great,' he said.

She realized he hadn't really been listening. He was still looking at her, query and longing bound up in his worshipful stare. What would he be like when he was eighteen? 'I'll do a deal with you, Fabian.'

'What?'

'If you take my bikini off, I'll pull your trunks down.'

*

Fabian's bedroom had been furnished with the same expensive care and attention lavished on the rest of the airship – an antique dresser, upholstered Nordic chairs, Chinese carpet, two pale still-life paintings in slim plain gilt frames. But the drawer had scratches, and a very odd purple stain that was still sticky; T-shirts, towels, and shorts hung all over the chairs; shoes and blade roller skates dotted that carpet; bawdy holograms of bimbo bands had been tacked up on the walls.

Fabian was a pretty ordinary teenager after all. One den the size of a small warehouse wasn't nearly large enough for all his rubbish.

Charlotte had only ever seen it when the light was low, in daylight it was even worse. She sat cross-legged in the middle of the bed, with her bikini back on, watching Fabian. He was squatting on his towel in front of the big wall-mounted flat-screen; it was tuned to French MTV, playing an old Rolling Stones track, the sound muted. But he was looking down at his cybofax, doing the London *Times* crossword with one hand, holding a choc-ice bar in the other.

She had never seen anyone do the crossword so fast. He would take a bite from the ice-cream and read the clues, then his fingers would dance over the keys. There was never any hesitation, no referring back to the cybofax's dictionary function. She was tempted to ask him about a bioware node again; but that would make an issue out of it. Besides, she didn't think Fabian had lied back at the pool yesterday. She didn't think Fabian would know how to lie to her about anything.

So how could he demolish the crossword like this?

'Doesn't the maid ever clean up here?' Charlotte asked.

Fabian looked round with bemused curiosity. 'The staff take my clothes and stuff to be washed. But I'd lose everything if it was put into drawers.'

She picked up a metre-long model of an old-style military tilt-fan. It was heavier than she'd expected. The miniature missiles looked very realistic. 'What can you do with this in-doors?'

Fabian flipped his lock of hair aside. 'Nothing, stupid. I fly it from the *Colonel*'s landing pad. Do you want to come up and try it? I'll let you use the remote, it's dead easy.'

'Maybe later. Where do you get all this stuff from? You must go on week-long shopping expeditions when the *Colonel Mait-land* reaches a town.'

'Oh no, I pick it all out from catalogue channels, and have it forwarded to our next airport. The Gulfstream collects it for me.'

'I see.' Jason Whitehurst hadn't been exaggerating when he said he kept Fabian on board the *Colonel Maitland* the whole time. She didn't approve of that at all. Not that she could ever say so.

'I'll have the maids clean it up if you don't like it,' Fabian offered generously.

'I don't think your father could afford the overtime bill.'

Fabian burst into gleeful laughter. 'How do you do that?'

'What?'

'Everything you say is always just right. The clothes you wear make you look utterly fantastic. You can swim well. You're a super dancer. You know about everywhere in the world, not just what countries look like, but their politics as well. You're like a superwoman, or something.'

'That's age, Fabian. When you're as ancient as me, you'll have learnt it all as well.'

Fabian dropped his eyes. 'You're not old.'

'You're very sweet.'

'You said you wouldn't call me things like sweet and cute again,' he said petulantly. 'Not now I'm your lover.'

'Sorry.'

'Charlotte?'

'Yes.'

'Can we do it again?'

He might be bright, she thought, but he had a grasshopper mind. 'I think we might, yes.'

Fabian scrunched up the choc-ice wrapper and lobbed it in the direction of the bin, then bounced on to the bed beside her. 'I forgot, you're incredibly sexy too.' He said it timidly, as though he was swearing in church.

'Thank you.' Charlotte straightened her legs, and lay on her side next to him. 'Remember what I like?' She kissed him, hand running over his belly. Her voice deepened. 'How to make me ask you for more?'

Watching her face closely, Fabian reached out and undid the bikini top. He smiled greedily as the triangular scraps of fabric came free in his hands, and began to stroke the length of her ribcage the way she'd taught him. 'What's it like in space?'

Charlotte groaned, the mood spoilt. 'Oh, heavens, Fabian. I've told you all I possibly can. If you want to know any more, you'll have to go there.'

'No. I meant, you know, *that* . . . freefall sex.'

'Oh. Unearthly delights.'

'What?' he choked.

'Unearthly delights, that's what the New Londoners call it.'

'Wizard! So what's it like?'

'I don't know. Never had the chance to try it.'

'No?'

She could read him like a book. He didn't believe her. 'No. But I admit I was thinking of it; I met a nice local boy while I was there. But I cut four days off the end of my holiday and came home early. So I never got the chance in the end. I expect it's overrated, tourist board propaganda.'

'You packed up a holiday in space early! Whatever for?'

Charlotte swore silently. This airship flight was affecting her more than she liked, her self-discipline was going all to hell. 'I had to get back for some business, and then there was the Newfields ball. Why? Would you rather I was still up there?'

'No! Crikey, Charlotte,' he said, genuinely indignant. 'Don't say things like that.'

She ran a hand over his chin, momentarily confounded by the lack of stubble.

Fabian drew a quick breath. 'Hey, listen, I've just had a tremendous idea. We can go up to New London together. Right? You heard Father say I could go in a couple of years. Well, I will. It'll be wizard. We could spend the whole time in freefall. Unearthly delights!' He giggled and clapped his hands exultantly.

It took a supreme effort to maintain her light smile. Dear

God, he was a besotted teenager who thought she was going to stay with him till death us do part, amen. Sex equals love, they all thought that at his age. How could she have been so stupid, getting herself into this situation? It could only ever end in heartbreak now.

Fabian was waiting, flushed and deliriously expectant.

'A couple of years is a long time to wait.' She took hold of his hands, and placed them firmly on her breasts. 'And I know some pretty good earthly delights.'

*

Charlotte let the shower's hot spray play over her back, soapy water running down her thighs and calves. It felt good, relaxing her. The sharp jets of water pounded into her skin like a scratchy massage. Steam swirled around, warming her all the way through.

What the hell was she going to do about Fabian? He wasn't a bad kid, certainly he deserved a lot better than her and his father. The obvious thing to do was cut and run as soon as she reached French Guiana. He was young, resilient, he'd get over her fast enough. Except she knew how much it would hurt him. How much *she* would hurt him.

She couldn't bear the thought of that trusting, mischievous face screwed up in misery. In itself an unusual, and disturbing, admission.

God damn Jason Whitehurst for not bringing up his son properly. And God damn Baronski for not knowing what Jason Whitehurst had wanted her for. The old boy was normally so careful about what he got his girls into.

Charlotte gave her hair a final rinse and turned off the shower. She wrapped a big towel around herself, then used another to dry her hair. The robe she'd worn over her bikini to walk about in through the gondola was lying on the damp tiles, soaking up the condensation the shower had thrown out. It could stay there now. The maid could clean it. Bitch.

She sat down in front of the mirror, and combed out her

hair. Her cabin hadn't got that stale stuffy taste in the air like Fabian's. It gave her room to breathe, room to move. Having her own cabin was the only real plus of this assignment. She liked the times she was on her own, an interval when she could be reflective, when every move and word wasn't an effort.

She looked at the image in the mirror, stretching, wriggling her toes. 'Gawd luv us, ducks. See 'ow grand we is nahdays.' She giggled. Funny, it was harder to do that accent now than the upper-middle-class one Baronski had patiently coached her in. The past really had died.

Charlotte got up and searched through her bedside cabinet. Her gold Amstrad cybofax was in the second drawer. She took it out and sat on the bed, curling her legs up. 'Phone function,' she told the wafer, then gave it Baronski's number. He probably couldn't help her out of her predicament straight away, but she could vent a lot of her frustration on him. It was something he was always good at, always there as a shoulder to cry on. Everyone needed someone like that, life would be unlivable otherwise. And in any case, she needed to tell him she wouldn't be going to Odessa. He liked his girls to keep in touch.

UNABLE TO ACQUIRE SATELLITE LINKAGE, the cybofax screen printed.

Charlotte stared at it. Unable? She climbed off the bed and walked over to the window. The jet-black solar envelope hull of the airship curved away above her like a medium-sized moon. No wonder the cybofax's signal couldn't reach the geostationary antenna platform.

There was a standard terminal on the other side of the bed, but she shied away. If she was going to have a decent rant at Baronski about Whitehurst she didn't want to do it on the man's own 'ware. More than one of her patrons had routinely recorded calls.

Charlotte began looking through drawers for her Ashmi jumpsuit. She could go up to the landing pad, the cybofax would work from there.

Maybe if she stuck out this assignment for another month, push Fabian away gradually. That might work, no hard feelings on either side, and a wonderful memory of first love for the rest of his life. But another month of this? At least in French Guiana there would be the beach bars, and some decent nightlife.

Charlotte was zipping up the jumpsuit when there was a rap at the door. The maid came in.

'Mr Jason would like to see you,' she said.

'OK, I'll be about twenty minutes.'

'He said now.' There was a definite gloat in the voice.

*

Fabian had shown her where his father's study was, in the midsection of the lower gondola deck, but they hadn't gone in. Now Charlotte found it was equipped with ultra-modern fittings, the first she'd seen on board. Walls, floor, and ceiling were a silver-white composite; flatscreens showed homolographic maps of the globe, coastlines glowing sharply, cities and ports tagged with ten-digit codes. Jason Whitehurst was sitting behind a smoked-glass desk that resembled a rectangular mushroom. She could see tiny red and green lights inside the glass top, squiggling like trapped fireflies. It was the only piece of furniture in the room.

The heels of her leather ankle boots clicked loudly as she walked towards him.

'Chair,' Jason Whitehurst said. A circle of floor in front of his desk turned grey. It extruded upwards, a smooth cylinder at first, then it began to flow, like something organic caught by time-lapse photography.

Charlotte sat tentatively in the curving scoop chair which formed. It felt as hard as rock under her fingernails.

'You attempted to use your cybofax to make an external call,' Jason Whitehurst said.

'Yes.'

'I must ask you not to do that again. I am conducting some very delicate negotiations at the moment.'

'I won't interrupt them. It was just a call to a friend.'

'You called Baronski.'

150

Charlotte began to wonder if it had been the bulk of the airship hull which had blocked the call, after all. 'That's right. He likes to know where I am, and as we're not going to Odessa—'

'He likes to know what you hear.'

'Pardon me?'

'Baronski deals in the information you supply him. That will not be the case on this voyage.'

'I wasn't going to say anything about you. I don't know anything about you.'

'Nor will you. I purchased you purely to provide Fabian with some amusement, nothing more. Now that is all.'

It took a moment for the dismissal to sink in. Charlotte rose on legs which were suddenly trembling. Once the door had slid shut behind her she rubbed her eyes. Her knuckles seemed to be very damp.

10

The Pegasus carrying Victor Tyo to Duxford settled on to the rooftop pad with a slight rocking motion as the undercarriage absorbed the plane's weight. The stewardess opened the belly hatch, and Victor trotted down the stairs. His bodyguard followed a few paces behind.

He supposed the necessity of having a bodyguard was an oblique compliment to his own efficiency. The latest generation of tekmercs tended to take failure personally, regarding their activities as something companies should tolerate, like fires or bad debts. If their deals got blown, it wasn't their fault. Like petulant children caught shoplifting.

It was a problem which meant simply blowing the covert operations they mounted against Event Horizon wasn't good enough any more. He had to root out the whole nest of them involved every time.

The current price for assassinating Victor Tyo was half a million Eurofrancs, offered by Eugene Selby after his attempt to snatch research data on magnetic logic circuits ended with his hotrods being backtracked and taken out by a couple of Foxhound missiles. The price for killing that assassin should he or she prove successful was a million Eurofrancs. A quarter of a million Eurofrancs could be picked up by anyone who cared to reveal Eugene Selby's present geographical coordinates.

Victor's life was nearly all tangled up in deterrent circles like that these days. It didn't particularly bother him. All part of the game. His choice to be a player had been made long ago.

Right back when he joined the security division, Morgan Walshaw had told him, 'Once in, never out; this job is for always.' He'd been young enough then to nod seriously and say, 'Yes, sir, I understand perfectly.' Understand, but not completely appreciate. Always was turning out to be a long time.

Lately he'd taken to saying the same thing to recruits himself. His division had grown in proportion with the commercial side of Event Horizon; it matched national intelligence agencies in size, possessing the tactical strike power equal to a couple of RAF squadrons.

The three major opposition parties at Westminster were constantly demanding enquiries into tekmerc-planted rumours of his activities, and even the New Conservatives were becoming nervous. If it hadn't been for the fact that ministers heeded Julia on their side over Wales, incidents like the Selby deal could well result in the police taking a more active interest. As if they had the capacity to deal with tekmercs, but try telling that to politicians. Event Horizon security wasn't the cause of problems, it was the result of them.

His staff were currently monitoring eighteen separate tekmerc deals being mounted against the company. There was definitely a leak somewhere inside the biochemical division, which even the psychics couldn't pin down. And now he had aliens coming at him.

I wonder what old Walshaw would make of that one?

It wasn't that life had been easier in his day, but at least the battle lines were a hell of a lot clearer.

It was hot outside the hypersonic, although Duxford was spared Peterborough's swamp humidity; that was something he'd never acclimatized to. The plane had landed on the roof of Building One at the Event Horizon Astronautics Institute. It was typical of the space industry to use that kind of nomenclature, he thought, reflecting the medium they dealt in. Cold, vast, and soulless.

Building One was a five-storey ring of offices and laboratories, eight hundred metres in diameter. The circular space they enclosed was covered by a domed solar collector roof, rising up beside him like a crack into space, sucking light and heat from the air. Looking the other way, Victor could just make out the stone buildings of Cambridge's colleges, trembling in the heat haze. The rest of the city was a pastiche of red brick and black solar panels. Hardly any modern buildings. It made a pleasant change.

Building Two was a clone of Building One, sitting a kilometre away, on the site of the old War Museum buildings, its green-silver glass wall bouncing spears of tinted sunlight at him. Building Three was the big brother of the first two, its outer ring fifteen storeys high, sixteen hundred metres in diameter. A mile, back in Birmingham where Victor grew up, where they still clung to the real England of pints and inches with the obstinacy of people frightened by the seemingly perpetual flux which the Warming had brought early in the millennium. Searching for the sanctuary of stability in erstwhile customs.

Spaceplanes hummed gracefully through the sky, big swept-wing delta shapes; arriving from the west and landing, departures racing away to the east. The long line of pads that accommodated them had been built along Duxford's old runway, he remembered. The War Museum's original geography was all very vague in his mind now. He could barely recall the lie of the land before Building One had gone up, seventeen years ago. Change hadn't stopped after the Greenhouse Effect plateaued, if anything it had redoubled its confusion.

Building Four was half completed, another one the size of Three; the first three storeys of glass already in place, as if the green-silver panes were organic, a crust that grew up the naked concrete and composite structure. And he knew that Julia had begun preliminary discussions with the bankers and finance houses for Building Five.

Even after all this time, after penetrating the Evans mystique, seeing her angry, frightened, sad, and drunk, he still looked on

Julia as a figure of awe. People were fascinated by her because of her money, blinded by it. Nobody understood, she had a thousand critics, snipers, detractors. All of them claiming they could do the job better. He knew different, Julia actually cared about the country. In that she was almost unique in an era of multinationalism, the abrasion of significant borders; but she insisted the critical divisions of Event Horizon were all sited in England. The software writers, the research teams, product designers, the factories which produced the 'ware chips. Other countries were given the assembly lines, the metal-bashing subsidiaries, but the heart of every piece of Event Horizon gear was built in England. That was where the real work lay, the real challenge, real money. The principal reason England's trade balance was permanently in the black.

And Duxford was the grand prize. Over half of the company's giga-conductor royalties had been invested here. The Institute pulled together every human engineering discipline, taxed ingenuity to its limits, gave England an unbeatable technological and economic edge over the rest of the European Market Alliance nations. Space hardware subcontracts were only placed with English companies. The external supply industry that had risen to support Julia's space programme provided secure jobs for over a million people, the Institute itself employed a hundred and fifty thousand at Duxford alone, and more in orbit and up at New London.

The money she poured into orbital materials processing modules and the New London project was frightening. She'd been doing it for a solid fifteen years without ever showing weakness or doubt. And only now was she beginning to get anything like a decent return. Nobody else had that sort of faith; in their own vision, in the scientists, technicians, and astronauts who'd captured the asteroid. Victor knew that if it'd been up to him, he would've abandoned space to the kombinates and government agencies a long time ago.

Without Julia Evans the world would be a much poorer place. She cared about people, and nobody appreciated it. Except him.

Victor put a halt on that line of thought. You ridiculous fool, he told himself.

Eddie Coghlan, the Institute's security division manager, was standing by the open stair door at the edge of the pad. Victor could see the man reviewing his own recent performance in his mind, desperately trying to think why his boss should pay an unexpected visit.

Victor shook Eddie Coghlan's hand. 'You can relax now, Eddie, I'm not here to chase you.'

Eddie Coghlan smiled crisply. 'That's something, you had me worried there for a minute.'

They went down the stairs, talking amicably. Eddie Coghlan was glad to have the opportunity to discuss a few points, and Victor listened readily enough, making suggestions. He didn't go for the intimidating approach, a fear figure. He knew there were some company security chiefs who ran their departments on those lines, and wasn't much impressed. Security was a delicate, complex job; bawling orders like a sergeant-major might look good for the board, but like all dictatorships it was ultimately ineffective.

Access Astronautics Institute Building One Floor Plan, he told his processor node. The three-dimensional glass image formed in his mind.

Display Route from Landing Pad Three to SETI Office. A red dot appeared on the landing pad, and extended a line down the stairs. Perspective shifted to keep the tip of the line in front of his perception point; directional graphics blinked up, naming the sections it was passing through.

When he came out of the stairwell on to the fifth floor's central corridor, he stepped unerringly on to a moving walkway. He was in an administrative segment, glass walls on either side showing him big open-plan offices with staff bent over desk terminals.

'There's going to be a rush of reassignment orders for the Institute's research staff coming through over the next few days,' he told Eddie Coghlan as they slid past the canteen. 'Top grades, the real thinker types. So I want you to blow Meterski's deal, and Kellaway's.'

'But we haven't identified all the team members,' Eddie Coghlan said. 'If we blow the ones we know, the rest will pull the cutouts and vanish.'

'Can't be helped. These reassignments are supposed to be ultra-hush, I don't want them to become open knowledge to the tekmercs. OK?'

'You're the boss,' Eddie Coghlan said glumly. 'When do you want it done?'

'Today.'

'Christ!'

'Sorry, but that's the way it goes. I'll see if I can assign some psychic empaths to you. Have them interrogate the tekmerc members you do nab, that way you should get a reasonably complete list.' He stepped off the walkway at an intersection, and started to ride an escalator down.

'Right you are,' Eddie Coghlan said. 'Is that why you're here, to supervise the reassignments?'

Victor liked that, no questions about what the reassignments were for. Eddie was a good security man. He started down the next escalator to the third floor. 'No, I'm here to see Dr Parnell, actually.'

Eddie Coghlan frowned, trying to place the name. 'Not the SETI project director?'

'Yes.'

'Oh, right.' He glanced at his watch. 'I suppose he'll be in by now.'

*

Dr Rick Parnell's personnel profile said he was thirty-seven, which surprised Victor. Himself apart, Event Horizon's divisional chiefs were normally in their fifties. When he accessed the Astronautics Institute's records he found out why. SETI was about the smallest project on Event Horizon's books, with only twelve members. Julia funded it out of the pure science budget; the project was virtually a token, she was simply covering all aspects of space research, however remote.

Victor certainly hadn't known it existed, not until Julia suggested he go and see if they could come up with any suggestions about how to find the alien starship. She was anxious that Greg's tenuous pursuit of the Newfields girl wasn't the only option of making contact with them.

The Search for Extra-Terrestrial Intelligence project had been allocated three offices on the inward side of Building One's ring; the usual array of desks and terminals and holographic display cubes, worn dark-green carpet squares. Victor was mildly disappointed, expecting something more elaborate for this kind of project, at least. His own office wasn't much different, larger with better furniture.

He left Eddie Coghlan to organize the tekmerc busts and went in. The SETI staff gave him and his bodyguard inquisitive stares; all of them were in their twenties, he noted. An attractive female secretary directed him to Rick Parnell's office.

The room looked out over the assembly hall, an incomprehensible mini-city of cybernetic machinery, its roadways heavy with little white carts and drone cargo flat-tops following buried guidance tracks. On the far side he could see a curving row of integration bays where standard payload pods were fitted out, each bay a buzz of activity. More pods were hanging from the overhead hoists, like a series of white moonlets drifting along rectangular orbital paths.

The wall behind the SETI director's desk was covered with holograms of satellites. To Victor's eye they were similar to the geosync antenna platforms, although he guessed the outsized dishes were radio observatories. There was one computer simulation of a mesh dish alongside New London; if he was reading the scale right it was over twenty kilometres in diameter.

Dr Rick Parnell had his feet up on his desk, drinking a can of Ruddles bitter as he watched a data display in his terminal's cube. He had been a varsity rugby player while he was at Oxford, half a head taller than Victor, with broad, sloping shoulders, and blond hair that was starting to thin. It looked like he worked hard to keep in trim. The body didn't really belong in a white shirt and suit trousers, Victor thought, more like tennis kit.

'Security chief?' he asked after Victor showed his card. 'What, you mean of the whole company?'

'That's right.'

'You come to evict us?'

'No. I'd like to talk to you.'

Rick Parnell suddenly realized he was drinking a can of bitter in office hours. He drained it in a couple of gulps, crumpled it, and threw it into the bin. Perfect shot. 'You don't look old enough to be a security chief.'

Victor sat in front of the desk. 'There aren't many old people in security. We don't survive that long.'

Rick Parnell managed a sickly smile. 'What did you want to talk about?'

'Firstly, let me remind you of the confidentiality undertaking you thumbprinted when you were employed by Event Horizon.'

Rick Parnell coloured slightly. 'Hey, now listen. I was told that was a formality. This project might not seem much to a guy like you, but we accomplish a lot, and most of that is because we're mainly a co-ordination centre. Half our budget goes on grants to universities and agencies, we arrange international conferences, publish datasheets. You start restricting our output, and there's no point to us even existing.'

'I'm not interested in restricting the flow of ideas, I simply ask that our conversation is not bandied about.'

'Otherwise I'm for the chop.'

Victor sat back in the chair and gave Rick Parnell a searching look. 'Tekmercs make threats, Mr Director. I work on the other side of the fence. We try and ensure that a dedicated researcher's life's work isn't stolen from under their nose, that the pension fund you've paid into for forty years doesn't get emptied by some hotrod with a smart decryption program. Now, you and I are employed by the same lady, and she suggested I ask your professional advice on a matter I'm involved with. Is that really so hard for you?'

Rick Parnell twitched in discomfort. 'No. Sorry, of course not. I'm just not used to the idea of the head of Event Horizon's security division walking into my office. I didn't think you people even knew we existed.' He lifted his head, as if he was sniffing at the air. 'Julia Evans herself told you to come here? *The* Julia Evans?'

'Yes.'

'For professional advice?'

'Yes.'

'OK, fire away.'

'Hypothetically, if there was an alien spaceship in the solar system, how would I go about detecting it?'

Rick Parnell opened his mouth, closed it, then started again. 'If an alien spaceship came into the solar system, believe me, you'd know about it. Something like that would be a bigger event than the Second Coming.'

Victor gazed thoughtfully at the hologram of the big dish. This was the second time he'd been told the arrival of aliens would be momentous. The prospect was beginning to worry him badly. 'In what way?'

'Spectacular. OK, look. There's two ways of travelling between the stars. In a small ship going very fast, say about thirty or fifty per cent lightspeed. Or a big multi-generation ship, something the size of New London, travelling at one or two per cent light-speed. Either way, it takes a colossal amount of energy to move them. If anything like that started decelerating into the solar system, the plasma from the reaction drive would scream like a nova across the radio bands. We'd spot it half a light-year out. It would stop radio astronomy stone dead across half of the sky.'

'What if they didn't use a reaction drive? What if they have some faster than light drive like the science fiction shows on the channels?'

'Christ, you're really serious, aren't you?'

'Yes.'

Rick Parnell put his elbows on the desk, and rested his chin on his clasped hands. 'Nick Beswick is the one you really should be asking about this, because it all fits in with quantum theory, but ... FTL means producing wormholes through space-time large enough for a ship to pass through. Now wormholes are theoretically possible, but we haven't got a clue how to open one.'

'An advanced technology might be able to achieve it.'

'Granted, an extremely fanciful technology could stress space to a degree that tears it open. However, even if you have that level of technology you still couldn't enter the solar system without being detected. If the terminus of a wormhole on this scale erupted near Earth, its gravitational distortion would be of epic proportions. To my knowledge there are three hundred and twenty functional gravity-wave detectors on this planet, fifteen of which are in orbit; astrophysicists use them to check out general relativity. They would have spotted it.'

'What about an FTL system that used something other than wormholes?'

Rick Parnell frowned sadly. 'You know, my problem is usually convincing people that aliens do exist. Now you come in, and I have to persuade you what you're saying doesn't make any sense. This universe is no different for aliens than it is to us, it obeys the same physical parameters ten million light-years away as it does right in this office. That includes relativity.'

'I was just trying to establish if there's a third method of aliens arriving in the solar system.'

'If there is, we can't conceive it. Which would make them roughly the equivalent of angels.'

'Fair enough. So just go back to my original question, we don't know the method they used to get here, and we didn't see them arrive. How do we locate them now?'

'These hypothetical aliens, are they on Earth?'

'No. We don't believe they could get past the strategic defence sensors.'

'Good point. But you're giving me a tall order here, you

know? The solar system is a big place, and that's just staying in the plane of the ecliptic. They could easily be in a high inclination orbit. If you take Pluto's orbital radius as the boundary, and extend your search to cover a spherical volume, that's a quarter of a million cubic AUs to sift through. An electromagnetic sweep is the only practical method, assuming they're emitting in that spectrum. There's a good chance of picking up random noise leakage from their onboard systems, certainly with the power levels a starship will need to employ.'

'Do you have that sort of equipment?'

Rick Parnell gave a low laugh. 'We've got six ten-million-channel receivers operating at the moment, although we only own them in partnership with various national science councils and space agencies. But they're all assigned to specific sections of the sky. It's the old nightmare, you listen to your section for eighteen months of deathly silence, then the day you move on to the next, there's a genesis pulse.'

'What's a genesis pulse?'

'Special message, a shout that says "Here we are!" to the universe at large. You use a dish like the Arecibo to beam a strong signal at a star cluster with a high quota of Sol-like stars. Put in plenty of data about local life and culture, star co-ordinates – you do that by triangulating with known quasars. We send out a couple every year. Give it a millennium, we might even get an answer.'

'So there's no way you can run a search for me, then?'

Rick Parnell swivelled his chair, and tapped the hologram of the giant dish. 'This is Steropes, we've spent twenty per cent of our budget and three years refining the design. You persuade our lovely lady boss to part with two billion pounds New Sterling and in five years I'll have it up and running for you. If you've lost a hydrogen atom inside the solar system, this beauty will be able to find it for you.'

Victor held back on the urge to shout. 'I meant, starting today.'

'God, no. No way, sorry.'

'Shit.'

Rick Parnell clenched his hands tight, as if he was praying. 'OK, I've been straight with you. Now, what have you got? What made you come in here and ask me this?'

'We are in possession of certain evidence which suggests that first contact has already been initiated.'

Rick Parnell's lips moved around the words, repeating them silently. 'Oh, God. What evidence?' he croaked.

'An artefact.'

'What fucking artefact?'

'A biological one.'

Rick Parnell lent right over the desk, fired by excitement and trepidation. 'High order?'

'Pardon me?'

'I mean, more advanced than the microbes?' His hands spun for emphasis, urging Victor on like a football coach.

Victor felt a real tingle of alarm. Greg had once explained to him how his intuition manifested itself, a cold that wasn't physical. This was something similar. 'Slow down. Which microbes are we talking about?'

Rick Parnell let out a groan and flopped back into his chair. 'After the turn of the century the Japanese NASDA agency sent an unmanned probe called Matoyaii out to Jupiter. It was designed to measure the near-Jupiter environment, from the ionosphere out to Io's plasma torus. That's a pretty active area, saturated with radiation, the planetary radio emissions; and then there's the magnetosphere, the flux-tube, small moons, the ring bands. Fascinating to see how they all interact. Thing was, when mission control manoeuvred the Matoyaii in close to a ring particle the on-board spectroscope started to register some pretty odd hydrocarbon patterns. Nothing conclusive, nothing final, you understand. Intensive analysis wasn't possible, the sensors weren't designed for microscopic examination. And the hydrocarbon deposits were minute. Specks really, like dust motes. If they were microbes, they could've been captured by the gravity field, and settled on the ring particles.'

'They were alive?' Victor asked.

'More than likely. The theory's been around since the middle of the twentieth century. High-order organic forms couldn't survive interstellar transit, they couldn't contain enough energy, not for the time-scales and distances involved. But something like a microbe or a germ, they might just make it. Go into a kind of suspended animation between stars, they're small enough to withstand freezing. The microbes were even put forward as an hypothesis for flu epidemics, literally a plague from space.'

'So there is life on other planets,' Victor said, half to himself.

'Now you question it!' Rick Parnell exclaimed in exasperation.

'What we found might have been a joke, an elaborate bioware construct. But not any more, not with you telling me this.'

Rick Parnell smiled affably. 'Well, we'll know about the microbes for certain when Royan gets back, of course.'

Victor looked up sharply, meeting a sincere expectant gaze.

11

The bishop was from the trendier wing of the Church of England, a Campaign for Orbital Disarmament badge prominent on his lapel. His wiry grey hair blew about in the light breeze as he stood at the microphone at the front of the stage. He kept slipping youth-culture sound bites into his speech in an effort to hold the younger members of the audience.

It sounded bizarre to Julia, like a Victorian toff getting enthusiastic about the lifestyle of New Age communes. Her early years had been spent with the First Salvation Church in Arizona; it was more cult than religion, but she had picked up a basic belief in Christian teachings and ethics which had never been discarded. She found the bishop squirm-inducing, almost making her feel ashamed about her faith.

She'd chosen to sit with the rest of the parents, in a plastic chair set out on the browning grass of Oakham School's playing fields. The governors had wanted her up on the makeshift wooden platform with the bishop and other dignitaries, or at least in the front row of the seats. She turned that down with a flatness which left them thinking they'd mortally offended her. Worried glances had flown like startled sparrows.

People were so stupidly sensitive. Did they think she was some sort of mafia princess who kept a black book?

There were about five hundred parents listening to the speeches and waiting for the prizegiving. The men in grey tropical-weave suits, putting a brave face on the bishop's verbal meandering; wives in light colourful dresses and elaborate hats, smiling brittlely.

She had deliberately fled into the middle of them, seeking anonymity; sitting with Eleanor in the hope she would blend in. Some chance. Between the two of them, she and Eleanor had six children to manage, then there were her seven hardliner body-guards. Her party had taken over an entire row of the hard chairs.

Eleanor fanned herself with the programme, glancing at her slim Rolex. 'He can't go on for much longer,' she muttered out of the corner of her mouth.

'No, they'll lynch him soon,' Julia agreed.

'Will the hardliners do it?' Matthew, her eight-year-old son, asked eagerly.

'Don't be silly,' Anita Mandel told him imperiously. 'Aunty Julia was being sarcastic. Don't you know what sarcastic is?'

'Of course—' Matthew began fiercely.

Julia and Eleanor silenced them before the argument got out of hand. Julia put her arm round her son, and gave him a hug. He resembled his father so closely, a constant raw-nerve reminder of all she was missing.

Eleanor took another look at her Rolex. 'They'll be in Monaco now.'

'I didn't want to ask Greg to do this, you know.'

'I know,' Eleanor said wearily. She put her hand on her belly and shifted uncomfortably in the chair.

Julia felt even more guilt crystallizing around her, it was like a prison cell she had to carry round.

The bishop sat down to a sharp burst of applause. The headmaster rose and began his introduction to the prizes. Julia gave Daniella a final check over to make sure her uniform was tidy. Daniella had won her year's history prize. Julia was secretly thankful it wasn't the economics prize; that would've been too much like Daniella bursting a gut for the subject she believed her mother wanted her to excel in. Not that she would be unhappy if Daniella showed a natural inclination towards the qualities necessary for a career in Event Horizon, she just didn't want the girl to feel constrained.

Julia leaned in towards Eleanor. 'It's foolish of me, in a way. I'm relying on Royan as a psychological crutch. Find him, and the world is going to be at rights again. Fat chance. Find him, and we find the flower's origin. Our problems will only just be beginning.'

'There's no going back now,' Eleanor said. 'Like it or not, the human race isn't alone any more.'

'Yes, but why all this secrecy? Why not just land on the White House lawn like they do in the channel shows?'

'The eco-warriors would laser them dead for bringing a million gruesome new varieties of bugs to the planet.'

'That's something,' Julia said thoughtfully. 'Suppose we never can meet in the flesh, that the risk of bacteriological contamination is too high. All we'll ever be able to do is trade information.'

'That's one answer for you, then,' Eleanor said. 'They aren't here to trade, they're listening, tapping our datanets and taking the information. The cosmic equivalent of data pirates.'

And who better to help them than Royan, Julia thought. 'Yeah, could be. Let's hope it is something that simple.'

*

The marquee was full of parents and pupils, standing with drinks in their hands, talking with animated voices. The sixth formers who were leaving were busy swapping addresses, promising faithfully to stay in touch. They had that slightly apprehensive air about them. Julia could remember the feeling herself: the day her grandfather had died, his body at least, and she was the sole legal owner of Event Horizon. The future was loaded with promise, but it was still totally uncharted, dark country. Scary at that age.

Eleanor's crack about contamination kept running through

her mind. Surely there must be some risk from unknown germs? Yet Royan had sent her a freshly cut flower. He couldn't have been worried.

She took a sip of mineral water from her glass, and pretended to study one of the paintings lined up along the back of the marquee, a hummingbird in flight, wings blurred as if in motion. It was part of the school art department's exhibition of work by the pupils.

Open Channel to SelfCores. *What did the genetics lab report say about humans picking up a possible infection from the flower?*

Virtually zero, NN core one answered. *In fact the problem is reversed. There was no equivalent to our bacteria in the flower. Appendix fifteen suggested that symbiotic bacteria, such as the terrestrial nitrogen-fixing rhizobia, have been incorporated into the parent plant's genetic code; and the natural resistance to parasites has evolved and strengthened to such a point where the parasites died off.*

Wouldn't the parasites evolve in tandem? she asked.

If they had, then the laboratory should have found some on the flower. There were none, ergo they have died off.

So we are a bacteriological threat to the aliens?

Possibly. There are three options. One, that contact with us would be extremely dangerous for them, that they will have no immunity to our primitive diseases. Two, their immune systems are so advanced that our germs and bacteria will be no threat at all. Three, that our respective biochemistry is so different that there can be no cross-infection. However, given that the flower's cell composition was so similar to terrestrial cells, for example the inclusion of cellulose and lignin in the cell membrane, the third option is the least likely.

So even if full contact is established, we may not be able to meet?

Insufficient data, you know that, NN core two chided.

Yes. Sorry, I just hate this floundering around in the dark.

We know, remember?

Two of you do, she countered, teasing.

They know, Juliet, but I care.

Thank you, Grandpa.

We have some good news for you, NN core two said.

Please, I could do with some.

Greg has discovered the name of the courier, a Charlotte Diane Fielder. She is one of Dmitri Baronski's girls.

Baronski? Julia knew the name, his operation, but he was very second-rate. Or rather, he made sure he stayed second-rate. Always targeting the idle rich and society figures. Never doing anything that would bring a kombinate security division down on him. A man who'd found his niche, feeding off parasites. *This is slightly out of his league, isn't it?*

Yes, if he is involved. Charlotte Fielder has been lifted from Monaco, and it was a very professional deal. Greg suggested that the same people who took a sample of the flower are now holding Fielder.

Where is he now? she asked.

On his way back to Monaco's airport. He is going to visit Baronski to see if he knows Fielder's current whereabouts.

OK, keep monitoring the situation.

'Marry me,' an American voice said. 'Marry me and let me take you away from all this.'

Julia turned from the hummingbird to see Clifford Jepson standing at her side, grinning ingratiatingly. The president of Globecast was in his forties with a round berry-brown face, thick black hair combed back, channel newsman smile. She knew it was all a forgery, cosmetic face and hormone hair.

Like Julia, Clifford Jepson had inherited his position; and Globecast had nearly doubled its share price in the eight years since he'd been its president. He also carried on his father's underclass arms trading, which was less welcome news. Julia had used him to supply the Trinities. And she'd questioned the wisdom ever since.

She really liked his father, her uncle Horace. But Clifford Jepson seemed to think that it was a friendship which he'd inherited along with Globecast. He hadn't, but his position made him just equal enough to talk without being stilted.

Julia glanced round, and saw Melanie Jepson talking to the

headmaster. She was a beautiful woman, early twenties, blonde hair so fine it was almost white, a spectacular figure.

'You've got it all wrong, Clifford,' she said drily. 'Middle-aged businessmen with midlife crises are supposed to leave frumpish old wives for dazzling young actresses, not the other way round.'

'Nothing frumpish about you, Julia. You know I've always held a torch for you.'

'Spare me, you'll be calling me a real woman next.'

He looked at the hummingbird painting. 'Not bad, sharpen up the colours, add some life to the eyes, could be the makings of a decent artist there. Nice to see the old forms being adhered to. Kids these days, all they do is talk to their graphic simulators.'

'Bloody hell, crook and art critic. Clifford, what are you doing here?'

He waved his glass in the direction of his wife. 'Getting the kids down for entry. I'm based in Europe more often than not these days. So we thought they could board over here, give them a chance of some permanency in their lives. Trouble is, the entrance list for this place is getting kinda full these days. Can't think why.'

That was another aspect of life Julia didn't enjoy. She'd chosen Oakham School because it was good, and near Wilholm, and Greg and Eleanor sent their children to it. Daniella and Matthew wouldn't be friendless when they arrived, nor would they have to board, a notion she couldn't bear. The arrangement had been confidential, but within a week of Daniella starting every entry place for the next ten years had been booked solid. Rumour had it that places for Matthew's year had been traded for over a quarter of a million Eurofrancs.

'Clifford, Sonnie's only two,' she said.

'Twenty months, and every bit as pretty as her mom.'

'Oh, well, I wish you luck. It's a good school, Daniella and Matthew enjoy it here.' She walked on to the next painting, a rusting petrol-driven car with a Coke bottle growing out of its roof. A couple of parents were engrossed with it. The woman nudged her husband who looked up, and gave a start when he saw Julia. She gave them a flicker of a smile.

'Julia, I was being serious about us.'

Why couldn't he take the hint? 'I'm a mother with two children, remember?'

'You're a single parent, who's been alone for eight months.' His face was sober.

'What do you know about it?'

'That he's a fool. That he won't be coming back.'

'He will.'

'Face it Julia, eight months.'

'Eight months or eight years, it makes no difference to me. I'll wait.'

Clifford Jepson gulped down the remainder of his drink. When she looked closely, she saw he was strangely apprehensive. Almost frightened.

'Can we talk?' he asked.

'Not if you're going to make any more indecent proposals.'

'It's important, Julia.'

The last thing she wanted was to talk shop. Oliver, Anita, and Richy had pulled Eleanor away to see the exhibitions various departments were staging, Matthew and his bodyguard had gone with them. Daniella and Christine were part of a big group of girls in a corner of the marquee, Daniella's bodyguard wearing a tired tolerant expression.

'Five minutes,' she said.

The sports field was almost deserted. A group of school maintenance staff had already started to dismantle the stage, ten boys were stacking up the chairs under the supervision of a master. Ahead of her, the first XI's cricket square was a bright strip of emerald, standing out from the rest of the field's parched grass. Over to one side the score board was still showing the result of the last match. It was one of the old-fashioned affairs, a small boxy pavilion dating from the last century, with junior boys scurrying about inside changing the numbers round.

171

Matthew had to explain how it worked the first time she and Royan came to watch a match. She was amazed at the primitiveness of it, the scorer even used a big paper ledger to keep the runs in. Royan, of course, had loved the idea. It'd been a good afternoon, she remembered, after the match they'd taken Matthew, Daniella and some of their friends to have tea at a café in the town. A big noisy party, where the children had all eaten too much cake. None of them cared who she was.

Julia sat on one of the wooden seats dotted around the pitch's boundary line, tugging the brim of her hat down against the glare. The air was dusty, tickling the back of her throat.

Clifford Jepson sat beside her, grimacing at the stains of ancient bird droppings on the cracked wood. A line of their bodyguards had fanned out behind them to form a phalanx against casual intrusion by any of the other parents.

'Marriage was only half the proposition,' he said. 'It's a start, an opening to something much bigger, grander.'

'Merging Event Horizon and Globecast so our children could take over the world. No, thank you, Clifford. You forget I could buy Globecast if I really wanted to.'

His PR smile turned tight. 'Will you hear me out? I'm not talking about Globecast. Right now, I'm holding something that's gonna grow and grow. It's big, Julia, the biggest. I'm offering you a partnership.'

Open Channel to SelfCores. *I think you three had better listen to this.* 'A partnership in what?' she asked.

'Something new. Something explosive. It's a whole new industry, Julia. The company that markets it is gonna win big.'

How interesting, NN core one said. *Not many days when we get offered two revolutionary partnerships.*

You think they're connected? she asked.

There's one way to find out, Juliet. Start name dropping, see how our Clifford reacts.

Right. 'This partnership,' Julia said laconically. 'Let me guess: you provide the data constructs of a rudimentary technology, and Event Horizon develops it to a commercially viable level? Is that the way you see it working, Clifford?'

He raised his hands, putting on a rueful grin. 'God damn, on the ball or what? After all these years, Julia, I'm still not in your class, nobody is. OK, let me lay it straight on the line for you. Event Horizon is one of several possible partners I'm considering. And I'd like it to be you, Julia, I really would. This operation of yours, you leave the kombinates standing. If we can thrash out a deal, make the numbers work, then it's yours. I'll be a sleeping partner, maybe a gate to some military contracts, but essentially it'll be your field.'

'This sleeping partner arrangement, I hope that's not intended literally, Clifford.'

'People like us, Julia, I mean, working close on this deal, spending time together, maybe you'll see more to me than you do now.'

'But I still have to put in the best bid if I want this new technology you're offering?'

'Yeah, you've got some stiff competition lining up for a slice of this pie. I'm not hiding that from you. But I'll show you what I'm offering on a confidential basis, and you can decide what sort of offer to make. I'm confident you'll come out tops. You'll understand what this means, you've got the kind of vision the kombinate boards lack. And this needs someone with vision behind it, Julia.'

Dear Lord, he makes you want to vomit, NN core two said. *So dreary and predictable.*

This all sounds very familiar, Julia said. *Do you think Clifford could be the one Mutizen stole the molecular structuring data from?*

If they did, then where did he get it from? NN core one asked. *Globecast doesn't employ a single physicist.*

Oh yes they bloody well do, my girl, Philip Evans said. *I told you there was something wrong about Globecast bidding to acquire the Mousanta labs.*

So you did, Grandpa. But they haven't acquired it yet. Which means Mousanta can't be the source. Did commercial intelligence come up with anything?

Sod-all! Idle buggers. You hit this Clifford, Juliet, hit him hard. Make him know he's a cheap nobody.

Behind Clifford Jepson a couple of umpires had walked out on to the cricket square. They began to set up the wickets.

'What's the matter, Clifford?' she asked. 'Hasn't Mousanta got the resources to hack the atomic structuring theory? Is that why you've come running to me and the kombinates to build the generator for you?'

'Motherfuck!' Clifford Jepson gasped.

It was all she could do not to laugh. His fall from oily confidence to bewildered fright was classic comedy. The lack of control surprised her, though, she hadn't been expecting that, not from a trained executive. Another demonstration that he didn't really have what it took. She could never understand why he carried on the arms trading. In his father's day it was different, the post-Warming world was unstable, astutely placed arms shipments could quite often shift the balance of power in small countries. But now life had calmed down again, the only people who wanted arms on the black market were the alienated, increasingly bitter and desperate radical political groups. It made Clifford Jepson little more than an extension of the terrorists he served.

'How?' he demanded.

'One has contacts.'

'Not for that. Atomic structuring is the biggest ultra-hush there's ever been.'

'Not so, apparently.'

Squeeze him, Juliet, go for the slam. You can dictate your own terms now. I never did like the little bugger, not a patch on his father.

'Do you still want to offer me a partnership?' she asked.

'I'll consider any bid you submit.'

'Good. Have your office contact Peter Cavendish. I'm sure we can come to some arrangement. I'll be generous, Clifford. The person who delivers the theory for a nuclear force generator to

Event Horizon will be a very rich person indeed. I hope it's you, Clifford, I really do. For old times' sake.'

My girl, Philip Evans said smugly.

Ask him about the source, NN core two said.

'Clifford.' He looked at her, not angry. Wary, though, she thought, a wounded animal, cornered but prepared to fight. 'If you provide me with your source, where you obtained the data from, I'll offer you forty-five per cent royalties, and we'll close the deal this afternoon.'

'No way, Julia. You want the generator, you deal through me.'

'As you wish.' She rose to her feet, brushing down her skirt.

'Hey, wait.'

'Call Cavendish, you have the number. I'll review what the two of you come up with; if I think it's good enough, I'll thumbprint on the dotted line. If not, your opposition get their big day.'

'Who are they? Who else is offering this?'

She gave him a sweet smile. 'No way, Clifford,' said with her old Arizona twang. Philip Evans's gusty laughter echoed through her brain, her cybernetic mind twins projected quiet satisfaction. She left an acutely flummoxed Clifford Jepson on the bench, and headed back to the marquee. Her bodyguards closed in to escort her.

An end-of-term-prankster had fastened a crude bra made out of pillowcases to the top of the flag-pole above the school's art and design block. It was flapping slowly in the breeze. The bishop and the governors had been facing it all through the speeches. Julia started to laugh.

12

The interest was trickling back into Greg's brain, like a hit that charged his neurone cells with a dose of raw energy, leaving the mind clean, thoughts flowing with cold perfection. He hovered on the razor's edge between satisfaction and dismay. Tracing the girl, and through her Royan, was supposed to be a duty, not one of love's labours. But it felt good, the way he'd made it all come together in Monaco. Most of what they had learnt was negative information; it was a challenge making sense out of that. Dropped straight into a premier deal after fifteen years out in the cold, and still managed to hit the floor running. Not bad at all.

He knew Eleanor had feared this the most, that he'd enjoy himself, remember the good old days, how it used to be, the excitement and the danger. When they met she'd been more than a little impressed by the romance of being a private detective. Even now, time tended to obscure the years before that, when he was out on Peterborough's streets; the brain's natural defence mechanism fading out the pain and anguish associated with the Trinities. But if he really thought about it, those moments were there, hiding in the shadows beyond the firelight.

Eleanor didn't have anything to worry about, he decided, not really. Chasing after Charlotte Fielder wasn't about to trigger the male menopause. In any case, there was something slightly unreal about this investigation; carried from location to location in millionaire style, every fact uncovered pounced on by Victor's division and Julia's NN cores, producing a flood of profile data. All very swift and painless.

In fact the interest would be purely abstract if it hadn't been for his eagerness to talk to Baronski, it was almost impatience. The Pegasus had to fly subsonically over land. He resented that, knowing how fast the plane could go.

There was something else fuelling his mood, though, something darker, his intuition imparting a sense of time closing in. He hadn't confessed that to Suzi yet.

The flatscreen on the forward bulkhead showed the Austrian alps slipping by underneath the plane. They reminded Greg of Greenland's coastline after the ice had melted, a range of lifeless rock, scarred and stained. He could see massive landslides, where the pine forests had died leaving the soil exposed to torrential rains. Thick white-water rivers snaked down every valley, tearing out more soil and flooding the pastures. Reafforestation was progressing slowly, the ecological regeneration teams had to build protective shields around their plantations. From the air they showed as green rectangles sheltering in the lee of the mountains, fragile and precarious. But there were new hydro-power dam projects everywhere, ribbons of deep blue water accumulating in the deeper gorges. Most of the electricity was sold to the kombinate cyber-factory precincts in Germany. Austria had little heavy industry of its own, although low taxes and loose genetic-engineering laws had attracted investment from the biotechnology companies after the Warming. Event Horizon had several research centres in the country, he knew, as well as its main clinic at Liezen. He'd spent some time there himself, recuperating after tracking down the people who squirted the virus into Philip Evans' NN core. It was where he had proposed to Eleanor.

He smiled at the memory, then turned back to his cybofax which was showing Baronski's data profile. Dmitri Baronski was sixty-seven, a Russian *émigré*, leaving his motherland when he was twenty-three as an exchange student and never going back. He'd spent ten years as a PR officer for the Tuolburz kombinate, only to be dismissed for creaming off too high a percentage on the girls and boys he was supposed to supply for visiting executives. After that there were some arrests for pimping, one for fencing stolen artwork. Then fifteen years ago he'd hit on the idea of providing escorts for the wealthy, going for quality rather than quantity. He gave his girls an education in deportment equal to a Swiss finishing school, and discreetly presented them to European society.

He ran about a dozen at any one time, and the snippets of information they provided from pillow talk earned him about three-quarters of a million Eurofrancs a year from the stock exchange. It could have been more, but he was surprisingly honest with the girls, giving them a percentage.

'Christ, will you look at this!' Suzi exclaimed.

Greg left Baronski's exploits to look over her shoulder. She was busy reviewing Charlotte Fielder's profile on her cybofax.

'What's up?' he asked.

'This girl has run up a medical bill that a hypochondriac millionaire would envy.'

'She's ill?'

'Neurotic, more like. There ain't much of the original Charlotte Fielder left, the biochemistry she's carrying around! Her piss'd rake in a fortune on the street.' She ran her index finger down the wafer's screen. 'Get this, vaginal enlargement! What's she been bonking, King Kong? Follicle tint hormones. Submaxillary gland cachou emission adaptation. What the fuck is that?'

'It's a biochemical treatment to alter her saliva composition,' Rachel said. 'Makes her breath smell sweet the whole time, even the morning after. Especially the morning after.'

'Jesus wept. Bigger tits, yes, I can understand that; but this lot . . .'

Greg enjoyed her growing choler; Suzi didn't show her real feelings often enough, keeping them bottled up in the mistaken belief that remaining unperturbed was more professional. 'What? You mean it's not natural?'

Rachel laughed.

Suzi started to snap at him, then grinned weakly. 'All right. But I don't know why we're bothering looking for off-planet aliens. This girl isn't anywhere near human any more.'

'It's just a tool of the trade, dear. You and Julia have bioware nodes, I have a gland, Fielder has beauty.'

Suzi turned the display off, and tucked the wafer into her shellsuit's top pocket. 'Yeah, maybe. But it's acid weird, wouldn't catch me doing it.'

'I'd hope not,' he muttered.

The Pegasus was over a large town, shedding speed.

'Is that Salzburg?' Greg called forward to Pearse Solomons.

'Yes, sir. And we've got landing clearance for the Prezda.'

'Fine.' They were losing height rapidly, the Pegasus pitching its nose up at a respectable angle. Outside the town, the ecological-regeneration teams had triumphed. Rivers had been given gene-tailored coral banks to halt erosion. They were lined by surge reservoirs, like small craters, to cope with the sudden floods inflicted by Europe's monsoon season. Valley floors were a lush green again, speckled with wild flowers; llamas and goats grazing peacefully. Dark green tracts of evergreen pines were rising up the side of the slopes once more. They were a gene-tailored variety, nitrogen-fixing to cope with the meagre soil, their roots splaying out like a cobweb, clinging to exposed rock with an ivy-derived grip.

He wondered how much it would cost to repair the whole of the country in this way, a Japanese water garden treatment.

The Prezda arcology had been built into a natural amphitheatre at the head of a valley, facing south. It was as if the rock had been ground down into a smooth curved surface and polished to a mirror finish. A cliff face of a hundred thousand silvered windows looked out down the valley, he could see the mountains and lush parkland reflected in them. The image wavered as the Pegasus drew closer, as though the windows were rippling.

Between the two silver arms of the residential section was a low dome housing the inevitable shopping mall and the business community, along with the leisure facilities. The cyber-factories were buried in the rock behind the apartments. Power for the city-in-a-building came from a combination of nearby hydroelectric dams and hot rock exchange generators, bore holes drilled ten kilometres down to tap the heat of the Earth's mantle.

'Ant city,' Suzi said as the Pegasus headed in for a pad above the western arm.

'You live in a condominium,' Greg retorted.

'Yeah, but I get out to work and play.'

The Pegasus landed on the roof, and taxied on to a lift platform at the edge. They began to slide down the side of the silver wall to the hangar level.

'Does Event Horizon have a contact in Prezda security?' Greg asked the two security hardliners.

'Not on the payroll,' Pearse Solomons said. 'But there is a commercial interests liaison officer, he deals with cases like data fencing, or bolt-hole suspects. He'll allow us to tap a suspect's communications, mount a surveillance operation, that kind of thing. You want me to call him?'

'No. We'll keep him in reserve.'

There was a swift rocking motion as the Pegasus rolled forwards into the hangar. Greg stood up and made his way to the front of the plane.

'You think Baronski is going to co-operate?' Suzi asked as she followed him.

'According to his profile he goes out of his way not to annoy the big boys. Besides, he's old, he's not going to blow his chances of a golden retirement over something like a client's identity, not when we start bludgeoning him with Julia's name.'

The belly hatch opened, letting in a whine of machinery and the shouts of service crews.

'Malcolm, you come with us this time,' Greg said.

The hangar took up the entire upper floor of the Prezda, nearly two hundred metres wide, curving away into the distance. Bright sunlight poured through its glass wall, turning the planes parked along the front into black silhouettes. It was noisy and hot. Gusts of dry wind flapped Greg's jacket as they made their way across the apron. Executive hypersonics and fifty-seater passenger jets were taxiing along the central strip, rolling on and off the lift platforms. Drone cargo trucks trundled around them, yellow lights flashing.

The back half of the hangar had been carved into living rock, the rear wall lined with offices, maintenance shops, and lounges. Biolum strips were used to beef up the fading sunlight.

Greg walked through the nearest lounge and called a lift. He held his cybofax up to the interface key in the wall beside it, requesting a data package of the Prezda's layout. 'Baronski lives seven floors down from here, and off towards the central well,' he said, reading from the wafer's screen.

Suzi pressed for the floor and the lift door shut.

Greg tried to get an impression from his intuition. But all he got was that same pressure of time slipping away.

The lift doors opened on to a broad well-lit corridor with two moving walkways going in opposite directions. It was deserted, the only noise a low-pitched rumble from the walkways. They stepped on to the walkway going towards the centre of the arcology. There were deep side corridors every fifty metres on the right-hand side, ending in a floor-to-ceiling window that looked out across the valley.

The eighth walkway section brought them to the central well. A shaft at the apex of the amphitheatre, seventy metres wide, zigzagged with escalators. It was twenty storeys deep, Greg guessed the roof must be the hangar above. Each floor had a circular balcony, two-thirds of which was lined with small shops and bistros, the front third a gently curved window. The rails of glass-cage lifts formed an inner ribcage.

It was a busy time, the tables in front of the windows were nearly all full, smartly uniformed waitresses bustling about.

People were thronging the concourse and the balconies, filling the escalators. Teenagers hung out. Strands of music drifted up from various levels, played by licensed buskers. Greg could see a team of clowns working through the window tables two storeys below, children laughing in delight.

'Baronski is back this way,' Greg said, and pointed back down the corridor. 'Couple of doors.' That was when he ordered his gland secretion, seeing a flash of black muscle-tissue jerking. His espersense unfurled, freeing his thoughts from the prison of the skull. Minds impinged on the boundary as it swept outwards, deluging him with snaps of emotion, of tedium and excitement, the tenderness of lovers, and frustration of office workers. One fragment of thought had a hard, single-minded purpose that was unique in the whirl of everyday life about him. He stopped and searched round, seeking it again, knowing from irksome memory what it spelt.

'Wait,' he said.

Suzi almost bumped into him as he halted. 'Now what?'

There was a flare of interest in the mind. And again, another one on the edge of perception, a couple of floors higher up.

'There's a surveillance operation here,' Greg said. 'I've got two people in range. Probably more outside.'

Suzi shifted her bag. 'Targeting Baronski, do you think?'

'Dunno. They're interested in us, though, the direction we're heading.'

'What now?'

'Malcolm, there's one on the other side of the well, opposite this corridor, not moving. Male. See if you can spot him.'

Malcolm Ramkartra turned slowly and leant back on the walkway, resting his elbows nonchalantly on the rail. 'Think so. Bloke in a blue-grey shortsleeve sports shirt, late twenties, brown hair cut short. He's outside a greengrocers, reading a cybofax.'

Greg looked down the corridor. A woman and her ten-year-old daughter were riding the walkway towards the well. Ordinary thought currents. There was no one else.

Two people in the well implied a sophisticated deal. They

couldn't stay there all the time, which meant a rotation, others held in reserve. Probably an AV spy disk covering Baronski's door as well. More people to trail the old man if he went down the corridor to a lift.

He realized he'd subconsciously accepted that it was Baronski who was the surveillance target. Not that there'd been much conscious doubt. The chance of this being a coincidence was way too slim.

'OK, this is how we handle it. Malcolm, you walk down the corridor to the first lift, call it, and hold it. When you've got it, Suzi and I will try and get in to see Baronski. If the observers start thinking hostile thoughts, we'll run for it, if not, we go in. Meantime, you get Pearse to contact that security liaison officer, go through Victor Tyo if it'll add more weight. But I want to know if that's an authorized surveillance. This might just be a police drugs bust, or something.'

'Bollocks,' Suzi said.

'Yeah, all right, some hope. But we check anyway.'

'Gotcha,' said Malcolm. He stepped on to the walkway that took him back down the corridor.

'We're running into a lotta heavy-duty shit for what was supposed to be a simple little track-down,' Suzi muttered. 'The Monaco lift, now this.'

Greg was watching Malcolm, who was talking urgently into his cybofax. 'Yeah, Julia didn't think this through properly.'

'How do you mean?'

'Why did the people who took that sample from the flower bother taking it in the first place? I mean if they knew what the flower was they wouldn't need to take a sample. If they didn't, then there'd be no reason to do it. The flower was a specific message from Royan to Julia, he knew she'd be curious about it because flowers are special to the two of them. But for anyone else, it would be meaningless, a beautiful girl carrying a token from a lover.'

'If they knew she was a courier they would have ripped her baggage apart to find the message. Analysed everything. Maybe even used a psychic to sniff out what she was carrying. You said the flower was giving off freaky vibes.'

'Could be,' he admitted. 'Especially if they knew she was carrying a warning about the aliens, a living example would be an obvious way of providing proof. But if they are working for the aliens, then why let a message about their existence get out at all? Why not snuff her?'

Suzi rubbed her forehead. 'Christ, Greg. I'm just here to hardline for you, remember?'

'I don't expect answers. All I'm saying is that this is weirder than it looks.'

'That's what I've just fucking told *you*!'

'I'm trying to think what kind of allies these aliens might have plugged in with. For a start, whoever it is has got to be rich enough to afford these kind of deals.'

'A kombinate, finance house, someone like Julia; Christ, take your pick.'

'There's no one else like Julia.'

'Independently wealthy, arsehole.'

'But why?'

'Like I said to Julia yesterday. Starship technology is worth a bundle. Antimatter drives, boron hydride fusion, high-velocity dust shields. Any one of those would be instant trillionairedom.'

'Right.' He was amused by her reaction. Suzi, a starship buff. He knew the English Insterstellar Society sponsored regular conventions, covering topics from propulsion systems down to the practicality of pioneers setting up homesteads in alien biospheres. And there was a large chapter active in Peterborough, naturally, the heart of England's high-tech industry. The thought of Suzi attending didn't fit his world view.

The observer on the other side of the well emitted a burst of annoyance. He began to walk away from his position, thought currents feverishly active.

Looking the other way, Greg saw Malcolm Ramkartra was holding the lift. The hardliner gave Greg a short nod.

Two new minds moved into his perception range, that same

steely intent as the first observer prominent amongst their thought currents.

'Bugger.'

'What?' Suzi asked.

'The observation team have realized we've seen them. Come on.'

At least Baronski was at home. Greg could sense his mind. Thought currents moving normally, their tension slacker than the people in the well, the way it always was with older people. Another mind close by was denser, brighter, filled with expectancy, a streak of suspense.

'He's got someone in there with him,' Greg said. 'One of his girls, at a guess.' He pressed the call button. The suspicion and interest of the observers rose.

'Yes?' Baronski's voice asked from the grille.

'Dmitri Baronski? Could we come in, please? We'd like a word.'

'I'm not seeing anyone today.'

'It is important.'

'No.'

'Just a couple of questions, I won't take a minute.'

'No, I said. If you don't go away, I shall call arcology security.'

Greg sighed. 'Baronski, unless you open this door right now, I'll come back with arcology security, and they'll smash it down for me. OK?'

'Who are you?'

Greg showed his Event Horizon security card to the key, there was a near invisible flash of red laser light. 'I'm Greg Mandel. Now can I come in? After all, you're not on our shit list . . . yet.'

'You're from Event Horizon?'

'Yeah, and one of your girls met with our boss in Monaco the other night. Are you getting my drift?'

'I . . . Yes, very well.' The door lock clicked.

Baronski's lounge was huge, its colour scheme navy-blue and royal purple. The chairs and settee were sculpted to look like open sea shells. Antique furniture cluttered the wall, delicate tables holding various art treasures, a genuine samovar, an ikon panel of the Virgin Mary that was dark with age, what looked suspiciously like a Fabergé egg, which Greg decided had to be a copy. The paintings were chosen for their erotica, old oils and modern fluoro sprays side by side. They were illuminated by biolum lamps in the shape of a tulip, grey smoked glass with elaborate gold-leaf curlicues. Vivaldi was playing quietly out of hidden speakers.

Suzi whistled softly as they walked in. Greg's suede desert boots sank into the pile carpet. He was conscious of his leather jacket again, Eleanor's disapproval.

Baronski and the girl were both in silk kimonos. There was a pile of glossy art books on a low coffee table in front of the settee. Two tall glasses full of crushed ice on Tuborg beer mats standing beside the open volumes.

The girl was black, about sixteen, with that same athlete's build that instantly reminded him of Charlotte Fielder. She was obviously going to be beautiful; her cheeks and nose were covered in blue dermal seal, but her features were so finely drawn it almost didn't matter. She stood beside the settee, perfectly composed, looking at him with wide liquid eyes, un-afraid.

Baronski was backdropped by the Alps beyond the picture window, a thin man with a thin face, nothing near Greg's simple mental image of burly red-faced Russian grandfathers. He was dainty, birdlike, longish snow-white hair brushed back, resembling a plume. But stress had marred his face, leaving bruised circles round his eyes, creases across his cheeks. His mind had such an air of weariness that it evoked a strong sense of sympathy. Greg wanted to urge him to sit down.

'What exactly is it you require?' Baronski asked stiffly. 'I'm sure you must be aware that I've never sought to infringe upon any of Event Horizon's activities. My girls have very clear instructions on this matter.'

Greg clicked his fingers at the girl. 'Best if you disappear.'

She glanced at Baronski.

'Go along, Iol. I'll call you when we're finished.'

She curtsied, and walked silently across the lounge to the hallway door.

Suzi watched her go. 'Give her a lot of artistic tuition, do you?'

The door closed.

'Miss . . .?'

'Suzi.'

Baronski appeared to chew something distasteful. 'Indeed.'

'I expect you know the routine,' Greg said.

'Remind me,' the old man said vaguely.

'Hard or soft. We don't leave without the data we came for. And I do have a gland, so we'll know if it is the right data. Clear enough?'

'My word, am I really that important? A gland, you say. You obviously cannot read my mind directly.'

'I'm an empath; you lie, and I know about it instantly.'

'I see. And suppose I were to say nothing?'

'Word association. I reel off a list of topics, and see which name your mind jumps at. But it's an effort, and it annoys me.'

'So what would you do should you become annoyed, beat it out of me? I imagine I would feel a lot of pain at my age. The old bones aren't very strong now.'

'No, I wouldn't lay a finger on you. That's what she's here for.'

There was a sharp pulse of indignation from Suzi's mind, but she held her outward composure.

Baronski studied her impassive face for any sign of weakness, then sighed and sat carefully in the settee. 'I suppose this day was inevitable, I just pushed it away to the back of my mind, always secretly hoping that I would be proved wrong. But I can honestly say that I never intended to upset Julia Evans. In a way she is an admirable woman, so many would have squandered what she has. Yes, admirable. You can see that I'm telling the truth, can't you?'

'I knew that before I came,' Greg said.

187

'Yes. Well, what do you wish to know?'

'Charlotte Diane Fielder.'

'Ah yes, a beautiful girl, very smart. I was proud of Charlotte. One of my triumphs. What has she done?'

'Where is she?'

'I genuinely don't know.'

Greg frowned, concentrating. There was a strong trace of disappointment in Baronski's mind. 'Do you know who she left the Newfields ball with?'

'It was supposed to be Jason Whitehurst. My problem is that I can't find out if she actually did or not. I haven't been able to contact her or Jason since.'

'This Jason Whitehurst, is he about fourteen, fifteen?'

Baronski gave him a surprised look, and picked up one of the beer glasses from the table. 'Good Lord no, Jason is in my age bracket. He has got a son, though, Fabian. Fabian is fifteen, perhaps you mean him.'

'Could be.' Greg pulled out his cybofax, and summoned up the memory of Charlotte and the boy leaving the El Harhari.

'Yes,' Baronski said, studying the wafer's screen. 'That is Fabian Whitehurst.'

'And this?' Greg showed him the chauffeur.

'No. I don't know that man at all.'

'OK, what does Jason Whitehurst do?'

'He's a trader, shifting cargo around the world. A lot of it is barter, buying products or raw material from countries that have no hard cash reserves, then swapping it for another commodity, and so on down the line until he's left with something he can dispose of for cash. There's quite an art to it, but Jason is a successful man.'

'Said it'd be some rich bastard,' Suzi said. 'Money lifted her over the border, no need for a tekmerc deal.'

'Yeah,' Greg agreed. 'Where does Jason Whitehurst live?'

Baronski took a sip from the glass. 'On board his airyacht, the *Colonel Maitland*.'

'What the fuck's an airyacht?' Suzi asked.

'A converted airship. Jason tends to the eccentric, you see. He bought it ten years ago, spends his whole time flying over all of us. I visited once, it has a certain elegant charm, but it's hardly the life for me.'

Greg sat heavily in one of the chairs. Wringing information out of the old man was depressing him. It was psychological bullying. Dmitri Baronski was a man who took confidentiality seriously. He'd built his life on it. 'Do you know where Whitehurst was flying to after Monaco?'

'Yes. That's why all the heartache. The *Colonel Maitland* was supposed to be flying straight to Odessa, so Jason told me. But there's been no trace of them, no answer to any of my calls. I tell myself it cannot be an accident. Airships are the safest way to travel; a punctured gasbag, or a broken spar, the worst that can happen is a gradual deflation. The *Colonel Maitland* would simply float to the ground. But it hasn't happened. Such an event would be on every channel newscast, rescue services all around the Mediterranean would be alerted by emergency beacons. Jason Whitehurst and his airyacht have simply vanished from the Earth. I don't like that. I always keep an eye on my girls, Mr Mandel, I'm very stringent about the patrons I introduce them to. There are certain members of my charmed circle who develop, shall we say, unpleasant tastes and requirements. I won't have that, not for my girls.'

'Very commendable. Did you try phoning Whitehurst's office?'

'He has several agents dotted about the globe, and yes I called some of them. It was the same answer each time. Jason Whitehurst is currently incommunicado.'

Greg looked at Suzi, who shrugged indifferently.

'Julia and Victor won't have any trouble locating something that size,' she said. 'There can't be that many airships left flying.'

'Yeah,' Greg acknowledged. There was something faintly unsettling about the way the world lay exposed to Event Horizon. A single phone call and someone's credit record was instantly available; a request to the company operating the Civil

Euroflight Agency's traffic control franchise, and Europe's complete air movement records would be squirted over to Peterborough for examination. If an Interpol investigator had requested the data, it would take hours or even days for the appropriate legal procedures to be enacted and release it. Companies and kombinates were developing into an extralegal force more potent than governments, but only in defence of their own interests. It was a creep back towards medievalism, he thought, when people had to petition their local baron for real action, when the king's justice was just a distant figurehead.

One law for the rich, another for the poor. Nothing ever really changed, not even in the data currency age. And why was he getting so cynical all of a sudden?

Baronski was sitting listlessly in the settee, face morbid. 'Please tell me, what has Charlotte done?'

'She hasn't done anything herself,' Greg said. 'It looks like she just got caught up in something a lot bigger. We're not angry with her, OK? But we do need to talk to her. Urgently.'

'Yes. I'll tell her if she gets in touch. Thank you, Mr Mandel.'

Greg stood up. There was a sharp twang from his intuition, an intimation that he was being sold short. He glanced sharply at Baronski, a shrunken figure lost in his own anxiety. The curse of intuition was its lack of clarity, he was never quite certain.

'Anything you want to ask?' he asked Suzi.

'Nah.'

'OK. If Charlotte does get in touch with you, ask her to call us, please. It will save everyone an awful lot of trouble.'

'I shall,' Baronski said. He put his glass down, and picked up a gold cybofax. Greg squirted his number over.

*

'Well?' Suzi asked as they left the apartment.

'Dunno. I get the impression he's cheating us somehow.'

'So why didn't you ask him about it?'

'Ask him what? Sorry, Dmitri, but what haven't you told us?

Fat lot of use that would be. You know my empathy is only good for specifics.'

'Yeah. Skinny little fart, wasn't he?'

'It's not a crime.' Greg saw Malcolm Ramkartra was still waiting by the open door of the lift. His espersense stretched out again. There were four observers in the well now, and that was just the ones within range. 'I think it's about time we found out a bit more about the opposition.'

'Suits me.'

Greg walked out into the centre of the corridor, and beckoned Malcolm Ramkartra.

'What did the liaison officer say?' he asked when the hardliner reached them.

'He didn't know the surveillance team were here. There's no police operation on this floor.'

'No shit?' Suzi said.

'OK. Malcolm, I want to talk to one of the observers. We're going back to the well; I'll physically identify one and we'll work a pincer on him. You go round the balcony clockwise, Suzi and I will take anticlockwise. If he backs off down a corridor, so much the better, he'll be isolated for a while. If you reach him first, then immobilize him, but make sure he's still conscious. Don't worry about visibility, tell you, this deal is important, OK?'

'Yes, sir, Mr Tyo explained that to us.'

'Right, and the name's Greg.'

Malcolm Ramkartra gave a quick smile, his thoughts tightening up. There wasn't any worry present, a true pro. Greg realized how little he knew about him, apart from the fact that he'd be the best. This deal was so bloody rushed.

'Let's go.' They began to walk towards the well. 'Two of them are sitting at a table in front of the window. The third is almost in the same place as the one Malcolm spotted earlier. The fourth is a woman, on the balcony above ours, hovering ten metres from the corridor on our left. So we'll take number three.'

'How long do you need with him?' Malcolm Ramkartra asked.

'About a minute.'

'Oh.' This time there was a flutter of consternation in his thought currents.

'And no, I can't read your mind directly.'

Suzi gave a wicked chuckle.

Two men stepped into the corridor from the well. The one in front had a pale face, wounded amber eyes, his ebony hair swept back and clinging to his skull. His suit was dark-grey, baggy trousers and a black belt with a silver lion-head buckle. Everything about him shouted hardliner.

The other was an oriental, his hair in braids ending in tiny ringlets. He possessed a surly confidence bordering on egomania.

Suzi stopped dead.

The first man gave a start, and put his hand on the arm of his partner.

His mind was the perfect twin of Suzi's, Greg saw. The two of them flush with loathing and alarm, ricocheting back and forth, building.

'Suzi,' said the man in the suit. 'The oddest places. Yes?'

'Leol Reiger, still trailing way behind as per fucking usual.'

'Depends what I'm after.'

'Baronski,' Suzi said firmly, and turned to Greg. 'Was he?'

The initial confusion in Leol Reiger's mind had twisted to sharp alarm at the mention of Baronski's name.

'Yeah, he knows Baronski.'

Leol Reiger's eyes never left Suzi. 'Who's your friend, Suzi?' he asked softly.

'Never seen him before in my life.'

'Chad,' Leol Reiger said.

The younger oriental man grinned at Greg. 'Hey, voodoo man, you do this?'

Greg was caught by surprise at the speed with which Chad's psi arose. Ordinary misty thought currents suddenly gleamed like chrome, rich with arrogant power. Chad's espersense unfurled, black daemon wings taking Greg into their implacable embrace.

The sensation was like a hot wet tongue slipping right through his temple, licking round his brain. Gone before he could harden his mind against it.

And he'd never even bothered to take the most elementary precaution. Jumped like a total novice. Chad must be loaded with sacs; themed neurohormones stored at critical sections through the brain, lifting the psi faculty from dormant to active like throwing a switch.

'Mr Greg Mandel is a gland psychic,' Chad said, his grin widening to mock.

'Really?' said Leol Reiger.

Greg could sense Suzi's annoyance, twined with a small thread of exasperation that she should be let down like this. He increased his gland's secretion, shame damping down as a cool anger surfaced in his thoughts; remembering the games the Brigade used to play in barracks. Squaddies' games, the kind played after days in combat, when life and dignity had been reduced to zero. The ones the Mindstar project directors had frowned upon, too dangerous for their valuable personnel to indulge in.

'And a Mindstar Brigade veteran as well,' Chad went on. 'A real top gun in his day. Like, a century ago.'

'So what is this?' Leol Reiger asked. 'You running a pensioner's outing, Suzi?'

'I'd hate to think you were treading on my turf, Leol. That'd piss me off real bad,' Suzi growled back.

Greg tried to keep track of the observers' reactions. They were alert and interested by the confrontation. Nothing to do with Leol Reiger, then.

'Back off, bitch,' said Leol Reiger. 'And you,' he flicked a finger at Malcolm Ramkartra, 'keep your hand away from that shoulder holster. I'll chop you into fucking dogmeat, else. Got it?'

'That's enough,' Greg said. 'You two aren't going to see Baronski, he belongs to us now. Fuck off, the pair of you.'

'Jesus, a geriatric control-freak,' Leol Reiger sneered. 'Chad, deal with him.'

Greg thought of a knife, bright steel shimmering, needle tip pricking the skin on the bridge of Chad's nose.

Chad began to laugh, his thoughts flaring as the sacs discharged again and the neurohormone dose hit his bloodstream. 'Gonna crack your mind open like an eggshell, war hero.'

Greg tensed his mind behind the imaginary blade, and—

—*reality flickered*—

—and pushed. Chad's thoughts were too hard, too closely packed. The knife slithered across their congealed surface, denied an opening.

'Best you can do?' Chad asked.

'Yeah.'

'Too bad.'

'That's why I always bring my little friend along,' Greg said, nodding at a point behind Chad.

Screams broke out in the well. People were pushing and shoving as they raced past the end of the corridor, terror in their faces. Display stands went crashing to the ground. One of the barrows was overturned, oranges and nectarines tumbling about across the tiled floor.

The beast was about the size of a lion, jet black, covered in an ice-smooth exoskeleton. Talons made skittering noises against the tiles as it padded round the corner into the corridor. Its head was a streamlined nightmare, eyes buried in deep recesses, razor fins on its crown, tapering reptilian muzzle.

Chad gaped at it, frozen in disbelief.

'Shit almighty,' Suzi squawked in panic.

Leol Reiger stumbled a step backwards, his pale face shocked. The beast screeched, a metallic keen that threatened to shatter glass. Chad threw his hands over his ears, yelling in fright. The sound cut off.

'Kill,' Greg said.

194

'No!' Chad wailed. He turned to run.

The beast leapt, forelimbs catching Chad's left shoulder, extended talons slashing. Blood squirted. Chad was flung into the walkway's handrail. He screamed at the pain as his mangled arm took the full weight of the impact. Tears squeezed out of his eyes. He doubled over, clamping his right hand over his left shoulder, blood bubbled through his fingers, staining his sleeve.

'Jesus Christ, call the fucker off.'

Leol Reiger went for his weapon, hand fumbling inside his suit jacket. Malcolm Ramkartra's arm moved with a smooth fast piston motion, as if his body was working in accelerated time; his Tokarev pistol pressed against Leol Reiger's neck. 'Don't,' he whispered happily.

The beast turned, head swinging round to focus on Chad. Its long muzzle snapped shut with a crack like a rifle.

Chad whimpered, cowering, staggering backwards. 'Please God, don't let it.'

He was bowled over by the beast, his head smacking on to the tiles. The beast's powerful muzzle opened centimetres from his face, and it let out a long undulating howl. A narrow gap in the exoskeleton between its hindlegs split open, grotesque genitalia arose.

Chad's mouth shrieked soundlessly, and—

—*reality flickered*—

—and he puked.

There was no beast, no blood, no shredded arm. Chad was curled up on the floor, hands wrapped round his head, sobbing quietly. The stench of vomit and piss curled the air.

Leol Reiger was staring down at him in amazement. 'What the fuck—' Amber eyes jerked up to fix Greg, betraying the wild flames of consternation that were burning in the mind.

'No expense spared, eh, Leol?' Suzi said. 'You always have the best on your squad.'

'Take him away,' Greg told Leol Reiger in a dead voice. 'And don't come back.'

'Shit on you,' Leol Reiger spat. He kicked Chad. 'Up, you useless bastard. Get up.'

Chad dropped his hands from his face, blinking tears from his eyes. He looked round in lost confusion. Saw Greg and flinched.

'Get up.'

Chad grasped the walkway rail, breathing heavily, and hauled himself to his feet.

Greg could feel the first twinges of the neurohormone hangover scratching away behind his temple. With the effusion level he'd used they would soon accelerate into stabs of white-hot lightning crackling round the inside of his skull. 'Bugger, but I hate eidolonics,' he muttered.

Leol Reiger and Chad turned the corner out into the well, Chad reeling like a drunk. Several shoppers watched their progress.

'I never knew you could do that,' Suzi said.

Malcolm Ramkartra was looking at him with a studied expression, respectful, and more than a little disconcerted.

'Oh yeah,' Greg said. 'But it costs.'

Each of the observers had become a whirlpool of excitement. One of them began to follow Leol Reiger.

'Who was that?' he asked Suzi.

'Leol fucking Reiger, real bundle of fun. Likes to think he's a premier-grade tekmerc, but he's just a jumped up hardliner with an attitude problem.'

'I thought the two of you were trying to out-cool each other to death.'

Suzi's face hardened. 'Listen, he might be a prize prick, but if he's in on this deal there's serious trouble brewing.'

'Yeah, he's not working with the observers for a start.'

'Oh, bollocks. A third group involved.' She sucked in air, letting it whistle through her teeth. 'Greg, I don't like this.'

'Tell you, me neither.'

Leol Reiger and Chad sank out of his perception range. They had taken one of the glass cage lifts down the side of the well.

'What now?' Suzi asked.

'I still want to talk to one of those observers. But first I think we'd better make use of the small lead we've got.'

'Are you going to warn Baronski?' Malcolm Ramkartra asked.

Greg thought for a moment. Leol Reiger's mind had been screaming for vengeance as he disappeared. 'No. Reiger has gone to regroup, that's all. We've got a small breathing space. Baronski isn't our concern. If we try and safeguard him, Reiger will come after us, and I don't know what he's loaded with.' He gave Suzi an enquiring glance.

'God knows,' she said. 'But he won't be travelling lightweight. He'll have hardline backup, and he'll have made sure it's enough to get him into Baronski's apartment.'

'So scratch Baronski, maybe the observers will protect him when they see Reiger coming back. Then, maybe not. Our advantage is we know about Whitehurst, let's exploit that.' Greg pulled his cybofax from his top pocket, and gave it Julia's number. He squinted at the screen when she came on; she was sitting in the back seat of her Rolls. The real Julia. 'How were the speeches?'

'Boring, I'll trade places with you next time.'

'Deal. Listen, are you up to date?'

'Yes, her name's Charlotte Fielder, and you're going to see Baronski.'

'Seen him. Trouble is, there's one very pissed off tekmerc here called Leol Reiger who wants to see him as well.'

'Do you need assistance?'

'No, he's gone now. But Baronski is being watched, and not by Reiger. That means at least two other groups are on the same trail we are.'

'Dear Lord. Who, Greg?'

'I don't know. I was hoping you could tell us.'

Julia sucked her lower lip in concern. 'No, sorry. I'll get my team on it.'

'You do that. But at least we've got a lead on Fielder from Baronski. He told us that she's gone off with someone called Jason Whitehurst, a trader. Do you know him?'

'Jason? Yes, I know him, I even do business with him. He places some of my gear in Africa and the Far East; he runs some complex exchange deals, but he's reliable. I've met him at a few functions. Quite a nice old boy. You'd get on well with him, Greg, he's ex-military.'

'No messing? Well, that boy who left the El Harhari with Charlotte Fielder was Jason Whitehurst's son, Fabian; so she's definitely with Whitehurst. The thing is, Baronski can't contact her. Apparently Whitehurst lives in an airship, and he's not answering calls. I need its co-ordinates.'

'Jason's son?' Julia asked.

Greg picked up on the puzzlement in her voice. 'Yeah.'

'I don't think so, Greg, Jason's gay.'

'Christ,' Suzi muttered. 'You said it, Greg, that old fart Baronski cheated you. How about we go back and find out who the kid really is?'

The neurohormone hangover was beginning to bite. He tried to concentrate. 'Irrelevant; Charlotte left with that boy, and Baronski believed he was Jason Whitehurst's son. So whatever this Fabian character really is, he and Jason are operating together. And Jason is definitely plugged in somewhere down the line; why else did he pull his vanishing act? Julia, assemble a full profile on Jason Whitehurst for us, and find out where the bloody hell that airship is.'

'OK, it's already underway.'

'Fine, call me back when you have something.' He tucked the cybofax back into his top pocket. 'Right, let's go and lift one of those observers.'

'I wonder who's paying Leol?' Suzi asked as they walked towards the well.

'One at a time, Suzi, *please.*'

13

'Haunted?' Fabian's eyes widened in delight. 'How can an asteroid be haunted?'

'I've no idea; it was only a rumour,' Charlotte replied idly. She hugged one of the den's cushions. It was fun doing it on the cushions, there were lots of combinations they could be used in, imagination and gravity the only limits. None of her usual patrons could have coped with her inventiveness; even with their expensive clinic treatments joints creaked, muscles soon tired. But Fabian was more than capable, and becoming increasingly proficient under her tutelage. 'How does anywhere get to be haunted?'

It was gloomy in the den, Fabian had turned the biolums off, leaving just the light from the fish tanks and the flat-screens to illuminate them. A black and white videoke scene they had recorded earlier was playing on the biggest flat-screen, showing Charlotte going through one of Charlie Chaplin's slapstick routines. Fabian had stolen a dinner jacket and trousers from his father's wardrobe for her to wear. They were baggy enough to complete the 'little tramp' image, but even after five goes she couldn't get the movements quite right. The holographic exoskeleton which choreographed her limb movements was inordinately difficult to follow. She was beginning to respect just how gymnastic Chaplin must have been.

'If something really terrible happens to a chap, like a murder or something, then his spirit is so heavy with grief that it lingers,' Fabian said. 'That's what I heard, anyway.'

'Hmm, don't think there have been any murders in New London yet. They used to say that shooting stars were the souls of emperors ascending to heaven; perhaps they all migrated into the asteroid.'

Fabian giggled. 'Napoleon, Caesar, and Queen Victoria all spooking up the habitation cavern together, they'd have a right old time.'

Charlotte counted that observation as quite a victory. The Fabian who'd leered at her during the Newfields ball would have launched into a lecture about how shooting stars were actually meteorites breaking apart in the atmosphere as they were coming down. So, stupid, how could they be spirits going up?

She wanted Fabian on her side, not that she had any choice when it came to allies. However, she did have some considerable advantages. He was a fifteen-year-old sex maniac, and completely in love with her. On top of that, he was fascinated with space. And she could satisfy each desire. Got him by the heart, balls, and mind. Poor old Fabian.

'Queen Victoria?' Charlotte enquired.

'Absolutely, she was empress over the biggest empire there ever was.'

'Oh, yes. I think we'd better scrap that idea, then. She would be pretty distinctive even as a ghost. The Celestials couldn't mistake her.'

'Celestials?' Fabian rolled over onto his belly, resting his chin on his hands. He flipped his hair aside. 'Who's that? Go on, tell me. You know you will.'

'All right. But you're not to tell anyone else. No showing off to your party friends that you know something they don't.'

'Promise. Really, Charlotte, I do.'

'All right. The Celestial Apostles are a group of about two hundred people who live up in New London without official clearance.'

'You mean like tekmercs?'

'No, not at all like tekmercs. Their name is a bit of a cover-all for all the illegals up there these days. But the original Celestial Apostles were founded as a religious community. From what I could understand they're waiting for something like the Second Coming.'

'Why can't they wait for it on Earth?'

'Revelation, chapter four, verse one: there is a door which opens into Heaven – presumably New London.'

'Oh, crikey!' Fabian whined in disgust. 'All the religious nuts always quote Revelation to back up their visions. It's pure junk, just like Nostradamus. You can read anything you want into it if you're stupid enough.'

'I know. Convenient, isn't it?' She flashed him a bright smile. 'Anyway, chapter four goes on to say: "Come up hither, and I will show thee things which must be hereafter." Which is why the Celestials chose to stay in New London, because that's where they'll see whatever it is that's coming. It does have a kind of internal logic.'

'I suppose so.'

'What started off as a fringe religious movement attracted more people when they realized it was possible to stay up there without Event Horizon's permission; the idealists who really believe in space, the old High Frontier dream. Construction workers mainly, ones whose contract with Event Horizon ran out after the main section of the colony was finished. A whole host of oddballs threw in with them, from research professors right down to maintenance engineers who'd been fired for negligence. All of them determined not to be flung out of what they see as the human race's greatest hope. So the Celestial Apostles preach two kinds of salvation now. Both wings of the movement expect New London to be a fulcrum in human events. I think they may be right, too, the technological Celestials. There are another four asteroid-capture missions in progress; it's the way the future's going. One day there could be hundreds of inhabited asteroids in orbit around Earth, and think how that kind of industrial capacity would boost the global economy.'

'But how could these Celestials stay up there if their contracts ran out? I thought only active workers were allowed to live in New London.'

'How would you find them, Fabian? There are fifteen thousand people living and working in New London, plus another four or five thousand tourists at any one time. How can you spot two hundred illegals in that crowd? Especially as there's only about seventy police officers, with maybe twice that many Event Horizon security staff. It would be a full-time job for the lot of them. And the Celestials hide good, Fabian. New London's habitat chamber, Hyde Cavern, has a surface area of twenty-three square kilometres, then there's the tunnels, hundreds of kilometres of them, and natural caves, fissures in the rock that Event Horizon has never mapped out.'

Fabian's expression was remote, junky eyes gazing at her. 'They live in caves?'

'Yes, most of them, or the unused apartments.'

'How come you know all this?' he asked suspiciously.

'I met a couple of them. They try and get round as many tourists as possible, asking us to join. They were very serious, almost evangelical. Everyone's welcome, they said. Not my cup of tea.'

'Crikey, you mean they're recruiting more people to join them?'

'Yes.'

'But you said there was over two hundred Celestials already. They'd never be able to buy food for that many, not in a closed environment. Besides, the banks would burn their cards. What do they eat?'

Charlotte laughed. 'Whatever they want. The only plant you can't eat in Hyde Cavern is the grass, the rest is all fruit and vegetable, every type you can name. A vegetarian's paradise. It looks spectacular, too. Most of the plants were gene-tailored, and the New London Civil Council insisted they were given decent flowers.' She drew a deep breath, remembering. 'And the scents! Fabian, there's nowhere on Earth that smells so fresh.'

He deflated in frustration. 'Bloody hell, I want to go there.'

She leant over and kissed the nape of his neck. 'I'm sorry, Fabian. I didn't mean to make you jealous.'

'I'm not. It's just . . . I wish Father would trust me more.'

'He's a busy man right now.' She moved her lips on to his spine, tasting warm saltiness. His downy hair brushing against her cheek. 'And New London is going to be there for a long, long time.'

'Oh, Father's always busy.'

'He told me he'd got some very important contracts to tie up this week.'

'Crikey, you're not kidding. I'm not even allowed to use my terminal's datalink to the communication platforms. How am I supposed to get hold of the latest VR games, and the new videoke releases?'

Charlotte stopped her featherlight kisses halfway down Fabian's back. She had been depending on him to provide her with a communication circuit to Baronski. Jason Whitehurst seemed to have thought of that too. God damn the man! 'Isn't that unusual?'

'I'll say so. There isn't a single satellite uplink free. I don't know what he can do with all the data that's being squirted on board. All of our cargo agents are plugged into the company management processor cores. He must be selling off an entire country.'

'Hey, can you see what they're downloading with all this gear of yours?' She made it come out casually, an impulse.

Fabian twisted his head to look back over his shoulder at her. 'Well, yes, I suppose I could. Technically, I mean. My gear could handle it.' He looked straight ahead again. 'I never have though.'

She started kissing his spine again. 'It might be fun.'

'Father tells me everything about the business.'

'Everything?'

'Think so.' There were shades of defensiveness and doubt jumbled together in his voice.

Charlotte reached his buttocks. 'Turn over, Fabian.'

*

Charlotte pulled on a broad white cotton halter top, and a pair of running shorts. They were tight, making her look as if she was about to burst out of them. Partly clothed always excited men more than being naked.

Fabian watched her getting dressed, wearing the serious face of someone at prayer. 'You're so beautiful.'

She knelt down and put her hand under her chin. 'You keep saying that.'

'Because you are.'

'And you're very chivalrous.'

He flipped his hair aside. 'Just saying what I think. I can do that, can't I?'

'The girls at Cambridge are going to go wild over you. Rich, young, clever, handsome, and a real gentleman; and that's before you take your clothes off.'

Fabian pulled away, staring at a science fiction saga on one of the flatscreens; wedge-shaped fighter-spaceplanes dog-fighting in the rings of a gas-giant planet. 'I don't want any other girls,' he said pertly. 'I've got you.'

She cupped his ears, and gently bent forward to kiss him. He had listened devoutly to everything she'd told him, and remembered it all. If only he wasn't so young, or she wasn't so bloody old. One of the fighters exploded in a brilliant concussion of white and blue flames, dousing them in a tide of phosphor radiance.

'There,' she said as the explosion shrank. 'See what kind of effect you have.'

'I love you, Charlotte.'

She gave his nose a quick kiss. 'Have you ever skinnydipped in an ice-cold mountain tarn while there's a full moon in the sky?'

'No. Never.'

'We'll try it tonight, then. I don't know about the moon and the ice, but the pool's there waiting.'

'Yes!' His head swivelled about, taking in the terminals and his miscellaneous 'ware modules, suddenly very determined. 'I'm going to see what Father's doing. He's got some pretty strange contacts, you know, for business, for making sure he gets delivery contracts and things. But he's never done anything like this before.' He tugged his outsize Superman T-shirt out from under some cushions, and fought his way into it.

'Oh, well, I'm already out of my depth,' Charlotte said. 'I can never even balance my card accounts. I'll let you get on with it.'

'Right,' he mumbled. Multicoloured graphics were already rising in the cubes of the terminal he was operating.

She arranged the cushions in a loose nest, slumping into a beanbag at the bottom. Her cybofax displayed the London *Times*; the headline article was on the upcoming Welsh referendum.

She couldn't concentrate on it. A mirage of Fabian shimmered above the little screen. It wasn't as if she hadn't formed strong bonds with a patron before. One of her favourites had been eighty-eight, Émile Hirchaur, a French count. There had never been any sex involved; he simply enjoyed watching her walk and swim and ride: she'd been a surrogate body for him. And she was an attentive listener, he could be quite funny. He had chortled delightedly at his scandalized relatives when *they* came to visit his chateau. Life had to be made fun at his age, it would have been so utterly pointless otherwise. He treated his senescence like a second childhood. Another real gentleman. She'd cried horribly when he died.

And there had been younger, hotter lovers. Never anything serious, just physical, a relief from the feeble, tremulous sex of her patrons.

But the two had never been combined. Not that Fabian could be called a patron, not really. He didn't understand the rules, the obligations. And she couldn't blame him for that.

Why couldn't he be a snot-nosed brat she could hate as easy

as breathing? Why a bright, shy, lonely boy? And most of all, why did he have to be cooped up on this bloody airship?

'Got it,' Fabian called.

One of the wall-mounted flatscreens was showing an accountancy display, thick columns of green numbers moving from top to bottom in jittery stop-start sequences. 'Oh, that's no use, hang on.' He began to type quickly. A narrow red line appeared along the bottom of the flatscreen, gradually moving upwards; as the descending numbers reached it some of them would contract, then expand out as tides. 'Decryption program,' he said. The red line reached the top of the screen and stayed there.

Charlotte put down her cybofax, and studied the neatly tabulated accountancy display. It was a big company, probably a kombinate, no one else had a monthly cash flow of two billion Eurofrancs. There were hundreds of subsidiaries, all tied together.

Another flatscreen lit, showing the same sort of tiling, a third.

'That's all kombinate finance,' she said. 'Look at the amount of money involved.'

Fabian flipped his hair aside and looked at her cannily. 'How would you know?'

'I can read, thank you, Fabian. And I've picked up enough money talk in my life.'

He blushed. 'Oh, yes, right.'

She walked over to him, and slipped her arms round him, resting her chin on his shoulder. 'I said I knew what it was, not that I could interpret it.'

'Oh, well, it's just a confidential monthly performance review, nothing breathtaking.'

'You mean your father shouldn't have them?'

'Anyone can get hold of them if they really want; that much data can't be kept hushed up. There are some commercial intelligence companies that actually produce nothing else but analyses of kombinates.'

'So what's he doing with them?'

Fabian shrugged inside her arms, and tapped a ringer on the

terminal's cube. 'One of our on-board lightware number crunchers is running a pattern-recognition program. I'd say he's probably running their finances through it, looking for money being spent on accumulating a stock of specific raw material, or invested in certain facilities.'

Charlotte ran the flat of her hands lightly across his chest. 'Why?'

'Placement. Father will have acquired some kind of rare cargo; and now he's searching for the best market.' He cocked his head to one side as another set of monthly performance figures began to roll down the first screen. 'You know, Charlotte, it must be a jolly important cargo for him to go to all this trouble.'

14

As far as Suzi was concerned the deal was souring rapidly. Leol fucking Reiger turning up, that was serious bad news.

She had planned on meeting Reiger again, sure, when she was in body armour, lugging some heavy-duty weapons hardware around with her. Be interesting to see how much the shit smiled then.

He hadn't been smiling much when he'd backed off, him and that psychic tit, Chad. She was still trying to make sense of that; it was like waking from a dream she knew had been bad, but there was no straight memory of it. The only clue was the shape lurking behind her eyes, never fully visible, some dark animal, similar to a gene-tailored sentinel panther, except this one was bigger, hard, like a gargoyle that had come to life. Freaky.

Greg had given her a double shock, first that he could do that, second that he would. Fifteen years of fruit farming stripped away, dumping him back on Peterborough's hot streets as if he'd never been away. One mean hardliner.

She hadn't been so close to psychics when they'd clashed before. And one sample of that backwash was more than enough. It was too much like black sorcery.

She snatched a glance at Greg as the three of them walked back towards the well. He was battling against his gland headache, face sliding back into remorse again. The soft years had returned to cloud him. But the old Greg was still there, buried under all that civilization. A good thought to hold on to if events freewheeled much further downhill.

That was what got to her, rode her hard into a micro-storm of worry, the lack of professionalism about the deal. The urgency. Bugger Julia for hustling her into it, using Royan for emotional blackmail. She was mildly surprised she could still be twisted like this, an unrealized chink in her armour-plated heart. First Andria, now old friendships; might as well walk into Leol Reiger's bedroom stark bollock naked.

Sharp cold sunlight fell into the well at a severe angle. Busy preoccupied faces swarmed past, a termite conveyor belt. There was something about arcology dwellers, clannish, almost cyborgs with smile circuitry. She could pick one out of a stadium rock crowd. The Prezda's well was just their kind of turf, all the primness and carefully calculated nookishness of the small franchise shops. Hardly surprising that visitors tended to use the big domed shopping mall outside.

Greg walked right over to the balcony rail, gripping the smooth brass with both hands, gazing across the well. She followed his line.

'There are two observers left on this level now,' Greg said. 'One straight ahead. And I tell you, he's getting jumpy. Male, thirty, ginger beard, wearing grey trousers, a mint-green polo shirt, sunshade band.'

She scanned the opposite side of the balcony. 'Got him.'

'Yes,' Malcolm said.

'OK,' said Greg. 'Haul him in.'

They turned right, walking round towards the window. Malcolm headed in the other direction.

'How you holding out?' she asked Greg.

'Bloody painful. I haven't used that much neurohormone for ten years, not since we had organized poaching teams invading the peninsula.'

'What, lemon rustlers?' There was the most ridiculous image in her mind.'

'No. Deer, as in does and stags. There's a good herd of them in Armley Wood now.'

He sounded so serious. 'Yeah, all right, Greg, spare me the juice. Point is, are you up to drilling this observer's brain?'

'Yeah. Don't fret yourself. I'll find out who hired him.'

They were halfway towards the observer, walking past the window tables. The alps outside were brown wrinkled teeth, small caps of snow a gritty grey in colour. Suzi kept a surreptitious eye on the observer with the ginger beard ahead of them. He was beginning to drift towards the corridor entrance.

She activated her cybofax. 'Malcolm?'

'Hearing you clear,' the hardliner answered.

'OK, checking.'

'Christ.' Greg blurted. He took two fast steps to the balcony rail and leant over.

When she joined him she saw he was watching one of the glass cage lifts rising smoothly. It was on the other side of the well, a couple of floors below. An escalator interrupted her view. 'Is it Leol?'

'Yep. And there's six others in there with him. Major hostiles.'

The lift emerged from behind an escalator. She looked directly at Leol Reiger, who saw her at the same time. His arms moved.

'Shit!' Greg's hand slammed into her shoulder. As she fell she saw white spiderweb cracks blooming across the glass of the lift. The distinct warble of an electromagnetic rifle cut across the well's bustle. She landed painfully on her shoulder, Puma bag thumping into her side. Already rolling.

A stipple sheet of orange flame erupted across the front of the delicatessen behind her. Fucking explosive-tip projectiles! Heat washed over the back of her neck. The toughened-glass windows of the delicatessen simply disintegrated, long, lethal crystalline shards raining down over the food displays and floor. Screams burst out all around the balcony, mixed with the crescendo of smashing glass. Terrified people around her diving for cover.

Cold fury boiled up. Leol fucking Reiger, like a conditioned lab rat, see her and shoot, never mind there were hundreds of civilians about.

A high-pitched alarm started to shrill. There was a man on his knees in front of the shattered delicatessen, hands held in front of his face, one of the shards transfixing his wrist. Blood was squirting out of the wound. Two young women in identical stewardess suits were clinging to each other, the fabric of their uniforms punctured as if they'd been peppered with buckshot, each hole the centre of a spreading red stain.

Suzi rolled again, on to her chest, bringing her legs up, trainers scrabbling for purchase on the smooth tiles.

'Corridor!' Greg roared above the bedlam. Another volley of electromagnetic rifle fire ripped the air. The plastic sign along the top of the delicatessen's window flared orange, then ruptured, showing the nearby section of the balcony with fragments of plastic and small chunks of smoking concrete. A fresh round of screaming broke out.

'Tell Malcolm!' Greg shouted. Then he was running, stooping to keep his head below the level of the rail. Moving surprisingly fast.

'Malcolm,' she yelled into the cybofax. 'The corridor, get into the corridor!'

Running was easier for her, she didn't have to bend over as much as Greg. She began to catch him up. An escalator was mindlessly delivering prone bodies on to the balcony; frightened men, women and children, sobbing, holding their hands over their heads. As if that would do any good. She dodged round the outside of the logjam of petrified bodies, nearly tripping on outstretched legs.

More electromagnetic rifle fire poured out of the lift. They were guessing where she and Greg were now. Projectiles twanged and whined off concrete and the metal of the escalators, bursting into bright fleurets.

Twenty metres ahead of her, she saw the ginger-headed observer scurry into the corridor. Beyond him, Malcolm was pressed up against the balcony rail, the Tokarev pointing towards

211

the lift railings. A dense ruby beam stabbed out of the pistol. She watched it strike the lift railings, just above the lift itself. There was a fantail plume of cherry-red sparks, a squirt of white molten metal. Suzi heard a grinding metallic shriek rising above the incessant alarm. It cut off with a crunch.

The shop windows behind Malcolm detonated into flame and scything fragments as the electromagnetic rifles opened fire on him. He hunched down low as glass daggers whirred through the air all around him. Streaks of blood appeared over his suit.

Suzi risked a glance over the balcony rail. The cage lift was stuck three metres below the balcony. She should have done that, fucked up the mechanism. Malcolm had done all right; security people normally played by the rules, but then, Malcolm was one of Victor's. Someone in the lift was swinging a rifle towards her. She ducked fast.

Greg had made it to the entrance of the corridor. He was looking helplessly at Malcolm, who was lying beside the balcony rail, his face screwed up in pain.

'Get him,' Suzi yelled. She jerked the zip on her Puma bag, spilling the contents on to the floor. Saw the Browning. Grabbed it.

Greg was edging cautiously towards Malcolm. Suzi flicked the Browning to rapid pulse, and twisted fast, hands over the railing, taking aim.

There was no glass left in the lift. Leol Reiger's team were climbing through the open frame, dropping on to the balcony below. Two of them had already made it. They were helping a third who was spread-eagled on the outside of the lift. The remaining four in the lift were covering the balcony with their rifles. Couldn't see which was Leol.

She let off three maser pulses; moving the Browning in a slow arc, the way Greg had taught her to use beam weapons in some distant age. One of the figures inside the lift fell backwards, arms windmilling. A small circle of intense flame flared on the back of the man climbing down on to the balcony. She couldn't tell where the third pulse hit.

Just as she dived back under cover she saw the man clinging to the outside of the lift begin to fall. She scuttled along behind the balcony rail, wincing as the electromagnetic rifle projectiles chewed at the shop fronts.

People were moaning now, rather than screaming. Most of the wounds she could see looked superficial, clothing and skin cut by flying glass, smaller deeper fragmentation punctures.

Greg had one arm around Malcolm, half dragging him towards the corridor. The hardliner's feet were skating about on the tiles, as if he didn't have full control over them.

Suzi lifted the Browning over the balcony again. The tekmercs in the lift had hunched down in the bottom. There was no sign of the two on the balcony. She got off six pulses, holding the beam on the lift. Then she saw one of the tekmercs on the balcony raising his electromagnetic rifle above the railing. She crouched down and raced for the corridor, blazing projectiles chiselling long gouges into the wall above her.

Greg and Malcolm collapsed on to the walkway leading down into the safety of the corridor. Suzi landed on the ribbed metal segments a couple of metres behind them. She realized how heavily she was breathing, air sucked into her lungs in fast gulps.

'You OK?' Greg shouted back at her.

'Yeah.' The walkway seemed to be crawling along, no speed at all. The corridor's curve was too gentle, she could still see the entrance into the well. The moans and whimpers were fading, but the alarm was still howling away. 'How's Malcolm?'

'Functional,' the security hardliner answered with a weak grin.

'Can you make out if Leol's team are coming after us?' she asked Greg.

'Not yet.'

Malcolm drew his cybofax out of his top pocket and muttered something to it. He studied the display. 'There's a SWAT squad on its way to the well, Prezda security think it's a lone psycho burner on the loose.'

'Can you break in and tell them it's a tekmerc team?' Suzi asked.

'Yes.'

'Do it; if the police go out there unprepared Leol's crazies will snuff the lot of them.'

Malcolm spoke into the cybofax.

'How bad does this Reiger hate you?' Greg asked.

'Bad enough. Sodding mutual it is, too.'

'Will he leave Baronski to come after you?'

'Doubt it. He's fucking insane, but not stupid. He knows he's got to get Baronski now, or he's blown his deal. I'll be around for a long time. We'll have our little chat later.'

Greg climbed to his feet, helping Malcolm to stand. Suzi looked back; the well was out of sight. She stood, yelling at the sharp unexpected pain in her left leg. When she looked down, the shellsuit was torn around the knee. A clump of glass needles were embedded in the flesh, blood flowing freely. Now her senses were calming down she was aware of other lacerations, arms, back, buttocks. Little tingle points, hot and sticky.

'Jesus wept,' she muttered.

They reached the end of the walkway. A group of people were milling about, numb and white faced as zombies. Some of them had cuts and nicks from the glass fragments. They looked balefully at Suzi. She realized the Browning was still in her hand, its red LED charge light winking steadily.

'Next set of lifts,' Greg said impassively. Malcolm was leaning on him heavily, limping. The back of his jacket was sodden with blood.

Suzi followed the pair of them through the silent group on to the next walkway. She hated the accusations in their stares. Wanting to explain, it wasn't me. Blame Leol Reiger. No use.

'What next?' she asked. The alarm's cry was reduced to a distant whistle now.

Greg's eyes were unfocused. There was blood on his face, oozing from small cuts on his cheeks, a deep one right next to his eye.

They'd been lucky, she knew. If Leol had thought about it, planned it out instead of letting his instincts rule . . .

'Tactical retreat,' Greg said. 'None of us is in any fit state to do anything. I've lost track of the observer. And chasing after the one back in the well is a definite no. Besides, if you're right about Reiger, our lead over Fielder is getting narrower by the second. Bugger, but I wanted to know who else we were up against.'

*

At the end of the walkway they took a lift up to the next floor, then switched. Malcolm slumped against the steel-panel wall, sucking down shallow breaths. Suzi was getting worried about the amount of blood he was losing. It was dripping steadily off his jacket, soaking the floor. He was muttering something in a slurred voice.

Greg tugged his cybofax out as the lift doors slid shut. 'Rachel, we're in shaft A17, lift five. Bring the Pegasus as close to it as you can, and come and get us. It's hit the fan, OK?'

'On our way, Greg,' Rachel's voice said out of the wafer.

Suzi's cybofax bleeped. She pulled it out of her top pocket with stiff fingers, knowing who it would be.

Leol Reiger's face filled the little screen. His corpse flesh was actually coloured, cheeks red. She could see one of Baronski's porno art paintings on the wall behind him.

'Two of my team, Suzi bitch. You snuffed two of them.'

There was a woman's scream in the background, Suzi thought it might be Iol. Leol Reiger never paid it any attention.

'You fucking well brought them here, Leol. You ordered them to open fire when there were civilians around, you paranoid rat prick. They were sitting ducks in that lift. Your screw-up tactics. Your fault.'

'I've got a deal to close right now, Suzi. But afterwards, you and I are going to say hello. First I'm gonna sprain your mind, show you a scene that'll make you scream; then I'm gonna snap your little kiddy body in two. You read me, bitch?'

'Bollocks. You're on the wrong side of this deal, Leol. I've got the fucking English Army behind me.' She savoured the

215

momentary flash of puzzlement on his face, then said, 'Say hi to the SWAT squad for me, Leol,' and flipped him off. The tremble in her legs was nothing to do with the glass fragments.

*

The lift opened into a passenger lounge, plastic chairs arranged in a zigzag pattern, hologram adverts of civil hypersonics slicing through clean sunny skies, departure information screens, a children's play area. An echoic tannoy voice was announcing a flight arrival. The first thing Suzi saw when the lift doors opened was Rachel and Pearse racing towards them, Tokarevs held ready. Waiting passengers scrambled out of the way.

Rachel's eyes widened in surprise when she saw them. 'Lord hellfire, anything serious?'

'Malcolm's out, can't walk,' Greg said.

'I got him,' Pearse said. He pulled Malcolm's arms around over his chest, and lifted him piggyback style. Suzi didn't notice any drop in speed as he began to jog for the lounge door.

The Pegasus was taxiing towards the lounge as they came out into the hangar. Greg went up the belly-hatch stairs first, then Pearse, Suzi followed with Rachel bringing up the rear.

Malcolm had been lowered into one of the chairs at the front of the cabin. A couple of wall lockers were open, aluminium first aid cases on the floor. Pearse was easing his colleague's tattered soggy jacket off. 'We'll have to cut the trousers,' he said. It was all very tight and professional, she thought.

'Fine,' Greg muttered, raiding the first aid kits for a diagnostic sensor and antiseptic sprays. He handed Pearse an infuser tube, which the hardliner pressed against Malcolm's neck.

The belly hatch slid shut.

'Where to?' Rachel asked.

'Out,' Suzi said. 'Now. We should have some co-ordinates coming from Julia in a little while. But just get us out.'

Rachel snatched up the handset.

Suzi started worrying about Leol Reiger's transport. Himself, a psychic, and at least six hardliners; whatever he'd arrived in it had to be big, and probably loaded with defence hardware, knowing Leol.

'Grab hold of something,' Rachel called.

The flatscreen showed the Pegasus turning towards one of the lift platforms. Suzi could hear the compressors surging. With a rush of childish delight she knew what the pilot was going to do. She sank quickly into one of the chairs. Her knee was giving her hell.

There was a push of acceleration, and the Pegasus began its run for the platform. Hangar staff rushed to get clear. She felt the drop as they shot over the edge, her belly suddenly freefalling. The grassy valley floor with its railway lines and twin autobahns filled the flatscreen. Then they were bottoming out, swooping up again above the Prezda's dome.

'Is this plane fitted with an ECM system?' she asked.

Rachel looked up from the handset. 'Yes.'

'Tell the pilot to use it, and fly an evasion pattern through the mountains. We might be followed.'

'Right.'

'Suzi!' Greg called. 'Take over from me, will you?'

She rose from the chair, the pain in her knee more acute. Malcolm was unconscious; Pearse had got his jacket and shirt off, and was spraying the wounds with antiseptic. The clear oily liquid mixed with blood, forming runnels across Malcolm's ribs, splashing on the chair fabric.

Suzi checked the data the diagnostic was displaying on its screen. Her guess about the blood had been right, he was losing too much. She found a plasma bladder, and pulled out its bioware leech patch. The patch resembled a flattened snail, a hard carapace with a soft spongy underside, connected to the plasma bladder with a plastic tube. She held Malcolm's forearm and pressed the leech pad against his skin. There was a soft sucking sound as it adhered. The pattern of yellow and green LED on the bladder's pump changed as the leech patch inserted its needle probes into his blood vessels, then it began feeding plasma into him.

Greg sat down gingerly in one of the chairs, and gave Victor Tyo's number to his cybofax.

Suzi heard the security chief say, 'Bloody hell, what happened to you?'

'Tell you, we're not the only people looking for Charlotte Fielder.' He started to fill Victor in on the events in the Prezda.

Suzi began spraying dermal seal on Malcolm's lacerations; the foam sizzled as it touched the skin, rapidly solidifying into a pale blue membrane. She was continually bracing herself as the plane banked and rose. Malcolm's back had been badly slashed by the flying glass. She had to use flesh tape on the wider cuts. Pearse was working on his legs, using a small sensor pad to find any buried glass fragments.

'Hey,' she said quietly. 'He did all right, your mate. Stopped those tekmercs dead.'

'Reason he was chosen,' Pearse grunted.

'Yeah, right.' Suzi heard Greg rounding up, and asked Rachel to finish for her. She limped back to where Greg was sitting. A glance at the bulkhead flatscreen showed a continual blur of rock.

'You too?' Victor asked when Greg handed her the cybofax.

Suzi sat heavily in one of the chairs, grimacing. The hand she was holding the cybofax with was filmed in dried blood, and not all of it was Malcolm's. 'Yeah. But you should see the opposition.'

'I know, Greg told me.'

'Listen, Leol Reiger, I know him. He's a prize turd, but the bastard's good.'

'I'm reviewing his profile now, Suzi. But I was aware of the name. Have you got any idea who employed him, any rumours?'

'Nope, sorry. Gave me a fuck of a shock seeing him there.' She stared at Victor's concerned young-seeming face, her instincts rebelling against confiding in him. Security man. But she had hardlined with him once, seventeen years ago, some weird case Greg was working on for Julia. It was just she hated opening herself to anyone. 'Victor, there's this girl. Name's

Andria Landon. She's in my apartment at the Soreyheath condominium; not a hardliner, not even tekmerc. Means she can't
look out for herself. So if Leol Reiger wants to hit me, she's
the obvious choice. You got a safehouse she can stay at till I get
back?'

'No problem, I'm dispatching a couple of my people, they'll
have her out of there in twenty minutes.' He said it all crisp and
efficient, which she figured was his way of not showing surprise.

'They've got to be good, Victor.'

He was looking at something off-screen, typing. 'They will be.
Call her now and tell her they're coming: Howard Lovell, and
Katie Sansom. Got the names?'

'Yeah. Thanks, Victor.'

15

Victor came down out of the Pegasus on to Wilholm Manor's lawn. He was greeted by a rich scent of honeysuckle in the moist air. The sprinklers had been on, drenching the lawns, keeping the grass lush and green. His shoes were swiftly coated in the artificial dew.

The Manor in front of him was a long classical grey-stone building, three stories high. It dated back to the eighteenth century, although it had undergone considerable modernization and refurbishment over the years. The last major overhaul had come when Julia and Philip Evans bought it, right after PSP fell, ousting the communal farmers and virtually gutting the interior before returning it to an opulence of a bygone age.

Wilholm estate was a rare enclave of gracious living, Victor always thought, out of sync with the present and all its digital bustle. A true English country house, basking in an eternal Indian summer. Birds always singing, flowers always in bloom. Time slowed down here.

Rick Parnell trotted down the stairs out of the executive hypersonic's belly hatch, carrying his suit jacket over his shoulder. When he was clear of the plane he turned a full circle, gawping at the grounds like an overawed tourist. 'Bloody hell, you mean somebody actually lives here? It looks like a theme park.'

'It's your boss who lives here, just remember,' Victor said.

Rick Parnell was staring at the trout lake at the bottom of the gardens; now the hypersonic's compressors had wound down the noise of the waterfall on the far side was clearly audible. Beyond the dark water was a dense stretch of woodland. Tall Chinese yew and virginciana trees were draped in a lacework of dark green ivy and clematis vines, clusters of plate-sized red and lilac flowers dangling. They had survived the spring hurricanes again, the few trunks that had keeled over adding to the rustic authenticity of the spinney. It was hard to believe that the grounds were only eighteen years old.

Paths crisscrossed the lawn, fenced by topiary drimys and japonicas, elaborate cockerels, dogs, bears, concentric spheres, and one giant pair of shears. A wide lily pond had a statue of Venus in the centre, shooting a fountain five metres into the air. Boxy orange drones crawled along the flower borders, digesting faded roses and forking out weeds.

Victor started off towards the manor, Rick Parnell following reluctantly. Daniella and Matthew were playing in the big out-door pool. They'd got Brutus, their sheepdog, in with them. Victor watched Matthew slide down the water chute along one side, nearly landing on top of the excited animal. Qoi, their nanny, was sitting at a table on the patio behind the pool, reading her cybofax, and occasionally glancing up to check on her wayward charges.

Victor liked the children; Julia had brought them up well, deliberately ensuring they didn't have the hauteur of their contemporaries. She had almost gone too far in Matthew's case, the boy could be a bit of a pain at times. Though what he probably needed was a father. Daniella was growing up along similar lines to her mother, tall and slim, through her hair was darker, and not worn as long. Nice kid, occasionally very serious, as if she was suffering bouts of premature adulthood. She waved, smiling, and shouted something at him. He guessed it was an invitation to join them, but the barking dog made it hard to tell. He gave her an exaggerated shrug and walked into the drawing room through open French doors.

'Open house here, isn't it?' Rick said.

'Oh no, nothing like. If you weren't with me you wouldn't have made it off the bottom step of the Pegasus. Julia just doesn't like the security hardware to spoil the look of the place.'

'I can believe that. What this place must have cost to build.'

Victor opened the door. 'She's entitled.'

They came out into a big hall hung with oil paintings. Victor led the way up a broad curving stairway and on to the landing. Rick struggled into his jacket on the way up.

The door to Wilholm's study was solid teak, with a simple polished brass handle. Victor turned it and pushed. 'Lion's den,' he said with a grin.

Rick gave him a thanks-for-nothing glance, and walked in still adjusting his tie.

The room was oak panelled, its lead-glazed windows looking out over the Manor's rear lawns. There was a long oak table down the centre, with ten black wooden chairs along each side. Julia sat at the head, studying the data displayed in the cubes of an elaborate terminal in front of her.

Rick's greeting died unspoken. Victor was expecting it, a reaction he had seen a thousand times before. Julia in the flesh did that to people. She belonged on channel newscasts, in gossipcasts, there was even a university which included her management of Event Horizon as part of its business finance course. She wasn't real.

'Dr Rick Parnell,' Victor said innocently. 'Your SETI director.'

Julia offered her hand. 'Do sit down, though I have to say I don't quite understand why Victor brought you.'

Victor pulled out a chair for himself, and sat on one side of Julia. 'I brought him because Royan's been playing silly buggers with our memory cores. Tell her about the microbes, Rick.'

Rick settled in the chair on the other side of Julia, his bulk filling it dangerously. Victor listened to him launch into an explanation of the Matoyaii probe, its unsubstantiated discovery in Jupiter's rings. Rick's usual bluster had vanished, replaced by a boyish eagerness.

Julia leaned back in her chair after he finished. 'Now you've jogged my memory, I do remember hearing about the flu theory,' she said slowly. 'Years ago, probably when I was back at school. But why do you assume these microbes come from the stars? I would have thought Jupiter itself is a more obvious choice. The chemistry and the energy exists to support microbic life forms in its atmosphere, surely some spoors could have leaked out to the rings, maybe even riding up the Io flux-tube.'

Victor watched the last of Rick's assurance crumple. Of course, an interstellar origin was so much easier for him to believe in, more important, more dramatic. It gave the whole SETI discipline that edge of certainty, respectability. The same reason people wanted to believe in flying saucers rather than swamp gas.

'The origin is irrelevant to our present situation,' Victor said. 'The point is, when he heard the microbes existed, or might exist, Royan had a probe built to investigate them.'

Julia looked at him blankly, as if the words he'd spoken had come out wrong. 'When?'

'He approached me about sixteen months ago,' Rick said. 'I expect that was because I suggested a probe to verify Matoyaii's findings as soon as you appointed me. It was turned down.'

Julia's expression became cool, she didn't say anything. Rick swallowed and went on, 'After Royan came to us, my office advised the design team on the kind of sensors required to locate the microbes.'

'There's no record of this,' Julia said. Her eyes were closed. Victor knew she was using her nodes, probably talking to her NN cores, running tracers through Event Horizon's memory cores. He had done it himself on the flight back from the Astronautics Institute, and drawn a complete blank. But if there were any bytes on the probe hidden in the company's memory cores, Julia would find them. He always thought it a considerable irony that the boss of Event Horizon was one of the greatest hotrods on the planet.

'I watched it being built,' Rick said, a shade defensively. 'It was assembled in Building One, you could actually see it from my office window.'

'A Jupiter probe?' Julia asked. 'Built in full view, and nobody said anything?'

'Best place to hide something,' Victor said. 'One more space project in an Institute that boots five thousand tonnes of hardware into orbit every week. Who'd notice, who'd even care?'

'Mr Tyo is quite right,' Rick said. 'Unmanned planetary exploration isn't of much interest to Institute personnel. Not since the Mars and Mercury landings. There was nothing special about Kiley, the components were all standard apart from the microbe detection sensors and sampling waldos.'

'Kiley?' Julia asked.

'Yes. Royan chose the name. It's a kind of boomerang,' Rick explained.

'A boomerang? You mean Kiley was a sample-return mission?'

'Yes.'

'Has it returned?' she demanded.

'I couldn't tell you. That would depend on how long it stayed in orbit around Jupiter. But I will tell you this, it was built for speed. The probe itself only massed about two tonnes, the propulsion section came in at over forty tonnes. It filled a *Clarke*-class spaceplane payload bay. There were five stages, throwaway reaction-mass tanks and giga-conductor cells. That raised a few eyebrows at the Institute. Whoever heard of throwing away giga-conductor cells? Royan was certainly in a hurry for it to get on Jupiter.'

The corner of Julia's mouth turned down. 'Nothing new in that, he was always in a hurry. So how long would it take to get there?'

'Launched at an optimal conjunction, ten weeks,' Rick said.

'And presumably the same time to return?'

'Yes, possibly a week or so less. The Sun's gravity field would accelerate it, you see.'

'Do you know when it was launched?'

'Not to the day, no. But Kiley was rolled out of Building One eight months ago, last November.'

Julia gave him a long hard look, holding her body immobile.

Victor knew her mood well enough, contemplative, but Rick was visibly wilting under such a direct contact.

'Did he ever say why he was so keen to examine these microbes?' Victor asked. 'What was so important about them?'

'No,' Rick said. 'He never confided in me. Sorry.'

Victor glanced enquiringly at Julia.

''Fraid not,' she shook her head fractionally.

'Care to guess?'

'I don't think I could. I'm beginning to realize how little of him I ever did know.'

Rick cleared his throat cautiously. 'Er, are we, the Institute, that is, in trouble for assembling the probe? Royan did have all the funding clearance, and we knew he's your husband—' He broke off miserably.

Julia favoured him with a thin grin. 'Oh, yes, he's mine all right. And no, I don't hold the Institute to blame. Royan has the authority to use whatever Event Horizon facility he wishes to.'

'Even if he can't be bothered to tell us,' Victor said. It came out with more feeling than he intended, and Julia registered a flicker of pain. Julia's choice had always baffled him, although he and Royan had always been careful never to show any animosity towards each other. If anything, they'd always been scrupulously polite, to the point of excess, it became a ritual. Perhaps the mistrust he felt was just a security man's instinct. But he always considered Royan a flaw in Julia's otherwise meticulous life; it was always her devotion, her money. All Royan had brought with him were his hotrod programs. Love was never reasonable.

'Something I'd like to ask,' Victor said, evading Julia's critical eye. 'Seeing as how I don't believe in coincidence: Royan builds

225

a Jupiter probe to investigate alien life, then he turns up warning us about alien life. Would it make sense for our aliens to use Jupiter as a base?'

'You mean, could their ship be in orbit around Jupiter?' Julia asked.

'Just an idea,' Victor said. It was one he'd had on the flight back to Wilholm. He had wanted to pursue it with Rick, but then Greg had called and he wound up getting sidetracked with safeguarding Andria Landon.

'A good one,' said Rick. 'However advanced their technology, a starflight would deplete on-board resources, certainly on a slower-than-light ship. Jupiter would be an excellent resupply point. Minerals and metal in its ring, ice on Europa, He_3 in its atmosphere.'

'Can you at least run a search of Jupiter for us?' Victor asked.

'I keep telling you,' Rick said irritably. 'SETI is not a hardware-orientated department. All we have is an office, and access to the Institute's lightware cruncher. That's it, the total, what we are.'

'Not any more,' Julia said. 'As of now, I am placing every deep-space sensor facility Event Horizon owns under the control of the SETI department.' Her eyes went distant. 'Your role will mainly be co-ordination, but then that's what you're used to. Tell the visible- and radio-astronomy departments what you require, I'll see you have the clearance by the time you get back to the Institute. You can also get the visible-astronomy staff to interpret any recent visual records of Jupiter. There's our own Galileo telescope, as well as the IAF's Aldrin. Victor, you handle any image purchases from the Aldrin. Go through some fronts, I don't want anyone to know Event Horizon is the end user, not at this stage.'

'This is all very sudden,' Rick said slowly. He kept glancing at Victor for confirmation of what was actually happening. 'Funny, nothing like the contact scenarios we were prepared for. We always assumed it would be non-material contact, almost archaeological, digging through the electronic remains of a culture, signals broadcast before the human race had even learnt how to knap flints. Now this, a starship finally arrives, then it hides from us. Crazy.'

'I'm sure you can cope,' Julia said, there was a line of steel in her voice.

Rick jerked back out of his daydream. 'Yes, of course, absolutely no problem.'

'Good. You're searching for two things. Firstly, any sign of an alien starship. Secondly, this Kily probe of Royan's. I want to know if it's still in Jupiter orbit, or if it's *en route* back to Earth. Got that?'

'Yes.' Rick bobbed his head.

'There's a third option on Kiley,' Victor reminded her. 'The most likely, that it's already returned.'

'How would we know?' Julia asked. 'Royan's wiped or guarded any reference in the company memory cores. Even I can't find any traces,' she added significantly.

'We do it the old-fashioned way. Ask people instead of machines,' he said with a slow smile. Investigative techniques, cross-indexing and correlating data, had been a part of his original training. Unused for well over a decade, ever since security simply became a question of correct data retrieval. It would be good to actually use his brain on a problem again, satisfying, that and being out in the field for a change. 'We can start with Rick here?'

'Me?' the startled SETI director asked.

'Yes.'

'But I've told you everything I know about Kiley, every byte.'

'Not quite. For a start, which bay the Kiley was assembled in?'

'F37, I think.'

'Right, Julia would you ask your team to access the records for that bay, see if they can work out how Royan glitched the cores to hide what he's been doing?'

'Good idea,' she said.

'In the mean time, Rick and I will get back to the Institute, start talking to the team that assembled Kiley, and more important, see if we can locate the spaceplane crew that launched it.'

'What for?' Rick asked.

'Because if it has returned, their familiarity with the system would make them the logical choice to perform the recovery flight.'

16

Julia watched the study door close behind the two men. Rick Parnell had been more or less what she'd expected, except for his physical size; an intellectual, socially out of his depth. Wasn't royalty supposed to be able to put anyone at their ease? That was one trick she had never mastered. It always took three or four meetings with people before they started to relax around her. Apart from Victor, of course, she couldn't think of a time when Victor had been reticent around her. Always honest, that was Victor's big attraction. And loyal, which went far beyond professional integrity. Julia quickly put a brake on that stray thought.

You shouldn't be so dishonest with yourself, Juliet, her grandfather said gently.

She hadn't realized the NN cores were still plugged in.

I wasn't being dishonest, just practical.

Poor Juliet, so many problems, so many unknowns.

You're getting quite dismally sentimental in your old age.

Listen, my girl. I know this is immortality, but it's tasteless, odourless, and numb; and it isn't going to get any better. Maybe I should have gone for the angels and demons deal after all.

You don't have glands, Grandpa, you don't need the outside world.

No, but I like it.

Oh, all right, anything for peace and quiet.

Load OtherEyes. She felt the package squirt into one of her processor nodes, it was a fragment of her grandfather, a sub-personality, formatting her sensory impulses and relaying them back to his NN core. In effect, he was riding her nervous system, a tactual tourist.

Happy now? Julia asked. She gave him access to her sensorium about once a week; he always claimed he needed to receive the physical sensations to stop himself going insane. Julia doubted it, her two NN cores never made the same request, and her grandfather had skipped the last four months of both her pregnancies.

'Too bloody weird, Juliet,' he had told her. 'Remember this is a lad who grew up in the sixties – the Beatles, Apollo moonshots, and black and white telly – that's my stomping ground, simple times. Looking round this brain-wrecked world half of me thinks I'm in hell already.'

That's better, thank you, Juliet.

His silent voice always sounded closer when OtherEyes was loaded, which was impossible. She stretched her arms, wriggling her fingers, then breathed in deeply.

Oh, terrific, that grand old smell of chilly conditioned air. Can't beat it. You live in a bloody spaceship, you do, girl.

She laughed. *I'll take a walk out in the gardens for you later. Daniella and Matthew are in the pool, I could join them.*

An eerie wisp of pride slithered through her brain at the mention of her children. Not hers, not the usual background of paternal pride.

They're good kids, they are, Juliet. My great-grandchildren. Even if they do keep taking Brutus into the pool.

Oh, not again! I've told Qoi not to let them.

There was a mental chuckle. *Brutus doesn't harm anybody, it's not as if he's got fleas. Besides, I remember a little girl who would have stabled her horse in her bedroom if I'd let her.*

If you're going to get all asinine maudlin, you can go back where you came from.

So cold and ruthless we are now, Juliet, how we've grown.

The communication channel widened to incorporate her two NN cores.

We've found Jason Whitehurst's airship, NN core one said. There was a brief impression of excitement. *We didn't even have to go extralegal. Stratotransit PLC holds the Euro-flight Agency franchise for traffic control, and Event Horizon owns twelve per cent of Stratotransit, so our request for a memory squirt was perfectly legitimate.*

Good, so where are they?

Stratotransit tracked the Colonel Maitland *leaving Monaco and flying west across the Mediterranean, then out into the Atlantic over the Straits of Gibraltar. That's where radar coverage ends, so we've been relying on our Earth Resource platforms to track her from there.*

One of the terminal cubes in front of her lit up. Julia recognized the Iberian peninsula and north-west Africa, both glowing in various shades of red. The sea was a light green.

You are seeing an enhanced infrared image, NN core one explained. The image expanded, centring on the Straits of Gibraltar. Julia could make out the drop flow, a tongue of emerald green that seemed to shimmer. A blue dot crept into the picture.

There they are. They crossed at night, which is significant. It was the only time they were in sight of land after leaving Monaco.

The image was expanding again, shifting west and south. The *Colonel Maitland* flew north of the Canaries, then out over the ocean.

The Colonel Maitland *is currently seven hundred kilometres due west of the Cape Verde islands, and holding station,* NN core one said. *That's the absolute middle of nowhere. For the last ten hours, all it's done is compensated for the wind.*

Julia stared at the blue dot, virtually equidistant from both landmasses, Africa and South America. *You mean only someone with our resources could locate the* Colonel Maitland *right now?*

Yes, for all its size, the damn thing is tiny on an oceanic scale. Unless you have access to the same Stratotransit and satellite data as we do, there's no way you could find it.

What about the usual communication links? she asked. *Call Jason Whitehurst up and locate him via a transponder.*

Jason is too wily for that; pulling transponder co-ordinates our of Intelsat is an ancient hotrod trick. There's no transponder response to his number.

You mean he's totally incommunicado?

Far from it; one of security's ELINT satellites has an orbit which passes close enough to scan the Colonel Maitland. *We waited until the latest results were squirted over to us before telling you we'd found Jason. It turns out the* Colonel Maitland *is operating some kind of localized jammer.*

Is that why we can't get any response from Charlotte Fielder's cybofax?

Could well be, if she's on board. But Jason Whitehurst certainly hasn't been struck dumb. He's using his own comsat to squirt data about among his cargo agents, and the bit rate is approaching maximum capacity. And the uplink to geosync orbit is a very tight beam; but the ELINT intercepted a portion while it was overhead. Jason Whitehurst is receiving a vast amount of kombinate finance reviews which his agents have bought from commercial intelligence companies.

Julia looked at the cube again, translating the blue dot into an airship drifting idly over the ocean. What had Victor said? No such thing as coincidence. And Greg said the same thing often enough.

Grandpa, do you notice the similarity here? I'm looking for this Charlotte Fielder girl, and I've also initiated a search through kombinate finance records because of the offers Mutizen and Clifford Jepson have made to me. Jason Whitehurst has got Charlotte Fielder, and what's he busy doing?

Spot on, Juliet. Notice something else as well?

What?

This atomic structuring technology cropped up more or less at the same time as Royan warned us about aliens. A technology that is so different it isn't even a breakthrough in the usual sense of the word, because nobody's even been working on it. A technology whose origins are bloody difficult to track down.

'Bugger,' she said out loud. He was right. Which was precisely what made him so indispensable, not just his experience, but an alternative viewpoint.

We should've realized that, she said to her two NN cores.

Yes, was the curiously hollow answer. A fragment of resentment.

Right, let's make up for the lapse. One of you contact Peter Cavendish, tell him to start putting some pressure on Eduard Müller and Mutizen. Explain to them that we've had a counter-offer for a partnership in atomic structuring, and they'll have to put in a revised bid if they want Event Horizon as a partner. Then I want one of our Atlantic antenna platforms reprogrammed to plug into the Colonel Maitland's satellite circuits. I want to talk to Jason Whitehurst, get him to accept a visit from Greg and Suzi.

No problem, said NN core two. I'm redirecting one of the dish foci now.

Fine. What about Jason Whitehurst's profile?

Interesting. I can find no reference to Fabian Whitehurst's birth certificate in any public memory core. The birth was simply not registered. However, I've been accessing recent gossipcats, the boy has been to several society parties over the last nine months.

The terminal's second cube came alive, showing her the image of a mid-teens boy with long, floppy dark hair. She could see some resemblance to Jason. The boy was a lively one, she thought, bright and sparky; years of trying to contain Matthew taught her the signs.

I wonder why Jason never mentioned him to me? she mused.

There was no need for him to tell you, her grandfather said. No reason why you should know.

Grandpa, if anyone I know has a child I'm given their age, school record, told they adore dogs and horses, and get shown their holo- gram, all within fifteen seconds. Anything that'll get them invited to *play with Daniella and Matthew. And this Fabian looks about the same age as Daniella.*

Jason Whitehurst isn't an arriviste.

Maybe not. But why isn't there a record of Fabian's birth?

Got me there, girl.

OK, I want a more detailed profile of Jason Whitehurst assembled, centred on his life sixteen, fifteen, and fourteen years ago. Finance, personal, the works, every byte. I don't know exactly how old this Fabian child is, but he's around that age. Find a trace of him. Look for unexplained payments to women, and possibly medical clinics as well. Given Jason's sexual orientation, I'd guess at an in vitro fertiliz-ation and a host mother.

You got it, Juliet.

I have established a link with the Colonel Maitland, *NN core two said.*

Jason Whitehurst appeared on the study's phone screen. He was sitting at some kind of desk, wearing a white shirt, open at the neck to reveal an MCC cravat. There was a window behind him, showing nothing by sky.

'Julia, this is a somewhat unexpected pleasure. I wasn't aware I was taking incoming calls.'

'I know, Jason, and I apologize for interrupting your communication circuits like this, but we do need to talk.'

'Certainly, I was going to call you today anyway.'

Julia felt a trickle of relief in her mind. At least they weren't going to play the euphemisms game. She tried to gauge his mood, which wasn't easy over a phone vid. But he was definitely riding an up.

She thought for a moment, unsure of what to say. What exactly was she asking him for? Charlotte Fielder, or should there be something more?

'I'm looking for someone, a Miss Charlotte Fielder. Apparently she left the Newfields ball with your son, Fabian.'

There was a slight tightening around Jason Whitehurst's mouth at the mention of Fabian. 'She left with me, that is so.'

Interesting, her grandfather said. *The old bastard's cagey about the tyke.*

Do you think I could use that? she asked.

Bloody hell, girl, don't you ever listen to me? Don't ever ask a question unless you already know the answer. How would you use the boy? Tell me that, hey?

Sorry, Grandpa. It was just that she was so used to negotiating from a position of strength. Spoilt.

'I'd like to talk to her, Jason.'

'There are several people who would, my dear Julia. But I'm sure you and I can sort out a deal.'

Bugger the man, her grandfather said. *Juliet, you have got to get that Fielder girl. She's not something he can sell twice. If she knows where the flower came from, then she knows where the alien is, and quite possibly all that atomic structuring technology. He's going to ask for a ridiculous sum, but pay it. You can't afford not to.*

Maybe, Grandpa, but we can certainly apply some pressure here.

Jason Whitehurst was regarding her with polite expectation.

'I'd like you to receive my representative,' she told him. 'He can be at the *Colonel Maitland* in an hour or so. And he's fully empowered to negotiate on my behalf.'

'I hadn't anticipated face-to-face meetings, Julia. My intention is to hold an auction. How else could I ascertain her true worth?'

'Perhaps you don't appreciate just how high the stakes are in this instance, Jason. I don't think an open bidding session would be to your advantage. Acknowledging that you hold Fielder could prove dangerous. Someone uncovering the location of the *Colonel Maitland* was inevitable. If nothing else, the amount of effort I've expended in finding you ought to tell you how deep you're in. Of course, you know you can trust me not to exploit the knowledge. But there are some parties involved here who won't hold your physical safety in such high regard.'

Jason Whitehurst pulled on his beard. 'Just the one man?'

'Absolutely, his name's Greg Mandel, and he'll have an

assistant with him. They'll arrive in an ordinary civil Pegasus. Your landing pad can accommodate that.'

'Very well, Julia. I'll see him.' He held up a warning finger. 'Nothing more. If your financial offer proves acceptable, he can take Fielder with him when he leaves. If not, you will have to compete with your rivals on a level pitch.'

Julia leant forwards, schooling her face into an earnest expression. 'Thank you, Jason. But please take care, at least suspend your dealings with anyone else until after Greg Mandel arrives. I don't want them finding out where you are, you're too valuable to me right now.'

'I appreciate the concern, Julia. Don't worry about me.' His image blanked out.

Julia let out a heavy breath, staring round the study, not really seeing it. Whenever she did have to work at Wilholm, she always used the study. With its dark panelling, chilly stone mantelpiece, and sombre glass-cased books it had the right air of sobriety. The decisions taken in here . . .

Atta girl, Philip Evans said. *Once Greg and Suzi get out to the* Colonel Maitland, *old Jason's going to find his options decreasing rapidly. You did exactly the right thing.*

Thank you, Grandpa. He always seemed to know when she was down. Although the mix of tension and depression that was wiring up her muscles must have given him a strong clue.

She fed the desk terminal the code for a secure link to Greg's cybofax. When his face appeared there were some small cuts on his cheeks, a splash of blue dermal seal near one eye. He was trying to damp down a scowl.

She sucked in her lower lip. It wasn't supposed to be like this. Not Greg hardlining. She had promised Eleanor that, promised herself. All she wanted was Royan. 'Dear Lord, are you all OK?' Victor had mentioned there had been trouble at the Prezda, a tekmerc called Reiger; but nothing about Greg being injured.

'Yeah, more or less. I don't know what sort of commendations Victor hands out, but Malcolm Ramkartra earned his today.'

She just nodded meekly at the screen.

Greg seemed to relent. 'I guess we were lucky, nothing a first aid kit can't patch up.' He dropped his voice. 'But you've gone and dumped Suzi straight into a blood vendetta. This Reiger bloke is a right fucking loony, and no messing. Two of his team were killed, and he blames Suzi for the whole shooting match. That's serious trouble, Julia. People like this, it ain't over till one of them's snuffed.'

'Whatever she needs, Greg, she's got it, you know that.'

'Yeah, but you know Suzi, she won't take it.' His voice was still low, almost inaudible.

'Then Victor will just have get rid of Reiger for her,' she heard herself saying.

'Right.' He looked loaded up with remorse, like she felt.

'I've got you the co-ordinates of Jason Whitehurst's airship. And more, he's agreed to meet you and Suzi as my representatives.'

'Hey, well done.'

She ordered the terminal to squirt the co-ordinates over to the Pegasus. 'Not entirely good news, Greg. When I called, he was getting ready to sell Charlotte Fielder to the highest bidder.'

'Christ. Just how many groups are we playing against?'

'I don't know. But you can tell Suzi that crack of hers about acquiring starship technology is starting to look uncomfortably true. I've been getting some pretty strange offers from kombinates and other major-league players today, all concerning some radical technology. Our alien isn't entirely the big hush we thought it was. I'd say the first one to reach Royan is going to hit the technological jackpot. That's why you're experiencing all this heat.'

'Great,' he said sourly. 'At least I know *why* I'm being shot at.'

'I don't care what price Whitehurst puts on Fielder, Greg. But you've got to come back with her. The ident card we gave you is linked directly to the company's main account, so pay him whatever he asks and don't worry about it. Besides, I don't think he really understands what he's gone and got himself involved in. Unless that airship is armed like a destroyer, he's seriously underestimated how eager we all are to get our hands on Charlotte Fielder.'

'OK, Julia, it's your money. And please try to find out who we're up against. If we know, we can watch them, find out what their moves are.'

'I'll do what I can.'

'OK, I'll call you after we get Fielder.'

She ordered the phone off.

Access Security File: Reiger, Leol; Tekmerc. She closed her eyes and let the profile open out in her mind. Victor had assembled a surprisingly large amount of information on the tekmerc, including a psychological report. Greg had been right, Leol Reiger's mentality bordered on sociopathic.

That's a mean-looking bugger, Juliet. What're you planning on doing about him?

Leol Reiger's deals seemed to glow like blue neon in the formless grey mist of the node interface; the number of fatalities involved, those confirmed plus estimates. Forty-eight in the last nine years. Rumours of more, when he was just an ordinary hardliner, before he came to Victor's attention as a deal maker.

Exactly what I told Greg. Turn Victor loose on him. But that'll take time, for the moment I want to know who's hired him.

Assemble Personality Package.

She was back in the isolation of the 'ware universe, the blank depthless emptiness. Her processor nodes were integrating the package, following the formula Royan had devised; freezing and copying specific segments of her thought patterns, digitizing them.

In its compressed, dormant, state she could access the composite's multiple data planes, all neatly folded in on each other; sequences of memory, response logic, identity, motivation. They were slices of her mind, the crucial portions; subconscious inhibitions and emotional reticence rooted out, discarded. It was a streamlined edition of her own mentality.

Julia formulated her instructions carefully, loading them into the personality package. She withdrew, leaving herself alone with Leol Reiger's sleazy profile. Her eyes flicked open, reducing the profile to a smoky shadow overlaying the warm browns of the study.

A representation of the personality package was floating in one of the terminal's cubes, a dark green sphere with a multi-segmented surface, reminding her of an insect eye.

She began to type on the terminal, summoning up a finance transfer order, then entered Leol Reiger's Zürich bank account number, reading it direct from his profile.

You're giving Leol Reiger ten thousand Eurofrancs? her grandfather asked.

That's right. She watched the representation of the transfer order form in the cube, a translucent blue starfish. *Easiest way I know of accessing the bank's mainframe.* The arms of the starfish were closing around the personality package.

Bloody hell, I don't know what the world's coming to.

There was no sign of the intricately rucked green sphere; its surface had been covered by a smooth blue shell. Julia tested the assembled composite with a couple of security probe programs. Its integrity held.

You know a better way? she asked.

No. A mental sigh accompanied the admission.

Right, then. She tapped the download key, and the data composite squirted into Leol Reiger's Zürich bank.

Julia made a brief kissing motion after it. There was a nostalgic thrill in watching it go. She hadn't done any serious hotrodding for years. If only the conspiracy theorists knew. Julia Evans's hobby was criminal data piracy. They'd have a field day with that one.

She could have routed the request through Victor's division, put pressure on the bank to squirt over Leol Reiger's account data. Corporate entities did co-operate to a reasonable degree, especially with regard to tekmercs. But Zürich banks still clung to their independence. It would take a lot of pressure, and time.

A hiss of compressors penetrated the window. She turned to see the Pegasus carrying Victor Tyo and Dr Parnell lifting of the lawn. The scene looked vaguely surreal, like something out of a five-star resort advert; all it lacked was a couple of smiling models posing at a table by the pool, sipping something potent and cool.

Julia ran her hands through her hair, and turned back to the terminal. Time to find out just how widespread the knowledge of atomic structuring was. With at least two other groups chasing after Royan, she was starting to wonder exactly how many routes there were to the alien.

The terminal accessed Event Horizon's main communication network for her, and she loaded a cut-off program at the junction. If anyone tried to backtrack her call the best they'd be able to come up with was English Telecom's Peterborough exchange. She entered the Gracious Services number.

There was no phone on the other end; England's hacker circuit had illegal catchment programs loaded into every exchange in the country. It pulled out her call and plugged her straight in.

There was a nervous flicker across her terminal's flatscreen, then it printed:

WELCOME TO GRACIOUS SERVICES.

WE AIM TO PLEASE.

DATA FOUND, OR MONEY RETURNED.

NO ACCESS TOO BIG OR TOO SMALL.

JUST REMEMBER OUR CARDINAL RULE: DO NOT ASK

FOR CREDIT!!!

PLEASE ENTER YOUR HANDLE.

Julia thought for a moment; she hadn't actually used the circuit from this side before. Royan had signed her on as a novice hotrod when he was teaching her to write dark programs, saying the experience would do her good. She had run several burns against various companies and government departments, competing against the other hotrods for the client's money. It was a race, the one who pulled the data first cleaned up, minus the umpire's cut. Competition sharpened her mind to a considerable degree.

She grinned furtively and typed: MARIE ANTOINETTE.

GOOD AFTERNOON, MARIE ANTOINETTE. YOUR UMPIRE IS
BLUEPRINCE. WHAT SERVICE DO YOU REQUIRE?

BULLETIN BOARD.

ALL RIGHT, MARIE ANTOINETTE, THERE ARE ELEVEN HOTRODS
PLUGGED IN, AND EACH OF THEM HAS A MEMORY CORE LOADED
WITH BASEBORN BYTES. WHAT DO YOU WANT TO KNOW?

ONE) HOW MANY COMPANIES ARE PLUGGED INTO ATOMIC
STRUCTURING TECHNOLOGY?

    TWO) ARE ANY OF THEM IN POSSESSION OF THE THEORY FOR
CONSTRUCTING A NUCLEAR FORCE GENERATOR?

    THREE) WHAT IS THE ORIGIN OF ATOMIC STRUCTURING
TECHNOLOGY? I WILL ACCEPT ORIGIN RUMOURS IF HARD FACTS ARE
UNAVAILABLE.

Her message stayed on the flatscreen for over a minute before it cleared.

I'M NOT QUITE SURE WHAT YOU WANT US FOR, MARIE ANTOINETTE,
SIX HOTRODS HADN'T EVEN HEARD OF ATOMIC STRUCTURING. AND
THOSE THAT DO SAY THEIR BYTES AREN'T GOING TO COME CHEAP.
ATOMIC STRUCTURING IS THE BIGGEST ULTRA-HUSH TECHNOLOGY
SINCE EVENT HORIZON CRACKED THE GIGA-CONDUCTOR.

'And don't I know it,' she murmured, then typed: I UNDERSTAND BLUEPRINCE. DEAL FOR ME, PLEASE.

OK, THEY DON'T HAVE MUCH, SO WHAT THEY'LL DO IS POOL WHAT
THEY HAVE GOT. I'LL TABULATE FOR YOU, BUT ITS A FLAT FEE. SIXTY
THOUSAND POUNDS NEW STERLING EACH, AND YOU TAKE THE RISK
THAT THE DATA IS REPLICATED FIVE TIMES. ARE YOU STILL
INTERESTED?

I'M INTERESTED.

YOU CHOSE YOURSELF A GOOD HANDLE, MARIE ANTOINETTE.
PLEASE DEPOSIT THREE HUNDRED THOUSAND POUNDS NEW
STERLING INTO TIZZAMUND BANK, ZURICH, ACCOUNT NUMBER
WRU2384ASE.

You're not actually going to pay them, are you, Juliet? her grand-father asked.

Her hands poised over the terminal keys. *'Fraid so. I need to know how widespread this knowledge is. And I need to know quickly. This is the simplest way. Whatever information is floating around, the circuit will have plugged into it. They're very good, you know.*

I wish I still had a bed. I wouldn't have bothered getting out of it this morning. Actually paying these criminals, bloody hell! In my day they would have been rounded up and forced to hand the information over. Cattle prods wouldn't come amiss.

Julia giggled and authorized the credit transfer from one of her Cayman slush funds.

YOUR CREDIT IS STAGGERING, MARIE ANTOINETTE. I HOPE IT WAS
WORTH IT. HERE'S YOUR BULLETIN:
    THE FOLLOWING COMPANIES ARE NOW KNOWN TO POSSESS
THE BEHAVIOURAL EQUATIONS OF THE STRONG NUCLEAR FORCE:
DASTEIN, JOHNATHAN-HEWIT, SEIMENS, BOEING, MUTIZEN,
MITSUBISHI, SPARAVIZ, RENAULT, GLOBECAST, HONDA, GENERAL
ELECTRIC, EVENT HORIZON, EMBRAER, SAAB, MIKOYAN, AND
ROCKWELL. IN ADDITION, THE DEFENCE MINISTRIES OF THE
FOLLOWING COUNTRIES ARE ALSO IN POSSESSION OF THE
BEHAVIOURAL EQUATIONS: AUSTRALIA, BRAZIL, CHINA, CANADA,
ENGLAND, FRANCE, GERMANY, JAPAN, RUSSIA, USA, SOUTH AFRICA,
AND TAIWAN. THE SENIOR STAFF OF ALL SEVEN MAJOR DEFENCE
ALLIANCES HAVE NOW BEEN INFORMED OF THE EXISTENCE OF THE
EQUATIONS, AND THEIR IMPLICATIONS.

Julia sat up in the chair, consternation acting like a static charge crawling over her skin. *Dear Lord, can you read that, Grandpa?*

Too bloody true I can read it, Juliet. What the hell do those prats in commercial intelligence think they're pissing about at? Are they on strike, for Christ's sake?

I don't know, she told him wearily. *We never heard even a whisper, nothing. And why hasn't the English MOD been in contact with us?*

AS TO THE ORIGIN OF THE ORIGINAL EQUATIONS: TWO-THIRDS OF THE COMPANIES LISTED ARE KNOWN TO HAVE BEEN APPROACHED BY GLOBECAST; THEY WERE OFFERED A PARTNERSHIP IN THE MARKETING AND PRODUCTION OF ATOMIC STRUCTURING TECHNOLOGY IN RETURN FOR GLOBECAST PROVIDING THEM WITH THE GENERATOR THEORY. MOST OF THE SUBSEQUENT DEALS BEING STRUCK BETWEEN COMPANIES ARE CONCERNED WITH SHARING THE DEVELOPMENT COSTS OF SUCH A GENERATOR. THIS WOULD IMPLY THAT GLOBECAST IS IN SOLE POSSESSION OF THE THEORY WHICH WILL ALLOW CONSTRUCTION OF THE NUCLEAR FORCE GENERATOR. I HOPE THAT'S WHAT YOU WANTED TO SEE, MARIE ANTOINETTE.

HOW LONG HAS GLOBECAST BEEN OFFERING PARTNERSHIPS FOR? she typed.

THREE DAYS. THE FINAL BIDS ARE TO BE SUBMITTED WITHIN TWO DAYS, AND THE HIGHEST BID TO BE ANNOUNCED TWELVE HOURS LATER.

THANK YOU, BLUEPRINCE.

PLEASURE'S ALL MINE. THE NEXT TIME YOU PLUG INTO THE CIRCUIT YOU ASK FOR ME, I'LL GET YOU THE BEST DEALS GOING. BLUEPRINCE SIGNING OFF.

The terminal screen reverted to its menu display. Julia focused on a spot just in front of the flatscreen, lifted out of time. She didn't even have to run the data through the logic matrix function of her processor nodes. Globecast was obviously being used as some kind of distribution agent, almost an auctioneer. Although it didn't have a monopoly, Mutizen proved that Eduard Müller wouldn't have offered her a partnership unless he could produce the generator theory.

Two sources. Two aliens?

She let the real world claim her back. Her personality package had returned to the terminal. She scanned the readout and laughed. It had squirted itself out of the bank's mainframe by transferring nine hundred thousand Eurofrancs from Leol Reiger's account back to Event Horizon's finance division. There was a total of fifty-seven Eurofrancs left in his account.

You have an evil mind, Juliet, even in its salami version.

And who did I inherit it from?

She began to read Reiger's account statement. The last deposit had been made two days ago, for two hundred and fifty thousand Eurofrancs. There was no name, just an account number for another Zürich bank, the Eienso.

We have a result from the memory core of bay F37, NN core one reported. There was a strange sense of confusion and high spirits in the tone. *You'll want to access this.*

Wait one, Julia said. She reprogrammed her personality package, and squirted it into the Eienso's mainframe. *Go ahead.*

There was a data package waiting in the manor's 'ware for her. Its guardian program was solid, no probe programs could break in.

Most of the files listed as stored in the assembly bay's memory core are fabrications, NN core one said. *According to the Institute's administrative records, bay F37 was being used to assemble a fish breeding pen filter for New London during the time Kiley was being built. But when we opened a channel direct to the bay's core to access the suspect files, we found the package stored inside. It squirted directly into Wilholm's 'ware, knew all the third-level access codes.*

Query identity? she shot at the quiescent package.

Request Snowy access, it replied.

'Royan.' She said it out loud, but she couldn't hear her own voice. *Sorry, Grandpa, I need the processor capacity.*

Yeah, all right, he grumbled. *But you still owe me a visit to the gardens, and a hug for each of the children.*

I won't forget. **Wipe OtherEyes.** She felt him go, a spectre slipping out of her consciousness. His absence left her with a slight taste of regret in her mind. **Initiate Processor Node One Data Isolation/Examination Procedure. Load Data Package.**

The package squirted into her processor node, and the interfaces sealed, isolating it inside. She had written the data-bus guardian program herself, if anything tried to broach the barrier the processor would wipe instantly. Her three memory nodes contained a vast amount of confidential data, as well as indexing the personal recollections she treasured, she wasn't about to risk any kind of virus attack.

Open Integrity Monitored Link to Processor Node One. It would mean a millisecond delay in communication while her second processor node analysed the package's output, searching the downloaded bytes for a Trojan program.

She ran a quick review of processor node one's management layout. The package had expanded to fill all the available capacity, but there had been no attempt to insinuate itself in the management routines.

Hello, Royan, she sent.

Snowy. His smile filled her mind, flooding her synapses with warmth and longing, triggering a cascade of poignant associations. She sagged in the study's chair, sniffing hard. He stood behind the smile, wearing the leather flying jacket she had bought for him. His arms lifted from his side in a gesture of helplessness, lips puckering up. The movement, like a lot of his mannerisms, had been copied from one of his physiotherapists who always shrugged like that when he asked how much longer he would have to stay in the clinic.

Well, here I am, trapped like a bug in amber, Royan said. *You write good guardian programs.*

I had the best teacher. I'm sorry I can't let you out. There are just so many unknowns about my current situation, I can't take the risk you are a Trojan. Not that you could do any real damage to my nodes, but I'd hate to lose the memories, and then there's the time it would take to write an antithesis to purge any virus. Do I sound paranoid?

I don't know what your situation is, so I can't judge objectively. Things getting bad, are they?

Yes. But I'm coping.

I wish I could help, but I've been in the assembly bay's memory core since April. No current data.

Why were you left in storage?

A fallback, a warning if anything went wrong. I presume something has, else you wouldn't have come looking.

I don't know. Wrong with what?

He smiled again, protectively. *My darling Snowy. There's so much to show you. Here, come fly with me.* He reached out with an open hand.

Impenetrable night folded about her, then the stars came out one by one. There was no horizon, when she looked down there was no ground. Drifting in space. Five slender silvery booms extended out from her, probing the vacuum.

These are the Kiley flight memories, Royan said. *The approach phase. There, see?*

In front of her was a bright orange-brown dot, its glow somehow malevolent. She could hear its cry over the radio bands, a crackling roar. Lonely, random.

A stillborn star weeping, Royan whispered reverently. *Can you imagine what we have missed? Can you imagine the beauty of a double sunrise?*

Kiley, it's back now isn't it? It came back.

Hush, Snowy. Watch, learn.

Jupiter grew, becoming a salmon-pink disc, distinct cloud-bands hovering or the edge of resolution. Moons expanded from dark stars to solid worlds, coloured grey and brown, mottled and streaked. New senses swept in, magnetic, particle, electro-magnetic, overlaying the basic image with bolder shadings. Jupiter nestled at the centre of colossal energy storms. Pellucid petals of blue and pink light whorled protectively around the gas giant, the white halo of Io's plasma tours, intangible sleet of ions blowing outward.

The electric gusts flowed around her, soothing her thoughts, lost in marvel.

What would our world be like, Snowy, if we could perceive it with these senses? How colourful and exciting,

Why did you come here? she asked. *And why alone? I would have shared all this, I would have been a part of it with you.*

Because it is I who was a part of you, Snowy. I have been since the day you rescued me. I guess I make a bad prince consort after all.

You had everything.

I had everything you gave me. This – Jupiter, Kiley – was my chance for the roles to be reversed.

To make it on your own?

Yes. To be your equal.

You always were.

No. Not really. With or without me, you would still have achieved what you have today.

You brought me the electron-compression data.

If not me, then your money would have found a way. It always does.

What did you hope to achieve? How would this space probe give you equality?

The microbes, Snowy. As soon as I heard of the Matoyaii results I knew they were genuine, that the sensor results weren't an aberration. They existed, I could feel it. Just like Greg and his intuition. They were real, alive, waiting for me. It was like being born again, I'd been given a purpose to live.

They were inside the orbit of Io now, Kiley sliding through the penumbra, falling in towards the gas giant. Perspective altered, Jupiter was definitely below now. Something so vast could never be overhead. Its curvature was flattening out, edges merging with distance, cloudscape expanding into an unending plane. If she looked up she could see Io; a volcano's mushroom fountain of sulphur just north of the equator belching upwards. A cold dragon flame cascading in glorious low gravity slow motion.

The stormband below Kiley was a pallid rust-yellow, ocean-sized elliptical cyclones and anti-cyclones of ammonium hydrosulfide grinding in conflict, buffeted by supersonic jet-streams. Clots of white cloud bloomed as whirlwind vortices sucked frozen ammonia crystals up from the hidden depths. They spilled into the churning cyclone walls like cream into coffee, diffusing and dispersing.

Then the terminator was ahead of them, a shadow straddling the nearly flat horizon. Firefly lights twinkled beyond.

Was I such a challenge to you? Julia asked sadly. *I thought you were the one person in the world who saw me as me, as Snowy, not some plutocrat bitch. I was alive then, when you held me.*

Your heritage is the challenge, the barrier. Not you. You, Snowy, you I love. Did you need to be told that?

I could give it all up. For you.

No, no, no.

No.

You are the one who is complete, Snowy. I envy you that. Me, I still have to find your peak. And I can. I can.

Kiley glided into the umbra. It was night below, but not dark. Lightning twisted between the imperious cloud mountains, tattered dazzling streamers that illuminated thousands of square kilometres with each elemental discharge. Comets sank down gracefully amid the storms, rocky detritus from the rings sucked in by the monstrous gravity field, braked by the ionosphere, flaring purple, spitting a tail of slowly dimming sparks.

Kiley began its deceleration burn, sending out a five-hundred-metre spear of plasma. The top of the atmosphere was only seventy-five kilometres below now. Julia could sense the massive flux currents seedling through the thin fog of molecules, glowing red veins pulsing strongly.

The burn ended abruptly. The image juddered as explosive bolts fired. Empty spherical hydrogen tanks and lenticular giga-conductor cells separated, tumbling away. Small chemical thrusters fired, stabilizing the modules which remained. Kiley began its coast up to the rings.

Do you see now, Snowy? The silent savagery of this place, its hostility. Yet amid all this, there is life.

Kiley found the microbes?

Oh, yes.

Is that all it found?

How could there be more?

A spaceship, a starship.

No. Is that what you are dealing with, a starship? Your trouble.

I don't know, Royan, I really don't. I've got people working on it, Greg, Victor, Suzi.

The old team. That's nice. They're good, they'll find you an answer.

They need to find you, Royan. Where are you?

I don't know. How could I?

Then why were you left in storage? What are you here to warn me about?

Potential. The potential of the microbes. But I was so sure. I had it all worked out.

Show me.

The rock reminded her of Phobos. It had that same barren grey-yellow colour, a battered potato outline. Except it was much smaller, barely a hundred metres long, sixty wide. Kiley hovered beside it, optical sensor images degraded by the dry mist of ring particles. Wavering braids of dust motes and sulphur atoms shimmered in the raw sunlight, moving sluggishly.

Jupiter's crescent eclipsed the starfield a hundred and twenty thousand kilometres away. Even from this height, the dancing lights of the darkside were easily seen. Like Earth's cities, she thought, the idea momentarily distorting scale.

Kiley's close-range sensors were stirring, focusing on the rock. It had worn down over the aeons, its surface abraded by the gentle unceasing caress of dust. Impact craters and jagged fracture cliffs smoothed down to soft curves. One end was scarred by a white splash-pattern of methane frost, tapering rays extending their grip over a third of its length.

Lasers swept the rock from end to end, building a cartographic profile within the on-board lightware processors. Cold gas precision positioning thrusters fired, moving the probe closer in centimetre increments. When it hovered a metre above the rock, microfocus photon amps telescoped out of their cruise phase sheaths, aligning themselves on the surface.

The image changed, a lunar mare strewn with boulders; Julia knew she was seeing the dust motes sticking to the rock. Kiley's lightware processors began to run a spectrographic analysis program. She watched the image alter, as if it had been overlaid with a grid of square lenses. Data began to flow back into the probe's lightware as the blurred squares were examined one by one.

Kiley's photon amps quartered a square metre of the rock's surface a millimetre at a time, then it fired its cold gas thrusters and moved to the next section. Again. Again.

The fourth time, one of the photon-amp grid squares flared red. The eight surrounding ones were immediately reviewed by the spectrographic program. It registered carbon, hydrogen, and various trace minerals.

The block of squares expanded to fill her vision, regaining their focus.

There, Royan said in awe. *In the middle of a desolation more profound than Gomorrah: life itself. And what life.*

The photon-amp focus was at its ultimate resolution, centred on a clump of microbes. They looked like a smear of caviare, tiny spheres, tar-black, sticky; they glistened with a dull pink light thrown by Jupiter's albedo.

Call it Jesus, call it Gaia, call it Allah, said Royan. *Whatever name you wish to bestow, but don't tell me God doesn't exist. The true miracle of this universe is life itself. Left to fate, to random chance groupings of amino acids in the primal soup, it could never happen. Never! We may evolve as Darwin said, man may not have been made in God's image; but that spark, that very first spark of origin from which we grew, that was not nature. That was a blessing. We are not a side product of an uncaring cosmos, a chemical joke.*

You're preaching to the converted, remember? She wasn't surprised by his outburst, nor its intensity; both of them had a strong quasi-religious background; her at the First Salvation

Church, him with the Trinities, it was another thread in their bond.

Kiley's sampling waldo slid out, micromanipulator claws closing around the clump of microbes. It retracted and placed them delicately inside the probe's collection flask.

Cold gas thrusters fired again, backing Kiley away from the rock. The lightware processors began to check over the propulsion systems.

You did this for me? Julia asked.

I did. Do you see now, Snowy? Do you see the why of it?

Kiley's chemical thrusters fired for a long time, lifting it out of the ring's inclination, into free space where the plasma drive could be used. Star trackers locked on to their target constellations, orientating the probe for its flyby manoeuvre burns.

No, she said, inexplicably humbled by the admission. She could sit and think, run a logic matrix, tear the problem apart. Answers never eluded her when she was in that state, a determined computer/human fusion. But somehow just the thought of expending all that effort inhibited her. Perhaps this appalling vastness of the gas giant's domain had numbed her into dormancy.

Kiley was shedding mass, discarding its primary mission modules, the sampling waldos, precision attitude thrusters, photon-amp booms, laser scanners, all peeling off like mounting scales. She watched them go, oblong boxes and spidery cybernetic arms, adding to the gas giant's ring. In a few thousand years vacuum ablation would reduce them to tissue flakes, a swarm of slowly dissipating metallic confetti.

The melancholia had really gripped now. The Kiley memory was its own Trojan, draining her.

It's like this, Snowy: the theorists, Rick Parnell and his merry band, they all say the microbes survived their flight between stars because they are simple primitive organisms. They're wrong. I know they're wrong. How could they be primitive? They are life's pinnacle, separated from amoebas by billions of years of evolution. These microbes, Snowy, came from a dying world, travelling Christ knows how far to get here – *certainly there are no burnt-out stars in our immediate section of the galaxy. Think of it, their planet, its sun growing cold, a freezing atmosphere bleeding off into space, oceans evaporated, mountains fallen. Anything that could adapt to survive such a decaying environment would have to be the toughest, most forbidding, most ruthless form of life imaginable. Then, when whatever it was that eventually triumphed – plant, or algae, or even animal – was all that was left, it made the final jump. It adapted to space. It abandoned its birthworld and achieved species immortality. That's what we all strive for, Snowy, deep down. Continuation, the biological imperative. It drives us, preordains our movements from before we are born, it is universal and irrefutable. That, if you like, is our spiritual burden.*

I think I see now, she said. *The microbes are a stronger form of life than any on Earth, more potent.*

And more, he said, eagerness swelling like a wave. *They live – thrive – in a vacuum. I want to tame them, Snowy. I want to put them to use, make them work for us. Extraterrestrial bioware, a kind of green space technology, and all at your disposal. My wedding present, at last.*

Kiley's plasma drive came on, a two-minute burn, nudging the probe in towards Jupiter and the flyby. A slingshot manoeuvre that would fling it out of the gas giant's gravity field and back to Earth.

Is that what you did when the microbes got back? she asked. *Manipulate them?*

So I believe, that's certainly what I intended when I left this package for you.

There must be more, then.

Yes. A diary. A daily package, so you could see my progress. And then if anything went wrong, you'd be able to see what I was working on before it happened.

Daily?

Perhaps not. But there will be accounts, lab notes, reviews, explanations, tables of results.

Where, Royan? I need them. Today. Now.

If you're following me, you'll find them.

Oh, God, she called out, furious, frightened. *What have you done, what are you doing? The chaos you've caused.*

The smile reappeared. *That's me, Snowy. The king of misrule. You know that's me. You loved that part of me, it excited you, as your power did to me. Opposites.*

God damn you! You've no right.

Don't cry, not for me. I'm not worth it. If I've screwed up, you'll put me back together again. You're so good at that.

When I find you, I won't patch you up, I'll tear you to bloody pieces.

That's my Snowy. He laughed.

Cancel Integrity Monitored Link to Processor Node One. Squirt Package into NN Core Two.

The study materialized about her again. The light pouring through the windows was oppressively harsh after Jupiter's gloaming. She blinked rapidly.

What do I want with him? NN core two asked peevishly.

Run a total review of Kiley's sensor memories.

Oh yes, Io's volcanos.

That sort of affinity had unnerved her for a week or so after the first NN core had come on line. Now she just took it for granted. The NN core would comb through Kiley's sensor memories, running comparisons against existing star maps. That was how Io's volcanos had been discovered, by accident, reviewing old Voyager pictures for a guidance plot. Maybe, just maybe, Kiley had recorded the starship.

Julia pushed the chair back, and pulled her shoes off. She walked over to the window. Daniella and Matthew were still splashing about in the pool. And they had got that damn dog in with them. The times she'd told them.

She pressed her cheek against the window, watching them. The worry which her entrancement with Jupiter had suppressed was beginning to rise. Microbes and starships. Which was she supposed to be looking for? And Royan, uncertain enough to leave her warnings, perhaps the most chilling aspect of the whole affair. He was always so cocksure.

It wasn't as if she could offload the burden, confess to someone. 'Bugger you, Royan,' she snapped.

The terminal on the desk bleeped for attention. Now what? She braced herself and turned.

Her personality package had returned from Eienso's mainframe. Clifford Jepson had paid the money into Leol Reiger's account.

17

The Pegasus was spiralling down towards the *Colonel Maitland*. Greg watched the vast bulk of the airship appear on the bulkhead flatscreen, its contra-rotating fans dawdling in a doldrum calm. Their shallow approach angle showed it as a large black oval above the glistening deep-blue of the ocean. He found it disconcerting, the absorptive black surface, sharp edges, it didn't seem to belong here at the centre of nature's passive domain, an intrusive foreigner.

'So why the guilty smile?' Suzi asked.

Greg clamped his lips together, he hadn't realized he was smiling. 'Nothing.'

He and Eleanor had taken their honeymoon on one of the *Lakehurst*-class airships, that was back in the days when all long-distance flights were made by airships. Two weeks spent circling around Greenland and back down Canada's east coast. A first-class cabin to themselves, day trips to resort centres, the eager buzz of third-class passengers on their way to a new life on homesteads springing up behind the retreating permafrost. The black shape was evocative, tripping his mind's gates, delicious memories spilling out along his synapses.

Above all was the gentleness, time spent entwined, time spent floating above fresh landscapes, above sunsets and dawns, gourmet meals, idle chatter, laughter. It had been stately.

He rued the day of the airship's passing, replaced with

hypersonic planes powered by Julia's all-pervasive giga-conductor. The last commercial trans-Atlantic airship flight had rated half a column in *The Times* one morning; he'd passed the cybofax over the breakfast table to Eleanor who quirked her lips in remorse. They had always said they would repeat the trip, but then there had been the kids, the groves to tend, responsibilities. Now all it ever could be was a sunny memory.

Greg had never really adapted to hypersonics, the second age of air travel; two-and-a-quarter hours to New Zealand from England; Japan a hundred-minute streak over the slushy remnants of the North Pole. Where could you escape in a world like that?

Jason Whitehurst had found the answer the hard way. The Pegasus had broken away from the Italian mainland over Genoa, hitting Mach eight above the Ligurian Sea. They were passing over the Straits of Gibraltar fifteen minutes later without slowing down, curving round north-west Africa to line up on the Cape Verde islands. Total elapsed time from Julia sending him the co-ordinates to arrival at the *Colonel Maitland* was forty-seven minutes.

'We've just been given landing clearance by the captain,' Pearse called.

'Fine,' Greg said. 'Take her down.' He stood up as Pearse spoke into the handset. Suzi got to her feet beside him. He noticed she used her arms to push herself up out of the deep chair. 'You OK?'

She pulled a face. 'Sod it, yeah, I'll do.'

The leg of her shellsuit was torn, stained with a ribbon of blood, blue dermal seal visible through the open fabric. And what would Jason Whitehurst make of that?

Greg's face still stung, but he'd checked it in the toilet mirror. Appearance-wise it wasn't too bad. His leather jacket had deflected a lot of the glass splinters. Out of the three of them, he had come off best. Even his neurohormone hangover had run its course.

Two converging lines of bright strobe lights were flashing along the top of the *Colonel Maitland*, leading them in towards the recessed landing pad. At the front edge of the pad a large blister rose out of the fuselage, which he guessed was a hangar for Jason Whitehurst's own plane.

Greg walked forward as the Pegasus descended, compensating for the inclined deck. The chair at the front of the cabin had been straightened and tilted horizontal. Malcolm was lying on it; all he had on were jockey shorts, his brown skin mottled with big patches of dermal seal. Diagnostic probes were stuck to his torso and the nape of his neck, the medical unit's screen showing an ecorche representation of his body, large sections coloured amber, two red pinpoints near his spine.

'Is he going to be all right?' Greg asked Rachel.

She looked up from the plasma bladder's LCD. 'Yes. Nothing critical punctured or broken, just blood-loss trauma. But we got the plasma into him in time. He might need some skin replacement for his back, otherwise fine.'

'Thank Christ for that.'

'Never thought I'd be doing this again.'

'Yeah, you and me both,' he said.

The Pegasus touched down with a slight tremor.

Greg shrugged out of his jacket. 'Pearse, give me a Tokarev and shoulder holster.'

'Right.' The hardliner went to one of the lockers. 'Suzi, do you want a holster for your Browning?'

'Nah, I stowed it.'

Greg glanced at her. The Puma bag had been lost in the Prezda's well. Her shellsuit wasn't all that baggy, though. He didn't ask.

Pearse handed him the holster. 'You want me to come with you?'

'No,' Greg said, velcroing the holster's straps. 'The deal is for me and Suzi. We shouldn't be more than half an hour, forty minutes at the outside. Buy the girl and bring her back. After that we zip Malcolm here straight to a decent medical facility.'

'Buy the girl,' Pearse repeated. 'That sounds so ... God, I don't know. Medieval?'

'Something like that.' Greg checked the Tokarev's charge before slotting it into the holster. 'But it's preferable to the alternative, for her and us.' He pulled his jacket back on, and pressed the belly hatch activation button.

There were two people waiting for them on the pad. Hardliners, dressed in dark grey trousers and light jade V-neck sweaters, as if they were cabin stewards.

Greg ordered a small neurohormone secretion. The hardliners were cautious, but not hostile.

They took a lift down to the gondola, riding in silence. A long windowless corridor, lit by a bright biolum strip, blank doors in either wall, and nobody else in sight. He thought the hardliners were leading them towards the prow, but it was difficult to be certain. A cleaning drone rolled past them going in the opposite direction.

He sensed the background shimmer of the crew's minds, a continual whisper of emotions. Reassuring to know the *Colonel Maitland* wasn't actually the ghost ship it looked.

The hardliners stopped outside one of the doors near the end of the corridor. It opened into Jason Whitehurst's clinically plain study. He was sitting behind his glass desk, playing with an old-fashioned gold Parker biro. The hologram display inside the desk top was angled so that it could only be read by him. From where Greg stood inside the door the symbology array was just an Expressionist laser frieze. Pretty, but meaningless.

A grey rectangle on the floor in front of the desk began to bulge up, silently sculpting itself into a settee.

'Please,' Jason Whitehurst opened his hand, gesturing at the newly formed settee.

Greg sat, sensing the two hardliners behind him withdrawing. Suzi plonked herself down beside him, her heels barely reached the floor.

'Do you require medical attention?' Jason Whitehurst asked Suzi. He was looking at her knee, the torn shellsuit leg. 'I have a doctor on board. Someone my age, it is advisable . . .' He trailed off with a dismissive wave.

'I've already had it patched, thanks,' Suzi said.

'Of course.'

'A hazard on our way here,' Greg said. He studied the mind before him. Jason Whitehurst put on a good front. Behind the bemused tolerance expression he was hiding a mix of fretfulness and expectancy. Greg recognized the mind set. Jason Whitehurst was a masterclass gambler, it was his out, his bang. He didn't merely play the game, he was part of the game.

'You see, we're not the only people looking for you,' Greg said. He wanted a reaction, see how Jason Whitehurst bore up under some pressure.

'I am aware of this,' Jason Whitehurst said. 'After all, the delectable Charlotte is in some demand, a valuable commodity. I simply did what I always do in such a case, and trade on it.'

'A pity you didn't think to warn Baronski.'

'Is he in some sort of trouble?'

'You judge. Suzi and I managed to escape the tekmerc team that was going to interrogate him about Fielder's location. That's where we picked up our little scratches.'

Jason Whitehurst pulled on his beard. Greg sensed the first traces of alarm rising into his mind, thought currents brightening.

'Baronski knew the risks,' Jason Whitehurst said bluntly.

'Baronski was a cautious man. He didn't know what Fielder has got herself involved in; if he had, he would have stopped her.'

'You have come all this way, by dint of considerable effort on the part of your employer, simply to remonstrate with me, Mr Mandel?'

'No. All I came for was Fielder. Just telling you this deal isn't all cosy advantage trading, that's all. Maybe you don't know how valuable this Fielder girl is.'

'I believe I have a fair idea of her financial status, or more precisely, the price of the information stored in that pretty little head of hers. Dear Charlotte is unique. And like all monopolies, she does not come cheap.'

'How much?'

'One hundred million Eurofrancs.'

'Bollocks,' Suzi snorted.

Greg had seen it coming, watching Jason Whitehurst nerve himself up. There was determination, but he was also testing, interested to see how important Fielder really was. It fitted Greg's initial impression. Jason Whitehurst knew he had something, he just wasn't sure exactly what.

Greg increased his neurohormone secretion. 'Did you know first contact has been made?' he asked.

Shadows of doubt flittered across Jason Whitehurst's mind. 'Whatever are you talking about, Mr Mandel?'

'First contact, with aliens.'

Jason Whitehurst's face registered impatience. Suspicion rose, his thought currents racing, then a slow dawn of comprehension which brought cold fright. 'That is the source of atomic structuring technology? Aliens?'

'Yeah,' said Greg.

'My God, of course, her holiday.' Jason did his best to recover his composure, physically he managed it, mentally his mind surged with phobic dread. 'Is Julia Evans really sure she knows what she is doing dabbling in this affair?'

'She's sure.'

'Very well. Then as I said before, if you are unwilling to pay the reserve price, dear Charlotte will be placed on the open market, available to the highest bidder.'

'Wrong,' said Greg. 'We will pay you sixty-five million for her.'

'Greg!' Suzi protested.

'Julia has been most foolish sending you,' Jason Whitehurst said. 'All you have done is simply confirmed dear Charlotte's worth to me. The reserve price stands. I must say, it's most unlike Julia to make this sort of mistake.'

'I told you about the aliens as a favour,' Greg said. 'That's the second one today. I'm trying to make you realize that you're in way over your head. This whole deal frightens me very badly, and I'm ex-Mindstar. Charlotte Fielder will be removed from the *Colonel Maitland* today; either by us paying for her, or by one of the tekmerc squads the kombinates have employed to hunt her down. And they're not far behind us, a few hours at most. If she comes with us, you will receive your sixty-five million. Wait until they arrive, and you can kiss goodbye to a lot more than money. That's the bottom line, Whitehurst. No third favour.'

Sparkling blue eyes fixed on Greg. 'The Mindstar Brigade?' Jason Whitehurst said it with reluctant admiration.

'Yeah. You want my advice, then leg it out of here as soon as we take Fielder. Head back to Monaco, where it's safe, and where you're visible, in a crowd. Tell the other bidders that Fielder's gone. Best I can offer.'

'I was in the King's Own Hussars, myself.'

'I know, I've read your profile. Good troops, the King's Own; they were in Turkey.'

'After my day. Mexico was my last campaign.' Jason Whitehurst sighed, dropping the Parker on the desk. 'Didn't know you were a brother officer. Sorry if I sounded off.'

'I really would like you to leave the *Colonel Maitland* after us.'

'Yes, quite. Good idea. Sixty-five million, you say?'

'Yeah, sixty-five.'

Suzi let out a disgusted hiss of breath, rolling her eyes.

'Very well, Mr Mandel. We have a deal.'

Greg fished around in his jacket pocket, and produced the ident card Julia had given him: pure white, except for the LCD display and a small triangle and flying-V logo filling the top right corner.

'You have the authority for the transfer itself?' Jason Whitehurst asked.

Greg scaled the card over the desk to him. 'No messing. Julia and I go back a long way. I help her out now and then.'

Jason Whitehurst picked up the card, glancing at it briefly. 'Event Horizon's central account, no less. You sound like a chap it would be a good idea to know.'

Greg stood up. 'Charlotte Fielder, is she on board?'

'Indeed she is, yes.' Jason Whitehurst's fingers sketched hieroglyphic symbols on the smooth surface of the desk.

Greg still couldn't make out the graphics, but they were changing below his hand.

'You really gonna?' Suzi asked. She had risen to stand beside him. Her mind appalled and fascinated. 'Sixty-five million?'

Greg imagined his own thoughts must be similar. Sixty-five million. He knew there was a tingle of magic in his relationship with Julia, but this kind of money wasn't chicken feed, even for her. He wondered who he would trust with that much, not many. There were levels of trust; Suzi would be utterly dependable in a scrap, but hand her sixty-five million for safekeeping and it would be a goodbye that would last beyond the end of the world.

'I have set up the credit transfer order,' Jason Whitehurst said.

The desk let out a piercing whistle. Greg saw a whole section of the incomprehensible graphics turn red and scurry into frantic motion. His cybofax bleeped, and he reached for it automatically.

There was the unmistakable crump of an explosion, distant and muted. The hazy blue world outside the study's broad windows remained unchanged.

Julia's face filled the cybofax screen, there was no background behind her, as if she was starless space. 'Greg!' she called. 'I'm registering an electronic warfare alert.'

Suzi was sprinting to the nearest window. The distinctive double thunderclap of a sonic boom rocked the *Colonel Maitland*. Greg could feel the vibration through his feet.

'Nothing here,' Suzi shouted. She was pressed up against the window, Browning in her hand. 'Shit, it must be above us.'

An alarm was shrilling in the corridor outside. The two hardliners burst into the study, weapons drawn.

'Put them down,' Jason Whitehurst said sharply.

They lowered the handguns reluctantly. Racal IR laser carbines, Greg noted absently, restricted to military sales only.

'What's happening?' he asked.

'Someone's thrown a jamming field around the airship,' Julia's image said. 'It's fluctuating, as if the source is moving. I can't get a message out.'

The desk stopped whistling. 'The plane that flew over,' Jason Whitehurst said; both his hands were pressed against the glass surface, almost as though he was communing with it. 'It attacked your Pegasus.' One of the homolographic maps on a wall-mounted flatscreen flicked off, replaced by a view from a camera on the *Colonel Maitland*'s tail fin, looking down the fuselage towards the prow.

Greg stared in horror at the ruined landing pad. The Pegasus had been ripped almost in two along the length of its cabin. It had collapsed on to the landing pad, spewing black oily smoke from its rear quarter. Intense flares of blue-white light writhed continually inside the buckled fuselage, the giga-conductor cells shorting out. As he watched, flames began to lick out of the gashes.

No one could have survived that blast. Through the shock, all he could think of was that he never even knew the pilot's name.

'The plane is returning,' Jason Whitehurst said with deliberate calm. 'Subsonic, and slowing.'

'Can the *Colonel Maitland* hold it off?' Greg asked.

'We have some ECM systems naturally,' Jason Whitehurst said. 'But this is not a warship. I consider my staff more than adequate to deter any normal kidnapping attempt.'

Greg was still gaping at the ruined Pegasus when a thin column of air above the landing pad seemed to sparkle for an instant. The hangar blister and whatever plane was inside disintegrated into a vivid plume of white fire. A shock wave thumped the wreckage of the Pegasus into the rim around the pad, flinging out a flurry of debris. The incandescent tumour of light swelling out of the ruptured hangar had turned the flatscreen image black and white. Large strips of the solar cell envelope all around the landing pad were curling up like autumn leaves, edges crisping, exposing the thin monolattice struts of the fuselage.

The sound of the blast rolled around the airship's flanks and hammered against the study's windows a couple of seconds later.

This time the *Colonel Maitland* juddered perceptibly. There was a long drawn out series of agonizing creaks and groans reverberating through the geodetic framework.

'Leol fucking Reiger,' Suzi said. She flinched at a loud metallic twang. 'Gotta be.'

'I think you might be right,' Greg said. He turned from the flatscreen to see Jason Whitehurst slumped nervelessly in his chair, a vein throbbing on his temple. 'Apart from the landing pad, how do you get on board?' he asked.

'There are access hatches on the top of the fuselage,' Jason Whitehurst said. 'I suppose they could break in there. The plane would have to hover, though. It would be difficult.'

'Not to tekmercs,' Greg said. He thought fast, no question that they were here for Charlotte Fielder, so there would be no indiscriminate shooting. Not until after they snatched her, anyway. 'What about escape systems? Lifeboats? Parachutes? Something to bail out in?'

'There's an emergency survival pod in every lower deck cabin.'

'It shouldn't come to that,' Julia's image said. 'My security crash team will be on the way.'

'You sure?' Greg asked.

'The Pegasus was in constant contact with Event Horizon's security division. As soon as that jammer cut the satellite link the crash team launched. I promised I'd back you up.'

'How long till they get here?'

'Twenty minutes, maybe a little less.'

'You hear that, Suzi? Twenty minutes' evasion and decoy.'

'Yeah. If these security people of Victor's are any use. So what do you wanna do about the girl, meantime?'

'Where is she?' Greg asked Jason Whitehurst.

'On board somewhere, with Fabian. Probably in his cabin. Get her away from him, Mr Mandel, get her well away.'

'Are you coming with us?'

Jason Whitehurst glanced round the study, blinking lead-enly. His thought currents had slowed drastically; the attack had shaken him badly, fissures of insecurity were opening in his mind, allowing subconscious fears to rise and clog his thoughts. 'Go where?'

'Shit. OK, order your crew into the emergency pods. That plane might try to puncture the gasbags, force everyone out so they can pick up Fielder.'

Jason Whitehurst debated with himself for a moment, then acquiesced. 'Yes, all right.' He stretched a hand out over his desk, stirring the light patterns. 'Fabian must get into a pod by himself; he'll be safe then. That's all that matters now.'

'Greg!' Suzi yelled frantically. She was pointing out of the window.

The plane was descending into view about two hundred metres away, a delta planform with a long bullet nose. Not easy to see, an elusive light-grey stealth coating seemed to slither when he tried to focus on it, pulling the uniform blueness of sea and sky around the flat fuselage like a cloak.

'That's a Messerschmitt CTV-663,' Suzi said grimly. 'Armed hypersonic military transport. Bollocks; Leol could be carrying up to twenty-five troops in that bastard.'

Greg watched it halt level with the gondola, then turn ponderously until its tail was pointing at him. The rear loading ramp lowered. Indistinct shapes moved inside. Something dropped off the end of the ramp, falling for a few metres then slowing, bobbing in midair. It began to rise. Human shaped, but bulky, dark. A second one fell from the ramp.

'Holy shitfire,' Suzi gasped. 'They're wearing jetpacks. Jetpacks and muscle-armour suits. The fuckers are gonna storm us.'

'Greg, I can't see what's going on,' Julia's image said. 'You must squirt me into the *Colonel Maitland*'s 'ware. I can help you from there.'

'Against them?' Suzi shouted.

'Where's a key?' Greg demanded.

Jason Whitehurst stared at him uncomprehendingly, shocked into stupefaction by the aerial assault.

'A bloody interface key!'

Five dark figures were hanging in the air between the Messerschmitt and the *Colonel Maitland*, wobbling slightly as they approached, picking up speed. Another two jumped from the plane's loading ramp.

The two hardliners in the study were fingering their carbines nervously.

'Don't shoot, for Christ's sake,' Greg told them. 'Lasers aren't going to puncture muscle-armour suits at this distance; all you'll do is pinpoint us for them.' He ran round the settee to the desk, and held up his cybofax. 'Try a squirt now,' he told Julia. The tiny lenticular key on the top of the cybofax winked with ruby light. There was an answering pulse from the middle of the desk. When he looked at the wafer's screen her face had gone.

Suzi had the tight-jawed expression he'd seen on squaddies in Turkey, the one put on just before combat, the one which said it wasn't going to be me, no way. Her nostrils flared. 'The girl?'

'Yeah. Find her and steer clear of the tekmercs. Twenty minutes, that's all, and this is a big ship.' He took a deep breath, psychological more than anything, and ordered up a full secretion.

The cold reptilian gland vibrated away, rattling his brain from the inside. His espersense swept outwards; a spectral silhouette of the airship filling his perception, a cobweb of struts enfolded by bottomless shadow. Minds glowed within, pure thought turning to light, fluctuating with emotion. He was bathed in an exodus of fear, and confusion, and hurt from the crew; their silent unbosoming. Soiling him; he hated people for their failings, he was always so careful to filter it out, pretend it didn't exist. The only way he could move through life.

He examined each of them, and found the mind he knew must be hers. It had the brightness of youth, tight thought currents that spoke of strong self-control, an underlying theme of resentment and longing. The silver-white study rushed back in on him. 'Got her.'

'Thank Christ for that,' Suzi said.

'Let's move.'

The two hardliners didn't try and stop them. He turned back when he reached the door, and saw ten armour-clad figures in the air. Jason Whitehurst's face was profiled against the window. 'Keep her away from my son, Mandel. Please. None of this is his doing.'

'You got it.'

The door slid shut.

'This way,' he said, and began to jog towards the stern. 'Fielder's up inside the fuselage, some sort of room near the tail. We need to be up. Look for some stairs, an inspection hatch, something.'

'Got it,' Suzi barked.

He nearly smiled. She was fighting off fear with action, needing orders, a goal. It wasn't such a bad idea. He began to scan the names printed on the doors.

They ran into an espersense sweep. It registered like a curtain of cold air brushing against his body. Goose bumps rose on his arms.

'Shit!'

'What?' Suzi's Browning came up in reflex.

'Chad.' Greg pulled the old Mindstar-training memories from his brain, looking for something he could use. This time Chad would be ready, and he was strong; Greg couldn't afford a straight trial of strength. He let loose the neurohormones, and—

—*reality flickered*—

—and Chad felt two familiar minds impinge on his expanded sphere of consciousness. He recoiled in alarm. Then, furious with himself, opened up the sacs' extravasation rate.

The neurohormone boost was almost a physical jolt, sacs acting like electrical terminals, hot and bright, charging his brain with energy, leaving his body buzzing inside the unyielding formfit grip of the muscle armour. His espersense pushed through the airship's hull like an eldritch radar, and closed around the two minds again. Contact made the skin in his palms itch.

He concentrated on the squirming thought currents, relating his espersense perception with his visual field. His view of the outside world was being relayed from the muscle armour's integral photon amp. The airship and its gondola had taken on a bluish-grey tint, overlaid with a tactical display – distance, speed, power reserves – the lower-deck target window was outlined in red. Numbers constantly changing.

'Squad leader,' he told the muscle armour 'ware. A green go-ahead dot appeared in the communication section of the tactical display. 'Leol. Couple of our friends on board. Suzi, and that Mindstar bastard, Mandel.' He was aware of Reiger's mental flare of excitement, the unclean glee.

'Yeah? Well don't fuck up like last time, my boy, or I'll kick your arse into orbit,' Reiger said.

'Not a chance. He pulled a fast one back in the Prezda, that's all, won't work twice.'

'OK, well, get this straight, that bitch Suzi is mine.'

'Sure thing, Leol.'

'Where is she?'

'Upper deck, twenty metres from the prow.'

'What about the Fielder girl?'

'Cabin on the lower gondola deck, right at the stern.' He heard Leol Reiger issuing a stream of instructions to the rest of the squad. There were none for him, Reiger was leaving him free to deal with Mandel.

He saw the first two squad members were about twenty metres from the gondola, actually under the bulk of the airship's vast fuselage. The leader lifted his Lockhead rip gun, and fired at the target window. The shot was like a rigid bolt of lightning, two metres long. A section of the gondola hull around the oblong window simply blew apart, leaving a jagged gap three metres wide.

The first squad member flew straight in, never even touching the sharp composite fangs round the edge of the gap. The rest of the squad were clustering round outside, passing through the gap one at a time, like black, hyped-up hornets, sliding into their nest.

Chad tilted his jockey-stick, veering off to one side. The jetpack nozzles behind his shoulders rotated slightly, realigning him. He brought his own rip gun up. The armour's muscle-band lining made the movement effortless. A targeting graphic traversed the side of the gondola. He halted the motion when it had centred on a window a couple of metres behind Mandel. He fired.

The window vaporized instantly, enveloped in a blinding fireball. Chad's photon lamp blanked out for a second, protecting his eyes from the violent light burst. He jigged about in the blastwave.

When his vision came back on line the window and its surround was a rough-edged crater. A jumble of broken struts and disfigured decking lay inside.

He twisted the jockey-stick for full acceleration, heading straight for it. Another coherent lightning bolt from the rip gun tore out a chunk of the cabin's interior wall. A cloud of scorched fragments fluttered round him and he slammed in through the hole he'd made. He jerked the jockey-stick back savagely, killing speed. His feet landed on the decking, and he ran at the narrow rent in the cabin wall ahead.

The wall seemed to be made out of kelpboard, his muscle armour punching through into the gondola's central corridor without even slowing him.

His photon amp penetrated the gloom beyond. Frail biolum light illuminated the corridor, flat sheer planes of floor, walls, and ceiling extending into ambiguous distance. For one unnerving moment his eyes tricked him into believing it went on for ever.

The beast was waiting. Snarling, Chad brought the rip gun up, target graphics zeroing its open jaw. The bolt overloaded his photon amp again.

It was Suzi, lying on the corridor floor, her chest torn apart by the rip bolt. The violation had blackened her flesh and singed her ribs, flinging her slight body backwards to sprawl against a wall. Flames licked at her shellsuit.

Mandel was standing behind her, yelling in torment at the sight. He looked at Chad, then turned and ran.

'No good!' Chad cried jubiantly. His armour's external speaker boomed the words down the corridor after the fleeing man. 'Nowhere you can hide from me, shithead!'

Mandel's mind gibbered in terror. He disappeared through a door at the end of the corridor.

Chad charged after him, rip gun blowing the door into splinters. There was another corridor behind; Mandel was half-way down it. 'You're not going to die quick, Mandel. It's going to take a long time after I catch you. A real long time.'

'I know,' Mandel said as he rushed through the door at the end of the corridor.

Chad shouted an unintelligible curse of rage. Fucking typical smartarse answer. He sent a rip bolt spearing into the door. 'I can see your mind, Mandel. You're scared shitless, and it hasn't even begun yet.'

There was another corridor waiting for him. He fired off a barrage of rip gun bolts, slamming them into walls and doors. Revelling in the unstoppable vandalism, the keening of terror in Mandel's mind at each shot. His tireless armoured feet pounded on the decking, leaving sharp indentations.

Mandel was disappearing through a door ahead of him. Just how long was this airship? The tactical display was wavering, out of focus, colours smearing together into an oil rainbow film over his vision.

Crashing through the door. Another corridor. Shorter this time, the door at the far end still closing. A blink of Mandel, face red, wheezing, stumbling on, energized by adrenalin alone.

'Going to catch you, Mandel. Real soon. And when I do it's going to be worse than you could believe.'

'I'm relying on it, Chad.'

The voice was sensed rather than heard, desperately weary.

'Shithead!' Chad used the armour's speaker like a sonic cannon. He hit the door full on, composite crumpling under the impact. The corridor was barely fifteen metres long. Mandel was shutting the door at the other end.

Chad sprinted for him, the armour's muscle bands whining softly. He was closer now, much closer, and Mandel was tiring. Past the door, so flimsy it was virtually unnoticeable. The next corridor, ten metres long. Five quick steps. Mandel's mind so near he could feel sweaty skin, labouring heart, burning lungs.

'Nowhere in this universe you can hide from me,' Chad crowed.

'I'm not hiding from you, Chad, I'm inside you. You've been running through your own mind, an eidolonic reality.'

Chad opened the door. There was a five-metre corridor in front of him. An armoured figure opening the door at the far end. What the fuck . . .? Mandel trying to fool him. 'Not good enough any more, shithead!'

'It's powered by your own anger, Chad. This is what you yearn for. I grant it to you, I surrender to you.'

The door behind Chad swung shut in tandem with the one he was looking at. He was alone in the corridor; walls shrinking, biolums dimming. 'Think I'm falling for that? Your last mistake, Mandel.'

'Stop hating me and you're free. Can you do that, Chad?'

Chad flung himself at the door ahead. Triumphant. 'Die, shithead!'

'I'm right behind you.'

The door shattered. It was like being caught between two

mirrors. Infinite multiples of a muscle armour suit jumping through the door, arms outstretched, legs bent, long composite splinters spraying out all around. The same ahead, the same behind. Slowing. Freezing—

—*reality flickered*—

—Greg staggered against a wall. A groan escaping from his mouth.

'Bollocks, hey, you OK now?' Suzi asked. Her taut anxious face peering at him through blood-coloured mist.

'Yeah,' he croaked.

'Sure, you look it.'

He swung his head about, focusing. A neurohormone hangover was burning like napalm inside his skull. They were at the end of a gondola corridor. The sign on the door ahead read DINING-ROOM. 'Where are we?'

'Upper deck, at the stern. I think. Jesus, Greg, I reckon I got corridor-phobia after that. Couldn't hardly tell if what I was seeing was real or not. What happened?'

'I suckered Chad into an eidoloscape, looped him in his own power fantasy. Think of it as cephalic judo.'

'Yeah, right. So where is he now?'

'No more hazard. You bring me up here?'

'Yeah. Like steering a sleepwalker. Been some shots below. Loud.'

'Rip guns, they've got bloody rip guns; Lockheeds, I think.'

'Good old Leol, just what you need to snatch a major hazard like an unarmed whore.' She grasped the handle of a door marked FUSELAGE.

Greg noticed the hesitancy in her hand as she turned the handle, afraid of what might be behind – a doorway into eternity. It was a narrow staircase leading up. A braid of thick ribbed hoses ran up the bare composite wall, a single biolum strip ran along the ceiling. The darkness above seemed to suck sound away. A gust of dry cool air blew down at them.

Suzi pointed her Browning up the stairs. 'This it?' she asked without any enthusiasm. 'Fielder up here?'

'Guess so. At least Reiger doesn't know she's up here.' He paused. 'Make that *was* up here.'

'Can't you check?'

'Give me five minutes, Suzi, OK?'

'Sure.' She started up the stairs.

Greg drew his Tokarev, snicked the safety off, and went up after her.

18

Fabian could actually play the guitar quite well. Discoveries like that didn't surprise Charlotte any more. Whatever held Fabian's attention long enough for him to develop an interest normally wound up being practised with a high degree of proficiency. The trick was getting him to notice something in the first place.

After lunch, he'd put on jeans and a studded leather jacket, white silk headband with scarlet Japanese ideograms. Grinning slightly self-consciously. The den's music deck was programmed to provide him with a support group, bass, rhythm, and drums. Unsurprisingly. Fabian favoured hard rock, one or two glam tracks. Thank heavens he didn't sing too.

She listened to him playing a couple of numbers, then walked over to the Yamaha piano.

'I didn't know you played,' Fabian said.

She gave him a disdainful smile, running through the intro to the Sonic Energy Authority's 'Last Elvis Song.' 'Doesn't everybody?' One of her first patrons had shelled out a small fortune on lessons for her. He liked what he called traditional evenings, no channels, no VR games, no nightclubs, just music recitals and poetry readings, sometimes a play or the ballet. She had enjoyed the piano lessons, one talent Baronski couldn't implant or graft on in the Prezda's little clinic. Although her knuckles had been reconfigured to give her fingers a greater dexterity, which was useful.

Charlotte gave Fabian the opening bars of Bil Yi Somanzer's

classic 'Dream Day Hi.' She had fond memories of Bil Yi; his albums were the first music she'd ever really heard after being taken into care. He was in decline then, but still the greatest, no matter what anyone said.

Fabian picked up the rhythm, strumming along in some private paradise. They cranked the deck up, and started jamming some Beatles and Stones, more Bil Yi, the two of them shouting the lyrics at each other over riffs that shook the den's heavy thermal insulation panels and rattled her gullet. The fish were going berserk in their tanks. She hadn't let her hair down like this for an age.

They were thrashing the hell out of 'Bloody Honey' when Charlotte heard the bang, thinking they'd blown a speaker. It took Fabian a minute to realize she'd stopped playing.

'What?' he asked. His face was flushed and sweaty. She didn't think she'd ever seen him smiling so brightly before, a natural high. It was nice to see.

'We've bust a speaker,' she told him, laughing. Her cotton top was damp and hot, contracting about her. There wasn't much air conditioning in the den. Somehow she didn't care.

'Aww.' Fabian pulled a face. He bounced over to the music deck, the guitar hanging round him. LEDs winked green and orange as he flicked switches. 'No, we haven't.'

'I heard something go pop.'

'Not us, not guilty,' Fabian's voice had a ragged euphoric edge.

'Oh well, I needed the rest.'

'Crikey, you were fantastic, Charlotte!' His eyes shone. 'I've never played with anyone before, only the deck.'

The breath was coming out of her in short puffs. 'Never?'

'No.'

'Pretty damn good, you were.'

'Really? Honest to God?'

'Yep. You've got a definite talent there, Fabian.'

His expression went all distant. 'Know what I dream? That I get a slot on MTV's garage access 'cast.'

Charlotte grinned. She'd seen that herself sometimes. Twice a week MTV turned over about ninety minutes of the death hours between two and four in the morning to unsigned bands. Any bunch of kids with an amp stack and a camera could plug into the channel. Wishful rumour said music biz suits sat glued to it, searching for new talent. Charlotte thought that was a load of crap.

Suddenly she had a vision of Baronski watching her and Fabian decimating 'Your Coolin' Heart.' She started giggling as Baronski's jaw dropped in stupefaction, every one of his precious sensibilities overloaded and fused.

'What?' Fabian asked.

She waved her hands helplessly. 'One of my friends seeing me on that 'cast.'

Fabian's nose twitched. 'Father seeing us on that!'

Charlotte whooped ecstatically, banging out a nonsense blast on the keyboard, aware of Fabian hooting wildly.

The door opened. Charlotte saw the maid framed in the gloomy light of the fuselage biolums.

'What do you want?' Fabian asked between gulps. 'Unless you've come to audition for drums?'

Charlotte laughed delightedly at seeing the sulky cow so thrown by the scene, which set Fabin off again. Although there was something peculiar about the maid's face, squinting as though she was drunk. Charlotte had seen that expression before somewhere. Couldn't quite place the memory.

The maid took two steps into the room. Fast steps.

'Hey—' Fabian began.

The maid hit him. It was a backhanded blow, she barely aimed it. Her hand caught him on the side of his face, lifting him off the floor. There was a moment of dead silence as he fell back on to the pile of cushions. Then the guitar made a clattering noise as it caught on the deck, and Fabian let out a dull grunt.

Charlotte yelled, 'Fabian!' and rushed over to him.

There was blood trickling out of his mouth, the side of his

face where the maid had struck was bright red. He was blinking in numb confusion, his arms struggling limply. One eye was already swelling, the smooth skin discolouring. She went down on the cushions, scattering some, and gripped his wrist. Her other hand went on his forehead. 'Don't move,' she whispered. The guitar neck pressed awkwardly into her belly.

'I—' he coughed. More blood sprayed out between his lips.

Charlotte sucked in a breath at the sight. Little specks of blood were staining her white cotton top. She stroked the side of his head anxiously, eyes watering. 'Don't . . .'

Fabian caught sight of the maid behind her. His face twisted into rage, and he surged up.

'No!' Charlotte flung herself on him, pinning him down on the cushions. 'No, Fabian. She's cleardusted.' That was the memory, the squint, the dazed crazed look. She'd seen some of her patrons' hardline bodyguards take the stuff. Cleardust was a synthesized derivative of the old angel dust, giving the manic strength and immunity to pain without the hallucinogenic effect.

'Very good,' said the maid. 'You're bright for a whore.'

Charlotte was centimetres from Fabian's face. Seeing pain and reflections of pain in his eyes.

A hand that must have been made of metal closed around her upper arm, and she was yanked up, squealing at the sudden pain. She stumbled for her footing. 'Please, Fabian, please stay down. Please.' It was all she could think of. He wouldn't understand. The maid would kill him.

He glared upwards, bloody lips parted.

'Please, for me,' she pleaded.

'Right,' his voice was distorted, as if he was chewing on something.

The pressure on Charlotte's arm increased, making her mouth part with the pain. She was turned to face the maid. The glazed eyes made her shiver inside. They didn't see anything in this universe.

'I will ask you some questions,' the maid said. 'You will

answer them for me, or I will start to snap all that expensive bonework of yours. Understand, whore?'

'Let him go. I'll tell you anything you want. But don't hurt him.'

Charlotte heard a muffled high-pitched crack from somewhere outside the den. She thought it sounded like some kind of weapon.

The maid gave a cyborg smile. 'You're a very popular girl all of a sudden. Lots of people want to talk to you. But I'm first. And last.'

The crack came again, men again.

'Who gave you the flower?' the maid asked.

It took Charlotte's wild thoughts a moment to work out what flower she was talking about. 'Let Fabian go.'

'The flower?'

'I don't know who he was, not his actual name. Please.'

'Liar.'

Charlotte's hand was grabbed. She screamed as two ringers were bent back. There was a pistol-shot *snap*.

Strangely enough, there wasn't any pain, not at first. She couldn't feel anything below her wrist, then a red-hot ache spread up her fingers, biting hard into her knuckles. There was bile rising in her throat. Her head began to spin alarmingly; for a moment she thought she was going to faint.

In horror she saw Fabian on his feet, lurching towards her and the maid. She lashed out with her free arm, knocking him back. His face was a mask of desperation and agony.

'Oh God no,' she wailed, tears swelling up. He was regaining his balance, going to try again.

'ENOUGH OF THIS. FABIAN, STAY WHERE YOU ARE.' The voice was an inhuman roar, loud enough to be painful. It was coming out of the music deck speakers, she realized.

Fabian ducked his head down in reflex, hands halfway to his ears. Even the maid was frozen.

The flatscreens came on, each one showing the same picture of a woman's face. Charlotte let out a choked cry as she recognized her. 'Julia Evans,' she gasped. It was her. Really her. Just like at the Newfields ball. That same compelling oval face.

Julian Evans smiled thinly. 'Hello, Charlotte. I think it's about time you and I had a talk.'

'Not a chance,' said the maid.

19

Julia's personality package was coded as a commercial intelligence summary, so the *Colonel Maitland*'s 'ware network-management program automatically assigned it storage space in the lightware cruncher Jason Whitehurst was using to analyse kombinate finances. Once it was loaded, the personality package immediately reformatted the command routines of the processing structure it was running in, isolating itself from the lightware's operating program and antiviral guardians. After it had confirmed its autonomy it sent out a series of instructions to the internal databuses, arrogating their handling procedures, shutting down the data flow.

With the lightware cruncher's processing operations suspended, the personality package began to wipe all the programs and files it found stored in the unit's memory. Access codes were changed. A new sequence of operating routines were loaded. The package's highly compressed data planes expanded into the empty lightware. Julia's reconstituted mentality came on line.

She started to assess the airship's 'ware architecture, spreading her presence through the datanet, burning into ancillary processor cores. The bridge's 'ware was her first priority, gaining complete command of her new domain. New channels were opened and safeguarded, data flowed back into the lightware cruncher.

The *Colonel Maitland*'s flight control systems were plugged into a broad range of sensors and cameras distributed throughout the fuselage. Radar and the satellite uplinks were useless, swamped by the tekmerc's jammer. She studied the optical circuits, pulling their codes out of memory cores, then started to look around.

∗

External camera, portside fuselage. The Messerschmitt hovered level with the gondola. A laser rangefinder pulsed every second, helping it to maintain its stand-off position exactly. Eight armour-clad figures were left strung out between it and the *Colonel Maitland*. Each of them identical, factory moulded; left hand controlling a jockey-stick, right hand holding a Lockheed rip gun. Two wavering columns of hot compressed air streamed out of the jetpack nozzles, behind and slightly below the shoulders. As she watched, one of them disappeared through a hole in the side of the gondola.

∗

Internal camera, gondola lower-deck crew lounge. The lounge had been ravaged by the rip bolt, loose chairs hurled at the walls, composite walls cracked and buckled, carpet smouldering. Glass lay underfoot, the door twisted in its frame.

Two of the armoured figures were standing inside, Lockheed rip guns raised cautiously, covering the open doorway. Helmets blank bubbles of metal.

A third swept through the hole, jetpack efflux stirring up a mini-hurricane of wreckage as he settled on the uneven decking.

∗

External camera, upper tail fin. The ruined landing pad, pitiful remains of the Pegasus spewing out thin plumes of smoke. Two of the *Colonel Maitland*'s crew, dressed in silvery fire-suits, were surveying the scene. They kept close to the edge of the pad,

281

giving the Pegasus a wide birth as they shuffled along, testing the deck sheeting before each step.

*

Julia called up a structural schematic and systems status review from the bridge's flight control 'ware. The central gasbag, below the landing pad, had been badly lacerated. Helium was escaping at a critical rate. The bridge crew had ordered a near-total ballast dump to compensate. Water from tanks and the swimming-pool was venting out of the gondola as fast as it could be pumped.

The *Colonel Maitland*'s geodetic framework was drawn in fine blue lines, gasbag suspension rigging a jumble of green cobwebs. A large, roughly oval, area of fuselage struts around the landing pad and hangar had turned red, fringed in yellow. The landing pad itself was mostly black; a lot of the stress sensors' optical cables had been cut in the explosions, leaving gaps in the picture. Maintenance drones were inching along the longitudinal frames, inspecting individual struts for fractures, supplementing and refining the data from the sensors, filling in the true status of the black zones.

The damage assessment was reassuring. The basic framework was bearing up under the redistributed loading. Power to the contra-rotating fans was being reduced, relieving as much pressure as possible until the upper fuselage frames could be repaired.

*

She accessed the bridge's memory cores and discovered that the maintenance drones communicated with the flight control 'ware via laser links; the entire geodetic framework was dotted with interface keys.

*

Internal camera, gondola stairwell. Greg and Suzi were moving to the upper deck. Suzi was brandishing her Browning in one hand, pulling Greg along with the other. She looked as if she was walking directly into a hurricane blast, face furrowed with concentration, teeth bared, every step an effort. Greg was moving like an unplugged junkie. Julia recognized the thousand-metre stare; his gland was active, dissolving the real universe.

*

Structural schematic. A patch of the gondola's upper-deck hull changed to red, shooting out a ripple ring of yellow. The red centre snapped to black. Another rip-gun bolt. Electrical lines were cut, fibre-optic links severed. Compensator programs assigned priorities and rerouted power and data.

*

External camera, portside fuselage. One of the armoured tekmerc squad had broken away from his colleagues, charging towards the gondola much too fast. He cannoned into a cabin through the gap in the hull which the rip gun had made, arm just catching the edge.

*

Internal camera, gondola upper-deck cabin. The armoured figure spinning chaotically, bouncing off walls and ceiling. Legs and arms thrashing about, splintering the composite. He wound up jammed into a corner, jetpack still firing, boots a metre off the ground. The Lockheed rip gun fell from his gauntlet. His legs began a running motion in midair, toe caps hammering deeply into the bulkhead.

Julia brought additional processing power on line for that. Armour malfunction? Some sort of flying phobia? There was no rational explanation.

*

Internal camera, gondola lower-deck crew lounge. The remaining nine members of the squad were all assembled in the lounge. Their movements were sluggish, forced, the same as Suzi.

283

One of them pointed his rip gun at the mangled door. Fired. Fire alarms howled in protest throughout the gondola.

The squad clattered out into the lower-deck central corridor, heading for the prow. A couple of the *Colonel Maitland*'s cabin crew were in the central corridor, a steward and a maid. Both of them listless and drowsy. They gawped at the approaching tekmerc squad.

'Where is Charlotte Fielder?' one of the squad asked. His amplified voice was loud in the confined space of the corridor, menacing.

The steward looked about, his face white. 'She might be with Fabian Whitehurst, in his cabin, or hers. I'm not sure.'

There was a momentary pause.

'Where is Jason Whitehurst?'

'In his study.' The steward pointed a wavering hand down the corridor towards the prow. 'That way.'

Four squad members stepped forward.

'You will show these four where Fabian Whitehurst's cabin is.'

The steward jerked his head in terror.

One of the squad reached out and grabbed the maid. She screamed.

'Be quiet. You come with us to the study.'

She began to snivel. The armoured figure jerked her along, nearly lifting her off the floor.

*

Julia accessed the *Colonel Maitland*'s radio gear, letting the raw signals flow directly into the lightware cruncher. The white-noise howl of the Messerschmitt's jammer dominated every frequency. She began to slot in filter programs. The tekmerc squad had to have some way of communicating.

She found a string of digital pulses in the UHF band, and refined the filter programs to kill the last of the jammer interference. A decryption program was loaded into the circuit.

*

Tekmerc squad inter-suit radio communication.

Tekmerc one: '. . . know what the fuck's happened to Chad. Those psychic freakos are beating the hell out of each other somehow. You know how it is with them.'

Tekmerc two: 'God, it's like my head's on fire. There are corridors everywhere, like a bloody maze.'

Tekmerc one: 'No, there aren't. Fight it, turn up your photon-amp brightness. There's only one corridor.'

Tekmerc two: 'Sure thing, Leol.'

Julia identified Tekmerc one as Leol Reiger. Her own abridged memories contained a concise security file on him.

She assigned the cause of the lone tekmerc's spasming run as due to Greg's psi effusion.

Tekmerc three: 'Shouldn't we try to find Mandel and Suzi?'

Leol Reiger: 'Suppose you tell me where the hell to look now Chad's weirded out.'

Tekmerc three: 'So how about helping Chad?'

Leol Reiger: 'How, you dipshit cretin?'

Tekmerc three: 'Sorry, Leol. Can't think with this psychic shit screwing my mind.'

Leol Reiger: 'Concentrate on finding the Fielder girl. And forget about the psychics, this corridor crap won't last much longer. They'll burn their brains out at this rate.'

*

Internal camera, study. Jason Whitehurst was sitting behind his desk cradling his head in his hands, rocking slowly back and forth, moaning, saliva bubbling from his lips. The two hard line bodyguards were covering the door with their Racal laser carbines, faces hard.

*

Gondola internal camera review. Snatched images flicked into the lightware cruncher as Julia shuffled through the inputs searching for Charlotte Fielder. The bridge with its crew, faces strained, hunched over their consoles, shouting hoarsely at each other.

285

Lower-deck corridor with the two groups of tekmercs walking away from each other, frightened blank faces of the steward and maid. Lower-deck cabins, lounges, gym, a sauna; all deserted. One cabin provisionally assigned to Fabian: a mishmash of toys and clothes sprayed about. Crew quarters at the prow, their small double cabins decorated with hologram pin-ups, a big mess room with a flatscreen showing mushy static, communal washroom, laundry. The crew members were curled up in their chairs or lying on bunks, woozy, afflicted by Greg's psi effusion. Greg and Suzi in the upper-deck corridor, directly above the crew quarters. Upper-deck cabins, beautifully furnished staterooms, a dining-room right at the stern, a swimming-pool, the water nearly gone, a terrific whirlpool in the centre.

*

Fuselage internal camera review. The cameras fixed to the geodetic framework were all black and white, providing her with pictures of the narrow dimly lit longitudinal walkways, the gasbags looming oppressively. Next came pictures of ladders and stairs pinned to the transverse frames. Cylindrical maintenance drones sliding along their rails, folded waldos at both ends, like cybernetic mandibles.

Someone was climbing up a ladder near the stern. A woman in a maid's dress, totally unaffected by the psi effusion. At three hundred metres she was too far away from Greg, the effect was localized, centring round the gondola.

Julia accessed the crew records, matching the face with a file image. The maid's name was Nia Korovilla, she had been a crew member for eight years. A Russian national, with good references from three hotels, a clean employment record.

There was no reason for her to be where she was. Julia assigned a subroutine to keep watching her.

*

Internal camera, gondola lower deck, Fabian's cabin. The tek-mercs with the steward broke in. They didn't bother with the lock, simply punching out the door. It swung inwards, buckled by the first tekmerc's kick. The four of them entered, rip guns held ready.

*

Tekmerc squad inter-suit radio communication.

Tekmerc four: 'Leol, Frank here, there's no one in the boy's cabin.'

Leol Reiger: 'OK, Frank, try the girl's. And ask the steward if there's anywhere else they're likely to be. Find her!'

Tekmerc four, identified, Frank: 'Will do.'

Tekmerc five: 'Hey! Hey feel that, it's stopped.'

Tekmerc six: 'Christ yeah.'

Tekmerc seven: ''Bout time.'

Tekmerc three: 'Hell, I can see properly again.'

Leol Reiger: 'Chad, Chad, check in.'

Tekmerc six: 'He had to win. Man, he's got some power, turn your brain inside out from half a klick.'

Leol Reiger: 'Chad, answer, fuck you.'

Tekmerc two: 'Come on, Chad!'

Leol Reiger: 'Right, scratch Chad. If he couldn't handle some fucking geriatric Army relic he's better off out of it. Don't make no difference to us, he was just a convenience. We go through all the cabins until we find the whore. Right out of the manual. Now let's see some action out of you bastards.'

*

Internal camera, gondola upper-deck cabin. Chad's jetpack was still pressing him up into the corner of the cabin, helmet pushing against the ceiling. His legs had stopped running, arms hanging limply. A phone mike was picking up the jetpack noise, a strident whine. The bed's counterpane had been caught in the efflux, blown towards the hole in the wall where it had snagged on the edge, flapping vigorously.

*

Internal camera, fuselage keel. Suzi had climbed up the stairs from the gondola, her Browning pistol pointing ahead along the walkway. Greg followed, looking enervated, the skin around his eyes baggy and dark; but he was alive.

Julia knew her flesh and blood self would be flooded with relief that he had beaten Chad.

Logically, if Charlotte Fielder wasn't in the gondola, and Greg and Suzi were heading up into the fuselage, then Charlotte Fielder must be in the fuselage too. Somewhere.

Julia reviewed the airship structural schematic again. Behind the last full-sized gasbag there was an engineering bay that held the giga-conductor cells, and heat exchangers. In the centre was a disused chamber that used to hold the MHD units. It was drawing power from the main electrical bus.

She plugged into the chamber's fibre-optic cables.

*

Internal camera, upper gondola deck cabin, provisionally assigned resident: Charlotte Fielder. The four tekmercs were inside. One of them walked through the wooden slat door to the bathroom, snapping it apart without breaking stride. Two more were ransacking cupboards and wardrobes. The fourth had his rip gun trained on the steward who was hugging his chest, jaw clenched.

'Where else would she be?' the tekmerc asked. He prodded the steward with the barrel of his rip gun. The man's cheeks bulged out.

'Pool, she used the swimming-pool a lot, or Fabian's den. He's always up there.'

'I've got the pool location loaded in my suit gear, but which room is the boy's den?'

'Not in the gondola,' the steward said. 'It's up in the fuselage, right back at the tail. Some sort of old engine room, he plays his music deck up there, stuff like that.'

*

Tekmerc squad inter-suit radio communication.

Frank: 'Leol, I think we may have her. The Whitehurst boy hangs out up in the fuselage tail, he's got some sort of den up there. We're going up to check the pool first, then we'll try the tail. It must be in the engineering bay.'

Leo Reiger: 'OK, I'm putting the squeeze on the old man. Let me know the instant you get anything.'

Frank: 'What if we meet the psychic? He must know where Fielder is, he and Suzi will be heading for her now.'

Leol Reiger: 'Snuff the psychic bloke, Mandel, but save Suzi bitch for me.'

Frank: 'Christ, Leol, I don't know, that woman, she's one major hazard. I see what she did to Nathe and Joely back at the Prezda. Two shots, that's all it took her. Catching her, that's maybe not such a good idea. It's complicated, Leol. We don't need it.'

Leol Reiger: 'Give the fucking verbals a rest. You got armour. You got stunshots for the Fielder whore, ain't you? Use 'em. Triple bonus for the one that wings Suzi bitch for me.'

Frank: 'All right, Leol. You say.'

Leol Reiger: 'I do.'

*

Internal camera, aft fuselage keel walkway. Greg and Suzi were approaching the tail section, moving at a steady jog. He seemed to be recovering from his gland-induced lethargy, limbs flowing in an easier, more fluid rhythm.

Julia used a key on a nearby transverse frame to plug into Greg's cybofax. It bleeped, and he pulled it out of his pocket.

'I wondered where you'd got to,' he said.

Suzi stopped and looked at the cybofax screen.

'I take it you're trying to find Charlotte Fielder,' Julia said.

'Yeah, she's somewhere around here. I sensed her earlier, I was just about to have another sniff round.'

'I believe she is in the old MHD chamber, along with Fabian Whitehurst. It's in the middle of the engineering bay; I worked

289

out a route for you.' She squirted the data into the wafer, lining the walkways and ladders they would have to use in red. 'You'd better get a move on. There is a woman in front of you, Nia Korovilla, one of the *Colonel Maitland*'s maids; I don't know what she's doing there, but she's closing on the chamber. And four of Leol Reiger's tekmercs are behind you, also heading for the MHD chamber.'

'Oh, great,' said Suzi.

'Once you get Fielder, I can keep you ahead of the tekmercs,' Julia said. 'I have them all under observation.'

'Thanks, Julia,' Greg said. 'We're on our way.'

*

Internal camera, study. Both of Jason Whitehurst's hardline bodyguards were dead. They lay on the floor, bodies torn open by rip-gun bolts, blood pooling around them. The maid Leol Reiger had hauled along had gone into catatonic shock, curled up against the settee in a foetal position, eyes squeezed shut.

Leol Reiger hadn't even bothered to use the door. There was a big rent in the wall, its craggy edges bent inward. He was standing in front of the desk, the four accompanying members of his squad fanned out behind him.

Jason Whitehurst still clung to an air of pride, defeated but not broken.

'Call your son, and have him tell us where Fielder is,' Leol Reiger's amplified voice said. 'That's all we want, Fielder. We get her, we leave. No more hazard to you and your crew.'

'And the alternative?' Jason Whitehurst asked. 'Aren't you going to threaten me?'

'Why? You already know the way it is. Snuff you, your crew, this ship. Your son. Especially your son.'

Jason Whitehurst glared at the armoured figure. 'I had agreed a price with your paymaster.'

Leol Reiger took a pace forward. 'I would hate to think you were stalling.'

Julia decided to intervene. She plugged into the study's

290

flatscreens, using an image-synthesizer program to reproduce her face. The camera showed five of her suddenly looking down on the scene, another face encased inside the desk.

'Jason isn't stalling,' she said out of the speakers.

Rip guns came up in alarm, the tekmercs turning in jerky agitated movements.

'Jesus, that's Julia Evans,' one of them stuttered.

'Oh yeah? Big deal,' Leol Reiger said. He tried for contempt, but the mikes detected a quaver in his voice.

'Good afternoon, Mr Leol Reiger,' she said.

'How the hell— What is this?' He levelled his rip gun on Jason Whitehurst.

There was the glimmer of a smile on Jason Whitehurst's lips, mocking. 'As I have met my match, so you have met yours.'

'Charlotte Fielder belongs to me, Leol Reiger,' Julia said. 'My team is on its way here to collect her. If you leave now, they will not pursue you.'

'Bluff,' Leol Reiger said. 'If they were coming you wouldn't try and make deals.'

'How do you think I'm talking to you? Event Horizon technology is capable of slicing straight through the Messerschmitt's jammer, and that is premier-grade military equipment. And I'll remind you that you're talking to a woman who's got her own stockpile of electron-compression warheads. Think about that.'

'Hot technology, my arse; I'll bet it's not as good as atomic structuring, I'll bet it doesn't even come close. Right?'

'Irrelevant. Atomic structuring is for the future, you are facing me now.'

'I'm facing a flatscreen. We're here, you're not. Fielder's mine. So fuck off, rich bitch.'

'Mistake,' Jason Whitehurst said gravely. 'That, my friend, was a big mistake. Nobody says that to Julia Evans.'

'Yeah? Well, I ain't been zapped by a lightning bolt. So now I'll take Fielder. Where is she?'

'Jason doesn't know,' Julia said. 'Nor will he be able to find out. My security programmers are in full control of the *Colonel Maitland*'s 'ware.'

'Leol,' one of the other tekmercs said, a woman's voice. 'Maybe we oughta listen—'

'Shut it.' Leol Reiger pointed his rip gun at one of the big wall screens, and fired. The flatscreen shattered, radiant pink fragments bouncing across the hard silver-white floor. Jason Whitehurst hunched down in his chair, hands over his ears. Leol Reiger swivelled to another flatscreen, fired again. Daylight shone through a hole the rip-gun bolt drilled into the gondola wall.

'You really are a complete fool, aren't you,' Julia said.

Leol Reiger demolished a third screen. He turned back to Jason Whitehurst, the muzzle of the rip gun coming down on the desk with a click. 'Time's up. Make your choice. Do you think the rich bitch is gonna save you, or you gonna hand Fielder over to me?'

Jason Whitehurst stood slowly, squaring his shoulders, looking directly at Leol Reiger's smooth armour helmet. The rip gun followed him up.

'Julia?' Jason Whitehurst asked.

'Still here, Jason. Tell him what you know, it doesn't make any difference. My team will get Fielder, and I don't want you hurt.'

'Julia, my dear, Fabian isn't my son, he's my clone, gene-tailored. A sort of an improved version, really. Bit vain, I suppose, but then that's human nature for you. Please look after him for me, there's a dear.' He smiled at Leol Reiger. 'Lost all round, old chap. Your sort always do.'

'You shit,' Leol Reiger bellowed.

'Don't,' Julia said.

Leol Reiger fired his rip gun. The muzzle was less than a metre away from Jason Whitehurst.

'I shall remember you, Leol Reiger,' Julia said. 'Do you hear me?'

Leol Reiger blew the last two flatscreens to shards. 'Come on, out. I want every cabin searched. Fielder will've gone to ground after all this shooting.' He led his squad out of the study.

*

The subroutine assigned to monitor Nia Korovilla reported that she had entered the MHD chamber.

*

Tekmerc squad inter-suit radio communication.

Julia: 'Don't think you can walk out on me, Leol Reiger. Life is not that simple, believe me.'

Leol Reiger: 'Christ Almighty.'

Julia: 'Jason Whitehurst was a friend and business colleague.'

Leol Reiger: 'Piss off, bitch.'

Tekmerc eight, female: 'How can she plug into our communications like this?'

Julia: 'Five million Eurofrancs for the one who kills Leol Reiger.'

Leol Reiger: 'You're dead, Evans. That's the only way out now. You and me, head on. The rest of you, get into these cabins. And if any of you are thinking of taking her up on that offer, you'd better make sure you get me with one shot. You're dead otherwise.'

Tekmerc five: 'Hey, come on, get real, Leol. No one's gonna loose off at you.'

*

The 'ware in the redundant MHD chamber was a confusing mess to unravel – a couple of ordinary terminals with custom-built augmentation modules, music deck, VR gamer gear – and all of it plugged together by a nonstandard web of fibre-optic cable. Julia recognized old hotrod-style programs protecting some of the 'ware cores. It took time to melt through and initiate her own command procedures.

The first coherent input she received was from the cameras.

Charlotte Fielder dressed in a white cotton top and shorts being held in an armlock by Nia Korovilla. Julia watched as Nia Korovilla broke two of her fingers. Charlotte's mouth opened in a scream of pain. Unheard; Julia couldn't find the microphone circuits. Fabian Whitehurst was charging at the two women.

Julia turned all of the lightware cruncher's spare capacity to interpreting the den's 'ware. She ordered one camera to zoom in on Nia Korovilla's face; her pupils were dilated; her grip on Fielder looked effortless. The woman was taking some kind of narcotic. Memory correlation assigned the highest probability to cleardust. Korovilla would be quite capable of killing Fabian Whitehurst and Charlotte Fielder with her bare hands.

Charlotte Fielder shoved Fabian Whitehurst away. He stumbled back, swaying for balance.

The den's circuits were defined, operational codes pulled out of the 'ware cores. Julia turned on the mikes, the flatscreens, the music deck speakers.

'Oh God no,' Charlotte Fielder cried.

Fabian was getting ready to charge again. There was blood running down his chin.

Julia rammed the music deck volume up full. 'Enough of this. Fabian, stay where you are.'

The three figures froze in surprise.

Julia activated a visual synthesizer program, plugging it into the flatscreens.

'Julia Evans,' Charlotte Fielder gasped.

'Hello, Charlotte. I think it's about time you and I had a talk.'

'Not a chance,' said Nia Korovilla.

'Your position is not a strong one, Nia,' Julia said. 'There is a tekmerc squad loose in the gondola, two of my agents survived the Messerschmitt attack, and an Event Horizon security crash team is *en route*. Whoever you work for, they'll have to fight through all those groups to reach you.'

'What's happening?' Charlotte Fielder implored. Her beautiful face was screwed up in pain. 'What attack?'

'The *Colonel Maitland* is currently under siege by tekmercs,'

Julia told her. 'You are the target, you possess some unique information which several people would like to obtain.'

'Not me, no I don't.'

Julia could see the girl was near to cracking up.

'Please, Mrs Evans,' Fabian Whitehurst called. 'Tell Nia to let Charlotte go. *Please*.' There were tears trickling down his cheeks, mingling with the blood on his chin, droplets spilling onto his jacket.

Nia Korovilla's free hand moved up to clamp around the back of Charlotte Fielder's neck. 'That isn't an option.'

*

Internal camera, fuselage keel. The four tekmercs under Frank's command had come up the stairwell from the gondola. They were clumping along in single file, helmets brushing the gasbags. The walkway hadn't been designed for armour suits, arms kept knocking against the hand rails, bending them. The grid mesh was creaking under their weight.

Julia sent out a string of instructions to the maintenance drones, directing them down the fuselage to the tail. They began to slide smoothly along their rails.

*

Internal camera, fuselage engineering bay. Greg and Suzi were stepping off the ladder on to the walkway that would take them to the MHD chamber. One side of the walkway looked out over the engineering bay, a circular lattice of girders like a metal spiderweb. Massive cylindrical heat exchangers, and chrome-silver giga-conductor cells were cocooned within it, concentric rings of metal eggs. Cables and thick pipes wound around the girders; the air carrying a steady thrumming from the machinery. On the other side of the walkway was the featureless shallow curve of the main spherical gasbag, ringed by one of the doughnut-shaped bags.

Greg consulted his cybofax. 'This is it,' he said. 'Straight ahead now.'

'Right.' Suzi's acknowledgement was strained.

Julia called them through the cybofax. 'Bad news, the maid, Nia Korovilla, is some kind of hardliner.'

'Jesus wept,' Suzi said hotly. 'Last time I ever take on an Event Horizon deal.'

'I'm sorry,' Julia said. 'I didn't realize what was involved when we started out. The situation is becoming very fluid.'

'Fluid,' Suzi snorted.

'What about the maid?' Greg asked.

'She's cleardusted, and using Charlotte Fielder as a shield.'

'So what do you want us to do?'

'The only viable option is to eliminate her. We cannot risk Fielder; and Korovilla has her hand round Fielder's neck, ready to snap it.' Julia squirted the den's camera image into Greg's cybofax.

Suzi craned her neck to look at it. 'Not good,' she said. 'We'll have to go straight in and sharpshoot. Korovilla won't be prepared. Even if someone does come in she won't expect them to fire right off. Everyone takes time to assess a new situation.'

'All right,' Greg said reluctantly.

'I do it,' Suzi said flatly.

'Oh yeah?'

'Yeah. It's what you brought me for. I can shoot straight, I'm familiar with the Browning. And you might hesitate, with her being a woman.'

Greg pulled a sour face. 'All right.'

'OK. Julia, is she carrying?'

'No, not that I can see.'

'That's something.'

'I'm negotiating,' Julia said. 'But I can't hold her much longer. And the tekmercs are two minutes behind you. I've arranged a delay, but I can't guarantee how long that'll keep them.'

'We're gone,' Suzi said. She began to run lightly down the walkway towards the MHD chamber, fifty metres ahead. The camera showed a hard grey fan of light spilling out of its door.

*

Internal camera, MHD camera. Charlotte Fielder clamped her jaw shut as Nia Korovilla's hand tightened. The skin of her long neck was showing white around the maid's fingers.

'Be logical,' Julia urged. 'My company's infiltration of the *Colonel Maitland*'s 'ware systems is total. Whatever questions Charlotte answers for you, whatever she says, wherever she is in the airship, we will hear them. There will be no advantage to your backers now. I offer you this: if you release her my security crash team will leave you alone, you may even have free passage to the destination of your choice.'

Nia Korovilla gave a guttural laugh. 'And I will tell you this. The whore is too valuable for anyone to risk harming her. Except for me, I'll have nothing to lose in a last resort. If anyone, you or the tekmercs, tries to interfere I will break her elegantly crafted little neck.'

Julia made her voice austere. 'You will not be allowed to leave with her.'

'You may not have her,' Nia Korovilla growled.

'Stop it!' Fabian Whitehurst wailed. 'Stop it, stop it. Let her go. Just let her go.' The creases down his cheeks were like an old man's.

'Don't get in anyone's way, Fabian,' Charlotte Fielder said, her voice was very faint. 'These people won't even notice you.'

'I revise my offer,' Julia said.

'I'm listening,' Nia Korovilla said.

'Contact your backers, we will explain the current situation, and I'll offer them an atomic structuring manufacturing partnership with Event Horizon.'

For the first time Nia Korovilla seemed uncertain.

Suzi stepped into the den. Her Browning pistol was held level with her face, one eye closed.

'If you—' Nia Korovilla began. Directly above her left ear a circle of hair one centimetre wide puffed into bright, almost invisible flame, singing the surrounding strands. She fell backwards, knees buckling.

Charlotte Fielder staggered forwards as the grip around her

neck and arm was relinquished. She twisted to look at the maid's body, lying with limbs akimbo on the decking. The eyes had rolled back, leaving only the whites showing.

Charlotte Fielder groaned, looking as if she was about to be sick. Then she found Fabian Whitehurst who was staring numbly at the body. They moved into each other's arms, and locked like magnets.

*

Internal camera, aft fuselage access way. The four tekmercs of Frank's squad had begun to climb the transverse frame ladder up to the midsection of the engineering bay. Eighteen mainten-ance drones were lined up along the side of the ladder. Another two glided down their rails and stopped.

Julia organized twenty separate drone-handling subroutines inside the lightware crunchers, loaded them with instructions, and plugged each of them into a maintenance drone.

The last tekmerc started up the ladder. The first was still twenty rungs from the midsection walkway.

*

Tekmerc squad inter-suit radio communication.

Tekmerc three: 'What is it with these drones?'

Tekmerc seven: 'Lacey, hey, Lacey, they're in love with you.' Kissing sound.

Tekmerc three, identified, Lacey: 'Go suck it cold.'

Frank: 'Come on, let's show some discipline here.'

Tekmerc seven: 'Hey, this one's moving.'

*

Julia's primary routine initiated the attack, handing over indi-vidual drone direction to the assembled subroutines. Welding lasers fired at the muscle armour suits' photon amps. Strut-repair waldos reached out and began drilling through the armour with monolattice carbon bits, aiming for wrist, elbow, ankle, and knee joints. Riveting guns punched metal pins into the jetpacks.

*

Internal camera, aft fuselage access way. A scene of terrorized chaos; machine versus machine. Metallic humanoids fighting vulpine robotic insects. The tekmercs thrashed and kicked as the drills penetrated; all the while desperately clinging to the ladder. Every time an armour boot hit a drone it would crumple the casing, smashing the hardware and hydraulic systems. Violent movement dislodged the waldos, but they would reach out again instantly, monolattice stingers blurring with speed.

Blood began to seep out of the drill holes, running down the outside of the dark armour. It mingled with hydraulic fluid, slicking the ladder.

The tekmerc below the leader lost his grip, dropping down a metre. He was halted momentarily by three waldos that had punctured the armour, but the force of the jolt ripped their drills free. He fell, rebounding off the fuselage framework, arms and legs flailing madly. Then he hit a clear section of the solar cell envelope head on, tearing straight through.

*

External camera, aft fuselage keel. The tekmerc was a black pinwheeling doll against the calm blue ocean. Shrinking rapidly. He must have tried to activate his jetpack. Whatever damage the maintenance drones had inflicted, it was drastic. The jetpack erupted into a shower of minute slivers, dismembering the rest of the muscle armour suit.

*

Tekmerc squad inter-suit radio communication.

Tekmerc seven: Continuous unintelligible shout.

Frank: 'Leol, the drones, the fucking drones. They've gone mad.'

299

Leol Reiger: 'What's happening?'

Frank: Screams. Shouting, 'Help us for Christ's sake. It's the drones. They're killing us. Blind. They've blinded me. Can't hold. Oh God, my hands—' Screams.

Tekmerc five: 'Holy shit, listen to them, it's likely they're being eaten alive.'

Leol Reiger: 'Shut up. Everybody, drones are hazards, shoot on sight. That goes for any other piece of mobile hardware. Ian, Keith, Denny, get up to that MHD chamber. Someone doesn't want us there. Help Frank if you can.'

Tekmerc eight: 'Jesus, Leol.'

Leol Reiger: 'Just fucking do it. Right? Snuff anything and everybody in your way, but do it. Now move.'

20

Charlotte Fielder really was astonishingly pretty. She was the first thing Greg saw when he came into the MHD chamber after Suzi, all dark-gold skin and tight white cotton. Nothing else registered at the same level, it was as though the background had suddenly become monochrome.

She and Fabian Whitehurst were clinging to each other. Greg reckoned a muscle armour suit would be hard pushed to prise them apart. They both stared at Suzi in trepidation.

'Don't piss yourselves,' Suzi told them, lowering her Browning. 'I'm one of the good guys. Right, Julia?'

'Yes,' Julia said, her voice booming out of speaker stacks. 'Greg and Suzi won't hurt you, Charlotte, nor you, Fabian, they work for me.'

Greg looked down at Nia Korovilla's body. She looked so tranquil in her prim maid's uniform. Hard to imagine her as any kind of hazard. Maybe Suzi had been right, after all. It irked him to think that she knew him better than he knew himself. But she certainly hadn't hesitated to shoot.

Nia Korovilla's presence kicked off a whole cascade of trepidation in his mind. Julia had squirted her data profile into his cybofax; according to that she had served on the *Colonel Maitland* for eight years. It meant she was a sleeper, a watcher keeping tabs on Jason Whitehurst. Which made no sense to Greg; if she'd been feeding someone with snatched bytes of Jason

Whitehurst's trading deals for eight solid years, then the old boy would have known. So if she hadn't been doing that, what was she on board for?

'Leol Reiger has dispatched three more tekmercs up here,' Julia said. Her face was replicated in six flatscreens, dominating one wall of the den. 'I won't be able to delay them, not now they have been warned about the drones being under my command.'

Greg glanced hurriedly round the MHD chamber. It reminded him of home, the kind of grotesque merger of gear and pets that the kids slapped together as various interests went through nova bursts of intense devotion, only to be abandoned a week or month later. It was an archaeological record of a boy's development. So much for his intuition telling him there was something out of phase about Fabian Whitehurst.

He tried to look at the MHD chamber from a tactical point of view. There was only the one door, and the walls behind the panels were solid alolithum. The tekmercs' rip guns could break through that easily enough. Suzi was prowling along the line of gear consoles below the flatscreens.

'Tell you, we can't stay in here,' Greg said. 'You got us a hidey-hole ready, Julia?'

'Not exactly, but I think I can keep you and the tekmercs apart until my crash team arrives. There's a lot of volume in this airship.'

Greg glanced at Suzi, who gave him a shrug.

'Sure thing,' she said. 'This is all so fluid.'

'Come on, Charlotte,' Greg said. 'We'll get you out of here.'

Charlotte and Fabian actually managed to hold each other even tighter.

'No,' Charlotte said. She was sweating profusely.

Greg noticed the discoloration on her hand. The skin around two fingers was swelling, puffy with blood.

'Charlotte, please, the tekmercs that are coming for you make Nia here look tame.'

She stroked Fabian's hair with her good hand. The boy's eye

had swollen shut, blood was drying on his lips and chin. 'What's happening?' she asked. 'Please, I don't understand any of this.'

'Julia,' Greg called.

Julia's face vanished from the largest flatscreen, replaced by a view of the *Colonel Maitland*'s landing pad with the gutted wreck of the Pegasus still smoking. Charlotte gasped.

'That's the plane we came in,' Greg said. 'There were four people on board when it was hit by the tekmercs. That's your alternative. Now will you please come with us.'

'I'm not leaving Fabian. Not if tekmercs are on their way here.'

Fabian looked up at her with complete adoration. Greg realized they weren't going to be separated. And he had promised Jason Whitehurst exactly that. Bloody wonderful.

'We're not asking you to leave him, Charlotte,' Julia said gently. 'One moment.'

There was a burst of static.

Jason Whitehurst's voice came out of the music deck speakers. 'Fabian?'

'Yes, Father?'

Greg's cybofax bleeped. He looked down at it.

'You stay with Charlotte and Mr Mandel,' Jason Whitehurst said. 'It'll be a lot safer for you. These damn tekmercs are all over the old *Colonel*. Bloody trigger happy brutes, they are. I'll catch up with you later, I must see the crew is all right first, *noblesse oblige*, and all that. You understand that, don't you?'

'Yes, Father.'

Greg showed the cybofax to Suzi. Her face remained impassive as she read the screen's message.

'Splendid chap; bit of an adventure for you. Charlotte, my dear girl, what can one say? I'm most dreadfully sorry about all this trouble. Julia will explain later. You take care of Fabian in the mean time for me, yes?'

'Yes, sir.'

'Jolly good.'

Greg pulled a first aid box off the wall, and found a local anaesthetic infuser. Charlotte didn't resist when he took her hand. He pressed the infuser tube to her wrist.

She gave a tremulous little sigh as the anaesthetic took effect.

'Careful you don't knock the hand against anything,' he warned her.

She nodded meekly.

Suzi was wiping Fabian's chin with a disinfectant tissue.

'OK,' Greg said. 'Let's move. Julia, which way?'

'Turn right outside, down to the hull, then head up towards the prow. I've loaded your route.'

He glanced at the cybofax, memorizing the *Colonel Maitland*'s blueprint with its superimposed red line.

It was cool outside the MHD chamber. The engineering bay heat exchangers constantly circulated the air in the gap between the hull and the gasbags, preventing the helium from becoming superheated and losing lift capacity. Greg thought it smelt vaguely of chlorine. It left an unpleasant tang at the back of his throat.

He led them along the walkway, the opposite direction to the way he and Suzi had come. Charlotte and Fabian followed him, holding hands; Suzi brought up the rear. The worst of his neurohormone hangover was lifting, but he wouldn't be able to use the gland again today, not after two psi effusions like that.

'Greg, a little faster, please,' Julia said out of his cybofax. There was an edge in her voice.

'Right.' He began to step out.

A rip gun was fired behind them, the sound of its shot rumbling round the engineering bay. It was the signal for a whole barrage to begin.

'What's that?' Charlotte asked, raising her voice above the clamour.

'Rip guns.'

'Crikey,' said Fabian, he squinted at Greg with his one good eye. 'You mean a neutral-beam weapon?'

'No messing.'

They reached the hull. A silent rank of drones was drawn up beside the transverse frame ladder. Greg didn't have time to question their presence. He turned on to the walkway that led towards the prow, sandwiched between the gasbag and the solar cell envelope. It curved away ahead of him, fading to grey.

The rip guns had stopped firing.

'Get going,' Julia said. The drones began to move out on to the engineering bay girders.

Fabian watched them go curiously. 'Do you have hotrods working for Event Horizon?' he asked.

'One or two,' Julia answered.

'Fabian, not now,' Charlotte said.

'Sorry.'

The walkway made Greg think of the eidolonic loop he'd left Chad in. The engineering bay had disappeared from sight behind, and more walkway kept unfolding in front, seemingly endless. They were moving at a jog now. Charlotte's panting was loud in his ears. His own breathing wasn't too good either.

There were five rip-gun shots fired in rapid succession. The sound barely audible.

'Last of the drones gone,' Julia said. The cybofax wafer was in his top pocket again, banging on his chest. 'The three tekmercs are covering all the options. One has gone down the transverse frame ladder, another is climbing up.'

'And the third's coming after us,' Suzi finished.

'Right,' said Julia.

'Run faster?' Greg asked.

'He'll still be able to catch you. You're only a hundred and eighty metres ahead of him.'

'The next transverse ladder?'

'No, you'd be sitting ducks on that.'

'Stand and fight. The Tokarev might penetrate the armour.'

'No,' Julia said. 'I've got your escape route mapped out. Keep going, twenty metres. Stop by the next doughnut gasbag.'

The only way Greg found it was because of the deep concave fold in the plastic where the two bags pressed together. He came to a halt, breathing hard. Charlotte stopped behind him, her face drained.

'Are you all right?' she asked Fabian.

The boy flipped some of his ragged hair off his face. 'Yes.' They still hadn't let go of each other's hands.

'What now?' Greg asked. He kept his nerves alert for the sound of the tekmerc, wondering if he should order another gland secretion after all.

'Start hyperventilating,' Julia said.

'What's this bollocks, you hustle us along here for exercise classes?' Suzi snapped. 'Have you glitched?' She was the only one who wasn't breathing heavily.

'No, listen,' Julia said. 'I want Greg to slice open the doughnut gasbag with his Tokarev. Then you hold your breath, and slide down the inside. You will stop right above the keel walkway. Greg cuts the plastic again, and you drop out.'

Suzi gave Greg an imploring look. 'If both of us fire at once, we can snuff that tekmerc.'

Greg wasn't so sure. Suzi's idea was all down to chance. Julia's had logic behind it. Machine logic, admittedly. And of course, she didn't have to do it herself.

'The tekmerc can just follow us down the doughnut,' he said.

'No,' Julia said. 'It'll tear like paper under the weight of the armour. He'd fall straight out of the airship.'

'All right, we'll try it.'

'Shit,' Suzi said. 'Fluid.'

Greg looked at Charlotte and Fabian. 'Do you two under-stand?'

They both nodded, both looked scared.

'Whatever you do, don't breathe in while you're inside the doughnut,' Julia said. 'Helium isn't toxic, but there's no oxygen. You'll asphyxiate.'

Greg got his breathing back under control, and drew the Tokarev. 'Everybody ready?'

'Do it,' Suzi said.

He aimed at a point level with his own head. 'Breathe in now, and follow me straight away.' He hoped to hell the two kids would do as they were told, Suzi would have trouble bullying both of them. Or maybe not.

The vivid red beam pierced the plastic, and Greg swung it down to the walkway, opening up a two-metre slit. With the Tokarev held in his right hand, he sat on the walkway grid, pushing his feet into the open gash. The blackness inside the doughnut was impenetrable, it almost seemed to slop out on to the walkway. He ducked his head under the hand rail, and pushed off.

*

The Messerschmitt exploded without warning. Julia had to replay the external camera memories to understand the sequence of events.

Two Typhoon air-superiority fighters arrowed in from the north, silver-grey needles with wings retracted, using the airship as a radar shield. Not that the Messerschmitt would have had many options even if it had detected them, not when they travelled at Mach eleven. One went over the *Colonel Maitland*, the second went under. Three Kinetic Energy Kill missiles slammed into the Messerschmitt at Mach seventeen. Then the fighters were gone.

A fireball enveloped the Messerschmitt, billowing out. It was slapped by the supersonic backwash from the two fighters; invisible hands compressing it back into a lenticular shape. Chunks of flaming wreckage spewed out from the ragged edges, spinning through the air, arching down towards the distant ocean.

The *Colonel Maitland* was shaken violently by the Typhoons' passage. Julia monitored the buffeting they inflicted on the already damaged fuselage framework. Stress sensors reported a dangerous amount of weakening in the midsection.

She sounded the evacuation alarm before the bridge crew had a chance to evaluate the situation; klaxons blaring out all through the airship. The hatches on the survival pods popped open.

The Messerschmitt's halo of ionized flame contracted, wrapping itself around the broken fuselage. The plane rolled lazily, then began the long fall towards the water.

*

External camera, starboard fuselage. Two Event Horizon transports were decelerating fast; big XCV-77 Titan stealth hypersonics with a cranked delta planform. They were virtually standing on their tails to aerobrake, underbellies glowing cerise; airflow vortices created spiral vapour trails that streamed off each wingtip, as if they were stretching out giant white springs behind them.

*

With the jamming blanket lifted, Julia opened a communication link to the lead Titan. Her living self was plugged into the transport plane's sensors, anxious for information. She compiled a summary of events since the Messerschmitt's attack, and squirted it over.

Get Greg and company back into the gondola, her living self said, *I'll brief the crash team to lift them.*

OK.

*

Tekmerc squad inter-suit radio communication.

Tekmerc eight, female: 'Oh, Jesus wept. The deal's been burnt. Event Horizon planes, big buggers.'

Leol Reiger: 'Ian, Keith, Danny, get back to the gondola. Move!'

Tekmerc five: 'Coming, Leol.'

Julia: 'Last chance, Leol Reiger. Put down your weapons, deactivate your armour. It's all over.'

Leol Reiger: 'Screw you. Everybody, Charlotte Fielder is to be snuffed. If you see her, kill her. How do you like that, rich bitch? You tell your people to stand off, I'll let her live.'

Julia: 'No deal.'

*

External cameras, overview. Both Titans were slowly circling the *Colonel Maitland* like prowling wolves, disgorging the security crash team from their open loading ramps. The hovering armour-suited figures formed an encircling necklace around the airship, electronic senses sweeping it for signs of tekmerc activity. When their deployment manoeuvre was complete, they began to close on the gondola.

Survival pods were dropping out of the bottom of the gondola, small white spheres with strobes flashing urgently. Two hundred metres below the airship their red and white striped parachutes bloomed, lowering them gently towards the ocean.

A rip-gun bolt, fired from inside the gondola, speared one of the approaching armour suits. The security hardliner disappeared in a plume of blue-white flame. Another bolt stabbed out.

The crash team let off a fusillade of plasma bolts at the gondola window where the rip-gun bolts had come from.

*

Internal camera, gondola lower-deck cabin. Leol Reiger was running from the bedroom, barging through the open doorway out into the central corridor. Plasma bolts smashed into the cabin behind him, igniting the furniture and fittings. An inferno was raging inside within seconds.

The armour suit's speaker emitted a demented peal of laughter as Reiger ran towards the stern.

*

Suzi wanted to scream. She was in freefall, hurtling through black eternity. The plastic surface of the doughnut gasbag had disappeared as soon as she jumped, the fissure of weak light from the gash drying up almost at once. There was nothing she could orientate on, no reference point. Time seemed to be expanding. It was like being plunged into sensory deprivation. Leol Reiger would be laughing his fucking head off if he could see her now, all panicky like this.

Standing and fighting would have made a fucking sight more

sense than this. They could have shot the walkway out from under the tekmerc, no need to penetrate the muscle armour, just flush him out of the airship. Too late now. And what the hell did some warped 'ware package know about tactics anyway?

A thunderclap penetrated the closed universe of the doughnut gasbag. The sound rumbled around her, a drawn out tortured roar. Explosion. Then came the multiple sonic booms, the grating sound of the airship's fuselage bending and flexing. Definitely some snaps of breaking frames. Christ!

Something flicked up her back. She began to spin. Then she was skittering and sliding down the curving plastic wall of the gasbag, totally out of control. Her injured knee twisted viciously as she reeled round, nearly making her cry out loud. It was all she could do to keep her mouth clamped shut.

There was an electric flare of deep vermilion light ahead of her. The scene it uncovered was weird, two-tone, red and black. A huge curved cylindrical cavern, slick walls printed with a black hexagonal web pattern, palpitating softly. Jonah must have seen something like this, she thought. She'd always liked that story back in the Trinities; their preacher, Goldfinch, could make it sound real somehow when he was delivering his sermons.

Fabian Whitehurst was visible ten metres in front of her, sliding down the bottom of the doughnut's curve, jouncing about madly. She stretched her arms out, trying to slow her speed. The light went out.

She could still hear the fuselage protesting loudly.

The angle of the gasbag's slope began to shallow out, reducing her speed. There was a stark slice of hoary light shining out of the floor fifteen metres away. She saw Fabian on all fours, scrabbling towards it. He vanished abruptly, as though he'd been sucked down.

Suzi came to a halt about three metres from the cut, and started crawling towards it. She could hear her heart pumping fast, the need to take a breath rising. Her knee was alive with stabs of pain as it pressed into the plastic.

She reached the cut, and grasped the melted edge with her

hands, pulling her body through and down. A half-somersault and she was standing on the walkway.

Fabian was on his knees, coughing roughly. Charlotte Fielder stood behind him, arm around his shoulder, looking anxious. Suzi let some beautifully clean air flood into her lungs.

Five metres down the walkway, three drones were working on the composite panels that made up the roof of the gondola. Greg stood over them, watching keenly.

'Cutting us a way into the cabins,' he said when Suzi went over to him.

'My security crash team has arrived,' Julia announced from the cybofax peeping out of his jacket pocket. 'They'll be inside any minute now.'

There was another groan from the fuselage framework, Suzi thought she saw a ripple run along the walkway. The drones lifted up a strut they had disconnected, and began to use their lasers on the composite.

'There are two tekmercs left in the gondola, both on the lower deck searching the cabins, and three more in the fuselage,' Julia said. 'They're operating on shoot-to-kill instructions now.'

'Where's Leol Reiger?' Suzi asked.

'He's in the gondola.'

'Forget it,' Greg said curtly.

She wanted to tell him where to shove it. But her knee was throbbing alarmingly now, and the fuselage was frightening the shit out of her the way it kept creaking and moving – though she wasn't going to admit that to anybody. Leol Reiger was toting a Lockhead rip gun, and fully armoured. Besides, she'd been running around in this creepy half-gloom with its clammy cold air for what seemed like hours. 'Yeah,' she said. But it was an expensive concession.

The circle of composite which the drones had been working on fell away with a clatter. A surprisingly bright shaft of light shone up from the cabin below.

Suzi heard a rip gun being fired, answered with the fast *zip* of a plasma-pulse rifle. A lot of plasma-pulse rifles.

'You go first,' Greg told her. 'Fabian, you're next.'

She slithered through the hole and dropped to the floor. Her leg nearly gave way altogether. This time she couldn't help the yelp as red hot skewers of pain pierced her knee.

It was a bedroom suite; dustsheets over all the furniture. Fabian's jeans and trainers appeared above her. She caught sight of armoured shapes racing through the air outside the window. The silhouette of a Titan transport in the distance.

Fabian dropped into the cabin, landing awkwardly. Suzi limped over to help him up. Someone in the gondola was firing a rip gun almost continuously. It was getting louder.

Charlotte's long shapely legs came through the hole; she landed easily, rolling as she hit. Suzi wondered where she'd learnt that. The girl's white top and shorts were streaked with dirt. Fabian caught her hand as she got up, and she smiled gratefully at him.

Two of Event Horizon's security crash team rose to hover outside the cabin's window; their jetpack efflux a steady thrum. One of them pressed a power blade to the glass. It sliced through cleanly, and the armoured figure tilted his jockey-stick, heading towards the stern, sliding the blade along as he went.

Greg landed in the cabin with a hefty thump, sprawling gracelessly on to his side.

'Ah, the old paratroop training, always useful.' Suzi grinned at him. The weary tension in her muscles was slackening off. Her knee was a solid knot of pain.

Greg stood up, shaking his head like a dog coming out of the water. 'Bloody hell.'

'Yeah,' she agreed. She was surprised by how glad she was that he'd come through OK. Every byte out of the combat manual thrown at him, and he was still upright. She should never have doubted, not Greg.

A big rectangle of glass fell outwards, letting in the full howl of the jetpack noise. The crash team began to fly into the cabin.

Suzi started to laugh, lost in a burn of elation as dustsheets took flight and her short hair whipped about, shellsuit trousers flapping wildly round her legs. It was always the same, relief at being alive at the end of the day boosting her higher than syntho ever could. Dangerously addictive.

Fabian and Charlotte were taken out first. She felt armoured arms close around her, and the security hardliner lifted her with a precision she could only envy. Then there were just the blues of water and sky, the giddiness which accompanied height.

*

Leol Reiger was *very* good. Julia hadn't expected that. Rip-gun bolts tore into cameras and fibre optic cable channels. Her coverage of the gondola's lower deck was being systematically broken down. Fire was spreading from the cabin her crash team had shot at. Halogen extinguishers in the ceiling came on, squirting out thick columns of white mist into the central corridor, degrading the camera images still further.

She relayed Leol Reiger's exact co-ordinates to the crash team.

*

Internal camera, gondola lower-deck central corridor. Dark smoke oozed along the ceiling, smothering the biolum strips. Flames fluoresced the halogen a lurid amber. She watched one of the crash team step out of Jason Whitehurst's study into the inflamed miasmatic cyclone, plasma rifle held ready.

Leol Reiger turned with a speed she couldn't believe. The rip-gun bolt was aimed with incredible accuracy, lancing straight into the security hardliner's chest.

If she had a stomach, she would have been sick at that point.

Leol Reiger stood still and amid the churning halogen smog, legs slightly apart, and pointed his rip gun up at the ceiling. He blew a wide hole in the composite, and kept on firing. His suit's jockey-stick deployed, swinging into place below his left arm. The jetpack compressor wound up.

He launched himself like an old-style space rocket, straight up.

*

Internal camera, gondola upper-deck central corridor. Leol Reiger came through the floor, and vanished through a hole in the ceiling.

*

Internal camera, fuselage keel. Rip-gun bolts had vaporized a three-metre section of the walkway, leaving the smoking ends drooping on to the gondola roof. There was a gaping rent in the spherical gasbag overhead. Leol Reiger flashed past.

*

That was where Julia's coverage ended. The only sensors she had inside the gasbag were the ones to detect temperature, contamination, and pressure levels.

The *Colonel Maitland*'s flight control systems reported a heavy helium vent from the gasbag Leol Reiger had taken refuge in. External cameras showed her rip-gun bolts flying out of the upper fuselage, leaving long breaches in the solar cell envelope.

*

Tekmerc squad inter-suit radio communication.

Leol Reiger: 'Scuttle it. Shred this fucker.'

Tekmerc five: 'You're crazy, Leol.'

Leol Reiger: Laughter. 'No way. They've blown it. The mayday beacons on board are shrieking so loud every emergency service on the planet will be picking them up. There's no jammer now. Air-sea rescue is going to be here in minutes.'

Tekmerc eight, female: 'Christ, he's right.'

Leol Reiger: 'Damn betcha, I'm right. Use your Lockheeds, blow your way into the gasbags, and deflate them. We'll ride it down to the sea.'

Tekmerc two: 'I'm with you, Leol.'

*

Julia watched the tekmercs in the fuselage burn their way into the gasbags. More rip-gun bolts began to tear through the solar

314

cell envelope. They left behind a growing static charge which snapped and sizzled across the geodetic framework. It jumped the power systems' circuit breakers and fused 'ware processors. Julia began to lose peripheral circuits.

Are you going to order the crash team into the fuselage after them? she asked her living self.

No. Reiger was right about the coast guard, the NN cores say three search and rescue hypersonics are already on their way from Nigeria. He's a dreadful annoyance, and he's certainly going to have to be dealt with at some stage. But our first priority is Charlotte Fielder. I'll let Victor Tyo sort him out later.

*

Charlotte knew she was dreaming. Her life wasn't like this – pain, horror, darkness, fear. Death. That tough little hardliner woman had killed the maid. Didn't say anything, didn't ask what was going on, just walked in to the den and shot her.

Was that part of the dream? It was all so vivid.

She rested numbly in the hard metal embrace of the machine-man, whizzing through bright blue space. The cold gnawed at her bare skin. There were lightning flashes and thunder grumbles behind her.

She was walking down long, deserted London streets again, cold from the rain, scared of the lightning forks that danced above the grey rooftops. Small, and hungry, and lost. Perhaps all of her life had been a dream? The finery, the wine, the laughter and bright, bright colours. Just figments spinning through her mind.

She wanted it back, that life.

The big plane hissed venomously at her as she swooped into the open end, above the ramp. She was coming to a halt inside a fat metalloceramic tube with yellow nylon webbing seats along the walls. Two biolum strips ran the length of the bare ceiling. Thick wires and composite reinforced tubes snaked over the floor, ending in bulky sockets clipped on to the wall by each seat.

A group of people in white jumpsuits were standing just inside the ramp, their arms waving like traffic policemen. The metal arms let go of her, and she was dumped into waiting hands. These hands were soft, made of skin and bone.

Hot urgent voices raged around her, firing off rapid questions. All she could do was stare back blankly. A silver shawl was wrapped round her shoulders, and she was eased into one of the webbing seats.

Plastic boxes were pressed against her arms and neck and belly, tiny coloured lights winking. A small tube that gave her a bee sting on her neck, swiftly turning to an ice spot, then evaporating altogether. The world really did lose all cohesion then, receding to a distant spot of silent frosty light.

She hung back from it for some time, letting her thoughts slowly come together. Then the light expanded again, bringing with it sounds and feeling, mainly of icy skin. She was light headed, which she knew came from the trank.

Jetpacks whined savagely as the crash team landed on the plane's ramp two at a time. There were liquid rumbles coming from the dark bulk of the *Colonel Maitland* a kilometre away.

'You OK now?' an earnest young woman in a white jumpsuit shouted over the bedlam. Her face was pressed up close. A red cross on each arm.

Charlotte nodded. 'I'm cold,' she said.

The woman smiled. 'I'll get you a thermal suit. But we'll be closing and pressurizing in a minute. You'll soon feel the difference.'

'Thank you.'

The man called Greg was sitting in a webbing seat opposite her, doing yoga breathing. He gave her a rueful grin.

Charlotte saw the motion long before the sound arrived. The *Colonel Maitland* was crumpling, prow and stern rising up, midsection splitting open. Long flames writhed out of the gondola windows.

'Father!' Fabian cried hoarsely. He was sitting next to her, she hadn't even noticed.

The *Colonel Maitland* began to sink out of sight. Not falling, but a slow idle descent down to the water so far below. People were standing on the plane's ramp, watching it go. She saw the little hardline woman among them, her fist punching the air. Smirking.

'Father!'

She put her arms round him as two of the white-clad medic team closed in. One of them was holding an infuser tube ready.

'Get away from him!' she shouted.

Fabian buried his head in her chest, sobbing uncontrollably.

'Just get away from him.' She rocked him gently, tears filling her own eyes.

The ramp hinged up.

21

The SETI office was livening up. Rick Parnell's original staff of twelve had been complemented with twenty people from the Astronautics Institute's astronomy department. The two teams were working together to realign Event Horizon's radio and optical telescopes on Jupiter. The SETI people were elated at the prospect of practical hardware-orientated work at long last, the astronomers coldly angry at having their observations disrupted. Tempers were getting frayed. It didn't help that Victor had called in Eddie Coghlan's security programmers to prevent any possible data leakage from the new linkages being established between the observatories and the SETI office.

Victor stood in the doorway to Rick Parnell's office, next to his bodyguard, and watched the shirtsleeved crew knuckle down. The tense hustle of activity was beginning to resemble a bank's trading floor. It was always the same routine: one of the terminal operators would sit up straight and wave a hand in some unknown sign language, then a knot of technicians and managers would form around them, arguing hotly. Tiger teams, loaded with authority and practical knowledge – in theory. There would be data requests fired into the terminal, thick folders broken open and consulted, cybofaxes performing simple calculations. When the decision was finally made the knot would break up, and another would form around a different terminal.

Victor was irksomely familiar with the scene, crisis management, or more often damage assessment and limitation. It was going to be a long afternoon for the SETI office, and an even longer night.

It said a lot for Julia's management that when something as outré as a search of Jupiter did spring up out of the blue, she could simply plug the appropriate division into the top of the company's command structure and get results. He was even mildly surprised at the way Rick had coped with the unexpected burden. Give the man his due, he hadn't started swaggering round like a mini-Napoleon.

Rick was sitting at his desk, jacket draped over the back of his chair, its collar getting more crumpled every time he leaned back. Both his terminal cubes were alive with whirling graphics. Every now and then he would nod encouragingly at them.

'What happens to the radio telescope data after you receive it?' Victor asked.

Rick looked up. 'It's squirted direct into one of the Institute's lightware crunchers. We've been sponsoring university groups to write signal analysis programs in preparation for Steropes. All we have to do is pull them from our memory core, load them into the cruncher, and run the raw signal data through them. Of course, establishing their integrity in the lightware cruncher is going to take time; but my people are on top of it. We should be ready to start in a couple of hours.'

'And the optical data?'

'Standard image comparison technique. Take two pictures of the same patch of sky a week apart, and see what's changed, if there's anything new appeared. We're in luck there. Aldrin did its last Jupiter survey five years ago, and it's all on file in the Institute's library. Galileo mission control is going to repeat that survey for me, starting in three and a half hours. So if your alien has arrived in the last five years, we should be able to spot it – providing it's larger than a hundred metres in diameter.'

'How long is the comparison going to take?'

'Virtually instantaneous, given the processing power we've

got available these days.' He held up a hand, palm outward. 'But the survey itself will take a couple of days.'

Victor didn't say anything. He'd been expecting the whole process to take at least a week. Astronomy had always seemed a glacial science to him; impressive incomprehensible machinery focusing on remote segments of the sky, providing building blocks for abstruse papers on cosmology. Arguments about how the universe was put together invariably went way over his head, but Julia thought it was important enough to finance to the tune of fifty million New Sterling each year.

'They were none too happy about that,' Rick said.

Victor roused himself. 'Who?'

'Galileo mission control. I've screwed up their observation schedule good and proper. There are items that were requested five years ago on that schedule.'

'Tough. We all work for the same lady, pure science departments are no different to anyone else. It's her telescope, it looks at whatever she wants.'

Rick clasped his hands together, grinning. 'Lord save us from these heathen hordes.'

Victor sat in front of the desk, staring up at the big hologram of Steropes. 'Is the data from the radio telescopes coming through all right? Requisitioning astronomical signals isn't exactly a familiar field for my people.'

'Yes, quite all right.' He put the cubes on hold and bent down to open a desk drawer. 'You want a beer?'

'No, thanks.'

Rick produced a can of Ruddles bitter. 'That Julia Evans, she's quite something.'

'Yes.'

'I mean, not just smart, attractive with it.' He tugged the can's tab back.

'Yes.'

He swallowed some beer and looked thoughtful. 'Do you think Royan is still alive?'

'He was a week ago.'

'Right.' Rick took another swallow. 'I want to ask you something. I meant to ask Julia Evans, but, well ... I didn't know quite where I stood with her. The thing is, I suppose she's assembling some sort of team to contact this alien when we find it.'

'I've no idea; but put like that, somebody will have to meet it.'

'I want in,' Rick said quickly. He bent forwards over the desk, knuckles whitening as he gripped the Ruddles tightly. 'Damn it, I'm loyal, I'll even keep quiet about it afterwards if that's what's needed. But I want to be there.'

'I'll tell her. I should think she would've included you anyway. Who else has spent a lifetime thinking about aliens?' He wondered if it had come out sarcastically; he hadn't intended it to.

Rick searched his face intently for a moment, then sat back. 'Thanks.'

Julia Evans Access Request, Victor's processor node told him. **Expedite Channel.**

Hello, Victor, how's it going? Julia asked.

Surprisingly well. The astronomy department won't be asking you to their Christmas party, their schedules have been shot to pieces; but the radio signal data is beginning to come in. Rick and his team are preparing to shove it through some kind of specialist analysis program. The optical review is going to take longer, couple of days, Rick says.

OK, fine, first the good news. Royan's Kiley probe is back, and it brought some microbes.

How did you find that out?

Your idea. There was a personality package waiting in bay F37's memory core.

One of Royan's?

Yes.

What did he say?

That he was going to modify the microbes into something useful. A more advanced form of bioware. And that he wasn't totally confident about the outcome, which is why he left the package, so that if anything goes wrong we'll be able to understand the problem.

There are more packages?

Yes, but he didn't say where. Have you tracked down that space-plane crew?

No, I've been organizing security for the SETI office, but I'll get on to it. Did Royan say if there was a starship orbiting Jupiter?

No, but the Kiley's sensors probably wouldn't have seen it anyway, they were attuned to the micro, not the macro. My NN cores are reviewing the star tracker memories. I don't hold out much hope.

This isn't making a lot of sense yet. At what point did Royan make contact with the starship aliens?

No idea, but we might find out soon. I've located Jason White-hurst, and he's agreed to meet Greg and Suzi. Get this, they can put in a bid for Charlotte Fielder.

A bid?

Yes. Jason was preparing to sell her to the highest bidder. Fortu-nately the auction hasn't started.

Ye gods. Anything else?

Leol Reiger is being paid by Clifford Jepson. And I think there's a connection between the alien and atomic structuring. It's too much of a coincidence having them both turn up at the same time, virtually the same day.

I can buy that. So we're in a race?

Beginning to look that way.

OK, Julia, I'll find that spaceplane crew, and your NN cores can access every memory core they ever plugged into.

Right. Let me know when you've got them.

Straight away, count on it.

I always do, Victor.

Cancel Channel to Julia Evans.

Rick was crumpling up his Ruddles can, head cocked to one side, giving Victor a shrewd stare.

Victor got up and went to stand by the window, looking down on Building One's assembly hall. 'Which is bay F37?' he asked.

The can landed in the bin. 'That one.' Rick pointed.

'Fine. Do you know the members of the assembly crew that put Kiley together?'

'Some of them, yes.'

'You'd better introduce me, then.'

*

The manager of assembly bay F37 was William Tyrrell, who told them it was the *Newton's Apple* which had boosted Kiley into orbit. Victor accessed the Institute's 'ware, and tracked the spaceplane down to Spaceplane Preparation Building Two where it was being readied for flight.

He and Rick took a personnel cart over to the big hangarlike structure. High bay twelve, where the *Newton's Apple* was being prepped, was a large white-walled chamber with overhead hoists and five large empty cargo pod cradles in the centre.

Newton's Apple was a *Clarke*-class spaceplane, a swept-wing delta planform with a span of fifty metres, sixty metres long. The fuselage was a lofriction pearl-white metalloceramic, gleaming brightly under the big biolum panels in the ceiling. Maintenance crews in blue overalls were checking round the undercarriage bogies. Red power cables as thick as Victor's arm were plugged into hatches in the underbelly, charging up the giga-conductor cells. The rear clamshell doors were already shut, its cargo pods loaded.

The flight cabin was small, with room for five people. They found the captain, Irving Diwan, at the pilot's console running through preflight checks.

People always gave Victor a fast distrustful glance when they were introduced to him. It was one of those things – royalty got bows, channel stars got asked for autographs, lovers got kissed, security men got nervous assessments. He had learnt to accept it, part of the routine.

It didn't happen with Irving Diwan. The captain had purple-black skin, a shaved scalp with a single dreadlock on top, worn in a flat spiral; when he stood up he was fifteen centimetres taller

323

than Victor, putting his eyes level with Rick's. He grinned with delight when Victor showed him his card.

'Head of security? What have we been caught doing, sympathizing with Welsh separatists?'

Meg Knowles, the payload officer, gave him a sharp accusatory stare. He shrugged back.

'I'm here to ask about the Kiley probe,' Victor said. 'Do you remember it? I need to know if it was recovered by the *Newton's Apple*.'

'Sure,' Meg Knowles said. She was sitting at the horseshoe-shaped payload monitoring console behind the pilot's seat. 'I remember the Kiley recovery, it was in early April. I had to snag it with the arm. I'd never seen space hardware in such a state before. Its particle-protection foam had taken a real pounding in Jupiter's ring.'

'What about unloading it?' Victor asked. 'Can you remember which high bay you used?'

'There are only five equipped to handle space probes. I think we used number seventeen,' she said.

'Great.' Open Channel to Julia Evans. 'How about after that? Do you know where the Kiley was taken?'

Meg Knowles paused, staring off into space.

NN Core One On Line. *Sorry, Victor, my flesh and blood self is dealing with Michael Harcourt right now. I can interrupt if it's important.*

No, don't bother. This is more relevant to you in any case. I've learned that Kiley was recovered this April by a Clarke-*class spaceplane called* Newton's Apple, *they unloaded it in high bay seventeen.*

Fine work, Victor, I'll plug into the spaceplane and the high bay's 'ware, see if there's another of Royan's personality packages waiting.

Right, and I'll see if I can find out what happened to it after it was unloaded. **Cancel Channel to Julia Evans.**

'Hey,' Irving Diwan protested. The payload monitoring console had activated itself, data was flowing through its four cubes so fast it was an unreadable blur. 'What the hell?'

'Leave it,' Victor ordered as Irving Diwan reached for the console's keyboard.

'But the flight 'ware doesn't respond to my node orders. It's malfunctioning.'

'No, it isn't. Leave it.'

The pilot exchanged a glance with Meg Knowles who had steeled her expression into tight-lipped pique.

'Did you do that?' Rick asked; he sounded more amused than anything.

'Sort of.' Victor turned back to Meg Knowles. 'The unloading?'

'Yeah, right. I have to stick around, you know. Not like these glam pilot jockeys. While a payload is on board, I'm responsible for it. That means I'm here for loading and unloading. I was interested in Kiley, the first sample from a gas giant. So I was surprised by the way it got played down, no channel news teams, no Institute planetologists. You'd think there'd be somebody. But there's just Royan and the regular high bay crew. I stuck with Kiley until it was in the payload facility room. They drained out the reaction mass and discharged the giga-conductor cells; then it was put into an ordinary commercial container and driven off.'

The data in the console's cubes froze, Victor saw a dark green sphere suspended inside one of them, a honeycomb tracery of minute folds furrowing its surface. It winked out. The console shut down. Irving Diwan swore softly, and shook his head.

'Did Royan say where he was taking it?' Victor asked.

'No, but the container was from the North Sea Farm company, its logo was on the side. You know, that daft one with the seahorse. That's why I remember it. I thought it was pretty odd, sending a space probe to a sea farm.'

'Yeah,' Victor said. A blank container would have been the obvious choice. So Royan had wanted it to be noticed. Laying a trail in bright flashing red neon. It was all a game, even something as momentous as alien microbes, a game, new and fascinating. He felt real anger then. Royan was risking everything Julia had built, and at the end, win or lose, he wouldn't particularly care. He'd just move on to whatever proved bright and glittery enough to capture his attention next, leaving everyone else to shovel up the shit.

His cybofax shrilled loudly. Emergency code. Victor pulled the wafer out of his jacket pocket, and scanned the security division status display rushing down the little screen. The crash teams had launched to rescue Greg and Suzi.

'Come on!' he called to Rick, and took the metal stairs out of the cabin three at a time.

22

Julia's nodes closed the channel to Victor after he finished briefing her on the SETI office's progress. Wilholm's patio sprang back into her perception; a broad rectangle of yellow-grey York slabs laid outside the library's French windows. There was a heavily tinted glass roof overhead, supported by thick stone pillars that were choked by the ropy branches of climbing fuchsias. Big orange and white puffball flowers shone like Chinese lanterns as they caught the bright afternoon sun.

Matthew was drinking his lemon juice from a tall frosted glass, looking at her in exasperation. 'You were talking to someone,' he accused.

''Fraid so.' She took a sip of tea from her cup. It had seemed like a good idea, tea on the patio with the children. Hot afternoon, cold drinks, excited chatter, and chocolate cake.

Deep down she knew she was grabbing the opportunity for herself. Charlotte Fielder would be brought to Peterborough this evening; there would have to be a decision over who to align herself with in the bidding war for atomic structuring; and Victor would soon find the spaceplane that had recovered Kiley. There weren't going to be many spare hours in the next few days. 'Bit of a flap on right now, you see.' Although when isn't there?

'Is that why Victor was here earlier?' Daniella asked.

'Yes.'

'I like Victor.'

'Me too,' Matthew said.

'That makes three of us, then.'

'Is it about Daddy?' Matthew asked.

'Matthew!' Daniella scolded. 'You said you wouldn't.'

He scowled rebelliously.

Julia patted her daughter's hand. 'It's all right. Yes, it is about Daddy. I've got a lot of people looking for him.'

'Uncle Greg will find him,' Matthew declared stubbornly.

'My word, nothing much escapes you two, does it?'

Daniella gave an awkward shrug. 'Christine said he was going to do a tracking job. He hasn't done that for years.'

'Daddy and Uncle Greg fought together in the war, you see,' Matthew said eagerly. 'People who do that will do anything for each other afterwards.'

Julia sighed. 'It wasn't exactly a war, dear.'

'What then?'

'A very sad time. Things got out of hand after the Warming, chaotic and unpleasant. It was just a very few people at the top who caused a lot of trouble for everybody else.'

'Daddy always said—'

'Can we drop the subject, please.'

'There, see,' Daniella said triumphantly.

Matthew slurped his lemon noisily.

'Uncle Greg will find him, won't he?' Daniella asked, her self-confidence suddenly collapsing.

'Your Uncle Greg is the best,' Julia said. She wanted to say yes, of course; but then she would have to produce Royan. She wondered if she was really doing them any favours sheltering them like this. When news of the alien hit the channel newscasts – and it would – there'd be temper tantrums and sulks because she hadn't told them about it. But in the mean time they could have a few more days running riot in Wilholm's grounds, a few more days of the childhood she never had, plenty of friends and no cares.

Her cybofax bleeped, and she sagged back into the chair. Was half an hour with the children so much to ask?

'Go on, Mummy,' Daniella said. 'Answer it. The only people who have your number are ultra-important. It's probably the King.'

'I don't think even William could help much with this one,' she mumbled half to herself as she took out the wafer. **Open Channel to SelfCores.** *Who is this?*

Michael Harcourt, NN core one answered. *It's an official call in his capacity as Minister for Industry, so we told Kirsten to let it through. The government has finally decided to contact you about atomic structuring. Apparently the inner cabinet has been in crisis session for most of the morning, ever since the Ministry of Defence briefed the PM on atomic structuring.*

Really. Stay on line, please, I may need some data interpretation.
Of course.

'Is it the King?' Matthew asked, trying to look serious.

Julia laughed. 'No. How about you two finishing your tea in the summer-house while I take the call?'

Matthew lunged for the chocolate cake, lifting its plate with both hands. Daniella picked up the tray with the jug of juice and the glasses.

'We don't mind, Mummy, not really,' she said.

Julia forced a smile through the guilt, disturbed by just how hard it was. 'And don't give any cake to Brutus,' she called after them.

Michael Harcourt was a New Conservative central office clone; all the party's cabinet ministers seemed to have been bred in a vat somewhere, she thought. The same vat, bloody nearly the same chromosomes. He was fiftysomething, old enough to inspire confidence but nowhere near past it, immaculately groomed, not too expensive suit, silver-grey hair, authoritative face, voice coached into classless inflection. Capped teeth smiled at her from the cybofax's little screen. 'Ms Evans, I'm very grateful to you for taking my call at such short notice.'

Smooth bastard, she thought; the channel current affairs casts had been hinting at a leadership contest recently: the New Conservative backbenchers were unhappy at Joshua Wheaton's handling of the Welsh problem. Michael Harcourt was a major contender to replace him. Something else she should have kept up with; the NN cores would know.

'My office coded your call as a priority,' Julia said.

'We consider it so, absolutely. The thing is this, Julia; this morning the government was informed of a rather valuable new technology being hawked round the market.'

'Yes, atomic structuring.'

'Ah.' Michael Harcourt's eyebrows rose a fraction. 'You do know about it. Excellent. The Ministry of Defence was contacted by both the Greater European Defence Alliance and the Globe-cast company, to tell them this atomic structuring was being offered for development. According to our analysis, and these are absolutely top-rate people I've got working on it, Julia, it's going to cause quite a bit of a stir. In fact, the word revolutionary has been bandied about, not altogether in jest.'

'My people say the same thing,' she replied.

'Good, I'm glad to hear an independent confirmation, always a relief. Can I take it then, Event Horizon will be putting in a strong bid for a partnership with Clifford Jepson?'

'Of course we'll put in a bid.'

Michael Harcourt's news bite smile dimmed slightly. 'Ah, well, that's a point of some contention in the Cabinet, Julia. You see, Event Horizon has such a prominent position in English industry, we really feel it's essential that you put in the winning bid.'

'If you know of a way to guarantee mine is the winner, Minister, I'd be delighted to hear it.'

'Well, obviously, Julia, I'd do anything in my power to ensure that Event Horizon wins. We really can't afford to have you fall behind on this one.'

'We?'

'The nation, Julia. As you know, the New Conservatives have

always supported you. Event Horizon is an inspiration and example to industrialists everywhere. You epitomize our policies and the success to be gained by following them. We want to make sure that continues.'

'Mr Minister?'

'Yes, Julia?'

'Would you mind leaving out the BQ, and get to the point.'

Michael Harcourt frowned. 'BQ?'

'Bullshit quota.'

That's my girl; always keep politicians in their place. And that place is down.

Either contribute constructively, or be quiet, Grandpa.

'Ah, yes, well, to be perfectly blunt, then, Julia, I'd like to offer my services as a negotiator between Event Horizon and Clifford Jepson. I might not have much weight in corporate circles, but for what it's worth, I'd like you to consider it at your disposal.'

It wasn't what Julia had been expecting. She took a sip of tea to cover her lapse, and embarrassment. Betrayed by her own cynicism. Of course all politicians were self-advancing autocrats.

'That's a very kind offer, Michael,' she said. 'Have you spoken to Clifford Jepson about it?'

'Certainly, I wouldn't wish to waste your time on impractical solutions.'

'How did you see the deal working?' she asked.

'I would act as a strictly unofficial conduit. Clifford Jepson has indicated he will allow me to see the other bids as they come in. I make a simple phone call, and you would be in a position to put in the highest bid. Their best offer plus whatever percentage you think would clinch it.'

'That sounds ... workable,' she admitted. And if all else failed, she really did have to obtain that generator data from Clifford. Strange that Michael Harcourt hadn't mentioned Mutizen, though.

'I'm delighted to hear it. It's always gratifying to know one can be of service.'

'Quite.'

'And of course, the government will be keen to back you up once you establish a partnership with Globecast. My department has a long tradition of encouraging new technologies, and a strong relationship in that respect with Event Horizon. I would want that to continue.'

'Indeed? Exactly how did you foresee this happy union progressing?' *This sounds like it's turning into favour trading. Run an immediate check on him for me, find what his angle is.*

Gotcha, Juliet. And I told you so. A smug ghost's chuckle.

Michael Harcourt never showed the slightest awareness of her irony. 'Obviously, we will offer a zero-tax start-up incentive for the new factories which will produce this technology.'

'You and every other national government.'

'I have it in my brief to extend the time defined as "start up" to a period we both find mutually satisfactory; it could even be measured in decades. There would also be considerable financial assistance in the form of R&D contracts for both civil and military projects.'

'You have thought this out well. I'm impressed.'

'It could even help us solve our current unfortunate siting problems.'

'Which are those?'

'Your new cyber-precincts.'

'Ah.' She experienced a feeling which was almost content-ment.

'Absolutely,' Michael Harcourt continued eagerly. 'Wales could receive both of those precincts now. Beneficial all round, we feel.'

'I don't quite see how that should be . . .' She affected a small puzzled frown.

'The Welsh would have the precincts, providing a great deal of badly-needed employment, and enhancing their local econ-omy, more than they currently expect, while England receives the atomic structuring factories, which are surely the larger prize.'

'I thought the New Conservatives were hesitant about seeing the cyber-precincts going to Wales?'

'Not if it were our policy to site them there, and our efforts which finalized the deal.'

'But it would be dependent on Wales remaining within the union?'

'That is the best solution for everyone, don't you think? These secessionists are so short-sighted. The larger the country, the greater its prospects and security, the more attractive it is for organizations like Event Horizon to base themselves here. Welsh independence would be a disaster for both the English and the Welsh.'

'North and South Italy both seem to have prospered since the split; and Germany is certainly doing well enough from devolving power to the regional governments. There are all three Californias as well. I could go on.'

'Yes, but it's a question of scale, Julia; both the Italies are large entities. We no longer have Scotland and Northern Ireland; if Westminster was to lose control of Wales, where would it end? Would Cornwall declare independence, Cambridgeshire perhaps? We cannot allow any further reduction, it is simply inconceivable. Besides, these ridiculous micronations may not pursue the kind of market policies we in the New Conservative party believe in so strongly. Can you afford to entertain that possibility?'

Lord, this is all I need right now. Those bloody Welsh.

Smart of him to tie his go-between offer in with Wales, her grandfather said. *And we do need him to find out what the other bids are. You'll not split his offer package, Juliet. He's not that stupid, this is his shot at the top slot; if it fails he won't get another.*

I'm not going to be rushed or bullied into making the Welsh decision now.

You may be running out of time on that particular issue, NN core one said. *I believe I've tracked down the reason for Michael Harcourt's sudden outbreak of apparent altruism.*

Go on.

It's rather mundane, really. The largest single employer in his West

Kent constituency is Globecast. Their European network hub is sited there. And it was Harcourt himself who was briefed on atomic structuring by Clifford Jepson, he had an appointment at eight o'clock this morning; I pulled that from the Ministry 'ware.

The bugger is Clifford Jepson's cyborg, her grandfather said bitterly.

And of course, securing Event Horizon the atomic structuring partnership with Globecast, as well as enlisting your help over the Welsh question, will effectively guarantee him the leadership of the New Conservative party, NN core two said.

Plus Clifford makes sure Event Horizon pays through the nose, Julia added. He would be in a position where he could virtually dictate whatever price he wants for the generator data.

Neat, Philip Evans conceded. Clifford's really pulling out the stops on this one. He gets you dancing to his tune, and his man in Number Ten.

The worst thing is, I don't blame him, Julia said. I'd do exactly the same. She couldn't help the cool bleakness that her world view had been correct in the final analysis. Michael Harcourt wasn't any different to the rest. Nobody acted honourably any more, everybody had to have an angle.

Why do I bother? she mused.

Somebody's got to, Juliet.

But why me?

My heritage, girl, Event Horizon gives you the power.

So it's your fault, then, Grandpa?

If you like. You could always sell it, turn it over to someone else.

To people like Michael Harcourt and Clifford Jepson, you mean? No thank you, the world is in bad enough shape already.

That's your answer then, girl.

Yeah.

She gave Michael Harcourt her ice maiden smile, enjoying the way he shrank back. Even over the phone people feared her. Stupid, but occasionally useful. 'Very well, Minister, I'd be obliged if you would proceed with your unofficial liaison for me.

I'll ask Peter Cavendish to contact you for the details, when to submit the bid and so on.'

'Excellent, so we can expect a statement from Event Horizon on the cyber-precincts; that they will only be sited in Wales if it remains part of England?'

'Yes, as soon as it is appropriate to make such an announcement.'

'I'll contact Clifford Jepson right away.'

'Thank you, Minister. It's always a joy to learn exactly who I can depend on. I certainly shan't forget what you've done today.'

Michael Harcourt gave a slight bow. There was no trace of his smile left. 'Whatever I can, Julia, you know that. Always.'

'Goodbye, Minister.' She made it come out like a pronouncement. Rewarded by his flash of alarm just before his picture vanished.

She should never have allowed this situation to arise; it was her own fault; if she'd kept on top of the political scene, been decisive about Wales, the prospect of a leadership contest would never have arisen, allowing openings for people like Michael Harcourt. In fact she should never have let a Globecast puppet become Minister for Industry in the first place. Attention to detail; once she'd applied the maxim ruthlessly. But there had been so many distractions lately, worry building like a spring stormfront. Funny the NN cores hadn't caught on to Harcourt before. Could they be afflicted by Royan's absence? They reflected her thoughts after all, amplifying them a thousandfold. Did that mean the loss they felt was a thousand times the intensity of hers?

Arrange a conference with David Marchant, she said. *I know we've left it late for damage limitation, but let's see what he can do. We can't have Harcourt as PM.*

Who left it late? her grandfather queried drily.

Ignore him. We'll get on to it, NN core two said. *Victor called while you were talking to Michael Harcourt. He's found the space-plane and the pay load facility room which handled Kiley. I'm accessing their memory cores now.*

Fine. The patio's fuchsia flowers were bobbing in the light breeze, utterly beautiful, something God's own origami artist had folded together. Several bees had found them, crawling inside their ruff of petals. Julia watched them while she waited for the results of the memory core search, remembering other flowers on the bluff behind the bungalow. They were artificial, too, not gene-tailored, but placed there, organized. All of her environments were organized, Prior's Fen Atoll, Wilholm, the Mahone Bay island, resorts. She spent her time in bubbles of perfection.

A brief flash of alien flower blossoming in Wilholm's borders. She almost had it, the impression was vivid, crystalline. Then the idea was gone.

We've found him, NN core two said.

*

This time the burst of emotion was absent as Royan materialized in her mind. Adoration would have been too painful.

Hello, Snowy. I suppose it must be getting bad. Tracking down this package means I screwed up, right?

I don't know. I'm looking for an alien starship.

His image appeared thoughtful. *Do you think I can help you?*

You warned me about it.

Sorry, I don't have any memory of that. It must be in my future.

When were you recorded?

June.

What have you been doing since the probe returned?

Made progress. Once I confirmed Kiley had brought back some microbes I had three more processor nodes implanted.

Oh, Royan, she said despairingly. How many times had they argued over implants? He had wanted them so badly after he was recovered and showing an interest in helping her with Event Horizon. She grudgingly paid for four, two processors, two memory stores.

I can handle it, he said calmly. *I knew you'd complain about that.*

I'm not going to argue with a package, she said. *What happened to the microbes?*

I loaded my implants with biochemistry and genetics data, and started to map their chromosomes.

The package squirted an image of the microbe's genetic structure. It looked like a Christmas tree bauble, a softly gleaming metallic-purple sphere hanging in the null-space of the node universe. As it grew larger she saw the surface was mottled with minute rings, it began to resemble a twined ball of chain.

Familiarity overwhelmed her. *Dear Lord, that's the same genetic structure as the flower.*

What flower, Snowy?

You sent me a flower, an alien flower. It has toroidal chromosome-equivalents stacked in concentric shells. Just like that.

I don't understand. The flower came from a starship?

I . . . Yes, no, something. Greg said there was something behind the flower, waiting. He must have sensed the starship. What else could it be?

And I warned you about it?

That's right. She thought furiously, summoning up a logic matrix from her processor node. The question was simple enough, trying to formulate a correlation between the microbes Kiley returned and a starship, it couldn't be coincidence. Her processor reduced the question to equations, naked digits, feeding them into the matrix's channels. The construct wasn't the kind of prismatic graphics a terminal cube projected, more an instinctive awareness of maths, the true properties of numbers. Colourless, almost without form, she needed the bioware to analogize it for her.

The equations flowed through the matrix channels, fusing, interacting, offering solutions. *Could the microbes have been part of a waste dump?* she asked. *If an alien starship has been orbiting Jupiter for any respectable length of time, the entire ring and moon system would be contaminated by now.*

No, I don't believe that's your answer, Snowy.

Why not?

I managed to identify some of the toroid sequences. I'll show you.

She watched the gleaming purple sphere turn. The chain was beginning to unwind. It was like a magician's trick, pulling a line of handkerchiefs out of one hat, a line that just kept coming. The chain spiralled round her perception point, forming a near-solid cylindrical wall, etched with a black groove.

This is just the outer shell, Snowy.

Dear Lord. The cylinder stretched out above and below her, there were no ends in sight. *And you thought you could tame this?*

It's all a question of processing power. Everything is solvable given time. I taught you that, remember?

So what have you solved?

Below her, the colour began to change. Fans of pale light were shining into the cylinder, as if slots had appeared in the wall of chain letting in the dawn sun. They began to build, moving up towards her. When they were level, she could see it was lengths of the chain itself that were brightening. Individual toroids in the lengths glowed, becoming translucent; in some cases there were only twenty or thirty of them strung together, in others there were over a hundred. They were filled with alphanumeric codes.

It's funny, Royan said. *Only the outer shell was active.*

What do you mean?

The genes which dictate the microbe's structure are all contained in the outer shell. The rest, the inner shells, are inactive. It's all spacing. Waste toroids, nonsense.

They have no purpose?

The inner shells aren't part of the microbe, no. In that respect this genetic structure is similar to human DNA. Ninety per cent of our DNA is rubbish, filling up the spaces between the active genes, the ones that make us what we are, give us our hair colour and height and blood type, every characteristic. But our active genes are strung out all the way along the DNA helix. Whereas in the alien microbe, they're only on the outside. And I can't think why.

Is it important?

I'm not sure. It doesn't affect the microbe in any way.

What's the significance of the sequences you have managed to identify? Why do they show the microbe isn't part of a waste dump?

It's not impossible, Snowy, I didn't say that, just highly unlikely. You see, I've found the sequences for the mechanism which breaks down minerals in rock. The genetic mother-lode.

A lot of the glowing toroids reverted to purple, the majority of the ones that were left were situated in a broad band of the cylinder above her perception point. *These ones,* Royan said. *It's like an osmotic process, but dry. The microbe envelope can be made porous to selected molecules, and gradually they diffuse across. And these—* The glowing toroids began to blank out, others came on to replace them, scattered the whole length of the cylinder. *These control its thermal absorption mechanism. The microbe becomes functional in a temperature gradient, one side hotter than the other. Perfect energy utilization for a space environment.*

She observed in silence as the identified toroids flashed at her like a mad nightclub lighting stack. Royan reeling off their functions, proud and possessive.

The point is, he said, *it lives in a vacuum, it's perfectly adapted for surviving interstellar transit, then multiplying on the asteroids and interplanetary dust orbiting a star. It's not a faecal parasite, Snowy. It's not something you have on board a starship.*

I'll grant you that, but there has to be a connection. Could it live on the starship's hull?

Hey, yes. That might be it. On the ball, Snowy, as always.

The cylinder dissolved around her, leaving only the lustrous purple sphere.

So what was this package recorded for? she asked. *What are you here to tell me?*

That I've cracked it. It's all there, just like I said, Snowy. The potential. Think of it; a clump of cells you can smear on an asteroid, they'd grow, cover the whole rock in a photosynthetic membrane, and inside they'll be grazing on the ore, fruiting pods of solid minerals and metal. You could seed a hundred rocks, a thousand, turn the entire asteroid belt into a living mine. Then we'd launch a fleet of

Dragonflight's cargo ships to pick up the pods, bring them back to Earth. Enough wealth for everyone to live like a king. Imagine that, Snowy.

Yeah. Imagine that.

Cancel Integrity Monitored Link to Processor Node One. Squirt Package into NN Core Two.

The patio shimmered into place around her. Matthew's damp towel was lying in a heap on the York slabs, she picked it up and hung it over his chair.

Same as last time, she told the NN core. *Review the package memories; but this time I want that microbe's genetic structure compared to the flower's. They obviously come from the same planet. See if you can find out how close the relationship is.*

Right.

Cancel Channel to SelfCores.

Being free of the electronic voices and pictures in her mind was like an escape from prison. She could hear the children laughing and yelling, Brutus barking. When she looked round the stone pillar at the end of the patio she saw they were playing with one of the big colourful inflatable balls on the lawn. It looked like a grand game.

Her cybofax began to shrill.

23

Listoel had changed since the last time Greg had visited, seventeen years ago, investigating his first Event Horizon case. Now he sat behind the Titan's pilot watching their approach through the cockpit windscreen. They were due west of Ireland, flying subsonically, descending slowly. Below him, the ocean was completely green. It was a ragged patch over a hundred kilometres wide, its shape varying according to currents and wind. Today it looked like a bloated comet, with a tail which streamed away to the south, broadening and diluting to invisibility three hundred kilometres distant.

He could see dirty-yellow specks floating at the centre of the discolouration, neatly arranged in a square formation, each one a couple of kilometres from its neighbour. That made the specks huge. Lights were twinkling on all of them as the sun sank towards the horizon.

Philip Evans had started the mid-Atlantic anchorage twenty-five years ago, a refuge for his cyber-factory ships. The old man had put together a rag-tag fleet of converted oil-tankers and ore carriers, even an ex-US Marine Corps Harrier carrier, all floating with legal impunity in international waters during the entire PSP decade. The household gear they manufactured was smuggled into England, helping to kick-start the country's black market, worsening the economy, weakening the PSP.

Kombinates had been swift to recognize the potential of the

tax-free anchorage, and more cyber-factories began to arrive. Investment poured in; banks and finance houses were running scared of the political and physical turbulence on mainland Europe. For a few brief glory-years Listoel was a centre of innovation rivalling Silicon Valley and the Shanghai special economic zone.

The cyber-factory ships had been equipped with thermal generators, sucking up cool water from the bottom of the ocean trench and running it through a heat exchanger, self-powering, virtually eternal. There had been pirate miners too, Greg recalled, scooping up the ore nodules that lay on the ocean bed to supply the cyber-factories. Marine harvesters, exploiting the bloom of aquatic life which the nutrient-rich ocean-trench water fuelled. But the most memorable aspect had been the spaceport; a floating concrete runway for the hydrogen-fuelled Sanger space-planes which ferried 'ware chips down from orbital industry parks so they could be incorporated into the cyber-factories' gear.

At its peak, Listoel had had the industrial output of a small European nation, exporting its gear right across the globe.

That all changed after the fall of the PSP. Philip Evans brought his cyber-factories ashore, beginning England's indus-trial regeneration. A new generation of giga-conductor-powered spaceplanes turned the Sangers into museum pieces overnight. The global economy started to struggle out of the recession which had followed the Warming, and kombinates found they could virtually dictate their own taxes as governments vied for their investment, making exo-national manufacturing redun-dant.

Listoel would have been abandoned if Julia hadn't recognized the enormous demand for electricity which the resurgent land-based industries would exert on national grids. Solar-panel roofing could supply the domestic market, but it was woefully inadequate for the new cyber-precincts and arcologies. She also faced the problem of powering revitalized transport networks; Event Horizon was counting on its new giga-conductor being incorporated in planes and cars and trains and ships and lorries. They all needed electricity to run. But no politician, bought or otherwise, was going to permit her to burn oil and coal to generate it. Fusion remained hugely expensive. A return to nuclear fission was out; too many stations had been sited on the coast, overrun by the rising sea. Salvage and decontamination operations had cost governments a fortune at a time when it was a struggle just to feed people. A large proportion of Dragon-flight's revenue still came from the Rad Run, lifting vitrified blocks of salvaged radioactive waste into orbit where they were attached to solid-rocket boosters and fired into the Sun.

The Titan switched to VTOL mode, coming down for a landing on one of Listoel's platforms. It was a triangle, two hundred and fifty metres to a side, made up out of concrete flotation sections bolted together. There were three ocean ther-mal generator buildings made out of pearl-white composite running along each side; the centre was clotted with an irregular collection of hangars, offices, maintenance sheds, and crew quarters, the blue rectangle of a swimming-pool. Nine large discharge pipes were venting brown water into the Atlantic from each generator building; there were other pipes, Greg knew, unseen, dangling kilometres below the platform, pumping up the icy water of the trench to cool the generator's working fluid.

A non-polluting and totally renewable energy source, for as long as the sun kept shining. Listoel supplied gigawatts of cheap electricity to England and mainland Europe via high-temperature superconductor cables laid across the ocean floor.

But despite its legitimate power industry, Listoel was still outside the jurisdiction of national governments. Greg knew one of the platforms housed the production line for Julia's electron-compression warheads. Another, or the same one, was Victor's principal hardline base. The whole anchorage was heavily defended; he'd seen the Typhoons flying escort on the two crash-team Titans, there were definitely null psychics shielding it. Rumour said there were submarines and strategic defence lasers, secret weapon labs, prisons, bullion vaults. He'd

343

laughed when he'd heard that on a tabloid newscast. Maybe he shouldn't have. The crash team was so effectively organized – Titans, Typhoons, super-grade armour and weapons, all of them on permanent stand-by. If Julia and Victor went to that much trouble . . .

The Titan settled easily on its undercarriage, and a section of wall on the generator building ahead split open. They began to taxi forwards.

Melvyn Ambler, the crash team's captain, tapped Greg on the shoulder. He had removed his muscle-armour suit during the flight, dressing in olive-green one-piece fatigues with Event Horizon's logo on his breast pocket. 'The platform's clinic has been alerted, we're all ready for you, sir.'

'Fine, thank you. How are Fielder and Whitehurst?'

'The medics gave the girl a second anaesthetic for her fingers and some treatment for the swelling. She's exhausted, but physically she's in good shape, nothing the clinic can't fix up. The boy is still in shock from the death of his father.'

Greg nodded, he'd let Fabian think Jason Whitehurst had died as the airship crashed, it was a lot kinder than knowing the truth. 'And what about Suzi?'

Melvyn Ambler couldn't quite keep his face straight. 'All right, though the doctor says her knee's going to need some work. She's been telling us about how tough it all was in the old days.'

Greg let out a small groan. 'Back when hardliners were real hardliners?'

'Yes, sir.'

'The name's Greg, thanks.' Sir reminded him of the Army.

'Right.'

Greg stood up slowly, pleased to find his neurohormone hangover had run its course. He thanked the pilot and followed Melvyn Ambler back through the Titan's fuselage. Charlotte Fielder was being helped down the ramp, she was wrapped up in a bright orange padded suit, as if she was wearing a polar sleeping bag. Fabian Whitehurst was walking ahead of her, his eyes dead to the world.

Greg watched Suzi being lifted into a wheelchair by a couple of the crash team. Her teeth were gritted.

'Just a flesh wound?' Greg asked innocently.

'Bollocks!' she shouted back, then shrugged. 'I landed wrong back there in the airship.'

'Never mind, Julia will pay for a new knee, no doubt.'

Suzi grinned. 'You finished with me for today? I've got me a date with good old Leol Reiger.'

'I think you'd better put that off for a day or two.'

'Come on, Greg, we've got the Fielder girl.'

'Yeah, and it's where she's going to lead Julia to that worries me, no messing.'

'Right. Suppose I'd better stick around, then. But, Greg, it's not going to be for ever.'

The generator building served as a hangar for several Typhoon fighters as well as three Titans. Greg saw a Pegasus parked at the far end as he came down the loading ramp. Julia and Victor were waiting for him, along with a large blond-haired man wearing a crumpled suit jacket.

Julia put her arms round him and rested her head on his shoulder. 'I didn't know it was going to finish up like this, Greg.'

'That's OK.' He stroked the long hair down her back. 'Tell you, I'm just sorry about Rachel and the other three.'

Julia nodded silently, giving him a lonely smile. 'Rachel's been with me for twenty years. I know her father and her brother. They were all so proud she was doing well for herself. Personal assistant to the mighty Julia Evans. Now I've got to tell them she's dead. She was out of hardlining, Greg. Clean away, then I made her go back.'

'This wasn't hardlining. Not really. It was just crazy. There was no need for it, the Pegasus wasn't armed.'

'We really have made a mess of today, haven't we?'

'I got you Charlotte Fielder. Nothing that important ever comes cheap.'

'Yes. Well, that girl had better bloody well start telling me what I want to know.'

'Tomorrow,' Greg said. Even without his espersense he could tell Julia was feeling the strain, and that was with all the protection the NN cores threw around her. Chasing after Fielder wasn't all this deal involved by the look of it. 'She's had a rough time of it this afternoon. So's young Fabian, come to that.'

Julia stepped away from him. 'Yeah, I know, I was there.'

'So you were.' Greg looked at Victor. 'Did Leol Reiger survive?'

'We don't know. We've been monitoring the air-sea rescue traffic. The Nigerian coast guard have picked up quite a few of the *Colonel Maitland*'s crew from their escape pods. I haven't got a list yet, my Lagos office will squirt one over in a couple of hours.'

'What about Baronski?'

'Snuffed, along with the girl who was with him. There were three people killed when Reiger's tekmercs opened fire on you in the Prezda well, another thirty-eight injured, seven seriously. I've never known anyone like this Reiger; he's a mad dog, absolute mad dog. I've been in touch with the Tricheni security chief, that's the kombinate which owns the Prezda, we're launching a joint search-and-destroy deal.'

The big man standing behind Victor was looking more and more uncomfortable.

'Good,' Greg said, surprised by his own anger. 'Did you find out who's behind Reiger?'

'Yes,' Victor said. 'We've got quite a bit to tell you about that.'

*

The conference room had a broad silvered window looking out over the rest of the oceanic energy field. It showed the other generator platforms as oblong ochre silhouettes on the darkening horizon, navigation lights winking steadily.

He sat with Julia, Victor and Rick Parnell at one end of a long black composite table, listening to Victor give a review of Royan's Kiley probe, and the waiting personality packages.

The office's three teleconference flatscreens were on, plugging the three NN cores into the discussion, two showing images of Julia, while Philip Evans filled the third. Julia's grandfather had synthesized an image of himself at fifty, a thin face with a healthy tan and silver hair.

Greg could see that Rick Parnell was having trouble coping with the NN cores, glancing up at the screens then back down at the table. The blunt hardline talk about Leol Reiger wasn't helping to settle him either. He wasn't quite out of his depth, but he was certainly having his world-view shaken today.

'If Clifford Jepson already has the data on the nuclear force generator, why would he want to find Royan?' Greg asked after Julia finished telling him about the two partnership offers she'd received. 'Especially, why go to this much trouble to find Royan? I'd say hiring Leol Reiger was almost an act of desperation.'

'To make sure Royan doesn't plug me into the alien, and do a deal direct. Clifford would be left with nothing then, Globecast can't develop the nuclear force generator by itself.'

'But Globecast doesn't have a monopoly on the generator data,' Greg said. 'Mutizen's offering you the same deal.'

Julia looked up at the screens, arching an eyebrow.

'Buggered if I know, girl,' Philip Evans grunted.

'It is odd,' Julia's NN core one image agreed.

Greg turned to Rick. 'Are we sure Royan's alien is the source of the atomic structuring technology?'

'No idea,' said the SETI director. 'It's conceivable that the microbes could live on the outside of a starship, that they were brought here rather than drifted across interstellar space. But that would mean the alien has been here a long time; a couple of centuries before the Matoyaii probe was launched, at least.

347

Remember, we've now inspected just two rocks out of all the millions which make up Jupiter's ring, and both of them had microbe colonies. No matter how vigorous they are, it would take a long time to spread that far.'

'Is that significant?' Victor asked.

'I think it must be,' Rick said. 'If the aliens have been here, been watching us for so long, why make contact now?'

'Because we discovered them,' Julia said.

'No, we didn't,' Rick said. 'Without all this hardline chasing around and the appearance of atomic structuring technology we would have cheerfully believed the microbes were interstellar travellers. There is nothing to make us suspect they came on a starship. And in any case, any aliens with starship-level technology could quite easily have tampered with Matoyaii. One very simple robot probe operating alone six hundred million kilometres from mission control, *we* have the technology to fool it. If there is a starship, then we were deliberately allowed to know about the microbes. But don't ask me why.'

'I think we have to assume Royan's alien is the source,' Victor said. 'There's just too much interest being shown in his whereabouts, by too many people, for any other conclusion.'

'No messing,' Greg muttered. He took a salmon sandwich from a plate on the table, surprised at how hungry he was. 'Have you come up with a proper profile on that maid, Nia Korovilla?'

'Not a thing,' Julia's NN core image said. 'The only data we have on her is the file my personality package squirted out of the *Colonel Maitland*'s 'ware. You saw it, it tells us very little.'

Greg finished the sandwich, and started on another. There was a jumble of impressions cluttering up his mind, all the knowledge he'd picked up today. There was no order to it, not yet. But there could be. He was sure of that. Intuition. Something would link it all together, a key, a connecting factor, some word or phrase. It was just a question of looking at it from the right angle, afterwards it would be obvious. Of course, he could force it, use the gland. One of the Mindstar psychologists involved with his training had called his intuition a foresight equal to everyone else's hindsight.

He swallowed the last of the salmon sandwiches, and started on the beef ones. It was almost completely dark outside now, the platforms had switched on floodlights to illuminate their super-structure. 'What about the observation team in the Prezda well?' he asked.

'I'm afraid you and Suzi are the only ones who saw them,' Victor said. 'Certainly Prezda security has no knowledge of them.'

'So we've no idea who this third party is?'

'None,' Victor agreed.

'Someone who can afford to keep a sleeper on the *Colonel Maitland* for eight years,' Greg observed pensively.

'Expensive,' Victor said. 'I wonder if her controller was behind the observers in the Prezda?'

'If it wasn't, then there's a fourth organization involved,' Greg said.

'Too many. You think Korovilla was tied in with the Prezda observers rather than Reiger and Jepson?'

'I would say yes,' Julia said. 'She was anxious to avoid contact with Reiger's tekmerc squad.'

'So who was she working for?' Greg asked.

'The organization that took the sample from the flower?' Julia suggested.

'Good point,' Greg said. 'It could be easily the same organ-ization. But then where does Jason Whitehurst fit in? He was obviously acting independently. Yet he knew how valuable Fielder was, that she was linked with atomic structuring, but not the nature of that link. He certainly hadn't heard about the alien. So how did he find out she was valuable?'

'Jesus!' The word came out like a bark from Rick. He looked round the table, his neck jerking mechanically. 'I'm sorry, but you people . . . You're making it all so complicated. Who's this bloke working for, these two are plugged in together, where does she fit in? It doesn't matter! There's an alien here, in our own solar system, making contact. God knows, it's a strange kind of contact, but it wants to talk to us. Just ask this Fielder girl where Royan is, and go. Where's the problem?'

'Atta, boy,' Philip Evans said. 'You tell 'em.'

Julia at the table, and the Julias on the screens all scowled together. 'Behave, Grandpa,' they chorused.

Philip Evans rolled his synthesized eyes.

Greg looked at Rick, knowing exactly how he felt. Itching to do something positive, to see some action. He'd been like that himself when he joined the Army. Physical got everything solved, and you could see it happening. That particular fallacy took a long time and a lot of grief to unlearn. 'It's like this,' he said sympathetically. 'Charlotte Fielder's in a bad way. She's a twenty-three-year-old girl who's known nothing but the good life for the last five years. All that got shattered today; she's been threatened, chased, shot at, had her fingers broken, seen her patron killed, and found out someone's snuffed her sponsor. Right now she just wants to curl up into a ball and shut out the outside world. If I start interrogating her now, she isn't going to co-operate, her mind will close up like a night-time flower. I'll miss things; good as I am, I'm not infallible. But if we wait until tomorrow, she'll have started to bounce back. She'll want to help, she'll want revenge on whoever terrorized her, she'll open right up to us. And when that happens, I need to know the right questions to ask her.'

'Listen to him, Rick,' Philip Evans said. 'He knows more about how people's minds work than a pub full of shrinks.'

Julia gave Greg an impish glance. 'And the fact that she's devastatingly beautiful has nothing at all to do with wanting to go easy on her.'

Greg flashed her a feline smile, and snatched another sand-wich. Victor was chuckling.

The tight fabric of Rick's jacket rippled as he offered a shrug. 'Sorry, I'm not used to this.'

'We need to go through it, Rick,' Julia said. 'I've got to have the complete picture before I decide what responses to initiate. And right now there are too many unknowns involved. There will be a common thread linking these faceless dealers. If we can correlate the data we've amassed so far we should be able to find it.'

Greg smiled inwardly. Julia was doing the same thing as him. Tearing into the problem from all sides until she came up with a solution. The only difference was that she used the logic her nodes supplied, he used intuition.

He ordered a tiny secretion from his gland, not enough for an espersense effusion, but just animating his grey cells, tweaking them above the ordinary. A dreamy calmness settled round him, almost a physical veil, dimming the conference room, muting the voices. He let the images of the day slipstream through his mind. There were faces and places, vaporous collages. An overwhelming sense of certainty rose.

'Russia,' he said. 'Russia is the connection.'

'How?' Julia asked.

'Tell you, intuition is always better than logic.' He cancelled the gland secretion.

'Greg!' she snapped.

'Spit it out, boy,' Philip Evans said.

'Nia Korovilla and Dmitri Baronski.'

Victor clicked his fingers. 'Bloody hell, they're both Russian *émigrés.*'

'No messing,' Greg swung his chair round to face the three teleconference screens. 'Run a search program,' he told the NN cores. 'Every profile you've assembled today, every person, place, and company involved. I want to know every and any link they have with Russia, however tenuous.'

'We're on it,' Julia's NN core two image said. She and Philip Evans froze.

'Thank you, Greg,' Julia said.

'I want Royan back too.'

A horizontal flicker line ran down the teleconference screens. The images returned to life. 'Greg was right. There are two more references, possibly three.'

'Go ahead,' Julia said.

'Thirty-two per cent of the Mutizen kombinate is owned by Moscow's Narodny Bank. And nearly twenty-five per cent of Jason Whitehurst's trade is with the East Europe Federation, half of that with Russia itself.'

'And the third connection?' Victor asked.

'It is somewhat more speculative, but the *Colonel Maitland* had originally filed a flight plan from Monaco to Odessa, it was changed the night Charlotte Fielder was lifted from the principality. Odessa is in Ukraine, also part of the East Europe Federation.'

'That fits,' Greg said. 'I should have thought of that one myself. Baronski mentioned it.'

'Fits how, exactly?' Julia asked.

'Tell you, we're up against a premier-grade Russian dealer here, right?'

'Yes.'

'OK, so he finds out about the Fielder girl somehow, that's she's a courier of some kind; so he takes a sample of the flower and discovers it's extraterrestrial. Assume Jason Whitehurst does business with him – God knows the kind of trading Jason does is complicated enough to need dodgy contacts – he owes the dealer a few favours. The dealer tells Jason Whitehurst to lift Charlotte Fielder from Monaco after she's completed the delivery to you, and bring her to Odessa where he can take over. That's where Baronski thought she was going, he arranged it, he was the go-between. But then Jason Whitehurst realizes how big a deal this is, and decides to play his own game. So he puts Charlotte Fielder up for sale. That's why there were watchers in the Prezda; our Russian dealer didn't know where she was either. And Baronski was the obvious link, we all wound up going to him. If there was anybody who knew where she was, it was going to be him. A pimp always keeps track of his girls.'

'Sounds feasible,' Victor said.

'What about Mutizen?' Julia asked.

'Dunno. Maybe that's where our Russian dealer found out about the alien.'

'Could be,' she said.

'Nia Korovilla still bothers me,' Victor said. 'Eight years is a hell of a long time in the hardline game. Any deal over a year is a long time for us.'

'You think she was a government intelligence agency sleeper?' Greg asked.

'Bloody Reds,' Philip Evans said. 'Never did trust the little buggers. Reagan was quite right.'

'Oh, Grandpa, don't be so paranoid; Russia doesn't even have a strong Socialist party in parliament any more, let alone represent a military threat. If anything they're more entrepreneurial than us these days.'

'This is what happens when you have thought routines that are formulated and frozen in the twentieth century,' Julia's NN core two image remarked, amused.

'Ha bloody ha, girl. Maybe they're not Commies, but they're still clannish, still hold the ideal of the Motherland close to their hearts. How far do you think they'd go to secure atomic structuring technology for themselves, eh? Every asset would be thrown in, corporate and state. Eight-year sleepers included.'

Julia sucked in a deep breath, obviously undecided. She looked at Greg. 'Well?'

'It could go either way,' Greg said. 'It's all down to Jason Whitehurst's trading. Somebody in Russia wanted to keep an eye on him. What did he export?'

'Gold, silver, and timber were the main cargoes from the East Europe Federation, along with some bulk chemicals, and ores,' Julia's NN core one image said. 'He tended to trade them for industrial cybernetics.'

'Who supplied the exports?'

'There are fifteen mining and chemical companies listed as his main suppliers, three in Moscow, two in Odessa, the rest scattered through the Federation republics. But he didn't limit himself to those. You know Jason, any cargo; and our lists will hardly be complete. I doubt there are official records of half of his transactions.'

Greg pulled his cybofax out of his jacket pocket. 'Squirt me a list of the companies, and as much financial profile as you've got on them, please.'

The wafer's screen lit, and he began to scan through the data.

'Cross-index the export companies with Mutizen,' Julia told the NN cores. 'See if they supply Mutizen with any raw materials.'

'Isn't the Narodny Bank state owned?' Greg asked.

Julia gave a tiny nod. 'Yes. After the USSR was dismantled, their industries went private, but the Russian parliament kept control of the Narodny. It was used like the Japanese used their MITI after World War II, providing money for targeted industries, unofficial subsidies really. It's been quite successful, too, done wonders for their car and heavy plant manufacturers.'

'You guessed that right,' Julia's NN core two image said. 'Twelve of those export companies provide material to Mutizen.'

Julia absorbed the news silently. But she looked worried, Greg thought.

'Could this hypothetical dealer be the Russian government itself?' she asked.

'It's a possibility,' Greg conceded.

'I don't have many assets in Russia,' Victor said. 'It would take a while to activate them and find out what's going down.'

'I still can't see where Mutizen fits in,' Julia said. 'Whoever he, she, or it is, the Russian dealer knew about the alien before me, yet Mutizen was the first to inform me about atomic structuring. By rights, they should have done everything they could to keep the knowledge from me.'

'Loose ends,' Greg said, half to himself. 'We still don't know enough about the Russian dealer to figure out what kind of stunt he's trying to pull.'

'He's trying to keep Event Horizon from developing a nuclear force generator,' Julia said. 'It's bloody obvious.'

'Maybe,' Greg said. 'But he's going about it in a very strange way, actually making you aware of its existence in the first place. We know he's used Mutizen to make you an offer. Would you take it up? I mean, does it have to be Clifford Jepson you take as a partner?'

'Certainly not.'

'OK, I might be able to help clear the air a little here. There's someone I know, a military man; I can ask him if it is the Russian government that's behind all this. If it is them, then maybe he can negotiate a deal for you, find out what it'll take to get them off your back. Don't forget, they must be pretty desperate for atomic structuring technology. We're close to Royan, now, that means you stand a good chance of acquiring the generator data without bringing anyone else in on it. If that happens, there will be three teams working on it, Clifford Jepson and his partner, Mutizen and their partner, and Event Horizon by itself. A straight race to turn those bytes into working hardware and slap down the patent. You with all your resources stand a pretty good chance of winning it anyway, but if you can arrange a combination with Mutizen and obtain the backing of the English and Russian governments on your own terms, you'll have Clifford Jepson in a box, and no messing.'

Julia clasped her hands, and rested her chin on the whitened knuckles. 'This military friend of yours, will he tell you the truth?'

'He'll be honest with me; either tell me, or say he can't talk about it. He won't lie. If he won't talk, you'll have to use the English Foreign Office to find out what's going on in Russia.'

'I'd be better off using Associated Press,' she muttered.

'But what about the alien?' Rick asked. 'If you're going to spend tomorrow chasing after someone in Russia, when can we go after it? I mean, once we've met it, you can just buy a nuclear force generator blueprint from it and save all that research and development money.'

'The lad's got a point there, Juliet,' Philip Evans said. 'If this alien's parcelling out data you could save yourself a tidy packet.'

'Unless the alien files a patent for itself,' Julia said.

'Interesting legal question,' Julia's NN core two image said. 'Would the alien be legally able to file a patent?'

'And what does it want our money for anyway?' Victor chipped in. 'Repairs? Set up a base in the solar system? What? You're the expert, Rick.'

'Jesus.' Rick's fists clenched and unclenched. 'I don't know. If we just go and *ask* it—'

'I won't be more than a couple of hours tomorrow,' Greg said smoothly. 'I'll go first thing, and after that we'll find out where Charlotte Fielder was given the flower.'

24

Greg watched the coast of Greenland sliding across the flatscreen on the cabin's forward bulkhead. A stark slate-grey line of rocky cliffs with grimy water churning against their base. Away to the north a fast-flowing river was spurting into the sea, spitting out irregular lumps of translucent white ice.

The Pegasus could easily have been the same one that he'd been using yesterday, the cabin had the same type of seats, same colour scheme, same tasteless air, the Event Horizon logo cut into each of the crystal tumblers behind the rose-wood bar. Except today there was only Melvyn Ambler sitting quietly beside him instead of Malcolm Ramkartra and Pearse Solomons.

He thought he'd learnt to deal with the memories of the dead. There had been enough in Turkey, and on Peterborough's chthonic streets. Hold on to the names, treat them with respect, and remember they'd be cheering you on.

He must have been out of practice, that or he'd softened down the years. The Pegasus had taken twelve minutes to reach Greenland from Listoel, and each lonely one had been spent thinking about the two security hardliners and Rachel. A sudden flare of light and heat swelling around them, penetrating the cabin. Maybe not even that. It had been very fast.

The sun hadn't risen yet, which made the dark undulating plains they were flying over seem even more forbidding, a barren expanse of grit and boulders, slicked with dew, features blurring as they lost height.

He couldn't work up any real enthusiasm about the meeting. It would be nice to see Vassili again, but talking about Event Horizon and the alien would sour the reunion.

The handset on Greg's armrest chimed. He picked it up.

'We've just lost our escort,' Catherine Rushton said.

Catherine Rushton was the pilot. The first thing he'd done after coming through the belly hatch was go into the cockpit to meet her. It was an overreaction verging on the childish, but it assuaged him, identifying her as a person.

'We're safe then, are we?' he asked with a hint of mordancy. Three Typhoon air-superiority fighters had escorted them from Listoel. It looked like he wasn't the only one overreacting this morning. Julia had been worried about the kind of weapons which Clifford Jepson could supply to Leol Reiger; an arms merchant and a tekmerc was a real bastard of a combination.

'Yes,' she answered. 'The Russian zone Air Defence Regiment command is tracking us. We'll be landing at Nova Kirov in two minutes.'

'Fine.' He pulled his leather jacket off an empty seat.

The flatscreen was showing a tract of emerald-green land below, marked off into square fields by wire fencing. Even with the high vantage point and anaemic light he could tell the vegetation wasn't grass, too low, too uniform, almost like a golf course fairway. And it was lumpy; whatever the plant was, it flowed over boulders and rock outcrops like a film of liquid. There were sheep grazing on it, though.

*

Nova Kirov was the Wild West reinvented for the twenty-first century, a frontier town in aluminium and pearl-white composite. There were no trees anywhere, Greg noticed. No timber for houses and barns. These pioneers weren't as independent as the ones who'd hit the Oregon trail two hundred years earlier. To set up a homestead in Greenland you either needed to be rich, or have rich sponsors.

The town was spread out over a kilometre along the rocky southern bank of a white-water river. He could see big lumps of glass-smooth ice bobbing about amid the spray and foam. A broad single-span bridge connected the town with a dirt road that ran parallel with the north bank.

There was a large patch of ground on the east of the town which remained free of the vegetation mat. Five An-995 subsonic heavylift cargo planes were parked on it, fat cylindrical bodies with a rear wing and canard configuration, all of them in blue and white Air Russia colours. A long two-storey office block sat on one side of the makeshift airport. Satellite dishes were scattered along its solar collector roof, pointing south; a tall microwave antenna tower stood at one end, an array of horns covering the surrounding countryside.

The Pegasus curved round the town and slid over the An-995s to land close to the office block. Greg caught sight of a small reception committee standing waiting. Dull grey dust swirled up, obscuring the camera image.

The belly hatch opened, and Melvyn Ambler stood up, zipping his blue and red check woollen jacket up to his neck.

'General Kamoskin and I will probably have a private talk in his office,' Greg said. 'You'll have to stay outside, OK?'

'Sure thing,' the hardline captain said easily.

Greg skipped lightly down the metal stairs. Powdery grey sand crunched below his desert boots. It was cool outside, a crisp clean humidity that came from morning ground frosts. Greg relished it for the sheer novelty value. His breath was turning to thin white vapour.

One day he'd have to bring the kids here, give them just a taste of the wind from ages past, how the world used to be. It would be terrible for them never to know.

General Vassili Kamoskin was standing at the front of the five-man reception committee, beaming broadly, his arms thrown wide. He was a solid stereotypical Russian, black hair receding from his temples, full face, thick neck. He wore his Russian Army uniform, dark green with scarlet epaulettes, knife-edge creases, five bands of medal ribbons. And they weren't show decorations, Greg knew, Vassili had earned them. Two of them in Turkey where they had served together.

He stepped into a bear hug, Vassili laughing in his ear. 'Gregory, as always it is too long. How is Eleanor?'

Greg released him. Vassili's hair was thinner than he remembered. It must have been five years since he'd visited Hambleton, just before Richy was born. They'd kept in touch because the kind of friendships formed in combat weren't the ones you could let go. There was too much pain and effort invested. 'Expecting again,' Greg said.

Vassili clapped him delightedly on the shoulder. 'You never sent word,' he accused. 'How many is that now?'

'This'll be the fifth.'

'You devil, you. Do you give lessons?'

'How's Natalia keeping?'

'Bah,' Vassili waved a hand dismissively towards the town. 'She's an Army wife, she doesn't complain. Sometimes I think she should.'

Greg looked at Nova Kirov. There was a cluster of warehouses behind the airport office block, tractors were already moving round them, tugging flat-bed trailers loaded with bales of wool. The buildings of the town proper were mostly single storey, spaced well apart, made up from standardized panels clipped on to a simple framework. An aluminium church stood by itself on a plateau above the river. Streets were wheel-rutted blue-grey mud. There were a couple of dogs running about.

Even without his espersense engaged, Greg could detect the buzz of optimism running through the place. The settlement was creating its own future, that always inspired.

'Looks pretty good to me,' he said.

'Gregory,' Vassili shoved out his arms theatrically. 'It's a retirement posting. They pushed me out to grass, the bastards.'

'Don't tell me you'd prefer to be shuffling bytes in Moscow?'

Vassili grunted. 'No. No you're right at that, Gregory. I have a responsibility here, some independence from our glorious knowledgeable Marshals. I'd never get the Defence Minister post anyway, I lack the politics. So here I am, tsar of sixty thousand square kilometres, even if three-fifths of it is still under the ice.'

The glacier was visible on the western horizon, a pristine white line disrupting the fusion of land and sky. It was beginning to shoot out orange-pink reflections of the rising sun. The image had a dream clarity about it. Greg stared, fascinated.

'Does it keep you busy, Vassili?' he asked.

'Bah, we're here to guarantee the zemstvo's boundaries until it's granted full independence by the UN. We've got the Indian zone to the north, and the French to the south. I don't think either of them is going to invade us, do you, Gregory?'

'No.'

'All we are is a glorified police force, saving the zemstvo from paying for their own. Not that the colonists could afford a police force, anyway. My troops spend their evenings stopping fights between drunks. That's all the farmers do, Gregory, plant their gene-tailored arable moss over this desolation during the day, and drink at night. They come out here with such high hopes, stars in their eyes. Then they see the true reality of Greenland. A desert of grubby shingle, and rivers of sterile water colder than yeti's blood. This land they have bought will take a century to transform into the garden they were promised. They expected freedom, and they've found they've indentured their children. Of course they drink, but I forgive them for it. What else can I do?'

'Dreams are never cheap, Vassili.'

'I know. But it saddens me to see so much heartache. They are so naïve. Never trust a man with stars in his eyes, Gregory. Never.'

Greg was still facing the distant glacier. There was a cool wind gusting off it, ruffling his hair. The air was so clear.

He knew Event Horizon had funded a couple of settlements

in the English zone. But Julia never mentioned them being a problem. Perhaps her smallholders had been equipped with drone planters. She did favour technological solutions to everything. But then colonizing Greenland was a very technical proposition. The idea behind the UN opening it up to settlers in the wake of the retreating ice was to turn it into a giant arable country. There was no ecology that would be destroyed by gene-tailored crops, no indigenous species to be usurped. Even the soil was devoid of bacteria. The farmers could use intensive cultivation techniques over every square metre with impunity.

He rubbed his arms. 'It's cold here. I'd forgotten what real mountain air could be like.'

'You English are wimps. It's too hot, it's too cold, it's too wet. Never satisfied.'

'Yeah, right,' Greg turned back to Vassili. 'At least we're allowed to complain.'

Vassili made a farting sound. 'Now we've found the glories of democracy, when do Russians ever do anything else?'

Greg glanced at the four young officers standing blank-faced behind Vassili. 'I need to talk with you, Vassili.'

'Bah, one phone call telling me you're coming. Then another from the Defence Ministry itself telling me to be vigilant this morning, there are to be no unaccountable accidents in my airspace. So I ask myself, all this for my old orange farmer friend?'

'I'm not farming right now. It's the middle of the bloody picking season, and I've been dragged away.'

'They never leave us alone, do they, Gregory?' Vassili said soberly.

'This isn't the Army, the English government, Vassili. I'm doing this for another friend of mine.'

Vassili's bushy eyebrows rose. 'This must be a tremendous friendship you have.'

Greg jerked a thumb back at the Pegasus. 'Julia Evans, the owner of Event Horizon.'

'The Queen of Peterborough herself? What circles we two poor footsore soldiers move in these days, Gregory. Come then, come and tell me how a simple Russian general can be of help to the richest woman in the world.'

*

Vassili's office was on the second floor of the airport building, taking up the entire western end, which gave him three glass walls looking out over Nova Kirov, the embryonic farms, and the glacier. There was a desk and high-back chairs, several bookcases, a long table for staff officer briefings. All the furniture was made from hard Siberian pine, with simple geometric carvings; it was old looking, cracked and worn, polished a thousand times. A battered samovar bubbled away on a table in the corner, its charcoal glowing rose-gold, filling the air with wisps of arid smoke. Polished artillery shells were lined up on bookcases and the desk. One wall had a row of framed pictures, beribboned generals Greg didn't recognize, Yeltsin, Defence Minister Evgeniy Schitov. One frame held a metre length of helicopter blade; there was a chunk missing, as though some animal had taken a bite out of it. It was from a Mi-24 Hind K. Greg had been in it, liaising with Vassili's troops, when it was hit by AA fire from the Jihad Legion. Thankfully, the pilot's autorotation technique had been flawless.

Vassili poured two cups of tea from his samovar as Greg sat at the long table. The tap squeaked each time he turned it. 'It's been in my family since before the Bolshevik Revolution,' he explained. 'I get the Air Force boys to fly my charcoal in. A general has some privileges.' He put the cup down in front of Greg. 'Have you cut yourself shaving, Gregory?'

Greg's hand went to the scar by his eye. The dermal seal membrane had peeled off during the night, but the new flesh was pink and tender. 'Did you hear about the *Colonel Maitland* crash?'

Vassili sat opposite him, frowning. 'The airship? Certainly, it was on the news channels last night. It caught fire somewhere over the Atlantic. Most of the crew got out. You were on board?'

'Yeah. Tell you, it didn't catch fire by accident.'

'Gregory, my friend, you are too old and too slow to be thinking of combat. Leave it to the stalwarts like that fine young man accompanying you. Please.'

'Christ, don't you start.'

Vassili chuckled, and blew on the top of his cup. 'So, what is it that Julia Evans wishes to know?'

'Is the Russian government mounting a covert deal against Event Horizon? And if so, she'd like to negotiate a peaceful solution.'

Vassili put his cup down without drinking any of the tea. 'Are you serious?'

'Yeah.' Greg didn't like the way Vassili was looking at him, almost hurt. He hadn't liked asking, either. Maybe coming here hadn't been such a good idea.

'You seriously think my government would do such a thing?'

'I don't think you would, Vassili. But someone inside the republic is going balls out against her. I need to know who.'

'Tell me, Gregory. Start at the beginning, and tell me all of it.'

Greg took a sip of tea, and started to talk.

Vassili's rounded face was thoughtful when he finished. 'No, it is not the Russian government that is doing this,' he said. 'I would know. I have been informed of this atomic structuring science. This Clifford Jepson you talk of approached Mikoyan two days ago with his development sharing proposition. Naturally as good Russians, Mikoyan informed the Defence Ministry. You'll see that I'm telling the truth, Gregory.'

Greg pushed his empty cup over the table to Vassili, meeting the general's eyes. 'I don't need to use my gland on you, Vassili.'

'Bah, so morbid and serious you sound, Gregory. I have been of some help to you, have I not? Would you not do the same for me?'

'You have my address, and I'm on the phone. I can't offer you air defence cover, though.'

Vassili slapped the table, laughing. 'So, we now need to know who is dragging my country's good name through the mud. Yes?'

'Yeah.' He thought for a moment. 'You said it was Mikoyan who informed your government. Didn't Mutizen approach the Russian Defence Ministry with its generator data?'

'No. I did not realize we owned a kombinate.'

'Only thirty-two per cent. But, yeah, it's as good as outright ownership.'

'If the government has a controlling stake, they would have made sure the generator data was used to their advantage. It would never be offered to Event Horizon.' Vassili stood up and took the cups back to the samovar. 'I don't like this, Gregory. The briefing officer they sent over explained some of the possible defence applications of atomic structuring. There will be a terrible scramble to acquire it. All or nothing, Gregory. What country could afford to be without it? A shield which can protect whole cities against nuclear weapons and electron compression warheads. The citizens of the world would demand nothing less from their leaders. And I would venture that offensive capabilities will soon follow. People are so very good at that kind of thing. And now you tell me there are unknown players on the field seeking a monopoly. No, this is not good, and not just for Julia Evans.'

Greg ran a hand across his forehead. Last night he had been too exhausted to give atomic structuring much thought. But Vassili's comments were opening his mind up to possibilities, few of them good. 'You think it'll mean a new arms race?'

Vassili refilled the cups and returned to the table. 'Arms race, economic upheaval.' He gave Greg a sad smile. 'And just when we were getting over the worse of the Warming.'

'Yeah. England's a good place to live in again, Vassili. You wouldn't know it was the same country that suffered under the PSP.'

'Do you have the names of the Russian export companies Jason Whitehurst was trading with?'

'Sure.' Greg pulled his cybofax out, and called up the data. He handed it over to Vassili. 'Mean anything to you?'

'Perhaps.' Vassili walked over to his desk and activated his terminal. Greg saw him squirt the export companies' profiles into the key.

'I have a scrambled link with the military intelligence cores in Moscow,' Vassili said. 'And through that I can access the Federal Crime Directorate memory cores. This won't take a minute.' He sat behind the desk.

The shiny artillery shells prevented Greg from seeing what data was in the cubes. He drank some tea.

Vassili suddenly let out a contemptuous grunt.

'What?' Greg asked.

'I'm surprised at you, Gregory. Mindstar gave you intelligence data-correlation training, did they not?'

'Three months of lectures and exercises, yeah. Why?'

'Shame on you, then. Do you not recognize that you are in familiar territory with this so-called Russian dealer? Have you no sense of *déjà vu*?'

'Familiar, how?'

'Private organizations that form a powerful national cartel, influencing government departments. Who do you know that duplicates that pattern, Gregory?'

'Shit. Julia. Do you mean we're up against the Russian equivalent of Julia Evans?'

Vassili sighed, and switched off his terminal. 'No, Gregory. Russia envies Julia Evans and Event Horizon. How could we not? A woman who devotes her wealth and power to nurturing her own country. Who does not abuse her position. An honourable person. No, Gregory, we have no equivalent of Julia Evans. Instead, this is something Russians are ashamed of. The other side of democracy's coin.'

'What is it?'

Vassili came back to the table, and sat heavily. 'Dolgoprud-nensky,' he spat.

'Never heard of it. Whatever it is.'

'Bah, of that I am pleased. I would like you to have the good memories of Russia only. But they exist. They are our Mafia, our Yakuza, our Triads. Organized crime, Gregory. These fifteen export companies are all owned by known Dolgoprudnensky members. Every one of them. What was it you were always saying in Turkey? There is no such thing as coincidence.'

'Right. And this Dolgoprudnensky is powerful enough to influence your government?'

'Influence is a strong word. They would not be able to buy our parliamentary cabinet members, not outright. But then, does Julia Evans actually hand over cash to make the New Conserva-tives do her bidding?'

'Point taken.'

'They are everywhere, Gregory, our bureaucracy is rotten with them. It is only natural, they are the Communist Party's succes-sors. They grew up in the party's shadows in the eighties and nineties. There were eight or nine of them in Moscow alone in those days, the Podolsk, Chechen, Solntsevo, others, but the Dolgoprudnensky was the largest even then. It was inevitable they would absorb the rest. Now there is only Dolgoprudnensky, stretching right across the republic. There had been criminals in the Soviet Union before them, but never so well organized, nor so brazen. Afghanistan was the start, the youths who returned from it were a breed the authorities had never dealt with before. The *Afgantsi*. They had no respect, no morals, no conscience. The war had burnt it out of them, they could see they were fighting for nothing, and worse, for a lie. Not all of them, of course, but enough, a hard core that turned to crime. Then the Communists fell, and the gangs began to fill the vacuum they left behind. The corruption, Gregory, the sheer misuse of power. Westerners still have little conception of how the Com-munists ransacked our country to maintain their personal status.

Dolgoprudnensky doesn't have their stature, but it is just as insidious, with its rackets and syntho vats, and prostitutes; its legitimate companies defrauding factories and farmers, and the bought officials sanctioning both. We fight them through the police and Justice Ministry, Gregory, fight and fight, until buildings burn and blood is spilt, but the best we can do is hold what ground we have.'

'I didn't know. I'm sorry.'

'No, it is I who am shamed. It is a terrible thing to tell someone this is the land I am sworn to defend, the kind of people I will die for.'

'We all have organized crime, Vassili. The number of people involved is so small you can't even call them a minority.'

Vassili handed Greg's cybofax back. 'But the trouble and misery they cause is vast. See what they've done to this old man, made him unable to look his friend in the face.'

'Can we help?' Greg asked. 'Hand over what we've got to the Russian Justice Ministry?'

'What have you got, Gregory? Fifteen companies traded with someone whose airship you say was attacked by tekmercs. Kombinates are jockeying for advantage over a new technology. How can this help us?'

Greg toyed with his empty cup, feeling stupid. 'Yeah, right.' For Victor Tyo it would've been enough, for a tekmerc it would've been enough. Circumstantial proof which condemned for all of time. How strange that illegality could accept what the law couldn't.

'I tell you this, Gregory, if you ever meet any of the Dolgoprudnensky face to face, then you shoot. That is the best help you can give us. Shoot. Shoot them down like rabid animals.'

'Is there a name?' he asked. 'A leader? I like to have a name for what I'm up against. I can form a picture that way.'

'Kirilov. Pavel Kirilov. The bastard, he lives like a merchant from the decadent imperial days, he flaunts his wealth and luxuries, he has many young girls to amuse him. But he is smart, cunning. Nothing ever holds against him in the courts, he laughs at the very best our prosecutors can do.'

Greg climbed to his feet. The sun was completely above the horizon now, casting long shadows. A thick blanket of mist had risen, glowing pink in the sunlight; it swirled gently above the cultivated land, filling Nova Kirov's broad streets. People and horses looked like they were wading through it.

'What will you do?' Vassili asked.

'Find out where Charlotte Fielder got the flower from, then go and meet the alien.'

Vassili gripped both of his hands. 'Gregory, if this alien turns out to be a threat, do not keep the knowledge to yourself. Do not become like the kombinates, and seek to gain advantage from it. It is the concern of all the peoples of this world.'

'If it's dangerous, I'll scream the house down, no messing. No matter what Julia Evans or Royan might say.'

'Good, for I confess, what you have told me about this alien has frightened me. This is very strange behaviour for a sentient creature. I am forced to say suspicious. Hiding like this, contacting weapons merchants before governments. Not good. You listen to me, my command network is plugged into the Chinese and Eastern Federation Co-Defence League's Strategic Defence platforms, and I am authorized to use them. I have the codes, and I am prepared to activate the systems, Gregory, on your word.'

'That's . . . quite a responsibility.'

'You are a soldier, Gregory, a true soldier. You will do what's right, I know you will.' Vassili let go of his hands, and clapped him on the shoulder again, grinning. 'Besides, since when did you go into battle without covering fire, eh? A soldier's most important maxim. Backup, Gregory. I will be your backup, once again.' He shook his head, grin turning to a mock scowl. 'Bah, listen to us. Two ageing warriors lost in the past. Portentous, are we not?'

'Very, but at least nobody else knows.'

Vassili laughed.

'One last thing,' Greg said. 'Can you run another name through the Federal Crime Directorate memory core for me?'

'Surely. Whose criminal misdeeds do you wish exposed now?'

'Dmitri Baronski.'

25

They told Charlotte about Baronski after she woke up. It was his death which finally cancelled all her links with the past. She had relied on him so much, which she hadn't realized up until then. But now there was nothing left for her, nothing at all; no one to call, nowhere to go.

So she made it her job to look after Fabian. The last promise made to a dead man. And Fabian needed looking after. His life had been fifteen years of luxury, of staff existing solely to run around after him, of any material possession he wanted a single phone call away. That was all he knew. He went into major sulks if his meals weren't ready on time. And now he'd seen his home and father fall out of the sky. Burning.

She was sure the Event Horizon medics didn't appreciate how deep it went. They had written him off as another shock case. Tranquillizers, a couple of weeks' therapy, a few months to recover, and it would all be over. They were used to treating combat casualties, not lost, traumatized teenagers.

He wouldn't even cry any more. They were given a room together in the platform's little clinic. She had woken some time after midnight to see him lying on his back, staring up at the ceiling. He spent the rest of the night nestled in her arms, dozing off in the early hours.

After breakfast the duty nurse found her some clothes; a pair of stonewashed Levi's, trainers, and an Organic Flux Capacity tour sweatshirt. She turned up the bottom of the Levi's to stop them from flopping over the trainers, and asked for a belt to pinch the oversize waist. Charlotte stared at herself in the bathroom mirror and shuddered. A Grunge disciple dressing down. At least nobody I know will see me wearing this, thank heavens.

Then it was time to wait again. None of the clinic staff quite seemed to know what their status was, whether they were guests or prisoners.

Suzi had been in the next room, her knee wrapped in bioware membranes, plugged into medical 'ware stacks with thick bundles of fibre-optic cable. Charlotte had thanked her for getting them off the *Colonel Maitland*, had a few words; but Suzi didn't know what was going on either. 'Greg'll be back soon,' she said. 'We'll find out what's going down then. And you'll have your big moment.' The casual way she said it chilled Charlotte, like she didn't have any choice but to tell them what they wanted to know, reducing her to a cyborg. Her life was being programmed by others. Nothing really new in that. But that didn't make it the same.

Delivering that bloody flower. Her one spark of independence in years. She knew she shouldn't have done it. But delivering a flower from a lover – it was just fun. Harmless fun. How could it possibly have ended like this?

Baronski would have known what to do next. In fact, he would have warned her off in the first place. If only she had confided in him.

In the end, Fabian's blank-faced suffering had got to her. She asked to go outside for a breath of fresh air. They even had to have a hardline escort for that.

Outside was heat, noise, and the smell. They walked along one side of the platform, looking down on the two-metre generator vent pipes peeing brown water into the ocean, it stank of salt and sulphur. The bass thundering noise of the cascades made her feel queasy.

'Pure shark shit,' said Josh Bailey, the crash team member who was with them. 'We have to live with it the whole time. I'm almost immune by now.'

'Lucky you.' Charlotte knew she ought to show an interest. 'Establish a minimum rapport with everyone you meet,' Baronski had told her. 'Try to understand where they fit into life, how they relate to you.' Except it all seemed a little pointless now.

Fabian leant on the rail and stared silently at the three waterfalls staining the green ocean. It was green, she saw, because of the minute algae flecks floating in it. Like thick soup.

She put her hand over his. 'He wouldn't have felt anything, Fabian.'

'You saw that gondola! He burnt to death. It's a *horrible* way to die.'

'He would have been unconscious from the smoke long before the flames reached the study.'

His head twisted round, eyes frantic for a moment, wanting to believe. 'Do you think so?'

'Whenever houses catch on fire, that's always the reason people don't get out; overcome by smoke.'

'Oh.' He dropped his head again to stare at the sloppy water. 'I've never lived in a house.'

'You'll get used to it.'

'Yes. I suppose . . .' He stiffened, speaking with brittle dignity. 'I suppose you'll be leaving me now.'

'No, not unless you want me to.'

He glanced up, too frightened to believe. 'But you're not being paid any more. And I heard them tell you Baronski is dead.'

'Fabian.' She turned him to face her, putting her hands on his cheeks so he couldn't look away. 'Your father's money never bought you the time we spent together.'

He started crying as his mouth parted in a smile.

'Oh, Fabian.' She cuddled him to her, kissing the top of his head. His arms tightened round her with desperate strength.

'I'm frightened,' he croaked.

'So am I. But it isn't so bad if you've got someone to share it with you.'

They embraced for a long time. Being that close, wordless but knowing, wasn't something she wanted to break. And she had told him the truth, fear was easier to weather this way.

She saw the Pegasus slide out of the western sky, three sharply pointed fighter planes enclosing it in a tight formation. It was heading straight for the platform. Charlotte watched it knowingly, a little twist of tension rising.

Josh Bailey's cybofax bleeped.

'Don't bother,' she told him. 'That'll be for me.'

*

Fabian tagged along automatically behind her. It could have been a problem when they reached the conference room, Josh Bailey looked like he was about to object, but Charlotte sent him a silent plea, and he shrugged, waving them both through the door.

That was when she finally met Julia Evans, in the flesh, shaking hands, actually saying hello in a voice that quavered alarmingly. The back of her legs trembled slightly, as if she'd run a marathon. But Julia Evans only smiled weakly, murmuring a few encouraging words. Charlotte virtually fled to her seat at the table in relief. There were none of the expected allegations, no hostility. Julia Evans didn't blame her for any of the trouble.

She watched unobtrusively as Julia Evans said something to Fabian, her finger tracing the shrinking bruise round his eye where the maid had struck him. The clinic medics had reduced the swelling to virtually nothing. Fabian just blushed and looked at the floor.

Charlotte was sitting next to Suzi who had come in ahead of them. The small hardline woman was in one of the Event Horizon security team tracksuits. There was a slight bulge in the fabric round her knee; but her stride had been natural enough.

Rick Parnell introduced himself, and promptly sat in a chair at the end of the table, just beating Greg to it. Greg seemed momentarily put out, but settled for the next chair down. Victor Tyo sat opposite her, activating the terminal in front of him.

Fabian took his chair beside her, fumbling for her hand below the table. She gave him a quick squeeze of reassurance.

The three flatscreens on the wall lit up as Julia Evans sat at the head of the table. One of them showed the face of an old man, the other two were of Julia herself, none of them had any background.

'They are synthesized images,' Julia explained. 'My grandfather and I have our memories stored in neural network cores.'

Philip Evans; Charlotte remembered him, Event Horizon's founder. She'd heard enough after dinner talk to know he had played a large part in the downfall of the PSP.

The whole concept was amazing. Julia could be in two places at once, three, four— No wonder Event Horizon worked so perfectly. Charlotte felt a smile of admiration building. It really was true, nobody could beat Julia Evans. Reality was actually greater than legend.

'That's how you burned into the *Colonel Maitland*'s 'ware,' Fabian said. He sounded impressed.

'Yes. And I'd be obliged if you two treated the knowledge of the NN cores' existence, and anything we discuss here today, as completely confidential, please.'

'Yes, of course,' Charlotte said. She nudged Fabian.

'Yes,' he agreed.

'Good. Now then, I understand Nia Korovilla was asking you about the flower, Charlotte?'

'Yes, she wanted to know who gave it to me.'

'A lot of people do,' Greg said softly. 'Will you tell us?'

This was where she had planned on doing her bargaining; a trade, money, and guaranteed safety for what she knew. But she didn't know what sort of price to ask for, and some hard little core of anger inside wanted something to be done about

Baronski, wanted justice. She strongly suspected that the kind of people who killed the old man weren't the kind who ever sat in courts to be tried. And Fabian would need protecting as well.

Julia Evans was the only person who could sort out those kind of loose ends for her. It would be for the best if she wasn't antagonized.

'Yes,' Charlotte said. 'He never told me his name, just that he was a priest.'

'Describe him, please,' Greg said.

'I suppose he was at least fifty-five, probably sixty; medium height, four or five centimetres shorter than me, very pale face, flabby neck, greying hair in a pony tail. He had a great smile, I mean, you just looked at him and knew you could trust him,' she trailed off limply. It sounded silly said out loud, but his smile had been the reason she agreed to deliver the flower.

'Not Royan,' Julia said.

'Would you recognize him if you saw him again?' Greg asked.

'Yes, absolutely,' she said. 'He was wearing a dove-grey jumpsuit, an old one, but it was clean. All the Celestials were clean.'

Victor looked up from his terminal. 'You mean this happened in New London?'

'Sorry, didn't I say? Yes. It was during my holiday.'

Julia and Greg were both grinning at each other. 'You went up to New London after New Zealand?' Greg asked.

'How did you—?'

'Tell you, Charlotte, you're a very important person. Victor here has a big profile on you.'

'Yes.' She swallowed. 'I took a flight from Mangonui spaceport.'

'With your patron?'

'No. I said it was a holiday. I went by myself.'

'How did you pay for it?'

'I didn't. It was a farewell gift from my last patron, all expenses paid. Baronski let me keep it. I normally have to hand the gifts over, but he could hardly sell it, so he let me go ahead.'

Victor let out a groan. 'No wonder we couldn't trace you through Amex. What was this patron's name?'

'Ali Murdad.'

'Did he send you up there to collect the flower?' Greg asked. 'Or any other kind of favour?'

'No. It was a genuine holiday for me.'

'I have confirmed the ticket,' one of Julia's images said. 'A regal-class package with Thomas Cook, booked by Aflaj Industrial Cybernetics – Ali Murdad listed as a director. A fortnight at the High Savoy, with a universal club and resort access card.'

'That's right,' she said.

'Tell us about this priest,' Greg said. 'Are you certain he was a Celestial Apostle?'

'Yes. There was a group of them working round the tourists at the fall surf beach. A couple of them spoke to me, they were about my age, they explained what the Celestials were. They were very devout, I don't mean silly like the Hare Krishnas or deadly dull like the Jehovah's Witnesses, they had a sense of humour, but they really believed our destiny lies out among the stars. They asked me if I wanted to stay up in New London permanently; they said it wouldn't be a hard life, not like the cults that exploit children down here, but it was fairly basic. That didn't seem to bother them, they believe it's only temporary, when this divine event of theirs finally occurs everything will change. I think they expect to receive a higher blessing than everyone else, or be the first people admitted into heaven, or something along those lines. Being a Celestial Apostle was certainly supposed to be a step up the ladder towards God.'

'But you turned them down?'

'Hell, yes. I can go up to New London any time I want. I'm not spending the rest of my life boring the pants off tourists with nutty creeds. Besides, they seemed a bit simple, you know? Dreamy types.'

'And was this priest one of the pair which spoke to you?'

'No, he came over when they left. He knew my name, though, that was the funny thing. I got the impression he was waiting for the other two to finish. He said he was sorry they had failed to show me the light, then he asked me if I'd do a friend of his a favour.'

'What was the friend's name?' Victor asked.

'He said he couldn't tell me for obvious reasons.'

Julia smiled as if she already knew. 'Go on.'

'He asked me to deliver something to you. He said it was a gift from your lover, but that no one must know. I thought – well, you already have a husband, you see, so there was this other secret man in your life. It was romantic and exciting, me being asked to be a go-between for you. I couldn't say no. You're ... well, you're Julia Evans, aren't you? I would have been involved in something delicious, I might even have been asked to do it again. So I cut short my holiday and flew back. Dmitri Baronski got me the ticket for the Newfields ball.' She stared determinedly at her finger nails, mortified. Whatever would Fabian think of her, acting like a schoolgirl.

'He knew your name,' Greg said in the silence that followed, 'he knew you had the contacts necessary to get into Monaco's social event of the year at a day's notice, and he knew you had the *savoir-faire* to deliver the flower. Some Celestial Apostle.'

'You think that's him, boy?' Philip Evans asked. 'The alien?'

'Alien?' Charlotte gasped. Fabian lurched upright in his chair, staring at Philip Evans's image.

Nobody said anything, they were all looking at Greg, waiting for him to speak, like he was some sort of guru or something, she thought. He blinked slowly, and focused on her. She shifted uncomfortably, feeling Fabian's hand in her own, the damp smooth skin tightening its grip silently. Greg didn't just look at you, she decided, he judged you. A psychic. The realization didn't make her any more comfortable. There were stories—

'You said you broke off your holiday to deliver the flower?' Greg asked.

'Yes.' Her throat was contracting.

'How much of it did you miss?'

'Four days, Ali's package was for a fortnight. But I changed my ticket for an earlier flight. The agent said there was no problem. I landed at Capetown then caught a connecting flight.'

''Ah.' A smile spread across his face. 'I think we'd better fill you in on a few points.'

26

Suzi sat dumb while everyone had their say. First Charlotte telling how some Celestial Apostle handed her the alien flower. And just what the fuck was a Celestial Apostle anyway? Then Greg on his Russian general mate, and how the Dolgoprudnensky were probably plugged in somewhere down the line. At least she knew about the Dolgoprudnensky, tough bastards. Julia started rapping about her starship supertechnology, and the heat she was getting from kombinates and microbes, and Royan being his usual monomaniac self. Royan always had to take apart anything new; split it open, figure it out, and put it back together so that it worked smoother. If Julia didn't know that about him then they weren't as close as she thought.

All heavy duty shit.

Charlotte and Fabian were sitting up straight like a couple of kids at school who'd been lumbered with the toughest master for a lesson, hanging on to every word. Charlotte's gorgeous face was crinkling from the effort of following details. Suzi glanced casually at the girl's profile. Not bad at all. Which reminded Suzi of Andria, who she hadn't phoned since the airship.

The rap went on relentlessly around her. It was something she hated, and she couldn't let them know. Silence implied wisdom, some bullshit like that. Let them think she was lost in deep thoughts, fully plugged in. This was Greg's scene, not hers. She could plan ahead, sort a deal down to the last detail. Good at it, too. But she could never pin the past down the way Greg could. He listened to what people said they believed had happened, thought about it, then explained what had really been going on. And it all made sense, like he was fitting a big jigsaw of events together in his mind, a map through what had been. Him and his warlock intuition.

She grinned at him.

He gave her a knowing look, then broke away. 'You see, Charlotte,' he said, 'you didn't know it, but you've actually been working for the Dolgoprudnensky since you left the orphanage. According to General Kamoskin, Baronski was plugged into them at a high level. That's why he always sent you and the other girls looking for financial gossip. He made some money out of it, certainly; but all the really smart data was squirted back to this Pavel Kirilov character. He's in a position to make a lot more use of it than Baronski ever could.'

The girl looked crestfallen. Suzi could see Fabian's hand locked in hers under the table, his thumb stroking gently.

'And you think it was the Dolgoprudnensky who asked Jason Whitehurst to lift her from Monaco?' Victor asked.

'Yeah.'

'Father did business with them,' Fabian said unexpectedly. 'It was sneaky stuff. Made us a heck of a lot of money, though.'

'Are you sure?' Julia asked.

The boy grimaced. 'Absolutely. Father explained it to me.' He smiled at Charlotte, flipping a lock of hair from his eyes. 'I said he told me everything.'

'Yes, you did,' Charlotte said. 'So how did it work?'

'It was the Dolgoprudnensky who made sure we were granted all our import-export licences with the Eastern Federation states. Licences are really tricky to get most of the time, unless you know the right people; those Eastern European states are still lumbered with huge civil service bureaucracies. All we had to do in return for the licences was use ships which the Dolgoprudnensky owned to carry our cargoes in and out of Odessa. It's simple really, most of our trade with Russia involves exchanging their timber for household gear and industrial cybernetics. So say if a Russian company comes to us and asks us for a particular piece of foreign hardware, we look round the global timber market and come back with a weight of wood which is equal to the cost of that hardware. Next, the Russian government's Timber Export Directorate authorizes the release of that weight from their stocks. They have millions of tonnes of dead deciduous trees left over from the Warming, it's a big national resource for them. The timber is shipped out of Odessa at ten per cent above the normal commercial carriage rate, and in return the company gets its hardware. Nobody queries the amount of wood being sold abroad which pays for that extra ten per cent in the shipping costs, because the Dolgoprudnensky have consolidated their control of the Timber Export Directorate. From the Director herself right down to the office cleaners, the entire staff is made up of Dolgoprudnensky members; it's like a closed shop, the personnel department will only employ their nominees. And the only merchants who are admitted to the Directorate's approved list to barter timber are the ones in on the deal. Like Father.'

'And timber is bulky,' Julia said. 'You need a lot of ships to transport it.'

'That's right. Only father didn't just supply single pieces of hardware to Russia, he shipped in entire factories.'

Charlotte reached out and smoothed the remaining strands of hair from Fabian's forehead. They both smiled at each other.

'OK,' said Greg. 'That confirms it. Jason Whitehurst was working for the Dolgoprudnensky, at least to start with. When he began to realize how valuable Charlotte was he decided he didn't need them any more. It explains why Nia Korovilla was on board, to keep a close watch on the Dolgoprudnensky's most valuable timber deal partner. And they were also the ones who mounted the observation on Baronski's apartment after the *Colonel Maitland* failed to show at Odessa.'

'But how did they know I was carrying the flower for Julia?' Charlotte asked.

'They wouldn't have known it was the flower specifically, not at first,' Greg said; he pursed his lips, gazing at the ceiling. 'Let's see. How long had it been since your last genuine by-yourself holiday?'

'I'm not sure, a couple of years at least, maybe longer.'

'OK, and where were you when you asked Baronski to get you in to the Newfields ball?'

'I was still up at New London. If he couldn't get me a ticket there wouldn't have been much point in coming back to Earth early.'

'And you specifically told him it was Julia you wanted to see?'

'Yes.'

'Good. That would make Baronski very suspicious. You break off a pre-paid holiday of a lifetime, all because you want to physically meet the woman who owns one of the largest companies in the world. There must have been a compelling reason, yet you didn't tell him, which is not only out of character, it goes against your whole arrangement with him. If I was Baronski, someone who lived off the kind of byte scraps dropped by people like Julia, I'd want to know exactly what you were up to.

'I'd say it went like this. After he found you the Newfields ticket he called the Dolgoprudnensky and told them something dodgy was going down. You either knew something about Julia, or you were carrying something to her. They would have been on to you straight away, probably before you left New London. Your luggage would be searched, which I'm guessing is when they took a sample of the flower. It was obviously something that had been given to you recently, something you'd brought down from New London. An empathic psychic would home on to that flower straight off. Tell you, it gives off some pretty weird vibes. And any pro tekmerc team would use a psychic on an observation mission. Suzi will tell you.'

She gave Charlotte a rough nod. 'Too fucking true. When we roll a courier, anything and everything they have with them is suspect until proved otherwise. Clothing, hair, luggage. We even pick up sweet wrappers out of the bin, half-eaten hamburgers, you name it, anything discarded. Using an empath is routine, it's the least you need. Me, I prefer a precog if I can get me one. They tend to be more reliable.' She held Greg's eye, taunting.

'The man at the airport!' Charlotte said in a fearful gasp.

'What man?' Suzi asked keenly.

'I saw him twice, maybe three times. He was waiting at Capetown when I landed, then he was at the Monaco airport, too. And I thought I caught a glimpse of him at the Newfields ball, but I couldn't be certain. He was dressed as a waiter.'

'Interesting,' Greg said.

'No such thing as coincidence,' Victor murmured.

'No messing.' Greg turned back to Charlotte. 'When did Baronski tell you to meet Jason Whitehurst?'

'He called me right after my flight landed at Capetown. I was still in the spaceport.'

'A day after he organized the ticket. Plenty of time for the Dolgoprudnensky agents to discover the flower. After that, after they had analysed it and discovered it was alien, they would have been very interested in exactly where in New London you obtained it, and from whom. They must have allowed you to go to the Newfields ball so they could confirm it was Julia you were delivering the flower to. Then Jason Whitehurst was supposed to take you straight to them for interrogation.' He shook his head in amused admiration. 'They must have been frantic when you dropped out of sight. I imagine they've had their agents searching New London for the last four days.'

'So if the Dolgoprudnensky haven't contacted the alien, why did Mutizen make their offer to me?' Julia asked.

'It wasn't a genuine offer,' Greg said. 'As far as we know, Event Horizon is the only company to be offered generator data by Mutizen. Everyone else has been approached by Clifford Jepson, including Mikoyan who loyally informed the Russian Defence Ministry. Consider the timing. Three or four days ago the Dolgoprudnensky learned about atomic structuring, either from contacts in Mikoyan or the Russian Defence Ministry. A technology so startlingly original it's frightened the crap out of every company and government that's heard about it. Then, at more or less the same time, they find out there could be an alien in the solar system. Just like you did, Julia; and just like you they drew the same conclusion. The two have to be connected. Since then, they have been doing exactly the same as everyone else, trying to find the source of atomic structuring, the owner of the generator data. Their advantage was that they were the first to know about both atomic structuring and Royan's alien together. They thought all they had to do was interrogate Charlotte and they would get to the alien first. But then Jason Whitehurst played his joker and isolated her. The Dolgoprudnensky started to panic. There's a definite deadline involved, because tomorrow Clifford Jepson is going to finalize his partnership. If they want in, they're going to have to find the alien before then. They're trying to get you and Clifford Jepson to do their work for them.

'Mutizen was ordered to offer you the joint development deal and production partnership. It's a complete phoney, but it made sure you knew about atomic structuring after you'd been given the flower. That way you would be bound to mount a major operation to chase after Royan, an operation that was naturally put together in a hurry. In other words, a sloppy one, one which would be easy for them to follow. And Mutizen's offer would also spur Clifford Jepson along, maybe even force him to visit the alien to ask how come Mutizen were also offering generator data. Certainly they slipped him the know about Charlotte and maybe Royan as well; that's why Leol Reiger appeared on the scene. The Dolgoprudnensky couldn't lose; they have their own agents searching New London, then they had Event Horizon and Clifford Jepson plugged in as well, three trails to follow. Vassili was right, that Kirilov is one smart bastard.'

'I've been used?' Julia asked quietly.

Suzi tried to tell herself she wasn't bothered by the ice-cool tone. But Julia had a way of speaking direct into the brain. And hearing her angry like this was daunting. All that power, safely bottled away by Julia's stuffy conventions and convictions, but what that woman could do if she ever lashed out . . .

'Yes, you,' Greg said lightly. 'And me, and Suzi, Victor,

Clifford. The Dolgoprudnensky loaded our programs, and we jerked about like cyborgs. The only one who didn't was Jason Whitehurst.'

Julia's face was perfectly composed, staring out of the window, swallowed by thought.

'The synopsis Greg suggests does seem to plug in to the profile we've been assembling on Mutizen,' one of Julia's screen images said. 'We were unable to find any reference to atomic structuring technology prior to two days ago. There have been no funds allocated to physics research teams, they don't employ any scientists capable of doing that kind of work. Your original assessment that they had obtained the data from someone else is the most logical solution.'

'Humm,' Julia turned to Greg. 'Is he still alive?'

'You know I can't answer that, but—' Greg's face went all slack. 'I don't get any bad vibes about carrying on the search. Maybe it'll be worthwhile. Tell you, I'm going to keep going.' He fixed Suzi with a bleary gaze. 'How about you?'

'New London next stop,' she said levelly. Then Leol Reiger.

'I didn't say I was going to stop.' Julia spiked Greg with a vexed glare.

'Good,' he said. 'New London is a big place, and the Dolgoprudnensky agents wouldn't even know where to begin.'

'And you do?' Julia asked.

'No. But Charlotte does. How about it? Will you come with us, Charlotte? Identify the priest for us?'

Charlotte gave a cautious nod. 'Yes. If you think I can help.'

'Thank you, Charlotte.' Julia showed her a warm smile. The girl's tension seemed to flake away.

'Are you sure New London is the source?' Victor asked. He struck Suzi as the only one round the table who wasn't entirely convinced abut Royan and the alien. Which was strange, he'd seen Greg's psi at work before.

'Only lead we've got,' Greg said. 'Unless the SETI team has found anything at Jupiter?'

'Sorry, not a thing,' Rick said. 'I've been updating this morning. There have been no detectable electromagnetic signals. Something might turn up on the visual search, but it's early days yet.'

Victor gave a dispassionate grunt. Definitely some tension there, Suzi thought.

'I want my hardliners with me,' Suzi told Julia. 'We came out of yesterday looking like shit. If we'd had some decent fire-power it would've been another fucking story. And if the Dolgoprudnensky have got some people up in New London, you can be sure they're carrying.'

'New London is a dormitory town and tourist resort,' Julia said. 'I'm not having you take a private army up there.'

'Take the crash team with you,' Victor said smoothly. 'You know they're good, yes? And Julia's right. We really can't permit armed tekmercs in New London, no matter how loyal to you or well disciplined they are. Highest bid, Suzi.'

She grinned. 'Sold. It sounds fluid enough.' The crash team would be OK; she'd been talking to them, putting on the old-time pro routine, surprising what'd kicked free.

'I hope you'll allow me to accompany Greg and the security team up to New London,' Rick Parnell said.

Suzi hadn't paid him much attention, a hunk in a bad suit. University man, who looked for aliens in the stars, his talk would be in the stratosphere. He'd been very keen to sit next to Julia.

'I want the Jupiter search supervised properly,' Julia said.

'It will be,' Rick insisted. 'But I'm not an astronomer. I couldn't contribute to that. You always say put the experts in charge. And I'd be best employed in contacting the alien. It's going to have a very strange psychology. I'm not saying I'll understand its motivational behaviour patterns, but, well, the SETI department has initiated some studies into—'

'All right,' Julia cut in. 'If Greg doesn't object to you tagging along.'

'No.'

Rick let out a quiet sigh of relief.

'Victor, you chase up Royan's next memory package,' Julia said. 'It ought to be at the North Sea Farm company.'

'We've already accessed every memory core at the Farm,' said one of the screen Julias. 'They're clean.'

'All the more reason for Victor to go in person,' Julia said. 'He can find what you're missing.' She looked round the table. 'Right, well if that's it, we'll start. Greg, your space-plane will be here in an hour.'

'Are you coming to New London with us?' Suzi asked.

'Not initially, first I'm going to try and sort out the atomic structuring situation with the kombinates and Clifford. But as soon as you locate the Celestial priest, I'll follow you up.'

'Right.' Suzi stood up. There wasn't even the slightest tweak of pain from her knee. The clinic's bioware bracing was the best she'd ever seen.

'What about the Dolgoprudnensky?' Fabian asked.

'Fabian—' Charlotte began warningly.

'No,' the boy said stubbornly. 'I won't be quiet. The Dolgo-prudnensky started all this, they got you all fighting each other. And that's why my father is dead.' He turned to face Julia Evans, eyes accusing. 'Why aren't you going to do anything about them?'

'I am going to do something about them, but this situation requires my full attention right now. They'll still be there in a week, after this is all over. And you'll be a big part of their demise, Fabian. We can pass on everything you know about their timber operation to the Russian Justice Ministry.' She gave him a modest smile. 'Good enough?'

He hunched his shoulders, looking belligerent. 'Yes. All right.'

'Thank you, Fabian. I know it's hard for you right now.'

'Can I go up to New London with Charlotte?'

'I don't think so. You'll be a lot safer here. Charlotte will be back in a couple of days.'

Fabian's sullen expression darkened, but he didn't push it.

Charlotte's arm had slipped round him, giving him a reassuring hug.

Suzi felt like cheering the kid on, someone who wasn't totally intimidated by Julia. Fuck knows, there were few enough in the world.

27

The sun hadn't quite risen high enough to burn the dew off Wilholm's lawns. Julia's Pegasus sent the pale grey and silver droplets scurrying in vast interference patterns as it landed.

She walked down the stairs from the belly hatch to be greeted with kisses and shouts from her animated children. Brutus barked at her, then started sniffing round her feet.

'You've been gone all night.'

'Where did you go?'

'Was it with Uncle Greg?'

'Do you know where Daddy is yet?'

She put her arms around both of them, hugging tight. They started to walk towards the manor together, Daniella skipping.

Julia took a deep breath. 'I'm sorry I had to rush off. It was Listoel. Yes. And, I think we might now.' She laughed at Matthew, his jaw had dropped as he tried to match answers to questions.

'Where do you think Daddy is?' Daniella asked.

'New London. Your Uncle Greg is going up there today to find out if he truly is. We should know by tonight. I might have to leave again.'

'Can we come?'

'No. If I find Daddy, I'll bring him straight back here. Promise.'

Daniella and Matthew exchanged a look, annoyed and half

relieved. Julia grinned at them. 'Come on, I've got a teleconference in a minute, but we'll have some elevenses together first.'

'No interruptions?' Matthew asked suspiciously.

'None at all.'

*

David Marchant had been the first New Conservative Prime Minister elected after the PSP fell, a position he held for twelve years and two further elections before finally standing down in favour of his successor, Joshua Wheaton. Julia had found herself regretting his decision with increasing frequency over the last five years. Wheaton was too much like Harcourt, an image merchant desperate for public support, a spin doctor's cyborg. At least Marchant had the guts to make unpopular decisions on occasion. These days he had settled into a cosy role of elder statesman and New Conservative grandee. Always on the channel current affair casts, ready with an opinion and a quip. Perceived as the power behind Wheaton's throne. An accurate enough assessment.

When his image appeared on the study's flatscreen she felt herself relaxing. There had been a lot of head to head sessions in the old days, hammering out deals to their mutual advantage. Nowadays it was done through an army of assistants and lawyers, departmental interfaces, industry and government working groups, advisory committees.

One reason why the whole Harcourt problem had arisen in the first place. No hands-on control any more.

'Hello, Julia,' he said. As always a rich resonant voice, instantly trustworthy.

'Morning, David. I have a problem.'

'Whatever I can do, Julia, you know that.'

'Choosing a better successor would have been a good start.'

David Marchant smiled wisely. 'Joshua is right for these times, as I was for mine. We needed strong leadership to recover from the Warming and the PSP, and now we need to loosen up a little, consolidate.'

'There's a difference between loose and falling to pieces. Wheaton has lost just about all of his authority, over the country and the party. And I have Michael Harcourt on my back because of it.'

'Michael is an ambitious man, admittedly.'

'Michael is a bought man.'

David Marchant laughed. 'You're just annoyed because it isn't you who owns him.'

'He isn't from your wing of the party. And if he does snatch the premiership from Wheaton, he'll purge the cabinet. You really will have to become a professional current affairs presenter if you want your voice to be heard after that. Trouble is, Jepson runs Globecast too. You'll be locked out. Give you a chance to get your golf handicap down,' she said maliciously. Marchant hated sports; when Peterborough United won the FA cup she had sat next to him in Wembley's royal box for the match. He had emptied two hip flasks of whisky. Out of boredom, he always claimed.

'If you'd given Wheaton some support over Wales none of this would have happened, Julia.'

'Life isn't as black and white as it used to be in your day, David. Politics isn't as simple, *nothing* is as simple. Which is a step to the good.'

'Hardly, Julia; complexity is a step towards chaos.'

'And simplicity makes control easy,' she countered wryly. 'It's oppressive.'

'The PSP was oppressive, Julia, never us. We created the economic environment you thrived in, you have a lot to be grateful for. And as long as we remain in Westminster, Event Horizon can go on expanding. You have *carte blanche*, you know that.'

'Event Horizon is already large enough, thank you. Besides, pure capitalism is as unsavoury as pure communism. I never favoured either extreme. There has to be a degree of regulation, and responsibility. A social market somewhere in the middle.'

'That's rich, coming from you. You know the gains to be

made from our policies. Without us acting in tandem this country would only be a second-rate European state, not the leading power we are today.'

'You people, you're always so hemmed in by geography, aren't you? It ruins your thinking. The rest of Europe, the rest of the world for that matter, needs to develop their economies to the same level as England. If for no other reason than if they're poor they can't buy our goods.'

'Nice in theory, Julia. You'll never see it in practice. Governments are too parochial, too protective. They have to be; it's how they get elected.'

She favoured him with an indolent smile. 'Unless they're Welsh governments.'

'*Touché.* So what did that little shit Harcourt offer you?'

'He claims a direct line to Jepson, which he'll use to tell me what the other bids are. That's his edge. The rest of it was a standard government to industry inducement package.'

'Hmm.' David Marchant rubbed the bridge of his nose, thinking hard. 'Well, of course, the inducement package will remain, that goes without saying. After all, my natural successors are placed in the Exchequer as well as Number Ten. That just leaves us with the problem of the actual bid. Fortunately, the PM can offer you Treasury backing for any offer you make to Jepson. In which case anything Harcourt tells you becomes irrelevant. I imagine Wheaton will consider a more appropriate position for him afterwards; Minister we can all blame for traffic jams, or somesuch. I take it you are arranging a suitable figure for Jepson with your financial backing consortium.'

'Yes,' she said grudgingly. Another bloody problem. Her finance division chief had briefed her during the flight from Listoel; the banks and finance houses were terrified by atomic structuring, running round like headless chickens. It was making business extremely difficult in the money markets.

'Good. Simply put in a figure you know the kombinates can't match. We will bridge the gap between that and the amount the banks will advance you. Blank cheque, Julia. And interest free.'

'It will run to tens of billions, if not hundreds.'

'So? Taxpayers are a bottomless source of money for governments. And they're not going anywhere.'

'As a taxpayer, I object.'

'Ah, but, Julia, you don't pay much tax, do you? New Conservative policies see to that.'

'What about Wales?'

'I'm sure that if you have a chat with Joshua Wheaton he'll convince you to see our point of view. Perhaps you could say a few words to that effect when you leave Number Ten, there's always a lot of reporters hanging around outside.'

'Tell me one thing, David. Why do the New Conservatives want to hang on to Wales?'

'A large country is a stable and strong country. Without Wales, we would be weakened, possibly fatally. I have no intention of allowing that to happen, to waste all we have built over the last seventeen years. It would be national suicide.'

'And you would lose your majority in Westminster.'

David Marchant gave a delicate shrug. 'If we lose, you lose, Julia.' The flatscreen went blank.

Going to be one of those days, I think, Juliet, her grandpa said.

Yes. And if I'm not extremely careful, it might be the last.

You should have told him about the alien.

No. I don't want people like him to make first contact; there's first impressions to consider as well.

And Royan is the perfect choice for that, is he, girl?

She couldn't answer.

*

Julia went upstairs for a shower after the teleconference. Wilhom's master bedroom was large, with a high ceiling, its windows looking out over the lake. A Paris design house had been contracted for the decoration, giving it walls of royal purple and emerald, a mossy cream carpet, gold fittings, heavy curtains that hung from the ceiling to the floor. A solid four-poster made from oak, with a plain white silk canopy.

On impulse she sat on Royan's side of the bed and opened the door of his cabinet. Inside she found a couple of bottles of aftershave, comb, a hardback set of *The Lord of the Rings*, AV memox crystal recordings of black and white films from the nineteen-forties and fifties, a cybofax that must have been ten years old, it was so bulky.

She took them all out and arranged them on the bed, lining them up according to size. Not much of a legacy. She remembered buying him the cybofax, the Tolkien books too, come to that.

Clothes? She slid open the door to his walk-through wardrobe. The biolums came on automatically. Dust filters kept the air clean. She walked between the two rails, her hand brushing along his shirts and jackets and waistcoats, setting them swaying gently. The shoe rack along the far wall was well stocked: cowboy boots, suede ankle boots, trainers, alligator shoes, hiking boots. Some of them hadn't even been worn. Then there were ties, belts, hats.

She let the styles and colours sink into her mind, seeing him in various combinations. He'd grown into quite a sharp dresser.

But what had he been wearing the day he left? She couldn't remember. There was no spare hanger.

The wardrobe, the bedside cabinet, they shook loose memories. Not her usual processor indexed recollections, real memories. Human memories. They were twinned with emotional responses. Messy.

She left the cube of clean silence, shutting the door behind her. He hadn't cared enough about the clothes to take them with him. They were hers as much as the manor and the company. He wore them for her, when he was with her. Plugging into the role she'd given him.

*

Kirsten McAndrews was waiting for her in the study, sitting behind a terminal on the long central table. A dark African vase had been placed in the middle, full of pale pink rose buds. They gave off a thin aromatic scent.

Julia took her own chair at the head. **Open Channel to Selfcores.** *I want you to run a search through patent office memory cores and see if Clifford has filed anything on the generator yet.*

He hadn't yesterday, we checked, NN core one said.

Well, check again, and assign a monitor routine to keep me updated. As soon as it's filed I want to know.

I see, NN core two said. *Why hasn't he filed one already?*

Quite. By telling people he has the generator data for sale he's exposed himself to every hotrod and tekmerc in existence running a snatch deal against him, not to mention us and kombinate security, probably certain defence ministries too with these stakes. All he has to do is file it with a patent office and he's covered.

He ain't got it, Philip Evans said.

That's what I'm beginning to think, Grandpa. Which means he's batting on a very sticky wicket. He must know that if I get to the alien before it squirts him the generator data I'll make it an offer that'll be difficult to refuse. Event Horizon has interests in every human discipline. Whatever it wants, I ought to be able to supply it.

Then why didn't it contact you in the first place, girl?

I don't know. More to the point, if it is up in New London how did it contact Clifford? That's something we've overlooked. It couldn't have been a direct broadcast from the asteroid.

We don't know what the alien's technological limits are, NN core one said. *I mean, how could it get into New London unnoticed in the first place? The strategic defence sensor coverage up there is just as good as the low Earth orbit networks.*

Ask Royan, she said bitterly. *He's the expert.*

Right, we'll keep you updated.

Cancel Channel to Selfcores. 'How is Peter Cavendish progressing with Mutizen?' she asked.

'Ah yes,' Kirsten typed rapidly on her terminal. 'Problems there. I've scheduled a meeting for ten thirty; he said they seem to be stalling.'

Julia allowed herself a moment of satisfaction amid the gloom. Greg was right, Mutizen's offer was a blind. God damn the Dolgoprudnensky.

*

Self Cores Access Request.

Expedite.

Sorry, girl, bad news.

What is it, Grandpa?

Victor's Nigerian office has just called in. Three of the survivors the coast guard picked up from the Colonel Maitland's *wreckage are now unaccounted for. It looks like they sneaked out of the hospital some time last night. Two nurses have been injured, and a porter's vanished.*

Bugger.

One of the missing survivors fits Leol Reiger's description.

I imagine he would, she said.

Victor is already putting a snuff deal together. Reiger won't hazard anyone for much longer, Juliet.

He won't have to, this situation is very close to being resolved, one way or another; twenty-four hours at the maximum.

You're probably right. Why don't you call Clifford, see if you can settle your differences peacefully?

I might.

Talking never hurt anyone.

Yes, thanks, Grandpa.

Always here for you, Juliet. And today's company status review is still waiting here with me.

Oh, Lord. All right, let's get started.

*

The sprinklers had risen out of Wilholm's lawn on metre-high metal stalks, like incredibly thin mushrooms wound with a spiral of flexible hose, pumping out long white plumes of spray. Julia stood by the study's window, listening to the faint *whup whup* sound of the water as it left the nozzles under high pressure. Puddles were forming in the indentations left by undercarriage bogies. Water was streaming off the wings of her Pegasus.

Matthew was back in the pool, practising his dives under Qoi's vigilant gaze. He could already do a forward somersault flip. Julia watched him try a back flip, landing on his side with a big splash, limbs flailing. He got out and tried again. Daniella was just visible in the paddock below the lake, riding her horse. Brutus trailed along after her, tail drooping in the mid-morning heat.

They normally invited their friends round to Wilholm in the holidays. Julia enjoyed the sound of the youngsters rampaging through the manor; they seemed to wake the old place up, breezy laughter blowing out the encroachment of dutiful solemnity. And the games they played roaming around the grounds gave the security team headaches. The defence hardware and gene-tailored sentinels all had to be reprogrammed to cope. Julia wasn't about to impose restrictions on the kids, childhood was too precious for that. And the shaggy woods and unkempt fields were a magical kingdom when you were that age.

But they hadn't asked anyone to visit today; or more likely Daniella had bullied Matthew into not asking his friends, mistakenly believing they'd be helping her.

There was a knock on the door, and Peter Cavendish came in, dabbing at his forehead with a navy-blue silk handkerchief. His face was heavily flushed, pure white hair damp with perspiration.

Julia turned away from the window and gave him a welcoming smile. If it hadn't been for the fact he was wearing a different suit from yesterday she would have said he hadn't been home, he certainly looked like he hadn't slept at all. 'Sit down, Peter, you look like you've been overdoing it to me.'

He slipped into one of the black chairs round the table, sighing gratefully. 'I don't understand it, Julia. Negotiating with Mutizen is like wrestling fog. We've had our contractual team sitting up with their Mutizen counterparts for eighteen hours solid, and every time we look like we're reaching an agreement, they throw us a blocker. I'd say they're deliberately stalling, but that doesn't make any sense. They came to us, remember?'

'Yes. But I'm afraid you're right, they are stalling. They are not in possession of the generator data, nor have they ever been in possession. The offer was purely an attempt to goad me into taking some hasty action.'

'Oh, for Christ's sake!'

'I'm sorry. I only found out myself early this morning.'

'Great. Hell, what now?'

'Fall back on Clifford Jepson and Globecast. How's that negotiation going?'

Peter Cavendish tucked his handkerchief back into his suit pocket. 'Second disaster. We've thrashed out a more or less satisfactory contract with Globecast's lawyers, but it hasn't been costed out yet. And it won't be until we submit it officially. We were waiting for Michael Harcourt to come through with the data on the other bids, like you said.'

'Oh, Lord ... Sorry, I haven't decided if I'm going to take Harcourt up on that yet. It turns out he's Jepson's cyborg, so we probably couldn't rely on his figures anyway. But David Marchant has made a counter-bid for our co-operation, quite a good one.'

He gave her a long look, then slipped a couple of centimetres deeper into his seat. 'Hell, Julia, I'm not sure if I belong here any more. Nothing stays stable long enough to establish a picture these days. I mean, we get a perfectly ordinary contract finalized. Then it's not just the goalposts which get moved, we're not even playing the same game we were when we started. I've got to have something that doesn't twist on me, Julia, a set of values I can depend on.'

She returned his mournful gaze. 'It's not us, Peter. We're not at fault.'

'Yes, sure, in a perfect world.'

'Something like that.'

'But in the mean time—'

'We do what we can.'

'OK, Julia, you win.'

'Just think how the other side must feel.'

'Some comfort. You want me to go ahead with the Clifford Jepson partnership, then?'

'Yes.'

'OK, how high do you want us to bid?'

'How high is up?' she murmured. 'I'll get the Finance Division to work out what sort of bid we can realistically afford, and commercial intelligence to provide estimates on the opposition's bids. Then we'll sit down this evening and decide what to offer Clifford. One piece of good news, I can have Treasury backing any time I want.' She didn't mention the price tag which came with it; Peter didn't need to know. Come to that, would he care about Wales?

'Right,' he said. 'At least that's something concrete.'

'Have you managed to bring any of the kombinates in on our side, put in a joint offer?'

He shook his head. 'Ha, no chance. There's no alliances in this war. Everyone wants atomic structuring, and they want it exclusively. You should see the Stock Exchange this morning. There's not a share moving. The floor's waiting to see what's going to happen after the bids are in.'

'Maybe nothing will happen. I have yet to be convinced Clifford Jepson has the generator data.'

Peter Cavendish held up his hand. 'No. Don't. I don't want to know.' He showed her a plaintive little grin. 'Win or lose, I'll be glad when this is over.'

'Yes.' Yet deep down in her mind there was an intuitive worry that this would never be over, that this alien was just the beginning. There were a hundred billion stars in the galaxy, each one of them waiting to pounce.

She remembered a newscast she'd seen on one of the channels, years ago; a drought-stricken village in Africa, Ethiopia, or the Sudan, somewhere that had never broken the poverty and drought cycle even in the twentieth century. And by the time the new millennium arrived they never stood a chance. A place where the Warming had killed even the dreams that there could be an end to suffering.

The village had been equipped with condenser mats, sucking precious drops of moisture out of the night air. They were pinned to the roof of every hut, the way European houses wore solar panels; a donation from some grandiose Bible-belt American Church charity. The inhabitants had been dying, now the flatscreen showed her healthy children, fat cattle, vegetables growing in hydroponic troughs. It was an oasis, surrounded by dead land, soil so dry it had long since crumbled to dust; the air was completely motionless, had been for years, a decade-long doldrum zone. There were bones out there beyond the huts; cattle, goats, chickens, bleached platinum-white, half buried by the slowly building dunes, they were circled by the skeletons of vultures.

The channel crew was there because the headman had killed the Church technician who'd installed the mats. A centenarian with wrinkled leather skin, protruding bones, a ragged old loincloth; the embodiment of land wisdom. He looked directly into the camera with cloned black eyes, undaunted and contemptuous. 'Why have you done this?' he asked. 'First you murdered the air with your greed, now you send us machines that bring water from nothing. You have stretched our agony across time. We live on the price of your pity, coins you have cast away. Miserable beggars whose piety and distress is our only weapon. We are reduced to eternal compassion victims. If you truly pity us, give us back our dependence on the weather. Bring back the rain and the wind. Then all men may be equal in our dependency again.'

She had understood what the headman had meant, how he felt. The insulting humiliation of relying on a technology he couldn't begin to understand, sent as a gift by people he did not know, reducing him and his relatives to little more than chattels. A primitive culture preserved by godlike science, a throw-away act of charity. He'd lost every shred of dignity, his entire existence subject to whims outside his control. Whims of a culture that had wrecked his land in the pursuit of its own comfort. Unforgivable.

Primitive cultures were always assimilated into advanced cultures. Values supplanted, and finally ruined. A fundamental law of nature. And her own genetics laboratories had said the aliens were billions of years more advanced than humans.

Atomic structuring was the condenser mat all over again, and now she was a peasant villager. Greg's Russian general had the right idea, she thought, the same one as the headman.

*

The Pegasus dropped smoothly on to the Hambleton peninsula's mudflats, finishing up at a slight angle, nose pointing up towards the Mandel farmhouse. Julia made a grab for Matthew as the belly hatch opened. 'Now listen, your aunty Eleanor is pregnant, and that means you're not going to cause the slightest trouble for her. You'll do exactly as you're asked, you'll do it without complaining, and without arguing. Understood?'

His face transformed itself into a picture of hurt innocence. 'Mummy!'

'Is that understood?'

'Yes.'

She narrowed her eyes.

'Really,' he said.

'All right.'

The groves were alive with activity, people and handcarts, tractors, smaller children running under the trees. Shouts and snatches of song carried down the slope to where she was climbing up the limestone chunks. Smells of cooking and cut grass mingled through the muggy air. Humidity next to the reservoir was wicked. She could see the travellers were all in hats and caps, men stripped to the waist. She was attracting quite an audience.

Oliver and Anita came down to meet them, accompanied by five other kids. Daniella and Matthew joined them, and they all took off towards the field where the cars and vans were parked; two security hardliners in casual clothes trailing along behind.

Three hardliners followed Julia up to the farmhouse, two of them carrying the children's bags. There was a sixteen-wheel lorry parked in the farmyard. A couple of men were busy loading it with white kelpboard boxes full of oranges. They glanced briefly in her direction as she came through the gate.

Christine drove a tractor in from the groves, its trailer piled high with more white boxes. She waved at Julia, but didn't get down. Picking was a serious business, Julia reflected. The girl started to back the tractor towards the lorry, grinding through the gears.

Julia rapped her knuckles on the kitchen's door frame as she came in. Eleanor was sitting in the carver's chair at the head of the long bench table, three cybofax wafers spread out before her. She glanced up. 'Come in, you're not disturbing me. Trying to get some byte shuffling done. Looks like we've got a good yield this year.'

'Thanks for having the children,' Julia said. 'I just hated the idea of my problems ruining their holiday.'

'They're no trouble.' Eleanor raised a glass to Julia. 'Help yourself. It's only Perrier: if I can't touch alcohol then you can suffer as well.'

'The odd glass of wine wouldn't hurt.'

Eleanor's hand fluttered irritably. 'Ha, you know what Greg's like. Bloody men. One prenatal clinic, and they're all qualified gynaecologists.'

Julia pulled out a chair, and poured some Perrier out of the bottle. 'Royan was the same. I suppose it's excusable in his case. After I had him stitched back together he was very health conscious – exercise, diets, screening cream. The works.'

'You miss him?'

'Course I miss him.' She rolled the glass between her palms. 'That's the problem, I think. The way I treated him. I made him, Eleanor, took him out of Mucklands Wood and turned him into my ideal man. So stupid.'

'Don't be silly, he had to leave Mucklands. You knew it, I knew it, Greg knew it. Royan did too, afterwards.'

'Yes, but I never let him go free, did I? I had it all planned out, his role in life. We were such good friends, you see, after he saved Grandpa's NN core from the virus. It was a dream for me. I had to go out in public and be *the* Julia Evans, talk contracts, deal with politicians, arrange finance with banks. Dear Lord, I was only eighteen. Then when all that company work was finished for the day, I could run away into my mind, and there he'd be, waiting for me. It was like having one of those imaginary friends children invent to keep themselves company. No one else knew he was there, no one else could see him. He was all mine; and we talked, and he sympathized with me, and I felt sorry for him. What we had was precious. I thought it would be the same after Mucklands. I wanted it to be the same.'

'He did too.'

'Maybe. But he never knew there could be anything else, not at first. He really was born again. A whole new and bright world. But I kept giving him things to do, hotrod for me, father children. That was it, all along, the one thing that was always in our way: I couldn't change, not with Event Horizon to manage. So he had to fit into my life. We could never begin together.'

Eleanor stood up, pressing her fist into her back as she straightened, and opened one of the wooden cupboards below the workbench. It was a fridge inside. She took out a bottle of white wine with a Kent label. 'So he felt smothered,' she said. 'Men always do around women like you.'

'Maybe. So how does Greg cope? You're not exactly a quiet obedient little housewife.'

Eleanor poured a glass of wine and handed it to Julia, a faint smile at distant memories playing on her lips. 'We worked it out. The gulf wasn't as big as you and Royan, mind.'

'Yeah. Do you know what he called himself, Royan? A prince consort. Says a lot about how much consideration I gave him.'

'Oh, come on, Julia, the whole world lives in your shadow.

He knew that right from the start, the failure isn't all down to you.'

She drank some of the wine, it was nice, dry and smooth. Eleanor understood, thank God; she was one of the few people Julia could really let her hair down with. They'd known each other long enough now; Julia had been the chief bridesmaid when she married Greg. 'He wanted to be my equal, that's what he said.'

Eleanor sniffed her wine and took a sip. 'And what if he fails? Had he thought of that? What was he going to do then? Find a different alien?'

'Lord knows. He's causing enough trouble with this one. Like a child really, he never learned to accept failure. Week-long setbacks are as close as he's ever come. Everything is solvable in the end.'

'Oh dear.'

'Yes.'

They smiled, and drank some more wine.

28

The waves were moving in irregular patterns across the North Sea, small, high white horses clashing in fast rucks, whipped up by submerged obstacles. The North Sea Farm Company wasn't as big as Listoel, there were only a hundred developed fields so far, but the water fruit it harvested raised a much higher price than krill. And tasted one hell of a lot better, Victor reckoned, but then what didn't?

Water fruit globes resembled pumpkins, a thick wrinkled yellow-brown rind enclosing an almost apple-like flesh. Victor always thought of them as tasting like salty melons. But they were protein rich, and popular throughout Europe. New varieties were introduced each year as the geneticists refined them.

They had developed into quite an important industry. Most countries had plantations dotted around their coasts. And the shallower southern half of the North Sea, with its warmth and low salinity, provided excellent growing conditions.

Julia had started the North Sea Farm Company twelve years earlier, assisted by a large Ministry of Fisheries grant. The division wasn't as large as some of the food combine farms which had sprung up in the North Sea, but it was turning in a reasonable profit now.

When the nodes squirted a profile of the Farm into his mind, he'd seen the organization was top-heavy with research personnel, and a lot of the fields were experimenting with new techniques. Julia covering her options again, he suspected.

It would have been precisely those research facilities which attracted Royan. The station's genetics laboratories were equipped to handle very sophisticated gene-tailoring operations.

Victor could make out the fields below the surface as the Pegasus began its approach run. Kilometre-long walls of brick-red gene-tailored coral formed a broad chessboard of squares. New walls were growing out from the edges, a tracery of spindly lines probing the stark sand. The colours of the water fruit crops planted inside the walls ran through every shade of brown.

There were various towers and platforms protruding from the water at regular intervals. Some he recognized as twentieth-century oil platforms. Waste not, want not. But the majority of structures were built up from the same concrete sections as the thermal-generator platforms at Listoel, mass-produced by Event Horizon's yards on the Tyne. Cargo ships were docked with the platforms, loading up. Squat, heavily laden barges crisscrossed the fields, small bright yellow submarines were visible underwater.

The Pegasus landed on one of the concrete platforms, and Victor trotted down the belly hatch stairs. Eliot Haydon, the Farm's director, was waiting for him, dressed in navy-blue shorts and a baseball cap with the Event Horizon triangle and flying-V logo on the peak.

Victor accessed his personnel profile: forty-seven years old, graduated from Norwich University with a marine biology degree, been with the company nineteen years, appointed as a divisional director five years ago, largely credited with making the Farm a profitable concern. Another of those smoothly professional Event Horizon premier-grade executives. He wondered if Julia classed him in the same category. Probably.

Eliot Haydon shook Victor's hand in a warm dry grip. 'Mr Tyo, not often we get a visit from your office.'

'Judy Tobandi is a good officer,' he said. 'The Farm's never been a problem from a security point of view. If people have their finger on the pulse, don't interfere, I say.'

Eliot Haydon smiled, showing four solid gold teeth. 'Well now, how about that? Enlightened administration, and at the highest level, too. You must have slipped through the personnel catchment net. What can I do for you?'

'I'm chasing after Royan. Do you know him?'

'Yes, of course. But I'm afraid you're too late if you want to talk to him, he left us three weeks ago. Didn't you check with our management cores?'

'That's part of my problem. We did check. There's no record of him at all.'

'What?'

'It's rather complicated, but he's covering his tracks very thoroughly. Can you tell me what he was doing here?'

'Yes, he was researching coral genetics, trying to improve mineral absorption rates.' A flicker of unease darkened Eliot Haydon's broad sunny face. 'Well, that's what he said. It was a temporary posting, of course. We get quite a few scientists visiting from other Farms and national marine institutes. Now the first rush of competition is easing off, we all find co-operation helpful.'

'Did you assign Royan a genetics laboratory?'

'Yes. He wanted one for himself. It's a bit unusual, but his authority rating entitled him. There were a few complaints when we reshuffled.'

'What happened afterwards?'

'After what?'

'After he left. Was there any equipment he left behind? Who moved into the laboratory? What happened to his research subjects?'

Eliot Haydon pulled his cybofax out of his shorts pocket and asked it a couple of questions. He consulted the screen, then gave Victor a thoughtful look. 'According to our records, his lab is still unoccupied. That isn't right at all, lab space is at a premium in the station. The management cores are programmed to reassign it as soon as it became available again.'

Victor had been expecting something like it, resentful of the way he was being led about like a cyborg. 'I'd like to see it, please.'

*

The little cylindrical submarine had a transparent hemispherical nose. Victor sat beside Eliot Haydon in the front as the farm director piloted them away from the platform, using a steering-wheel which could have come from a car. It was designed to ferry twenty people down to the Farm's main underwater station, but there was only him and his bodyguard on board.

The water was surprisingly clean. Eliot Haydon explained that the water fruit itself was responsible, its matted root system holding down the sand. A variety Event Horizon's geneticists had developed.

Ripe globes of fruit hung a metre above the sea bed, suspended on a twisted ropy chord, like a squadron of tethered balloons. They were swinging rhythmically in the slow pulse of currents. Thirty Frankenstein dolphins, with long dextrous flippers, swam among the rows. He watched one wriggle underneath a water fruit, its powerful snout cutting clean through the cord. It gripped the globe with its flippers, and carried it to a big net bag at the end of the field, dropping it through the open neck with the accuracy and panache of a basketball player.

The main station loomed beyond the fields, a fat yellow-painted saucer sixty metres in diameter, with portholes round the rim. It stood fifteen metres off the sea bed on three sturdy cylindrical legs. Eliot Haydon steered the sub underneath it, manoeuvring up to an airlock set in the keel. They docked with a loud clunk. Pumps started to whirr.

'We keep the station's internal pressure at one atmosphere,' Eliot Haydon said, as he ran the powerdown program through the sub's control 'ware. 'That way once we're docked, we stay docked. Opposite of spacecraft.'

'What exactly goes on in this station?' Victor asked.

Eliot Haydon stood up and walked back down the sub to the airlock set in the ceiling. He checked the seal display before

409

starting to turn the lock wheel. 'Some practical work; investigating sea bed growing techniques, methods of harvesting. Several of the food combine farms use drones to pick the water fruit; we found the Frankenstein dolphins are just as efficient. But mainly it's a genetics research facility. We improve the water fruit species, modify fish. One team is working on coral; we wanted to give the field reefs small caves, like Swiss cheese, so we could breed crustaceans in them. The pilot scheme is quite successful.'

The circular airlock opened with a hissing sound. A small shower of water sprinkled down on Eliot Haydon's head. He started to climb up the metal ladder.

*

The laboratory was GD7, a rectangular chamber on the edge of the station. Three portholes looked out over the fields and reefs, some chemical aspect of the thick material turning them a deep blue-green. Fans of jade light poured in, dancing across the white-topped benches which ran along the wall.

GD7 appeared to be a standard set up. The benches were crowded with specialist terminals and composite equipment modules, long crystalline glassware arrays and culture vats. A rack of empty aquariums stood along the back wall. There was a section given over to an electron microscope. All of it was clean, unused, switched off. Waiting, Victor thought.

Kiley was resting on a pedestal in the centre. An octagonal framework two metres in diameter, half a metre high, its side panels covered in crumbling, grey thermal/particle protection foam. Thimble-sized cold gas thruster nozzles poked out above the foam, along with three sets of star-tracker sensors, a couple of slim conical omnidirectional antennas, tarnished-silver electrical umbilical sockets, and an interface key. Seven corners sprouted a square dull-copper thermal radiator fin. The eighth had a long grapple pin for the remote manipulator arm on *Newton's Apple* to grab during retrieval.

A metre-high truss structure on top had held the probe's collection flask. It was empty now, mounting points trailing a spaghetti tangle of severed power lines and fibre optic cable. Above that was the communication dish, a gossamer-thin umbrella of silver foil, badly crumpled and torn.

Victor looked round, and saw the collection flask on one of the benches, a titanium rugby ball, split into two halves. Empty. There was a plain white card resting against it. He picked it up.

I'll bet it's you, Victor.

The handwriting was Royan's. He crumpled it into a tight ball. It was a superbly equipped lab. What had Royan done here?

'What is this thing?' Eliot Haydon asked, he was walking cautiously round Kiley, staring. 'A space probe?'

'Yes. A Jupiter sample return.'

'Gods, what's it doing here?'

'That's a bloody good question.'

Open Channel to Julia Evans NN Core. *I've found Kiley, or at least what's left of it.*

Great. Where?

It's in the Farm's main underwater station, laboratory GD7. That's a genetics lab. But there's nothing else left, he's cleaned it out.

Hang on, I'll access that lab's memory cores again. They've already been reviewed once.

Victor thought he detected a hint of resentment in the soundless voice. 'When Royan left, what did he take with him, can you remember?' he asked.

Eliot Haydon was still looking at Kiley, left hand stroking one of the thermal radiator panels. 'Just a standard air cargo pod.' He brought his hand away, rubbing his fingers together. 'Oh, and a plant. Funny looking thing, like a cross between a cacti and a palm. He was carrying it when he got on the plane, that's why I remember.'

Victor felt a tingle of alarm. 'Was it flowering?'

'Was it . . .' Eliot Haydon trailed off into uncertain bemusement.

'Flowering? Did it have any flowers?'

'I don't think so, no.'

411

I still can't locate anything, Victor, NN core one said.

He turned a full circle. The personality package had to be here. Royan would expect him to work it out, to come in and see the obvious.

Start with the basics, he told himself. A data construct has to be stored in 'ware. And it has to be obvious. Royan wasn't hiding anything, they were supposed to be warnings. A location proof against accidental discovery, but not obscure.

He wanted Greg and his intuition here in the lab. Greg would have seen it straight off.

Victor turned slowly and looked at Kiley. The tiny glass eye of the interface key stared back at him. He pulled his cybofax out of his inside jacket pocket and held it up.

29

The armoury was a long windowless concrete room, metal lockers along one wall and weapons racks along the other. There were ten tables running down the middle, fitted with test rigs and the various cybernetic tools the armourers used. The sight and warm oil smell of the place took Greg right back to his squaddie days. Even the pre-mission chatter of the security crash team was the same, brash with that unique brand of strained humour.

He was sitting on a bench watching Suzi being kitted out by Alex Lahey, one of the armourers. He had found a muscle armour suit small enough for her, and now he was programming it to accept motor neurone impulses from her implant. A thick bundle of fibre-optic cables ran from the 'ware interface socket on the suit's chest to the terminal he was operating on the table. Only the helmet had been left off, leaving Suzi's head sticking out of the black barrel-like torso.

'First there's healthy paranoia,' Greg said. 'And then there's obsessive psychosis. The dividing line is pretty thin.'

'Bollocks. Leol got out of that hospital in Nigeria. You think he's going to give up on Charlotte now?'

'No. But how's he going to find her?'

Suzi gave a disparaging grunt. 'The bastard's good, Greg. Give him that. And he's got Clifford Jepson's money behind him.'

'Victor's better. And we've got Julia's money.'

'Yeah, sure.'

Alex Lahey looked up from the terminal he had plugged into Suzi's armour suit. 'Could you raise your left arm, please.'

She moved it up slowly until it was level with her shoulder, then it suddenly shot up to point at the ceiling. 'Fuck's sake!'

'Sorry,' Alex Lahey said. He studied the terminal cube, muttering to himself.

'Hey, can I lower it, or what?'

Alex Lahey didn't look up. 'Yes, yes.'

'This personalized tank, bit over the top, isn't it?'

Suzi's gauntleted left hand slapped her torso, producing a hollow thud. 'I can face him now, Greg. No more running, no more evasion and decoy. Christ, that was fucking humiliating. You should try a suit out, gives your confidence an orgasm.'

'No thanks, muscle armour was after my time. I'll stick to what I've got. Good old mystic intuition. It's kept me alive this long.'

'Yeah? So what does it say about Royan?' Suzi asked.

'Tell you, he's up there.' He surprised himself. The words had come out without any conscious thought, he hadn't ordered a gland secretion, either.

'Huh,' Suzi grunted.

'Would you touch your toes, please,' Alex Lahey said.

Greg kept his amusement in check at the slightly ridiculous sight of a muscle armour suit doing callisthenics as Suzi tested each limb's articulation. The rest of the crash team started to check out their weapons from the rack.

Suzi's armour suit split open down the side of the torso, and she began to wriggle her legs out. Her tracksuit fabric was heavily creased where the suit's spongy internal lining had contracted about her.

Alex Lahey began to unplug the fibre-optic cables. 'Your knee shouldn't be a problem,' he said as Suzi emerged. 'The suit will support it.'

'Great.' She dropped lightly on to the floor, and promptly flexed her leg, rubbing at the bioware sheath.

'Could you thumbprint this, please?' He proffered a cybofax. 'It's the release authorization for the suit.'

Greg looked at the bare concrete of the ceiling, offering up a small prayer.

'You betcha.'

Suzi was smiling acid sweet as she pressed her thumb against the cybofax's sensitive pad. She eyed the weapons rack. 'I'd like one of those Honeywell pulsed plasma carbines; a Konica rip gun, plus eight power magazine cells; five Loral fifteen-centimetre pattern-homing missiles, programmable from my implant; and ten directed lance charges with timed and remote detonators. And have you recharged my Browning?'

Alex Lahey sagged in place, his watery eyes giving Suzi a disbelieving stare.

'What's up? Do you need another thumbprint?'

'Whatever the lady wants, Alex,' Melvyn Ambler said in a pained tone. 'Put it all in with the rest of our gear.'

'You're a gent,' Suzi grinned.

Greg turned round to see the crash team captain standing behind him.

'The spaceplane will be here in five minutes,' Melvyn said. 'We'll load our gear and launch straight away.' He held up two maroon flight bags. 'I've got your shipsuits. Put your clothes in the bag, you can wear them again in New London. Do either of you need an anti-nausea infusion for the flight?'

'Not me,' Greg said. 'I've been in freefall before. Didn't suffer then.'

'I'll take one,' Suzi said brightly.

'Right.' Melvyn Ambler hesitated. 'Are we likely to meet a hazard up there?'

'I'll give you a full briefing on the spaceplane,' Greg said. 'But you're along mainly for your deterrence value.'

'Thank you. Mr Tyo said you are in complete control of the operation.'

'He's got to be fucking kidding,' Suzi muttered.

*

Spaceplane shipsuits seemed to have improved. The last time Greg had gone into orbit the rubber garment they gave him looked like it was sprayed on. You needed to be a mesomorph to wear one with any dignity. This time Melvyn had provided him with a comfortable, fairly loose, ginger-coloured one-piece with elasticated wrist and ankle bands; the wide pinned-back lapels taken straight off the kind of jacket a nineteen-thirties flying ace would've worn. A multifunction 'ware wafer was clipped into its pocket on his upper right arm, monitoring his physiological functions, along with the atmospheric pressure, temperature, gas composition, and radiation levels.

He carried his maroon flight bag out to *Anastasia*, the *Orion*-class spaceplane that had landed in the centre of the generator platform. The twenty-strong crash team were trooping into the airlock in front of him, all of them in the same ginger one-piece, a cyborg army. Charlotte and Fabian walked behind, talking in low tones.

Anastasia was a simple delta shape, twenty-six metres long, built around a pair of induction rams; convergent tubes which compressed incoming air, heated it with a battery of radio-frequency induction coils, and blasted it out through expansion nozzles. A simple, clean propulsion system which took over from the fans at Mach seven and boosted the spaceplane up to orbital velocity. There was also an auxiliary reaction drive fitted which made her capable of lifting twenty-five tonnes of payload direct to New London. Her pearly lofriction fuselage glinted bright and cool under the mid-morning sun. Big scarlet dragon escutcheons were painted on the fin.

A convoy of five small drone lorries had drawn up under-neath, and the crash team's armourers were loading pods of equipment into the rear cargo bay through hatches in the tail cone.

Greg ordered a small neurohormone secretion as he waited at the foot of the airstair. His intuition didn't say much about anything, a grudging sense of inevitability was the best it could manage. He always thought of the ability as being slightly timeloose, a weak form of precognition. That ought to mean death should ring out loud and clear.

'Anything?' Suzi asked. She knew how he relied on it.

'No. Not a thing.' He turned to Charlotte and Fabian. The ginger shipsuit looked stunning on the girl. 'Time to go,' he told her.

She bent down and gave Fabian a long, lingering kiss.

Greg shifted uncomfortably; Suzi chortled and started up the airstairs, swinging her flight bag jauntily.

Charlotte eventually broke off the embrace. 'This won't take long,' she murmured in a voice so quiet Greg could barely make out the words. She and Fabian looked as if they were being parted for eternity. Fabian flipped some hair out of his eyes. 'Come back to me,' he pleaded mournfully.

'You know I will.' Charlotte planted a final kiss on his brow, and went up the stairs in a hurry. Greg tugged his cap on, a close-fitting padded dome that came down over his ears, protection against hard corners when he was in freefall. He followed Charlotte up the stairs; when he looked back Fabian was sprinting for the crew quarters, a hardline bodyguard in pursuit.

＊

Anastasia seated forty passengers in her cabin. It was compact, but not cramped. The walls were covered in a quilt of grey padding, even the deck was slightly springy as Greg walked down the aisle. A biolum strip ran along the centre of the ceiling, fabric hoops hanging on either side, reminding him of the handholds for standing passengers on a bus. At the rear of the cabin was a galley and a couple of toilet cubicles. He eyed them warily, a series of unwelcome memories surfacing, painfully tight tubes and suction holes that pinched. Best to wait until New London.

There was no separate cockpit. The pilot sat behind the narrow curving windscreen, dressed in the same kind of ship-suit as Greg, except his was silvery grey. He didn't even have a flight console, no controls of any kind. Sitting with arms neatly folded across his lap, eyes half-closed in some zen-like contemplation. Multicoloured geometric spiderwebs rolled across the windscreen itself. Greg guessed the pilot must use a processor node to interface with the spaceplane's flight 'ware.

He didn't enjoy the idea. When he was in the army he used to fly parafoils and microlites; direct physical control, you shifted your weight and the wing banked in response. It was something you could feel, solid and dependable. Real flying.

Surely the spaceplane must have some kind of manual fall-back? The pilot would probably laugh if he asked. He looked young, mid-twenties; a generation that wasn't so much 'ware literate as 'ware addicted.

The crash team were choosing their seats noisily, like a small-town rugby club on their way to a match, all jokes and laughs. Two stewards helped to stow their flight bags in the lockers under the seats.

Suzi was sitting in one of the seats behind the pilot. Greg claimed the one next to her, where he could see out of the graphic-etched windscreen. He touched the activation stud on his armrest, and the seat cushioning slid round his legs, gripping gently.

Charlotte and Melvyn Ambler were sitting across the aisle from them, Rick in the row behind. The security captain leaned forward. 'That's everyone,' he told the pilot.

'OK. Flight time will be about three and a half hours, we should rendezvous with New London somewhere over South America.' The airlock hatch closed, cutting off the thrum of the platform's thermal generators.

Greg heard the compressors wind up. There was a tremble of

motion, and the corner of the thermal generator building was dropping out of sight through the windscreen.

'You told Eleanor where we were going?' Suzi asked.

'Yeah. She'll worry about it, but she'd worry more if she found out and I hadn't told her. I said the crash team was providing hardline cover now. That ought to help.'

'Mean she'll be happier that you're not dependent on me no more.'

Anastasia shifted to horizontal flight mode, deck tilted at fifteen degrees as it climbed, pushing eastwards, aiming for the Bay of Biscay. Greg sniffed at the air; the pervasive sulphur smell of the thermal generator vent pipes was missing, filtered out by the life-support system. The spaceplane's purified air was curiously empty, an absence of scent more than anything.

'Why do all the women in my life give me such a hard time?' he complained.

Suzi laughed. 'Eleanor's not a problem. You two, fucking lucky, you are.'

'I don't know what you're moaning about. Andria seemed like a nice girl.'

Suzi glanced over at Charlotte and Melvyn Ambler, her voice dropped. 'The greatest, Greg. No shit. Me and her, it's happening. Funny, I mean, what I am, who'd want me? But she does.'

He didn't need his gland to see how earnest she was. Suzi taking life that seriously would take some getting used to. 'You'll have to bring her out to the farm some time.'

'She's pregnant.'

'So's Eleanor. They'll get on all right.'

'Right.' She whistled through her teeth. 'Greg? I'm gonna get out after this. For the kid, you know? So, like, if you hear of anything coming up on the market, pub or something, let me know.'

'Sure.' He ought to have a word with Julia, see if she could find a likely club, sell it to Suzi through a front. He settled back into the seat. Attention to detail, that's what it was all about. He'd put a note in his cybofax, later, when Suzi couldn't see.

Anastasia switched to her induction rams three hundred kilometres south-west of the Scilly Isles. Greg heard a crackling roar build until it was loud enough to block ordinary talking. He was pressed down in the seat, estimating the G-force at about one and three-quarters. There was a disorientating sensation as the deck began to level out once they reached thirty-five kilometres altitude, yet at the same time the growing acceleration effect made it seem like the angle was increasing. Perhaps he should have taken that infusion after all.

The pale azure sky began to darken beyond the windscreen.

It took seven minutes after the induction rams came on to reach their orbital transfer trajectory, slicing cleanly through the mesosphere and into the rarefied lower chemosphere where the power-to-thrust ratio decayed drastically. The induction rams cut off over Egypt. *Anastasia* was doing Mach twenty-nine, coasting gently upwards.

The stars had come out, burning steadily in the night sky. Earth was a fringe of blue-white light along the bottom of the windscreen.

Greg let out an alarmingly damp burp as the nearly forgotten sensation of freefall buoyed his stomach up towards his sternum.

'We'll be performing our New London flight trajectory burn in eighty seconds – mark,' the pilot said.

The silence Greg had been expecting was punctuated by sharp snapping sounds of the induction ram linings contracting as they shed their thermal load. Electrohydrostatic actuators whined on the threshold of hearing.

Suzi pulled a sour face. 'Bollocks, three more hours of this.'

'Isn't the infusion working?' Greg asked.

'Yeah. But that only holds your gut together, it doesn't stop this whole scene from being a major downer. Floating about like this ain't right, Greg. I'm not a fucking fish.'

A small portion of his mind was secretly glad there was something he could handle better than her. Of course, he'd done a lot of flying in his Army days, burning the nausea out.

'It took me a day to get up to New London last time,' Charlotte said. 'I went up on a transfer liner.'

'I was in one of the low Earth orbit stations for a week,' Rick said. 'Checking out a radio telescope before it was boosted out to Ell Two behind the moon. It beats the hell out of dieting, I must have lost a couple of kilos.'

'How about you, Melvyn?' Greg asked. 'You ever been up here before?'

'Sure. Victor Tyo likes us to familiarize ourselves with every possible environment we're likely to operate in. I get rotated up to New London for a month every two years.'

'That sounds like Victor,' Greg said.

Anastasia's reaction-control thrusters fired suddenly, a rapid burst of pistol shots. Greg saw the Earth's coronal haze slide off the bottom of the windscreen.

'Stand by,' the pilot called out.

Greg tried to make some sense out of the graphics scrawling across the windscreen, flexible holographic wormholes of blue and green, red cubes rotating, yellow lines in wavering grid patterns. Nothing was bloody labelled.

The auxiliary reaction drive came on. A pair of bell-shaped nozzles in *Anastasia*'s tail. Water was pumped into their vaporization chambers where it was energized directly from the giga-conductor cells. It emerged from the nozzles as a brilliant flame of ions.

Greg was pushed back into his seat again. *Anastasia* appeared to be standing vertically. The G-force was much lower this time, about a third.

*

New London followed a slightly elliptical orbit high above the Earth, with an apogee of forty-five thousand kilometres and a perigee of forty-two thousand kilometres. *Anastasia* rose out towards it in a long flat arc.

New London was visible from Earth even during the day, a

fuzzy oval patch of light, far brighter than the Moon. During most of the approach it was a sharp-edged nebula, building in size and magnitude.

Greg spent the last hour in his seat, watching the rock and its attendant archipelago resolve. The angle of their approach, virtually straight up, meant that the archipelago grew longer the whole time, stretching out along the rock's orbital track. At first it looked like the rock was the head of a strangely stable comet, one possessing a solid diamanté tail; then he began to make out the individual orbs.

The asteroid Julia had chosen to carry the torch of her new world industrial order was sixteen kilometres long, with an irregular width varying between five and eight kilometres, one end flared out into an asymmetrical bulge. One of her Merlin probes had surveyed it fourteen years ago; until then it had been a smear of light in a telescope, and a catalogue number: 2040BA. A fleet of the little robot prospecting craft had been amassing compositional data on the Apollo Amour asteroids for nearly a decade. It was a project Philip Evans had started even before the PSP fell; he had predicted the development of the space industry, and wanted to use the probes to give Event Horizon a data monopoly. Julia had carried on with the Merlin project after his death, launching up to fifteen a year. 2040BA was her reward for persistence; a nickel-iron asteroid orbiting two hundred million kilometres out from the Sun, no different to a hundred others the Merlins had examined. Except at some time in the distant past it had struck a carbonaceous chondritic asteroid. The collision had deposited a thick smear of shale, eight kilometres long, down the flank of 2040BA. It was a sticky tar, rich with nitrogen and carbon and hydrogen, millions of tonnes of them.

They were the chemicals which made New London possible. By itself a nickel-iron asteroid was worth trillions for the metal contained in its ores, but the cost of supporting the teams of miners and refinery operators would have been prohibitive. Every consumable would have to be lifted into orbit for them;

even with giga-conductor spaceplanes it would be a marginal venture. To make the investment attractive, a mining team would have to be self-sustaining. At the lowest level that meant hydroponics and vat-grown-meat. At the other end of the scale, space activists dreamt of capturing both nickel-iron and carbonaceous chondritic asteroids and using them in combination to build cylindrical O'Neill colonies, twenty kilometres long, orbiting Gardens of Eden, revitalizing the Earth physically and spiritually.

2040BA allowed Julia to compromise between the two.

The relays of astronaut crews she sent out to 2040BA took two years to capture it. They detonated strategically-placed ten-megaton electron-compression devices at its bulbous end, altering its orbital track and increasing its long-axis rotation.

'I wanted to use nukes,' Julia had confided to Greg and Eleanor once the mission was underway. 'Use up all the old superpower arsenals. That would have given people something they could understand and appreciate. The old age visibly going out in a blaze of glory to usher in the new. Now wouldn't that be a sight?'

She needn't have worried. People interpreted the asteroid's arrival as the symbol of the new age. It brought hope to a psychologically leaden world. A technophilic *coup d'état*, signalling the end of the worst aspects of the Warming. When you looked up you could see that there was somebody who had the guts and the drive to achieve something again, instead of just muddling through the way things had been going for nearly two decades. The somebody being Julia. It was the capture mission more than anything else – her inheritance, the giga-conductor monopoly, Peterborough's incredible renewal – that catapulted her into the global public limelight.

The last three months of 2040BA's journey became the greatest spectator event in human history. Greg had always wondered if it was coincidence that the final electron-compression device was detonated above night-time Europe. Julia working a subtle PR ploy, or Royan crowning their achievement with a typical brass neck gesture? Whichever, after that Julia's kudos hit the stratosphere.

He could still remember the Last Blast party, it was country-wide. New Year's Eve plonked down in the middle of a sultry cloudless August night. Hambleton had hosted a street barbecue, the whole village sitting round trestle tables in front of the church. Christine had been about five, but they'd let her stay up.

Eleven thirty-seven: the time was tattooed in his mind. 2040BA was a star brighter than Venus, then the last electron-compression device went off, stabilizing its orbit. A ten-megaton explosion, jetting out an incandescent plume of vaporized rock. The discharge had lasted for about a minute, growing as broad as a full moon before fading to violet and dispersing. They had all watched in silence, children, adults, pensioners, looking straight up; Greg inanely waiting to hear a distant rumble from the explosion.

The mining machines Julia sent up to Earth's new moonlet cut out a cylindrical chamber five kilometres long and three in diameter, Hyde Cavern. Rotation gave it an Earth-standard gravity. Solar furnaces liberated oxygen from New London's rock. Event Horizon crews collected the shale smear, shoving it through giant distillation modules, refining all the chemicals necessary for a working biosphere.

Hyde Cavern was given an atmosphere, water, light, warmth, gene-tailored food plants, insects, and soil bacteria. Engineering teams from Event Horizon and various kombinates' space indus-try divisions moved in, and began refining the ore in earnest. Microgee-processing factories were boosted up from their low orbit to swarm in attendance; it was cheaper to use New London as a dormitory for the operating crews than costly habitation stations.

Greg could see New London itself through *Anastasia*'s wind-screen, a dark head to the archipelago of high-albedo orbs. The rock's long axis was orientated north/south, so that it rolled along its orbit. A counter-rotating docking spindle extended a kilometre and a half out of the southern hub, supporting a diamond-shaped solar cell array four kilometres square. The northern hub had a similar spindle, ending in a concave circular solar mirror five kilometres in diameter. It was built up from hexagonal sections a hundred metres across, with a speckle pattern of tiny black spots showing the holes that had been torn in them down the years. A focusing mirror hung two kilometres over the centre, sending the collected beam back down through an aperture in the middle. As he watched, one of the orbs peeped slowly over the mirror's rim like a small sun rising above the horizon.

The orb was part of the excavation from the second chamber which was currently being hollowed out. A larger one than Hyde Cavern this time, eight kilometres long. The mining machines which cut through the ore crushed it into a residue of fine sand that was a mixture of metal powder and rock dust. It was impelled along the northern hub's spindle into the foundry plant at its tip, where the mirror focus was aimed. The intense heat combined the rock and metal into a glutinous magma which the foundry crews called slowsilver. It was done for convenience, in freefall any liquid was easier to control and direct than a river of sand, and after mining came the problem of storage.

The slowsilver was pumped through one of a bagpipe array of extrusion pipes out into space in the shadow of the mirror, where it was allowed to accrete until it formed a globe fifty metres in diameter. Then after the outer shell had cooled and solidified the pipe disengaged, setting it loose. The foundry produced a hundred and forty orbs a day, a constant emission of metallic spawn.

Julia had no option but to store the second cavern detritus in this fashion, New London's refineries and microgee materials-processing modules could only consume a fraction of the mining machines' daily output. So the orbs accumulated in the archipelago, tens of thousands of them, like an elongated globular cluster staining space behind the asteroid. Some of them were nearly pure silver, others had abstract rainbow swirls frozen into their surface where exotic salts and minerals had curdled and reacted from the heat.

Refinery complexes floated round the fringes of the archipelago; big cylindrical modules, two hundred metres long, forty wide, hanging behind a kilometre-wide solar mirror. Perspective was difficult out here, part of his mind saw the refineries as chrome water lilies drifting on a velvet ocean. Almost an op art canvas. Space hardware had an inherent harshness, he thought, every square centimetre was functional, precise, there were no cool shades nor half colours, white and silver ruled supreme.

There was an annular tug departing one of the refineries, an open three-hundred-metre-diameter ring of girders with a drive unit at the centre, starting its three-month inward spiral to low Earth orbit. Ten foamedsteel lifting bodies were attached to the outside of the ring, blunt-nose triangles, massing three thousand tonnes, but with a density lighter than water. Space-born birds which would be dropped into the atmosphere and glide to a splashdown by one of the two permanent recovery fleets on station in the Pacific, or the one in the Atlantic.

Anastasia was heading in for New London's southern hub. This end of the asteroid was covered in long thermal-dump panels, radiating out from a central crater like aluminium impact rays. Two spherical Dragonflight transfer liners were docked halfway down the spindle. A steady flow of small tugs and personnel commuters was berthing and disengaging, carrying crews and cargoes between New London and the clusters of microgee modules holding station south of its main solar panel.

Greg tried to draw the image of New London inside his mind, to capture its essence, sketching out the crumpled dusty surface, small high-walled craters. Hyde Cavern: gaping emptiness surrounded by thick shadow folds of solid rock, the second chamber, mushroom shaped, unfinished. Shafts and rail tunnels knitted the two chambers together, black gossamer lines cutting through the two-kilometre rock barrier, looping underneath the valley floors in complex twists; there were buried fresh-water reservoirs and surge chambers, caverns housing reserves of oxygen and nitrogen.

The ghost image turned slowly behind his closed eyes, pulsing with the slow rhythm of life. Hyde Cavern a warm heart, a kernel of expectation and promise. He could sense the strength and determination it housed, a hazy aural glow spun out by the combined psyche of its inhabitants. The asteroid nestled at the centre of a spectral whirlpool of human dreams.

He felt it then, a solitary discrepant thread impinging on the communion, not a contaminant, but aloof from the consensus, different. Alien.

Anastasia's cabin trickled back into existence around Greg as his mind let the phantasm slither away. 'It's here,' he said. The asteroid's southern end was sliding by outside the windscreen, ribbed thermal-dump panels pinned to the brown-grey rock by enormous pylons, a maze of yellow and blue thermal shunt conduits laid out underneath.

Suzi cocked her head, her cap making her appear strangely skeletal. 'What is?'

'The alien, it's inside New London.'

'Shit. Where?'

He tried to shrug, but the muscle movement simply pushed his shoulders away from the seat back. 'You want specifics, use a crystal ball. My espersense is good for about half a kilometre if I really push it, and solid rock blocks it completely.'

'So how the fuck do you know it's there?'

'Intuition.'

She opened her mouth to shout. Reconsidered. 'How about Royan? He there too?'

'Dunno.'

'Great. So what do we do?'

'Stick with our original scenario. Find Charlotte's priest.'

'Hmm.' Suzi waved her cybofax wafer. 'Been updating on these Celestial Apostles. Beats me why Victor doesn't just flush them out the airlock. Fucking weirdos.'

'I think I detect Julia's hand in that. She always allows a little looseness in human systems. The Celestials are harmless, and they support her long-range aims, if not her methods. As long as they don't get out of control, why bother?'

'You think they're the ones in contact with the alien?'

'It's as good a guess as any. The psychology certainly fits. They'd treat it as a messiah. The only group of people who'd keep quiet about it, if it asked. Which prompts the question "How did it find them?"'

*

New London's southern hub crater was a kilometre wide and three hundred metres deep, the walls perfectly flat. It had been cut out by the mining machines; the electron-compression devices had all been detonated at the northern end.

Anastasia glided over the rim and its picket ring of radars. The floor below was a near solid disk of metal, massive circular bearings in the centre supported the two-hundred-metre-diameter spindle, outside that were tanks, lift rails, observation galleries, airlocks, three concentric rings of lights illuminating the rim walls, bulky incomprehensible machinery.

Anastasia's reaction-control thrusters fired. Greg's visual orientation began to alter as the spaceplane turned. The crater floor tilted up slowly to become a wall, the rim wall shifted to a valley floor curving up to the vertical and beyond. There was another sequence of drumbeat bursts from the reaction-control thrusters as the pilot changed *Anastasia*'s attitude again.

Greg heard the unmistakable metallic rumbling of the undercarriage lowering. The crater wall curved up out of sight in front of *Anastasia*'s nose; it was moving, he could see a strip of small white lights running round the circumference, New London's rotation carried them down the windscreen and under the spaceplane. To Greg it looked as if *Anastasia* was flying low above a smooth rock plain.

There was a final burst from the reaction-control thrusters, and *Anastasia* began to descend. It was like touching down on a runway, the difference being *Anastasia* was stationary and the crater rim was moving. They landed with a gentle bump. Electric motors accelerated *Anastasia*'s undercarriage bogies, chasing New London's rotation.

Suzi's jaws were clamped shut, her cheeks very pale, staring rigidly ahead. Greg could feel the spaceplane racing forward, yet their speed relative to the rim was visibly slowing. The starfield and spindle began to turn.

'Down and matched,' the pilot announced.

Greg started to register the low gravity field. Blood was draining from his face, that annoying fluid puffiness abating.

Anastasia taxied towards the circular wall of metal and a waiting airlock.

*

They came out of the airlock tube into a rock-walled reception room. Greg walked carefully in the low gravity field, very conscious of inertia, each step carried him a metre and a half.

New London's Governor was waiting for him, flanked by two assistants. A tall, spare man who smiled expectantly, holding out his hand. Greg stared, frantically trying to place a name to the distantly familiar face.

'Greg Mandel, good to see you again. It's been over fifteen years, yes?'

Now the memory came back. Sean Francis, one of Event Horizon's younger generation of executives, a disturbingly ambitious one, if memory served. He was also superbly efficient, and keen, giving his total attention to every problem and request, no detail was too small to be reviewed. It was an attitude Greg had enjoyed the first time he'd met him, Sean Francis in person inspired confidence. Then after five minutes' exposure, the unrelenting effusiveness began to grate.

Greg shook his hand. 'Seventeen years, would you believe? Seems like you've done all right for yourself. I'm surprised Event Horizon let you go.'

Sean Francis grinned brightly. 'I haven't left. I'm just on

sabbatical. You see, the English Government had to have a trained executive who was also completely conversant with the space industry in the hot seat, so Julia Evans loaned me out. Simple, yes?'

'Yeah.' Even after all this time Julia's political expediency still never failed to gain his admiration. New London might be a Crown Colony on paper, but in *realpolitik* it was hers, and no messing.

Sean Francis introduced his assistants. The man was Lloyd McDonald, an Afro-Caribbean, one of Victor's people, whose job description was New London's corporate security chief. Greg suspected his responsibility extended further than that, given the administrative hierarchy. The woman was Michele Waddington, the Governor's secretary. Another on secondment from Event Horizon.

'We've prepared a barracks facility for your team in the security quarters,' Lloyd McDonald told Melvyn. 'My people will take your gear down to it.'

'Fine,' Melvyn said.

'Are you anticipating trouble?' Sean asked.

'There is a possibility,' Greg admitted. 'I'd like Lloyd McDonald here to step up his screening procedures for new arrivals. In particular for a man called Leol Reiger. He's a tekmerc, very dangerous. And he might just be stupid enough to try and follow us up here.'

'Reviewing visitors is the responsibility of the Immigration office,' Sean said. 'But I can have company security personnel deputized as backup, that's within my brief.' He turned to Michele Waddington. 'Get the authorization lined up, please.'

'Yes, sir.' She entered an order in her cybofax.

'Got a profile of Reiger?' Lloyd McDonald asked.

Greg held up his cybofax, and squirted the data over to McDonald's. The security chief glanced at it. 'There are three more flights scheduled for today. I'll make sure the passengers are isolated and identified before they're allowed into the colony.'

'If Reiger does come up he won't be alone,' Melvyn said. 'Make sure your people are armed.'

'Anything else?' Sean asked.

Greg looked at Melvyn, who shook his head.

'Just somewhere for us to get changed,' Greg said. 'We'll start hunting after that.'

'Certainly,' Sean said. 'I've had some rooms prepared in the Governor's Residence for you.'

'I'll see my team to their barracks then join you,' Melvyn said.

'Right, bring a couple of them back with you,' Greg said. 'Carrying, but nothing heavy, the Tokarevs will do.'

'Sure thing.'

Greg picked up his flight bag and followed Sean into a circular lift, along with Charlotte, Suzi, Rick, and Michele Waddington. It started to descend slowly, Greg's feet nearly left the floor. Gravity built steadily.

The doors opened on to another smooth tunnel carved through the living rock, a pair of moving walkways ran down the middle, two broad biolum strips were fixed to the ceiling, brighter than usual. Gravity felt normal. Greg looked along it, expecting to see it curve up out of sight, but there was a corner about eighty metres away, and another one behind him. The floor might have been slightly curved, it was hard to tell.

They took a walkway down to the corner, then another one. The layout reminded Greg of the Prezda arcology, people slotted neatly into regulated accommodation space. Hive mentality.

There was a policeman sitting behind a metal desk outside the door to the Governor's Residence. He stood and saluted as Sean showed his card to the door.

The Governor's Residence changed Greg's mind about conformity. The interior seemed to have been lifted straight out of some eighteenth-century colonial trader's mansion, a formal European layout, with modern Asian and Oriental furnishings. The rooms were spacious and airy, with high ceilings and white

431

walls, pillars and arches dominated the architecture. He wondered how much it cost to lift all the wood up from Earth.

Suzi stood on the parquet floor of the hall, and whistled appreciatively. 'Not half bad. You pay rent?'

'No, this is my official residence. It comes with the job. The King and Queen have slept here, and the PM.'

'No shit? Now us.' She nudged Greg playfully.

'Tell me about the Celestial Apostles,' he asked as Sean led them up the stairs to a broad landing.

Sean put on an unconvincing smile. 'Bunch of religious nuts, mostly; though some technical types threw in with them. Their creed decrees space as the turning point in human destiny. No specifics, surprise surprise. Just generalities: space will save us, expand our spiritual horizon. Same kind of crap most loony cults spout. The main difference is that the leadership don't live off the acolytes. By all accounts they're quite genuine in their belief. They all live in the disused tunnels and empty storage chambers. I wouldn't call them dangerous, exactly; but personally I'd just as soon send the police and security teams into the tunnels to round them up and deport them, yes? I mean, what happens in a real emergency situation, a pressure loss? Or an epidemic, how would they get vaccinated? I'd have to risk my people trying to help them. But of course they never consider that.'

'So why don't you?' Greg asked.

'The police do catch a few. But Julia Evans says let them be, no big trawling operation. It's not as if we'd drain the Colony's police budget.'

Greg gave Suzi a satisfied grin, he'd known that kind of sentimentality was one of Julia's traits. Suzi just rolled her eyes.

The bedroom was decorated in red and gold, with ornate hardwood marquetry furniture. Painted fabric screens had been used to partition off the bathroom and jacuzzi with forest scenes, black backgrounds with tall spindly trees, pale leaves. Metal-framed French windows opened out on a balcony with iron railings, a row of potted ferns was lined up along the front edge.

Greg dropped his flight bag on the bed, and pushed the windows open. Hyde Cavern's air was warm, humid, ozone rich, and smelt of fresh blossom. He was looking out over a small deep valley, with a blunt dark massif of rock blocking the far end. A slim tubular sun blazed with blue-white virulency overhead, its glare haze blocking out any sight of what lay behind it. He followed the sides of the valley as they rose upwards, curving in like two giant green waves about to topple. If he used his hand to shield his eyes from the tubular sun, he could just make out the landscape directly above. By then he was ready for the impossible sight. He'd been intellectually prepared for it, of course, but ground as sky was still a dismaying sight. The physical mass, pressing down. He wasn't quite sure what to call the involuntary phobic shudder running down his back, but it seemed as though the little cylindrical worldlet was about to constrict, crushing him at the centre.

He dropped his gaze again. The first four out of the five kilometres between him and the other endcap was lush green parkland. Hyde Cavern's rock floor had been shaped with gentle undulations, silver streams meandered through the coombs, low waterfalls feeding calm lakes. There were copses of young saplings, tree-lined avenues of yellow pebbles wandered like serpents across the grass. White Hellenistic buildings were dotted about, each at the centre of its own garden. They were the focus of New London's social life – theatres, restaurants, clubs, pubs, reception halls, churches, two sports amphitheatres. People didn't live out in the Cavern, groundspace was too valuable; instead the lower fifth of the southern endcap housed the warren of living quarters, offices, light engineering factories, and hotels.

The last kilometre of Hyde Cavern was filled with the miniature sea, a band of salt water running round the foot of the northern endcap, its parkside coast wrinkled with secluded coves and broad beaches of white sand. Tiny islands studded the middle of the sea, covered by a dense shaggy thatch of vegetation. Just looking at it made Greg want to run over and dive in.

He gripped the balcony rail and peered over. They were about twenty metres above a broad rock roadway running round the base of the endcap; people in light clothes strolled about idly, the far side was a bicycle lane, nests of café tables with bright parasols sprawled out directly below him. Balconies stretched away on either side, vines with huge heart-shaped leaves twining round the iron support columns, long mauve flower clusters formed a fringe above his head, bunches of green grapes dangled on either side. He picked one; it tasted sweet, succulent, and seedless.

Suzi, Rick, and Charlotte had come out of the bedroom to join him. And even Suzi was quiet as she looked round.

'Where were you when you met the Celestial priest?' he asked Charlotte. The girl hadn't put ten words together since they'd lifted off from Listoel. Her thought currents were tightly wound, slow but deliberate, there was a lot of concern and guilt accumulating inside her skull.

She frowned lightly, searching the shoreline. 'There.' She pointed to a point high up on the right-hand curve. 'It's the fall-surf beach near the Kenton station.'

'Ah, tourist zone,' Sean said. 'The beaches round there all have bars and sunbeds, game pits, that kind of thing. It's popular with the younger ones.' He smiled at Charlotte.

'Do the Celestial Apostles often try recruiting there?' Greg asked.

'They vary. Routine would trap them, yes? But they do tend to prefer the tourist zones.'

Greg turned his back on the distracting vista of Hyde Cavern, gathering his thoughts. 'OK, I want every available policeman assigned to foot patrol. Have them cover the kind of public areas the Celestials frequent. I'm looking for any kind of activity by the Celestials, recruiting, picking the fruit, whatever. Specifically, they're to look out for older male Celestials. If they see anything they're to report in, but under no circumstances apprehend. The last thing I want now is for them to go to ground.'

'All right,' Sean said. 'It'll take a while to organize.'

'No problem, but I want it started this afternoon. We'll take a look ourselves in a little while.'

'I'd like something to eat, please,' Charlotte said.

'Good idea,' Greg said. 'We'll get changed, have a bite.' He checked his watch. 'Meet back here in an hour, half-past three. OK?'

'Yes, thank you.' Charlotte gave him a quick courteous smile.

'I'll have the cook rustle something up for you,' Sean said.

'Send Melvyn Ambler and Lloyd McDonald straight in when they arrive,' Greg said. 'And Charlotte.' She looked round, eyes wide and sad. 'Don't go anywhere without your hardline guard. You're the single most important person on New London right now.'

He got a brief flustered nod.

'I'll show you your room,' Michele Waddington said, opening the door.

Suzi winked. 'I'll stick with her till the hardliners arrive.'

'Fine, thanks Suzi.' He ran his hands back through his hair, it was sweaty and tangled after four hours of that tight-fitting cap.

The jacuzzi came on at his voice command, and he began to take off the hot shipsuit.

30

As soon as Royan shimmered through the protective programs Julia had thrown round her processor implant she could tell he was excited, face all tight and bright.

Snowy, how's it going?

Not good. I've got you mucking about with microbes. Event Horizon is under threat from superior technology. My hold over the New Conservatives is slipping. Greg's off chasing after an alien. And Victor's furious with you for hiding this personality package in Kiley's 'ware. He had to go out to the Farm in person.

Some of his infuriating bonhomie faded, the image turning translucent for an instant as the features reshaped themselves into a more serious attitude. His sympathetic expression offered concern.

That was him all the way through, knowing exactly which buttons to press. And she always bloody let him.

I'm sorry, Snowy. Truth to tell, I'm surprised you needed to access this package at all. It's been going so well, really. I was right about the microbes, they are the greatest discovery since America, since . . . the wheel. God, Snowy, they're magnificent. Truly. They're going to make you mine again, Snowy. They'll bring us back together. Equals and lovers. He gave her a lopsided smile. *Fated, it's written in the stars.*

Once he'd been able to make her smile and dance and blush with his romanticism. Fifteen years ago, when the peace of a beachside bungalow and whole days spent making love were more important than anything. When just the touch of him lit a fire in her blood.

The only thing I see in the stars these days is how much New London has cost me, in red figures a thousand kilometres high. And only mental cripples leading futile lives believe in astrology, as you so often told me. Now what the bloody hell have you been doing? Have you stitched that space plant together yet?

There was no movement in the pixels that composed his face, no show of hurt, which just made it worse. Julia responded with her own front of stubbornness, refusing to be bullied.

I discovered something about the microbe genetics, Royan said. *Did my earlier recordings tell you about the inner toroid shells being inert?*

Yes.

Well, I did a bit more work on them. A second project, alongside my asteroid dissemination plant. I was curious that only the outer shell contained active gene toroids; so I removed the outer shell from one sphere, and used the remainder as the basis of a clone.

You did what?

Cloned it.

His image dissolved. The cell which replaced him was a sac of white shadows, foggy inside. It reminded her of a flaccid jellyfish. The nucleus was a dark ovoid core at the centre, surrounded by a snowstorm of white organelles.

Her perception point drifted through the cell wall, carrying her up to the nucleus. She stopped just outside, observing the internal structure through a smoky membrane which gave everything a rusty tint. At the heart of the nucleus was the sphere of alien chromosomes. She felt like a small child pressed up against a shop window, complacent and dreamy.

I used an ordinary moss cell as a base, Royan said. *I removed its terrestrial DNA, and replaced it with the modified alien gene sphere. I studied the sphere's reproduction process, it's very similar to DNA replication. Cell division starts with a generation of ring-like threads, chromonemata equivalents, which anneal to the toroids, facilitating duplication; then the two sets of toroids are split apart and regroup at separate ends of the cell, ready for the division.*

Chrome-black rings tumbled through the nucleus, swooping towards the toroid sphere. They began to cluster over the surface, dropping down sharply to mate with a toroid. A fuzz of molecules began to build round each one. The outer shell of the gene sphere split into thirteen crescent segments, and opened like a flower. Rings started to fall in towards the second shell. The process was repeated with each of the shells, accelerating with each layer. As the shell segments continued to unfold the nucleus membrane dissolved, allowing them to spread through the cell like the wings of a dark bird.

Julia could see the duplicate toroids building, swelling out of the rings which had latched on to the originals. The last shell opened to expose a single molecular globe at the core, individual atoms arranged in what resembled a geodesic framework. Then all the twinned toroids were peeling apart. Two complete sets of the unfolded genes were now diffused throughout the cell. She thought it looked as if the membrane had been filled with a pair of crumpled oil stains, unable to merge, slithering endlessly round each other. Then they began to contract. It was the unfolding in reverse, shell segments recombining with bewildering speed, weaving round each other in a perfectly synchronized dance, snapping shut.

She let it all happen without protest, absorbed by the complexity and dynamics. Life reduced to fundamentals, its fabric more grandiose than any human cathedral. Royan was right, it was hard to believe nature, chance, could produce this chemical mechanism unaided.

When it was finished there were two gene spheres with nucleus membranes gradually thickening around them. The cell began to elongate, the separate nuclei pulling apart. A pinch began halfway between them. Then there were two cells, just touching.

Fascinating, isn't it? Royan asked; he used a hollow tone.

I've seen terrestrial cell duplication. This is no different. Evolution obviously results in the simplest solution to the problem each time. *A galactic constant.* She observed the two cells; their organelles seemed firmer now, more compact. Black rings were beginning to flood each nucleus again.

You've grown very cynical, said Royan. *The point of all this is that the second shell pattern is a viable one. I only initiated the first division; as you can see the reproduction mechanism carried on.*

And it grew into a plant, she said. *One that looked like a cross between a fern and a cactus.*

How did you know?

You carried it with you when you left the North Sea Farm.

Oh. Trust Victor to find that out. He's keen, that one.

What's all this supposed to prove? she asked.

Come on, Snowy! The second shell was a completely new species. Doesn't that strike you as being incredibly neat? The alien genes are arranged in a numerical sequence. Since when has mathematics governed nature?

Life is chemistry, she said. *Everything can be reduced to numbers and formulae in the end. That's what genes are, ultimately, chemical numbers. The microbe's genetic structure is neater than ours; that's only to be expected in something a couple of billion years more advanced than we are. The second shell plant is probably the form the microbe evolved from. Human DNA contains all sorts of vestigial codes – tails, pelts – and we still haven't got rid of our appendix.*

No way, Snowy. Nothing as complex as a plant could devolve into a microbe in one generation.

There's all that garbage in the outer shell's toroid sequence. How much did you say, ninety per cent of it? That will represent the intermediate stage, the devolution process; the garbage has to come from somewhere, after all.

Possibly, but it's still very strange.

What about the third shell? she asked. *Did you try cloning that?*

Not when this recording was made, I haven't had the time. Perhaps I'm a little bit afraid. That plant unnerved me, Snowy. It shouldn't exist, it really shouldn't.

Did it flower, Royan? Did the bloom remind you of us, how we used to be?

There was a bud forming when I left the Farm, that's all I know.

You sent me a flower.

Because I love you.

No, it's a warning, like all these packages. What could you be warning me about? The asteroid disseminator plant? What happened to that project?

Success, I think. I used modified microbes in symbiosis with gene-tailored landcoral.

He flipped the image again. She was tiring of his pixel virtuoso act, her teeth pressing together somewhere outside the void of this node generated universe. Patience was the one quality she always cherished, like water it could erode any resistance, a weapon she could always rely on. But now she wanted all this settled, finished, over with.

It was the microbe again, that same black tacky globe Kiley had scooped up. But different this time. Flattened slightly. And the surface texture was silkier, she was sure. A second appeared beside it; egg shaped. This one was even darker. They turned slowly below her perception point, giving her an all-over view.

This is what I was after all along, Snowy. The flat one has had its mineral absorption process beefed up. While the ovoid's thermal conversion efficiency has been enhanced by a factor of five. I combined them with landcoral in a sandwich arrangement. The landcoral will act as a basic organic framework, growing a crust over the asteroid which provides a skeleton for the microbes to grow on. Its outer surface will support a layer of the thermal conversion microbes to energize the polyp's nutrient fluid, rather than photosynthesis, while on the inside, the other microbes gobble up the rock. I had to sequence in a second capillary network to transfer the dissolved compounds to the discharge pores. Later I'll add collection pods, and hopefully some kind of filter mechanism so you get pure deposits in each pod. Gases might be a problem, though. But this will do for now.

This symbiosis arrangement is a bit crude, isn't it? Julia asked.

440

Somehow, wholehearted praise would have seemed like surrendering.

It's only a proof of concept prototype, Snowy. The first generation. I'm not even sure if it will work externally, exposed to a vacuum. Maybe we'll have to gnaw at asteroids from within. Once I've demonstrated its viability, we can get the research divisions to work on refining it. Top-grade geneticists should be able to splice all this into a single genetic structure.

Event Horizon genetic research divisions, Julia thought privately. She reviewed the arrangement again, implications sleeting through her mind. If Royan was right, if the microbe's traits could be loaded into landcoral cells the way he said, producing a single space-adapted bioware organism, then there really would be rivers of metal pouring into the global economy. Enough to support Western-level consumerism right across the globe. Nice idea. No, nice theory, she corrected herself sharply; she'd had too many dreams stall and degenerate into mediocrity to believe in technology based Utopia ideals now.

For all his determination, Royan wasn't rooted in the real world. The central concept was sound, but the ancillary industries – the fleets of spaceships needed to pick up the metal and minerals, the industrial modules necessary to convert it into foamedsteel landing bodies, more recovery fleets, more factories to use it, the energy they would need – that would take time and money to organize. Besides, New London had cubic kilometres of ore in reserve already; and there were four more asteroid capture missions currently underway. Taken together, just those five asteroids would produce enough exotic metal and raw material to supply global demand for another twenty years.

Sounds too good to be true, she said carefully. *Have you considered what it would take to put it into practice?*

Nothing else, he said. The answer she knew he would give her.

Don't you see, Snowy? The asteroid disseminator plant is a living machine. The very first. I'm on the verge of creating nanoware here, Snowy, the most powerful technology there is. Once you've cracked this you can do anything, it's pure von Neumannism, self-replicating,

441

and capable of producing anything you can supply a blueprint of. After they've been developed properly the cells can be programmed to dismantle an asteroid, or carve out a chamber like Hyde Cavern; they can be grown into an O'Neill colony or a teaspoon and anything in between; you can put together minute specialist clusters that'll float through the human bloodstream repairing tissue damage, airborne spores that can break up the world's carbon dioxide, reverse the Warming. Nanoware rules the micro and the macro, Snowy. And this splice is only the beginning.

She wondered how that would square up against atomic structuring technology. Were the two complementary, or antagonistic? If she didn't get the nuclear force generator data for Event Horizon, could she counter with asteroid dissemination? Save the company that way. More questions, problems.

And who would benefit? The turmoil from one new revolutionary technology was bad enough, introducing two that were this radical would produce utter chaos. She remembered what had followed Event Horizon's success with the giga-conductor; whole companies becoming obsolete overnight, workers thrown on the dole; it had redefined economies all over the planet. And that was in a time when the power and transport industries had declined to virtually nothing.

But right now the global economy was powerfully upbeat, expansion was running at nine per cent, there was investment, confidence, stability. The planet was in better shape than it had been for decades.

In any case, present-day cybernetics was a form of large-scale von Neumannism. And at least with cybernetics there was room for people – designers, maintenance crews, civil engineers who built the factories. Their hierarchy might be top-heavy with 'ware-literate staff, but there were still jobs for the semi-skilled, semi-literate, some dignity, keeping them off the dole. What would they do in a world where you could get a ten-bedroom mansion just by planting a nanoware kernel in the ground, then watch it grow like a flower?

Should I suppress this before it starts? Do I have the right, or even the wisdom? That's what it boils down to. Another bloody decision I have to make. Always me.

She felt the blood hot in her cheeks. *All right, you've modified the microbes in the laboratory. Does this arrangement actually work in practice?*

It has up until the moment I was recorded, he said. *I grew a small prototype in the Farm laboratory's clone vat, checked that the two modified microbes functioned the way they were supposed to. I had to do a bit more tailoring, a few modifications. But the penultimate stage is completed. That's why this recording exists, to tell you I'm ready to see if the asteroid disseminator plant works, if the polyp and the microbes will operate as an integrated unit. I'm going up to New London to run some field trials.*

Then something must have happened, she said.

The image of the microbes popped, Royan was standing before her perception point. *Snowy, if it has, if I've screwed up, then do whatever you have to.*

Yeah.

I love you, Snowy.

I'll remember.

He hung his head, and vanished.

Calculated, she reminded herself sternly, a coldly logical emotion.

31

The arcade was cut seventy metres directly into Hyde Cavern's southern endcap; there was no moving walkway, just a broad floor of green and red stone tiles. Hard cavernlight shone through a rosette of stained glass above the entrance, casting a colourful dapple over the shoppers milling near by. Big shiny brass fans spun slowly above the hanging biolum globes, circulating the air. It was cool, quiet and relaxing.

The small shops reminded Charlotte of the ones she had toured in Rodeo Drive, exclusive and exquisite. If they had a fault, it was the sheer monotony of tastefulness; everything blended, colours and shapes. It would be so easy to get sucked in. Designers had built their reputations on those interiors.

Some of the names were familiar. Parent companies treating New London as a prestige showcase. After all, there were a lot of their clientele who came up here for casinos and low-gravity hotels, simply for the cachet of having left Earth. But seeing a 300 k.p.h. Lotus Commodore for sale in a space colony that didn't even have roads appealed to her sense of the ridiculous.

She walked past the car showroom window, almost smiling. Teresa Farrow, her bodyguard from the crash team, gave the streamlined, royal-purple sports car a fast glance, shaking her head. There was something about the hardline woman, a sort of vagueness, which convinced Charlotte she was another psychic. Her mind vigilant on some unknown level, alert for trouble.

But she hadn't objected when Charlotte said she wanted to come down to the arcade. It was practically underneath the Governor's Residence anyway.

The American Express office was halfway down the arcade on the right. Charlotte pushed the glass door open, walking straight into the reception area. It looked like the office of some ancient legal partnership, dark wood panels and shiny red leather chairs.

'You're going to think me terribly silly,' she said, in her gushy voice, to the uniformed girl behind the desk. 'But I left my card on Earth. I must have forgotten it when I changed into my shipsuit.'

The girl smiled brightly. 'That's quite all right, madam. We're here to help.'

Obtaining a replacement didn't take long. A data construct to fill out. A thumbprint check, the company's memory core on Earth confirming she was who she said she was, that she had an account with them. Cancelling her original card, wherever it was by now. Being nibbled by perplexed fish, presumably.

Two minutes later she was back out in the arcade, heading for a Toska's store she had noticed earlier. It had fluffy white carpets, purple marble pillars, huge gilt-framed mirrors, a thousand choices. And best of all the assistants understood, they knew the best ranges for her age group, what suited her hair and figure.

She sat on the ashgrove chair sipping a mineral water, and watched the life-sized hologram of herself as it ran through permutations – tops, trousers, shorts, skirts. The assistants made suggestions about colours, possible accessories.

She wound up taking a body-hugging top with a modest neck line, made out of cloned snakeskin. The material was dry and thin, but stretched like rubber, its grey and cream scales had a wonderful matt shine, and it was so soft. The hologram flicked through a catalogue of skirts and shorts, and she chose a cornflower-blue mid-thigh skirt to match. It was a sportsy combination, light enough for Hyde Cavern and showing off without posing. Consummate, she decided; Baronski would have been proud, God bless him. Just looking at herself in the mirror was a heady boost. Her life righting itself again. It was a shame about having to wear tights, the skirt was great for her legs; but running round the *Colonel Maitland* had given her a lot of scratches and not all of the dermal seal had flaked off.

She paid with her new Amex, adding a pair of Ferranti shades as a last thought. The appalling shipsuit went into a Toska's bag, and she carried it out into the arcade, resisting the temptation to leave it behind.

Back in the arcade she looked longingly at an Arden salon, wishing she had time to do something about her hair, the cap had simply killed it dead. Tomorrow, she promised herself.

*

It was ten past three when Charlotte got back to her room in the Governor's Residence. Suzi's room was on one side, Rick Parnell's on the other. Thankfully there was no one about to see her. It wasn't that Greg had forbidden her from going out, but the implication was there. The sensation as the door closed behind Teresa Farrow was reminiscent of the one she used to have sneaking out of the care home, a giddy relief.

Her room had black and green walls, an elaborate jungle print; the Scandinavian furniture was cut from redwood and. left unvarnished, giving it a raw feel. The paradise birds in the large white cage by the balcony doors started to shrill wildly.

Charlotte blew them a kiss and picked up her flight bag from the bed. 'Just going to clean up,' she told Teresa Farrow, and skipped into the bathroom.

She was in two minds whether or not to call Fabian. She felt as though she was exploiting him, deliberately abusing his grief to help her achieve her revenge. But when she had suggested they get even with the Dolgoprudnensky, the two of them alone in their room at the platform's clinic, she'd seen that insouciant spark return. The prospect of retribution had animated him. It wasn't the sort of hope she particularly wanted to see in him, but it was hope of a kind. And that number-cruncher brain of his had rapidly cooked up several possible scenarios. She'd made suggestions of her own, helping to refine and fine-tune the idea. But now the time had come to actually commit herself, doubts were rising.

No battle plan ever survives contact with the enemy. More than one of her patrons had told her that; surprising how many of them were ex-military. And this wasn't something they'd ever have a second chance at. It had to work first time. It was risky.

Charlotte raised her hand, the bioware sheath was like a two-fingered glove, flesh coloured; there was a constant warm itch underneath. No, she couldn't forget what Nia Korovilla had done, what she'd been *ordered* to do, and by whom.

She put the seat down on the toilet, sat on it, and unzipped her flight bag. Below the Levi's and neatly folded Organic Flux Capacity sweatshirt was her gold Amstrad cybofax. Heaven alone knew how the wafer had stayed inside her shorts pockets while she was charging around the *Colonel Maitland*, but there it was, the only possession she had left that was truly hers.

She entered Fabian's personal number, then ran the scrambler program. The Amstrad's screen fuzzed with static, then stabilized to show Fabian's face. He was smiling nervously.

'Crikey, Charlotte, I thought you were never going to call. *Anastasia* docked an hour ago.'

'I've been busy.'

'Any sign of the alien?'

'No, none. We're going to go out looking for my Celestial priest in quarter of an hour.'

'Oh. Well, good luck.'

'Thanks.'

'Are we going to do it?'

'Yes, Fabian, we're doing it.'

'Terrific! Switch to conference mode and call Kirilov. Have you still got the number?'

'Yes,' she said with some exasperation.

She pulled the number he'd given her from the cybofax's memory, and entered it in the phone circuit. The Amstrad's screen split in two, Fabian on one side, the other remained blank.

'Yes?' a male voice asked, a heavy Slav accent.

'We want to speak with Mr Kirilov,' Fabian said.

'There is nobody of that name here.'

Fabian flipped his hair aside impatiently. 'Rubbish. Tell Pavel Kirilov that it's Fabian Whitehurst and Charlotte Fielder calling.'

Names put a coolness in her belly, names meant there was no going back. And she was pretty sure Pavel Kirilov wouldn't be happy discovering his identity was being bandied about.

A man's face appeared on the cybofax screen. She studied him closely. There was nothing exceptional about him, late forties or early fifties, thinning hair, gaunt cheeks, in fact – she almost smiled – the man bore a more than superficial resemblance to Lenin.

Pavel Kirilov gave them a tight-lipped smile. 'So, it is you, young Fabian. You've grown, I think, since we met last. And Miss Fielder, of course, I recognize you from your picture. May I say how glad I am you both survived the *Colonel Maitland* crash. The reports I received on the incident were most confused.'

'My father's dead,' Fabian said.

'Yes, I know. I'm sorry. He was a valued client.'

'And I inherit everything.'

Pavel Kirilov inclined his head. 'Indeed.'

'So I want to carry on with the timber shipments, and the ship charters from Odessa. Just like before. The company agents will handle the details.'

'That's very astute of you, Fabian. I'm sure we can come to some arrangement with your father's estate.'

'Good.'

'May I ask you how you escaped from the *Colonel Maitland*?'

'I have friends,' Fabian said. He smirked.

Charlotte hoped Fabian's confidence wasn't going to overload his prudence. Perhaps she should've insisted on dealing with Kirilov by herself. Too late now.

'I see.' Pavel Kirilov pulled at his lower lip. 'Well, as long as you're safe now.'

'I want to do a deal,' Fabian said.

'What sort of deal, Fabian?' Pavel Kirilov asked.

'We know where the alien is.'

'Which alien is this?'

'Nia Korovilla is dead as well,' Charlotte said. She caught Pavel Kirilov throwing a glance at someone off-camera.

'You seem remarkably well informed, Miss Fielder.'

'I've picked up a lot in the last few years I've spent working for you, Mr Kirilov.'

She was surprised when all Pavel Kirilov did was laugh. 'I'm afraid that I know where the alien is as well. But I thank you for your offer.'

'No, you don't,' said Fabian. 'You just know the contact point is New London. Only Charlotte knows exactly where the flower came from.'

'I have all the information I require,' Pavel Kirilov said.

'Are you sure?' she asked. 'Really sure? Remember, we already knew that you know the flower was handed over to me in New London. Why would we phone if that was all you needed? The fact is, you require a lot more data if you want to find the alien.'

Pavel Kirilov hesitated. 'This additional data, you are offering to sell it?'

'No, we're offering you a partnership.'

'In what?'

'In atomic structuring technology. We secure the construction data for a nuclear force generator. You market it to a kombinate as you originally intended. And we take a percentage. Simple.'

Pavel Kirilov patted his hands together in front of his face. 'My God, a child and a— You really know what you're talking about, don't you?'

'You got it,' Fabian said triumphantly.

'Are you interested?' Charlotte asked. She was jamming her knees together to stop her legs from shaking. 'If not, we can always call Event Horizon or Clifford Jepson, offer them the generator data.'

'What sort of percentage?' Pavel Kirilov asked impassively.

'Five. And as a guarantee, Fabian and I are to be named on the patent application which you and the kombinate file.'

'I'm interested. No doubt you have devised a foolproof method of handover.'

'Yes. We're up in New London now.'

Pavel Kirilov raised his eyebrows. 'You have the generator data already?'

'We'll provide it for you,' she said. 'But it does have to be you, in person. No one else. I don't mean come alone or anything.'

'How very gratifying.'

'We have our own hardliners with us. So we'll meet here, on neutral territory, and we'll explain how we want to handle the actual transfer.' She held her breath.

Pavel Kirilov gave her a reluctant nod. 'Baronski would be pleased to see the way you've turned out. You're a credit to him, Miss Fielder, if not to me. Where exactly in New London do you wish to meet me? Should I wear a carnation in my lapel, knot my tie in a certain fashion?'

She tried to ignore the sarcasm, but there was a lot of weight behind it; one of the largest crime lords in Europe focusing on her. Displeased.

'The more important they think themselves, the greater the disdain they feel they must show,' Baronski had told her. 'They can only intimidate you if you allow yourself to believe in this charade. None of it is real, they are acting. Imagine yourself as a channel critic and watch for the flaws in their performance.'

Charlotte said nothing.

'Well?' Pavel Kirilov asked.

He wanted to know, he needed them. God bless you, Dmitri, she wished silently. 'Phone me exactly one hour before you dock,' she said. 'I will tell you where to wait, you may bring up to four hardline bodyguards for your personal safety. But if you phone after you arrive, if you send someone else in your place, if there are more than four hardliners, then the deal is off.'

'Very well, Miss Fielder, Fabian. I agree.'

'All right!' Fabian grinned.

'But. If you are unable to provide me with the generator data, or if you try and sell the data to my rivals, then you will wish you had stayed on board the *Colonel Maitland*. Do I make myself clear? This is not a game. If you genuinely know what is going on, you will understand this.'

'We understand,' Charlotte said.

'Good. I shall make arrangements for a flight, expect me within six hours.' His image disappeared from the Amstrad's screen.

Charlotte's muscles felt drained, her palms were damp and sticky.

Fabian was laughing like a mad thing. 'What a team! What a team! We did it, we nailed the bastard.' His face jiggled about on the screen.

'Oh, Christ,' she murmured. The enormity of what she'd done was beginning to register.

'What's the matter? It's over. We did it. We won!'

'It's only just started, Fabian.'

'Rubbish, stupid. He's on his way. That's all we needed. Once he's phoned you and confirmed he's docking, we'll tell Julia Evans.' His lip curled up. 'She'll have to act then. There's no way she'll allow Kirilov into New London, not with you and the alien and that Royan chap all up there together. And there Pavel Kirilov will be, in a spaceship, all alone. A sitting duck. I mean, do you know what kind of Strategic Defence weapons they've got up there?'

'No, Fabian, I don't.'

'Hundreds and hundreds; masers, lasers, particle beams; and everyone knows Julia's got her own electron-compression warheads too. Ten megatons apiece. Scrunch! She'll dissect him.'

Trust Fabian to know about heavy duty weaponry, something in the male make-up drew them to it. Small boys and shiny warplanes went hand in hand, big boys too, come to that. 'And then us, I should think,' she said quickly.

'Oh come on, Charlotte. We're doing her a favour. You heard her say she'd hunt Kirilov down afterwards. Well, we've gone and saved her all the trouble. We've given him to her on a plate. And she won't be able to shirk off this time. All she has to do now is give one order, and Kirilov is a cloud of hot atoms.'

32

There were seven of them in the group that emerged from the public lobby below the Governor's Residence. They stood clustered together on the lava-like surface of the ring road which ran round the base of the southern endcap, looking across the open parkland, not quite sure where to go first. Very touristy, Greg thought, not that he was particularly concerned with stealth. But they did give the impression of a booked party. No need to draw unnecessary attention. Charlotte and Suzi were with him, of course; along with Rick and Melvyn; while a couple of the crash team, Teresa Farrow and Jim Sharman, completed the group. Lloyd McDonald had set up a dedicated mission office in the security centre, where he was reviewing reports from the police and his own personnel from inside the Cavern.

'Where we headed?' Suzi asked.

'Not sure. Lloyd will call us as soon as someone spots a Celestial Apostle.' He sucked in some air, glancing round Hyde Cavern. A tiny secretion struck up a certain restlessness, but there was no call towards any particular part of the cylindrical landscape. 'But in the mean time, we'll try the beach. The one where you met the priest, Charlotte.'

Charlotte nodded. 'All right.'

Other pedestrians were glancing at her as they passed. Greg had to admit she looked sensational. Perhaps he ought to have asked her to wear something less conspicuous.

It isn't her clothes, he told himself, it's your hormones.

Rick had stuck close to her side on the way down from the Residence, making small talk, absolutely not looking at the top's scoop neck. The way she dealt with the attention was a frictionless wall of politeness, nothing that would encourage, nothing to take offence at. It was a neat trick. Poor old Rick.

He took his cybofax out of a jacket pocket, and pulled a map of New London's train network from the colony's memory core. There were stations every two hundred metres round the endcap. He started walking towards the nearest one.

'I've just heard from Sean Francis,' Melvyn said. 'Julia Evans is on her way up.'

'When will she be here?'

'Three hours.'

'What's the matter, doesn't she trust us?' Suzi grumbled.

'Give her a break,' Greg said. It came out flatter than he intended. 'She needs that atomic structuring technology. Once I confirmed the alien was here she didn't have many choices.'

'Yeah,' Suzi said. 'This alien thing, knowing it's here somewhere, ain't helping calm me. Why doesn't it show itself?'

'It hasn't demonstrated any hostility,' Rick said.

'Not yet,' Suzi said knowingly. She patted the Browning in her shoulder holster.

Rick gave a despairing sigh.

The vine-roped balconies gave way to sheer rock cliff, and the road bowed out from the base. They walked over a gently curved mock-stone bridge across the neck of a lake. A waterfall emerged from a cleft in the rock a kilometre above; Greg had to tilt his head right back to see its apex. The crinkled rock behind it was thick with creepers and slimy algae. He tracked the ragged white plume as it curved sideways through the air, thundering into the lake twenty metres away. The air was full of a fine spray, leaving the side of the bridge permanently slicked.

'Freaky world,' Suzi said above the noise.

'Yeah,' Greg called back. The endcap rose vertically for the first hundred metres, which was as high as the balconies and windows went, above that it sank into a slight depression of blank rock, with the lighting tube sprouting out of the centre. He could see another five of the exotic Coriolis waterfalls spaced round it at regular intervals.

The train station was on the other side of the bridge, below ground. They took an escalator down to a white-walled, spotlessly clean platform. Greg asked the station 'ware for a private coach. There was a rush of dry air from the tunnel, and the bullet-nosed aluminium cylinder glided out, hovering a couple of centimetres above the single rail. They all trooped in, and Greg showed his Event Horizon card to the driver panel, requesting the Kenton station.

*

The fall-surf beach was spread out along one side of a deep horseshoe-shaped cove which hugged the foot of the northern endcap. This time there was no cliff of balconies at the base, the endcap was a simple shallow hemisphere carved out of the rock. The six Coriolis waterfalls were replicated, but lacking the severe drop of their southern endcap counterparts. They flowed down channels cut in the rock, clinging to the curve. One of them emptied into the cove with a dramatic foam cloud of spray. Thin rainbows swirled inside it.

Greg watched in amazement as a woman on a surfboard shot out of the mist, flying across the cove. Another followed her. He looked up.

The fall-surfers were dotted at fifty-metre intervals all the way back up the waterfall. Where it jetted out of the endcap, a kilometre above him, he could just make out a small metal platform like a broad diving-board. A tiny dark figure leapt off it, descending almost vertically to start with, low gravity only just managing to provide the stability for a lazy glide. The tail of the long board barely touched the water. Then gravity took hold, building constantly as the curve of the endcap increased underneath the surfer. His speed began to pick up. By the time he reached the bottom he was travelling at a hellish velocity.

They all heard a gleeful whoop as he exploded out of the waterfall's foam cloud and flashed past, slicing out a long creamy wake. He had almost reached the end of the cove before he slowed to a halt and began paddling back to shore.

'Now that is something else,' Suzi muttered in admiration.

Greg knew what she meant, his immediate reaction was: I want to try that.

Charlotte stared up at the waterfall with a fond smile. 'It takes a lot of nerve to kick off the first time. But after that it's addictive.'

'You've done it?' Suzi asked, slightly envious.

'Oh, yes. Fall-surfing is one of their greatest tourist traps. It looks wild, but actually it's very safe.'

'I'm sure it is,' Greg said. 'But it isn't on our agenda.' He led them along the path towards the cove, Suzi grumbling behind him.

The beach itself had a Riviera look, organized, colourful, and crowded. Bars that were little more than wooden planks under dried-palm roofs lined the bluff above the sand. Behind them was a more substantial row of restaurants. Regimental squares of sunbeds covered the top half of the beach, competing for space with netball pitches. The powder-fine sand was dazzlingly white. Waiters in white shirts and dark-green bow ties scurried between the bars and sunbeds, carrying trays of drinks.

Greg walked along the crumbling sandy soil of the bluff. There was a steady drift of families coming up the steps from the beach, carrying their bags and towels, small children with tired-looking faces.

Suzi stayed at his side, looking out over the bodies lying on the sunbeds. Rick and Charlotte were still together, locked at the centre of a protective triangle formed by the three hardliners. Greg was pleased with their unobtrusive professionalism.

Teresa Farrow was a psychic, equipped with sac implants; he could discern her espersense pervading the beach and the bars, alert for hazards. She had told him she possessed an empathy similar to his, but no intuition.

Jim Sharman was one of the crash team's tech specialists. All of the team members had one or two fields of expertise.

'Can you see him?' he asked Charlotte.

She was standing at the top of some stairs. 'No, he isn't here. Sorry.'

'I didn't expect to find him first time,' he said, and gave her a reassuring smile.

They walked on.

Greg's cybofax bleeped. It was Lloyd McDonald.

'I think we've got something for you,' the security chief said. 'A couple of bobbies saw three people distributing leaflets outside the Trump Nugget casino. Two men and a girl. One of the men is in his late fifties, they say.'

'Great,' Greg said. 'Tell the bobbies to keep watching, we'll be right over.'

*

One of the bobbies was waiting for them in the station, barely able to keep his excitement contained. His name was Gene Learmount, a boyish freckled face and ginger hair; Greg thought he was about twenty, terribly naïve.

He told Greg how he and his partner had seen the suspected Celestial Apostles, and immediately taken a table in the casino's beer garden where they could watch without being seen. The search for the Celestials was the biggest deal for New London's police in months. Did it mean the Governor was finally going to do something about them?

Greg gave a noncommittal shrug as they rode the escalator up from the station to the park.

Victor had told him that the police were there principally for the tourists; company security handled the workers and possible tekmerc deals. He wondered how the police felt about that, but the kid seemed happy enough deferring to his Event Horizon card. It was his tradecraft, or rather lack of it, which was worrying. The Celestials must have developed some kind of watcher routine.

The escalator brought them out under a small marble rotunda. The Trump Nugget was fifty metres away, a three-storey Disneyland fairy castle with tall circular turrets, a moat, drawbridge, and portcullis. Flags were fluttering idly at the top of turret spires. It was ringed with young apple trees in full blossom, white and pink petals coating the grass like dry snow.

Gene Learmount muttered into his cap's comset. 'They're still in the quadrangle,' he said.

'How do we go?' Melvyn asked.

Greg looked at the portcullis and drawbridge again, letting his espersense expand. There were a few people coming and going, it wasn't a busy time for the casino. Too early. He caught the watcher's steely wakefulness, completely out of phase with the passive thought currents around him. When he looked he saw a young man in scarlet shorts picking small yellow fruits from a bush above the moat.

'Bugger,' he muttered. The watcher would have seen Gene Learmount walk from the casino to the station. 'Is there another way out of the quadrangle?' he asked the bobby.

'Yes, certainly. If you go into the castle, there's a goods delivery subway, and a couple of footbridges over the moat.'

'OK. Charlotte, Suzi, and Teresa come with me. The rest of you stay here, but be ready to move.'

They walked out into the open. Greg kept his espersense focused on the watcher, waiting for any sign of alarm, but the man just showed a mild interest in their approach. He carried on filling his net bag with the fruit.

'Tell you, we're being watched,' Greg said to Suzi.

'Yeah, I know,' she said. 'Stud in the red shorts. I clocked him when we came up the escalator.'

'Oh. Right.' He turned to Charlotte who was staring at the watcher. 'Don't be too obvious.'

She grimaced and looked away quickly. 'Sorry.'

'This is the way I want you to handle it,' he said. 'When we get into the quadrangle just look round and see if you can spot him. Take your time, make certain. If he's there, point him out to us, and walk over to him, say hello. We'll be with you the whole time. If he makes a run for it, don't try and follow. Leave that to Suzi and me.'

'Thanks,' Suzi muttered.

'Teresa, you stick with Charlotte the whole time.'

'Yes, sir.'

His cybofax bleeped when they were twenty metres from the drawbridge.

'Got another one for you,' Lloyd McDonald said.

'Oh, Christ, now where?'

'Sports arena. There's a tennis exhibition tournament this week; the Jerome Merril and Lemark Pampa match. One of my people has seen a couple of Celestials talking to some spectators.'

'OK, same procedure. Keep them under observation until we get there.'

'Affirmative.'

The castle really was made out of stone, one-metre cubes of a rusty-brown colour that had been quarried out of the asteroid somewhere. Greg had been expecting jazzed-up composite.

The quadrangle had three levels. A sunken corner given over to an ornamental water garden, the main lawn with several large brass and granite freeform sculptures from the organic school, and the beer garden running along one side, overlooking the other two. Greg squashed a groan when he saw the second bobby sitting at one of the tables, diligently observing the people threading their way round the sculptures.

Greg spotted one of the girls straight off, a smiling blonde in a halter top and long swirling skirt.

Teresa Farrow nudged Charlotte, and nodded to a man coming up from the water garden. He was about sixty, a thick sheaf of leaflets was sticking out of an open belt pouch. Greg wrapped his espersense round him, finding a peculiar mix of alertness and satisfaction.

'That's not him,' said Charlotte.

'Shit,' Suzi said. 'You sure?'

'Absolutely.'

Greg felt something being thrust into his hand, dry and light, cylindrical. He closed his fingers round it instinctively.

When he turned, there was a slim Oriental girl standing behind him, wearing a black string vest tucked into cutoff jeans.

'Your future lies among the stars. I hope you'll join us tomorrow,' she said, deeply serious, then smiled and walked away.

He followed the denim-painted backside as she walked through the archway towards the drawbridge.

'Just your type, huh?' Suzi asked. She was smirking lecherously.

'Committing her to memory, that's all.' He looked down at what she'd given him. It was one of the leaflets, rolled up.

Tomorrow a new dawn will rise.
Tomorrow the road to the stars will be thrown open.
Tomorrow man will not be made in God's image.
Tomorrow our suffering and fear will end.
Tomorrow we will no longer be alone.
Tomorrow the Earth will be cured.
Tomorrow we shall be free.
Tomorrow is now.
Join us in Tomorrow.
The Celestial Apostles will hold a Blessing.
Ushering in the age of Redemption.
The All Saints Church Hyde Cavern.
Noon Tomorrow.
All Welcome.

Greg showed it to Suzi. 'Yeah, very deep,' she said. 'I didn't know copywriters ran away to be Celestials when they grew up.'

'Tomorrow, Clifford Jepson is officially going to announce, atomic structuring to the world,' Greg said.

She sniffed, and read the leaflet again.

'Some of those connotations are pretty strong,' he said.

'Could be,' Suzi admitted grudgingly. 'You want to snatch one of them and run your word-association gimmick?'

'No. They'd all go to ground, and we can't afford that if I'm wrong.' He folded the leaflet and stuck it in his jacket pocket. 'Come on, let's go see the tennis match.'

*

Greg rode the escalator out of the Slatebridge Park station into another of the ubiquitous rotundas. There was a police sergeant waiting for him, Bernard Kemp, whose stomach was bulging over the regulation belt holding his shorts up. Greg was glad to see him, obviously an old hand. His phlegmatic greeting made a pleasing change from his colleagues' breathless enthusiasm.

Slatebridge Park was the ninth sighting of the afternoon. After the casino there had been the tennis match, an orchard, a beach, shopping arcade, another beach, a gallery – Hyde Cavern seemed to be suffering from a plague of Celestial Apostles, all of them distributing the same leaflet advertising the blessing ceremony. 'They've never been this blatant before,' Lloyd McDonald said. 'It's almost like they don't care about stealth any more.' And after Slatebridge Park there were another two sightings waiting to be investigated.

The visibility of the Celestial Apostles was worrying him. He was sure the Dolgoprudnensky would have agents up here. Would they connect the leaflet with the alien? His intuition was mercifully silent. They couldn't have found Royan or the alien yet. But not even Royan could hide for ever. He was growing increasingly aware of how finite New London really was. And the Dolgoprudnensky had a four-day lead.

Greg looked over Bernard Kemp's sagging shoulders at the Globe. It was an open-air amphitheatre, cut into the side of a hillock, circled by a lonely rank of fluted Greek pillars. Tiered ranks of stone seats looked down on a simple open circular stage; the only backdrop was the long still lake at the foot of the small valley.

About a quarter of the seats were filled. Three actors in white togas were on the stage. Greg was too far away to hear the dialogue, but guessed at *Julius Caesar*.

Bernard Kemp used his police-issue cybofax to verify Greg's card, something none of the other bobbies had done.

'Company man?' the sergeant said sourly.

Greg recognized the mind tone, resentful and weary. Bernard Kemp wasn't a man who enjoyed his beat being interrupted for political reasons. Greg felt a degree of sympathy. As a policeman Kemp was infinitely preferable to André Dubaud. Pity he himself was the irritant. 'Not quite, no,' Greg said. 'But it's a good enough description. So where's our man?'

Bernard Kemp stabbed a thumb at the Globe. 'Annoying the audience. There's a couple of them in there. My partner's watching.' The thumb moved, lining up on the pillars at the top of the seats. 'Their look-out is skulking about up there.'

A black woman in an Indian poncho was sitting with her back to one of the pillars, her knees drawn up to her chin. The position gave her an excellent view over the surrounding parkland.

Bernard Kemp was the first person to spot a watcher. Greg wasn't surprised.

They walked up the slight incline to the amphitheatre. Greg detected the stirrings of alarm in the black woman's mind as she saw the group of them. She climbed to her feet, brushing grass from her poncho.

Charlotte stood on the side of the seats, looking round the audience. She blinked, leaning forwards. 'It's him.' She sounded dubious. 'Really.'

Greg looked at the man walking up one of the aisles. Charlotte had been generous when she said he was in his late fifties, Greg put his age closer to sixty-five. Other than that he fitted her description: rotund, thinning hair drawn back into a pony-tail, albino skin. He was playing the joker, handing out the leaflets with a bow, smiling broadly, mocking himself. The technique was good, people took the leaflet without protest.

'All right,' Greg said. 'Charlotte, you lead. Just walk over to him. Teresa, keep an eye on the watcher.'

Charlotte started to thread her way along the seating. It wasn't quite the surreptitious approach Greg had wanted, too many heads turned to follow Charlotte's progress. When they were halfway towards him, the Celestial caught sight of her.

Greg watched the emotions chase across his mind, the surprise that came from recognition, interest then concern. When he caught sight of Greg the concern tilted into agitation. Resignation was last, after he'd looked round, sizing up his chances of making a run for it. He gave a half-hearted shrug, and stuffed the leaflets back in a satchel.

The black woman by the pillar had disappeared by the time Charlotte reached him.

'Hello again, Charlotte,' the old man said. 'I didn't expect to see you up here again so soon.'

Charlotte gestured awkwardly, not saying anything.

'Good afternoon to you,' he said as Greg stepped into the aisle. 'You'll be wanting a leaflet?'

Greg grinned. 'Thanks, I've already got one.' Charlotte had been right about the warmth of his smile.

'Ah well. I'll be going, then.'

'I've come all the way from Earth just to see you,' Greg said.

'What, this little sack of skin and bones?'

'Yeah.'

'I'm sure you must have the wrong person.'

'No.' He was aware of the people sitting by the aisle watching him. 'You want to go somewhere where we don't disturb people?' He pointed to the top of the amphitheatre.

The old man glanced round with pointed slowness. 'Well now, what do you say, Charlotte? Should we stop distracting these good people from this rather mediocre performance? I could never resist the wisdom of a pretty girl.'

'Please,' Charlotte said quietly.

'Ah, now that's the word to use. Please.' He began to walk up the slope.

Greg saw Rick, Teresa Farrow, Jim Sharman, and Bernard Kemp walking up the side of the seats to meet them at the top.

'Is that a member of the constabulary I see?' the old man asked.

'Yes,' Greg said.

'Am I to be taken away in chains, then?'

'Not unless I tell him to,' Greg said lightly.

The Celestial shot him a fast appraising glance, then squared his shoulders and carried on. Suzi gave an evil chuckle.

'The look-out scooted,' Teresa Farrow said when Greg reached the top of the hillock. 'Do you want her back?'

'No. Not important.'

'All this effort,' the Celestial said. 'I'm quite flattered.'

'Want to tell me your name?' Greg asked.

'I'll show you mine if you show yours.'

'Greg Mandel, Mindstar Captain, retired.'

'By all that's holy, a gland man.'

'No messing.'

'The name is Sinclair, for me sins. Pleased to meet you there, Captain Greg.' He stuck out his hand.

Greg turned to Bernard Kemp. 'Thanks very much for your help. We'll take him from here.'

'I figured you might,' the sergeant said. He paused. 'Sir.' He adjusted his cap, taking his time, then walked back down the aisle.

Greg just heard him mutter: 'Glory boys.'

Sinclair's smile was fading as they all looked at him, he dropped his hand back to his side. 'Ah well, I had a grand run. Not that it particularly matters any more, of course. Not after tomorrow.'

Greg realized the light was dimming. The idea was perturbing, it had remained constant the whole time they'd spent chasing round Hyde Chamber after the Celestials; an eternal noon, casting virtually no shadows. He looked up, round, instinct calling him to the southern endcap a couple of kilometres away.

The waterfalls had gone. Instead, six huge plums of dense snow-white vapour were shooting out of the openings in the rock. They swept across the sky, heading towards the northern endcap, already several hundred metres long, twisting round the alighting tube like bloated contrails from an aerobatic display team.

'What the hell is that?' he asked.

'Hyde Chamber's irrigation system,' Melvyn said. 'They turn it on every other night, once in the early evening, and again just before dawn.'

'You mean it rains in here?' Suzi asked.

'Yes. The lighting tube's infrared emission is turned off, and the cloud condenses, just like on Earth. It's a whole lot cheaper than laying down a grid of pipes and sprinklers, and it flushes any dust away as well.'

Suzi squinted up at the clouds. 'I'll be buggered.'

Greg watched the head of each plume mushroom out, merging into a broad puffy ring. The cavernlight had changed subtly, he could feel it on his upturned face, it was still as bright, but the pressure of warmth had gone from the rays. A second, identical band of cloud was reaching out from the northern endcap.

He shook off the distraction, and told Sinclair: 'I need to know about the flower you gave Charlotte.'

'Ah, well now, you see, that's a private matter, Captain Greg. A very delicate matter, to be honest. I'd be betraying a trust.'

'Tell him,' Suzi said. 'He'll only rip it bleeding from your mind, otherwise.'

What was left of Sinclair's smile became fixed.

'Julia Evans and I know Royan sent it,' Greg said. 'We just want to know where you got it from.'

'Is that true what your charming companion just said?' Sinclair asked. 'About minds and blood, and other things ladies shouldn't know about?'

'I can if I have to,' Greg said. 'Although there's no physical pain involved. But I'd rather not. How about you?'

'Julia Evans?' Sinclair asked. 'Julia Evans sent you here looking for me?'

'That's right. The very same Julia Evans who tolerates you

465

and your mates running about like mice, stealing her food. Now I think it's about time you started paying her back for that kindness. Not to mention Charlotte here, who was nearly killed because she took the flower down to Earth.'

'Is that true, young Charlotte?'

She pursed her lips dolefully. 'Yes.'

'I wasn't told that,' Sinclair said thoughtfully. 'I wouldn't have asked you if I'd known it was dangerous. No, I wouldn't.'

'I believe you,' she said.

They were suddenly engulfed by a shadow. The leading edge of the southern cloud ring was directly overhead, blotting out the lighting tube. Its bottom layer had dropped down to barely three hundred metres, looking disturbingly solid. Small vortices swarmed over its surface, there was a hint of darkness inside. The northern cloud was racing to meet it. Only a narrow band of light was left shining down in the centre of the cavern.

The Globe's audience were looking up, some of them began to take out umbrellas.

'Royan?' Greg prompted.

'Now there's a strange lad for you,' Sinclair said. 'We found him. Or I suppose you might say we found each other really. Fated to meet, we were. Outcasts, but very different. He was with us for a few days.'

'When was this?'

'About a month ago, maybe three weeks. We don't concern ourselves with time as much as you fellows do. Everything's scheduled for you. That's part of what we are, you see, throwing all that away, keeping life calmer. I don't think the lad was really cut out for a life with us. He was wound up terribly tight inside, you know? Bit like you, really, Captain Greg.'

Greg ignored the crack. 'He was with you, then he left?'

'Ah, sharp as a knife you are. I can see I'll keep none of my dark hoarded secrets from you.'

'Did he say where he was going?'

'No. That he didn't, I'm afraid.'

'All right, so what about the flower?'

'Do you believe in ghosts, Captain Greg? I do. Spirits at any rate. Spirits that possess. Spirits that drive you. There's a spirit in New London.'

'There's an alien in New London,' Rick said.

Greg shot him an annoyed look.

'Is that so, now?' Sinclair asked in amusement. 'Well well, fancy that.'

'You're not surprised,' Greg said.

'Aren't I, Captain Greg?'

'No.' He wasn't. In fact, Greg could sense some of his thought currents racing with gratification. 'You want me to go deeper?'

'Thank you kindly, but no. You see, this strapping young man here—'

'Rick.'

'Pleased to meet you, Rick. You see, Rick here, he calls it an alien. I call it a presence. A guiding light, Captain Greg. An angelic being come to grant us the sight. We'll be shown our own souls in all their nakedness. Do you think you can withstand that? You who entomb yourself in the physical world?'

Intuition deluged Greg abruptly, as it so often did; like cards snapping down on the table, everything laid out and visible. 'You founded the Celestial Apostles, Sinclair,' he said. 'You're their preacher and their leader.'

'Ah now, Captain Greg, you're becoming a sore disappointment to me. You said you weren't going to peek. And you an officer and a gentleman, and all.'

'Tell you, I didn't peek,' Greg said. 'It just happens that way sometimes.'

'Perhaps it was the spirit who showed him the truth,' Suzi said, feigning complete innocence.

Sinclair wrinkled at her. 'You could be right at that. Anyhow, this flower you're so keen about, it was brought to me.'

'Who brought it?' Greg asked.

'Why, one of the little people, Captain Greg.' Sinclair gave him a cheery smile. 'About so high, they are.' His hand prodded the air half a metre above the grass. 'All dressed in orange and black, he was, very smart, his little antenna wobbling about.'

'A drone,' Greg said.

'Your word, Captain Greg, so crisp and functional. Suited to what you are.'

'What I am is an orange farmer,' Greg said, and had the enjoyable sight of Sinclair's face slapped by perplexity. He brought out the leaflet, and tapped it with an index finger. 'What about this? What about tomorrow?'

'The simple truth,' Sinclair said. 'Oh, Captain Greg, come now, can you not feel it? And you with your marvellous second sight as well. It's like a thunderstorm sent by the Creator himself; one that builds and builds away on the other side of a mountain range. You can't see it, not with your eyes, but oh dear mother Mary, you know it's there, and you know it's going to come sweeping over the tallest peaks to remind you of nature's raw power. That's what tomorrow is. A storm to wash away our tired terrible perception of the world. We'll see everything in a new, clean, and golden light. The coming of Revelation.'

As if on cue, the first drops of rain began to patter down around them.

33

We have a data alert situation, NN core one said.

Exit VentureCost Package. The three-dimensional accountancy lattice slipped out of Julia's mind. Event Horizon's finance division had put together a preliminary estimate of how much money she could raise to bid for the generator data. The numbers were ridiculous. At this level it wasn't even money any more, just digits in a memory bank. Risk and estimates; you were worth only what people thought you were, how you'd proved yourself. It was all so incredibly cynical. Yet it made the world go round.

She used to think she would prefer a life where wealth was a good solid nugget of gold. Nothing ephemeral about that.

But now she actually had Event Horizon tabulated and defined, some of it quite creatively. Banks and finance houses were reviewing their position, finalizing their figures, coming together in a consortium to back her. Market rumour said there were only three real contenders, Event Horizon, a Mitsubishi/General Electric partnership, and Jonathan-Hewit, with a Boeing/SAAB bid as a dark outsider.

The finance consortium members had a lot of confidence in Event Horizon's potential. And, of course, the intangibles. Mainly herself, and what she would do to them if they failed her.

She found herself thankful for her reputation again. The second time in one day. Must be a record.

What's the problem? she asked.

Charlotte Fielder has been issued with a replacement Amex card.

Oh, Lord.

Quite. We've been running constant monitor programs on all the critical units of this deal to see if there has been any movement. Charlotte applied for a replacement card through a New London office, but her identity was verified by the company's memory core on Earth. She followed that by buying clothes at Toska's.

Clothes? At a time like this?

Yes.

Idiot girl! And if we know . . .

Correct. Leol Reiger, the Dolgoprudnensky, and Clifford Jepson are all hunting her. The hotrods will be running monitor programs similar to ours. We must assume one of the three will be told, if not all of them.

Bloody hell! What does Greg think he's doing?

Perhaps he doesn't know.

Well, he ought to. She opened her eyes. The study was as depressingly sober as always. Wilholm without the children had little appeal. She might just as well be in the office.

Open Channel to Victor Tyo.

Where are you? she asked.

I'll be landing at Prior's Fen in five minutes.

Forget that. Come direct to Wilholm; you and I are going up to New London.

I'm sure Greg and Melvyn Ambler can handle the situation.

Ha! She told him about Charlotte's Amex. *That gives us three reasons to join them. Greg says the alien is there. Royan told me he's gone up there to test his prototype nanoware. And now everyone and their mother knows Charlotte Fielder is up there. I'd have to go up eventually, might as well be now.*

All right, Julia. But I still don't see how Royan and the alien can be tied together. Not now we've established that he grew the flower himself, that it didn't arrive in the solar system on a starship. In fact, I'm not entirely convinced that there is an alien any more.

Greg says he sensed it.

I know. Julia, I've known him as long as you, remember? But, well, I admit his espersense is perfection. Hell, I wish I had psychics half as good in security. It's just this intuition of hi—

You don't believe him.

I'm sceptical, that's all I'm saying. Especially when you should be concentrating on the bid for the generator data.

There's no such thing as coincidence.

That's one hell of a bon mot *to gamble your entire future on.*

She sighed and gave a half-smile. Thank heavens for Victor, always gave his opinions straight.

What do you three think? she asked the cores.

I think Greg knows what he's talking about, Juliet, her grandfather said. *This atomic structuring is just too odd.*

Yes, we concur, said NN core two.

Unanimous, then. *Sorry, Victor, you've just been outvoted.*

All four of you?

'Fraid so.

OK, Julia. I'll be at Wilholm in seven minutes.

Fine. In the mean time, I'm going to phone Clifford Jepson.

Whatever for?

A truce. I want this hardlining to stop. There's been too much already.

*

Clifford Jepson was behind his desk in the Globecast office, dressed in an expensive light grey German suit. His round manufactured face gave her a vicious smile. 'Julia. Gonna make your bid?'

'No, Clifford. I want to ask you a favour.'

He lounged back in a high-backed leather chair, toying with a pearl-textured light-pencil. 'A favour? Changing your tune, aren't you, Julia? Coming down to Earth with the rest of us?'

Burn the conceited little shit, Juliet, Philip Evans raged.

No, Grandpa. And please don't interrupt unless it's a relevant observation.

That was a relevant observation in my book, girl.

Behave, NN core two said.

'My bid will be in tonight, Clifford. But I'd point out that you haven't filed a patent on the nuclear force generator yet.'

'It'll be filed. Don't you worry about that.'

'If you say so. But in the mean time, I'd appreciate it if you put the brakes on Leol Reiger.'

The light-pen pointed rigidly at the ceiling. 'Goddamn, Julia, it was your people at the *Colonel Maitland.*'

'Only after Reiger went on the rampage. I think your judgement in selecting him was execrable, Clifford.'

'Not your type, huh? A bit too direct for you, Julia? I've got no complaints.'

'Well, you ought to have. After all, what has he accomplished for you so far? And Jason Whitehurst was a friend of mine.'

'Yeah.' A muscle twitched under Clifford Jepson's right eye. 'I couldn't help that. Reiger wouldn't have done anything if Whitehurst had seen reason. The old man told his bodyguards to shoot Reiger's squad. He didn't leave Leol with any choice.'

'I was there, Clifford, and what you're saying is absolute tabloid. You have no control over Reiger, he's as much a danger to you as anyone else.'

'What do you mean, you were there?'

Julia gave him a level stare, then accessed her personality package memory files in Wilholm's 'ware and pulled the recording taken from the camera in Jason Whitehurst's study. She squirted it over to Clifford's terminal. He watched the scene as Leol Reiger confronted Jason Whitehurst. The rip gun fired.

'Motherfuck.' Clifford Jepson winced, lips peeling back from his teeth.

'I know Reiger got clear of the hospital in Lagos,' she said. 'Call him off, Clifford, pay off his contract and dump him.'

Clifford Jepson raised his gaze to a point above the camera. Julia watched the shadows of doubt forming across his face, she imagined cogs turning behind his too-smooth skin.

'And then what?' he asked faintly.

'Sorry?'

'What happens after that? I mean, let's not fuck around here, Julia. You've got the Fielder girl, right?'

'She's under my protection. I won't let anyone harm her, least of all you and Reiger.'

'That's just it, Julia. This goddamn AV recording; lifting her out from under Reiger's team like that; and now I'm told Harcourt might get blown away in a cabinet reshuffle. Jesus, Julia, how do you do that? You're just laughing at me. Reiger was one of the best, and he barely gets out alive. I mean, nobody's that good. It's goddamn frightening the way you operate. I'm fighting for my life here, Julia. You know what I mean: the Fielder girl. She could screw me. My contact is playing a very elusive game, I'm not hiding that. You go barging in there with Fielder and that freak Royan, and I'm flushed. I ain't gonna roll over and let that happen. No way.'

Julia watched the light-pen being tapped on the edge of the desk, it was hypnotic. The pressure was starting to get to Clifford Jepson.

And he's not the only one.

'Risk you take playing in this league, Clifford. So I'll make you an offer. In return for giving me your source and dumping Reiger, I'll cut you in on forty per cent of the profits from atomic structuring.'

'No.' He shook his head. It was paper defiance, she thought.

'If I get to the source first, you won't get a penny.'

'I play to win, Julia. I'm not backing out now. You're just as worried as me or you wouldn't have called.'

'Don't count on it,' she said, and broke the circuit.

He hasn't got the generator data yet, her grandfather said. *We could come out of this holding the trumps.*

Providing we secure the generator data first, NN core two said. *Clifford knows he's going to have to produce it tomorrow to satisfy the bidders. He must be reasonably confident about that. That doesn't give us much time.*

Are we all agreed that the alien is the source? Julia asked.

Yes.

Looks that way, girl.

And it's currently up in New London?

Concurred.

Right then. Let's see if we can prevent it from squirting the data down to Clifford.

Sean Francis's face formed on the study's phone screen. His shoulders straightened when he saw who was calling.

'Good afternoon, ma'am,' he said respectfully.

She smiled, showing him he was in favour. Sean Francis took life a mite too seriously, but he was the best executive in the company. Even so, she considered forty-five thousand kilometres was just about an ideal separation distance.

'Afternoon, Sean. Has Greg Mandel's team settled in?'

'Absolutely fine, no problem. They've just left the residence to go and look for Miss Fielder's Celestial Apostle.'

'Excellent. I'll be joining you myself in about three hours. In the mean time I want you to cut New London's communication links with Earth.'

Sean Francis looked as though he'd misheard. 'Cut our communications?'

'Completely. I want New London isolated from Earth. Leave the company security link, but shut down all business, private, and finance links. And all the channel linkages as well, please. We have the franchise from English Telecom, it shouldn't be difficult.'

'But what can I say, what reason? And there's the spacecraft traffic, yes? They'll need guidance updates from flight control.'

'I was just coming to that. Turn back all vehicles on their way up from Earth, their docking clearance is revoked as from now. Keep the local communication frequencies open, of course, we don't want any accidents with the commuter pods and tugs. But the direct relays to geostationary platforms must go; tell them it's solar flare activity, or the exchange 'ware has crashed. Nobody will believe it, but cover yourself. It's only until tomorrow.'

'I suppose I could,' he said unhappily.

'You're my representative up there, you've got the authority. I'll take full responsibility. But unplug New London, now.'

*

Victor was waiting on the lawn outside the library's French windows as she hurried out, still sealing the front of her topaz-coloured shipsuit.

'How did it go?' he asked.

'No use. Clifford's scared of me. But he's more scared of losing out on atomic structuring.'

'Pity.'

They walked over to the CHO-808 Falcon spaceplane sitting between the two Pegasus hypersonics. It looked like a stretched version of the executive jets, slightly fatter, a lead grey in colour, with a single induction ram intake protruding from the under-belly. There was something coldly daunting about its lines, an impression of hidden power.

Event Horizon produced the marque: it was a rapid response vehicle for the RAF, and the Greater European Defence Alliance. They used it primarily to investigate new satellites, checking to make sure they weren't kinetic harpoons. It could also carry six technicians and a two-tonne payload up to geostationary orbit.

Might as well concrete the lawn over, she thought as she went up the Falcon's composite airstair. It's used as a landing pad more than anything else.

The small cabin had seating for seven including the pilot, Maria Garrick. She was an ex-RAF officer who had flown Julia around for eight years, highly competent, and loyal. Julia liked her, one of that rare breed, like Victor, who gave an honest opinion when asked.

Julia ducked her head to avoid the low ceiling as she walked over to the seat behind Maria. The Falcon had none of the padding and trimming of commercial spaceplanes, apart from the active cushioning of the seats. A functional composite cave.

'Take us straight up to New London,' Julia said. The seat cushioning flowed round her legs, gripping them like a vice made of sponge.

Maria twisted round, giving her a bright stare. 'How straight?'

'Fast as we can, please.'

'Right-oh, one purple corridor coming up.' Maria turned back to the graphics on the heavily shielded windscreen slit.

Pilots were all the same, Julia reflected, can't resist a dramatic race against time.

The cabin hatch slid shut, its actuators drowned out by the sound of compressors winding up. They lifted with a jolt, the cabin tilting up thirty degrees. Acceleration pressed Julia down into the seat, rising quickly to two Gs. The Falcon was already doing Mach two when it passed over Yaxley and charged out over the Fens basin.

*

There was a rush of giddiness when the induction ram cut off abruptly, dropping Julia into freefall; with her eyes closed she could believe she was diving headlong through space. There was nothing to be seen through the curving windscreen, a few stars and the diffuse rose-pink glow of the friction-heated nose. It faded to nothing as she watched.

'I can't establish a datalink with New London,' Maria said. 'Inmarsat says their microwave antennas have shut down. Solar flare activity.' She turned her head, glancing back over her shoulder. 'That's pure bullshit, you know that.'

'Yes,' Julia said. 'Use the company security link, you'll get through that way.'

'You're the boss.'

'Did you unplug New London?' Victor asked.

'Yes. I want the alien isolated until we've made contact.'

'It might not like that.'

'I thought you didn't believe in it?'

'If it exists, it might not like that.'

Somehow Julia couldn't raise a smile. 'I don't like the way it's messed me around.'

*

Twenty-five thousand kilometres up, and the Earth was a gibbous white and blue apparition beyond the windscreen. Julia watched the terminator crawl across Italy and Africa, igniting a multitude of city lights in its wake. Apart from the equatorial band, she noted. That remained ominously dark.

'We've got company,' Maria said.

'What sort?' Victor asked sharply.

'Spaceplanes. One is three thousand kilometres behind us, the other another ten behind them. Both on a New London intercept trajectory. I wouldn't mention it, but neither had clearance, not with Inmarsat's linkage still down.'

Open Channel to Falcon Command Circuitry. Access External Sensor Feed.

The starfield wrapped itself around her, Earth dominating one quadrant, the silver splash of New London directly opposite it. There was the beginnings of a faint necklace in geostationary orbit, bright sequins strung out in a fragmented loop, the vast commercial communication dishes interspaced with strategic defence platforms from all five major defence alliance networks.

The high-orbit platforms were an act of mass political paranoia which always rankled, despite the fact that Event Horizon earned a great deal of money from supplying the Greater European Alliance with platforms, and components to all the other networks.

Over half the global armaments budget was spent on low Earth orbit SD platforms to guard against the possibility of sneak attacks. Since the West African slamdown war, kinetic bombardment from space had been the number one public bogeyman. Anybody with a spaceplane could launch harpoons at any target on the planet. A ten-tonne projectile protected against re-entry ablation, travelling at orbital velocity, was a thousand

477

times cheaper than nuclear or electron-compression weapons. And there was no worry about radioactive fallout if the intended victim was a neighbouring country.

It resulted in the five independent defence networks, assembled more or less along regional groupings rather than the political combinations which dominated the previous century. A triumph of practicality over ideology, Julia always thought, with nominally hostile neighbours co-operating. She had drawn a lot of comfort from that at the time; political commentators were hoping it would lay the foundations for a more stable world order. There were even discussions of combining some of the networks into a single global defence system under the control of the UN. But so far nothing had come from them.

The geostationary platforms were a good reminder that for all the progress made in defusing the worst international tensions, there was still a long way to go. There was so much commercial hardware in geostationary orbit, along with national military communications satellites, that the aerospace-force generals and marshals had worried about harpoons being hidden among the antenna platforms. Squadrons of sensor satellites from the Asian-African Pact and the Greater European Alliance had been positioned in geostationary orbit to watch for clandestine harpoon launches. They were swiftly followed by similar spysats from the Chinese and Eastern Federation Co-Defence League, and the Pacific Treaty Nations. The Southern and Central American Defence Partnership brought up the rear three months later. And after the sensors came the weapons platforms. Strictly for defensive interception duties, the network chiefs said.

Julia observed them glimmer in the raw sunlight with a feeling of sad resentment. How little the politicians change. Watching you watching me; the old Cold War slogan resurrected and given fresh respectability. It was bandied about quite a lot on the current affairs 'casts these days. Pure governmental machismo.

As well as the capability to attack other systems in geosynchronous orbit the high-orbit platforms could also launch an assault on New London. She had seen confidential intelligence assessments about New London and the other four asteroids currently being manoeuvred into Earth orbit. Military intelligence was always defined in terms of potential, and what was worrying the generals was the sheer mass of rock available: enough to flatten every city on the planet a thousand times over if it was ever flung down.

Potential.

Possible threat.

Theoretical capability.

I was right not to warn the government about Royan's alien.

Superimpose Radar Return.

Two stars turned red, and the 'ware assigned them five-digit codes, followed by velocity readings, size, and projected course vectors.

NEGATIVE TRANSPONDER RESPONSE, the Falcon's 'ware reported, printing it over the image.

'They don't want us to know who they are,' Maria said.

Exit Falcon Command Circuitry.

Julia looked over at Victor. 'Coincidence?' she asked archly.

'There's no need to get nasty. The question is, which two?'

'Clifford Jepson and Leol Reiger are tied in together, so one of them has to be carrying Reiger. Whether Clifford would come up with him, I don't know. He was pretty desperate for that generator data.'

'I'm not having Reiger inside New London,' Victor said flatly.

'No,' she agreed. 'Maria, can I have a communication channel to Sean Francis, please.'

Maria unclipped a handset from her chair, and handed it back to Julia.

'Yes, ma'am?' Sean Francis said.

'There are two spaceplanes on a rendezvous trajectory with New London.'

'Yes, we know. We've been tracking them.'

'Open a datalink to them, and order them to stop outside your flight-control zone. If they come inside, use the defence

479

systems to kill them. Under no circumstances are either of them to dock with New London.'

'Yes, ma'am.'

'Good enough?' she asked Victor.

'Yes. I wish we could find out if Reiger really is on board one of them.'

'Not without X-ray sight.'

'Can you get an ident on the type of craft?' Victor asked Maria.

'I'll run a comparison program on the nearest, see what the 'ware's best guess is. But the furthest one is well outside sensor definition range.'

The handset bleeped.

'Yes?' Julia asked.

'No reply, I'm afraid,' Sean Francis said.

'Put the message on repeat, and keep sending it until they violate New London's flight-control zone.'

'Yes, ma'am.'

'No good,' Maria said. 'It's jamming the sensors. I can't burn through their ECM at this range.'

'Well, that confirms they aren't legitimate,' Victor said mordantly.

'Yes, there is that,' Julia said. But it did clear up a lingering doubt about ordering Sean Francis to use New London's defences.

34

There was more to Julia's cautious walk than the one-third gravity field. Victor knew her well enough to see how shaken she was by the two unidentified space-planes following them up to New London. By now every major player would know the alien was in the asteroid. Isolating New London bought Julia some time, but there was the question of what the opposition would do next.

The confined titanium airlock tube gave way to the VIP reception room; noise, light, smells, and people registered again. It was a sharp transition from the isolation of the Falcon's cabin. Sean Francis, Lloyd McDonald, and three hardline bodyguards were waiting for them.

'Are you all right, ma'am?' Sean Francis asked. He was even more hyper than usual, pale and anxious.

'Yes, thank you, Sean.' Julia gave him a tired little smile.

'What are the spaceplanes doing now?' Victor asked Lloyd McDonald.

'The first one altered its trajectory as soon as our target acquisition radars burned through its ECM and locked on. It matched orbits with New London, and it's holding station five and a half thousand kilometres ahead of us. Outside the defence perimeter, you'll note. We identified the model as an Alenia COV-325; so with its capacity it could be carrying up to thirty hardliners. The second spaceplane is fifteen thousand kilometres out, and closing. And just to add to the situation: all five Strategic Defence networks placed their geostationary platforms on amber alert status as soon as we targeted the Alenia and powered up our weapons platforms.'

'Have there been any transmissions from the spaceplanes yet?'

'None. We're monitoring continually, of course.'

'Good. I need to know who's on board. If Reiger is in one of them he must be snuffed immediately.'

'Difficult,' Lloyd said. 'We don't have any kinetic harpoons; our platforms are all equipped with energy weapons. It really is a defensive system.'

'Politically expedient not to base offensive weapons here,' Julia said with a hint of regret. 'Sorry, Victor.'

'Five hundred kilometres beyond the defence perimeter,' Victor mused. 'That's not much of a margin for them.'

'We're geared to halt incoming hostiles,' Lloyd said. 'You start shooting outside the perimeter and you run slap bang into the inverse-square law. The nearest platform to the COV-325 is over a thousand kilometres away, the lasers wouldn't even melt plastic at that distance.'

'So move one of the platforms in range,' Victor said automatically.

Lloyd looked at Sean, who nodded thoughtfully. 'Could do, yes?'

'OK,' Lloyd said. 'But the platforms aren't equipped with high-thrust engines. It'll take time.'

'Time we have plenty of,' Victor said.

'Just as long as they can't get in,' Julia said.

'They won't,' Sean said. 'Our hardware is the best, yes?' He gestured to a waiting lift. 'Greg and his people are in the security centre. They've just got back.'

'Did they find Charlotte's Celestial priest?' Julia asked.

'Absolutely, yes. He's a funny old bird, though. Don't know what you'll make of him.'

Julia stepped into the lift. They all crowded in around her,

Lloyd talking into his cybofax, organizing the platform realignment.

'How are you coping, Sean?' Julia asked as the lift began to move down.

'Pretty good, considering. I've declared an official bio-hazard alert, which I think added to the Strategic Defence commander's jitters. But it gives me the authority to quarantine the colony without any legal comeback. Shutting down the communication circuits is stretching the principle a little, mind.'

'But our lawyers can fight it if anyone objects,' she finished for him. 'Good. Well done.'

*

Victor reckoned that if he ever got lost in New London's southern endcap complex his processor implant would be the only thing to save him wandering through the labyrinth of corridors for the rest of his life. There was a kilometre and a half of rock between Hyde Cavern and the hub docking crater, a termite nest of housing, offices, tunnels, corridors, hydroponic farms, fish farms, light-industry factories, and chambers full of environmental support machinery. It wasn't that he was claustrophobic, but there was so much smooth featureless rock, and very few windows.

Sean Francis led them through the security centre without any hesitation. But then of course, everything he did was perfection. One of the reasons nobody felt quite at ease with him, not even Julia, and that was quite an accomplishment.

The briefing room had a window-wall looking out into Hyde Cavern. Heavy drops of rain trickled down the glass. All Victor could see outside was a solid sheet of bleak mist, tinted by a slight orange-pink fluorescence.

There were active holograms on the walls, illuminated landscapes, all of them pre-Warming. A circular table of brown smoked glass stood in the centre of the room; most of New London's furniture was glass and metal. Tourist zones could afford to import wood, the security budget didn't stretch to that. Suzi and Melvyn stood in front of the window, silhouetted against the mist, talking quietly. Greg, Rick, and Charlotte were sitting in the aluminium-framed chairs around the table; a couple of the crash squad hardliners he didn't recognize were in the chairs lined up along the wall.

Julia pulled her shipsuit cap off, letting her hair fall loose. Greg gave her a quick peck on the cheek.

'You found him all right?' Julia asked.

'Charlotte's contact, yes; his name is Sinclair. Royan is proving a little more elusive.' Greg sighed. 'I had hoped he'd contact me. He must know I'm here, he'll have monitor programs loaded into every 'ware core in New London by now. I know Royan.'

'He'll know I'm here too,' Julia said. She turned and gave Charlotte a long stare.

Charlotte dropped her gaze, looking fixedly at the olive-green carpet squares. Victor almost felt sorry for the girl, a cool Julia Evans was a daunting prospect. And of course Charlotte wouldn't have known not to access any datanets, even at second-hand through the American Express office. The oversight was as much his fault as hers, she should have been fully briefed.

'Can we get on with the problem in hand?' Victor said. He pulled a chair out for Julia.

She turned from Charlotte and sat down, giving him a private sly grin. 'Male hearts and fallen angels,' she murmured in a tiny voice.

Victor could feel the warmth creeping up his face.

'Royan used a drone to hand the flower over to Sinclair,' Greg said. 'If we want him, he'll be somewhere in the tunnels and caves the Celestial Apostles use.'

'Intuition?' Victor asked.

'Not really. Royan spent a couple of days with the Celestials, that means he'll have learnt all about their set-up, what they know about the caves, the ones they use. Once he cross-referenced that with security and police procedures he would have found himself a totally secure location for his trials, safe from anybody interrupting, just in case anything did go wrong. Presumably that's where the alien is as well.'

'So what do we do?' Lloyd asked. 'Conduct a mass search? I'd hate for any of my people to stumble on this alien. If you say it exists, ma'am, then I'll believe you. But you're not going to convince everybody.'

'Tell you, there's no need for a search,' Greg said. 'Sinclair will take us into the caves and show us where the drone gave him the flower. We'll see what we can find there. Another personality package maybe. Royan has to have left some method of guiding Julia to him.'

'Sinclair!' Suzi grunted. 'You're going to rely on that over-microwaved fruitcake? Jesus, Greg, he's totally brainwarped.'

Amusement and annoyance chased across Greg's face. 'Sinclair's not exactly rational,' he said slowly. 'But neither is he insane, no way. I think he might be slightly timeloose.'

'Trust you to stick up for him then,' Suzi said.

'Sinclair is a precog?' Julia asked.

'He has some ability along those lines, certainly. Although the talent seems somewhat erratic. He's very aware that there's a big concentration of events and interests focusing on New London right now. It's what he's been predicting all along. Quite a formidable prescient vision, really. Given that he's been up here for seven years.'

'All right,' said Julia. 'If you think Sinclair is reliable enough, then we'll try it.'

Victor groaned inwardly. He'd known this was coming. One whiff of Royan and she'd charge off without thinking. She was so methodical and prudent about everything else in life; the man was a dangerous blind spot. 'Julia.' The quiet, purposeful way it came out made everyone look at him.

Julia's eyes narrowed challengingly. 'Yes?'

'If you go into the caves then you wear proper protective gear, and the crash team goes with you. You don't go in otherwise.'

Suzi chuckled in the dead silence that followed.

'Will Sinclair buy that?' Julia asked Greg.

'It's not up to him,' Victor said.

'Victor's right, I'm afraid,' Greg said apologetically. 'That flower was a warning, after all. And *I* know the alien's here even if nobody else quite believes.'

Julia raised her hands in good-humoured capitulation. 'OK. The crash team it is.'

*

Charlotte stayed with him. It made sense, her part was over, and Greg didn't want her with him in the caves where she'd be a liability. She said she didn't fancy spending the night sitting in the Governor's Residence with a hardliner. He certainly wasn't going to let her go out into the cavern again. So the security centre it was.

Besides, Victor thought, she was so bloody easy to look at.

They were in Lloyd McDonald's office, an impersonal standardized cube with two glass walls and two of rock. One of the glass walls gave him a view across the Cavern, the other showed a secretary's office on the other side. The hardline bodyguard Lloyd had assigned to him was lounging in one of the reception area chairs outside.

Charlotte had curled up on a low black leather settee, chin on her hands, looking dolefully out into Hyde Cavern. She still seemed nervous, always glancing at her watch. It had stopped raining now, allowing the mist to clear away. The lighting tube had dimmed to a sylvan glimmer, a lone moonbeam threaded between the endcap hubs. Buildings across the parkland were picked out by floodlights, a weird mix of architectural styles, the best classical representation of each era, scattered about without thought.

New London always put him in a contemplative mood. The eye-twisting geometry and the determination with which the residents pursued life insisting on introspection.

He was sitting in front of Lloyd's desk terminal, watching the intricate jockeying of the Strategic Defence platform as it inched towards the Alenia COV-325. New London's electronic warfare satellites were blocking the spaceplane's sensors, preventing it

486

from observing the manoeuvre. It would be within laser range in another ninety minutes.

The spaceplane pilot must know. It was the obvious tactic. They would have to pull back.

COV-325 performance perimeters streamed through Victor's processor node. He reckoned the spaceplane had another thirty-two hours' life-support capacity left before they would have to de-orbit and head back to Earth.

The Typhoons from Listoel would catch it. A spaceplane lumbering down through the atmosphere would be no match for front-line fighters.

Charlotte shifted round on the settee. It was distracting. Her legs belonged to someone at least three metres tall.

He started to enter the code for Listoel into the terminal, then the alarm went off.

'What's that?' Charlotte demanded.

'Status one security alert,' he said.

Access Security Centre Command Circuit. Query Alarm.

New London Strategic Defence Operations Room Violation. Five Possible Penetration Agents. Sector Isolation Procedures Activated.

'Bloody hell,' Victor blurted. He made for the door, Charlotte scrambled to her feet behind him.

'Stay here,' he ordered. 'And you,' he told the bodyguard, 'stay with her.'

Charlotte looked like she wanted to protest, but the strength in his voice stopped her. Her shoulders slumped.

Display Security Centre Floor Map. As the outline squirted into his mind he drew the Tokarev pistol from his shoulder holster and flipped the safety off. A rush of adrenalin buzzed in his veins when he came out into the broad central corridor. Security personnel were ignoring the moving walkways, half-running past him, grim faced. They all seemed to know what to do, where they should be going. The alarm was still blaring away.

Victor saw a lift opening, and ran for the doors.

*

There was a press of people at the head of the corridor T-junction. Two drone stretchers slid past Victor as he arrived, black bodybags zipped up. A couple of meditechs in white jumpsuits followed them down the corridor.

Lloyd McDonald watched them go with an expression of controlled fury. 'Tekmercs, hardline fucking tekmercs active in New London,' he said. 'Hell, Victor, I'm sorry, this is one almighty great cock-up.'

'Damage assessment?' Victor asked. It was the only way to do it, job first, shout and mourn later.

'They're inside,' Lloyd shook his head disbelievingly. 'They got into the Strategic Defence Ops Room. They loaded a top-grade virus into the screening 'ware, and shot their way in. Now they're holed up in there but tight. My people think they winged two of them, with one possible fatality. But there are still three confirmed actives left.'

The corridor was four metres wide, three high; walls, floor, ceiling were solid rock, a single biolum strip ran along the ceiling. A lead-coloured slab of titanium/carbon alloy had risen out of the floor ten metres past the T-junction, solid and irresistible. Lloyd's people were already working on it.

The lock panel on the wall had been unscrewed, hanging on springs of coloured wire. A slim grey plastic case containing a terminal and several customized augmentation 'ware modules lay on the floor below it, fibre-optic cables plugging it into exposed circuit blocks. Suction-cup sensors were clinging to the edge of the door. Three security division technicians were standing round the case, talking in low, worried tones, ignoring the data displays filling the unit's small flatscreens.

Victor walked right up to the giant slab; estimating the gravity in the corridor at two-thirds standard.

'They glitched the entire lock system,' one of the technicians said. 'We think they've physically burnt out the 'ware. If we want in, the door will have to be broken down.'

'Can you use a rip gun on it?' Victor asked.

'No, sir, this is over a metre thick. We're going to have to set up a cutting beam, and that's going to take time.'

'How long?'

'Quite a while.'

'Be more specific,' Victor said forcefully.

'Ninety minutes, maybe two hours, before we can start. You see, we'll have to bring in environmental equipment to cope with the heat and the atmospheric contamination which the beam will generate. That will all have to be plumbed in to the colony life-support systems.'

'It gets worse,' Lloyd said. 'This is only the first of three doors. All identical.'

'How about blasting through?' Victor asked.

'We'd have to use shaped charges to blow the rock round the doors,' said the technician. 'And they're all countersunk; that means three or four blasts per door. It would take virtually the same amount of time as cutting, plus the blowback would ruin this entire floor of the security centre, and the environmental damage couldn't be contained as easily.'

'Bloody hell.' Victor rapped his knuckles on the alloy. 'What exactly can they do in there? Can the platforms be retargeted to shoot out the solar panels and industrial modules?'

'Not at all,' Lloyd said. 'They can't activate a single platform, not without the authority codes. And Sean Francis is the only person who's got them.'

Victor gave Lloyd a sharp look. 'He's not in there, is he?'

'No. First thing I checked, he was having a meal in the residence. Should be here any minute.'

Victor turned back to the obdurate door, trying to visualize what was going on behind it. 'Have you got a psychic that can see inside?'

'I'm afraid not. There's two hundred metres of solid rock between here and the Ops Room, and the corridor zigzags. It was deliberately designed that way to stop any psychics from seeing inside. Not even a super-grade like Mandel could perceive it.'

'So what the bloody hell are they in there for?' Even as he said it he knew the answer. 'Shit. With the platforms inactive, there's nothing to stop the spaceplanes from docking now.'

Lloyd punched a fist into his palm. 'Of course. But who are they? They've obviously been up here for a while.'

'Dolgoprudnensky,' Victor said automatically. It fitted, they'd known about Charlotte coming down from New London right from the start. Greg had suggested that Kirilov would probably send agents up here to search for the alien. They must have attacked the Ops Room in order to allow their spaceplane to dock. But why? He couldn't think what could be on board that was so important it forced them into breaking cover and abandoning their search to make sure it got into the colony.

'We'd better check on those spaceplanes,' Lloyd said.

*

They arrived at the command post at the same time as Sean Francis. Victor showed his card to the door and went in, with Lloyd bringing Sean up to date behind him.

The security command post was at the bottom of the security centre, where the gravity was virtually normal; a circular cavern cut into the rock, twenty-five metres in diameter, with a domed ceiling. It had three concentric console rings of terminals and communication stations, plugged into every part of the colony. The shirtsleeved desk jockeys operating them behaved with unruffled competence, filling the chamber with a sustained grumble of restless chatter. He was pleased to see there was no panic, just a smooth co-ordinated response to the alert status. Specialist technical and hardline teams being readied, transport priorities re-allocated, police and security personnel preparing to perform joint civilian control duties, keeping tourists and residents out of the way in case of an escalation, emergency services being brought to full stand-by status. He could remember the long hours spent finalizing contingency plans for the asteroid, that would be just after he was appointed Event Horizon's security chief, everything from biohazard procedure enforcement to full-scale evacuation.

Theatre-sized flatscreens were spaced round the walls, showing grainy green and blue images from photon amps dotted around Hyde Cavern.

Victor gave them a fast sweep, receiving a collage of rolling parkland, secluded gravel paths, small scurrying creatures, black glassy lakes, couples arm in arm, glaringly bright walls of illuminated buildings. It was New London at its usual pace, designer nightlife, providing an artificial fulfilment. There was no sign of any more tekmerc activity.

A large cube hung down from the centre of the ceiling like a boxy obsidian stalactite. New London floated at its centre, rotating slowly, shadowless, every crag in the rock beautifully detailed, with the flame-shaped silver stipple of the archipelago twisting upwards. A shoal of spacecraft glided round the outside, cool blue spheres, projecting green vector lines that wrapped the whole colony in an undulating net. The four englobing sentry layers of Strategic Defence platforms were flashing an urgent amber, as was the outer shell of passive sensor ELINT satellites.

'Where are the spaceplanes?' Victor asked Lloyd.

'Bernie Parkin will know,' Lloyd said. 'He's the duty commander tonight.'

He walked down to the outer ring of consoles, and patted one of the desk jockeys on his shoulder. The man glanced over his shoulder, giving Victor a glimpse of a fifty-year-old face with rough leathery skin and thick lips, crinkled frown lines spread out from the corners of his grey eyes.

'What's the spaceplane situation?' Lloyd asked. 'Any movement?'

'Sure thing,' Bernie Parkin said. He reached over to one of the three keyboards on his console and tapped in an instruction sequence one handed. The image in the big ceiling cube began to shrink. A red dot swam into view with a green vector line extending right up to the southern end of New London.

'That COV-325 pilot knows his stuff,' Bernie Parkin said. 'As soon as our targeting radar shut down they loosed off two missiles, probing the defence perimeter. Of course, the platforms didn't respond, so the spaceplane performed a four-G burn. It's heading straight for us.'

'So it's definitely armed?'

'Yes, sir.'

'When will it get here?' Victor asked.

'Assuming a four-G deceleration burn, it'll rendezvous in another eight minutes. Give it time to manoeuvre, and it'll be putting down in the southern hub crater in quarter of an hour.'

'Is there anything in the crater we can use to intercept it?' Victor asked.

'Not a damn thing,' Lloyd said.

'OK. Assume it puts down in the crater,' Victor said. 'The tekmercs will enter the colony, probably in search of the alien. That means they'll be armed, suited-up as well.'

'Well, Christ, Victor, we're not equipped to handle muscle-armour suits,' Lloyd said. 'I've got a total of five rip guns in the armoury. But the tekmercs would just shoot back at any snipers until they've been blown to pieces. You'll have to call the crash team back to the docking complex, let them ambush the tekmercs.'

'I wonder,' Victor mused. 'Clifford Jepson had to know where to get in contact with the alien. And it must be done tonight if he's to sign up his industrial partner tomorrow.'

'You mean let them in unopposed?' Lloyd's voice rose an octave.

'The crash team has got to fight the tekmercs somewhere, why not in the caves where there'll be minimal damage to the rest of the colony? And they'll have the advantage of surprise.'

'If it is carrying tekmercs, and if they go into the caves. That's a big assumption.'

'We'll wait and hope, because one of those spaceplanes is carrying Reiger. I know it. And allowing his squad into the caves is the only chance we'll have to fight them on our terms. If not, it'll be a running battle in Hyde Cavern. And that will be bad, Lloyd.'

'Yeah,' Lloyd massaged the back of his neck with one hand, his face registering harrowing indecision. 'Maybe, Victor. Christ, I don't have an alternative. But how do we find out which one is carrying Reiger?'

'I don't know. I wonder if Greg could identify him for us?' Typical. He'd mistrusted Greg's intuition all along. But now he actually needed miracles performing . . . 'Where's the second spaceplane?' he asked Bernie Parkin.

'Just reaching the defence perimeter now, five thousand kilometres out. Still on a standard approach vector. ETA, twenty-five minutes. They're not in the same hurry as the COV-325. That timing is interesting.'

'Oh?'

'The COV-325 was stuck out there for seventy-five minutes before the Dolgoprudnensky agents made their move on the Ops Room. And we initiated colony quarantine procedures four hours prior to that. The Dolgoprudnensky agents could have launched their assault at any time since the quarantine started. But they waited until the second spaceplane was nearing the defence perimeter. What I'm saying is: it looks like the platforms were shut down specifically to let that second spaceplane through.'

'And the Dolgoprudnensky agents in the Operations Room couldn't stop the first one from coming in either,' Victor said.

'Right.'

It had to be Reiger in the first spaceplane. But he still couldn't imagine what was in the Dolgoprudnensky space-plane. 'Get your people to evacuate the entire southern crater docking complex,' he told Sean. 'I don't want anyone in the way of those bastards when they come in.'

'Absolutely,' Sean said.

'Lloyd, your teams and the police are going to have to keep people clear of the tekmercs. We'll monitor their progress from here, and update as we go.'

'Right.'

What Victor actually wanted to do was concentrate on snuffing Reiger. He could almost justify the risk of exposing the snipers; kill the brain and the body becomes irrelevant. But he had the residents and tourists to consider. That was what security was about. And now, when it came down to it, he found he was just too dedicated to the ideal.

The crash team would have to take out Reiger. Suzi would get her chance after all.

'Sir.' One of the desk jockeys at a communication station was waving for Victor's attention.

'What is it?'

'There's a call for you from Listoel, coming over the company secure link. Priority rating.'

'Put them through.' Victor pulled his cybofax out of his pocket. The face that formed on the screen was familiar, one of the crash team hardliners.

'What is it, Bailey? And be quick,' Victor said. The man seemed very edgy.

'Sorry, sir, but it's Fabian Whitehurst. The boy's just found out about New London being unplugged from the commercial communications circuits. Quite upset about it, he is; says he needs to talk to you or the boss. Says there's a spaceplane *en route* for New London you should know about.'

35

Greg could feel his skin cooling slowly. The energy-dissipater suit he wore was made from thermal-shunt fibres intended to absorb and deflect maser and laser energy, and they continually pumped out the heat his body generated. It was a one-way flow through the suit's inner insulation layer, making sure he didn't cook in his own juices. But it could get uncomfortably chilly when he wasn't moving.

The hood, with its gas filters and integral photon amp, was slung over his shoulder. A cap with a throat mike and earpiece plugged him into the suit's 'ware and communication circuits.

He watched the biolum strips on the subway tunnel wall slide by, throwing pulses of pink-tinged light through the coach's windows. Sinclair was always the first to get caught, sitting up in the front, his pale face suddenly printed with deep shadows, like an undertaker's doll.

Julia was next, lines of exhaustion brought into unkind relief. She was also wearing one of the black form-fitting energy-dissipater suits, its hood hanging down her back. Her eyes were open, showing her adrift in her own thoughts.

Rick was twitching continually, unused to the cloying grip of the dissipater suit's fabric. Tension pulled his expression down into doubt, a big contrast to the anticipation shining in his eyes.

After that, the fans of light swept along the row of motionless muscle-armour suits standing in the aisle. There were nine of them, dull black metalloceramic humanoids. The background hum of their internal systems sounded bleakly oppressive in the small coach, an ominous reminder of how much power each of them contained.

The only one Greg could recognize for sure was Suzi. The smallest, standing at the head of the line, with a Honeywell carbine and a Konica rip gun clipped to the waist of the suit, four Loral missiles in slim launch tubes attached behind her shoulders.

The other twelve members of the crash team were riding in a second coach, directly behind them.

Sinclair hadn't liked that. 'I'll not be having these demon heathens in the caves, Captain Greg. They'll be frightening the children for sure,' he'd complained when the muscle-armour suits had marched into the security centre train station.

'Tough,' Greg had said. 'We need them. Besides, you might wind up being glad of them. We've no idea how the alien is going to respond to our contact.'

'Oh, come on now, Captain Greg, all I said was I'd show you where I was given the flower. You never said nothing about this invading army.'

'They won't lay a finger on any of your followers,' Julia had said. 'You have my word on that.'

Sinclair had gaped, features twisting into delighted astonishment. 'By all that's holy. 'Tis really you.'

'Yes, it's me.'

'Well now, me darling, I can hardly doubt your word, now can I?' He had bowed as far as his portly frame allowed him.

The train drew into Moorgate station, just behind the foot of the northern endcap. Greg stepped out of the coach, finding himself in a large oblong rock chamber, with six platforms laid out in parallel. It was obviously a staging area for the crews digging the second chamber. Rails disappeared up four smaller tunnels in the north wall. Beyond the last platform there was a collection of heavy machinery laid out like a small town; lorry-sized electrical transformers, big spherical tanks, and the ribbed cylinders of turbo-pump casings. A crisscross grid of two-metre pipes, heavy-duty plastic tubes, and thick power cables led away from them into eight service tunnels.

Moorgate station was deserted except for Bernard Kemp and a youngish WPC who were standing waiting on the platform.

Bernard Kemp's mood hadn't improved, Greg observed. The sergeant gave Sinclair a look of undisguised contempt, then started when Julia emerged from the coach. The WPC came to attention.

Julia lifted her hand in an airy gesture. 'There's no need for that,' she told the woman.

'We've secured the station, sir,' Bernard Kemp told Greg as the crash team piled out of the coach. 'And the transport controller has shut down this line's traffic: there'll be no more coaches in. All the construction and mining crews in the second chamber will use the Lancaster Gate station when they come off shift.' He watched the coach carrying the remainder of the crash team glide to a halt. 'Exactly what is going on, sir, ma'am?'

'Just like the Governor says, a biohazard alert,' Greg said.

'A biohazard?'

'Yeah. But not a biology we know much about. OK?' Greg didn't even want to tell him that, God alone knew what kind of rumours it would start, but he felt he owed the sergeant something for all the inconvenience.

'Yes, sir,' Bernard Kemp said reluctantly. His eyes kept wandering back to Julia.

'Right, now you two take one of our coaches, and report back to your headquarters,' Greg told the sergeant. He waited until the door slid shut behind them, then turned to Sinclair. 'OK. Where now?'

Sinclair looked at the crash team and sighed. 'The Celestial Apostles, we had something . . . good. Nothing grand, I do declare, no Utopia, but we got along fine. The only quarrels were the quarrels that people should have, little things by the by. We all believed together, you see; that was enough to bind us.'

'But that was all due to change tomorrow anyway, right?' Greg asked.

'Ah, now, Captain Greg, there you go again. Spoiling the rhythm, just when I was working up a fine head of indignation. You're a hard man, you are. No respect.' He gave Julia a mocking smile. 'I'm surprised at you, a lady with a vision past mine. You shouldn't be associating with the likes of him. Terribly bad for you, it is.'

'No, it isn't,' Julia said. 'Greg's one of my real friends.'

'Oh, Holy Mary, and I'm to deliver us into your tender hands, am I? Lord forgive me.' He dropped over the side of the platform with surprising ease, and started walking down the rail towards the north wall.

Greg landed lightly behind him, then turned to help Julia. The crash team began to jump down, the resonant hammer blows of their boots hitting the rock echoing round the silent chamber.

Sinclair looked round, and muttered a despairing, 'Jesus.'

Greg took the lead as Sinclair led them past the rail tunnels, heading towards the heavy machinery at the end of the chamber. A small secretion awoke his intuition, and allowed him to expand his espersense. The three psychics in the crash team had used their sacs to activate their own psi abilities. They all exchanged mental grins of acknowledgement.

It was going to be one of the service tunnels that carried pipes and cables up to the second chamber, Greg decided. He whispered a request for a link to Melvyn Ambler into his throat mike. 'Melvyn, I'll go in on Sinclair's heels, but I want two of your tech specialists behind me. I'll know if we're heading into anything lethal, or if Sinclair's brewing up trouble. But there are bound to be sensors.'

'Roger,' Melvyn acknowledged. 'Carlos, Lesley, up front. Ms Evans, could you and Rick move into the middle of the team, please?'

Greg sensed the beginnings of resentment rustling round in

Julia's mind. He ordered the communication circuit off. 'Best place,' he said, and held her eye.

'Yeah, all right.'

Sinclair walked into one of the service tunnels, a simple tube three metres in diameter. Inside was a remote, basic world; walls scored by the blades of the mining machine which had cut it, a metre-wide pipe fastened to the rock at waist height by solid metal brackets, cables strung from the ceiling in long hoops which made him duck every few metres. The rock was cold, leaching warmth from the air, minute beads of condensation clung to every surface. Long oblong grids had been laid down to give a narrow level floor. Dim biolum panels were stuck to the wall every five metres. Greg could see a tiny silver trickle of water underneath the metal grid.

He reckoned they'd gone about seventy metres when Sinclair halted.

'Would you be so kind as to give me a hand here, Captain Greg?' Sinclair asked as he bent over. 'Me back isn't what it used to be.'

He stuck a couple of fingers through the grid, and fished up a wire hoop. 'Here we go. Just tug on that. It'll come up like a trapdoor.'

Greg sensed a tingle of satisfaction in Sinclair's thought currents, nothing malicious.

'I'm registering some magnetic patterns,' Carlos said. 'They came on when Sinclair picked up that loop. This section of the tunnel is wired. Something just above you, sir, small and delicate. Probably a photon amp and mike. I'm jamming the processor.'

'Will they know that?' Greg asked.

'Not unless it was military grade hardware; it should just seem as though the hardware is down.'

Greg couldn't believe the Celestial Apostles would use military 'ware. They'd know someone was coming, but not who. He got a grip on the hoop, and pulled. It was heavier than he expected.

The grid came up with a loud squeak, revealing solid darkness. He slipped the energy dissipater suit's hood over his head, feeling the wet lick of the photon amp adhering to the skin round his eyes. His universe shifted to a weathered blue and grey grisaille, and the darkness receded.

There was a large crack running along the bottom of the tunnel. It had been widened below the grid, chiselled away with some kind of power tool. The jagged hole was over a metre wide, rough-hewn steps leading downwards. He bled in the infrared, adding a faint pink hue to the image. But there were no hot spots, no sign of life.

'Is there anybody on duty below?' Greg asked.

'Certainly not, Captain Greg. What would we be wanting with look outs? We're not criminals, we're believers.'

Greg hopped across the hole to Sinclair. There wasn't room in the tunnel to get past anyone. He probed round with his espersense, the crash team invading his consciousness, a complicated *mélange* of emotions. Nobody else.

'Melvyn, it's clear for the first fifteen metres.'

'Roger. Carlos, Lesley, secure the entrance please.'

The first armoured figure waddled gracelessly up to the lip of the hole, massive in the restricted width of the tunnel. Infrared picked out ruby shimmers around its joints, fluctuating at each movement. Greg wondered if any of them would be able to fit down the steps.

Carlos held out an arm and dropped a thick ten-centimetre reconnaissance disk down into the hole. Greg watched the miniature *UFO* swoop into the cave, its motor glowing, tracing a crimson line that curved through the air like a bent laser beam.

'No hazards visible,' Carlos reported. He started down the steps. His arms scraped the rock on either side, sending up a burst of vivid orange sparks.

Greg winced.

Lesley followed with more grinding noises.

'I see you don't intend on creeping up on my folk,' Sinclair said.

'Is it all this narrow?' Greg asked.

'No. And you'll be going to thank the Lord for that this next Sunday.'

'I might just do that.'

*

It was unlike any cave Greg had ever seen on Earth. The rock had been split along natural fracture lines, crystalline weaknesses, stress lines, veins of metal in the ore. Greg imagined a tracery of hairline cracks spreading down from the electron-compression blast crater, cancerous shadows eating through the rock. Pressure differences clashing at each shock wave. Some of the internal structure around the fractures must have compacted, while others had wrenched apart in a parody of tectonic faults, creating vast empty fissures.

For every sheer surface there was a corresponding plane above, razor-sharp ridges had left torn gauges, the angular root-pattern of shining metal veins was perfectly twinned. It was the most intricate three-dimensional jigsaw puzzle ever made. And for the first time in his life, Greg felt claustrophobic. Floor and ceiling so obviously fitted together – they belonged together. Jaws of a vice, waiting.

Sinclair waited until all the crash team came down the steps from the service tunnel, then took a torch out of his pocket. 'Now then, would you be so good as to close the grid above you there?'

The light of Sinclair's weak beam was picked up by Greg's photon amp, illuminating the cave like a Solaris spot. He saw a couple of power cables trailing out of the crack next to the steps, snaking away into the gloom. The Celestials must have spliced them into the lines up in the service tunnel.

'We'll reel out an optical cable as we go,' Melvyn said as the last team member pulled the grid back into place. 'Keep our communications with the security centre open.'

'Yeah, OK,' said Greg. He gestured at the red power cables. 'Is this your power source?' he asked Sinclair.

'One of them, Captain Greg. Space is awash with energy. The

light, the radiation, the wind from the sun. Bountiful it is. I'm sure Miss Julia here doesn't begrudge us this mere trickle.'

'Sure she doesn't. So where were you given the flower?'

'This way.' He started following the red cables, stepping lightly over the crumpled rock.

The cave turned out to be about fifty metres across, its floor a gentle upward slope. Sinclair was heading for a bottleneck crevice opposite the stairs. There was no dust, Greg noticed, none of the little drifts of soil and bat droppings that contaminated natural caves.

His initial feeling of claustrophobia was fading. Bubbling up in its wake came a twinge of expectation. Foolishly he felt bright to the point of being cheerful. It wasn't quite his usual intuition, more like instinct. On the right path and getting closer. The same blind compulsion a salmon feels as the unique surge of fresh water from the mouth of its birth river finally flows around it.

The alien.

Was this the bewitchment Sinclair experienced? God knows, it was cogent enough to be mistaken for divine guidance.

A grin tugged at his lips. You're enjoying this, you idiot.

A glimmer of light was shining out of the crevice ahead of him. He pulled his dissipater-suit hood off, initially confused by the monochrome gloaming he found himself immersed in. A swirl of air cooled his sweaty face. The light coming from the crevice was blocked out as Sinclair moved into it. Greg hurried after him.

There was a horizontal oval passage leading away beyond the entrance, its sides crimping together. Biolum globes dangled on slim chains from the roof. Their radiance was decaying into greenish blue, giving the wrinkled passage a biotic appearance, as if it had been grown, the inside of a giant root. Sound would carry here, Greg knew, the rough clanking of the crash team's boots against the rock rolling on ahead of them.

'Is it worth it?' he asked Sinclair. 'Living like this, hiding in caves?'

'Well now, Captain Greg, we walk the park in the day, sun ourselves, dance in the rain, take our children to the beach. Nobody starves; to be sure, I even weigh in a little over the odds meself. And here we are, with Miss Julia Evans herself coming to see what it is that attracts us here. 'Tis only due to people like you that we can't live in the southern endcap. Men and women have a right to live in space. We shouldn't be persecuted for exercising that right.'

Greg grunted and gave up.

There was another cave at the end of the passage, a big lenticular bubble of air. They came out halfway up one side, looking down on a forest of sharp conical outcrops. Someone had left a cluster of biolum globes sitting on the top of the spires near the centre. Sinclair led them down to the bottom on a path which had been hacked into the rock, then straight into another passage.

'Christ, Julia, this is one badly fucked asteroid,' Suzi said. 'This many catacombs, it's gotta be leaking air all over the shop. Did you know it had so many busted rocks?'

'Seismic analysis showed there were eight major fault zones,' Julia answered. 'All of them occur where different strata intersect. There were five deep in the interior, two of those got excavated to make room for Hyde Cavern. This is the third, the fourth will be excavated for the second cavern, and the last is down at the northern end of the second cavern. We had to vitrify a square kilometre of Hyde Cavern's floor after it was excavated, because it bordered on an external fault zone. And we'll have to do the same thing to the second cavern when it's finished. But New London's integrity is sound.'

And Royan would know about all the seismic analysis and the fault zones, Greg thought, probably more than the Celestials did.

He heard the water when he was still twenty metres from the end of the passage, a suckling sound that grew with each step. The passage opened out into a cave about fifty or sixty metres across. Greg thought it must have had a deeply concave floor, the surface of the dark lake which filled it possessed the kind of stillness which he associated with depth. On the other side, a streamer of water oozed out of a fissure near the roof, slithering down the wall, making the sounds he'd heard. Ripples spread out from its base, dying away before they reached the middle of the lake.

'We're below the Cavern level,' Melvyn said. 'There must be a leak in the freshwater streams.'

'Integrity, huh?' Suzi murmured.

Greg trailed after Sinclair along a crescent-shaped shelf of rock that served as a shore, running three-quarters of the way round the side of the cave. A row of bright biolum panels on the wall above him fired harsh pink-white beams out across the lake. Serpents of reflected light twisted over the damp black walls.

A flick of movement caught his eye, and he turned in time to see a ring of ripples out on the lake accompanied by a quick *chop* as the water came together.

'Hey, it's got fish in it,' Greg said.

'Indeed there is, Captain Greg, some of the finest rainbow trout this side o' heaven. I thank the Lord for his providence every night.' Sinclair stood right by the edge of the water, and crossed himself. The darkness of his thought currents were a clue to just how seriously he meant what he said. 'I found this lake, Captain Greg. It was shown to me, like Moses and his burning bush. I heard the call, and brought me friends down here to sanctity and solitude where we wait for the new dawn.'

'Tomorrow?'

'Don't mock me, Captain Greg,' Sinclair said smartly. 'You know it's truth as much as I do. All of us are guided, one way or another.' He raised his voice. 'Isn't that right, Miss Julia?'

The crash team had been filing out of the passage behind. Greg saw Rick and Julia emerge, both pulling their hoods off.

Julia took in the cave with a stoic glance. 'I came looking for my husband,' she said, 'Nothing more.'

'And yet this edifice you call New London cost you billions.

More billions than you'll ever see returned to your corporate balance sheet. Now why is that, I wonder? Do you see beyond the physical, Julia Evans?'

She shrugged.

Sinclair carried on round the shore towards a brightly lit archway. This time the passage was much shorter, ten metres, with a sharp right-angle turn at the end. A wave of warm humid air blew straight into Greg's face as he turned the corner, bringing a thick, living smell of vegetation with it. Bright, hazy red light dazzled him.

When he blinked the moisture from his eyes, he found himself standing on the top of a broad stone staircase, looking down on the biggest cave yet, easily eighty metres across, twenty high. A village of reed huts was clumped together on the far side. A ring of ten big Solaris spots on the ceiling shone with a strong gold-pink light, fluorescing the thin water vapour around them into hemispherical nimbuses. A Hollywood sunset, Greg thought.

The floor had been levelled and covered with gene-tailored arable moss, reminding him of Greenland. Rows of circular troughs had been built around the huts for more substantial plants, young fruit trees were already flourishing, trellises supported grape vines, yellow melons hung over the edges. A herringbone network of irrigation hoses lay on the floor between the troughs, the pattern barely visible under the tide of moss.

A broad square pedestal had been set up in the centre of the village, supporting six large flatscreens in a hexagonal arrangement. The two facing Greg looked almost completely black, though they could be showing some tiny silver smudges, he was too far away to be certain.

Children were playing around the pedestal. Adults walked about, tending to the troughs, working in an area that was obviously a communal kitchen, with aluminium tables and benches. Greg guessed at about a hundred and fifty people all told. He wasn't prepared for it. Commune-mentality Greens in sleeping bags, candles and camp fires, huddled into dark clefts, chewing cold fruit, zombie pupae. That was the theory he'd built.

But this ... This was designer underclass. Or perhaps not. Perhaps New London's innate perfection carried on even down here, a natural extension of the philosophy which suffused Hyde Cavern. Julia's principle of success with style.

The Celestial Apostles did believe in the future, after all, however it diverged from the mainstream. And some of them were tech-types.

Sinclair started to descend the stairs, stretching out his arms, laughing wildly. 'I'm back. I'm back. 'Tis me returned to you all.'

The Celestials nearest the staircase turned to look, smiles turning to alarm as armour suits clumped out of the passage. Yells and cries went up.

'No, no,' Sinclair shouted. 'You've nothing to be afraid of. Tomorrow is come. I've brought it to you.'

He reached the floor of the cave and started to gather Celestials to him, ruffling the heads of the children, embracing the adults. An archetypal tribe father.

'Look,' he said. 'Look.' And pointed.

Julia was halfway down the staircase as the murmur of astonishment began. It spread out in a wave; the Celestials edged towards the foot of the staircase, ignoring Greg and the others. The children were shy and curious, adults incredulous. Two of the crash team moved protectively in front of Julia.

'She knows the dawn we await is real,' Sinclair said. 'She came to us because our path is right.'

'You should shut the old prick up,' Suzi's voice said in Greg's earpiece. 'The daft sods will want miracles next. And we can't deliver.'

'Too late,' he whispered back.

Sinclair folded his arms across his chest and faced Julia. 'Behold, my kingdom. Yours to command.'

Julia studied the faces in front of her, they were all quiet, waiting for her to speak. Greg sensed a curious calm settle in Julia's mind.

'You have all waited a long time for this day,' she said. 'And it hasn't been without its trials. But tomorrow the change we all expect will come.' And she smiled warmly.

'Oh, bollocks,' Suzi said as the Celestials started to applaud. 'She's flipped. She's totally fucking flipped.'

Tears were forming in Sinclair's eyes. There were calls of 'How?' coming from the crowd.

Greg left them behind and walked into the middle of the village for a closer look at the flatscreens; the move was intuitive. All the screens were showing images of space, taken from cameras on the outside of New London as far as he could tell. There was the archipelago, and Earth, the Moon, silver flowers of industrial modules.

'I didn't know who you were before,' said a voice behind him. It was the Oriental girl in the black net top who had handed him the leaflet in the Trump Nugget castle quadrangle. She was carrying a baby, about eighteen months old, who looked at Greg with wide brown eyes.

'A lot of us saw you in the Cavern this afternoon,' she went on. 'We thought you'd stolen Sinclair from us.'

'I was just looking for him. Julia Evans wanted to see him.'

The girl smiled pertly. 'I can't believe that's really her. Even though I believed in Sinclair. But it's actually happening, isn't it? All the things he told us. How is she going to save us?'

'It's a bit complicated. All plugged in to alien technology.' He moved on round the flatscreens, searching. There was something to see here, something to watch for. The impulse was irresistible.

'An alien?' the girl asked, intrigued. 'Are you making fun of us?'

'No, I'm perfectly serious.'

'Sinclair always said that our souls would be liberated by a celestial angel; and that we would be safe up here while stars fell upon the Earth and smote it. And there would be locusts and plague, too. I was never really sure. Could your alien be the same thing as Sinclair's angel, do you think?'

He gave the gently zany girl a sideways glance. 'I've no idea, theology and xenobiology aren't my strong points. What are these flatscreens for?'

'So we can watch for the dawn of change to emerge from the stars.' The tone wasn't quite self-mocking, but close. 'Perhaps your alien's star.'

'The images are real-time?'

'Yes. Tol plugged the flatscreens into the colony's datanets.'

'Who's Tol?'

'A brother.'

Greg stopped in front of a flatscreen showing a view of the southern hub crater, the docking spindle covered a third of the screen. 'He must be a very technical lad.'

'Yes, he is. He knows everything there is to know about the asteroid's communication networks, he used to belong to one of the big channel companies.' She giggled. 'He's been with Sinclair almost since the beginning. I don't think he really believes in the Celestial Revelation, but he contributes as much as anyone. Five of the children are his, as well. Including Zena here.' she bounced the softly cooing baby on her hip.

'Busy man,' Greg said. One star was brightening, edging across the screen. He stared at it, and *knew*.

'Melvyn,' he called.

'Greg,' Melvyn's voice was equally urgent. 'Victor's on line. He reckons there's a tekmerc squad on the way.'

*

The Celestial Apostles didn't like it.

'The time for running and hiding is over,' Sinclair protested plaintively.

'Nobody is asking you to run,' Melvyn's voice clanged out of his suit speaker. 'We just want you safely out of the way.'

508

'This is our home, now, Mr Ambler. We live here. We built this place with the sweat of our brows.'

'You may live anywhere in New London you wish after this,' Julia said. 'That's what you told me you wanted.'

'That I did, yes. But why do you have to wait until these monster criminals come down here? Why not waylay them somewhere else?'

Greg listened to the argument with half an ear. The collective mind tone of the Celestials was nervous. And a fair proportion were practical types. They'd go. What he and Julia wanted was for Sinclair to carry on and show them where the drone had been. He suspected Sinclair was angling for concessions.

'They'd better get a move on,' Suzi grumbled. She was standing beside him as he watched the spaceplane approach New London.

'Yeah. You going to stay here with the ambush team?'

'Fucking right I am.'

'Well, don't annoy Melvyn, OK? He doesn't need it.'

'Oh, thanks for the confidence. I'm fluid enough to take orders when I have to.'

'Sure you are; I can read minds, remember?'

'Bollocks. All you know is that I'm pissed off with Leol fucking Reiger. Don't take no genius.'

'Reiger's squad are bound to be in muscle-armour suits. How are you going to know which one is him?'

''Cos the bastard walks with a swagger. Even in a suit, Greg, he walks with a swagger. I'll know him when I see him.'

The spaceplane's auxiliary reaction drive came on, a vivid white spear of plasma extending across half of the starfield.

Sinclair started shouting orders, spurred by the sight. The Celestials were running round, collecting children, picking up flight bags stuffed with clothes.

Sinclair grabbed one of the girls. 'Where's Tol?' he demanded loudly.

'I haven't seen him,' she said.

'Holy Mary, the lad's probably off in the caves with a girl. All he thinks about, you know,' Sinclair told Julia. 'Terrible it is, but his heart's in the right place.'

'You'll have to put someone else in charge,' she said.

'Right you are there. Marcus!' he bellowed. 'For the love of Mary, Marcus, where are you?'

One of the Celestials rushed over to Sinclair; Greg recognized him as a member of one of the afternoon's leaflet teams.

'I'll send a couple of the crash team with them to make sure they get out all right,' Julia said.

'That's very kind of you,' Sinclair said.

Greg smiled. Even down here, Julia was automatically in charge.

Eventually the Celestials were shepherded into a single agitated group. Some of the younger children were crying.

Sinclair stood on the rock staircase to talk to them, Julia at his side. 'You can't use the Moorgate station, take them out through the Whitechapel entrance,' he told Marcus. 'It's the quickest from here.'

'There will be some of my company security people waiting for you,' Julia said. 'Not the police, all right? They'll put you up in a hotel for tonight. After that, we'll sort out where you're going to live permanently.'

The spaceplane's plasma drive cut off, revealing a small grey triangle floating beyond the end of the docking spindle. Pinpoint twinkles of blue light flickered around its nose, and it began to turn in towards the crater.

'Come an' get it,' Suzi said.

Greg's intuition seemed to have dried up. He watched the spaceplane manoeuvring round the spindle, free of any presentiment.

Rick joined the two of them on the pedestal, giving the spaceplane a sober glance.

'You joining us?' Greg asked.

'Yes. It's what I came for. And I haven't been much use so far.'

'Nobody expects you to hardline, Rick. Your job starts after we make contact.'

*

The crack was slanted over at a good twenty degrees, one of several around the village cave. Sinclair had to clamber a metre off the arable moss floor before he could squeeze into it.

'Down here?' Greg asked.

And Sinclair actually seemed embarrassed about it. 'That's right, Captain Greg. The, er, younger folk use it quite a lot, if you take me meaning. The walls on the huts there, they aren't very thick.'

'Got you,' Greg said.

'It opens up a bit further down,' Sinclair said encouragingly. 'Your tin men'll be all right after that.'

'Right.' Three of the crash team were coming with them, Teresa Farrow, Jim Sharman, and Carlos Monetti. He took another look at the narrow crack. If they did meet anything hazardous in there, then targeting it would be a brute. 'Hold it, Sinclair; Carlos, you go first. I want fire-power available if push comes to shove.'

'Yes, sir,' Carlos said gladly. He clamped his gauntlets on the side of the crack and walked himself up. Little splinters of rock spilled down.

Someone had found the controls for the Solaris spots. They flared white, throwing everything into sharply defined contours.

Melvyn was busy organizing his crash team, sending them ranging into the village, and exploring the other cracks and fissures leading out of the cave.

'Hey, Greg,' Suzi said. 'Give Royan's arse a kick from me, OK?'

'No messing.'

Sinclair wriggled into the crack after Carlos. Greg levered himself up. The aliens' presence was a cold burning star ahead of him, exerting a gravity which acted on his thoughts alone, pulling him on. He sucked in his belly, and slipped into the crack.

36

The empty corridors were faintly unnerving. Before the alarms
had gone off the security centre had been a bustling, lively place.
Now the moving walkway rattled hollowly in the deserted main
corridor as the hardliner escorted Charlotte to the security
centre's command post.

They stepped off the end of the walkway in front of a bank of
seven lifts, the two at the far end were big service shafts. Security
personnel were struggling with large flat-bed drones loaded with
bulky machinery, trying to fit them through a service lift's doors.
They were the first people Charlotte had seen since leaving Lloyd
McDonald's office.

'What's all that for?' she asked the hardliner as they waited
for their lift.

'Cutting gear by the look of it,' he replied.

He'd been polite the whole time. Naturally. His eyes switching
between her legs and her face. But he didn't know what was
going on any more than she did. Nothing good, she knew, not
with those alarms going off.

The lift arrived, and they descended.

There were three guards outside the command centre's door,
all of them armed. He had to show his card to a cybofax one of
them carried before they were allowed through the door.

Inside was a big circular room with rings of consoles, large
flatscreens round the wall, a giant cube at the centre of the

vaulting rock ceiling. She picked up on the current of worry infecting all the people sitting behind the consoles, their serious faces, strained voices.

'Over here.' Her hardliner gestured at a glass-walled office. She could see Victor, Sean, and Lloyd inside.

Just as she got to the door she saw Fabian's face on a phone flatscreen, her legs almost faltered. Then Victor's expression registered. She wanted to turn and run.

'Fabian here has just told us that the pair of you managed to convince Pavel Kirilov to come up to New London,' Victor said.

'Yes,' she whispered.

'I don't bloody well believe this. You let him know you survived the *Colonel Maitland*, and then invited him up here? He will do anything to obtain the generator data, including ripping it out of you. And I do mean rip.'

'Kirilov started all this!' Fabian shouted from the phone's speaker. 'My father is dead because of him.'

'And Julia Evans told you quite plainly that he would be dealt with,' Victor said.

'Oh, sure. Sometime,' Fabian said petulantly.

'What's that supposed to mean?'

'We did it so we could be certain,' Charlotte said.

'What do you mean, certain?'

'You didn't seem interested. I thought ... well, I wanted to be absolutely sure Pavel Kirilov was dealt with. Dmitri Baronski was killed too,' she added lamely.

'Didn't you listen to a word said at Listoel?' Victor demanded. 'We have got other, more urgent, problems right now. Third-rate crime lords have to wait their turn. But we would have got round to Kirilov, nobody screws Event Horizon about like he's done and gets away with it. You were given Julia Evans's word on it. What more do you want, a thumbprinted contract?'

Charlotte rubbed her bare arms, suddenly chilly in the air-conditioned office. The disgust and contempt in Victor's voice was almost unbearable.

'Just one shot from a Strategic Defence platform,' she pleaded.

'That's all it needs. Pavel Kirilov is going to call me before his spaceplane docks, we'll know when he's in range.'

'No, he's not going to call you,' Lloyd said. 'And we're not shooting anyone right now. We can't, thanks to you.'

She gave him a fearful glance.

'Screen six,' he said, and pointed through the glass.

The delta-wing spaceplane was inside the lip of the southern hub crater, hanging below the docking spindle. Small blue flames stabbed out of the reaction-control nozzles, lining it up for a landing on the crater wall. Two sets of doors had hinged open on either side of the dorsal ridge. Black thermal-dump panels had concertinaed out, and folded back parallel with the wings, making way for silvered dishes and framework racks to rise out of their recesses. Charlotte peered forwards. There were squat cylinders nestling in the racks, their front ends were like insect eyes, a multisegment hemisphere of black chrome lenses, a large bell-shaped nozzle protruded from the rear. Now she knew what to look for, she could see the gold-foil covered boxes of lasers on telescopic arms rising above the dishes.

'That's Kirilov?' she asked, her voice had become a croak.

'Oh no,' Victor said. 'Kirilov is still on his approach phase. That's Leol Reiger. You remember him? The two of you almost met on the *Colonel Maitland*.'

She bit her lower lip, fighting the tears building behind her eyes. Nothing. Nothing she ever did turned out right.

The office's terminal bleeped. Lloyd picked up a handset and listened for a few seconds. 'It's Leol Reiger,' he said. 'He says he wants to talk to Julia.'

'Talk to him, Sean,' Victor said. 'Stall him if you can.'

Lloyd opened up the communication circuit. The flatscreen remained blank. Charlotte edged well out of the camera's pick up field.

'This is Governor Francis,' Sean said.

'Where's Julia Evans?' Leol Reiger asked.

'Unavailable. I'm all you're going to get.'

'OK, Mr Governor, you and I need to come to an arrangement.'

'You have no docking clearance, Mr Reiger, and I'm not authorized to make deals.'

'Never learn, you people, do you? Your SD platforms are fucked, otherwise you would have snuffed us ten minutes ago. We're coming in. Now how much damage we cause to that very delicate biosphere of yours in the process is down to you.'

'How so?'

'I want Charlotte Fielder.'

Charlotte let out a soft moan, the sound of her heart pounding was very loud, all the glass walls of the office were suddenly rushing towards her. Hands clamped round her upper arms, guiding her into a chair as her legs buckled.

'Have her brought to the docking bay,' Leol Reiger said.

'Never heard of her,' Sean said.

'Wrong. She's been on a bit of a spending spree in your shops today. She's up here. Find her and bring her to me.'

'Otherwise?'

'We come hunting for her. And you know me, that will become very messy. Guaranteed.'

'What do you want her for?'

'She knows where to find something I'm looking for.'

'Don't,' Charlotte gulped. 'I don't.'

Lloyd knelt down beside her, 'Shush,' he said softly. 'It's all right.' His arm went round her shoulder.

She hated herself for being so weak, especially in front of Fabian.

'She tells me where it is, and I pick it up,' said Leol Reiger, 'then I leave. Nobody comes to any grief that way. Simple.'

Sean looked helplessly at Victor. The security chief threw his hands in the air.

'We don't hand people over to tekmercs,' Sean said. 'I suggest you refer back to Clifford Jepson if you want to know where the source of atomic structuring is located, yes?'

There was a brief pause.

'Gotta hand it to you people,' said Leol Reiger. 'You're well plugged in. So you know what'll happen if I don't get that little fuck-dolly. Think about it. You've got five minutes.'

Victor's fist came down on the desk top. 'Bloody hell. Why hasn't Clifford Jepson briefed Reiger on how to contact the alien?'

'Do you want me to recall the crash team back to the airlock complex?' Lloyd asked anxiously.

'Looks like we'll have to,' Victor said. 'Do we know if Reiger's spaceplane has a datalink with any of the geosync communication platforms?'

'I'll get Bernie to run a check on their data traffic,' Lloyd said.

'Do that. If not, we'll offer to plug him in to Jepson direct.'

'He'll want to know why you're making that kind of offer, yes?' Sean said.

'Yeah,' Victor growled. 'Maybe we can spin him something about not being able to find Charlotte. Hell, we've got to give him something.'

Lloyd picked up a handset, then frowned. 'Now what?'

Charlotte turned to look into the command post. There was a commotion round one of the consoles, its operator shouting into his headset mike. Two supervisors stood behind him, leaning over his shoulders.

Lloyd raised the handset to his face. 'Bernie, what's going on?'

Charlotte instinctively checked on the spaceplane. The undercarriage had unfolded. As she watched, it touched down on the crater wall. The wheels blurred with speed.

'There's someone in the docking complex,' Lloyd blurted.

'Not one of my people,' Sean said. 'They were all taken out.'

'I wonder,' Victor said thoughtfully. 'Lloyd, put the intruder on this screen.'

Lloyd muttered into the handset. The desk terminal's flatscreen lit up. It was another of the southern endcap's interminable stone-walled corridors. Someone was walking along it, dressed in a blue maintenance division jumpsuit.

'Run an ident check on him,' Victor said.

Lloyd typed hurriedly on the terminal keyboard.

The spaceplane had finished its acceleration run. Its nose began to turn in towards the southern endcap.

'Got him,' Lloyd said.

Victor bent over to scan the data flowing down the flatscreen.

'His name is Talbot Lombard,' Lloyd read. 'Aged forty-one, got his communications technology degree from Hamburg University. Came up to New London eight years ago, employed by Globecast, worked setting up their franchise in the southern endcap. Fired seven years ago for pirating programmes. His return ticket was never used, no record of further employment in New London.'

'A Celestial Apostle,' Victor said. 'One who'd know all about Clifford Jepson's arms trading. And how to get in contact.'

'You think he's the interface?'

'Has to be,' Victor said. 'And he'll take Leol Reiger straight down into the caves.'

'If Reiger doesn't shoot him first, yes?' Sean said.

'So cynical,' Victor muttered with a grin. He straightened up, pointing two fingers at the big flatscreen outside, and shooting. 'Got you, Reiger.'

'What about the Dolgoprudnensky spaceplane?' Sean asked. 'They're due to reach us in another ten minutes.'

'I'll call Pavel Kirilov,' Charlotte said. 'If you want. Explain that I haven't really got the generator data.' She thought of facing that cold clinical expression again, and shivered; but she desperately wanted to do something right, try and repair a little bit of the damage.

'I think it's a bit late for that,' Victor said.

'That's not the answer, anyway,' Fabian said. She heard the old sneer in his voice.

'No?' Victor asked.

'Course not. It's simple, stupid. This is your story: The second spaceplane is assaulting New London, it's already knocked out your defences; and the Governor officially requires assistance in dealing with it. So call Greg's Russian general friend, the one that's authorized to use the Co-Defence League's Strategic Defence platforms, and explain exactly who's inside that space-plane.'

Charlotte watched Victor and Lloyd exchange a nonplussed glance, then gasped. On the big flatscreen behind them, black armour-suited figures were emerging from the spaceplane and bouncing in long steps across the crater wall towards the docking complex.

37

The Celestials' village gave Suzi the fucking creeps. A jungle village buried inside an asteroid, mega-primitive sophistication. It was a real sense tripper. Twenty billion tonnes of rock above, and a vacuum infinity below. Bad.

She worked hard to block out the conflict.

Melvyn was doing his job properly. Sending scouts into the surrounding catacombs, building a detailed picture of the zone. Major fault zone – why the fuck did Julia have to call it that? And just how many minor zones were there, exactly?

She sidestepped her way along one of the cracks leading off from the village cave. At least that tit of an armourer back at Listoel had been right about her knee, the suit carried it well. The crack opened into a dry cave with a long fissure along its sharply sloping bottom. The rock glittered in the infrared beam her helmet lights gave off. Tiny flecks of metal frozen in silica. She couldn't see the base of the fissure, and it was too thin for anyone to climb. Not even the Celestials had used the cave.

She used her rangefinder laser to map the cave accurately, and spliced the result in with her inertial guidance unit data. When she scuffled her way back into the village cave the package was added to the composite Melvyn was assembling. He updated her own 'ware in return.

The catacomb map was superimposed over her photon-amp image. Cumulus clouds of solid light – reds, blues, and greens –

caves, passages wide enough for a suit to traverse, dangerous cracks, the lake. Maybe fault zone was right after all. The surrounding area was rotten with cavities, as if the rock was mouldy.

Then there was Dennis Naverro to cultivate, one of the crash team's remaining two sac psychics. Melvyn had wanted to widen some of the cracks leading off from the cave to give the team greater tactical positioning. She'd teamed up with Dennis, the two of them blasting away awkward chunks of rock with their Konica rip guns, kicking the debris out of the way. Turning the crack into a corridor an armour suit could run down. She would need Dennis later; he didn't know it yet but he was going to pinpoint Leol Reiger for her.

The flatscreens in the middle of the village allowed her to monitor the spaceplane's progress. A squad of tekmercs had disembarked, penetrating the airlock sector.

Victor and Lloyd McDonald squirted over the images from security cameras in the southern endcap docking complex. She watched the image with her right eye, leaving the left free to pick the rock pinnacles that needed clearing from the crack. The images interlaced, both ghostly, transparent, her attention wandering between the two. Concentration would give one a solidity, banishing the second.

She saw Talbot Lombard standing in a corridor, hands raised above his head as the tekmercs boiled out of a space-plane reception room. Lockheed rip guns were levelled at him.

'Hey, what is this?' A handsome tanned face registered genuine bafflement.

He was flung against the wall, two tekmercs gripped his arms and pinned him there, feet twitching twenty centimetres above the ground. An armour-suited figure walked ponderously down the corridor, and stopped in front of him.

Leol Reiger. Had to be. Going for pose, as always. Crap artist.

'Listen, man,' Talbot Lombard yelled frantically. 'Where's Jepson? Which one of you is Jepson? I've got a deal, man!'

'Congratulations, you just asked the right question,' Leol Reiger said. 'You get to live a few minutes more.'

'Did Jepson send you?'

'That's right. Who are you?'

'Tol, they call me Tol.'

'Well, they call me Tol, where can I find the nuclear force generator data?'

'Down in the cave. He'll bring it, he said he would. I was supposed to take Jepson there tonight, after he'd put together a deal to manufacture atomic structuring technology.'

'You're the interface?'

'Yes.'

'Between Jepson and who?'

'I don't know, man. He runs a drone, real smart hardwired. I couldn't backtrack its interface.'

'So you've never actually met this person?'

'No, never.'

Leol Reiger stepped back, making room for another tekmerc. This one stood so close to Talbot Lombard the suit helmet virtually touched his nose. Talbot Lombard closed his eyes and began to whine, fingers scrabbling against the rock wall.

Suzi felt her belly rumble. The guy in the suit must be a psychic. Not that she was squeamish when it came to using them. Had to be done most deals these days. But there was no way to fight something like that, nothing to get hold of, nothing to kick. Fucking spooky, rutting around in someone's mind.

The two tekmercs holding Talbot Lombard let go, he dropped to the floor, legs collapsing. His breath was coming in huge judders.

'The truth. Well done,' said Leol Reiger. 'Where are these caves of yours?' His boot nudged Talbot Lombard. 'Where?'

'Northern endcap, they're under the northern endcap. I swear.'

'Show us.' A gauntlet grasped Talbot Lombard's upper arm and pulled him to his feet. He flopped about like a rag doll.

'Now,' said Reiger.

The tekmerc squad marched off up the corridor, with Talbot Lombard scrambling to keep up. Twenty-five of the shits. Suzi wondered if she knew any of them. Most likely.

'There are four coaches waiting for them in the docking complex's station,' Victor said. His voice was wonderfully smooth, audio silk. Him and Leol, mirror men, the same on opposite sides.

'Are the Celestial Apostles clear?' Melvyn asked.

'Yes, we collected them from the Whitechapel station; they're being parcelled out around the hotels. The tekmercs are all yours. I don't want them loose in Hyde Cavern, Melvyn. Snuff them.'

'Yes, sir.'

'Suzi?' Victor asked.

'Here.'

'This is Melvyn's show, OK? I know you want Reiger. So do I. But it's a collective kill. Dead is dead.'

'What is this? You been rapping with Greg?'

'I know you, Suzi.'

She smiled unseen in her helmet. 'Bollocks. I'm not gonna screw Melvyn's deal. Hell, I'm gonna make him an offer when this is over, plug him into my catalogue. Too fucking good to waste his time with Event Horizon.'

'Take care, Suzi.'

'Yeah. I was kinda planning on it.'

*

Give him this: Melvyn knew his tactics. She advised when he asked for her opinion, knowing how Leol ran his hardline deals, probing with expendables – the whole world was expendable to Leol. But figuring out the combat routine was down to Melvyn.

Leol Reiger was heading for Moorgate station, using three of the coaches. It meant they'd be coming in through the lake cave. Two of the crash team were rigging sensors and setting charges to seal the lake off once the tekmercs were inside. There'd be no way out except through the village, and that was where Melvyn was concentrating his fire-power, the killing ground.

The security captain stood on top of the staircase, directing the crash team into position. There were ledges up near the roof, in the cracks, behind the piles of rock rubble produced when the Celestials levelled the floor. Even a couple of them lying in a small cave above the ring of Solaris spots. Climbed up there like a pair of spiders.

Suzi and Dennis Naverro were in one of the cracks which led back to three deep caves.

'Suzi, Dennis, back a metre,' Melvyn said.

She took two steps back.

'OK, that's where your infrared signature cuts off.'

'Got it.' She loaded the co-ordinate into the suit guidance 'ware, then pushed her thumb into the flinty rock and scratched a line. 'Hey, Dennis, you got any intuition loaded in your skull?'

'No, sorry about that, Suzi,' Dennis said. 'All I got is esper-sense, see? Handy enough for our kind of work.'

'Yeah, right.' He had the most gentle Welsh lilt, almost purring. She couldn't visualise his face, must have seen it back at Listoel and on the *Anastasia*, though.

Whoops and cheering came over her earpiece. When she looked back out into the cave there was a rust-coloured dog dashing round the huts, three armour suits in pursuit, their boots tearing long gashes in the thick carpet of moss. She would have just zapped the fucking thing.

One of the team caught up with the dog. It howled as the gauntlet clamped round its hind leg.

'Lock it in one of the huts,' Melvyn said.

Suzi called up the feed from the security centre. It was a roof camera in Moorgate station. The last two tekmercs were disappearing into the service tunnel. Quarter of an hour, maximum.

She felt the hot calm of a combat high building inside. Checked round the cave. The two tech specialists rigging the lake cave charges had finished, walking down the staircase with Melvyn.

Melvyn ordered the Solaris spots to be turned down. They were reduced to a vague ginger glimmer, filling the cave with dusky shadows. Her photon amp cut in, washing away the murky outlines with opalescent blue and grey silhouettes.

She could hear Melvyn's footsteps as he made a final inspection round, clumping on the rock, then the softer wet thuds as he walked over the moss.

'Radio silence until after we blow the charges,' Melvyn said. 'You know the form once they enter the kill ground. Get to it.'

'Amen,' Suzi mumbled. She plugged her suit's interface socket into an optical lead the tech specialists had laid out, careful not to tug the thin fibre with her gauntlets. The suit's 'ware meshed the image from the lake cave sensors into her photon-amp feed. It seemed to be working OK.

The only noise left was a regular gurgling coming from a pump. It was directly opposite her, to one side of the staircase. Water from the lake was seeping through hairline splits in the rock, dribbling down the wall where it was collected in a rough pool that the Celestials had chopped into the floor. The pump fed their irrigation pipes, and supplied the communal washroom.

She couldn't hear the dog any more, not even with the suit's external mike boosted up to full sensitivity.

Dennis tapped her on the arm, and pointed back down the crack. She gave him a thumbs-up and retreated down past the scratch on the wall.

*

The image from the lake cave wasn't particularly clear, the sensor was sitting behind one of the biolum panels, looking down on the entrance which Leol's squad would come through.

Twelve minutes. The prick was taking his own good time.

Weapons Check.

Symbology zipped through her mind. Everything was on line, rip gun magazines charged, hardware functional, targeting sensors operative. Just like the previous eight times.

Something moved in the lake cave. A reconnaissance disk,

skipping erratically through the air like a clockwork bat. Sensors picked up its datalink emission, high-pitched cluttering.

The first tekmerc came through the entrance, rip gun tracking round the cave. There was a burst of coded radio pulses. The rest of the squad began to move in.

Suzi crossed herself, and started counting the tekmercs. Talbot Lombard was hustled along by the eighth squad member. He looked terrible, white, sweating, little spasms running down his spine.

More coded radio chatter was exchanged. The reconnaissance disk coasted along the passage towards the village cave.

Fifteen, sixteen . . . Suzi realised she was mouthing the numbers silently as the tekmercs emerged, and jammed her teeth together.

She switched inputs to the village cave sensors. The tekmerc's reconnaissance disk darted nervously out of the passage, hovering above the first stair. A couple of the squad followed it, spinning out of the entrance in a fast, well-practised motion, crouching down, rip guns swinging in wide arcs.

The flatscreens in the middle of the village suddenly flared white, casting a wintry glow over the huts circling the podium. A star was erupting into a phosphorescent nebula with a dense arc-bright core.

Looked like the Co-Defence League's kinetic missiles had snuffed the Dolgoprudnensky spaceplane. Clean and sweet.

Eight tekmercs were in the village cave. Four of them descending the staircase. Talbot Lombard stood on the top of the stairs, looking round in trepidation.

The first charges in the lake cave detonated. Suzi heard the explosion through her suit pick-up mike. The ground trembled.

A tekmerc was punched out of the passage by the blast-wave, somersaulting through the air. The pair holding on to Talbot Lombard lost their footing and went tumbling. Lombard landed heavily, mouth wide, screeching unheard torment.

'Go,' Melvyn said.

Suzi cancelled the optical sensor inputs, and headed forwards.

The second set of charges in the lake cave went off. She wished they'd brought enough charges to bring the whole fucking roof down on the bastards. Would have made life a bloody sight easier.

She reached the mouth of the crack as the first glare flares ignited. Small nova-bright spheres soaring out of shoulder launchers on the tekmercs' suits, swarming like a miniature galaxy above the village. Black overload spots ruptured right across her photon-amp image.

Tekmercs were coming out of the lake cave passage so fast that for one moment she thought they were equipped with jetpacks again. They were diving for cover, behind troughs, into crannies. The crash team opened fire, rip gun bolts slamming out from the walls, furious dazzle streaks that boosted the light intensity to a near-universal glare sheet. Her photon-amp image dimmed alarmingly, greying out to protect her retinas. She saw the bone-dry huts catch fire as a sleet of glare flare embers rained down. A tekmerc was speared by two rip gun bolts, disintegrating into a jarred purple corona of ionized molecules. Her pick up mike had cut out, she could feel the suit vibrating from the sonic battering. The energy pouring into the cave had turned the air into a cloying orange haze, fast gusts were roaring past her down the crack as the pressure build up escaped into cooler areas. Temperature displays were flashing amber caution warnings. The suit's heat exchanger was already operating near its safety margins, and she was partially sheltered. It wouldn't take long before heat alone snuffed the tekmercs.

Activate Weapons Suite.

Target graphics materialized over the burning huts, graded scarlet circles. She brought the rip gun round. Dark, humanoid figure running with inhuman speed, spitting starpoints of intolerable light. Framed by red circles. Her rip gun discharged short beams of solid sunlight, the muscle armour thrumming as it compensated for the jackhammer recoil. She wiped the segmented line across the fleeing figure, watching the suit outline crumble.

Then her reflexes were automatically flattening her back against the rock. 'Shoot and shift,' Greg had told her, down in Peterborough and a long time ago. 'Stasis is death.'

A fusillade of tekmerc rip gun bolts chewed the mouth of the crack. Molten rock sprayed out.

'Dennis, where's Reiger?'

He was crouched down, firing up at the staircase. 'I can't . . .' His voice dissolved into a roar of static as the tekmercs cranked up their ECM. He jumped back fast as lava pebbles splattered his suit.

'Shit!' she screamed.

There was a lull in the firing. The air in the cave was choked with glare flares. All they had to do was wait until the tekmercs ran out of chaff.

One of the crash team up above the Solaris spots opened fire with his plasma carbine, pulses jabbing down and splashing open against the floor, violet ripples expanding on the edge of visibility. Two pulses hit an armour suit, flinging it into the air, spinning madly; its legs were missing. Tekmercs answered with a deluge of rip gun bolts from around the cave.

It was a knock-on effect. Every bolt revealed someone's location. The crash team fired on exposed tekmercs who shot back.

Melvyn ordered a round of airbuster grenades into the cave. They exploded five metres above the ground in a blaze of ragged plasma, lightning tendrils lashing down, grounding out through tekmerc armour suits.

Suzi squeezed off a couple more bolts. One of them catching a tekmerc head on. Total detonation. This time there was no return fire.

The ECM jamming blanket ended abruptly.

'Suzi? You OK, girl?' Dennis asked.

'Yeah. No problem. Snuffed two. Can you spot Reiger for me?'

'I'll try.'

'Did any of them get out?' Melvyn demanded.

'Isaac here, chief. Thought I saw two of them make it to Dean's cave.'

'Dean? Dean, respond please.'

'One was heading for Neil's cave, chief.'

'Snuffed him,' Neil called.

'Dean, respond.'

The glare flares were definitely thinning out. She saw explosions away on the other side of the cave, orange fireballs splattering against the rock.

'Robbie, Lilian, get a reconnaissance disk down Dean's cave fast,' Melvyn ordered.

Another bout of rip gun bolts ricocheted round the cave. More explosions smothered the rock opposite her. This time she caught the black darts flicking through the air before the blasts.

'Hey, the pricks are using missiles,' she cried.

The pump casing was torn open, glowing metal fragments whirling away. A narrow jet of water fountained horizontally out of the rock wall above the pool; chunks of rock flaked away from the gash that had opened, skittering along the blackened smouldering moss. New cracks multiplied across the wall with frightening speed.

'Take out those fucking missile launchers,' Melvyn shouted.

Tekmerc rip gun bolts mauled the wall, splintering the rock, concussion clawing the cracks apart. Two more spouts of water gushed out. A third formation of missiles impacted.

Suzi knew the rock wall was going to collapse under that kind of onslaught. 'Dennis, where is that fucker?' She had to fight against crushing the rip gun butt she was wired so hot.

'Left of the stairs, behind a trough.'

She swivelled like something mechanical. Five possible troughs. Infrared was no use, the whole cave still crawled with energy. The rip gun smashed the first trough apart. There was nobody behind it.

Then the rock wall shattered.

38

The first cave was a small one, with a single red-tinged biolum globe jammed up between the saw-teeth rock snags of the roof. Rosy light made it seem warmer than it was. Someone had hacked a circular depression in the floor, four metres across; it was full of some transparent gel with a tough flexible plastic sheet stretched across the top.

Greg tested it with his hand, and watched a sluggish ripple ride across to the other side. Eleanor would like to hear about this, she adored waterbeds. He smiled furtively, wondering what she was doing right now. New London was on Greenwich Mean Time, which meant they would have finished the day's picking by now. She would probably be sitting outside by the camp's range grill, supervising the evening meal.

The clump of Teresa's boots as she climbed down out of the crack broke his train of thought.

'Tol,' Sinclair called. 'Tol, me boy. You're all right, 'tis only me.' He looked at the other two openings in the cave walls, and grimaced ruefully. 'Ah, well. I was hoping the lad would be down here. Your tin men, they won't be going shooting at civilians, now will they?'

'No,' Greg said. 'If he does wander back into the village cave, he'll be quite all right.'

'That's fine, then. He's a good lad.'

Julia and Rick were already down in the cave, Jim Sharman was bringing up the rear. Julia ignored the gel bed.

'Where now?' she asked.

Sinclair pointed to one of the openings. 'This one. It goes into one of our storage caves.'

'Carlos,' Greg said. 'Lead out.' He could hear faint whines and thuds coming along the crack to the village cave. Melvyn getting ready. He wished Suzi had come with them.

The passage sloped downwards. Greg watched the rock grow darker, from burnt ochre at the entrance to a deep slate-grey; it was harder, too, more brittle. Almost like flint, he thought.

By the time they reached the store cave his breath had become a white mist. There was a sprinkling of hoarfrost on the walls. It was a small cave, barely more than a wider section of the passage, with an uneven floor. A rough lash up of metal shelving stood along one side. Composite cargo pods were stacked opposite them, the names of various shops and New London civil administration departments stencilled next to long bar codes. There was a weak vinegar smell coming from the apples and plums on the shelves. The globes of fruit were large, gene-tailored, their skins crinkling.

Carlos walked past the end of the shelves, helmet lights picking up the thicker rime covering the rock.

'This is it?' Greg asked Sinclair. 'The drone was here?'

'That's right, Captain Greg.'

'Dead end,' Carlos said.

'You knew that,' Julia said. 'And you still brought us down here.' Her mind boiled with weary frustration.

''Tis what you wanted,' Sinclair said sullenly.

'It's all right,' Greg said. They were in the right place, he would have known otherwise. There were levels of intuition, and this seemed to be the most intangible, yet perversely the most resolute. He reckoned that if he shut his eyes and started walking he would wind up standing beside Royan and the alien. Close, it was close now.

'Wait there,' Greg told Carlos. He ordered up a secretion, the neurohormones acting like a flush of icy spring water in his brain. His thoughts seemed to lift out of time as he walked down the cave towards Carlos, mind flicking methodically through the impressions of his sensorium, searching for evidence of Royan, that unique spectral imprint his soul discharged in its wake.

The rock walls beyond the shelves were lined with small holes and slender zigzag clefts. Tiny splinters had flaked away where water had penetrated hairline cracks and expanded as it froze; the result was as if someone had taken a chisel and meticulously chipped a million pock scars into the walls.

There was a horizontal gash, about four metres long, varying between half a metre and a metre wide, level with Greg's head. He stood squinting into it, listening to the silence it exuded. The alien's siren song. 'Bring some of those pods over here,' he said.

'You can't be expecting me to go in there,' Sinclair said as Greg stood on the pods and shone his torch into the gash. It was flat for about five metres, then angled upwards. ''Fraid so. It must get wider past that slope. Carlos, can a suit get in·there?'

Carlos sent a fan of green laser light into the gash from his shoulder sensor module. 'Tight fit, but we can get through.'

'Any electronic activity in there?'

'No.'

Nerves fluttered back to hound him as Greg levered himself into the gash. It had an uncomfortable resemblance to a pair of lips, plates of the mouth waiting to bite down.

Stop it!

He lay on his back, and shifted his buttocks sideways, shuffling towards the slope at the rear. His breath was melting the hoarfrost on the rock above him, tiny beads of oily water flowing into droplets that fell onto his face.

When the floor began to lift he stopped and shone his torch up. It seemed to be some kind of kink in the gash, rising up a couple of metres, then levelling out. Growing narrower, though, maybe two metres long at the top. Sighing, he began to work his way up.

He could tell there was a cave just beyond the top of the kink.

The air had the right deadness for an empty space, sucking up sounds. Exertion was leaving a layer of sweat all over his skin which would quickly turn clammy cold as the suit's shunt fibres kicked in and drained the heat out. The temperature palpitation was bloody irritating.

There was a shelf at the top of the slope. He rested on it, and shone his torch into the cave. The ledge was about two metres long, ending abruptly. All he could see were the nondescript curves and angles of more dark grey rock. It was too much effort to wrestle his hood into place and use the photon amp, so he inched over to the lip and shone his torch straight down. The floor was a metre below. He swung his legs out.

This cave was much smaller than any the Celestials used. He prowled round it as the others squirmed their way out of the gash. There was very little frost on the walls.

'Where now?' Rick asked. There was no scepticism in the big man's tone. He had accepted Greg's talent as genuine. Even Jim and Carlos had no qualms, but then, three of their team mates were sac psychics.

Greg led them on, down a passage whose walls slanted over at thirty degrees. Selection was automatic. Seductive whispers in his mind.

They walked for about two hundred metres. In one place the walls and floor contracted, forcing them to crawl on all fours for five metres. Then Carlos said his sensors were picking up magnetic patterns ahead.

'Can you identify them?' Greg asked.

'It's a single structure containing several processors, power circuits, and some kind of giga-conductor cell.'

'The drone,' Greg said.

'Could be.'

It was waiting for them in the next cave. A dull-orange oblong box, with a wedge-shaped front, a metre and a half long, seventy centimetres wide. There was a sensor cluster at each corner, two matt-black waldos folded back along the sides. He saw a small triangle and flying-V printed on one side near the rear.

'Its sensors are active,' Carlos said. 'It's seen us.'

'Any datalink transmission?'

'Yes.'

'Hello, Snowy,' the drone said. It was Royan's voice all right, or at least a pretty good synthesis.

Julia let out a muffled gasp. There was a powerful burst of emotion from her mind – anger, but mostly worry.

'Greg, thanks for coming,' said Royan. 'I knew you wouldn't let me down. You never do. Good job, too. The alternative would have been dire all round.'

'What alternative?' he asked.

'Clifford Jepson.'

'You do know about atomic structuring, then,' Julia said.

'Yes. There's no such thing.'

'*What?*'

'I have a lot to say, a lot to show you. And you're not going to thank me, Snowy. Not for what I've done. Sorry.'

*

The drone's six independently sprung tyres made easy going of the bumpy rock floor. Greg and Julia followed it, the others close behind. He was painfully aware of the conflicting thought currents in Julia's mind: guilt, relief, and that consistent fiery thread of anger, compressed so tightly it was almost hatred. Flipside of love. He knew there was nothing he could say. They would have to sort that out for themselves.

And he liked both of them; he and Eleanor, Julia and Royan, they'd all been through hell and golden days together. Not exactly the happy reunion he'd been anticipating at the start.

They turned a corner, and saw a blue-green light at the end of the passage. The air was a lot warmer. Long tongues of glaucous fungal growth were probing along the passage walls. It wasn't a true fungus, he decided when they drew level with the tips of the encrustations, it was too wet, too solid.

'Is this your disseminator plant?' Greg asked the drone.

'One version. Its internal structuring was quite successful. It's flexible and fast growing, but it couldn't operate in a vacuum. I was thnking of using it to bore out living accommodation similar to the southern endcap complex.'

The cave which the passage opened out into was a perfect hemisphere, completely covered in the plant; there were five equidistantly spaced semi-circular archways piercing the walls. A line of bulb-shaped knobs protruded from the wall at waist height, glowing with a soft light. When Greg touched a wall, he felt the growth give slightly below his finger; it had the texture of a hard rubber mat. Yet to look at it could have been a polyp, it had that same minute crystalline sparkle. Something poised in the gap between vegetable and mineral, then.

It gave off the most unusual psychic essence. Of waiting. Endless, eternal waiting. He felt an age here that made the centuries of human history fleetingly insignificant.

'When did you grow this?' he asked.

'About a fortnight ago.'

He recognized it then: affinity with the origin microbe; drifting halfway across the galaxy in frozen stasis. A second eternity orbiting Jupiter, a life stretched beyond endurance.

Greg shivered inside the dissipater suit.

The drone trundled straight into one of the tunnels. The plant here was slightly different; a marble-like band ran along the apex, radiating a phosphorescent blue light; wide flat blisters mottled the walls. After twenty metres the tunnel began to curve, rising upward in a long gentle spiral.

'Well, look at all this,' Sinclair said. 'Right beneath us the whole time, and we never even knew. You've been a busy lad, young Royan.'

Julia's head was thrust forward, mouth bloodless. God help a granite stalagmite that got in her way, Greg thought.

'The gaps already existed when I came here,' said Royan. 'The disseminator plant modified this section of the fault zone for me. But there's nowhere to shove processed rock, so it just redistributed the space available. Reamed out the centre, and filled in the edges, so to speak.'

'Did you manage to refine the metals and minerals out?' Greg asked.

'Some, yes.'

The blisters were becoming darker. Crisper, too, Greg reckoned; they could even have been dead. A faint tracery of black veins was visible under their delicate cinnamon skin.

'There's some power sources up ahead,' Carlos's voice said in Greg's earpiece. 'Electromagnetic emissions, magnetic patterns. The works.'

Greg nodded once, without turning round. His mind had felt it already, a slackening of psychic pressure. The eye of the hurricane.

Red-raw tumours were bulging out from the tunnel walls, fist-size, as if the disseminator plant was suffering an outbreak of hives. Some of them had distended up through the blisters, puncturing the skin; waxy yellow fluid had dripped down the wall below them, pooling on the floor.

The drone stopped, and extended a waldo arm. Metal flexi-grip fingers closed round one of the tumours, chrome-black ceramic nails cutting into the plant flesh. Severed from the wall, the tumour looked like a ripe apple.

Greg nearly dropped it when the drone handed it to him. It was impossibly heavy. He peeled the mushy flesh away to reveal a kernel of whitish metal.

'Pure titanium,' Royan said.

Greg passed the nugget to Rick, who whistled.

'Is it worth very much?' Sinclair asked hopefully.

'You'd need a lot more before you can buy a desert island full of geishas,' Royan said. 'But the system which produces it is priceless. Though not in monetary terms. The value comes from what it can provide.'

'A plant, you call all this?' Sinclair looked round the tunnel sceptically.

'It was to start with.' The drone turned sharply, heading up the tunnel again.

Sinclair tucked the nugget into a pocket, and gave the tumours a long, measured assessment.

They came into another hemispherical cave, with just the one tunnel entrance. The disseminator plant had grown scales of rough pale-brown bark around the walls, only the floor was clear of them. A thick tangle of hairy creepers was clinging to the bark, like an old grape vine which had been allowed to run wild. Some of the free-hanging loops were swaying slowly. But there was no air movement. They must have some kind of sap inside, Greg decided. Greenish light was coming from a circle of knobs overhead; they lacked symmetry, as if they had melted at some time, drooping under gravity. Very fine creepers had spread across them, making it look as though they were hanging inside string bags.

A couple of hexagonal cargo pods lay in the middle of the floor, seals flipped open. One of them had a plant on top, growing out of an ordinary red clay pot. There was a central corm sprouting five tall flat leaves with tapering tips; their edges were serrated and ruffed, lined with small furry buds. The ones near the bottom had bloomed into long trumpet flowers, coloured a delicate purple.

Greg and Julia exchanged a glance.

'Where are you?' Julia said.

There was a drawn out splintering sound as part of the bark wall split open, revealing a tunnel.

'Just you and Greg, Snowy.'

'Hey,' Rick protested. He ignored the filthy look Julia threw him. 'You can't keep me out of this, Royan. Not if the alien is here. I helped you with Kiley. Damn it, I want to meet the alien. You owe me that, at least.'

'I'm not sure you can handle the disappointment, Rick,' Royan said.

'It's not here?' Rick asked, appalled.

'Oh yeah, it's here all right.'

'Then I want in.'

'OK, but I warned you.'

Greg turned to the three crash team members. 'Keep monitoring us. And if I shout, come fast.'

'Yes, sir,' said Jim Sharman.

'There's no need for that,' Royan said.

'I taught you better,' Greg said.

'Yeah, sure, sorry.'

Greg went first, letting his espersense flow ahead of him. Royan was there all right, his thought currents wound into a compact astral sphere. Greg perceived all the familiar themes, the deep injury psychosis, buoyant self-confidence, bright notes of arrogance and contempt. It was all shrouded by a grey aura of resignation, the scent of failure.

Then there was the other, the alien. Not a mind as Greg knew them, nothing remotely human, there was no focus, just a hazy presence wrapped around Royan's mind. But for all its ethereal quality, it possessed a definite identity. And it was brooding.

The tunnel was circular, high enough for him to stand in, and this time it was easy to believe he was inside a living creature. It was made from convex ring segments stacked end to end, translucent amber, as smooth and hard as polished stone. Fluid was circulating on the other side, a clear gelatin with shoals of orange-pink blobs floating adrift, like dreaming jellyfish. Either the walls or the fluid beyond was giving out a soothing phosporescence, there were no shadows as he walked along.

It opened into a simple rock chamber. The disseminatory plant had been at work here, but something had halted it in the middle of the conversion. Long strings of rubbery vegetation twined their way round the rock walls and ceiling, anchored by a root skin similar to lichen. White dendritic reefs flowered in the interstices. A tenuous silver-hued weave of gossamer fibres had crept up the lower half of the wall; underneath it, the sharper ridges and snags had been digested, smoothed down, while cavities had been filled with a cement-like paste. He could see the start of the curve that would end with a domed roof.

537

There were dense knots of the vegetative strings along the top of the weave, baby light knobs were germinating inside, silk-swaddled imagoes, casting whorl shadows all around.

The floor had already been levelled, coated in the usual grey-green mat of cells. Various hardware modules were scattered about, linked with power cables and fibre optics; there was a customized terminal, a couple of lightware memory globes, domestic giga-conductor cells, a hologram projector disk, some white cylinders that he didn't understand, tall circuit wafer stacks with nearly every slot loaded. All of it top-range gear, sophisticated and expensive. The only things he was really certain about were the four silver bulbs fixed to the rock roof: gamma-pulse mines. The military used them for urban counter-insurgency; the energy release, converted to gamma rays, would sterilize an area two hundred metres in diameter. Completely wiped of life, including soil bacteria down to a depth of two metres. They were in the top ten of the UN's proscribed weapons list; production and trading carried automatic life sentences.

Four of them in a cave barely twenty metres across was a typical Royan overkill.

But when he saw what was in front of him, Greg was swamped with the terrible conviction that this time they might just be necessary. The skin chill of his dissipater suit reached in to grip his belly.

Royan and the alien were in the middle of the chamber. The alien was shaped like a single gigantic egg; elliptic, fat, four metres high, three wide. It had a pellucid shell which seemed to be vibrating; watery refraction patterns slithered around it, clashing and merging. The first layer, the white, was a clear band of cytoplasm about a metre thick. Inside that was the nucleus, ice-blue, contained within a rumpled ovoid membrane.

Royan was encased within the nucleus. A solid-shadow adult foetus, naked, legs apart, arms by his sides, head tilted back. Greg peered at the silhouette; Royan had no feet or hands, his limbs tapering away to nothing. The nucleus matter about them was thicker, cloudy, preventing full resolution. There was something wrong with his face, the eyes and nostrils were too large, he had no hair left. Large sections of skin were missing, along with their subcutaneous layers. Greg could see several naked ribs, and most of the skull.

'Jesus!' Rick grunted in shock.

A moan escaped from Julia's lips, a sound of pure anguish and horror, forced up from deep inside her chest. Her hands came up impotently, and she took a couple of hurried steps towards the alien.

'Do not attempt physical contact,' a voice said from the terminal on the floor. It was perfectly clear, without any inflection, a neutral synthesis.

Julia stopped dead. 'What happened?' she squealed. 'Oh, darling, what . . .'

'Confidence and carelessness,' Royan said, his voice coming from the terminal. 'Or to put it bluntly: hubris. Good word for my life.'

'Are you hurt?' Julia asked.

'Only my pride.' The terminal chuckled.

Julia swung round to face Greg. 'Is that truly him talking?'

Greg nodded silently. The mental activity matched, and the bitter spike of humour.

'Let him out,' Julia said.

'You are unaware of the implication inherent in that statement,' the bland voice said.

'Royan?' she pleaded.

'The Hexaëmeron is correct,' Royan said. 'That's why you were summoned.'

Rick tilted his head on one side, frowning. 'Hexaëmeron? That's a human term, biblical, the six days it took God to make the Earth.'

'I have no language of my own. Obviously I have to use human terms. Royan seemed to think this was appropriate.'

'What are you?' Rick asked, his voice raised.

'My planet's evolutionary terminus, and progenitor,' said the Hexaëmeron.

'And that's the problem,' said Royan.

'Did you come on a starship?' Rick asked.

'No.'

Rick let out a hiss of breath. 'Then how did you get here?' it was almost a shout.

'By my mistake,' said Royan. 'Have you reviewed the personality programs I left for you, Snowy?'

'Yes.'

'Then you know my original edit for the disseminator plant was a symbiotic arrangement; terrestrial landcoral and the alien microbes working in tandem.'

'You said it was a prototype, and that geneticists could splice together a single genetic structure once you had proved the concept.'

'Yeah. The prototype started to work out pretty good. You saw what I've done with the fault zone. Then something happened.'

'Consciousness initiation,' said the Hexaëmeron.

'Too bloody true,' Royan said. 'The alien microbes achieved a rudimentary kind of sentience. I said nothing like that gene sphere could exist naturally, and I was right. It was designed, for fuck's sake, a very deliberate design. The core of the sphere doesn't have anything to do with genetics, it's a molecular circuit with a function similar to a neurone, but considerably more sophisticated. And there's a threshold level; clump enough of the microbes together and they develop a processing capacity. For want of a better description, they start thinking for themselves. And of course, I grew them in their billions for the disseminator plant.'

'Dear Lord,' Julia gazed at the alien. 'This is it, the sentient microbe cluster?'

'No, unfortunately. The thought-processing organism is only stage one. That's where the real trouble starts. These aliens have the ability to control their own genetic heritage, they can consciously switch individual genes on and off. Christ knows where that ability comes from. Whoever heard of instant evolution?'

'I am protean by nature,' said the Hexaëmeron. 'Internal cellular modification to fulfil a specific function requirement is inherent, what I am.'

'Yeah, right,' Royan said. 'Anyway, this was the chamber where the microbes went critical. After that, the Hexaëmeron started to grow entirely new types of cells for itself, and shifted its consciousness into them. That's what you're looking at now, a protean entity capable of fashioning itself to operate in any environment.

'I thought the disseminator plant was mutating at first, some kind of transgenic process with the microbes infecting the landcoral; which actually was a pretty good guess. You get that in really complex bioware sometimes; chromosome deletion or translocation, the growth pattern is distorted out of recognition. That's why I rigged up the gamma mines, as a last resort. Christ, alien cells with an exponential growth rate, who knows what it would have ended up as. A cancer the size of an arcology eating its way down Hyde Cavern. I could just see me trying to explain that away to you, Snowy. I was trying to track down the nature of the mutation so it could be isolated when the bugger went for me.'

'You would have destroyed me,' the Hexaëmeron said impassively.

'Maybe,' said Royan. 'But not straight away. I want to learn, to understand. Barbarians destroy without reason. We might not be as far along the evolutionary scale as you, but I'd like to think we're above that.'

'What do you mean, it went for you?' Greg asked.

'Exactly what you see, Greg. Every protean cell this new consciousness had produced coagulated together like God's own amoeba, and swallowed me whole. It was going to crush me into a pulp and digest me, use me as food for new protean cells.'

Greg gave Julia a quick glance. She had turned pale, staring up at Royan's shaded face. Waves of guilt and revulsion were punishing her mind. The idea was making him feel pretty queasy as well.

'So how did you stop it?' Rick asked.

'Hey, you're talking to Son, you know,' Royan said with his old swagger. 'I was one of the best fucking hotrods that ever plugged into the circuit back home. When the Hexaëmeron pulled its Jonah stunt, I glitched its command procedures. See, any sentient entity, however freaky, functions in the same fashion: observation, analysis, response. Intelligence is the processing of data, that means networks and routines. Which in turn means it can be disrupted with the right sort of disinformation. With 'ware it's easy, viruses have been around as long as integrated circuits. Organic brains are a little trickier to break; high-frequency light can induce epilepsy, but that's crude; psychics use eidolonics to corrupt memories and perception directly; the military have developed a whole range of disorientation techniques. It was just a question of finding something appropriate.

'The Hexaëmeron was processing data in a homogeneous cellular array, halfway between a bioware processor and a neural network. I loaded in my glitch virus, and stopped the cells which were attacking me dead in their tracks. Then I substituted my own management routines and took control. Trouble was, I didn't get all of the cells in time. The main Hexaëmeron consciousness saw what I was doing, and isolated all the cells I'd usurped, cut them straight out of its command procedure. So now I control the cells directly around me; I've organized them into a life-support mechanism, feeding me nutrients and oxygen, siphoning out piss and carbon dioxide. But the Hexaëmeron retains its integrity throughout the other cells, those are the ones surrounding mine. What we've got here is a very delicately balanced stand-off.'

'Which you hope we can break,' Greg said. He'd been studying the Hexaëmeron, it would be easy enough to kill with the rip guns; the trick would be extracting Royan alive. Maybe they could set the Tokarev lasers to longburn, char the outer layer of cells away. He wondered how the Hexaëmeron would react if they started doing that.

'You have already broken our stasis,' said the Hexaëmeron. 'As we intended you to.'

'Summoned,' Julia murmured. 'You said we were summoned.'

'You and Clifford Jepson,' said the Hexaëmeron. 'That is correct. Our situation outline is a simple one: Royan can still trigger the gamma mines, destroying all life in this chamber, and I retain the capacity to physically ingest the cells under his authority. Neither of us is capable of dominating the other. Mutual suicide is all we can achieve by ourselves. Clearly, this cannot be allowed to continue.'

'Clearly,' Julia said.

'We came to an arrangement,' Royan said. 'Each of us would call someone who would terminate the stand-off in our respective favour. I chose you, and used Charlotte Fielder to deliver my warning message.'

'How did you find her?' Greg asked.

'I'm still plugged in to New London's datanet,' Royan said. 'So I knew who was up here, and of course she's listed in Event Horizon's security files as one of Baronski's girls. Simple cross-referencing gave me her name.'

'If you're plugged into the asteroid's datanet, then why didn't you just phone us, for Christ's sake?' Greg demanded.

'I will not permit that,' the Hexaëmeron said. 'I will not allow my existence to be compromised prior to negotiations. Humans have a dangerously xenophobic nature; your leadership would find it difficult to resist public pressure concerning me. If Royan had tried to open a direct communication link with his allies, then I would have been forced to initiate my consumption routine.'

'And if that happened, I'd have no choice but to use the gamma mines,' said Royan. 'What we needed was a throw of the dice, a method of breaking the stand-off which gave us an equal chance of coming out trumps. Logically, such a stand-off had to be interrupted by an external factor. So we gave each other one opportunity to call for help. A sharp game, but the only one in town. I believed in you, Snowy, I knew you'd come hunting as soon as you received the flower. The Hexaëmeron thought Clifford Jepson would have the edge – which makes it quite a judge of human character; Victor's file on Clifford isn't very complimentary, a real low-life. Talbot Lombard was given the atomic structuring data, and promised more tonight. If Jepson's people had arrived before you, the Hexaëmeron would have made a deal with them.'

'But you said atomic structuring technology doesn't exist,' Greg said.

'No, it doesn't, not in hardware form. The equations make sense, but they're just a thought experiment, problematical: what could be done if a strong nuclear force generator did exist. It was a lure, the mythical dragon's hoard. Designed to be irresistible to the right sort of mind. Clifford Jepson would do anything to get the generator data, and that includes setting the Hexaëmeron free. It was love against greed. The two human fundamentals. I trusted to love, Snowy.'

'Why not simply let it go?' Rick asked. 'Are you so xenophobic?'

'The Hexaëmeron should have called for you, Rick,' Royan said. 'Trusting and naïve. There's nothing people can't solve by sitting round a table and talking rationally. Right, Rick? I can't let it go. There's the third stage to consider.'

'The flower,' Greg said automatically.

'That's right,' Royan said. 'The Hexaëmeron can edit its own genes, decide which toroid sequences to activate. Do you understand now, Rick? Why I call it the Hexaëmeron? The reason the alien gene sphere is so large in comparison to terrestrial DNA is because the shells contain the genetic codes for over six thousand different species – plants, insects, animals, sentient creatures. Survivors of life's endgame. The Hexaëmeron is an intermediate stage, an artificial midwife. Left alone, it can engender an entire planet's ecology. That's its sole purpose; what it was *designed* for. Where would you put it, Rick? Where would you let it loose to breed? Earth? Cambridge maybe? Mars? Put it on Mars, and what happens in a thousand years' time after the planet's been bioformed? When the aliens have run out of expansion space? And they will, Rick. Their metabolism is orders of magnitude above ours, efficient, strong, potent. We wouldn't stand a chance, Rick.'

Greg didn't like the implications rising out of his subconscious. Scare images, every third-rate channel horror show he'd ever seen. The gritty conviction in Royan's mind acting as reinforcement to his own paranoia. When he reviewed the Hexaëmeron's vaporous thoughts he found only detached serenity. A long time ago, when Philip Evans's thoughts had been shifted into his NN core, Greg had tried to use his espersense on the new bioware entity. He had got the same composed aloofness then, an inability to become involved, not emotionally, anyway. Problems were an abstract. He wasn't sure the Hexaëmeron qualified as a living thing.

'If it came to that,' Greg said slowly, 'Clifford Jepson's people reaching you first – surely you'd use the gamma mines anyway. I mean, they'd kill you to set the Hexaëmeron free, so by using the mines you could at least take it, and some of them with you.'

'Maybe. That's one of the reasons I'm bloody glad it's you and Snowy who arrived. You see, you only really need one cell, no, one complete gene sphere, and the whole thing starts over. That's what you must understand before you make your decision.'

'Decision?' Julia asked in a dead tone.

'Yes, Snowy. It's all or nothing. If you chose against the Hexaëmeron, then the entire disseminator plant must be destroyed. Every cell and microbe. If not, then the Hexaëmeron will be resurrected one day. Maybe not intentionally, but it'll happen. That's why the gamma mines are a last resort; they wouldn't end the problem, only the more immediate part of it. Of course, if I had triggered them, I hoped you'd question why

545

I felt I had to. That way you'd exhibit a lot more caution with the disseminator plant cells that were left. After all, it's only my stupidity with this one-man-band act which has put everyone in such a ridiculous situation in the first place.'

'Yes,' Julia drawled.

It wasn't the answer Royan wanted, he was looking for sympathy. Greg could sense the anguish peak in his mind.

Abruptly, he was aware of another mental voice, a cry of pain and rage, toxic with shock. Suzi.

39

Suzi saw the rock wall lurch forward, then disintegrate into a thousand flying chunks. The wave behind it held together until it was halfway across the village cave. She was dropping to the floor as soon as the first motion began, grabbing the mouth of the crack. Her photon amp gave her a single glimpse of the debris ploughed up by the leading edge of the wave, a line of foam, stones, muscle-armour suits, scorched saplings, and burnt remnants of the huts and their furnishings, all bearing down on her at a terrific speed.

It hit, blinding her sensors. She was suddenly, frighteningly confined in a padded iron maiden, unable to see, unable to feel, unable to hear. Something solid cannoned into her, a very muffled thud. The suit shifted position slightly. Yellow and green graphics winked up, an outline of the suit, showing her the damage on her left side, the metalloceramic had been weakened by the impact, there was a dent, some of the chest muscle bands were inoperative. Her implant began a suit systems-status review. She clung to the details, using them to fight off the hot claustrophobic panic erupting at the back of her skull.

A timer was counting off the seconds below the suit outlines. Five seconds so far, it couldn't be such a short time. A minute at least.

She could feel a movement, something giving below her arms. It developed into a full-blown slide. The rock around the mouth of the crack was giving way. She lost her hold.

Instinct made her want to curl up, tuck her head into her chest; but the armour prevented that. She ended up bending her knees as far as the muscle bands would allow, and folding her arms across her torso.

Her inertial guidance display showed her she was jouncing back down the crack, impacts rattled her teeth and spine. The feed from the photon amp turned a deep grey, as if she was wrapped in pre-dawn mist, then there were flashes of blue, crimson streaks as the water threw her about.

She bounced to a halt against a sharp corner, and the water sank down around her. It was smooth and fast flowing, icy black. She struggled against the current and made it on to all fours. Water was trickling down her left leg, inside the muscle bands.

The suit 'ware was pushing out a fast sequence of status graphics. Suzi coughed, feeling sour creamy liquid in her gullet. Tight snaps of pain in her chest made it impossible to focus on any of the graphics. Her knee was hell; she thought the bioware sheath had torn.

'Call in,' Melvyn said.

There was a string of responses, names and curses.

'Suzi?'

'Yeah, here, Melvyn.'

'OK, everyone into the village cave. There were still some tekmercs left.'

She climbed to her feet. There was very little light in the gash. Her infrared helmet beams came on, showing about five centimetres of water sloshing around her ankles. Where the hell had it all gone? It had looked like a small sea crashing into the village cave. Greg must be up to his neck in it. Wherever the fuck he was.

The graphics were coming into focus now. Nothing seriously wrong, not with the suit; three muscle bands dead, power reserves OK, two sets of sensors on backup. The suit 'ware was already calculating new load paths for the remaining muscle bands. She could move, she could fight.

Her mike picked up the blast of rip gun fire.

'Two of them,' the radio squawked. It sounded like Robbie. 'Cave 3B, hostile and active.'

'Got 'em.'

'Isaac, let's have some airbusters in there.'

'Coming up.'

'Lilian, launch a reconnaissance disk down 4C, Isaac thought he saw a hostile in it.'

'Could be one of ours.'

'No answer from Harris.'

Suzi realized her rip gun was missing. She started to walk towards the village cave. The suit responded stiffly at first, almost as if she had to carry the weight herself. Then the 'ware finished reprogramming the muscle bands, and she began to pick up speed. It was a lot easier on her knee.

'Dennis?'

'No response from Dennis yet, Suzi,' Melvyn said. 'Did you see him?'

'Didn't see shit after that wall went.'

The wave had scoured the village cave clean. The only thing she recognized at first glance was the stone staircase. Where the wall had blown out was a pile of big boulders. It looked like half of the lake cave beyond had collapsed. Two Solaris spots were intact, one of them swinging on the end of its wiring, rocking shadows across the walls. All that was left of the village was a line of burnt splintered wood and soggy reeds along the wall opposite the lake. Water was lying a couple of centimetres deep. Torn sheets of crumpled, saturated moss floated past. Fish were everywhere, jumping and flipping about.

Melvyn was marshalling his remaining troops. She counted thirteen others surviving. Plus another two medic cases. One was already out of his armour, Neil, bruised and bloody. Three of the team were working to extract the second casualty from under a rockfall which had crushed his legs.

There were eight dead tekmercs lying about, their armour inert. They looked as if they had been battered by the wave, the metalloceramic was badly scratched and dented. She saw Talbot Lombard, face down in the water, his jumpsuit charred, blackened flesh underneath.

She walked over to Neil. 'What happened?'

'Boulder,' he said. 'Bastard rolled over me.' She guessed he'd been given an infusion, his mouth had the slack look, face grey with pain.

'Use your rip gun?' she asked.

'Sure, help yourself.'

It was lying next to his bent armour suit. She picked it up. **Weapons Integration: Konica Neutral Beam Rifle.**

The key on her left shoulder began to interface with the rip gun's 'ware. Red target graphics appeared. She was whole again, size and strength no longer a disadvantage, equal to the rest of the world.

It was time for the last deal with Leol fucking Reiger.

Melvyn was handing out assignments, sending the active crash team members down into the caves and cracks, scouting for tekmercs.

Suzi pulled the guidance package out of her suit 'ware, and used it to place the five troughs. There was no sign of them, not even when she went over to check, boots splashing the thin layer of water. All she found was flat rock. She stood where the third one had been, amid the contortions of dying fish, and looked back to the broken lake cave, trying to work out the angle the wave had hit the troughs. If she carried the line on, Reiger would have been swept against the wall thirty metres away. There were two possible caves there, 6B, and 7B. According to her suit 'ware they joined up in a big cavern fifty metres back, another wide cave leading off from the junction.

'Melvyn, I'll check 6B, OK?' She got it in before he could assign her one.

'Roger, Suzi. Do you want anyone with you?' Something in his tone suggested he'd guessed the reason.

'Nah,' she said. 'I'll solo.'

6B was a pinched oval passage, just under two metres high, five wide, laced with veins of tarnished copper. Her helmet scraped the roof as she walked towards the junction. The rock was slick with water, a steady rain of large drops pattered down from the roof. Light from the village cave illuminated the entrance, but the passage curved, and after ten metres she had to switch to infrared. The water level crept up her legs; she could see fish racing away ahead of her.

She called up the map package, and bled in her suit's inertial guidance read-out. When she was fifteen metres short of the junction, she killed the infrared beams, using the photon amp as a passive sensor. The image showed her pitch-black passage walls and faint neon-blue water, even the fish were blue blobs. No hot spots, but her field of view was very limited. If Reiger was in the junction cavern, the shit would make sure he couldn't be detected from the passage.

She took an airbuster grenade from the retainer loop on her waist, a seamless metallic cylinder fifteen centimetres long, six wide, with a locking ridge running along its length. It slotted into the latch rail on her left forearm with a solid *click*.

Expedite Grenade Launch Program.

The red targeting circles turned white. She brought her left arm up until the circles interlocked over the junction cavern entrance. Grey droplets were still falling from the roof, hazing the photon-amp image.

Disengage Safety Lock. Set Fuse for Twenty Metres.

The targeting circles turned violet and started flashing.

Fire.

The airbuster grenade streaked into the cavern, exploding into a seething energy cloud a metre below the roof. Stark white light stabbed back down the passage. She saw lightning tendrils whipping violently backwards and forwards, clawing at the rock outcrops above the water.

The spent grenade canister was flipped off her forearm latch rail, spinning away. She moved into the cavern at a run, pushing her recalcitrant left leg hard.

There was nobody inside. Little columns of steam were rising into the air. Dead fish bobbed on the surface of the water.

'Not that easy, Suzi bitch,' said Leol Reiger.

She jumped with shock. He was using a general broadcast frequency. Her electronic warfare gear couldn't locate the radio transmission source; rock did weird things with radio, bouncing it or absorbing it. But not much, he couldn't be far away. She checked passage 7B quickly. Empty. That meant the cave at the back of the junction cavern.

'I know it's you, Suzi bitch. Because you know I'm in here, that's why you let off the airbuster.'

She clipped a fresh airbuster grenade on the rail.

According to the map, the rear cave twisted to the left after fifteen metres. There was no data after that. She primed the grenade for twelve metres, then fished around for a loose rock.

'Always hiding, Leol,' she said. 'But then, running scared is your scene. Right?'

She crouched down, and lobbed the rock high across the entrance of the rear cave. Two rip gun bolts pulverized it in midair. But she was already diving underneath, twisting.

Fire.

She landed on her side, momentum rolling her, knocking the breath out of her lungs. Then she was up and racing for the cave, suit boots kicking up sheets of foam. The airbuster's energy cloud was flaring, fingers of vivid white light pouring out of the entrance. As it began to dim she fired the rip gun up the cave, hosing the bolts around at random until the magazine was drained.

Leol Reiger didn't shoot back. She smacked a fresh power magazine into the rip gun, and walked forward. The cave walls were covered in bright infrared scars where the rip gun bolts had struck. Runnels of lava dripped into the water, sizzling loudly. Long twisters of steam rose up all around her, licking at the roof.

There were two ways she could do it; rip gun firing the whole time, chewing up the cave walls and triggering any anti-personnel mines he'd scattered; or the quiet way. But he knew she'd be coming, that gave him an advantage.

'Did Julia Evans get the nuclear force generator data, Suzi? Or is it still up for grabs?'

'Don't tell me,' she said. 'You and I can deal, snatch it for ourselves. Right?'

The cave ended ten metres in front of her, a narrow jagged opening into another cavern. All the photon-amp image gave her was blackness, as if the universe ended beyond the opening. Reiger was in there, waiting; and he knew she had airbusters. She tried analysing it from his position. Hide under the water? It was almost up to her knees, and getting deeper. A side cave that gave him a line of fire on the opening she'd come out of?

'You see anything wrong with that, Suzi? It's worth billions. And you and I, we haven't got a quarrel, not really. We just got hired by different people, that's all. Did what we got paid for, shot the shit out of each other. We don't have to do that no more, we can buy them with atomic structuring. Evans and Jepson, we can own them, Suzi.'

The roof? Was he clinging to the roof? A muscle-armour suit could hold him up there effortlessly.

Arm Loral Missiles. Target Image: Muscle-Armour Suit.

She smiled. The Lorals could just give her the edge; he'd be expecting another airbuster.

'Who said I was getting paid?' she asked.

'What? You do this for free? Like crap you do, Suzi.'

She fed a flight path into the Lorals' 'ware: into the cavern, then a loiter manoeuvre while the smart seeker heads performed their target acquisition, scanning with microwave radar and infrared. Once they locked on, Reiger would have to shoot them, revealing his position. If he didn't, he'd be dead. Either way, she'd nail the shit.

'Fuck no, not free, Leol. Something you don't know.'

'Oh yeah, like what?'

'Friendship.'

'Load of bullshit, Suzi. All tekmercs have is deals. You a real tekmerc, Suzi? You want to deal over atomic structuring? Or do you want to die?'

'Bollocks to you, Reiger.'

Launch Two Missiles.

A blast of compressed air pushed the missiles out of their tubes, small triangle fins unfolded, then the solid fuel motors ignited. Her infrared image was momentarily overwhelmed by the twin exhaust plumes.

'Shit, you bitch!' Reiger shouted.

Suzi was two seconds behind the missiles as she went through the opening into the cavern. The infrared radiance from the rocket motors lit up the interior like a pair of glare flares. She saw a roughly semicircular space, ten metres across. Above her, the roof was made up from giant cuboidal stone blocks, as if steps had been carved at some crazy inverted angle. Water came up to mid-thigh, slowing her movements.

She saw the missiles curving upwards. There was a red corona shining out from behind one of the rock cubes, Reiger's infrared signature. Her photon amp caught the squat black cylinder tumbling down. Airbuster grenade. Stupid! her mind yelled. Bitterness and fury welled up. She flexed her knees, and started to fling herself flat, the water might shield her from the worst.

The airbuster detonated just as she hit the water. Her sight went from misty blues and reds to glaring white, then black.

There was no pain, no real feeling of anything. Her thoughts were sluggish, full of worries; about getting Reiger, and whether or not Greg had made it to the alien, and Andria who was far too innocent to be left to fend for herself alone. All of them mixed up, faces twisting together in a crazy kaleidoscope whirl until she wasn't sure who was who any more. Shit but that airbuster must have fucked her brain good and hard.

Suzi?

She knew it was Greg. He was bringing pain back to her, suffering. Greg was crying in her mind.

I screwed up, she told him. *Reiger got me with an airbuster.*

Suzi, Suzi, I taught you better.

Sorry, Greg. She could see the weirdest egg, translucent, white and pale blue, dark shape at the centre. Julia's face, frightened and angry. *Is that the alien?*

Yeah.

Don't look much.

Julia's getting it sorted, no messing.

Great. Then the image began to slip away.

Arm Loral Missiles.

That was strange, she certainly didn't have the mental strength left to load orders into the implant. But somehow her thoughts were being pushed up a very steep hill into her processor node.

Target Image: Muscle-Armour Suit.

Greg, was that you?

Sure thing, we're going to get Reiger yet, you and I, no messing.

Launch Two Missiles.

She couldn't tell if they had fired or not. Even the memory ghosts had fled. There was only blackness, without form. *Greg, don't let my kid grow up like me.*

Oh, Suzi.

Promise me, Greg.

—

Greg?

—

Bollocks.

40

The gothic-biology fabric of the chamber seemed an appropriate setting, Julia thought, as she listened to Royan. Neither one thing nor the other, rock or disseminator plant, both gone awry, stalled and incomplete.

Her anger had drained away, as it always did when she concentrated on assimilating the intricacies of a problem. But this time, that cool logical state of reasoning she exercised, the famed Evans rationality, was in danger of crumbling away. Her eyes couldn't linger on Royan for more than a few seconds at a time. Royan, trapped inside this creature, this grotesque chimera. The deliberate physical ruining of his body. Once again. She knew exactly how much that would tyrannize his soul. And all her guilt from knowing it was because of the gulf between them that he had been driven here, to this ignominy. If they had never met, if she hadn't tried to bind him to her, if . . .

Her mind was going through the routine at a virtually subconscious level, processor nodes analysing the data she was hearing, coding it, assigning it storage space in her memory nodes. All ready to be run through a logic matrix when the time came. Her decision. But all she really wanted to do was take Royan in her arms and hold him. To be free of all this punishing pressure, and live. Just for once, escape from what both of them were.

God, or fate, never seemed to give that option to an Evans.

Greg moaned, eyes widening in shock. His knees sagged, and Rick just caught him before he fell.

'What is it?' she demanded.

'Suzi,' he said, voice coming from the back of his throat. His features clenched in effort.

'What do we do?' Rick asked.

'Wait,' she said. 'It's all we can do.'

Greg moaned again.

She glanced at the Hexaëmeron, wondering whether to call the crash team hardliners in. But it didn't seem to be doing anything; its surface was awash with shimmering refraction patterns. She'd been relying on Greg to provide any advance warning in case it turned hostile.

'Dead,' Greg said numbly. 'Suzi's dead.'

'How?' Julia asked.

'She went after Leol Reiger; they tangled in the caves somewhere.'

'Is Reiger dead?'

'Dunno. We loosed off Suzi's missiles. Might have got him.' He steadied himself against Rick, and straightened his back ponderously.

'Reiger,' said Royan. 'I've heard of him. Tekmerc with a high hazard rating. Is he Jepson's agent?'

'Yes, he's Jepson's.' She gave the Hexaëmeron a long stare. 'The one you summoned. Do you have a reason why I should allow you to live?'

'I am not a hazard, Julia Evans, to you or your world,' the Hexaëmeron's smooth voice said. 'I am, as stated, simply a midwife. When the species I contain have birthed, my time will be over. Royan is guilty of judging me by his own human standards. My planet's life is sturdy, yes, but also highly organized. It is not as competitive as terrestrial organisms.'

'What do you mean organized?' she asked.

'Plants supply animals with all the nourishment they need. Animals are non-carnivorous, they do not prey on each other as is the common practice on your Earth. Our life harmonizes.'

'Fascist Gaia's world,' Royan said. 'Everything knows its place, and stays there. But where would our place be?'

'Is that it?' Julia asked. 'Some kind of shared consciousness? An insect mentality?'

'Not at all. Organization is different from obedience. Animal and insect forms have all evolved high social orders. Clannish, if you like. Once established in a territory they will not venture outside.'

'That sounds detrimental to me,' Julia said. 'You'd need a certain amount of cross-breeding to continue species viability.'

'Naturally, each clan maintains contact with its neighbours, and major species have a degree of conscious control over their own germ plasm.'

'I still find that trait quite incredible,' Julia said. 'Perhaps the most frightening aspect of all. Even if I believe you can vouch for the non-belligerence of the individual species you contain, what is to prevent them from altering beyond recognition within a few generations? If they react and adapt to their environment, they'll have to undergo considerable alteration, physical and mental. And I have to ask myself how they'll react to humans. For we are not saints. Nor are our animals. Let loose on Earth, aliens would have to protect themselves from the ignorant, the frightened, not to mention the ideologically inclined. Can you guarantee that these species of yours will not grow horns and fangs, will not hit back?'

'No, of course not. Not if those circumstances arise. That is why I suggested Mars to Royan. It would be worthwhile to consider; I offer to purchase Mars from the human race. You would act as my agent, profiting accordingly. Negotiate for me, Julia Evans, I do not lay claim to that skill, and you are the world's acknowledged expert. You have the material and political means to bring about this arrangement. In return, I will multiply myself and function as a fully-operational asteroid disseminator plant. One that will respond only to you. In addition, Venus could be terraformed. I contain the genetic codes for an algae which would digest Venus's atmospheric carbon dioxide. With the resources and wealth that asteroid dissemination would make available to you, the algae's production in sufficient quantities would pose no problem. Accelerating Venus's rotation to a twenty-four-hour period would probably be beyond my ability to supply. But I would provide Event Horizon with a human chemistry compatible food crop which will thrive in days that last four Earth months. I can bloom, Julia Evans, if you let me.'

Julia hesitated for a moment. She didn't doubt the Hexaëmeron could back the offer with solid bioware – alien bioware – and if any word of the offer leaked it would snowball, become irresistible. Politicians would welcome the Hexaëmeron with open arms; the wealth it could provide was enough to fulfil any manifesto. She either stopped it, killed it, now, or events would be ripped beyond even her ability to control. Intelligent benign aliens on Mars, the asteroids converted to bullion vaults, Venus tamed. So very tempting; she could play Midas to the Hexaëmeron's Dionysus.

And look what happened to Midas.

She glanced round. Rick had an overawed, slightly beleaguered expression on his young face, dazed and doting. Greg was gaunt, lost in his own torment over Suzi. Consulting Royan was an impossibility; she knew he'd never give her any advice on this, saying, 'Look where my expertise has got us.' Even if she had been blind to everything else between them, she was sure of that.

It made her frightened for what would happen afterwards; with the Hexaëmeron free or the Hexaëmeron destroyed, the two of them would still be left to resolve whatever they had. And how wretched he was going to be, not only at failing his one chance at equality, but for creating such a danger and quandary, for disappointing her, making her angry, and stressing her virtually to breaking point. It might even be pushing her love too far. She was afraid to think about that. Instinct and concern had brought her this far, but what was left?

'If you can do this,' she said carefully to the Hexaëmeron, 'if you can provide so much, why did you call for Clifford Jepson? Why not just ask for me in the first place?'

'But I did,' said the Hexaëmeron. 'You or Clifford Jepson, both of you are similar, both of you with the right political contacts, both of you in positions of direct influence. You both make your own decisions without consultations or reference, and you are not afraid to make those decisions even if they go against what is seen as being in the public interest. Had Clifford Jepson arrived first, I would have offered him the same as I now do to you. Either way, I win.'

'The whole world hates a smart-arse,' Royan said.

Julia walked right up to the Hexaëmeron's quivering shell, stopping with her nose almost touching. 'Is it telling the truth, Greg?'

'Yeah, as far as I can tell. At least it's very earnest.'

Now she was close she could see Royan's nose had been eaten away, there were no lips left, and his eyes – she was sure they were missing. The Hexaëmeron had done that, in a moment of fear and panic Royan had said. Could what was virtually a machine intelligence fear and panic? 'Keep scanning it, I have a question to ask. I must know if the answer is honest.'

'OK.'

'Was the microbe spliced together, or was it natural?' She held her breath. Had they been deliberately manufactured, set loose on the universe with the intent of conquering?

'That is a null question,' the Hexaëmeron said. 'There were no laboratories involved, no instruments nor machines. All that was left alive contracted to this. What I am. The sentience coadunation molecule at the centre of the gene sphere was a product of necessity. Designed, perhaps, though you would call it being driven. There was no free will involved. Primordial life originated as a microbe, as was the first, so is the last. The difference is the genetic codes. Six billion years of history. Do you consider you have the right to extinguish that, Julia Evans?'

'Nobody should have to decide this,' she said, almost to herself. 'Not something like this.'

'Anyone who has the ability to decide, will decide. This is inevitable. If you were unable to decide, you would not be here, Event Horizon would not exist in the form it does. There can be no abrogation of your position.'

'Royan?' she appealed.

His deliquescent face remained devoid of emotion. 'You already know the answer, don't you, Snowy? The Hexaëmeron is God's creature. Why it's here, I don't pretend to understand. But I'm sorry I wasn't strong enough to decide in your place, I would do anything to spare you this. But I guess this is His test for you.'

She gave Greg a forlorn look.

He returned a sad smile. 'Tell you, Julia; this, you, it's all way out of my league. But the alien is right, if anyone's to decide, it should be you. I'd rather it was you.'

'There is one thing I can add,' Rick said quietly. 'A third option.'

'Go on.'

'Send it back.'

*

There were no NN cores to consult. And it had been a long time since she hadn't had a second and third opinion on every topic under the sun. She carefully cancelled the waiting logic matrix in her processor node. Then there was just her, alone.

Julia made her choice.

*

It was a standard personality package, configured to establish control in whatever system it found itself operating in. She had to add a few modifications first.

When the squirt was complete it checked its own integrity, then began to re-format the command routines of the cellular array it was stored in. This time there was a difference; as well as altering the processing structure's programs, it could change the actual physical nature of the network itself. Protean cells elongated and joined together, forming a complex new topology, their membranes' permeability altered.

Julia's mentality unfolded into the new neural network. Satisfied she was now in total control of a clump of cells over a metre in diameter she sent a go code to her flesh-and-blood self.

Memories streamed in, of Peterborough and Wilholm and Event Horizon and the children and Royan; regressing, Grandpa alive, school in Switzerland, Mother and Father – she hadn't thought of them for over a decade, childhood in the desert sandstone warrens. Not just the visual image, but sounds, tastes, smells, textures, raw emotion. She grew from the present back down into the past. Complete.

Her sensorium was different, three-hundred-and-sixty degrees spherical; optical reception extending from infrared up into high ultra violet; vibration acceptance was so sensitive she could actually hear the big mining machines cutting out New London's second chamber; the magnetic and electromagnetic spectrums were strange; as was the chemical reception. She began to modify cells and compose filter programs. Chemical reception was easy to translate into smell, once she'd tagged the molecular formulae. Magnetic and electromagnetic she translated into black and white, seeing the giga-conductor cell in Greg's Tokarev laser shining brightly. It was the all-directions-at-once panorama which gave her the most trouble; she began to adapt her sensory reception and interpretation routines, enlarging the associated neurone structure. Her attention stopped flicking round nervously, and started to accommodate the whole view.

'Have you confirmed your operability?' the Hexaëmeron asked.

'Yes.'

'Very well, Julia Evans, I defer to your authority. This idea goes against every instinct I possess. I am the micro, destined to timeless embrace of the cosmos. This brash voyage goes against nature. Gambling all on one risky flight. What strange, hasty creatures you are.'

'It's just youthful enthusiasm, the inability to resist challenge. We dream, that is our flaw, and our beauty. Your strength is physical, ours lies in conviction of self.'

She felt the Hexaëmeron's consciousness fading into dormancy. Her control routines extended out through the remaining cells as it retreated.

'Royan, darling? I'm here with you now.' She said it without a hint of trepidation; the emotion mechanism still existed, but she had superseded it, becoming the Julia Evans everyone always thought she was. A minor pulse of amusement trickled through the prohibition, and she sent a smile image at him.

'You sure, Snowy?' The tone was cautiously welcome, sceptical rather than contemptuous.

'Yes. Watch.'

Cells flowed. A pseudopod distended from her ovoid shell, the tip flattening out. Fingers and a thumb appeared, the human hand took its final shape and gave the three startled people in the chamber a thumbs-up.

'All right, Snowy, I believe you.'

She worked in tandem with Royan to transform a section of the cells he commanded into a neural network.

'Like old times, Snowy. You and me, working like this.'

'Yeah, old times.'

Her internal perception tracked the neural network forming. When it was complete Royan squirted in his personality package.

'Are you operational?' she asked the mini-entity.

'Yeah.'

Royan began to download his memories.

Julia resumed control of the cells Royan had converted into his life-support system, and began to digest the remains of his ruined body. She left the brain until last, a closed-circuit loop supplying it with re-oxygenated blood from a small haematopoiesis saccate.

'Ready?' Julia asked.

'Memories intact,' Royan said. 'More fun to travel than arrive, so let's go go go.'

The protean cells broke his brain apart, gorging on the raw chemicals they released, reproducing as they went. Julia felt round inside herself until there were no more intrusions; then opened a channel to the terminal in the chamber. 'You'd better leave now,' she told Greg, Rick, and her flesh-and-blood self. 'Go down into the cave where you first met the drone, and wait until I've gone past. There may be tekmercs about.'

She watched her flesh-and-blood self quirk her lips in silent acknowledgement. Some of the tiredness seemed to have gone. She was glad, body and mind had been subjected to far too much pressure over the last three days. Almost maxed out.

'It worked, then,' Greg said, his voice had the sluggishness she knew came from a neurohormone hangover.

'Yes,' she said. 'The Hexaëmeron won't be coming back.'

'*Bon voyage*, the pair of you.'

Julia began to send tendrils of herself out into the floor mat, breaking down and digesting the disseminator plant. She watched Rick, Greg, and her flesh-and-blood self scurry down the connecting passage as a circular bulge rippled out from her base.

The tendrils' inner core of protean cells absorbed the chemicals that the outer layer had dissolved and processed, fissioning rapidly. Individual tendrils met and merged into a single consumptive wavefront. It reached the chamber walls and rose up hungrily.

Once the last of the chamber's rubbery strings had been converted, Julia pulled the skirt of protean cells back, and began to alter her shape, becoming more pliable. She headed towards the passage, her movement a combination of rolling and slithering. When she reached the entrance she extended a ring of herself that melded with the translucent walls, and began to digest them. She sent a second ring of cells swelling fluidly over the top of the first, then a third. Her main bulk moved forwards, soaking up the engorged rings as she went. More rings were formed and sent on ahead. Specially formatted suckers fastened on to the rock beneath the disseminator plant, and began to leach out various minerals the cells needed.

By the time she squeezed out of the end of the passage she was a globe over seven metres in diameter, almost touching the hemispherical chamber's apex. Her weight crushed the composite cargo pods into blade-like splinters. She covered the whole chamber in a digestive layer, and moved on into the next passage, pushing a tube of cells ahead of herself as she followed the spiral down. The titanium nuggets in the tumours were ingested and pulverized, the motes held in suspension. She would need all the metal she could get later.

In the bottom chamber she waited for the new cells to catch up with her, at the same time sending fresh tendrils out into the four remaining passages to suck in still more organic matter.

She could perceive Greg and her flesh-and-blood self standing at the far end of the passage, consternation on their faces. The three crash team hardliners had taken their Konica rip guns from their armour suits' waist clips.

'Do we run?' Rick yelled.

'No,' Greg said. 'But it'd be a good idea to stand back against the wall when it comes, no messing.'

'It's still her?'

'Yeah.'

'Jesus.'

'You wanted to come,' her flesh-and-blood self said. There was a ripple of light laughter in her voice that had been missing for quite some time. 'Insistent, you were.'

Rick grunted in dismay. They flattened themselves against the passage walls.

Julia's alien body began to coalesce. The chamber wasn't going to be big enough to accommodate her; Royan's disseminator plant had been more extensive than she'd expected – another five of the hemispherical chambers, nearly a kilometre of connecting passageways. She shaped herself into a serpent form a couple of metres in diameter, hardened and roughened her external layer for traction, and surged down the passage.

'My Lord!' Sinclair shouted. 'The Beast! The Beast is come.' He fell to his knees, clasping his hands in prayer. 'And when they shall have finished their testimony, the Beast that ascendeth out of the bottomless pit shall make war against them, and shall overcome them, and kill them.'

'Oh, shut up,' Rick said.

The security hardliners' rip guns were aimed at her in fear as her questing tip slithered past.

'Down,' her flesh-and-blood self ordered in an iron tone. 'Put those guns down. It won't touch us.'

Not that it mattered even if they did fire. She could absorb the bolts without any real damage, and take their guns away as any mother would from errant children. Yes, Royan had been right to fear the Hexaëmeron. She regarded the knot of cells that held her lover's slumbering consciousness tenderly. They would be together again one day, and truly free.

Her tip split into two as it emerged into the catacombs, then those tips branched again. She started to probe the fissures and passages of the fault zone. A tide of cohesive oil penetrating every cranny; some of her extremities were thinner than leaves, barely five cells thick.

Caves and passages were observed, oppressively miasmatic in the low infrared band. Rock formations revealed their composition and weaknesses; ores were assayed. She watched freshets coursing through the bleak ragged cavities, several thin waterfalls splattering down isolated clefts, their volume visibly decreasing; and guessed at the lake next to the Celestial Apostles' village being breached.

She started to siphon the water into herself, opening up a plexus of capillaries to distribute it evenly.

Bodies in muscle-armour suits were lying above the sinking water, jammed into tight rifts, or caught on jutting rock fangs. Little clumps of jetsam bobbed along. In one passage she discovered a dog, its fur badly singed, barbecued flesh peeling away. She sent out a pseudopod, and digested it.

Suzi was floating face down in a crescent-shaped cave where the water had pooled, long scorch gouges down the back and legs of her armour. Rip gun bolts had gouged molten scars in the rock, glassy beads dribbling down the walls like wax from a candle.

Julia ingested the water, then pushed a large lump of herself into the cave, inflating it like a bubble until every square centimetre of the rock's surface was covered with a thin skin of cells. Four missiles had detonated, she could taste the bitter chemicals of the warheads imprinted on the walls. Minute particles of metalloceramic were detectable, along with composite and plastic fragments. Leol Reiger had been hit.

She retracted her far-flung body from the more distant sections of the fault zone, and concentrated on examining the area around Suzi's cave.

Footsteps betrayed him, she could hear the crash team blundering about in and around the village cave, but discrimination procedures quickly eliminated them. She heard it then, a monotonous clumping, one foot moving slowly, coming down hard.

She infiltrated the passage behind him, sprouting exploratory tentacles into the wall cracks. They discovered a labyrinth of narrow chinks behind the surface, dislodged ore veins, rock and metal torn apart. Her body oozed in, filling every cranny. The leading edges passed round him in silence, slithering on ahead. Ten metres in front of him, she seeped back out into the passage, forming a solid clot like cold brimstone.

The armour suit was limping, left leg grating loudly at each movement. One infrared helmet beam shone weakly ahead, swaying from side to side. Two of the thermal dump panels on his back were dead, the third glowed strongly in the infrared. Her magnetic-sensitive cells picked up shivers of energy from the muscle bands. Air filter intakes on the helmet growled asthmatically.

Leol Reiger stopped, his rip gun raised to point at the smooth protoplasm barrier. Julia sculpted a relief of her own face, a metre high, and extended it out of the integument. A green laser fan from the suit's shoulder sensor pod swept over her.

Julia opened her mouth, and used the cells inside as a diaphragm. 'I warned you before, Mr Reiger, I would not forget you.'

Leol Reiger's suit speaker clicked on. 'Julia Evans. Gotta hand it to you, this is some stunt. You wanna deal?'

'No. I want you to know it was me.'

'Yeah? Then you'd better be good, rich bitch, you'd better be fucking supreme. Because I told you once already, the only way out now is you and me.'

'Yes, that you did.'

Leol Reiger fired, walking forwards. Rip gun bolts tore into her outsize face, clawing it to cinders. Steam and carbon particles spewed back at him as cells died in their hundreds of billions.

Julia started to expand her cells, filling the cavities around the passage. Osmosis impelled the water through her, bloating every capillary. She felt it as a peristaltic contraction, muscles straining at their limit. The rock screeched in agony as hydrostatic pressure began to close the passage. A violent shudder threw Leol Reiger to his knees. The rip gun clattered away. He rolled on to his back, and stuck his arms up, pushing against the roof as it descended. The metalloceramic armour buckled.

Julia kept on squeezing long after it was necessary, wringing every wisp of air out of the compacted rock.

41

Greg pressed himself against the rough surface of the passage wall as the alien behemoth squirmed past. He could almost believe neuorhormone abuse had sprained his synapses into hallucinosis, abandoning him in a universe of the mind's whimsy. In a way he wished it were true, that would mean the alien wasn't real.

Two metres in diameter, a skin like coarse leather, coloured sable-black, gruesomely supple, and possessing more inertia than a rampant dinosaur. Shadowform thought currents purled along its length, distorted human idiosyncrasies, anything but reassuring in their metamorphosis. Human without humanity.

'A serpent of the night,' Sinclair cried. 'Satan incarnate.'

Strong eddies of air whipped past Greg's face, bringing a scent of corruption, of ripe fruit mouldering on branches. He coughed, eyelids blinking against the acridity.

'Hail Mary, for all me sins I beg your forgiveness,' Sinclair said. His eyes were tight shut.

'It won't hurt you,' Julia said, her voice raised above the rasp of alien skin slithering over rock. Her thought currents had a self-assured tranquillity Greg envied.

'Not this,' Sinclair cried. 'I didn't want this. You've let loose the beast. I wanted an end to madness, the start of justice.'

'It's harmless,' Rick said. 'Believe me. That's what we've done, neutered it. You'll never see it again.'

Sinclair opened one eye, and shivered.

Greg wondered just how big the alien was now. There must have been a lot of disseminator plant to give it this much bulk.

'Is it an angel or a demon?' Sinclair asked.

'Neither,' said Julia. 'It's hope. A very noble sort of hope.'

'For who?'

'Maybe a lot of people. The whole Earth is going to be given proof we're not alone in the galaxy, and never have been. They'll see it written in the sky tonight. And God knows this world deserves to be touched with wonder.'

'You're a religious woman, Miss Julia?'

'Yes, I suppose I am.'

The tail of the alien rushed by. Swallowed by the darkness in seconds. Greg hadn't really appreciated how fast the bloody thing was moving. Muscles unknotted, his legs were shaking.

Circles of light from the helmet spots on the hardliners' suits shone on the opposite wall. He stepped out into the middle of the passage. The alien presence was dwindling, a dawn-washed star at the back of his mind. Julia was staring into the gloom after it.

'Regrets?' he asked.

'Not one. It was all I could do.'

He put his arm round her shoulder, and gave her a little hug. Doubts were still cluttering the peripheries of her mind.

'I said you were the best when it comes to decisions,' he told her.

She grinned up at him. 'Thanks, Greg. And you, too, Rick. I'm deep in your debt; I would never have thought of that by myself.'

'No,' Rick said. 'There's nothing to thank, this was the zenith of my professional life, I've justified fifteen years' work and dreaming, and you made it possible.' He was solemnly intent, nearly entreating. Julia's grin became a little laboured.

'Come on, I think we'd better get going,' Greg said.

'Yes,' Julia said. 'I must get in touch with Victor and Sean, there will be the most awful panic if I don't inform them what's about to happen.'

*

Greg had half expected to meet the alien again in the caves. Two or three times he thought he could hear something rumbling, a sound like boulders being slowly ground together. But the only sign of its presence was an oval tunnel which had been bored into the storage cave, saving them from wriggling along the narrow crack. The rock had been sheered clean, giving it a polished-marble finish.

'Is it ahead of us?' Greg asked Julia.

'No. I want to get back to Hyde Cavern quickly.'

'So it made this opening for you?'

'Yes.'

Shelves and cargo pods had been smashed against the rear wall of the storage cave where the wave had flung them, walls and ceiling were dripping wet. There was no sign of any of the fruit.

'The hardliners must have breached the lake,' Greg said.

'So where did all the water go?' Rick asked. 'We never saw any, and we were lower down than this.'

'Used up,' Julia said without hesitating.

'Are you in contact with that thing?' Greg asked.

'Not exactly, but there was some feedback when I squirted my memories over. I know what it can do, and I know how I'll use it. The water is only the start. It needs a lot of organic chemicals.' She sighed. 'I hope it leaves enough hydrocarbons to germinate the second chamber's biosphere.'

The extent of the damage in the village cave surprised Greg. It must have been a brute of a fight. The crash team were splashing about through ankle-deep water. He counted seventeen armour suits laid out in a row. One of them was small, badly scored.

Suzi had been so young when they first met, barely a teenager, frightened and determined, emotionally scarred. One of the best Trinities he had ever trained, soaking up every word, bright and quick. She never had a childhood, not the kind his kids at Hambleton were getting. Instead he taught her how to kill, then threw her straight into the front line. She hadn't known anything else, her entire life moulded by a bunch of drunken Party militia, a random fling of the dice. If they had turned down another street, ransacked someone else's hotel, it would've been so different. Suzi was smart enough to have made it in any field. Never had the chance to try. That was what they'd fought for together, back in Peterborough, so that the next generation could live real lives again. And they'd been right, Julia and her achievements proved that.

He turned to Julia as she picked her way over dead fish, button nose wrinkled in dismay. She recoiled from the heat in his expression.

'Are you quite sure you and the alien dealt with Leol Reiger?' he asked.

She nodded hurriedly, eyes dark with emotion. He hadn't seen her that vulnerable-looking for seventeen years.

Greg's earpiece hissed with static, then Melvyn was talking in a breathless voice. 'I was about to send out a scout party for you. I was worried the water might have trapped you.'

Three of the suited figures were walking towards them.

Julia fumbled round in her hood, and found the small mike. 'Do you have a communication circuit with Victor?' she asked.

'Not a chance, our fibre optic went down in the combat.' He paused. 'Greg—'

'I know,' Greg said.

'We're leaving now,' Julia said. 'Get your team together.' She started for the staircase.

'But there's still five tekmercs unaccounted for,' Melvyn protested.

'Are all your people here?'

'I detailed four to take our wounded out, but the rest are here, yes.'

'Then get them out.'

'Yes, ma'am. What about the tekmercs?'

'Leave them to the alien, they won't escape.'

'You found it?' Melvyn asked. Greg heard a thousand questions in his voice.

'Yes,' Julia said.

'Lordy, me boy, you should have seen the beastie,' Sinclair said. 'A kilometre long, it was, black as hell.'

'Where's Royan?' Melvyn asked.

Julia's step faltered. 'Gone.'

*

Fragments of data traffic bounced down the service tunnel as Greg led them out into Moorgate station, his earpiece picking up snatches of shouting voices. Half of New London's security staff were waiting for them. He could see paramedics easing the crash team casualties into a hospital coach, the four armour-suited members standing close by.

Victor came at a dead run as they emerged from the service tunnel. He stopped short half a metre from Julia, looking her up and down. 'You're all right,' he said, he sounded scared.

Julia smiled. 'Yes, Victor, I'm all right.'

Victor cleared his throat, and glanced back down the service tunnel. 'What about Royan, did you find him?'

'Yeah,' Greg said. 'But he's not coming back, not with us.' He sat down on one of the big pipes next to a turbopump casing. Now the tension and adrenalin drive were abating, the exertions of the last two days were making themselves felt. The immediacy was lost; always the same after combat, and that's what this had been, even without the physical side. His neurohormone hangover was nagging, cutting him off from the emotional by-play of the security staff, Victor and Julia, Rick; Sinclair's doolally inspirations. And he didn't care. He wanted out of his dissipater suit, then a bath, a drink, and a call to Eleanor. Maybe the other way round.

'And the alien?' Victor asked.

'It's agreed to leave,' Julia said. 'Have you got your cybofax on you?'

Victor handed it over.

'Get all these people out of here,' Julia said as she entered a code into the wafer. 'And clear all the other northern endcap stations as well.'

'Why, what's happening?'

Her eyes glinted challengingly. 'There's going to be a slight adjustment to New London.'

Victor appealed to Greg.

'Don't look at me, she made the deal.'

'What, with the alien?'

'Yeah.'

Victor glanced back at Julia. Like a teenager hit with first-love blues, Greg thought.

Sean Francis's face appeared on the cybofax screen. 'Ma'am. You're all right, yes?'

Julia sucked in her cheeks. 'Yes, so it seems. Sean, order a complete evacuation of all personnel in the second chamber, miners, technicians, supervisors. Absolutely everyone, they are to use the emergency capsules. I want them out fast.'

Sean looked shocked. 'What's happening?'

'The alien will be entering the second chamber soon. And while I think of it, make sure the orb foundry plant crew evacuate as well. Then clear every spacecraft within a five-hundred-kilometre radius of New London, and that includes all the cargo tugs and personnel commuters. Everything, understood?'

'My God, if it's that dangerous shouldn't I order a full-scale evacuation?'

'It's not dangerous,' Julia said quickly. 'Just very, very big.'

'Big,' Sean mouthed silently. 'All right, I'll initiate the procedures now.'

'Thank you, Sean,' Julia said. 'And have Maria power up my Falcon. We'll be at the southern hub docking complex in five minutes.'

'You're leaving?' Sean asked. It wasn't quite an accusation.

'Certainly not. I'm reserving a grandstand seat; after what we've been through we've earned it.'

'Yes, ma'am.'

Julia sat beside Greg, and slipped her arm through his. She was effervescent. It was a lovely sight, he thought, like watching time in retreat, her face smoothing out.

'How about you boys?' Julia glanced up at Rick and Victor, tip of her tongue caught between her lips. 'You coming?'

Victor and Rick exchanged a nervous glance, not quite sure how to react to this teasing, girlish Julia.

Greg chuckled at them, and allowed her to haul him to his feet. Muscles creaked in protest, but she was right, he couldn't miss it. At least somebody had got what they wanted out of all this.

*

Space was full of bright orange sparks, a wide cyclonic circle spinning out of New London's northern hub like some giant Catherine wheel display. The Falcon glided smoothly towards them, maintaining a steady two-kilometre separation distance from the bulk of the asteroid.

'Just how many people have you got building the second chamber?' Rick asked. He was floating parallel to the cabin roof, gawping out at the pyrotechnic armada of emergency escape capsules.

Julia clucked her tongue, concentrating on the data her processor nodes were feeding her. 'About three and a half thousand all told. The capsules can hold up to eight people. They've launched most of them.'

Maria snorted. 'A thousand vomit comets, the mind boggles.'

Greg tightened his grip on the back of her chair. Maria had been grumpy since they left New London's southern hub docking crater. He got the impression she didn't like being crowded out like this. The four of them hanging on behind her, peering out through the slim, graphic-laden windscreen.

'How are we doing, Sean?' Julia asked.

'The emergency capsules are all clear,' Sean's voice reported. 'But there are fifteen reported cases of broken limbs, and numerous minor injuries. We very nearly had a panic situation after all the rumours which have been circulating. Our second chamber schedule has been ripped to pieces. It'll take weeks to get back to full operational efficiency. Some of the gear just isn't designed for instant shutdown, yes?'

'There is no schedule any more, Sean. So don't worry about it.'

'If you say so, ma'am,' he said in a tired voice. 'We've suspended traffic movements around the asteroid, apart from yourself. How soon before we can start picking up the emergency capsules?'

'As soon as they pass the five-hundred-kilometre limit.'

'Yes, ma'am.'

The sparks around the edge of the expanding circle were dimming and going out.

'Where do you want to watch from?' Maria asked.

'Take us round to the northern hub crater,' Julia said. 'But not too close.'

A flurry of purple lines swept across the windscreen. Greg heard the reaction control thrusters fire. The Falcon was sliding up level with the shoal of emergency capsules, the sunlit length of the mirror spindle crept into view round the northern end of the asteroid.

'I've got damage reports coming in from the second chamber's environmental maintenance section,' Sean called. 'Five hydrocarbon storage tanks have been breached, massive fluid loss.'

'Don't send any repair crews down to them,' Julia said.

'But—'

'None, Sean.'

'There's another three tanks gone,' a note of frustration was clogging Sean's voice. 'We're going to lose them all.'

'You won't,' Julia replied, imperturbable.

'Jesus Christ, the command centre reports a rotational instability. The centre of gravity is shifting in the second chamber.'

'Sean, please. Nothing is going to harm New London.'

'Yes, ma'am.'

'Julia—' Victor began.

Her hand came down on top of his. 'It's all right, Victor, really.'

'OK.' He nodded with obvious reluctance.

Greg wanted to say something, do something to reassure Victor and the people back in the asteroid. Julia's faith was unshakeable, but it was all internal, noncommunicative. He'd believed himself, of course, when the alien had slithered past him, although there was no real way to convey his conviction. Just hang on and pray Julia could deliver, once again.

The emergency capsules' solid rockets had all burnt out, leaving their white and green strobes winking against the backdrop of stars as they deserted New London.

Another burst from the reaction-control thrusters halted the Falcon's drift. They were keeping station fifteen hundred metres out from the mirror spindle. It sliced the starfield in half, an open silver-white gridwork six kilometres long, with the tubular sand duct running down the centre. The foundry plant at the end was a shadowy profile lost in the mirror's umbra, red strobes flashing silently around its empty capsule hatches.

The Falcon rotated around its long axis, bringing the northern hub crater into view.

'Now,' Julia said reverently. Her hand was still clamped over Victor's, dainty knuckles whitening.

Greg could see right down into the crater; it was larger than its southern hub counterpart, a couple of kilometres across, a deep conical bite out of the rock. The sides were smooth black glass, streaked with ash-grey rays. It was inert now, but it must have been a good approximation of hell while the electron-compression devices had gnawed it out.

A backscatter of stale light from the big mirror illuminated the sloping walls. The concave floor was three hundred and fifty metres wide, covered with a ribbing of pale metal braces that held down the spindle bearing, a fat gold foil-covered ring containing the superconductor magnets which suspended and rotated the spindle. The sand duct ran straight through the middle of the ring, disappearing into a jet-black bore hole in the crater floor.

'We've lost every datalink into the second chamber,' Sean said. 'And that includes the foundry plant. But something is tapping the power lines, the load is one hundred per cent capacity. We're having to powerdown some of Hyde Cavern to cope.'

'Thank you, Sean,' Julia sang. 'It's important you maintain the power supply. The drain will only be for a few hours.'

Greg couldn't move his attention from the spindle bearing. Intuitive expectation was building up inside him, despite the vestigial neurohormone hangover, the rosy glow before the dawn. Maybe Sinclair wasn't so brain-wrecked after all.

Just outside the spindle bearing ring a small circle of the crater floor cracked open, palpitating like a minor earthquake, then crumbled inwards. Greg's shout died in his throat, his view was inverted, which threw him for a moment; but the floor of the crater was vertical to the asteroid's rotational gravity. The debris should have rolled down the crater wall and fallen out of the lip, instead it had fallen horizontally.

'It's started,' he said meekly.

'Where?' Julia hissed.

'Base of the spindle.'

A white worm of alien flesh was rising out of the new hole, waxy and pellucid, its tip swaying slowly, as if it was searching. He thought of a maggot clawing out of an apple, then the scale hit him.

'Bloody hell,' Victor mumbled.

Julia just giggled.

A second hole fell inwards. Cracks were spreading across the crater floor. The worm's tip began to expand, engulfing the nearby section of the ring bearing. More white tips were reaching blindly out of the ruptured rock.

'What's it doing?' Maria asked.

'Finishing off the second chamber for me,' Julia said. 'That was part of the deal. I'll have to ship up a lot of hydrocarbons to replace what it's soaked up, but I'll be saving money on the mining operation. Swings and roundabouts, it ought to show a profit in the end.'

The white bulk of the alien had completely enveloped the spindle bearing ring. In fact, Greg saw the whole of the crater floor was now a single expanse of undulating white mire. There was no sign of the bracing ribs. A tremor ran up the spindle.

'I hope it won't warp,' Julia said in concern.

Greg thought the alien was flowing up the spindle, until he realized it was the spindle itself which was moving. With a cumbrous inexorability that made him wag his head in disbelief, the girders began to slide past the Falcon's nose. The alien was pushing the spindle up out of the crater.

Light and shadows shifted round in the cabin as the huge foundry mirror was impelled away from the asteroid. Nobody had spoken for some time; even Sean Francis had remained quiet. Greg began to relax, soaking it all in; he would never have to buy another round in Hambleton's pub again. *I was there.*

A white column of alien flesh was mounting below the base of the spindle, guiding it away. He guessed it was about three hundred metres high when the top peeled open, releasing the gold ring of the bearing. It must have imparted a final shove, because he was sure the spindle picked up speed. The white column sank back into the crater. For a moment the floor of the crater was covered by a lake of white flesh, then a dimple formed at the centre and began to deepen.

'You say it's going to hollow out the second chamber for you?' Rick asked.

'Yes. Mine the rock, and refine it. Exactly what Royan dreamed of. You see, he was right. In the end.' The grin dropped from her face, and she glanced at Victor for reassurance. He gave her a narrow smile.

All that was visible of the alien was a thin white rim around the base of the crater wall, the rest of it had sunk out of sight, leaving a gaping shaft. A dove-grey globe, three hundred metres in diameter, levitated up out of the centre. The scene reminded Greg of an active-hologram poster he'd bought Oliver for his eighth birthday, time-lapse Earthrise from the Moon. Sedate and unstoppable. They watched it in silence.

'I wonder what that one is,' Julia said after the grey globe left the shaft. 'It can't be a metal, not with that albedo.'

The spindle bearing ring had cleared the top of the crater, with the globe a kilometre behind. A second globe emerged from the shaft, a light metallic blue this time.

'You mean they're all going to be different?' Greg asked.

'Absolutely, yes. Minerals and metals all separated out, with a purity our large-scale refineries can't match. That's something else which will save me a bundle.'

A third globe was emerging, another metal one, its mirror-bright surface reflecting warped constellations.

*

Greg watched the alien disgorging globes for over three hours. Fatigue only affected his body, shutting it down. His mind remained alert, fascinated at the slow carnival of elements riding by outside. The majority of globes were either iron or silica, three hundred metres in diameter. But there were smaller globes, the rarer minerals, dark greens and yellows and blues. Eight batches of them had emerged in clusters at the same time as the ordinary globes, like satellite moons swarming round a gas giant.

It took a while for the end of the procession to register. The last globe, a brick-red colour, which Julia said was probably zircon, had travelled halfway up the crater before he noticed the alien flesh dilating out from the rim to recover the shaft.

'Is that it?' Maria asked.

'This is the last phase,' Julia said. 'The cells will be regrouping;

they've been spread pretty thin around the second chamber for the mining and refining. It's a big area to cover, I'm glad half of it was complete before the alien started.'

'Last phase?' Victor queried.

'Departure.'

*

Greg wondered if it was fate again that put New London over the middle of the Atlantic while Europe was still in darkness, awaiting the dawn. The asteroid would be visible from four continents: Europe, Africa, and North and South America. All of them with perfect viewing conditions.

Did people make the era, or did the necessity of the time throw up the right people? Either way, Greg thought, God had singled out Julia, and no messing.

They had listened to some of the channels while the globes had risen out of the crater. The whole world knew something was going on up at New London, that the Co-Defence League's geosynchronous Strategic Defence platforms had been used for the first time, that Julia Evans herself was up there, that she'd ordered an evacuation.

She told Sean to plug the asteroid back into the communications net, mainly to try and reassure people that the emergency wasn't life-threatening. The Globecast franchise office had been transmitting pictures of the refined globes back to Earth ever since. Greg could taste a sweet irony in that. What would Clifford Jepson be thinking?

Maria turned the Falcon again, pointing its tail at the northern hub. Greg could see the seemingly infinite line of sunlit globes stretching towards Polaris, like multicoloured stars raining down from heaven.

A bulge rose in the middle of the alien flesh, quickly distending, lengthening. It formed a conical spike six hundred metres high, then stopped. The tip began to lean over, tracing a widening spiral as the asteroid's rotation carried it round.

Greg could sense the anticipation flooding out of the alien, a mix of excitement and fear. Julia's personality had given it emotions, it could feel, and it was scared, nerving itself up.

Nothing lasts for ever, he told it sorrowfully.

The alien jumped. A vast spasm rippled down its flanks, hitting the base of the crater wall, and it let go. It was changing shape almost at once, contracting into a sphere four hundred and fifty metres in diameter.

Greg reckoned it was travelling a lot faster than any of the globes; its trajectory taking it away from New London's rotation axis and the line of globes. When it slipped above the crater rim and into the direct sunlight the flesh changed colour, darkening to ebony.

'Do you want to follow it?' Maria asked.

'No,' Julia said. 'We can see from here.'

New London was seven kilometres behind it when the alien began its metamorphosis. The flesh flowed again, flattening out into a lentoid shape. Greg saw a circular silver stain emerge at the centre and split into six arms, spreading out to the rim.

'That looks like metal,' he said.

'It is,' Julia agreed. 'Titanium motes that are only a few atoms in diameter. The cells can manipulate them to form a surface coating quite easily.'

Greg gave her an uneasy glance, wondering again just how much of a union existed between them.

The alien was still expanding, a disk two kilometres wide now, the titanium completely covering one side, facing the sun full on, painfully bright to look at.

'I did the right thing, didn't I, Greg?' Julia asked.

'Yeah, both ways. I've had to sit back and endure what happened between you and Royan, my friends. That hurt, Julia. And this thing,' he waved a hand at the windscreen. The alien was retreating from New London, still growing, ten – fifteen kilometres across now, at least. That made it hard to believe it was leaving. It was such an overwhelming presence, breaking down his conviction of a neatly completed deal. 'Look at it. We couldn't have let that loose in the solar system. It's too powerful.

You can't ignore it; either it would have engulfed us, or we would have abused it, little people twisting it to serve parochial needs. And there are a lot of little people in the world, Julia. Maybe that's why you stand out so much.'

'Maybe.'

Size was the killer, forcing him to accept his own insignificance. New London was big, but the asteroid was something that had been tamed, he could admire that. But now he could finally appreciate Royan's internal defeat, his broken soul. Royan had known what was at stake, that was why he'd been prepared to use the gamma mines.

The alien had become two-dimensional, a veil of titanium atoms that lacked the substance of a mirage. He guessed there must be a net of cables to support the sail and provide some degree of control. But they were probably no thicker than a gossamer thread. Invisible and irrelevant.

A hundred and twenty kilometres in diameter, and it didn't even seem to be slowing down. A flat white-hole eruption.

Maria backed the Falcon eighty kilometres away, a leisurely thirty-minute manoeuvre. When they stopped, the alien was two hundred and sixty kilometres in diameter.

The measurement had to come from the Falcon's sensors, its dimensions defeated the human eye. Such vastness perturbed his comfortable visual references, cheating him into believing the sail was *down*. In his mind it had become a featureless silver landscape; not an artifact or a living creature. Logic warring with belief. He was truly in alien country now.

Four hundred kilometres in diameter. The sail engulfed half of the universe; powerful waves of sunlight would roll across it, washing over the Falcon and dazzling Greg before the wind-screen's electrochromic filters cut in.

He experienced the figment kiss as the sail reached five hundred kilometres in diameter. A strand of thought spun out from the knot of cells at the centre of the sail, the one he couldn't see, but knew was there. Julia's teasing lips brushed his.

And he was standing on a beach of white sand with the deep

blue ocean before him, stretching his arms wide in primal welcome to the rising sun, soaking his naked body with its warmth. He dived cleanly into the water, striking out for the shore beyond the far horizon, abandoning the past with giddy joy.

The ghost haze of solar ions gusted against the alien sail, beginning the long push out to the stars.

42

The Frankenstein wasp crawled round the metal bar of the conditioning grill, and poised on the cliff-like edge of copper paint facing into the office. Greg could make little sense of what it saw, just smeared outlines, as if he was wearing a glitched photon amp. But the wasp was aware of the empty space ahead, and somewhere out there were flowers, pollen. Sugar tugged at it like a tidal force.

Greg used his espersense to locate the mind he wanted; four metres from the wasp, slightly below. He pushed the wish into the insect's instinct-governed brain. A need to fly towards the man sitting at the desk. Wings blurred furiously.

'You just want the stinger changed?' Jools the Tool had asked Greg curiously that morning. He was a small man, dressed all in black. Round gold-rimmed glasses shielded his' damp eyes with pink-tinted lenses. His chalk-white skin looked unhealthy, though Greg wrote it off as partly due to the time of day. The sun hadn't risen when he rang the pet shop's bell.

'Yeah,' Greg said. 'That's all.'

'So how are you going to control it?'

'I'm a gland psychic.'

Jools the Tool nodded a grudging acknowledgement, and led him past the cages of sleeping animals to his cubbyhole surgery at the rear of the shop.

The operation hadn't taken long. Greg stood behind the little

Frankenstein surgeon, watching the microscope's flatscreen over his shoulder. It showed the wasp, magnified to thirty centimetres long, held down with silk binding sheaths. Micro-surgical instruments delicately amputated its stinger, and stitched in a wicked-looking hollow dagger to replace it. Blades and clamps danced with hypnotic agility around the yellow-and-black striped abdomen, responding to the waldo handles which Jools the Tool was caressing.

'I've primed it with a shot of AMRE7D,' he told Greg as the artificial stinger was filled with a clear fluid. 'It's a neurotoxin, one of the best. Once it's in the bloodstream, you've got a maximum of twenty seconds before death occurs.'

The back of the man's head was distinguishable now, hair like a logjam, lunar mare of skin. Greg guided the wasp down to the nape of the neck, allowing the insect's own instincts to take over for the landing. When the warmth of the skin pressed against its legs, his mind shouted out the compulsion. The wasp thrust its composite stinger into the skin, expelling the AMRE7D in a single blast.

Clifford Jepson's hand swatted the wasp, his yell of surprise and pain rattling round the office.

Greg focused himself on the boiling thought currents. *I want you to know something before you die, Jepson,* his mind whispered. *I want you to know why.*

Clifford Jepson's muscles had locked rigid, maybe from terror, maybe from the neurotoxin. Greg looked out through bugged eyes, feeling throat muscles like iron bands, hands clawing at the chair's leather arms.

You were offered an honourable chance to end the madness over atomic structuring. You refused it because you thought you could squeeze more money from the deal. You were greedy, Jepson. And that greed killed my friend. It might have been your psycho-cyborg Reiger who pulled the trigger, but you loaded his program, you ran him. Now you're going to die because of it. I'm glad, and I hate you for that as well.

Greg cancelled the gland's secretion, and opened his eyes. He was sitting in the passenger seat of a navy-blue Lada Sokol, parked in the shade of a Japanese umbrella pine in a big open-air car park. Fifty metres in front of him, the ornate carved stone of the stately home which Globecast used as its European headquarters burned brightly in the mid-morning sun. A flock of white birds were flying through Kent's cloudless azure sky overhead.

'Did you close the deal?' Col Charnwood asked.

'Yeah.'

'Good.' Col Charnwood flicked the Lada Sokol into gear and drove carefully out of the car park.

*

Some time after midnight Charlotte pulled on a white silk robe and went out on to the balcony to enjoy the cool breeze that blew in from the Fens basin. It was so refreshing after the sweltering heat of the day. She let it ruffle her hair as she gazed up at the night sky. The alien solar sail was definitely smaller tonight. It had been crawling away from New London over the last few days, now it was low in the south-east, while the fuzzy patch of the asteroid's archipelago glowed above the western horizon.

According to the channel newscasts, light pressure from the Sun was constantly accelerating it. She hadn't known that light could exert pressure; apparently it could. A tiny pressure, but the sail's surface area was the size of a small country, making the overall force colossal. In another twenty days it would reach solar escape velocity; after that it could go wherever it chose in the galaxy. Several times since returning from New London, Charlotte had found herself thinking what it must be like having that much freedom. What a wonderful thing to be able to roam the universe at will, searching out wonders and horrors. And to voyage so majestically, sailing on a sunbeam.

She had never seen a star so gloriously radiant. It was

probably bright enough to cast a shadow at night; but Peter-borough's permanent light haze made it impossible to know for sure.

They had a good view of the city from their penthouse in the Castlewood condominium, especially the futureopolis of Prior's Fen Atoll. The day they moved in she spent hours on the balcony staring out at the mega-structures that seemed to float on the green-hued swamp.

She thought it strange that she had never visited Peterborough before; after all it was an incredible focal point for wealth. But after she arrived, she realized it ordered a different sort of money to the type she was used to. Peterborough's money was active money, it was finance consortium muscle, corporate power, political influence; the only gambling here was the venture capital backing industrial research lab. Nobody hoarded money in Peterborough, they worked it; the static, emasculated trusts which enabled her patrons to drift indulgently through life shrank from this city's vitality.

Prior's Fen epitomized the new culture, bold, purposeful architecture sticking two defiant fingers up to the dead past. The antithesis of Monaco.

It had been a long journey between the two cities, and the physical distance was the least of the gulf she had bridged. But now she'd found it, she knew she wouldn't be leaving.

There were stockbrokers to see in the morning. A new chapter of life to begin.

Victor Tyo had brought Dmitri Baronski's private memory cores with him when he returned from the Prezda with her furniture and clothes and trinkets. 'I figured you were the best person to sort through the bytes,' he had told her. 'The rest of Baronski's girls should be told where they stand. And somehow I don't think they'll be too keen on hearing it from me.'

She'd given every piece of that clothing to a charity shop in Stanground, along with the cheaper jewellery. The other girls she had called one at a time, telling them the way it was now, arranging for them to pick up their cut from Dmitri's Zürich account. But the rest of the data, the finance and industry gossip the old man was supposed to squirt over to the Dolgoprudnensky, that was interesting. She could see some valuable deals opening up if the knowledge was exploited properly by Fabian's cargo agents.

The breeze was growing chilly now. She went back into the bedroom, sliding the glass door shut behind her. Fragments of the city's street lighting leaked round the edges of the curtains, giving the room's white furniture a phosphorescent hue.

Fabian was asleep, sprawled belly down across the double bed where she'd left him. She wondered if it was illegal for a guardian to sleep with her ward. More than likely. If only he wasn't so terribly young. But he was hers for three whole years, until he was eighteen. Nothing in her life had lasted three years before. And after three years, well . . . Dreams were part of Peterborough too.

She smiled down at him, and slipped the robe from her shoulders. He stirred as she slid on to the bed beside him.

'Fabian,' she called softly.

His eyes opened drowsily, and he grinned up at her. 'Am I dreaming?'

She kissed his brow. 'What do you think?'

*

Julia combed the sweat-damped hair from his eyes as he lay back on the pillows. He really is very handsome, she thought. Funny I never noticed before. Or was that never wanted to notice before? It would have been complicated.

Then she frowned, and peered at his face. 'I don't believe it! You're looking guilty already.'

'Certainly not,' Victor protested. 'What you're seeing is plain relief. I thought—'

'What?' she asked eagerly. It was fun teasing him, she hadn't been free to tease a man like this for a long time. It was fun having him in bed too. Nothing astonishing, but that would come with time. She intended there would be a lot of time from now on.

Victor shrugged. 'Rick.'

'Oh, him. No. He was sweet, and hunky too, of course.'

'Thank you very much, ma'am.'

She giggled. 'Not my type, though. Outside of his work, there's nothing of interest about him. Sad really.'

'My heart bleeds.'

She waited a while. 'I'm extremely grateful to him, though. I would never have thought of flying the Hexaëmeron away. Lord, the thought of having to make that choice still makes me feel cold.'

'It won't happen again.'

'Thank heavens.' She rested her head on his chest. 'I'm going to reward Rick, show him just how appreciative I am.'

'How?'

'Give him his radio telescope, that Steropes he's forever whining about.'

'You serious?'

'Yes. We know it's not a pointless search any more. That puts a whole new perspective on SETI. Now people have been convinced there is life in the galaxy they'll expect a follow-up. And I want Event Horizon to maintain its leadership in the field.'

'There isn't going to be much doubt about that, I'm afraid. Greg certainly isn't going to come forward to claim any credit for what happened up at New London. And Sinclair is already a channel celebrity with his religious 'cast; telling the world how you tamed the Beast and liberated the New Jerusalem. So that's another brick firmly cemented in the wall of legend. Julia Evans, superwoman.'

'Bugger.' She hadn't thought of that aspect. Perhaps Greg . . . No, that wouldn't be fair at all. 'Oh well, at least Steropes won't put a strain on my finances now.'

'Too true. That second chamber is quite something, even if

the miners didn't appreciate losing their jobs five years ahead of schedule.'

The two of them had walked the length of the second chamber the day after the alien left, their boots kicking up puffs of arid dust. It was a landscape of rock turrets and deep zigzag canyons, delicate arched stone bridges reinforced with cores of solid iron. Instant geology; she'd seen the smoothness of water-etched curves, run her spacesuit glove over weather-chewed redstone outcrops. Yet for all its pristine state, the solid cyclo-rama engendered a sense of déjà-vu. It was the landscape of her childhood, a composition drawn from memory. There had been few nights when she hadn't sat on the rocks above the First Salvation Church warren and watched the sun set above the desert.

'All part of the deal,' she said. 'The alien was me, after all, remember? A completed second chamber gives Event Horizon a considerable financial boost. What did you expect?'

'Was that really necessary?' he asked quietly. 'Showing your memories to that thing?'

'It was the deal, Victor. How else could we be sure the Hexaëmeron would leave? And not just leave, but travel a long way before it resurrects its planet's species. The Centauri system would be no use. Our own ark starships will be there in less than a century; perhaps even sooner if Beswick ever does work out how to open a wormhole. But with my personality loaded in, I guarantee it won't stop for fifty – sixty light-years. Good enough, I think.'

'Not much of a deal for the alien. We're free of it, you make a profit. What did it get?'

'It got to live, Victor. Death was the only other option. And that would have been a monumental crime. Planetary genocide. I'm not sure I could have sanctioned that. But it can wait for a couple of millennia until it finds a barren star system to colonize, it's already waited billions of years.'

'If you say so,' he said reluctantly. 'And what about us? What sort of combination do we make? You build it and I protect it?'

There was a tremble in his voice, slight though, well concealed, it wouldn't register with many people. Do I know him that well already, or have I always known? 'Something like that. I don't think you're cut out for life as a househusband.'

'That's true enough.' His arm came over her back, hand stroking the side of her ribs. 'Funny how the Hexaëmeron knew us so well it cut straight to the heart of our society. It knew all along that people like you and Jepson were the real powers in the land.'

'I've been thinking about that. And it was wrong. Jepson and I were simply the most appropriate people, not the most powerful. That's the way the world works today. A million different interests, all competing, all clamouring for a voice. I told Marchant the world is becoming more complex, and the Hexaëmeron proved that to me beyond a shadow of a doubt. Simple political systems don't work any more; that two-party, two-ideology confrontation is behind us now. We need a system valid for the data age, a world where total information is available and no two places are physically more than ninety minutes apart. Parochialism is dead, long live parochialism.'

He gave her a long look. 'I don't get it.'

'Think about Wales. As part of England it was failing; above-average unemployment, mediocre social services and infrastructure. To New Conservative politicians in Westminster it's just another special interest grouping, like education policy or tax levels. They invest minimum resources compatible with a maximum return of votes; double the investment and they certainly don't double their votes. So it's automatically marginalized. That's why there are such powerful regional secession movements evolving. Not just here, but right across the globe; the Californias, Italy, Germany, even China's decentralization is the same thing with a different name. Small but forceful local governments, providing they are democracies, can always look after their people more effectively. What they lacked in previous eras was the strength and stability resulting from size, which is what Marchant was so worried about England losing. But now access and membership to large-scale organizations is profoundly simple; they're virtually spoilt for choice. Autonomous regions will become nodes in the global networks; and there are hundreds of them, thousands, each of them separate, but every one interlocking; financial, commercial, strategic defence alliances, corporate, pure data, trading markets, all of them networks of some kind or another. Event Horizon itself is a network; my factories are so widely distributed now any product you buy has components made all over the place, there is no single source.'

'So you're going to back the Welsh Nationalists' bid for independence?'

'Yes. But first I'm going to dump the New Conservatives. Not dramatically, but they'll get no more money or patronage from me. They were necessary after the PSP fell, rampant capitalism is always a good way to build quickly, and we needed that then, we'd fallen so far. But unless you're very careful, that kind of economy becomes a runaway shark, always having to move to eat, to survive. You get unemployment in the name of efficiency, suffering in the name of market forces. That's over. We've rebuilt, we've gathered all we lost; now we need to consolidate. If the New Conservatives can't accept that, then they deserve to go; if they're smart, they'll adapt their policies. Whatever they do, it isn't important to me any more. They don't matter. England will benefit from Welsh secession as much as the Welsh.'

'So it will be you who decides Wales's fate after all. Doesn't that place you outside these networks you have so much faith in? Doesn't that make you the controller the Hexaëmeron thought you were?'

'I neither control nor dictate. I see the trends which evolve, I'm good at that, damn good; it enables me to go with the flow. That's why Event Horizon functions so smoothly, that's what makes it such a powerful network. In this case, I'll nudge a little. But even if I didn't, and this referendum kept Wales under Westminster, the next or the one after would see them breaking free. It's happening, Victor. Separatism is evolving as the single most powerful political movement this century. And evolution is always stronger than imposed solutions.'

'You really think that's the way we're going?'

'Yes. It's right for this age. It'll work. Not for ever, but it'll do until the children want to change it.'

His hand began to stroke her ribs again. She snuggled up closer, looking over his chest at the bedroom's window. Wilholm's grounds were bathed in a combination of moonbeams and cool sail light. The woodland and lakes were quite enchanting like this, she thought, kissed by magic. It was the same the world over, the human race holding its breath in awe. Police had reported a drop in crime, politicians were quiet for fear of looking utterly foolish. Everybody busy gazing at the stars. Pity it wouldn't last.

*

The Pegasus lifted from the reservoir's mud flats while Greg was clambering up the limestone rocks. It rose straight up for a hundred metres, then peeled away to the east. He watched it blend into the darkening sky before extending a hand to help Andria up the last couple of metres.

A bonfire was blazing in the middle of the Berrybut estate away on the other side of the reservoir, its reflection dancing off the grey water. As he headed up the slope to the farmhouse he could see the pink and blue glow of charcoal on the pickers' range grill; thin streamers of smoke were spurting upwards as meat juices dripped through the soot-blackened metal mesh. People milled about in the camp field, little groups of five or six sitting on the dusty grass, passing a bottle round as they waited for the meal. A few figures were still wandering through the groves, organizing stacks of white boxes ready for tomorrow's picking.

He hadn't realized just how much he'd missed it all. The three days away were so unnatural compared to this, like something he'd watched on the channels. If it hadn't been for Suzi—

'They don't bite,' he said as Andria hesitated on the doorstep.

She flashed a nervous smile. Her eyes were still slightly red from crying.

The hall's biolums were on. Greg walked in to the familiar battered oak chest, the hat stand, churchwarden mirror, ancient tiles with fresh muddy footprints. He could hear rock music playing somewhere upstairs, the mechanical twangs and squeaky voices of a cartoon from the open lounge door.

'Dad!' Christine shrieked. There was a blur of motion as she flew down the stairs.

Eleanor stuck her head out of the kitchen, and smiled. Christine flung her arms round him and kissed him before he could reach Eleanor. Oliver, Anita, and Richy piled out of the lounge yelling and whooping.

'Were you really there, Dad?' Oliver asked, his eyes were round and incredulous. 'Up in space when the sail unfurled?'

Greg blinked as Christine let go. 'Why are you wearing your nightie?'

She laughed and did a twirl. 'Do you like it? It's my new party dress.'

'The channel newscasts said Aunty Julia was up there,' Oliver insisted. 'They never mentioned you.'

Christine's shiny black dress was held up by two thin straps at the front, its back dropping almost to her rump; the skirt hem rode well above her knees.

'This is Andria,' he said distractedly to the three younger children. 'She'll be staying with us for a while.'

Richy was chewing one of his toy cars. He tilted his head to one side, and looked up at Andria. 'Why?' he asked.

'Because she's a friend, and it's nice here.' Which was true enough, the farm was the best place he knew to bring up a kid, but he was going to have to come up with a better reason than that. He would try and explain about the extra baby tomorrow.

Though maybe it would be better coming from Eleanor. Yes, excellent idea.

'Do you mind?' Andria asked.

Richy shook his head shyly.

Greg managed to kiss Anita.

'Missed you, Dad,' she whispered.

'Greg told us you used to work at a shipping office,' Eleanor said.

'Yes,' Andria nodded.

'How are you at accounts?'

'I shuffled some finance bytes when I was there.'

'Good.' Eleanor gave Greg a quick kiss and began to steer Andria towards the kitchen. 'You can help me with our figures. I'm afraid I'm way behind this year.'

Greg gave Oliver a strong hug. 'Yes, I was up there, and so was Aunty Julia.'

'The sailing star is an aspect of Gaia, isn't it, Dad?' Anita asked urgently. She threw a contemptuous glance at Oliver. 'One of her angels come to show us the path to redemption.'

Christine smoothed down the front of her dress. 'I'm going to wear it to the dance at the Victoria Hall on Saturday. Graham's asked if he can take me. Mum said I'd have to ask you first. But it's all right if I go, isn't it, Dad?'

'Who's Graham?'

Eleanor smiled sweetly. 'Supper will be late, sorry.' She and Andria vanished into the kitchen.

'It's an alien monster, and Dad stopped it from eating New London,' Oliver said hotly, and glared at his twin. 'That's right, isn't it, Dad?'

Greg scooped up Richy, who smiled angelically and wrapped his arms round Greg's neck.

'Dad! Can I go dancing with Graham or not?'

EPILOGUE

Julia opened her eyes to pure whiteness, a smooth translucent material centimetres from her nose with sunlight shining through. She stared at it while her thoughts coalesced, as if she was waking. But there had been no sleep, she was sure of that.

Memories rose, coldly bright, every aspect of her life recalled in meticulous detail, the joy and pain undimmed by time. That was so unfair. Time was supposed to heal human angst. And there had been so much time. Centuries.

The whiteness brightened, splitting open to show a cloudless sky. She was lying inside an oval cocoon which had a texture of resilient rubber. Sunlight warmed her skin and heavy moisture-laden air rolled in. There was the distinctive sound of waves breaking on a beach. She sat up.

It was a beach, a long, curving cove with gingery sand and beautifully clear water. She could see a rocky headland about three kilometres away to her left; on the other side there was a dark line of cliffs stretching into the distance. The bluff behind her was littered with big boulders, narrow wind-blown buttresses of sandy soil gripping them tight. Blades of tough-looking reed grass struggled for a toehold above the sand, growing into a thick wiry mat at the top of the bluff. Beyond that was a band of dense vegetation. The trees were unusual, each of them had five equally spaced slender grey trunks, gradually curving inwards, their tips meeting at the centre of the pentangle. A clump of mossy indigo foliage foamed out around the conjunction, with long ribbons dangling down to the ground. She shivered in dark delight at the sheer alienness of the world.

Five metres away was another cocoon. She waited as its top dilated, then Royan sat up.

They embraced on the sand between the two cocoons, spending a long time just looking at each other, hands constantly touching and stroking for reassurance. Finally she held his gaze, and screwed her face up. 'That was a bloody silly thing to do. Didn't you ever read *War of the Worlds*?'

He grinned. 'Brought us together in the end, didn't it, Snowy?'

She groaned in mock-outrage, and hugged him tighter.

He craned his neck, searching the sky.

'There.' She pointed back over the jungle. A brilliant star hung above the tree tops.

'Where it will go now?'

'I'll find it a world of its own, that was the deal. The SETI division had compiled quite an extensive list of local stars confirmed to possess planetary systems. I accessed the file before we left New London.'

'Good old Rick.'

'Yes.' She took another look round the beach, and rubbed her arms absently. 'It's going to be cold at night.'

'The nanoware will make you some clothes, they'll make you anything as long as they've got the right raw material to process.'

She glanced down at the white organisms. Both of them had closed up, shrinking slightly now there was no body to accommodate. If she concentrated she could feel their presence in her mind, an obedient animal-sentience, waiting for orders.

'I wonder what happened to me . . . her, afterwards?'

'We can always go back and see.'

'No,' she said with a sigh. 'It was just a dream. This is our world now.'

Royan slipped his arm around her waist. 'Shall we take a look around?'

The image of a planet seen from space filled her mind, strange continents, deep oceans dotted with long island chains, and large dazzling white polar caps. She had always adored the recordings of Earth's ice-bound continent, ruing the fact she would never see it.

Exploring this planet would take a lifetime. The two of them would do it together, alone, and free of any obligations. The way it could never be on Earth.

'Sounds good,' she said.

They started to walk along the beach towards the headland. After a minute, the nanoware organisms stirred themselves, and began to slither dutifully after them.

Read on for an excerpt from

GREAT NORTH ROAD

by Peter F. Hamilton

Coming from Del Rey Books

Friday, February 1, 2143

Most of the expedition pilots were toxed up with HiMod to keep them sharp and push them through their natural sleep cycle without the chembuzz of a street stim. Ravi Hendrik didn't bother with analeptics. No need, not even now he was pushing fifty. As to why so many of his fellow pilots had turned users, he didn't understand at all.

How could you not stay fresh and focused on this world with this mission?

Right now the ass-end of a Daedalus C-8000-KT tanker variant was a hundred meters ahead of him, wing flaps extended to keep it just above stall speed. The refueling hose had wound out of its port wingpod, holding fairly steady in the slipstream.

The refueling probe of Ravi's European Aircraft Corporation CT-606D Berlin heavylift helicopter was fully extended now, and he eased the big machine forward to make contact. Up ahead, the traffic lights below the tanker's refueling pod switched from red to double green. The long receiver pole that had telescoped out from just below the Berlin's nose thrummed in the downdraft from the contrarotating coaxial blades, powered by twin high-speed, high-temperature turbines a meter above and behind Ravi's head.

He lived for this. A man in tune with his machine, flying with a purpose. Ease the shaking brute forward, anticipate the slipstream oscillation, match it, don't forget the unwieldy inertia from the 'dozer dangling seven meters beneath the fuselage and . . . squeeze the ergo-joystick to slide that fucker in. Three blue lights shone bright on the windscreen display as the locks engaged.

"Got it," he told the fuel supervisor on board the Daedalus.

"Roger that. Seal confirmed. Beginning transfer."

Ravi's free hand flicked a gang victory sign at the lumbering plane in front. Oh yeah, the old master scores a first-time clean entry. Again. Symbols on the screens showed him the JB5 biav flowing into the Berlin's depleted tanks.

He monitored the stress on the receiver pole through an icon in his netlens glasses grid. The weight of the new fuel would change the Berlin's performance and balance, and with that 'dozer playing hell with his drag, he couldn't afford to slacken off. Now this, *this* was the kind of true flying you just couldn't hand over to some bastard autopilot, no matter how much poncy AI code you crammed into its silicon.

Grinning wildly, he took a glance out of the curving cockpit to check how Juan-Fernando was doing. The other Berlin was closing on the starboard refueling hose. Below the helicopter, hanging on near-invisible cables, was a bright yellow JCB compactor, looking utterly surreal as it zoomed over a StLibra jungle at close on 250 kph.

Juan-Fernando missed his first attempt.

"Oh yeah." Ravi flicked another sign at his pathetic loser of a colleague. "Say my name, dipshit, say my n-a-m-e," his voice called above the voluble cabin noise. He could just imagine Juan-Fernando's dismay. The other two Berlins in the flight, waiting their turns to suckle at the Daedalus, would have seen the miss also. Ravi's fellow pilots would be buying him a lot of drinks when they got back to civilization tomorrow night.

The ferry flight had made more than half the distance from Abellia to Edzell, the first advance base that was being carved out of the jungle 2,700 kilometers straight north of Abellia. Eight hundred kilometers left to go, and Ravi would be lowering the 'dozer down into the clearing. An overnight stay and then tomorrow a fast flight back to Abellia to pick up more outsized equipment.

First priority for the HDA engineering corps at Edzell was to use the 'dozers and compactors to carve a runway out of the wild ground for the Daedalus planes, whose design allowed them to land on some pretty rough surfaces. Once that strip was established, the big planes would take over supplying the base and expanding it to full operational status, but until then it was all dependant on the Berlins. Ravi and the helicopter pilots were the pioneers everyone else was depending on to pull off this truly wild schedule. The whole expedition, from the vice commissioner down to the catering staff, was following this flight in real time, admiring their ballsy skill. Right now his neurons were pumping him a high no tox could match. Oh yes.

The Berlin's tanks filled to their capacity, and Ravi disengaged, sending the Berlin curving away, making room for Greg in the number-three bird, who was carrying another of the five-ton 'dozers.

The weather radar display shining across the cockpit canopy showed the afternoon storm as a giant red wave sweeping in from the southeast. If nothing went wrong they should just be able to outrun it. Any kind of weather forecast on StLibra was a boon. Without satellites they were as close as Ravi had ever been to flying blind. Thankfully the e-Rays provided some coverage along the flight path to Edzell, but this zooming-into-the-unknown form of piloting was all part of the great game.

"Smooth," Tork Ericson called above the turbine whine and gearbox growl that saturated the cabin—military birds weren't big on soundproofing. He was an aviation engineer, sitting in the copilot's seat today to help with the abnormal load.

"Riding this gig is cool," Ravi told him as the Berlin settled down to its cruise speed of 275 kph, considerably lower than its usual because of the 'dozer.

"But not as cool as a Thunderthorn," Tork supplied.

"You got it." In his glorious youth Ravi Hendrik had flown SF-100 Thunderthorns, the HDA's first line of defense against Zanthswarms. And Ravi had been a newly qualified pilot, eighteen months out of HDA flight school, when the New Florida Zanthswarm began. He'd flown mission after mission above that doomed world. Nothing in his professional or private life since had come close to matching the sheer terror and exhilaration of those three weeks.

The HDA had reassigned him away from his beloved SF-100 when he was in his late thirties. Younger pilots were coming through the academy, boys and girls with hunger to kill the Zanth, with faster reflexes and more up-to-date systems knowledge than that sad old-timer Ravi Hendrik. They didn't have the real-life experience, but that counted for shit in these days of virtuals. So Ravi was assigned to support flying duty as the clock ticked down to pension time—still extremely important work, his squadron commander insisted, even though he was older still and knew exactly what a load of bullshit he was feeding to resentful sidelined ex-hero pilots.

It was a Bad Thing, he knew, but Ravi wanted every day to be a Zanthswarm day, allowing him to fuck the enemy with D-nukes that *he* launched, that *he* detonated amid the terrifying rifts through spacetime. The universe's greatest power trip.

But even he had to admit this crazy expedition was pretty hot. A good swan song for his career.

The alien jungle stretched out to the horizon in all directions, lush glaucous vegetation clinging to every hill and ravine. The plants possessed a unique vitality, clogging tributaries until they swamped, forming clifflike sides along the deep, faster-flowing rivers. Giant, palmlike trees stabbed upward, towering thirty to forty meters above the main canopy like green impaling spikes waiting for the Berlin flight to make one mistake. Vines festooned the gaps over steep gorges. Bubble-bushes, a pink-hued scrub that grew in clusters across any sodden area, thronged the folds creasing the mountainsides where misty streams trickled downward. Waterfalls spewed white from rock precipices, falling for an age into deep pools. Thick tattered braids of cloud meandered along valleys and around peaks. Away to the west, the land rose in a vast massif that created an even more rugged-looking plateau country beyond—as yet unnamed. Who had the time?

"Man, this is one mean bushworld," Tork said.

Ravi nodded. He got it. Traveling like this, low and slow over land where no human had ever been before, and likely as not never would again once the expedition was over, made him very conscious of how far they were from civilization. More important, how far from help if anything went wrong. The expedition had some Sikorsky CV-47 Swallows, including a fully equipped medevac version. But even Ravi had to question how useful they'd actually be at plucking casualties out of this remote verdant wilderness.

The last Berlin finished refueling, and the Daedalus retracted its multitude of flaps neatly back into its wings, returning them to a clean supercritical airfoil lifting surface. It started to climb to a more comfortable altitude, banking hard to starboard as it did so, heading back to Abellia.

Far below, Ravi and the other three helicopters flew onward over the unending jungle. Communications to Abellia were routed via relay packages in the six e-Ray AAVs (Autonomous Airborne Vehicles) that were strung out across the gulf between Abellia and Edzell, flying tight, high-altitude loiter patterns. It had taken four days to position the e-Rays, which had gone on to perform preliminary scans to plot out the basic features of the land. Once the expedition had some rough cartographic details to work with, a squadron of the smaller Raytheon 6B-E Owls had flown out to begin a more detailed examination of the area with specialist ground-mapping sensors.

A two-kilometer flat zone close to water and with low bush coverage had been found with relative ease. Once conditions were confirmed by the Owls, a couple of Berlins had flown out to drop preliminary camp equipment and a detachment of engineers—along with a full Legion squad for protection. None of the Owls had detected any alien animals, not even insects, but Maj. Griffin Toyne, who was head of expedition security, wasn't taking any chances. They were here to find potentially hostile aliens; he didn't want them finding the expedition first.

After eight straight hours of flying, and placing more trust than Ravi found comfortable in their inertial guidance system, he spotted the lake. It was at the base of a wide gentle valley that was clear of jungle, with just a few lone bullwhip-trees standing among the wispy amethyst-shaded grass. Sunlight shimmered on the long serpentine patch of water fed by a river at the head and leaking away into a broad swamp six kilometers away at the lower end. The cluster of silver domes above the lakeshore made an incongruous sight amid the pervasive color wash of StLibra's abundant flora. Two Berlins were sitting beside the shelters. Legionaries patrolled the loose perimeter of the camp, including the eighty-meter stub of raw earth that a lone 'dozer had cleared.

Clouds were already crawling across the sky as Ravi brought the Berlin to a hover over the end of the infant runway. Ragged shadows slipped toward him across the valley. HDA engineers scuttled underneath the big helicopter, holding their sun hats in place against the downwash. The senior loading officer on the ground guided him down, and the 'dozer touched the earth. Tork released the cables, earning a thumbs-up from the ground crew. Ravi peeled away to find a landing site.

Later, after he'd had a rest, he'd help unload the remainder of the equipment and supplies the Berlin had brought, along with the fresh food. They could barbecue the burgers and sausages this evening, enjoying a tropical sunset without the usual insect attack that plagued most of the transstellar planets. As he settled the big copter, he saw the blades on the parked vehicles start to turn as the turbines were fired up. The crews were desperate to get airborne before the bulk of the storm hit Edzell. They had at best seven hours of daylight left, including a refueling rendezvous with the Daedalus tanker, so they'd be finishing the flight back to Abellia in darkness. Ravi grinned approval at that—more skilled flying required.

He throttled the turbines back and initiated the general power-down sequence. Raindrops began to splash across the bulging cockpit windscreen. It was growing dark outside; the twirling mass of cloud had already veiled the sun. Tomorrow he'd be sitting about waiting for the next Berlin flight to arrive before he could leave. That gave him several hours to scout around and get a feel for the territory. Maybe the engineers would allow him to drive one of the 'dozers. It was a grand time to be alive.

For news on when Great North Road *will be released, send a blank email to sub_peterhamilton@info.randomhouse.com.*

ABOUT THE AUTHOR

Peter F. Hamilton is the internationally bestselling author of numerous short stories and novels, including the Void series (*The Dreaming Void, The Temporal Void,* and *The Evolutionary Void*), *Judas Unchained, Pandora's Star, Fallen Dragon*, and the acclaimed Night's Dawn trilogy: *The Reality Dysfunction, The Neutronium Alchemist*, and *The Naked God*. He lives in Rutland, England, with his family.

DON'T MISS
ANY OF
PETER F. HAMILTON'S
UPCOMING TITLES
FROM DEL REY BOOKS

Send a blank email to
sub_peterhamilton@info.randomhouse.com
to subscribe to the
Peter F. Hamilton email list.

Don't miss Peter F. Hamilton's eBook short story collection

MANHATTAN IN REVERSE

Featuring a brand-new novella starring detective Paula Myo, the genetically engineered police investigator whose single-minded pursuit of justice clashes with a postwar citizenry eager to forget old crimes. This and six other thrilling short stories round out the collection—and showcase Peter F. Hamilton's ability to weave scientific speculation into very human storytelling.

Coming to your eReader in Spring 2012 from Del Rey Books!